Legacies

Quest Academy

Book 4

Brian J. Nordon

CONTENTS

CHAPTER 1: RETURN

"Don't be silly, Sal, you're just back. I don't expect you to help out when you're finally on a break. Your mother and I are more than capable of handling an auction by ourselves. We've been running them without you for a while now." Petro laughed as he tried to reassure Sal. Smiling, he placed an ornate ceramic cup in front of his son, before moving back to the coffee machine with his own. "Besides, you'd probably slow us down. Going to be hard talking to clients if they're too busy fawning over the top-ranked student in Quest Academy." He added a wink over his shoulder to show he was joking.

Sal smiled as he looked at the espresso in front of him. "Come on, don't be like that. I just want to get back into the swing of things, and it's going to be a while before everything arrives."

With a shake of his head, Petro slid his cup out from the tray, chuckling. "We both know that if you start working, your mother will take it out on me. You're to rest up and then we can make a plan of attack. Deal?" He stared at Sal meaningfully as he pulled out a stool at the granite island in the center of the kitchen. Sitting down, he spread his hands, his silver eyes locked onto Sal. "Your mother has made it very clear that I will be smothered in my sleep if I try to force you into Crafting or put you to work in the auction."

"You made an entire workspace for me in the Argento Auction House, but you won't show me. And now I'm not allowed to use it until I rest?" Sal shook his head, laughing. "Talk about mixed signals. I just want to see what you've set up."

Petro drummed his hands against the table, grimacing. "I'm really excited to see what you think. Your mother and I worked hard on it, but I just want to make it clear that there's no problem if you're disappointed. We're just a family business and unlikely to be able to compete with the likes of Quest Academy. But we wanted you to have a place for yourself between semesters."

Sal faltered as he looked at his father in astonishment. "Dad, it could be a table in an empty room and I'd be delighted. It's the thought that counts, so don't talk about being disappointed, okay?"

Petro smiled as he drained his own cup. "It's going to go cold if you keep staring at it." He gestured at Sal's espresso. "As for the workspace thing, let me talk to your mother. She'd kill me if you saw it without her—she wants to see your reaction."

Sal sighed with a slight shake of his head. "And you'll talk to her about tonight's auction? We could call it research since I can use my ability to make blueprints of whatever I see?"

Petro thought about it for a moment before shaking his head. "Nah, we'll go with the angle that you miss spending time with us. Sentimentality goes further than practicality when it comes to your mother."

Sal nodded in agreement. "And after that, would we be able to sit down and talk about the new Guild?" When he had tried to bring it up over the last few days, he was stonewalled by both of his parents, insisting that it wasn't the right time to talk about it. He wanted to talk to them about the vision that Divinity had showed him about the Argento Auction becoming Argento Plaza. It was just a possibility though, and when it came to business, his parents worked with facts.

Petro looked at Sal for a moment before sighing and offering a shrug. "We're working on a few things behind the scenes, Sal. I've had a couple of conversations with Quest and Grant, but it's all too vague. They're optimists and believe things will work out because they're giving their support. To make this a successful venture, you need more than just promises and assurances. Trust us and give us a little more time, and then we can have a more productive conversation about it."

"That wasn't a no. I'll take it." Sal smiled as he pointed at his father, who threw his hands up in mock surrender.

"Of course it's not a no. We want you to be happy, but we also want to ensure that this is something you actually want. Take it from an acclaimed Appraiser— when the guilds see value in you, they'll make every promise under the sun to get you on their side." Petro gave Sal an encouraging smile.

"It's about knowing your value, son. You've got so many avenues open to you because of your power and accomplishments, and it would be ridiculous to jump at the first thing that looked appealing. Your mother and I just want what's best for you, and in this case, it's practicing caution and pushing the Guilds Association and Hunter Bureau into making their moves. Let them make this concept a guaranteed success, and then we come to the table."

Sal nodded in understanding. "It's a little daunting, but I'm glad to have you on my side for all of this." He drained his own cup of coffee before getting to his feet and placing it in the sink. "I just don't want to make a mistake or end up getting a bad deal. There are a lot of heavy hitters involved who want this to work, but so much of it hinges on me. It's a lot of pressure."

Petro snorted. "Pressure is for tires, Sal. You've been negotiating since you were a child. The only difference this time is that you're not impartial. It's all about you, and the investments you could get from these people could guarantee you a very comfortable future." Petro got to his feet and plucked his suit jacket from a rack by the door. He threw it on with a fluid movement before fastening a single button.

"It comes down to what you want. We're going to support you every step of the way, and we'll shield you from the expectations that everyone else puts on you. Now, are you certain that you want to come over to the auction today?" There was a twinkle in his eye as he held up his keys.

Sal just grinned as he slid his stool back under the granite worktop. "Yes! Can I drive?"

Petro chuckled as he pretended to think about it. "I'm already risking my life by going against Sophia's wishes, so no. Tell you what—you can make a fancy blueprint of the car and make your own. How does that sound?"

Sal sighed as he shook his head. "I'll add it to the list."

When Sal got out of his father's prized classic car, the modified Panther De Ville, he stood at the entrance to the Argento Auction House. It was at the heart of the commercial district in Silver Sanctuary, and only a short drive away. Although there were multiple towering buildings, none of them held the same charm as the auction house. It was an old railway station that had been completely renovated over the years, with a modern style that still retained a lot of the classic architecture. Aged red brick created an imposing archway, with a prominent clock tower overhead. His father had constantly fought against the pressures of the residential committee to remove the clock and plant a turret there instead. It was great to still see it in place.

"You coming?" Petro started to walk across the paved courtyard, pocketing his keys as he did so.

Sal nodded as he followed his father, looking at the display windows on either side of the pathway. They typically refreshed the stock every few weeks, but there were a few old reliables in place, secured by reinforced glass. Certain weapons and armors that had a nostalgic value, like collection pieces. There was a helm that was a few hundred years old, and although it looked like it would probably work on a battlefield against the demons, it held absolutely no benefit other than aesthetics.

Petro looked over his shoulder, smiling. "Recognize some of the exhibits? You Appraised a few of them for the Reavers Guild. It was surplus stock they didn't have much interest in moving themselves, so we took it off their hands."

Sal frowned. "You sure they're mine? They don't look that familiar." Either his father was mistaken, or Sal had really underestimated how tired he was when he completed that massive order for them.

Petro shrugged. "Could be wrong. The Reavers' stuff might be in the main hall, or in storage." He approached the massive double door that was made from steel and polished wood. To the left was a handprint reader, which Petro used with a sigh. "We've got a lot of surplus lately, so hopefully we can move a chunk of it tonight."

Sal perked up at that. "Sounds like you could use some help." He didn't bother trying to hide the hopeful tone in his voice. The Credit floor, bazaar, and Scavenger Network had been fun, but it wasn't anything to the electric pace of the Argento Auction House. Sal desperately wanted to get back into it.

Petro's face broke into a smile as he lifted his hand from the reader, looking at Sal with a raised eyebrow. "You trying to make some commission? We've got a few new members of staff to help on the sales floor, and having you competing with them would only disgruntle them."

Sal winced at that. If he were to get successful sales, it would help the auction, but alienate the staff. "Okay, then what about slotting me in as an Appraiser? Help you get some of the stock lists updated?"

Petro thought about it for a second before shaking his head. "You know, if you want to keep your mother sweet, you should probably offer some Restoration services instead."

Sal groaned inwardly. Restoration was nowhere near as fun as the Appraisal station, and his mother was more of a perfectionist than anyone else. If she was standing over his shoulder, he'd have to do Restoration meticulously rather than brute-forcing the whole thing. "Okay, wait…different compromise. How about an Upgrade station?" Sal laughed at the suggestion, knowing his father would dismiss it completely.

Petro gave his son a level stare. "Our insurance wouldn't cover that. Even Restoration is a nightmare to navigate. Upgrading equipment would be so much riskier as you could potentially destroy a valuable piece in the process." He looked at Sal for a few more seconds before pulling the unlocked door open.

"Now, ground rules. You're not to go near the workspace we're making for you. It's not ready yet. Someone decided to come back from his semester early and caught us off guard. If you want to be helpful, and earn some goodwill, you can help your mother on the Restoration station, or you can do some cataloguing. Lastly, no distracting the staff. We've got the event tonight, and we're going to be flat-out."

Sal gave his father a mock salute. "Understood, sir."

"Repeat the rules back to me. Just so I've got some plausible deniability when your mother comes for me." Petro smiled, rotating his hand as though asking Sal to be quick about it.

"Don't look at the workspace, do some cataloguing and Restoration, don't annoy the staff." Sal mimicked everything back to his father. "I'll stay out of the way, and just help out where I can."

Petro chuckled. "Good. Now go say hello to your mother. I'll catch up with you later." He paused as he looked at Sal a little more carefully. "By the way, do you need a new uniform for tonight? You've filled out a lot more and I doubt that your old one will fit anymore."

Sal waved his hand like it was nothing. "I'll make some adjustments to the old one. It'll be fine. I picked up a bit of tailoring."

Petro nodded slowly before he eventually sighed. "Tomorrow, we're going to sit down and you're going to write out everything you've learned so far at Quest Academy."

Sal watched him walk off to his office, muttering something about upgrading and tailoring. When he moved farther into the Argento Auction House, he smiled. There were three members of staff standing along the glass walkway overlooking the large display hall. They were adding listings onto an old-school blackboard with chalk, highlighting the minimum bids for exclusive pieces and special offers on older sets. On the ground floor, there were a few uniformed staff with aprons who were polishing up the glass display cases, while other workers set up cordoned-off areas.

Sal turned to look at the office spaces to find his mother. It was an open plan space, with a mezzanine that had its own private glass walkway, set against a red brick wall. The style was that of an old American loft, with various historical Argento family pictures lining the walls and the various stages of the auction house over the years. A large glass window opened into an area with a half dozen tables, covered with tagged exhibits. His mother was already at work on small-form restorations, her hair tied back in a ponytail and her glasses resting low on her nose. The other members of staff gave her a wide berth as she worked, which brought a smile to Sal's face.

Lifting his eyes to the next floor up, Sal could see Petro wearing his waistcoat as he stood with a fresh coffee in hand. A series of displays were open in front of him, relaying catalogue information and attendee lists for the auction happening in the evening. Both of his parents were already hard at work as dozens of people moved efficiently from space to space, getting everything ready for the big event.

Sal took it all in. He was finally home.

CHAPTER 2: PETTY

As Sal made his way into his mother's workspace, he smiled as a few of the employees looked up in surprise.

Sophia followed their gaze and saw Sal at the entrance. She took off her glasses and glanced at the employees who had stopped their work. "No talking to him about Quest Academy until lunchtime. Understood?" She waved a hand as though dismissing their frowns. "None of you will get a thing done when you hear about him taking down a hulker."

The reactions of the staff were priceless as they whipped around first to look at Sophia in utter shock, before whirling back in a comical double take to stare at Sal.

Sophia smiled wryly at Sal. "Sorry, that was supposed to be a secret, wasn't it?"

Sal smiled as he shook his head, giving his attention to the stupefied employees. "It was mostly down to the equipment. Some of the staff made me Epic-grade armor to wear. Don't go thinking that I'm a front-liner or anything like that." His words did little to dissuade them from fawning over him. There were countless questions thrown at him, and when he turned toward his mother, he could see a playful smile on her lips as she hunched over a small watch that was laid out on her worktable in multiple pieces.

When Sal finally excused himself, promising to tell them all about it in the break room later, he approached his mother. "Thanks for that," he muttered under his breath, looking closely at the dismantled watch. It would have been easy to just fix it without having to dismantle it, but that wasn't his mother's style at all.

As though sensing his line of thought, Sophia turned the backplate of the watch around, showing him a dull engraving of initials. "Can't afford to Restore this and lose the sentimental value. Needs a little more finesse." She gave him a wink before turning the plate around and adjusting it so that it was back in line with the markings on her work mat.

Sal nodded slowly. "So, are there any non-sentimental things you might want me to Restore? Dad said I was allowed to help, as long as I stay out of everyone's way."

Sophia considered it briefly before slightly shaking her head. "We'll be able to manage. No need for you to be working on your break."

Sal stared at the mound of boxes behind her. "Do you want me to just sit here and feel guilty?" He pointed at the boxes. "Or are you going to let me help with those?" It was odd for there to be so much of a backlog in Restoration. His mother was ruthlessly efficient, and she knew how to manage workloads better than anyone. There had to be a reason for her to be so behind. *Had there been a massive haul that came in last minute?*

Sophia followed her son's gesture and smiled. "Don't worry about that. Those aren't going to be in tonight's event, so we're working on a more exclusive list."

"That's Auctioneer talk for limited," Sal countered as he moved around the table to examine the boxes. "Come on, either I'll work on these with your approval or without. What's it going to be?" He didn't know what the circumstances were for his mother to be so behind, but he had the ability to help, and that's what he was going to do.

With a resigned sigh, Sophia waved at them. "Okay, you can set up on that table beside me. I want to check everything you work on, though. No shortcuts, understood?"

Sal nodded as he lifted the first box over to the table. "Understood. Starting to think that you and Dad don't trust me to work in the auction these days. Got a lecture from him earlier, too."

Sophia smiled as she stretched her back. "You get the same treatment as all employees when you're here. You know the rules." She pulled at her sleeves that had slipped over her elbow, ensuring that her forearms were free to work. "There's no telling what bad habits you might have picked up from Quest Academy, so we need to ensure you're still able to work our way when you're here."

Sal opened the box and placed the wooden lid to one side, carefully pulling away the foam that kept the piece secure. "It's too early for you to be goading me." Sal smiled as he inspected the contents of the box. "Nope," he exclaimed before putting the foam back and placing the lid on top of the box, securing it completely.

"What was it?" Sophia laughed, trying to peer into the box before it was sealed off.

Sal lifted the box and set it to one side of his table before moving back to the pile to pick up a different one. "It's one of those creepy dolls, with the ceramics." He suppressed a shudder as he placed the new box on his table, repeating the process of pulling back the foam to get a better look. "This is perfect."

Sophia gave a resigned sigh as she watched Sal pluck out a battered breastplate from the box. "You know, you won't get better at Restoration if you just default to the pieces that make you comfortable."

Sal gave his mother a bright smile. "Which of these exhibits are more likely to sell during a demonic invasion? Creepy doll, or a piece of armor?"

Sophia held her son's gaze before letting out an exasperated sigh. "Cultural value is important, too. It's very likely that the doll could earn a lot more than that breastplate. Just depends on the buyer."

Sal shrugged. "I don't disagree, but this is a domain I'm much more familiar with. Appraisal and Restoration are much easier on something you understand. I can leave the finesse to you and your specialists." He looked over at the employees, who gave him a set of smiles. Even though he could work just like his mother, and Restore things perfectly, it was a tiring process when you had no interest in the project. By claiming incompetence, he could work on more fun items and give the employees some praise at the same time.

Sophia chuckled as she shook her head. "And there's the flattery. Go on then, work on all the crude pieces of armor and weaponry. We'll take care of the *specialist* pieces."

Her emphasis on that single word told Sal that she knew exactly what he was doing. Sal began to laugh as he got started on the breastplate. A quick Appraisal had told him that it was Uncommon grade and held three broken runes. It was similar in style to the one that Marcus from the Harmony Guild had worn, the Hunter they had "saved" on the second floor of the tower.

Sal frowned as he studied it. It was over a decade old, and had been Crafted by someone. The name of the breastplate had been lost when the primary rune was destroyed. Restoring it would just bring it back to a Rare grade, and although that was good, it could have been better. The other two runes that were inscribed were wrong, and likely had never activated even when it was in perfect condition. One of them was essence absorption, and because it wasn't done correctly, it meant the total charges for the Reflect rune were finite. It had likely been used a few times before it broke down. The third rune was for Barrier, and it hadn't ever activated either. Looking at the back of the collar, Sal saw a recess, likely for the core that was never slotted into the breastplate.

"I'm surprised." Sophia glanced at Sal thoughtfully. "I was half expecting you to flood it with essence to get it back to pristine condition, but you're studying it diligently."

Sal flinched, startled by her voice. "Ah, yeah…was just looking at the design choices that went into it. It's pretty much a disaster, with two out of three runes never activating because of small mistakes."

Sophia nodded as she moved over to examine the slip of paper attached to the lid of the box. "Your father had this one marked as preferable salvage, but the Delvers brought it in and wanted a Restoration. Considering it's Shade, I think that it's worth just doing the basics rather than going the extra mile. He'll likely back out of payment when he realizes it's flawed."

Sal frowned as he ran his fingers across the rough metal. "What if it turned out as Rare grade? I could fix the runes and the damaged area. Would he pay for that?"

Sophia considered it for a moment before a smile appeared on her face. "If it was Rare grade, we'd be able to hold onto it until he settled his debts on the other work that's outstanding." Her smile faltered before she laughed and shook her head. "Ah, but you're not allowed to go into that workspace yet. It's not ready, and there will be no exceptions…not even screwing over Shade."

Sal smiled as he raised his gloved hand. "I have everything I need here. Dad said that insurance for upgrades would be a nightmare…are you sure it'll be okay?"

Sophia laughed. "He talks like he's the one who handles the paperwork for that. Restoration is a very vague term when we don't know what we're Restoring." She winked at Sal. "Like, to me…that clearly looks like a Rare grade with three active runes that needs to be Restored. The paperwork will reflect that, and the Appraisal will be done afterward. The one your father completed unfortunately got lost."

Sal grinned. "Who are you, and what have you done with my mother?" He hadn't seen this side of her in a while, which told him that she was clearly in a good mood.

Sophia turned on her son and gave him a mock shocked expression. "Excuse me, but I could be saying the exact same thing. My poor innocent child went off on a train and came back as a part of the Savior class." She smiled before giving his hand a reassuring squeeze. "Can't a mother be curious about what her son has been learning?" She added that last part in a conspiratorial voice.

Sal chuckled as he looked at the breastplate. "Okay then, step back for a second. Do you want to see something cool?"

She nodded curiously as she stepped back to her own bench. "Just don't break anything."

Sal sent a surge of essence into his right glove, causing it to transform into a mechanical claw. It caused a series of gasps in the workspace, with the employees gaping at him in astonishment. Only Sophia stared at the claw intently, a smile on her face.

Without wasting any time, Sal started to work on the breastplate. He had the Perfect weave active as he poured his internal essence into the metal, causing it to become softer like putty. His clawed fingers guided the essence-infused metal to the gaping hole in the center of the chest. The edges of the hole reached outward in small tendrils of metal, creating an almost web-like lattice across the space, before blossoming and removing the hole entirely.

The newly formed metal had cut off a segment of the Barrier rune, so Sal blended the metal to erase the rune entirely from the breastplate. When it was clear, Sal used his index finger to etch out the Barrier rune across a wider space. The previous design would have allowed a barrier to only protect the user from the front, whereas Sal's design would allow for it to also protect against the sides and back of the user.

Mythcrafter had taken on the role of his mother, noting each of his inefficiencies as they occurred, while Perfect took his intentions and executed them. It meant that all his runes were adjusted in real time until they were perfectly carved into the malleable metal. The rune itself didn't look very remarkable, especially after Sal had seen the effects prowler blood could have on their construction. It would have to do, though, as Sal was making all these changes without any additional materials.

The self-replenishment rune came next, which Sal had to completely erase and start over from scratch. Essence absorption was tricky, and nobody knew that better than Sal. His first attempt at making this rune had almost killed him, using Fabi Maccles's design no less.

Sal created the rune for self-replenishment around the collar of the breastplate, removing the recess for a core as he did so. Three runes working without a core was going to be inefficient, but it didn't matter. It didn't need to be perfect. Recharging this thing with atmospheric essence would take an absolute age. Mythcrafter seemed to agree, and when the amended blueprint appeared in Sal's vision, he dismissed the suggestion for adding in a core.

With that option gone, Mythcrafter adapted and made a new suggestion to increase the size of the self-replenishment rune. Sal didn't question the choice and expanded the rune to cover most of the breastplate. The downside was that it took away the available space for the Reflect rune, but that would have to do. It hadn't worked on the original, anyway.

When both runes were done, Sal adjusted the metal to even it out. There were a few small changes he made to the shoulders to add in some flexibility, but overall, there weren't that many improvements he could really make. It was only when he was finishing up that Mythcrafter insisted that he add in a third rune. *Was it because he had used the evolutionary runes so regularly?* Sal saw the evolutionary rune layered over the interior of the breastplate. It didn't really make much sense, and Sal wasn't exactly sure the breastplate would ever absorb enough of a surplus of essence to fuel the evolution. It didn't have a core.

Ignoring his own concerns, Sal carried out the instructions of Mythcrafter and added in the rune. On the upside, it meant that he now had three runes on the piece. The downside was that it wouldn't really be that useful in combat. There were so many better options out there.

When it was finally done, Sal stepped back and paid special attention to transform his mechanical arm back into the glove. The breastplate was glowing, and Sal knew it would take a while for it to settle. He looked over at his mother and was shocked to see her staring at him with her mouth wide open.

"What?" he asked, looking between himself and the breastplate to see whether there was anything obvious he had missed. When his eyes landed on the breastplate, he realized that the glowing had stopped. It hadn't taken more than a few seconds this time around, and it had morphed due to his influence. Even if the design itself hadn't changed, the glowing self-replenishment rune, combined with the polished hue of the Restored steel, made it look like a high-end piece of equipment.

Sophia stepped forward and inspected the breastplate before turning on Sal with a wide grin on her face. "Screw the insurance. How much of this crap can you fix up?" Her eyes practically glittered as she looked up to a section of the ceiling. "Can someone get hold of my husband, please? We've got a potential game-changer on our hands."

Sal smiled at his mother. "Come on, it's not that impressive. You don't have to make a whole song and dance about it." It felt nice that he was able to show her his Mythcrafting ability, but she was humoring him a little too much.

Sophia laughed as she shook her head. "No, Sal. You're confusing things…I want you to fix up every piece of trash that Shade has given us. We're going to flaunt all of it at tonight's event. He owns no claim to most of it because he hasn't paid his bills, and it's going to absolutely torture him to see all this equipment going to someone else."

Sal's jaw dropped as he stared at his mother. "You can't be serious?" There was no way she would be this petty. Sure, both of his parents had an incredibly tense relationship with the Delvers guildmaster, but this was going a little too far, right?

Sophia clapped in excitement. "He's going to be sick to his stomach with this."

CHAPTER 3: BRIBE

"Prowler blood?" Petro repeated in confusion as he entered the term into the search bar. "I doubt we have any in stock, but I could call around to get an express delivery. Is it really that important?" He scratched at the back of his head as he moved through the different listings. "It wouldn't cost much. Maurice likely has some," he muttered as he thought about it out loud.

Sophia looked at her son. "And that's all you'd need to work on the other pieces of equipment?" She sounded skeptical, but the smile hadn't left her face since seeing the breastplate.

Sal nodded in response. "Prowler blood and prowler hide give equipment Stealth attributes. A friend of mine made a whole set and it was perfect for an ambusher. If you really want to twist the knife with Shade, why not do it with attributes he'd desperately want?" He was going to continue, when his mother's arms wrapped around him in a hug.

"I always knew he was my son. Silver eyes be damned." She laughed as she gave Petro a wide grin. "It'll remove the pressure on the backlog if Sal makes a few more pieces for us to add to the auction. How long has it been since we had surprise exhibits? Most of the attendees are likely bored with the status quo. This could be an exciting new collection that builds up some chatter."

Petro sighed as he looked at Sophia. "A Rare-grade breastplate is one thing, but there's no guarantee that Sal will be able to have the same effect on everything else." He paused as he turned his attention to Sal. "I trust you, and believe you could pull it off, but there are a lot of risks involved. Despite what your mother told you, Shade still brought in those pieces of equipment. We need him to write them off as losses, and if we offer to shoulder the cost, then he'll likely jump at that."

Sophia frowned as she cocked her head to one side. "He'll be suspicious if you do it that way."

Petro smiled. "Not if I ask him for a favor. I can tell him that I'd prefer if he didn't chase after Sal for his Appraisal ability. And give him a clean slate, and a few preferential slots in the future. He'll likely jump at it."

Sal raised a hand at that. "Wait, no. Don't give him more of your time. I could make an entirely new set of equipment rather than forcing you to work with Shade." He didn't want his father to be tied to the Delvers Guild any more than was necessary.

Petro snorted as he shook his head. "Don't worry, Sal. Shade is the type of person who will run to the Guilds Association and the Hunter Bureau if I ever try to stop working with him. The amount of bullshit antitrust accusations we've had to shoulder because of him is, frankly, ridiculous." He made an offhand gesture as though it were nothing to worry about. "Besides, if you just made good equipment, then he wouldn't learn a thing. What your mother desperately wants is for him to regret not paying his bills. All the junk pieces he abandoned here, being sold off as incredible pieces that were discovered with a new Restoration technique? It'll kill him."

"New Restoration technique? Is that what we're going with?" Sal chuckled. "All it would take is an Appraisal to see that there is Mythcrafter essence as a component."

Petro laughed at that and placed a hand on his chest. "Sal, trust me when I tell you if Shade isn't paying me, he's sure as shit not paying any other Appraiser for a second opinion."

Sophia finally let go of Sal as she moved off to one side, dusting herself off and adjusting her sleeves. "Gentlemen. As exciting as this is, we do have an auction tonight." With her attention squarely on Petro, she pointed at the screens behind him. "Put through an express order with Maurice for the prowler blood. If Sal says he needs it, then we'll get it for him."

"I can pay for it," Sal offered with a smile. "If they take Q-Cred, I mean."

Sophia turned to her son. "Absolutely not. You're humoring our personal grudges, so obviously we'll be the ones to fund it. Besides, you're going to be working on a few Restoration pieces. Could you have a look through the marked boxes and see if you can make a semi-cohesive set? If we could package it as a full set, then it would really drive up the prices."

Petro winced at that. "Selling it off piecemeal will aggravate him more, though."

Sophia laughed as she shook her head. "We're getting ahead of ourselves. Even with just the breastplate, it's enough. Anything more than this is a bonus for a bit of fun." She looked at Petro for a moment, a thoughtful expression on her face. "What do you think… should Sal get a twenty-five percent cut for all this?"

Petro scoffed at that as he looked between them. "Are you trying to bankrupt me? Fifteen percent is already a generous cut of the markup." He spread his hands as though he were genuinely remorseful. "We've got Restoration and Upgrade costs to factor in, so I can only justify the fifteen percent of the final price."

Sal's eyes widened slightly. "Wait. No, I'm doing this as a favor. Don't go making up fees for the work I'm doing." He looked at his mother for help, but she only offered a weak shrug.

"Sorry, Sal. You do the work, you get the fee. That's the rules." She smiled as she looked at Petro. "Still worried that he's going to wipe the floor with the new sales staff?"

Petro laughed as he moved over to clap Sal on the shoulder. "This is a compromise I'm very happy to make. If you're upgrading the equipment from Shade, then we've got little to worry about in terms of the stuff breaking. When we sell it at a profit, the team gets their commission, and our Crafter gets his cut. I think it works perfectly."

Sophia's smile was bright as she looked at Petro. "Can we show him the workspace? I know it's not ready, but I think it's only fair if we're putting him to work already."

Petro faltered as he looked at Sophia in surprise. "Really? From the woman who threatened to gut me if I even gave him a clue?"

Sophia shrugged. "I changed my mind. Come on, let's show him."

Sal looked between them, smiling. "You know you didn't have to make anything for me. I can work beside you in the Restoration room. There's no need for a dedicated space."

Petro laughed. "Okay, I'm on board. Let's show him."

Sal followed his parents to the back of the Argento Auction House. Since it had been an old railway station, it had a lot of Restored parts from the original train line. None of the tracks led anywhere anymore, as the place had been decommissioned well before the demonic invasion. When they walked down a series of steps that led to the underground line, Sal was surprised to see natural light at the base of the stairs. *Had they installed windows or something?*

"I can see the gears working in your head." Sophia chuckled as she squeezed her son's elbow. "Remember, there's no pressure if you don't like it."

Sal smiled at her and nodded. "I'm pretty sure I'm going to love it. Just trying to figure out how you managed to get sunlight in an underground tunnel."

Petro chuckled from ahead of them. "At great cost. Pulled in a few favors for this project, because we wanted to make a place that you'd be happy to come back to." He looked over his shoulder, grinning. "Now that you're crushing it at Quest Academy, we needed to step up our game."

Sal frowned as he continued down the stairs. The underground area of the Argento Auction House had only been used for storage in the last few years. After the Hunter Bureau collapsed most of the tunnels around the city, in the name of preventing dungeons from forming, the tunnels existed as private spaces. What had previously been a gloomy and cold storage area had been transformed into something extraordinary.

Sal's jaw dropped as he looked up to see a massive skylight in the ceiling. It stretched out with a dozen giant panes of glass, each of them twice as tall as him. A faint blue tinge to the glass told him that they were protected by a barrier. He was certain if he looked at them closely, he'd see the etched runes carved into the glass. The sunlight washed over the entire room, highlighting all the changes that had taken place. A metal stairwell led up to a mezzanine that overlooked the train tracks. One of the old train carriages was wide open, revealing a completely modernized interior.

"Ah, I should have taken a picture of that face," Sophia remarked with a laugh. "I think he likes it, Petro."

A wide smile crossed Petro's face. "Come on, I want to show you the inside of this thing." He gestured for Sal to follow him over to the train carriage that was permanently parked on a strip of railway. Petro pulled at the metal door that slid all the way to the left, revealing more of what was inside. "We heard from Quest that you spend a lot of time in the workshop, making all sorts of things. We wanted you to have a special place like that when you were home."

Sal was speechless as he looked at an array of tools and machinery laid out along the side of the cabin. Just standing in the center of it would put everything you could possibly need in reach.

Petro pointed at the machines from left to right. "We saved a fortune by taking in broken or outdated equipment. Your mother has been working on Restoring it all for months. This one is a 3D printer that does all sorts of fabrications. It's set up with that terminal on the wall, and can read blueprints that you scan on the top workbench." He pointed through the wall of the container to where the mezzanine was. "Your sketching area is up there. We managed to get you one that's a slightly newer model than what they use at the Academy. I don't know if it's all set up properly, but you should be able to draw up basic things and get the printer to start making them."

Sophia cleared her throat meaningfully, causing Petro to falter, before a guilty smile crossed his lips.

He gave Sal an apologetic smile. "Ah, the next one…it's an engraving laser. Uses the drawings from your workbench and will cut them into whatever you're making." Smiling, Petro moved his hand to the next machine. "This is a refiner. Removes impurities from salvaged materials, literally hits it with lasers and separates the components. Any junk you pick up can be thrown in there and it will break it down into materials you can use for Crafting."

Sal just stared at the machines. He had only used the printer with Martin's guidance in the workshop. The refiner was like a large freezer with a transparent window. The printer and engraver also had transparent screens that would let him watch the process in real time. Despite his father saying that the machines were cheap, there was no way it was true. Even if his mother had Restored it all up to being brand-new, there was no way they didn't spend a fortune on all of this.

"Early inheritance," Petro joked as he looked at Sal's expression. "We had a talk about this, and it's the most fun we've had in a long time, getting this set up for you. We asked all our Crafter contacts for their perspective on the best equipment to use, and more than a few of them donated their old equipment. Half of Silver Sanctuary has given something to this project, because you're a part of this community and they want to see you succeed."

Sophia stepped forward to hug Sal from behind. She placed her chin on his shoulder as she looked around the carriage. "Just don't drag any demon corpses down here to chuck into the refiner. We'll know if you do."

It was incredible how she could make such a sentimental moment sound like a threat.

Petro continued with the tour, pulling out shelves and opening cupboards. "We've filled these with the nonperishable materials that our friends said would be good. All your textiles are hung up in this closet. There are bolts of fabric somewhere else…don't ask me where. We honestly made this layout up on the spot. You'll need to organize it to your own needs." He placed his hands on his hips and looked at Sophia. "Do you want to show him upstairs?"

Sophia nodded as she disengaged from Sal. "Absolutely. Come on." She almost danced toward the stairs, hurrying Sal and Petro to follow her. "I didn't like how clinical and cold the place was. I wanted it to be warm and inviting, but still a place you could do your work," Sophia explained as she moved up the stairs. "You've got your own coffee machine up here. We gave you our old one, and upgraded ours to something nicer. There's a little kitchenette over here." She gestured at an empty wall with a broad smile.

Sal stared at it for a few seconds in confusion before his eyes widened. "No way. You didn't."

Sophia laughed as she shook her head. "Your father insisted that you'd love it. I think it's silly, but I can see he was right." She moved over to the empty wall and pushed against it, causing the fake wall to make way, and reveal the secret room with a small kitchen and a double bed. "This way, we don't need to worry about you spending late nights here and walking home alone."

"Soph, he killed a hulker," Petro reminded her in exasperation.

Sophia shrugged. "It's a mother's job to worry about her child." She turned around and gestured for Sal to come inside and take a look. "What do you think?"

Sal was genuinely speechless. They had created a workspace that was so far beyond his expectations that he didn't even know where to start with thanking them. It was like the place had been future-proofed, giving him equipment that he'd be able to use as he improved his skills. Having his own personal space inside the Argento Auction House was exciting as hell. He'd be able to walk out of his workspace and Appraise a range of new equipment that would be passing through storage. "It's just incredible. I don't have words."

"Try to find some. We worked really hard." Sophia laughed as she beamed at Petro. "You're our favorite son, and we wanted you to be happy when you came home."

Petro chuckled. "It's also a massive bribe so you'll continue to visit us regularly."

Sal just looked around him, smiling. "I think you'll regret saying that someday."

CHAPTER 4: UNIFORM

"Is that the last of them?" Sal came down the metal staircase, his eyes locked onto the most recent box that had been added to the large pile near the entrance to his new workshop.

George gave him a quick nod as he slapped the top box. "All the listings we have under Shade's name are in these boxes. Your father asked me to bring down the package from Maurice when it arrives. Want me to bring them up to you when they get here?" He untwisted his Argento Auction House apron and retied it behind him, smiling. "Good to have you back, Sal. I didn't get to chat with you, but the break room was on fire earlier."

"Ha. I promise we'll have a chat about the first semester. I just have a lot of stuff to get through before the auction tonight. If you could just bring down the package whenever it arrives, that would be great." Sal smiled as he pulled the wooden lid off the top box of the pile. By his estimate, there were around fourteen different pieces of equipment to work with. He didn't have time to stand around and chat, and he was eager to get back into Crafting.

"I'll leave you to it. Just give me a call if you need anything else." George lumbered off with a slight limp in his left leg.

Sal watched him leave before turning his attention back to the box in front of him. It was the lowest percentage of quality he had seen in a long time, at just two percent remaining condition. How it survived the journey to the storage area was beyond Sal, but he figured it would likely be more effort than it was worth. He put the lid back on the box and moved it to a section of the workshop that he mentally marked as his rejection area. When he moved back to the pile and opened the second box, he was greeted with a set of plate boots. It was a portal artifact, and looked to have an assortment of broken runes and a partially shattered core in each heel. Definitely something he could work with. Sal moved that one to a separate section that he'd carry up into the train carriage.

This process continued for the next twenty minutes as Sal quickly Appraised each of the items in the boxes, and sorted them by time commitment and how easy it would be to get a good result. It felt somewhat arrogant to look at a piece of armor for just a few minutes and determine whether he could make it better with minimal resources.

Of the entire selection he had been given, the one he was most excited to work on was a frayed cloak…which was a kind assessment, considering it resembled a clump of rags more than anything—a fabric tunic that held an unfamiliar crest on the center. He'd do his best to restore the symbol, but he'd need to drastically improve everything else about it. It was a mess of runes and was missing the entire left side. He'd need to reconstruct it completely.

That tunic was the reason he was excited for the broken pauldron. Aesthetically, they didn't match at all, but Sal intended to combine them into a single piece.

There were no pants in any of the boxes, unless he counted the garish yellow breeches that were stained with multiple smears of blood, both human and demonic. If he assembled those pieces as a collection and left them as they were, there was no way in hell that anyone would want to buy them. Nothing in the list was higher than Rare grade in terms of potential, with everything falling into the broken Common grade or barely functional Uncommon grade. The ones with Rare grade had been abused to the point that they were falling apart, telling Sal a lot about Shade's treatment of the gear.

Sal finished with the sorting and carried the pieces into the carriage. He placed each of them on the Restoration mats that his mother had undoubtedly supplied from her office. While the left wall was completely covered with machinery, the right had surfaces for him to work on. The drawers under the countertop were filled with fastenings, buttons, and small chunks of metal. It was perfect.

"Should I leave this out here, Sal?" George asked from outside the carriage.

Sal poked his head outside the door and saw George grimacing, trying to hold a massive container in his arms. It was a lot more prowler blood than Sal expected, or needed for that matter. *Did his parents think he wanted to submerge the equipment in it?* Rushing out to meet George and give him a hand, Sal placed his hands underneath the box and helped George bring it across to an empty space outside the carriage. "Here is fine, George. Thank you so much."

"Not sure if it's supposed to clink that much. You should check to see if it's broken, because it sounds like something shattered in there," George said with a worried expression as he steadied himself against the carriage door. He had been an employee of the auction house since Sal had been a child. Although many might have thought he was clumsy because of his impairment, Sal knew better.

Taking a knee, Sal opened the box and grinned when he saw stacks upon stacks of obsidian glass glittering in the sunlight. "This isn't the prowler blood, but it's the start of a much bigger delivery from Quest Academy."

George's face paled. "Wait—so all of that stuff that just came in is for you?" He swallowed as he looked back at the stairs leading up to the auction house. His worry was clear on his face.

Sal smiled at him and shook his head. "Don't worry, I don't expect you to bring down all of it. Just have the delivery guys place it in the normal storage bay area, and I can come up and pick a few things to take down. Sound good?"

George's relief was immediate. "I'd be happy to do it, but it's just that there's a lot of stuff that needs doing before tonight." He bit his lip as he looked at the stairs again. "I could get it done after the auction, and have it all down here for you tomorrow?"

"Absolutely not, George," Sal insisted. "You've already been an incredible help with these boxes. I've got it from here, so you can relax for a bit." He really didn't want to see the older man exerting himself.

When George finally agreed to not push himself, Sal thanked him again and got back to work. He didn't need to create a full set with the Stealth attribute, maybe just the boots and the cloak. That would allow him to spend more time working on the pauldron, tunic, and breeches. With the bracer being in there too, Sal was tempted to create it all as a single piece of equipment.

Turning around, Sal moved to the closet to see what fabrics he'd be able to use to potentially substitute the missing pieces of the cloak. If there was dreadcloth, he'd be a very happy man, but he tempered his expectations. He'd make do with whatever was there. As soon as he opened the door to the closet, he was greeted with a familiar outfit. It was his uniform for the Argento Auction House. A sticky note was attached to it in his mother's handwriting, telling him not to forget to make the alterations before the auction.

With a chuckle, Sal looked over his shoulder at the collection of broken equipment and shook his head. So much for having a relaxing break before heading back to Quest Academy. It looked like he was back into the bad habits of overworking himself. But the excitement welling in his chest told him that he wouldn't have it any other way. It was a challenge, and rather than doing it for some arbitrary reason, it was for his family. Sal was going to do everything in his power to ensure they were happy with the results.

Sal cheated. There was no way he was going to do a few alterations to the uniform for the auction house. He had access to a ridiculous range of materials and fabrics, and he had an incredible blueprint in his head of the tower uniforms Blathnaid had helped make. Even better, all the stylistic choices that went into those sets were saved onto the Mythcrafter blueprint.

"This is insane," Sal breathed as he loaded his blueprint into the scanner up on the mezzanine. All he had to do was confirm the engravings that he wanted and where it was to be located. To his absolute surprise, it asked whether he'd like to incorporate a logo with a separate stitching. The Argento Auction House logo was already preloaded, which told Sal that his parents had used this device to make some branded merchandise at some point.

Sal put the logo on the back of the waistcoat, silver stitching against the black satin material. The rest of the material was dreadcloth, because Sal found an absolute trove of it in the closet. After a few confirmations and suggestions from Perfect and Mythcrafter, Sal was left waiting for the engraver to finish the job. The 3D printer was already fashioning a set of buttons from a couple of shards of obsidian glass. He was going to use the residue from the cuttings to add a shimmering effect on the back of the waistcoat.

The pants that he made were a straight cut, with a deliberate crease going straight down the center of each leg. Dreadcloth had a slightly violet hue to it, and rather than working out that color, Sal decided to keep it. His white shirt would be freshly pressed, and he already knew that it would look great against the violet-charcoal color of his ensemble. His dress shoes still fit perfectly, and they were already polished to perfection. Sal was excited to see how it would all come together.

The dress code wasn't strict at the auction house, but it required a logo to show who was a member of staff, for easy identification. It also needed to be formal attire and sharp. Sal's new outfit was going to tick all those boxes, and worst-case scenario, if his mother sent him back to the drawing board, he'd do the alterations.

Sal looked down at the carriage and wondered how long it would take for the uniform to be done. It was a definite distraction, and he was happy that he couldn't see the progress from his place at the workbench upstairs. It allowed him to move onto the next phase of the project: his idea for combining the different pieces of Shade's collection. After a lot of deliberation and a few different designs, Sal had finally landed on something he was happy with.

The pauldron was going to be attached to the left shoulder of the destroyed tunic. Sal was going to reinforce it and make it a seamless part of the armor. An obsidian collar was going to secure the frayed cloak to the pauldron and tunic, and the bracer would be fashioned into a half vambrace, leading into the pauldron. Sal had gotten the idea from the armor he purchased for Barry. It would mean that only one side of the armor was protected, and would likely require the user to wear it to one side. It would look good, though, which was a big part of making it a hit for the auction.

Sal had dismissed so many suggestions from Mythcrafter to replicate the design on both sides. It was a silly thing, but Sal thought that it added far more character for it only to be on the left side. All of it was going to end up being Uncommon or Rare grade, so it didn't really matter. It needed to look flashy, be in good condition, and have a few runes that could activate. That was the baseline, and Sal was more than capable of delivering on that.

When the blueprint was done, Sal smiled and sent the information into the queue. The printer would get to work on the attachment pieces, using some void metal and steel. It gave him a little bit of time to work on a plan of action for the breeches. They were gaudy as hell, so Sal decided to recreate them in a different fabric, but kept all the runes and etchings in the same style. Rather than having them stop below the knee, Sal extended the cut to snatch at the ankle instead.

He looked at the pauldron for a moment before silently compromising again in the name of style. Blathnaid would have either been proud or furious with him. He wasn't really sure as he started ideating on knee guards that matched the style of the pauldron. *Something that would allow the user to use their knees as a weapon? Or just something that looked good?*

Sal spent far too long overthinking that one design piece when the sound of beeping behind him pulled him back to reality. The 3D printer had finished, and Sal could see a collection of smooth buttons resting on a metal plate at the base of the machine. Beside them were two sections of the obsidian collar that would hold the cloak. He already knew the tray underneath the laser held all the obsidian fragments he'd be using later.

Sal withdrew the tray and dumped the fine dust into a container, making sure to cover his mouth and nose in the process. He didn't want to accidentally inhale any of it. When it was all secure, he popped the tray back into the machine and loaded it up with void metal and steel, wondering whether it would create a new type of alloy by mixing the two. It didn't matter, though. He could forcibly refine it with essence if it screwed up at some point throughout the process. The machine whirred for a few moments before emitting a happy beep and locking the hatch. When the lasers started up, it was enough to cause a series of flashes in the carriage interior, mimicking a small lightning storm.

With a smile on his face, Sal moved back to the workspace in front of him and started working on the tunic. The machines were saving him a lot of time, but there was still a lot for him to do before he was even close to being finished. As he looked at the pieces together, he realized it was the first time he had tried combining a load of prefabricated pieces. The excitement welling up inside him made him curious about what would happen when he Appraised the result.

CHAPTER 5: UNKNOT

Petro had to do a double take when he noticed Sal walking into the room. He held a tablet in his hand and had been talking to one of the floor staff when he saw the new uniform Sal wore. His eyes started to glow as he silently used Appraisal on the waistcoat. "Give me a second, Morgan." He excused himself from the auction employee as he walked over to Sal, who had a wide smile.

"So, this is either going to be a very good reaction or a terrible one. I'm ready for the verdict." Sal laughed as he gave an about-turn so his father could see the engraving and stitching on the back. The shimmering effect had worked out beautifully and contrasted perfectly with the violet hues and black satin. It created an effect that looked like a sprawling cosmos with a collection of glittering stars. It was still somewhat muted unless you focused on it, as your attention would inevitably be drawn to the connecting lines that built out the runes.

Petro gripped his son's shoulders and stared at the back of the waistcoat with wide eyes. His silver irises glowed as they took in each detail of the materials and the runes. "How on earth…" He turned to face Sal's front. His reaction upon seeing the buttons was priceless, with both his eyebrows shooting up in surprise. "Obsidian?"

He said it like it was a question, but Sal knew he was just discovering the full specifications of the new uniform.

"And the Feather attribute? But this one on the back…I can't for the life of me understand what it means. It looks similar to the interior of the breastplate, but altered somewhat."

Sal smiled as he gave his father a reassuring nod. "Correct. It's an evolutionary rune. Means that the uniform will evolve over time as it absorbs essence in the atmosphere. I've been adding them to pretty much everything lately, including that Rare-grade breastplate. What do you think? Is it too flashy or am I able to wear it on the shop floor?"

Petro laughed humorlessly as he shook his head. "I'm more inclined to ask you to make some for me and your mother. This quality is exceptional. How did you manage to do this with alterations to your uniform? I can't detect a trace of the original materials."

Sal smiled as he offered a slight shrug. "I might have gotten excited when I found the dreadcloth. It's all completely new. I got the shipment of obsidian glass from Quest Academy. It was the remnants of the hulker that we took down."

Petro looked at Sal as though he were crazy. "Dreadcloth on a uniform? That feels like a monumental waste…but, you could sell something like this in a heartbeat. The details are extraordinary." He traced his finger along the edge of one of the obsidian buttons. "It's a Rare grade, isn't it?"

Sal nodded, the bright smile not leaving his face. "Yes. Feather and Reflect are the main features, but there's also Attune in there too. Combined with the two runes, for self-replenishment and evolution. It's in the upper tiers of Rare grade. Should allow for me to pick up heavy boxes with ease, and if someone attacks, it will be sent straight back at them."

Petro stared at Sal before shaking his head. "I don't think I've ever come across the Attune attribute. What does it do?"

"Essence refinement and control. Increases both of them, helps people fine-tune their outputs." Sal gestured at the waistcoat. "It's a set with the pants, which gets synergy and boosts the output of all the attributes."

Petro put a hand to his face as he continued to shake his head. "We just left you for like three hours. How did you manage to make something like this in such a short space of time?" A moment of silence passed between them before Petro's eyes widened. "Wait, would that work for your mother? The Attune attribute?"

Sal put up his hands to calm his father down. "Wait now, before we launch into stuff like that. I wanted to have a chat with the two of you. It's about my Skill Master ability. I'm obviously incredibly happy to make whatever gear you want, and I can do a lot more than that…but now isn't the right time to talk about it."

Petro grimaced as he looked over his shoulder to where the staff were getting the last pieces ready in the display cases. "Come on, give me the short version then. What's the 'more' that you're talking about?"

Sal looked at his father dead in the eye and kept a straight face. "I learned how to unknot the weaves of other people, in a safe manner. It means I can help people unlock more of their powers, without harming them."

Petro stared at Sal for a moment. "You're joking, aren't you?" He sighed as he looked at the main centerpiece. "Should we put the breastplate there? If it has the evolutionary trait like you've said, then we're going to blow a massive hole in Shade's wallet in an hour." Petro looked back at Sal and gave him a reassuring squeeze on the shoulder. "I know you were excited about making a new uniform, so don't worry about all that other stuff. The breastplate is already more than enough."

Sal's face broke into a wide smile. "Sure you don't want to come down and have a look at what I was working on?"

Petro faltered. "You didn't…" Without so much as another word, he dropped his tablet onto a nearby display and set off toward the corridor leading to Sal's new workplace.

Sal followed him, laughing. "Careful, you'll hurt yourself if you rush."

Petro didn't even glance back as he took the stairs two at a time leading down to the former storage. "Keep talking like that and we'll find out if your Reflect ability can stop a slap." When he got to the base of the stairs, he straightened and looked around in confusion. "Where am I supposed to be looking?"

Sal moved past him and pulled at the door to the carriage. "In here. But you might have a bit of an issue with the Appraisal."

Petro chuckled as he peered into the carriage. "You're really testing me today, aren't you? I may be getting older, but I can still Appraise—" He stared at Sal's project in utter disbelief. One factor probably was because Sal had combined each of the pieces into a single entity. But the likely reason Petro was lost for words was because he couldn't Appraise it.

Sal smiled as he leaned against the side of the carriage, enjoying his father's reaction. "So, we can make a secret deal here. If you're open to it."

Petro's attention snapped away from the piece and he looked at Sal in confusion. "What sort of deal are you scheming up?" A smile crept onto his face. "Did you put some sort of blocker on it that stops Appraisal?"

Sal shook his head. "You told me before that you can't Appraise higher than the mid-tier of Epic grade." He nodded meaningfully at his creation. "But my deal would allow you to Appraise it. You just need to trust me."

Petro looked between the gear and Sal, frowning. "Of course I trust you. Just tell me what I need to do." He let out an exasperated sigh. "If this is an elaborate prank, I'm going to kill you and confiscate that uniform. It would probably fit me." He added that last part with a smile.

Sal activated his Skill Master ability and looked at his father's internal weave. He had it memorized from a young age, and he was sad to see that it had somehow managed to regress slightly in the months since he had seen his father. A few additional knots had formed, likely cutting off Petro's ability to properly Appraise. It had been years since he had done a Legendary-grade Appraisal, and now he was struggling to identify the Epics. If it continued, the Argento Auction House's prospects would suffer severely.

With a gentle smile, Sal tried to reassure his father. "I'm not going to do anything too dramatic. I just want to dust off some of the cobwebs." After confirming that his father was willing to see it through, Sal got to work with unknotting the recently formed knots on the edges of his weave. A memory of his conversation with Divinity back on his first day popped into his head. The ability he had replicated from his father wasn't Appraisal, but something called All Sight. It meant that his father had a much stronger ability than what he was using it for. Which also meant that by undoing a few small knots, it would give him a stronger capacity with Appraisal, without opening the other aspects of All Sight.

Just as Sal was going to stop with the second knot, his Perfect weave made some suggestions. It was an instinctive thing, and Sal followed the process because he agreed with what it was highlighting. All the practice he had with the simulation orb had made these minor changes incredibly easy.

Petro gasped as he clutched at the carriage door. His other hand moved to his collar, where he pulled at his tie to give himself more space to breathe. When he looked at Sal in shock, his eyes were flickering between colors. The best comparison Sal could come up with was the tempest that was present within the obsidian shards. Petro's eyes seemed to contain a storm with lightning sparking between the irises.

Sal realized that he might have gone a little too far. "If it hurts or it isn't manageable, let me know and I can undo that!"

Petro shook his head. "Don't…you dare try to take this away." He gasped as he blinked repeatedly, gazing up at the glass panes above. "What the fuck is happening?" There was no anger in his tone as he started to laugh, looking at everything around him as though seeing them for the first time. "This is…extraordinary. Is this what you experienced when you used my Appraisal? Seeing information on people, too?"

Sal's heart froze at those words. His father was describing Analysis, not Appraisal. "What did you say?"

Petro pointed at his eyes, laughing. "I can see a jumbled mess of information, but I'm making sense of it…it'll just take me a few minutes. Like, I'm getting this whole threat profile when I look at you. You've apparently learned some martial arts in the last while?" He shook his head in wonder as he studied his son.

His once silver irises no longer flickered, but instead held the stormy feature permanently. "You weren't lying…you can help people with their powers?" He turned around until his eyes locked onto the piece Sal had made. "Whoa."

Sal smiled. "Glad you're able to Appraise it. Should we bring it up and put it on the central display? You can run through the Appraisal live for the audience. I wouldn't want to steal the limelight."

Petro readjusted his tie, pulling it back into place with a wide grin. "Salvatore, I cannot put into words how I feel right now." He looked over at Sal with a proud expression. "This makes up for all the terrible Father's Day gifts over the years."

Sal smiled along with his father, but his brain was firing on all cylinders. *His father was somehow able to use a version of Appraisal and Analysis? Threat profiling was only a thing with the Analysis ability, and his father was not only able to use it, but could also control the overwhelming amount of information being thrown at him? Was it because it was his natural ability that he had a higher level of mastery?* Every thought resulted in more questions for Sal, but there were no regrets. He glanced at his father and it was clear that he was elated by the changes to his weave.

Petro clapped his hands together. "I think I need a drink. There's no way I can do this auction sober. Want to join me?"

Sal gave his father a sideways glance. "Are you really trying to get us killed? You know that she'll find us and murder us if we start drinking."

Petro grinned as he gave Sal a playful nudge. "Come on, it's not every day that your son makes an Epic-grade piece of equipment to annihilate his father's enemies, while simultaneously giving his dear old dad a massive power boost. How long does this last, by the way? Will it wear off after a few minutes? Would be great if you could do it again just before the auction kicks off."

Sal stared at his father. He realized he needed to start telling people in advance that it was a permanent change. "It won't wear off. It's a permanent improvement."

Petro's face blanched at the sudden understanding. He stared into the empty space in front of him before a nervous laugh escaped his lips. "Yeah, I definitely need a drink."

"One drink," Sal corrected as he crossed his arms, smiling.

Petro looked at him blankly before chuckling. "I wonder how long I'll be able to keep this a secret from her."

Sal winced slightly. "Eh, probably not for very long. Your eyes are a different color now."

Petro reached into the carriage to pull down the hook holding the new equipment. He gave Sal an almost delirious smile as he gestured with his head toward the stairs. "To the bar, my son. We need to celebrate my new powers and mourn the sexy silvers." With that, he marched proudly toward the stairs.

Sal closed the door to the carriage and followed his father, laughing. "Could be worse…mine turn purple when I'm Crafting."

CHAPTER 6: CONCERN

"Does it hurt anywhere?" Sophia asked as she gripped her husband's head with both of her hands, peering into his eyes as though it might uncover some terrible truth that they hadn't noticed before.

Petro tried to shake his head, but it was locked in the vise that was his wife's hands. "No, Soph. I promise, I feel better than I have in years. It's like a blockage has been cleared in my head and I can finally see much clearer."

Sophia shook her head as she looked over at Sal. "Are you insane, Salvatore? You can't just test your powers on your father. Did Quest give you the go-ahead to use it on people like this?" She finally let go of Petro as she placed her hands on her hips and looked at Sal with gritted teeth. "And can you undo it? If he gets some sort of reaction to it, can you bring him back to normal?"

"I can undo it if necessary. I can also replicate a Healing ability that would let me heal any damage that happened, but I can assure you that it's perfectly fine. I unknotted Upgrade's weave and she was in a much worse condition than Dad. Even Divinity and Blathnaid. Quest didn't ask me to undo any of the changes as they worked out for the best." Sal sidestepped the question about whether he had Quest's permission to perform the weave adjustments, and instead just hit her with all the other facts. "They have me working on a simulation orb to create new weaves and learn how to use Skill Master, helping hundreds of students reach their potential. I just wanted to help the people I care about most."

Okay, that last part might have been laying it on too thick, but behind Sophia, Petro gave him a wink and a thumbs-up. The effect was immediate; Sophia's expression softened as she looked off to one side.

"I'm sorry, Sal. I didn't mean to snap at you. I just wasn't prepared for…" She gestured wildly at their new exhibit that he Crafted, then his uniform, and finally at Petro's new eye color. "All of this! It's a lot to process, and I let my nerves get the better of me." She took a steadying breath before looking at Sal calmly. "Just please be more careful and talk to me before you do anything like that again, okay?"

Sal nodded and tried to look reproachful. If he smiled too quickly, she'd end up killing him. "I was telling Dad that I want to do the same for you, if you're up for it. Maybe give it time to let Dad settle into his new powers and then make your decision. It's still a very closely guarded secret that I can do this, so we can't really tell other people about it."

Sophia smiled as she looked at Petro with a raised eyebrow. "I can already tell that this oaf is going to pretend he's fine even if it's torturous. Let me have a think about it, and I'll get back to you. I wouldn't say no to a wardrobe change though. I love the color you got with the cloth." She shook her head before looking at Sal with a sigh. "And this simulation orb thing…are they paying you for it or taking advantage of your goodwill?"

Sal smiled and spread his hands. "Got a royalty deal for every student who uses one of my improved weaves. Was sitting on close to twenty thousand Q-Cred before I started spending on preparations for the tower."

Sophia nearly choked as she looked at Sal in shock. "Twenty thousand? You could buy a house with that!" She turned to look at Petro. "Did you know about this?"

Petro nodded, but when he saw his wife's face, he turned it into a shake instead. "No, first time I'm hearing about it." He glanced at Sal, smiling. "Well done on the royalty part, son."

Sophia sighed in exasperation before she moved toward the door. "We're opening in twenty minutes. Could you wear glasses or something to disguise the fact that your eyes are literal pools of lightning?"

Petro perked up at that. "Do we like the new eye color?" He used a playful voice that didn't improve Sophia's mood in the slightest.

She shook her head and left, leaving father and son in the room together.

"I think that went reasonably well," Sal started before his father burst into laughter.

"Good call on not going to the bar. That would have been worse." Petro chuckled as he lifted his tablet to check his own reflection. "I'm not even angry. The new color looks pretty damn good. Won't need to change up my suits." He gave Sal a sly wink. "Don't worry about your mother. She's just concerned because she doesn't understand what's happening. I don't think you want to know what sort of threat levels I was reading during that conversation."

Sal smiled in return. "You know that you've somehow picked up the Analysis ability, right? That's not an aspect of Appraisal." He paused for a moment, not sure how to bring up the topic. When he saw his father's curious expression, he decided to just be honest. "When Divinity showed me the future of my Skill Registration, I was using your ability…but instead of Appraisal, it was a different name."

"All Sight?" Petro guessed with a raised eyebrow. "That's the term they put on my registration years ago. I told them that it only manifested as Appraisal, and that was good enough for the Hunter Bureau. They needed people to value the goods coming out of the portals, so it was easier than trying to push me into other areas of Support."

Sal just stared at him. "You knew? How come you never said anything about it?"

Petro smiled at Sal. "Well, when you started talking about seeing weaves in people, I was certain that you had All Sight, just like me. When my ability first manifested, I was able to see all sorts of stuff, like lights and patterns in people. It didn't make much sense at the time, and I ignored it to focus on mastering Appraisal." He gave a playful wince. "And then you started replicating weaves and I was no longer certain about us having the same power. But I'm pretty sure it was because of All Sight that you're able to see patterns so clearly."

Sal shook his head. "But I was using your weave without any of the knots, and it didn't give me any of the Analysis stuff. Like, it was just really advanced Appraisal."

Petro grinned. "Just like I taught you. All the control techniques I showed you likely shifted your perspective to never look at what the ability fully offers." He chuckled as he spread his hands wide. "But seriously, Sal. Don't listen to me…I haven't a clue when it comes to Skill Weaves. You're likely learning far more about them than I'll ever know."

Sal wasn't sure how to process that information. *Had he been conditioned to only use some aspects of his parents' powers?* In a way, it made sense, but Sal wanted to put his parents' weaves into the simulation orb to see what information it gave. He'd need to wait until he was back at the academy, unless they sent over the equipment to his new workspace. Grant had been eager to get him working on more weaves, but Quest had run interference on that, insisting Sal have some time to himself during the break.

"Are you going to stare into space, or are you going to help us get ready to open? We're going to have to mingle in the bar for the early arrivals." Petro laughed and reached over to squeeze Sal's shoulder. "And seriously, don't worry about me, okay? The moment I feel anything out of the ordinary, I'll let you know, and you can revert the changes. Deal?"

Sal smiled as he looked at his father. "Deal."

"Excellent. Now…are you ready to prime some rich bastards?" Petro asked with an excited clap of his hands. "We need to put in the groundwork to build excitement for our main exhibit!"

"Let's go." Sal pulled the door open for his father. "And we can have a little drink to mourn the sexy silvers."

Petro laughed as he led the way to the bar. "I don't know, I think she's a fan. There's hope of you having a sibling after all these years."

"An Epic grade?" Felix Hawne asked in a conspiratorial whisper, his eyes locked onto Sal in disbelief. "And Petro verified the claim?"

Sal gazed around warily before nodding slowly. "I saw it myself and couldn't believe it. It's like an entire set combined into one piece. Seems to really favor an Offense style, but I can't be certain. You can check it out at the center display, and I think you'll agree that it looks fabulous. I don't want to steal my father's thunder, but I managed to Appraise some of the attributes…and it's ridiculously good."

Felix stepped closer and gestured with his right hand for a person to come and join their conversation. A slender man joined the rotund Felix, looking slightly perplexed at his summoning. Without missing a beat, Felix turned to the new-comer. "Looks like we might need to combine bids to push out the competition. Young Argento here is telling me that there's an Epic grade on the card for to-night! Offense style, too."

The newcomer's eyes widened as he pulled his shoulder forward to close the gap and give them some privacy. "That does sound very promising. Is there a reserve from the seller?"

Sal smiled at him and shook his head. "This is the crazy part. There's no out-side seller on this piece. It was part of a collection that had been written off by Shade. He didn't see the value in Restoration and didn't pay the fees."

Sal pretended to look somewhat conflicted as he looked around. He knew Shade wasn't there yet, but still wanted to put on a performance. "Turns out, my parents have been working on a new Restoration technique, and they found out that the set transformed when put together. They got some assistance from a

Crafter, and the end result is the piece on display. It's completely owned by the Argento Auction House…but since it's such a sensitive topic, I'd ask you not to mention it to Shade. He'll likely be devastated to know that the pieces he walked away from ended up being an Upper Epic-grade set."

"Upper?" Felix repeated in shock, turning to look at the slender fellow with a nervous laugh. "And you're positive it was goods from Shade's portfolio?" The laugh became less nervous and turned into something a lot more devious. "Serves the bastard right."

Sal nodded emphatically. "Did I not mention it was Upper Epic grade? Oh, my apologies… It likely slipped my mind in the excitement. Yes, we double and triple-checked the set. Each and every piece is something from Shade's defaulted portfolio. When my father contacted him to see if he'd like to honor his payments, Shade insisted that we keep them to mitigate the costs of Restoration and Appraisal. I doubt he's aware of what he's just thrown away."

The slender man shot out a hand to Sal. "Theo Graten. An absolute pleasure. I work with Felix from time to time on acquiring collectors' items. We've been big fans of the Argento Auction House for years now, and would love to arrange a private viewing, if that would be okay?"

Sal nodded, smiling. "Of course. You likely have met my mother, Sophia? She's over there. If you tell her that you were talking to me, she'll make sure you get a private viewing with my father. He'll walk you through the full Appraisal. You need to promise me that you'll tell me what you think of the Stealth attributes…they look incredible."

"Stealth attributes?" Felix paled as he looked at Theo with wide eyes.

Sal smiled as he apologized hastily. "Ah, sorry…didn't I mention that? I was sure I talked about it. Or was it with someone else?" He looked over at another group of people with a conflicted expression.

Felix followed his gaze and visibly gulped. "Excuse us. We're going to set up that meeting with your father. Thanks for your help!" And as fast as he could manage, Felix Hawne moved over to Sophia, dabbing at his forehead with a napkin.

Sal grinned as he looked around the room, picking out the next batch of people to drive up the bidding war. Spreading the information about Shade was also going to inevitably get back to him, which would result in a number of people bidding out of spite as well as desire. It was going to be a fun night.

CHAPTER 7: OPPORTUNITY

"Ladies and gentlemen, I just wanted to thank you for your extraordinary patronage. We have not had such interest in an exhibit in years! Many of you have become wise to our secret piece that we were going to hold on until the end of the auction…but with how much excitement there is, we'll move it up on the list. Your private bids have been secured, but we'll be showing it off before the intermission to give everyone else a fair chance of putting in their own offers." Petro was in excellent form as he stood on a makeshift stage in the center of the main hall.

"Now, before we start off with the pieces that are listed on your cards, I think it's only fair to tell you that our last piece is also worth sticking around for. I'll only say two words relating to it." Petro smiled at the crowd, who stared at him in expectation. Holding up his hand, he extended a finger in time with each word. "Evolutionary. Rune."

A collection of gasps moved through the crowd, and consortiums grouped together to discuss bidding strategies. It was clearly the consolation prize for the main piece that Sal had Crafted with all of Shade's discarded items. The Raregrade breastplate wasn't going to be a showstopper, but it would still showcase to the attendees that the Argento Auction House was capable of putting out quality pieces of equipment.

Sal smiled at his mother. "Doubt we'd get that reaction for the creepy doll." He took a quick step to the side to avoid the swipe of her hand. A playful smile was on her lips as she looked at him sideways.

"Well played with Felix and Theo. They were practically frothing at the mouth. Minimum bid is up at half a million, in no short part thanks to you." Sophia congratulated her son with a wink. "Your father thinks he can stoke the fires to get more, but I think he should settle for the five hundred thousand." She left the sentence there as though asking for Sal's perspective.

Sal looked at the crowd for a few moments before shaking his head. "If it was a flat auction, then I'd likely agree with you. These people are out for blood, and I think they'll happily drive the price up if they think Shade is going to top the bid. Even if they can't win, they can make him bleed all the way to the finish line."

Sophia smiled. "Nice to see you haven't lost your touch. Good insights. The real question is whether Shade will make a scene and secure his fate, or whether he'll play it professional."

Sal frowned as he continued to observe the crowd. "Do you mind if I put on my visor?"

Sophia made a reluctant noise before sighing and giving him a nod. "Knock yourself out, but don't make a habit of it. You're perfectly fine at Appraisal without one, and we don't want people to think that you're losing your touch."

Sal reached down to his invisible belt and withdrew the tracker that popped into view. He didn't pause before slipping it over his right eye, activating it and studying the crowd. Deduction and Insight were going to be very useful when gauging their sentiments. It also helped him determine who was who as it cross-referenced all the databases that had been loaded onto the tracker.

"Something else you made in twenty minutes?" Sophia asked in disbelief as she looked at the tracker on Sal's head. "Don't suppose you plan on mass-producing them? Would definitely reduce your father's workload."

Sal ignored her as he moved through the crowd, looking for his target. It only took a few moments before he found him. "Shade is here. He's in a transparent state, up on the glass walkway."

"He's using his ability at our auction?" Sophia's voice held an edge that Sal recognized all too well. "Give me that."

Sal didn't hesitate as he unclipped the visor and handed it to his mother. He was curious what she was going to do with that information, but he was sure that she'd play it cool.

Before Sal or Sophia could react, Petro clapped his hands together from the stage. He raised his hand and pointed to the walkway. "Apologies, Shade. But we don't allow guests to lurk in the shadows. If you wish to partake in the auction, you'll need to join everyone else down on the main floor."

"Oh fuck." Sophia spoke before quickly covering her mouth to stifle a giggle. "He's panicked. Like, I can see it on his face, but this thing is telling me what his body language means." She took it off and handed it back to Sal with a delighted expression. "I want one of those. Screw appearances—that thing is a gold mine!"

Petro stared at Shade defiantly. "Yes, I can see you. Now please, come down and join everyone else. We're about to start the auction."

When Sal put the tracker back on, he could see that Shade had repositioned to the bar area. He picked up a glass of wine from a table before deactivating his ability, revealing himself with a fake smile.

"Ah, I heard my name mentioned." He laughed as he raised a glass. "Hopefully you weren't saying anything untoward." His entrance from the bar confused a number of people, but Petro just smiled.

"Nothing untoward, Shade. We were just talking about auctioning off all the equipment you never paid for. Shall we start the bidding on entry number thirty-two?" Petro dramatically pulled a silver cloth off one of the display cases at the front. It revealed the Rare-grade breastplate that Sal had fixed up in the Restoration office.

Sophia chuckled under her breath. "Your father is definitely riled up. So much for keeping that last piece as a surprise."

Smiling, Petro gestured at the breastplate. "First up on the defaulted products from the Delvers Guild, we have a destroyed breastplate with two incomplete runes, a missing core, a broken rune, and a gaping fissure going through the stomach section." He paused for a moment as he raised a finger. "Well, that's what it was before our team got their hands on it. Having been told to salvage it to recoup our service fees, we decided to fix it up instead. You're now looking at the Breastplate of the Unyielding, a Rare-grade breastplate, with a perfectly functional Barrier rune. Protection from every direction, including your blind spots! But Petro, you said there was no core embedded into it? That's why we've fixed it with an essence replenishment rune, taking atmospheric essence to charge itself up." Petro told the story of the piece with a modulation of his tone, going from a whisper to a crescendo, capturing the audience's attention with every word.

"So, we have Barrier, Reflect, and it can recharge…big deal, right? Well, how good do you think it will be after it evolves? What will it look like when it gets to Legendary grade? Oh, yes. You heard that right. We've Appraised this extraordinary piece and can see it going through Unique, Epic, and into Legendary grade. Conservatively, we're looking at an addition of at least one new ability with each evolution, but our staff thinks it could be as much as two. So, shall we hear some bids for the Breastplate of the Unyielding…a piece that will eventually be a Legendary grade?"

The entire floor descended into chaos at the mention of evolution. This wasn't even the premier exhibit. Everyone took out the tablets they were issued and input offers. Their funds would be locked for the purposes of bidding, before being refunded if they were unsuccessful.

Petro sighed deeply as he looked at the numbers on his tablet. "If we don't see higher numbers than this, I might be forced to withhold the item for my son. He's the top rank in Quest Academy and training to be a Hero. Show me some offers that will make me have no regrets."

Sophia snorted as she shook her head. "I knew he'd find a way to boast about you." She smiled as she showed her tablet to Sal. "Evolutionary truly changes the price point…the promise of future potential really gets them excited."

Sal stared at the number in surprise. "Still, isn't two hundred thousand a bit ridiculous for something like that?"

Sophia shook her head again. "Not at all. You can't put a price on hope." She looked over at Petro with a smile on her face. "I haven't seen him enjoy an auction so much in a long time. Thanks for this, Salvatore."

Sal looked between his mother and father. "I'll be honest, I'm kinda tempted to run down to the workshop and make another one of them. This thing is going to go on all night, so might as well milk them dry if they're willing to spend stupid amounts of money."

Sophia blinked in surprise. "You can make them from just raw materials? I thought you had to rework existing stuff."

Sal pointed at his tracker and pulled out the gun from his holster. "Both of these were made from just materials. Oh, and the belt. It turns invisible so nobody asks too many questions about me walking around with a gun." Sal laughed sheepishly at that last part.

Sophia stared at the gun before she slowly looked back up at his face. "How much time do you need? I can make this thing drag on for hours."

Sal shrugged as he thought about it. "Honestly, if it's just another breastplate with the same design…maybe just under an hour. I can brute-force it with essence to speed things up. Is there something that is always in high demand? I could make something else."

Sophia thought about it as she clicked her fingers. After a few seconds, she looked at him as though she had an epiphany. Then she frowned before shaking her head. "I was going to say something ornate or ceremonial. They usually jump at mysterious objects like that, but it's not really a huge earner. Evolutionary runes seem to be a massive hit." She looked at the tablet and smiled. "It's already over three hundred thousand!"

Sal thought about everything he had made so far. *What would be the quickest thing to make that could look good, and potentially carry an evolutionary rune?* He was running through the options when the obvious answer took hold. "Oh. I think I've got it."

Sophia didn't even have time to ask him what he was talking about, because Sal was already rushing off in the direction of his new workshop.

It was obvious what he needed to do. The first time he had come across the evolutionary rune had been on Blink's dagger. The obsidian glass was brittle, but sturdy enough to hold an evolutionary engraving. That would tick the box for ceremonial and non-practical. With a little trickle of essence into the blade, it would have a stormy appearance and look great. Combine that with the fact that it came from a rare form of hulker that primarily existed in lava dungeons, it was almost like a fairy tale for them to sell. Best part was that Sal could replicate the order if it proved to be successful. They could just sell stock based on the prototype, and he could manufacture the rest afterward.

When Sal got to his carriage, he opened the door and plucked a wide and long shard of obsidian glass before starting his concept stage. With Blink's Siphon blade's blueprint in front of his eyes, he started to pour essence into the shard itself to see whether he could make it conform to the design he saw in his head.

With his free hand, he opened the drawer and looked at all the fastenings and small chunks of metal. One of them looked similar enough to gold, so he picked it out. There was also a scrap of satin from his waistcoat pattern. He used that too. All he wanted to do was blend them together with his essence, and then he could take care of the finer details like the engraving.

Just as he was about to add the chunk of metal to the mix, Sal paused. The obsidian was naturally brittle, so he wondered whether he could use hellfire titanium to add in some durability. It also worked more thematically if he used hellfire titanium with a product only available in lava dungeons. With that thought in mind, Sal decided to use the red and black metals for the grip. It wouldn't appear ornate, but it would look menacing. All he needed was an appealing blade, and everything else wouldn't really matter.

With a flick of his wrist, Sal activated his mechanical arm and cut at the side of the glass to create a jagged edge. At the same time, another finger finely ground the blade to increase the sharpness. As more and more of his essence seeped into the blade, the dark glass started to light up with an internal storm. Flickers of lightning made the whole thing come to life, and it looked beautiful.

With a wide smile, Sal rummaged through the chunks of metal in the drawer until he found a jet-black one with red stones embedded in it. Most metals that Sal had worked with became malleable with just a few minutes of massaging it with essence. Hellfire titanium seemed to hate him with a burning passion, as it resisted for nearly twenty minutes. His perseverance eventually won out and he was finally able to create a grip for the obsidian dagger.

As Sal performed all these rapid movements and changes to the dagger, Mythcrafter seemed to be going insane as it tried to keep up. Perfect was also trying to catch up to everything Sal was attempting. Their influences were still welcome, as Mythcrafter made suggestions to improve the overall design, like removing the jagged edge and making it just a sharp blade. It also showed him how to lace the satin into a nice design that made the dagger appear more ornate and professional. The weaving was like a braid, and Perfect had him master it in under five minutes.

With the hellfire titanium already set and cooled, and the satin crossing in a pattern that revealed segments of the glowing red rocks, complete with an obsidian button molded into a small pommel…Sal was ready to start the engraving. He could have used the engraver, but it felt like it would take too long. Instead, he pulled up the design from the Siphon blade and started to etch it into the blade with careful scratches. Each of the grooves that he made into the obsidian was white, that he assumed could be polished out at a later point. Sal poured his essence into the runes as he made them, hoping that it would save time at the end.

Another twenty minutes passed as Sal performed a series of checks, making small adjustments with his essence to make final tweaks. There were so many things that were invisible to the naked eye, like balance and sharpness. Perfect and Mythcrafter were able to adjust those values with essence, and Sal gave them full rein. When he stepped back from the dagger, it continued to glow with a low hum of vibration.

Nodding in satisfaction, Sal left the carriage and ran up the stairs to one of the storage rooms. He needed a nice container, and he knew they kept some ornate boxes for jewelry in there. It took him only a few seconds to find a black box with a white cushion interior. It was perfect, especially with the Argento Auction House logo on the lid in a beautiful polished white. The contrasts were perfect and would really draw the eye to the dagger.

With a grin, Sal tucked the box under his arm and made his way back to the carriage. The dagger was still glowing, so rather than waiting for it to cool down, he put it in the ornate box and closed the lid. He'd have to wait for it to settle on the way back to the auction.

He just hoped that he hadn't taken too long.

CHAPTER 8: DAGGER

When Sal got back to the main hall, he saw that the stage was empty. There was a momentary panic before he heard the sounds of laughter and chatter in the bar. With a heavy sigh of relief, Sal walked in that direction, cracking the lid of the box open to see whether the dagger had settled. A bright glow pierced through the edges in the dim lighting, causing Sal to grimace.

Just as he was about to step into the bar, a figure appeared in front of him with a hand extended, holding the edge of the box.

Sal glanced up in surprise, only to see the guildmaster of the Delvers Guild staring at the box intently.

Shade eventually looked up at him with a curious expression. "What on earth creates a glow like that?" His lips curled into a smile as he pulled at the lid, which revealed the light again. "Perhaps another memento of mine that has been repurposed?"

With a polite smile on his face, Sal placed his palm on the top of the lid and closed it gently. "This isn't for sale, I'm afraid." He didn't elaborate on what was inside, or the nature of the glow. Instead, he nodded politely to Shade before sidestepping him.

The guildmaster reappeared in front of him. "I don't think I made myself clear. I would like to know what is in that box. This is an auction house, so I would imagine that anything dressed up in a decorative box has a price." He looked off to one side as though thinking about his next words. "I'm sure you've heard from your parents that we've had a strained relationship over the years. I'd prefer to have a good one with the Argento Auction House, be it the current generation, or the next."

He offered a warm smile to Sal as he tapped the box with his finger. "I've been found chasing my tail this whole night, and watching from the sidelines as everyone takes out their frustrations on me. Yet, it looks like I'm the first person to see this exhibit."

Sal was about to insist that the item wasn't for sale, when Shade interrupted him with a raised hand.

"Don't." His warm smile twitched for a moment before he continued. "I'd like to leave here with some shred of pride. So, would you please humor this old man and let me buy this piece?"

Even without the tracker, Sal could see that the entire thing was a front. Shade was far from helpless. He also didn't value things like dignity or pride. A guild with a massive casualty list, all throwing themselves to their deaths to get loot for Shade. It wasn't a compelling narrative. No amount of pity garnering would change Sal's opinion of him, and that was without any of the bias that came from his parents and their business dealings with him.

Shade was the guildmaster of the place that ruined Vanessa's career. He was also the one trying to recruit Anna Sakura with a half-broken Rare-grade gauntlet. Sal had no intention of ever dealing with this man.

"Unfortunately, I don't have the authority to make deals like this. You'd need to speak with my father if you'd like to bid on any items outside of the auction selection. This piece still needs to be fully Appraised, and I hoped to get it completed during the intermission. If you'd like to arrange a private viewing, you can arrange it with my mother, Sophia." Sal was professional and layered his words with an apologetic tone. He said all the right words, but both men knew that the other wasn't genuine.

Shade straightened his back as he looked Sal in the eye. "I was curious to know what type of person could get the top spot in Quest Academy. I thought it might be an overwhelming strength, but it looks like you're just a devious bastard." He smiled as he tilted his head slightly. "Sweet words filled with malice. How many necks did you need to step on to claim the top spot?"

Sal's smile didn't falter in the slightest. "Any chance of you going back to snooping around in the shadows? It was a more relaxed atmosphere when you were hiding." He moved again, this time walking more purposefully toward the bar before a thought struck him.

Turning around to face Shade, he smiled. "Also, we have an open bar for this event. Please don't steal the wine glasses from the other guests. I don't care if it's to protect that precious pride or dignity…stealing isn't a good look for a guildmaster."

Shade's laughter sent a chill down Sal's spine, but he didn't dwell on it. With another creak of the lid, Sal saw that the glow was still emanating from the dagger. It was certainly taking its time. Sal glanced around the room. His father was talking to a number of people in an excited voice, clearly telling a story about one of the exhibits or building rapport. His mother was helping the bar staff with the drink orders of the attendees. There was a small stage to the side that was empty. Usually, it was for showcasing raffle lots, but they weren't hosting anything like that this evening.

Sal smiled as he moved over to the stage area, catching his father's eye as he passed. When he got to the stage, Petro had disengaged from the group and followed him.

"Should I ask what you have cooked up?" Petro asked in a hushed tone, not able to keep the mirth from his voice.

Sal grinned as he placed the box on the podium. "How do you feel about a mystery box event? How many of these people are familiar with a Crafting cooldown period?"

Petro chuckled as he shook his head. "Excellent angle. My guess is zero. You're taking lead on this one, though. Show me what you've got."

"Thanks, Dad." Sal stood behind the box, looking over at his mother meaningfully and gesturing at the lights. She took the hint immediately and dimmed them, causing the guests to look around in confusion. Sal opened the box in front of him, causing the glow of the still vibrating dagger to fill the room.

"Good evening, everyone. My name is Salvatore Argento, Petro and Sophia's son. I've had the pleasure of speaking with some of you tonight, and I got the distinct impression that there was some disappointment." Sal started off slowly, putting on a pained expression as he shook his head regretfully. "It's a hard fact that only one person leaves with the winning bid for the special items, so I wanted to level the playing field somewhat. We have a new supplier who has given us an extraordinary offer…that we'd like to share with our best patrons."

Sal gestured at the glowing dagger that was still as vibrant as ever. The crowd had started to gather around it, looking at it in a mixture of confusion and curiosity. Some had expressions of outright awe, and Sal made a special note to remember who those people were. "We've secured a supplier who has not only gone to the depths of the deepest lava dungeons, but have gone a step further and hunted down the rarest of deep-dwelling monsters…the obsidian hulker. Famed for their storm-infused skin, our supplier has taken that glass and fused it with only the finest hellfire titanium. A touch of satin to show the delicate elegance amid a raging storm. Only ten of these daggers exist."

Sal smiled as he looked at their faces. "But I can read your thoughts almost plain as day. It's just another dagger, Salvatore. We've seen stuff like this everywhere; what is the gimmick this time?" He raised a hand, with the smile becoming wider. "Well, to quote a famous man in these hallowed halls…two words."

Petro chuckled as he shook his head, smiling. "Bastard," he muttered under his breath.

Some of the more attentive guests locked onto the clue immediately and moved closer to the box with an opening bid, but Sal wanted to make sure everyone was on the same page. He held up his fingers just as his father had done earlier. "Evolutionary. Runes."

With an abrupt clap of his hands, he seemed to snap everyone out of their stupor. "Each dagger is made specifically by our new supplier. They've committed to giving us ten in total, with this being the first iteration. As it's the first one, and you've all been incredible sports, we'll raffle off this first blade. The other nine can be bid on through your tablets once my father sets up the requisition order. Appraisal information will follow."

A smattering of applause welcomed Sal back to the floor when he came down from the small stage. As though timing its debut, the dagger stopped glowing just before Sophia was going to turn up the lights. The infused essence within the obsidian blade caused a series of white flashes to pour through the darkness as it lay menacingly on the white cushion. The rough edges that Sal had worked on were nowhere to be found. It was genuinely beautiful—so much so, that Sophia refrained from turning up the lights. Everyone stared at the box, as though transfixed by what they were seeing.

Name	Storm Strike
Origin	Crafted
Age	New
Grade	Rare

Materials	Refined Mythcrafter Essence | Hellfire Titanium | Obsidian | Perfect Essence
Attributes	Shock: Paralyzes targets cut with the blade. Nullify: Cuts off essence flow when embedded into a target. Thunder: Emits a thunderous sound when thrown, causing fear effect.
Abilities	Shock | Nullify | Thunder
Runes	Essence Replenishment Rune Evolutionary Rune
Power Source	External Essence
Evolution	Yes - 0%
Quality	Perfect
Condition	100%
Value	Est. $125,000.00 – $160,000.00

Sal unconsciously let out a whistle as he started to Appraise the dagger. It wasn't bad for a rushed job, but he knew that without Perfect, Mythcrafting, and great materials like hellfire titanium and the obsidian, that it would not have worked out nearly as well. The main relief was that it hadn't been a complete failure. If the thing had just broken down or turned out to be a shitty Common or Uncommon piece, then he would have humiliated himself and his parents. It would have involved a lot of bullshitting to get them back from something like that.

Petro just looked at him, grinning. "Your mother sent you off just over an hour ago. I'm pretty sure you're going to absolutely destroy the economy of this city." He laughed as he shook his head in disbelief. "I will be there with popcorn every step of the way."

More than a few of the attendees looked at Petro expectantly, as though waiting for him to start off the proceedings. He didn't leave them waiting long as he hopped onto the stage and lifted the dagger for everyone to get a closer look at it.

"Preliminary Appraisal has this piece at a Rare grade. With the excellent materials of obsidian and hellfire titanium, combined with the masterful craftsmanship of our supplier…my judgment is that these daggers could easily pick up an extra attribute when they go through the sub-tiers. You heard me, that's two attributes per grade. If this went all the way to Legendary grade, you could be looking at an additional five or six attributes, on top of the three existing ones!"

Petro held up his three fingers and let it sink in. "We have Shock, Nullify, and Thunder…one dedicated to paralysis of targets, another for taking away the target's essence, which is deadly to demons…and lastly, an area of effect ability that causes fear to targets that hear its scream. The versatility in just a single dagger, that has the capability to evolve into something exceptional…how could you put a price on that?"

He waved at the crowd. "And to think that ten of you here could own one of these fabulous daggers. Or…one of you could own all ten. I said that it would be hard to put a price on it, but we'll put a buy-in of twenty thousand for the raffle. If we don't hit the reserve price from our supplier of four hundred thousand, then we'll need to hold it back, I'm afraid. One ticket per person, and the tablet will randomize the results. You all know the drill." Petro smiled as he held up his tablet. "You'll see it marked down as item number forty-one. The bidding for the remaining nine blades will be at the end of the auction after our main exhibit. Good luck to you all."

Petro stepped down from the stage and approached Sal, smiling. "Simply extraordinary. Loved your pitch, by the way. The whole lava and hellfire thing was inspired."

"Thanks. I learned from the best." Sal laughed as he looked at close to forty people staring at their tablets and talking in hushed voices to their friends. "Four hundred was a little excessive, don't you think?"

Petro shook his head. "The breastplate you made sold for five hundred and forty thousand. The dagger will go higher, and the special exhibit will beat that, too."

Sal just stared at his father. "You know, what I said earlier about not wanting to take a cut from family…"

Petro chuckled as he shrugged. "Between the three pieces that you've worked on today, you've pretty much paid for that special workspace in full." He looked at Sal meaningfully. "You'll get your pay. You know the rules."

CHAPTER 9: THREAT

Sal managed to avoid Shade for the rest of the evening. The guildmaster had been lurking, and using his powers from time to time, as if to test whether Petro could really see him. He had made a few choice comments to the other attendees about the obsidian daggers, claiming that there was no point in joining the bidding process, as he would be taking all of them for the Delvers Guild.

The excitement throughout the auction house was electric. Groups of people were taking turns to inspect the obsidian dagger from every angle. The intermission had to be extended because there was still a line for people waiting to take a look at it. By having a raffle instead of an auction, it got a lot more interest than the intermission events they held in the past. There was a statistically higher chance of winning a bid, just by locking out the big spenders in only allowing them a single ticket.

Petro was busy talking to a few attendees Sal didn't recognize. Their suits weren't the typical formal black-tie style, but were a whole range of different colors. One of the men had wispy white hair and wore a baby-blue blazer. His white shirt had an open collar, but the most attention-grabbing piece was the ornate walking stick in his hand. It was jet-black with an ivory handle. Sal Appraised it for fun, and was delighted to see that it contained a sword. Concealed weapons were up there on his list of favorite things, beside the fake walls and secret rooms. He was delighted that his father insisted on creating one of them in the private workspace.

"Someone might think you're avoiding me." Shade smiled as he suddenly appeared beside Sal. "I was talking to a few of the employees earlier, and George told me something interesting." It was clear that he wanted Sal to ask what the interesting thing was.

Sal stared at him for a few seconds before shrugging. "I'm not the one who can teleport with the shadows. Should I stand near shaded areas to make life easier for you?"

Shade ignored the comment and tapped at his chin with a smile. "George said that you only got that obsidian order in today. That there was a whole big fuss about your homecoming, making sure that all the Crafting equipment was ready." Shade's smile turned into a grin, as though he had just discovered something incredible. "Which tells me that your exotic Crafter, who is delving into lava dungeons…is none other than you. Did your father plant that bullshit story about the hulker?"

Sal returned the smile. "Even if that were true, and I could Craft all those weapons…what makes you think that it would benefit you?"

Shade laughed as he tapped the side of his nose. "Secrets can be quite valuable. Keeping them, especially. Wouldn't want to ruin your little charade here. How many of the guests here would be willing to buy this equipment if they knew it was being made by an eighteen-year-old?"

"All of them," Sal said, genuinely surprised. "Unless you have a good threat up your sleeve, you should probably go. You're only going to embarrass yourself." He gestured off to a dark corner. "Look, it's perfect."

Shade's expression froze for the briefest second before it darkened. "Listen here, you little shit. I'm trying to offer you a hand here, and you seem hell-bent on spitting on it. You're a Support, and your prospects are going to be close to rock bottom when you graduate. If I were in your shoes, I'd start networking with people who can help you in your future as a Hero. The Argento Auction House won't be around forever."

Sal laughed as he shook his head. "Apologies, but I don't want to make deals with someone who can't pay what he owes. I also have my own personal reasons for not wanting to interact with the Delvers Guild. I hope you'll understand." Sal smiled at him before clicking his fingers. "Oh, and if you want to start spreading rumors that I'm Crafting weapons and armor, go for it. Those daggers are only Rare grade…they're nothing to be excited about."

Shade's right eye twitched as he opened his mouth for a second, before closing it and shaking his head. "Only a fool would make an opinion of a person before having a conversation with them. This is our first time meeting, and yet you seem to have your mind made up about me." He spread his hands wide as though he was about to go for an embrace. "All I want is to set up a mutually beneficial agreement. A little Appraisal here, and some Crafting there…and I can ensure you get an officer position in the Delvers Guild. It's not an official offer just yet, but it's not outside the realm of possibility for the next few months. If you apologize for your behavior up until now, then we can talk about drawing up a contract. I respect the abrasive attitude and your principled nature. Us joining hands could be a fresh start for your family and the Delvers, so just think about it."

Sal stared at him as if he had two heads. "I have no desire to join the Delvers Guild. Thanks for your consideration. I need to get back to the auction, so I'll leave you here. I hope you enjoy yourself." Sal shook his head as he walked away. It was ridiculous how out-of-touch Shade was, and how he expected Sal to succumb to such a weak threat. Then, when it didn't work…Shade complimented him and offered an officer track in the guild. It was honestly insane. Sal had thought that Shade was a competent and evil man, but it turned out he was just an idiot.

"Have fun chatting to Shade?" Petro clapped Sal on the shoulder, smiling. "You looked like you were either going to storm off or punch him in the face. What happened?"

Sal laughed as he thought about it. "You know the way they say that you should never meet your Heroes?"

Petro nodded in confusion.

Sal hiked his thumb over his shoulder. "Well, I think this is a case of never meeting your Villains. He threatened me, switched tactics, tried some extortion, then complimented me and offered a non-contract with the Delvers Guild. I can't get my head around it." Sal continued to shake his head in shock. "Honestly, if it wasn't for the fact that he's led teams to their death in the portals, I'd almost feel sorry for him."

Petro shrugged it off as he looked around the room. "Did you check out the concealed sword in the cane? I very nearly asked him where he got it." He pointed at the guy Sal had noticed earlier with the blue blazer and the walking stick. "Lawrence Baron, a very good man to know if you're looking for exotic supplies. His collection is one thing, but it's the supply chain and logistics that are incredible. You throw him a vague term for a piece of material, he'll have it for you the next day."

Sal's eyes widened. "Next day? That can't be possible…like, Maurice is across the street and I doubt he'd be able to get it over here in that space of time."

Petro gave Sal a light slap to the back of the head. "Hey, Maurice got us that prowler blood…be grateful—and with an express delivery, no less."

Sal sighed. "Don't worry, I'll thank him when I next see him."

Petro nodded. "Even though you didn't end up using the prowler blood. I was kinda looking forward to seeing what you came up with. But I'm not going to lie—that obsidian dagger is fantastic. It's the perfect harmony between a beautiful piece and having useful attributes. Usually there's a compromise, but this is perfect on all accounts. Having an evolutionary rune for selling them on the future…it's just magic, Sal." He smiled warmly at his son. "Any idea what you'll do with all your money? There's no way that you'll leave here tonight with less than a million."

Sal chuckled as he shrugged. "We could go with the old reliable and invest it back into the company?"

Petro frowned at Sal. "I know you can't take any wealth from the real world when you go back to Quest Academy. They've got that Q-Cred system." He looked thoughtful for a few seconds as he gazed at Sal in frustration. "Investing in the auction was just a method to give you something to do with the money you earned over the years. I think that you should start looking at using the money for the things you actually want. If it's an entire catalogue of exotic materials from Lawrence Baron, we can arrange that. If it's to buy up the tunnels to your new workspace, then we'll arrange that. Hell, if you want to buy a flying car and get yourself a launchpad…you guessed it, we'll arrange it."

Sal thought about the question as he looked at the room of excited businessmen. "Is there any property for sale in Silver Sanctuary?" He had heard of some of the prices from Barry, of the buildings out in the Reclaimed Zone…but Silver Sanctuary was a private residential area. A gated community that was incredibly protected and had its own economy. The population of the community was close to ten thousand people, which put pressure on the land prices, Sal was sure.

Petro's eyebrow shot up. "Property investment? Are you thinking residential, or considering something like a guild headquarters? Residential, you'd already have enough to get yourself a nice apartment in any of the districts. Commercial is a much harder one to calculate. You could have a storefront and rent it out to businesses. But…I'd just be throwing useless numbers at you if I was to answer now. Leave it with me, and I'll come back to you tomorrow."

Sal smiled. "Thanks, Dad. I was just exploring my options, as a part of me was thinking of buying property in a Reclaimed Zone…but after coming home, I started wondering if I could afford something here."

Petro nodded with a warm smile. "We'll have a chat with your mother tomorrow. There are a few things we need to sort out, including all of this." He pointed at the exhibits that Sal had contributed toward. "Lots to talk about."

The man Petro had identified as Lawrence moved over to them with a wide smile. "Ah, Salvatore. A pleasure to meet you." He held out his right hand, which Sal accepted.

"The pleasure is all mine, Mr. Baron." Sal smiled. "I'm quite taken with that cane. Would you mind me asking where you got it?"

Lawrence just shook his head. "You're as bad as your father. It's a custom piece that was Crafted by a good friend of mine. When it comes to finesse weapons, he makes some excellent stuff. I could pass on your details…maybe even get you a work order. My treat."

Sal's jaw dropped at that. "That's incredibly generous. I couldn't possibly accept something that valuable for free, though." He let go of Lawrence's hand as he looked at his father to get a read on the situation.

Lawrence chuckled as he shook his head. "Heavens, no. It wouldn't be for free at all. You can get yourself an exquisite cane-sword for a vastly reduced price…and I would leave here with that obsidian dagger. Of course, you'd get the price of my ticket," he added with a conspiratorial wink.

Sal smiled. This was the key difference. Both Shade and Lawrence wanted the same thing, but they had wildly different approaches to getting what they wanted. Lawrence was trying to entice him with a potential work order for the cane, and Sal was very tempted to take him up on it. He decided against it in the end, and when he looked at his father, he could see that it was the second time tonight Lawrence had been rejected by an Argento.

"Actually, Mr. Baron…would you allow me to do a quick Appraisal of the item? I'll be very honest with you, though…I'm going to ask our special Crafter to mimic the design. See if we can challenge your finesse expert." Sal gestured at the cane-sword. "Naturally, I absolutely expect failure. You'll be the first person I'd show, of course."

Lawrence tilted his head. "Why would I humor you in such an endeavor, as all that would be achieved is a cheap copy? I'm not insecure enough that I need to see terrible impersonations to value the piece."

Sal pressed a hand against his chest. "Well, you've already been quite taken with the obsidian dagger. I was just curious what it would look like if we made your cane with obsidian and hellfire titanium. Our Crafter is quite versatile, and in constant need of a challenge." He looked at his father, smiling. "I know we said that there would be ten daggers…but what if it was ten daggers and a single cane?"

Lawrence's mouth opened as he looked between father and son, before a smile crept onto his face. "Oh my, you two are indeed a dangerous duo." He focused on Sal. "A truly interesting way to say that you've got no interest in having a cane-sword made for you. You're instead looking to impress me, which makes me curious as to what I could do for the young Argento?"

Sal held up his hands and offered a slight shrug. "Let's treat it like a trial run. I've heard that you're a top dog when it comes to exotic materials. I tend to need things like that from time to time." He took out his tracker and handed it to Lawrence. "This one took a bit of time because of the scarlet screen and—"

"Moonsilver," Lawrence finished as he turned it over in his hands, before giving it back. "So you're even acquainted with Doc Ameye? Okay…I'll bite." With a laugh, he threw his cane to Sal. "Appraise it to your heart's content. When you have something to show me, we can talk about getting you listed on the books for the Material Exchange. But be warned, you'll have a steeper hill to climb if you fall at this hurdle. My curiosity is piqued—don't squander it."

Sal held the cane in his hands, his eyes already taking it apart. "I won't, sir."

CHAPTER 10: BULLY

Sal sat at the edge of the bar with a wide smile on his face. It had been so long since he had enjoyed the thrill of an auction with his family. Just sitting alone and watching the sales staff doing their work was enough for him in that moment. He plucked the tumbler of whiskey from the bar and took a lengthy sip, enjoying the burning sensation flowing down his throat. The lots for the obsidian knives had managed to be a resounding success, and Sal wasn't worried about replicating the design. If he was honest with himself, he was more entranced with the concept of making an obsidian cane. *Maybe he'd be able to use Prestige's one as a reference point?*

"You look happy," Sophia said with a warm smile as she sat on the stool beside him. She looked around the room before a laugh left her lips. "I still can't believe it. There hasn't been this much buzz in years, and I haven't seen your father this enthralled in even longer."

Sal nodded as his gaze locked onto Petro, who was still chatting with a group of somewhat inebriated men. It was clear from their looks of awe that his father was talking to them about the Argento Auction House's mysterious new supplier. A few mentions of commissions had been thrown around, likely from anyone who had been talking to Lawrence Baron. The little wager that they had made was apparently something that tickled the owner of the Material Exchange, and he was happily informing his friends of the bet.

"I am happy," Sal answered his mother finally as he turned on his stool to look at her. "It's certainly a change of pace now that I can bring more to the table. I can't help but think about how much will change for the auction house."

Sophia chuckled as she shook her head. "I won't hear you say anything bad about the work you did before heading off to Quest Academy. There's a reason we needed to protect our current sales staff when you came home." She winked at Sal before gesturing at the small stage. "While your skills are truly unbelievable, you're still just our Sal. We want to support you as much as we can, and not be a burden to your plans in the future."

Sal sighed as he looked at her carefully. "Even if I wanted to go off and create a guild?" He wasn't sure now was the right time to discuss the guild creation, especially as the auction was still ongoing, but he felt like it wouldn't blow up in his face.

Sophia hesitated as she folded her hands on her lap. "If that's what truly makes you happy, and you want to do it for the right reasons…then neither your father nor I would stand in your way." She smiled softly. "You just need to be very sure about why you're doing it. You're a gentle boy who will give a stranger the shirt off your back, and I don't want to see you being taken advantage of."

Before Sal could say anything in response, Sophia raised her hand and gripped his shoulder. She looked him squarely in the eye as her grip tightened. "If anyone takes advantage of you, they'll have to deal with me." She stated it as a fact. If her demeanor was equitable to capability, then not even Prestige would have been an opponent for her.

Sal laughed as he nodded. "I get it. Thank you." Sal thought back to the excursion, when he had first spoken to Prestige. "By the way, Prestige seems to know you…"

Sophia's eyes widened before a guilty laugh escaped her lips. She brought her hand up to her face and shook her head as though ashamed of herself. "Ah, we knew each other when we were young."

Petro chose that exact moment to appear in front of them with a wide smile. "Tell him the truth."

Sal looked between them in confusion. "Is there a story here?" He was more curious than ever, especially with how uncomfortable his mother had become.

Petro nodded as he gestured at Sophia. "Go on, tell your son who used to bully Prestige." He seemed delighted by the topic of conversation as he looked at Sal excitedly. "She was like a force of nature. I thought she was an Offense class when I first met her. Family life calmed her down."

Sophia's glare was petrifying, and it was aimed directly at her husband. "Petro."

Petro grinned as he shrugged nonchalantly. "Hey, it's better he hears the truth from us rather than Prestige. Hopefully she didn't take out her frustrations on our poor boy, because you had a temper." It was clear that Petro was enjoying himself as he continued to poke fun at Sophia.

Sophia rolled her eyes before turning back to Sal. "Don't listen to your idiot father. I grew up not far from Prestige, back in Barrier town. It was one of the few places that kids were allowed to play outside, and everyone from those blocks knew each other."

Sal stared in shock at his mother. "You bullied Prestige?"

Sophia groaned as she resumed her glare at Petro. "Seriously? You're going to make him think I was some kind of delinquent. It was just kids being kids." She waved her hand to the area behind Petro. "And is this really the best time to be reminiscing? You've got an entire floor of eager buyers out there waiting on the last exhibit." Her tone was exasperated, but it was clear she was trying to change the subject.

Petro shook his head. "Building suspense is a part of the gig, and the longer I'm here, the more they'll think there's a private buyer who has us conflicted." He pointed at Sal meaningfully. "Those knives have managed to exceed all expectations. First one closed over six hundred thousand, and we're only on the sixth blade now…" Petro checked his tablet before chuckling. "And the fear of missing out is clearly killing them. The current bid is seven hundred and twenty thousand."

Sal's jaw dropped, and he had to quickly hide his expression from any curious guests. Staring at his father, he couldn't find the words. Sure, he was used to the sale prices being ridiculously high, but this was beyond excessive. Each of those blades would only take up to an hour to Craft, and he already had the materials that he needed. Was the story and design that important to the sale? He already knew that it was, but it was still a shock when he was the Crafter behind each piece.

Petro smiled as he handed the tablet over for Sal to take a look for himself. "So, with the previous bid becoming the precedent, every subsequent one is going up. The first few were smaller increments, but they're really getting worried. I wouldn't be surprised if we hit close to a million, just from the conversations I've had with the guests."

Sal looked through the numbers and saw that his father was right. The prices were really rising as the scarcity increased. "I honestly thought the first blade would have the highest amount because of the raffle system. But for it to increase?" He looked up at his father in confusion.

Petro nodded. "These guests want surety rather than chance. If they spend money, it's to leave with something…and it looks like Shade hasn't managed to secure a single blade of the five that sold so far."

Sophia sighed in relief as she leaned back in her chair. "Well, that's just the cherry on top, isn't it? By the looks of those numbers, what's your estimate? Even if they all sold at the reserve price, then we'd be looking at four million. By my guess, it looks like it might be closer to seven."

Petro shook his head as he took the tablet back from Sal. "Best guess would be closer to eight, but it will really depend on how the rest of the bidding goes. I was worried they might question the chance of the blade being replicated to perfection, but that seemed to be in vain. They're quite literally begging for me to add more blades to the auction." He chuckled as he pocketed his tablet. "They've asked for a calendar of all our upcoming auctions. I think we're going to have a lot more guests for the next few events, even if we don't have anything from Sal to play with."

Sophia quickly looked at her son. "Don't start thinking you need to keep this up. This was a one-off, and we're delighted with the result. We can manage expectations going forward, so there's no need to put any pressure on yourself. You've got time off between now and your next semester, so don't even think of pushing yourself. Got it?"

Sal laughed as he looked between his parents. "Okay, that's a deal. I promise to only work as hard as you two. That's fair, right?"

Sophia frowned but Petro let out a hearty laugh.

His father clapped him on the shoulder as he looked between them. "Ah, Soph…you can't be angry with him. We raised him, after all."

Sophia sighed as she got to her feet, sparing only a moment to look at the tumbler of whiskey in Sal's hand. "Just pace yourself. I know it's exciting, but we're not done yet." With that said, she moved off to speak with the guests, a fake smile on her face.

Sal watched her leave with a shake of his head. "She just had to give some motherly advice, didn't she?"

Petro nodded as he sat in the vacant seat. "Sometimes she confuses the role of a parent, with thinking that she needs to be the bad cop. You're an adult now, Sal…and I can't believe I'm saying it, but I think Quest Academy was the right choice for you. Both of us do, even though it's been surreal to say the least." He reached over and plucked the tumbler from Sal's grasp. "To Salvatore Argento, a Savior in Quest Academy." He shook his head with a chuckle before downing the remainder of the whiskey in one go. "Now, I think it's time we moved on to the grand finale."

Sal stared at the empty glass in his father's hands before registering his words. "Wait, don't you want to finish up with the blades first?"

Petro shook his head as he stood and placed the empty glass behind the countertop of the bar. "Nope. A third of the audience hasn't touched the bidding for the blades. They're sticking around for the final exhibit, and drawing it out isn't good for us." He smiled as he straightened his waistcoat. "Let's give them what they want, and we can close out with the remainder of the blades."

Sal got to his feet and mimicked the gesture of straightening his own waistcoat. "What do you need me to do?"

Petro pointed at the covered exhibit. "If I handle the showcase, do you want to take on the Appraisal? It's been a while since we teamed up."

Sal grinned as he moved toward the center of the auction floor. "Too long, if you ask me."

Petro clapped as he smiled at Sal. "Then let's get started." He turned his attention to the nearest guests, who reacted at the sudden sound. "Everyone, I'd like to invite you all to the main hall. Please, follow me." Petro spoke loudly as he followed Sal, gesturing at the glass case that was covered with the trademark silver cloth of the Argento Auction House.

Sal stood on the platform surrounding the glass case and placed his hands on the edges of the cloth, waiting for his father to get the other side. It was a strange feeling for him because he didn't really care about the exhibit all that much. The cause for his happiness was seeing his parents' delight and the overall atmosphere of the auction.

Just looking around him, he could see the excitement of the guests. *How long had it been since they had such a reaction?* Indifference and skepticism had been their usual fare, but now they were dealing with over a dozen pieces that were Rare grade at a minimum, with all of them holding an evolutionary rune, too. It was a massive difference from what the guests were used to, and was very much the start of an Argento Auction House renaissance.

"Got it?" Petro gripped the opposite edges of the cloth. When he saw Sal's nod of approval, he smiled and turned to the crowd. "Are you all ready to see the main exhibit?"

A smattering of applause and shouts were the response, but Petro wasn't satisfied. "I asked if you're ready to see something extraordinary. Don't give me that lukewarm reaction, because what is underneath this cloth puts every blade you've bid on to shame." He tested them with a barb, but the smile on his face was enough to keep everyone at ease. A few laughs emitted from the crowd as Petro asked again, "So are you ready?"

A roar came back from the crowd, even if it was just to humor Petro. With the height of the cheer, Petro started to lift the cloth, with Sal following suit, until the glass case was completely revealed to the crowd.

Petro stepped forward and gestured at the full armor set. "Ladies and gentlemen, I'd like to introduce you to our Upper Epic-grade, Wraith Walker set."

CHAPTER 11: BIDS

"Wraith Walker is an incredible piece that was reformed using advanced Restoration and Crafting techniques within the Argento Auction House," Petro began dramatically as he pointed at the set of armor.

Name	Wraith Walker
Origin	Crafted Portal Artifact (Reforged)
Age	New
Grade	Epic (Upper)
Materials	Refined Mythcrafter Essence | Void Metal | Obsidian | Perfect Essence | Dreadcloth | Spectre Silk | Prowler Hide | Umbral Ingot | Arachne Thread
Attributes	Stealth: Allows user to conceal their presence by staying still. Potency increases within darkness. Shadow Strike: Allows user to shoot invisible projectiles. Range and damage increase within darkness. Shadow Step: Allows user to teleport from one shadow to another. Range increases within darkness. Spectre: Allows user to create an illusory copy of themselves that can imitate movements.
Abilities	Stealth | Shadow Strike | Shadow Step | Spectre
Runes	Essence Replenishment Rune Evolutionary Rune
Power Source	External Essence
Evolution	Yes - 0%
Quality	Perfect
Condition	100%

Value	Est. $720,000.00 – $950,000.00

The helm was jet-black with a wispy white smoke emitting from the visor. The cloak, which had previously been a clump of discarded rags, had been completely transformed. The tattered nature was now stylized, and its frayed edges floated gently behind the armor. When it came to the tunic, the emblem was completely restored, showing a glowing skull surrounded by the evolutionary rune. It had a menacing vibe that really matched the overall tone of the set. The plated boots were also black, much like the bracer and pauldron attachment. Flecks of blue and silver could be seen as faint hues within the black, a likely result of the void metal used in the Crafting.

Petro grinned at the crowd's reaction as he gestured for Sal to take over. "Salvatore will be conducting the Appraisal, so listen well. You won't want to miss this."

Sal smiled at his father before starting. "Wraith Walker…it's a fearsome name. What thoughts are conjured when we think of the Wraith? Transparent…deadly? Well, both are true. Our first attribute is Stealth, allowing our successful bidder to pass unseen and unheard. Complete invisibility within darkness. It's an excellent attribute for the set, but it's no slouch when it comes to offensive capabilities." Sal paused to watch the crowd's reaction. Nobody was looking at him as their eyes were locked onto the armor. With a smile, he continued.

"Shadow Step is the next attribute, allowing excellent traversal. Our winner will be able to teleport from location to location, with a much higher range in darkness, able to reposition to a more strategic location, and strike from the shadows…with Shadow Strike!" Sal raised his voice as he spoke excitedly. "Invisible blades made of essence, with a large range within darkness. You can attack your enemies before they ever realize you're there. But…what if they detect you?"

Sal let the question hang in the air for a moment before he clapped and pointed at the armor. "Well, not when you send a replica of yourself into the battlefield to distract the enemy. Spectre is the final ability of the Wraith Walker set. It allows for the perfect illusion of yourself to misdirect your opponent."

Sal let the words sink in, before he raised a hand to gesture at the center of the tunic. "This glowing series of symbols surrounding the skull emblem is the evolutionary rune you've been hearing about all night. We believe that this piece could reach the highest points of Legendary…and perhaps even beyond. I don't say those words lightly. The material quality and composition are so impressive, there is a very high chance that every component in this set will pick up an attribute each. If it doesn't have six attributes when it breaks into Legendary, then I'll buy it back at twice the cost you pay for it now. That's an Argento Auction House guarantee."

The audience was surprised by that, and for the first time, a number of them tore their attention away from the armor set to stare at Sal in disbelief.

Sal smiled as he nodded. "You heard that right. I'll buy this back at twice the cost you pay for it now, but just know…that its potential isn't limited to how many attributes it has. The potency of each attribute is exceptional and all of them are specialist skills. When the fifth and sixth ones come through, then we are almost guaranteed to see more Assassination-based skills. Perhaps even some undiscovered ones."

Sal decided that it was time to wrap things up and hand it back over to his father. "The Wraith Walker set has the capability to transform its wearer into the greatest Assassin-style Hunter in the entire bureau. Guilds will fight over it, but they're not here right now. You are." Sal brought his hands together before gesturing to his father. "Thank you for your time. Over to Petro."

Petro looked at the faces in the crowd before raising his tablet. "We're not here to waste anyone's time. Let's skip the facade where we pretend that this piece could go for a steal. I'm starting the bidding at one point four million. Who wants to make a bid?"

It took everything in Sal's power to keep his poker face in place. His father had started them off at nearly double the estimated value.

Petro looked at his tablet. "Really? I expected more than five people to be in the running for this one. Should I mention the elephant in the room?" He looked over at Sal with a conflicted expression that was feigned. "Do you think our esteemed guests should know the origin of this armor?"

Sal smiled as he looked back at the group. "Much like the Breastplate of the Unyielding, each of the pieces you see here were brought in by Shade of the Delvers Guild. A portion of the winning bid will be used to offset the losses the Argento Auction House has faced over the years from that mandated collaboration."

"Mandated is a cruel word to use, Salvatore." Petro chided his son. "The Hunter Bureau and Guilds Association asks us to help people like Shade, even when it means we don't get paid. Unfortunately, that business model means we need to increase our prices to stay in the black. This Wraith Walker set was constructed using a variety of discarded pieces Shade left with us. If it wasn't for our new artisan, we'd be facing a substantial loss…but with their incredible skill and work, we're able to present you with an unparalleled piece of equipment. I hope you'll all show your support in the Argento Auction House by participating."

Sal smiled inwardly at the theatrics they had to employ. Just the mention of Shade was enough to get some of the more reluctant buyers interested, even at the ridiculous asking price. When Sal caught sight of Sophia at the side of the room, he wanted to laugh. She looked positively delighted. It was obvious why.

Rather than lurking within the shadows as he had done before, Shade stood in the center of the room with his arms crossed. He didn't say a word as he kept his eyes fixed on the tablet in his own hands. From the movements of his fingers, it was clear that he was making bids.

Sal could have sworn that Shade would cause a ruckus or start demanding that it be returned to him. There was nothing of the sort as the guildmaster kept his calm. Was it the fact that the Wraith Walker was so impressive, or was he trying to look composed in front of all the guests? Either way, it was a welcome sight to see him playing by the rules.

"One point seven?" Petro looked at his tablet. "You're telling me that this Wraith Walker set is the price of three Rare-grade obsidian blades? Stop trying to wait each other out. Nobody is going to be getting a bargain with this one. This is an investment in the future of a Hunter, Hero, or guild. Salvatore already told you how much it can change the landscape, and I trust him. He's the number one-ranked student in Quest Academy and a member of the Savior Class."

Sal could see his mother face-palm from her side of the crowd. It was funny how Petro managed to slide his pride into each of his pitches. It wasn't something Sal was embarrassed by, because he knew that his parents were proud of him. Any angle they could use to give credibility to the pitch was what mattered, and Petro's words seemed to be doing the trick.

Petro looked down at the tablet. "That's better, but we're still in bargain territory. I'm not trying to tell you how to spend your money, but how do you think this set of equipment would fare if we took it to the Hunter Bureau Gala? Do you think Robert would let any of you have it?" He posed the challenge to everyone in the room. "This is a perfect fit for Phantom. Anyone who gets it will have the attention of the president of the Hunter Bureau. Is that status worth one point eight million?"

Sal wanted to stare at his father, but he kept his composure in check. *He was throwing Robert's name into the mix?* It was like he had a death wish. Yet, by the expressions of the group, it hadn't fallen on deaf ears.

"Welcome to the bidding war, Mr. Baron." Petro greeted Lawrence with a smile from the stage. "Shade seems very intent on picking up the Wraith Walker, so I wish you the best of luck. Same to Master Hawne." Petro spoke to them individually as he watched from his place on the stage.

Highlighting the bidders was a great way to incite competition between the guests. Even if they didn't have any need for the set, or an audience with the Hunter Bureau…many of them would be incentivized to see their competitors fail. The best example of which was Shade.

His calm demeanor had started to break. Likely from the sideways glances that were aimed at him from the other guests while they placed their bids. His fingers twitched over the tablet screen, as though hesitating to confirm a new bid.

Sal watched as Shade glanced up quickly to lock onto Lawrence Baron, before returning a half second later to his own tablet. It confirmed to Sal who the biggest fish was in the auction, and who Shade was worried about. Just as Sal was going to move over to Petro, he saw his father tilt his head slightly in Shade's direction, as if to ask if he was seeing the same thing. Sal wanted to laugh. Of course his father knew what he was doing.

Petro laughed as he lifted his hand with the tablet in it. "Just to put our own cards on the table…we've crossed the two million mark. The Argento Auction House would be happy to let go of the piece for that number, so it's all down to who closes the bid. You're only betting against yourselves now."

Lawrence looked up at the stage with a wry smile. "I'll return that transparency in kind." He raised his voice as he turned on his heel, his cane tapping against the ground as he looked at the guests in the room. "I can comfortably go to four million for this. Robert and I go way back, so I thought it would be a nice little something to pick up for him."

Petro chuckled as he looked at the tablet. "Are you setting that as the new bid, Lawrence? Or just trying to scare off the competition?" With a slight shrug, he looked over at Sal. "We might need to stop Mr. Baron from coming to our future auctions. A big fish like him will scare everyone away." He said it loud enough for the other guests to hear, which resulted in a chuckle from Lawrence.

"Don't paint me as a villain, Petro. Ah—" Lawrence frowned as he looked down at his own tablet in confusion.

"Five million!" Petro exclaimed as he looked directly at Shade in the center of the room. "Thank you for your bid."

Sal was surprised. Shade had used a plethora of excuses over the years about how he couldn't afford to pay the Appraisal fees, and yet he had five million to bid on an auction. The main cause of surprise wasn't Shade, though; it was the professionalism of Petro. There was no edge to the words as he thanked Shade for his bid, just an affirmation of the transaction.

Petro smiled brightly as he looked at the group of bidders. "I guess we're going to close it here? Looks like Shade is going to be taking home the Wraith Walker set. Thank you all for participating. We'll just wait for the countdown timer to finish up before confirming it. Just another thirty seconds to go."

Lawrence tapped at the tablet for a few seconds before looking at Shade with a tight smile. "You'll remember I said that I could comfortably go to four million. I never said anything about how uncomfortable I was prepared to become, Shade."

"Mr. Hawne! Could you be the deciding factor in this war of bidding?" Petro turned his tablet around for everyone to see. The leading bid, at five and a half million, had just dethroned Lawrence Baron's entry at five point two. It was a shocking moment for the guests who had bowed out. Many of them looked at Felix Hawne in a daze.

Felix glared at Petro from the auction floor as he waved his tablet. "The theatrics are a part of the process, I get that. But I don't appreciate the insinuation that there are only two real bidders in attendance." He huffed as though it were a chore to get the words out. Looking between Shade and Lawrence, Felix shook his head. "The piece will stay in Silver Sanctuary, where it was made."

That statement managed to rile up the crowd far more than anything Petro could have said or done. Rather than making it about the Hunter Bureau, it was made about territory. Sal had to readjust his impression of the portly man. Felix Hawne wasn't someone remarkable, and the conversation he had with him earlier hadn't been anything incredible. The fact that he was also from Silver Sanctuary was a surprise. Their private community had nearly ten thousand people, but the Hawnes were an unknown to him.

Petro frowned slightly as he looked at the guests. "Let's not make personal attacks. The Argento Auction House is proud to call Silver Sanctuary its home, but the doors are open to anyone who has money to spend. We're happy to facilitate the transaction to whoever wins the bid, be they you, Mr. Hawne, Mr. Baron, or even Shade. We don't play favorites here."

"Then stop running down the damn clock by talking," Shade snapped from the center of the room as he lifted his tablet. "My bid isn't going through because you've not accepted it."

Petro glanced at his tablet before a smile graced his face. "Ah, that's not how this works. It appears that you lack the necessary funds to complete your bid. I'm surprised you haven't noticed the message before, since you claimed the same fault every time it came to Appraisal payment."

Sal nearly choked. The gloves were off as Petro stared at Shade with a bright smile.

CHAPTER 12: TENSIONS

Petro stepped down from the podium and moved into the crowd, his eyes not leaving Shade. "Your funds have been returned to you. As this is the last item on the docket, there's no need for us to maintain appearances. I'd ask for you to leave the auction house."

Shade's eyes widened as his hands fell to his side. "Kicking me out? Are you sure you can handle that, Petro?" He looked around him to see whether anyone else saw this action as ridiculous. The incredulity on his face was quite visible.

Petro nodded slowly. "Due to your track record, we don't feel comfortable having you learn which bidder secures the Wraith Walker set. A piece going for such a large sum of money needs to be guaranteed by the Argento Auction House, and I'd feel terrible if our successful bidder was waylaid because of the greed of another."

Shade's jaw dropped. "How dare you! I'm a guildmaster! You can't throw accusations like that at me." He looked again around the room for support, but found none. With his fists balled, he laughed humorlessly as he stared at Petro. "You've just made a massive mistake. I can take a few slights here and there, but this…this is crossing the line. The Hunter Bureau and Guilds Association will be hearing about this."

Petro nodded. "I'm sure they will. Tell them that we've got pieces at the auction house with evolutionary runes, and the capacity to get to Legendary grade. See what happens." With that said, Petro looked over his shoulder at Sal and gave him a smile. When he looked back at Shade, his smile vanished. "I'd also appreciate if you stopped trying to recruit my son."

Shade tapped at the tablet to log out of his profile before throwing it to the side, letting it clatter against the marble floor. "Suit yourself, Petro. You've crossed the line, so don't blame me for what happens next. Your little artisan might make you think you've got a trump card, but everyone has a price. How deep do the pockets of the Argento Auction House go?"

Petro bent at the knee and picked up the tablet from the ground. He lifted it and waved it a bit. "Deeper than the Delvers Guild, apparently." He laughed as he gestured for the door. "So, if you don't mind…get the fuck out of my auction house."

Shade stared coldly at him, and then at the other attendees as though memorizing everyone's face. "I'll remember this." With a burst of black smoke, Shade disappeared from view for everyone except Petro.

Petro didn't move from where he stood. His eyes were locked onto a location on the other side of the room. Reaching down to his tablet, he tapped a few buttons without looking. The lighting in the auction changed abruptly as every wall suddenly glowed in a deep red, and was accompanied by a pained gasp.

Shade materialized on one knee, clearly out of breath. The red lights had all converged on a single wall behind him.

"Restraining crystal?" Sal whispered, wondering when his father had them installed as a security measure.

Petro looked around at the startled guests. "I apologize for any discomfort. We'll remove the essence blockers when our intruder has been dealt with." With a click of his fingers, three security staff moved to pick up Shade, who shrugged them off.

"I'm leaving!" He pulled at his black jacket and shot a baleful glare at Petro before turning on his heel and pushing his way through the double doors to the courtyard. His figure stalked away, not daring to burst into shadow again.

Petro let out an exasperated sigh. "Some people just can't stand to lose." He undid the restraining crystals, and the lighting in the room changed back to the warm colors from before. Petro pocketed his tablet and moved back up to the podium. "I hope none of you will look upon the Argento Auction House too harshly for our actions. We just want to ensure that all our bidders and artifacts are given absolute protection. Even if the perpetrator is a guildmaster, we don't give special treatment."

"Hear, hear," Lawrence Baron said with a tap of his cane, a wide smile on his face. "I was about to kick him out myself if you hadn't stepped in."

Petro smiled at the comment. "I'll consider the auction very lucky that you didn't. There's a limit to Sophia's Restoration abilities." He winked before bringing his hands together. "Would we like to now conclude the sale of the Wraith Walker set? I've reset the clock and can open it back up to bidding."

Felix Hawne gave a curt nod, while Lawrence Baron gave a smile as his consent.

Sal looked across the room to where his mother stood. Her gaze was on the door, a frown on her face. She looked worried by the turn of events, but it was clear she was conflicted. If anyone wanted Shade to be kicked out on his ass, it was her. But she was likely considering all the consequences of their actions.

Petro chuckled. "Mr. Gauss…welcome to the bidding."

The reaction was immediate as both Lawrence Baron and Felix Hawne whirled around to see a slender gentleman with a glass of wine and a smile on his face.

"Couldn't have Shade painting a target on my back. I hope you can understand." He raised his glass in salute to Petro. "Fabulous work on knowing he was still here. I had my suspicions."

Petro gestured at his eyes. "They can see a lot more than Appraisal information, but I rarely have need to use them." He lied so smoothly it sounded as if he had always had the capability Sal had granted him. Petro gestured over his shoulder at Sal. "I keep telling him that he got his good genetics from me, but Sophia won't hear a word of it!"

The crowd laughed and the tension in the room dissipated, all except for Felix Hawne, who looked positively peeved by the new entrant to the bidding war.

Lawrence just looked amused as he glanced down at his tablet. "I must confess, my main goal was depriving Shade…so I will call it here. I wish both gentlemen good luck in their bids." He gave a polite bow in both of their directions.

Felix softened at that as he looked over at Gauss. "You planning on gifting this piece to Robert?" It was clear what his worry was.

Mr. Gauss just shook his head. "Gift for my kid. She's a first-year and having quite a time on that tower trial." His eyes flicked over to where Sal stood and he smiled. "I want to give her as much of a chance as possible when it comes to getting into the Saviors class."

Felix frowned as he looked down at his own tablet. "Then I'll also call it with this bid. I'm at my limit." He put through a new bid before looking up with a smile. "Good luck."

Mr. Gauss paused for a few moments as he looked at his own tablet. "She's never getting another penny from us." He sighed with a chuckle as he tapped the tablet. "Thank you both for your forthrightness with your bids." He looked at Lawrence and Felix with genuine warmth.

Petro watched as the winning bid came through. "Congratulations, Mr. Gauss. For seven point two million, you've just secured yourself the Wraith Walker set!"

Sal nearly choked when he heard the closing bid price. With a quick calculation in his head, he realized that the final price was the equivalent of over a hundred and forty thousand Q-Cred. It was an insane number to get his head around, and all he could think of was how much time and effort had gone into the Wraith Walker set. Sure, it had a few artifacts to work as the basis, but for it to be worth that much was insane. *Was it just because there was so much scarcity of good equipment on the market?*

Petro brought his hands together. "Thank you all for coming tonight. I don't want to make any promises, but I have it on good authority from our resident artisan that it won't be long before we have another showcase with even more surprising pieces on display. Sophia will be in touch with all of you to find out what your personal shopping list is for auction pieces. If you'd like to be informed of future evolutionary collections, please register your interest."

He gestured back toward the bar area. "You're more than welcome to help yourselves to some refreshments at the bar while we get this place cleaned up. Doors will be locking in a few hours, so you've got plenty of time to enjoy yourselves."

With that, he hopped off the podium and moved over to Sophia. Shooting Sal a meaningful look, he jutted his chin toward his office on the above floor.

Sal didn't waste time as he made his way up the glass-and-steel staircase to his father's office. The transparent glass door led straight into a technological marvel of modern design. Screens were placed all around the desk and on the brick feature wall to the side. Display cases of beautiful weapons and equipment rested on ornate pedestals around the room. A plush couch with multiple button indents was fixed against the wall, beside a coat rack that held several suit jackets. The artwork in the room was historical in nature, with old pictures showing the Argento Auction House in its first years, but also the beautiful landscapes of Italy. A collection of paper books was preserved in glass and mounted to the walls like picture frames.

"Perfect," Petro said as he saw Sal in the room. He stepped inside and held the door for Sophia, waiting for her to enter before closing it behind her. "That was one hell of a rush!"

Sophia just stared at him with her arms crossed. "You humiliated Shade in front of everyone, and promised that we'd have more evolutionary collections.

Petro, are you insane?" She waved her hand at Sal. "You didn't even ask for Salvatore's opinion on making more pieces like this. We've got no idea how much this takes out of him to do these sorts of projects." She pinched the bridge of her nose. "And Shade isn't going to take this one lying down. We play the back-and-forth with him, but this was more like a declaration of war. What were you thinking?"

Petro turned to look at Sal. "You said you wanted to start looking into properties? This is how you do it." He lifted his tablet to show Sal a set of figures. "Take a look at that and tell me what you'd like to do."

Sophia looked between Salvatore and Petro as she shook her head. "What are you two scheming about? Properties?"

Sal looked up from the tablet with a smile. "I've got a meeting with the Arc Guild and wanted to understand a bit more about property before I went to it. If we're going to be making a guild, then I'll need a headquarters for it."

Sophia moved over to the couch and plopped down on it. "So, we're having this conversation now, are we?" She looked at Petro meaningfully. "We were going to have it as a family, so now should be as good a time as any."

Petro scratched at the back of his head. "I wasn't conspiring with him or anything. It was just a topic he brought up with me. Obviously we're having this conversation as a family. No backroom deals, I promise, Soph."

Sophia nodded slowly. "Like how he upgraded your ability? Was that going to be a conversation too?"

Petro faltered at that as he leaned against his desk, folding his arms. "Shade got what was coming to him. I thought we were pretty aligned on that, but I guess I went too far. I'm sorry for that, Soph."

Sophia pointed at Sal. "You should probably apologize to your son, who you've essentially indentured to the Argento Auction House with that last stunt. How could you offer his Crafting without even checking with him?"

Petro looked like he forcibly bit back whatever retort came to mind. Instead, he took a breath and looked at Sal with a sigh. "I'm sorry, Sal. I shouldn't have whored out your talents like that."

Sophia put her hand to her face. "Petro!"

Petro grimaced and a tight smile graced his face. "He knows what I meant." An exasperated sigh escaped his lips when he stood up. "Why are we not celebrating? This is the biggest haul the Argento Auction House has had in years, and the costs are rock bottom. Even just the obsidian stuff would have put us in a healthy position, but the Wraith Walker set has pretty much smashed our annual goals. This is a good thing!"

Sophia stared daggers at her husband, but he just raised a hand and started talking through his logic.

"Okay, let's say that between the daggers and the armor sets, it's ten million. I know it's more, but let's call it a round ten million." He gestured at his index finger. "Now, since we had already absorbed the costs of the artifacts from Shade, they were written off and seen as surplus stock. Restoration, Crafting, and Appraisal were all handled by Sal. Overheads are already factored in, because we were hosting the auction anyway. Material cost was his own stuff from Quest Academy and the few bits and pieces we got for him in the workshop…are you seeing where I'm going with this?" Petro asked as he looked at Sophia expectantly.

Sophia stared at her husband for a few moments. "I'm delighted that he's managed to earn a lot for himself. That's not what I'm annoyed about. Since Quest got in contact with us about the auction aligning with a starter guild, you've become erratic and you're losing your edge."

Petro clapped his hands together. "Soph, this is our new reality. Salvatore is able to make Mythic-grade equipment, and we need to scale up the Argento Auction House alongside him. If we truly want to protect him, we need to become an absolute powerhouse of an institution." He pointed at himself as he stared at his wife. "I'm not losing my edge. I've never been sharper…it's you who seems hell-bent on living in some reality where we maintain a status quo and hope for the best. Sal isn't dropping out of Quest Academy. He's not going to be coming back to work with us. This is his new life, and we need to adapt."

Sophia got to her feet and moved to the door. "Well, it sounds like you two have a lot to discuss. I'll go and check in on the staff." Her voice was devoid of emotion, but the force with which she opened and closed the door was a much better indicator of her feelings.

Sal wanted to say something, but the door closed before he had a chance to speak up. He looked uselessly at his father. "That could have gone better."

Petro let out an aggravated growl as he looked at the ceiling. "I'll talk to her. She just needs a bit more time to process all of this. You should go and get some rest." He moved toward the door but paused to clasp Sal on the shoulder. "You did extraordinary work today, Sal. I'll make sure not to fall short." And with that he was gone, moving down the stairs to catch up with Sophia.

Sal stayed in the office, feeling hollow on the inside. Looking down at the tablet in his hands, he saw a single cell that was highlighted. It was the profit from the auction.

"Holy shit," Sal breathed as his hand started to shake.

CHAPTER 13: EPIPHANY

Sal learned that his mother was excellent at holding a grudge. She managed to maintain a frosty persona for two full weeks, before she eventually sat down and spoke with Petro. The local florist was likely kept in business with the amount of apology bouquets that littered the auction house. Although his mother did love flowers, she preferred a husband who was on the same wavelength as her. Sal wasn't there for the conversation, but he got the highlights from his father.

"Your mother understands that we need to move forward, but not without your consent. She felt like I was rushing you to make a decision on your own future, without having spoken to you," Petro admitted as he sat across the table from Sal. "I thought she was reluctant to challenge the guilds, but she didn't really care about any of that. It was more the fact that you upgraded my power, and then she felt my behavior was erratic in the auction. We found a good compromise though, so everything is fine now."

"And the compromise was?" Sal asked out of curiosity, wondering whether his father would tell him. "You aren't being forced to sleep on the couch in your office, are you?"

Petro chuckled and shook his head. "No, nothing as drastic as that. She wasn't aware that you wanted to purchase property in Silver Sanctuary. Her stance on it being an idiotic investment and too rash did a complete one-eighty when she realized you'd be closer to home. She's fully invested in you building a base here."

Sal smiled at that and just looked at his father. "Come on, it couldn't have been that easy?" His mother was a much more logical and reasonable woman than that. Sure, it would be great being closer to them, but he was certain that it wasn't worth two weeks of frostiness.

Petro smiled guiltily. "She wasn't a fan of how I spoke with Shade. She called me an Offense-class brute, and told me where to sign up for the front lines if I wanted to fight someone that much. That's what you get when you build a legacy of using words to do your battles—the moment you square up to someone, you get ridiculed relentlessly." He sighed as he crossed his arms and rested them on the table. "But, she understood why I did it…she was just worried that it might have put a target on you. That's why she was furious. Me glossing over her worries didn't help the problem when we spoke in the office."

"I'm glad that you guys made up. Is she okay with me, too? Do I need to apologize?" Sal looked up at his father earnestly.

Petro scoffed as he shook his head. "Why on earth would you apologize to her? She's the one who's been unreasonable with you, just because she was angry with me. You've got nothing to be sorry for. I'd expect her to be the one apologizing to you."

"So, what do you think…is it time to start working on a cane for Lawrence Baron?" Sal tapped his pen against the sketch in front of him.

Petro frowned as he looked at the pages. "Ah, he can wait awhile. It's not like you need anything from him just yet. Everyone got their daggers, so you don't need to worry about them. What other projects are you hoping to complete before heading back to the academy?"

Sal thought about it for a second. "Well, I wanted to make myself a new set of armor clothing. The last set was Epic grade and saved my life against the hulker, but it's not really going to be future-proof. I was going to make something with an evolutionary capacity that will work with me for the rest of my time at the academy."

Petro nodded. "Sounds reasonable. Any prototypes that don't make the cut can be sold at the auction, by the way." He winked at that last part.

Sal laughed as he thought about the other projects. "I wanted to create a machine that would create elixirs. Sort of like a vending machine, that used a Growth ability to create the ingredients internally. I was going to use Alchemize with it, maybe Refine, too." He winced slightly as he thought about those weaves. He wasn't sure he had records of all of them to be able to put them into his Crafting. Maybe Grant would send him the weaves if he requested them.

Petro stared at him for a moment. "What do you need elixirs for? Don't get me wrong, it sounds like an incredible invention and very difficult to make, but what is your end goal?"

Sal looked at him strangely. "To sell, and make money. Elixirs are expensive and it would be self-sustaining. Upgrade told me that Doc Ameye made his fortune through automation, so I was going to try to do something similar. If the machine can make elixirs without me being there, then I could passively earn a fortune."

Petro frowned. "And you think you can make something like that?"

Sal paused before nodding. "Yeah, but it will take a lot of time…and there's so much I don't know. I'd need to commission a few other people to make some of the trickier components."

Petro looked over his shoulder at the carriage. "Hear me out for a second…"

Sal followed his gaze. "Go on."

Petro paused for a few seconds before looking at Sal with a quizzical expression. "What if you did that for equipment and weapons instead?" He got to his feet. "Like, if you made a few presets of drawings that would be made, you could send them to the machines down there and they could make it for you?" He looked at Sal. "Am I being ridiculous?"

Sal got to his feet and followed him over to look at the carriage below. "So, like…a vending machine for weapons and armor? It would be impossible to store all the materials in the machine. That's what I was going to use the Growth ability for. Making a few seeds grow is easier than storing a factory's worth of hellfire titanium."

Petro tilted his head to one side. "Not if they had to bring their own materials. You put in the amounts required by the design you've picked and it does the rest. Now, *that* would be something remarkable." He looked at Sal and immediately put up his hands. "Sorry, I wasn't intending to discourage your elixir idea…I just thought about if I was in the same situation as you. Automation for weapons and armors would be a revolutionary piece of technology. I have no idea how you'd make something like that, though."

Sal considered it for a few minutes, looking down at the machines he already had available. "That is…a very cool idea." He had expected his father to encourage him to work on something less complex, but the inverse had happened and Petro was suggesting something seemingly impossible. "Let me work on some sketches and I'll see if it can work. I tried in the past to make a Crafting visor, similar to my tracker, for a friend…but it didn't work. I wasn't able to give the visor my ability."

Petro nodded in understanding. "But none of those machines have a Crafting ability. They just follow instructions you input from up here…" He looked at the workbench and the interactive screen.

Sal stared at it, feeling as though they both had come to the exact same conclusion. "Hypothetically, if I tried this and it failed…all of the machines would be pretty much ruined."

Petro bit his lip. "Unless you want to have divorced parents, you'll tell your mother this was your idea completely. I personally have full faith in you, but…I also have no idea what you're planning, because we never had this conversation."

Sal chuckled as he shook his head. "And you're sure this isn't just an angle so you can have more products to sell when I go back to the academy?"

Petro shrugged as he leaned against the railing. "I know you didn't ask for my advice on this one, but I think it's a tragedy that people are so ill-equipped for the ongoing war. In what world is it okay for the Wraith Walker set to sell for that much money? I'd rather see a day where it's sold for a fraction of that price, and that we have a ridiculous amount of supply. Your ability could make that future a reality, and an equipment vending machine…or whatever you want to call it…would free up a lot of your time."

Sal contemplated it as he looked between his father and the carriage. "Leave it with me. Like I said, I'll do some sketches to see if it's something that's within my abilities, but don't get your hopes up. This is absolutely something that Upgrade would kill me for even considering."

"I like the sound of her already." Petro chuckled as he moved toward the stairs. "Just don't push yourself—well…not an unhealthy amount. I'll keep that coffee machine stocked and you get to work. Any materials or equipment you need, just call for me and I'll get it delivered."

"Guess you'll be taking it out of my earnings?" Sal said dryly with a smile on his face.

"Naturally. We're not a charity, Sal." Petro laughed as he descended the stairs with a visible spring in his step.

Sal watched him leave before he let out a sigh. He hadn't been expecting that sort of reaction from his father. Rather than trying to talk him out of something borderline impossible, his dad had encouraged him to give it a shot…while keeping it a secret from his mother.

Moving back to the workbench, Sal cleared away all the sketches of the elixir device and decided to brainstorm the concept for this new weapon vending machine. It was a ridiculous concept, and Sal was very sure that the design would be riddled with errors…but he'd try it so he could at least face his father and tell him that he did his best.

In the briefest of moments before Sal's pen touched the fresh piece of paper, he paused. Looking up from the bench, he sighed and got to his feet, moving over to the secret wall. When he pushed it and moved into the bedroom area, he could see the small crate that Vanessa had procured for him. The Grand Design, as Alex had called it—Kakushin for everyone else. The elixir that would help him with breakthroughs. It had given him all sorts of grief the last time he had used it, but this time his head was firmly locked onto the Crafting challenge.

Sal brought a single bottle of it out to the workbench, where he took his seat again. Unscrewing the cap, Sal took a quick swig of the liquid, holding it in his mouth as he screwed the cap back on and placed it off to one side. A moment later, he swallowed the elixir and immediately realized that he had fucked up. The Perfect ability that was almost like second nature to him was still active, and it had just been given an essence-rich treat to play with. Sal tried to focus on his weave to deactivate the thread, but it was too late…the images pierced his brain at a ridiculous pace, flooding his mind with creative concepts.

Sal's hand shook as he picked up the pen and focused his thoughts on the challenge at hand: the vending machine for the weapons. Perfect was allowing his hand-strokes to recreate the images in his head to perfection, while Mythcrafter flickered in front of his eyes. It was an overwhelming amount of information that coursed through his brain. Despite closing his eyes to drown out the Mythcrafter ability's influence, Sal could feel his hand moving and drawing, even without his eyes guiding it.

A vision of the small screen device that Grant had used in the private meeting room. It was highlighted as the perfect interface for the machine. Sal tried to consider the workbench, but his brain discounted it for over a dozen reasons, listing them off in painful detail…showcasing to Sal that his instincts were fundamentally wrong. The laser engraver was broken down into components and restructured with a whole list of materials, and Sal was like a passenger as Mythcrafter, Perfect, and Kakushin essentially went into autopilot and created a game plan for how to build up the best components. It was like a mental checklist that was acquiring components using Sal's memories, like Grant's glass tablet. The simulation orb was discounted immediately because it wasn't good enough. The refiner at Quest Academy was discounted next, and Sal had to force the one in the carriage into consideration. It was a ridiculous amount of effort to fight against the logic of his brain, but it was possible.

Well, he thought it was. His mind broke down the machine and created a whole new task list to build it from scratch. Making all the components from raw materials, and programming a new set of instructions to make it a suitable component in his build. This repeated for all the machinery in the carriage, and Sal realized that his goal of just stacking them together and flooding them with essence wasn't going to yield any sort of result. He thought about Fabricate, Evolve, or even Invention as abilities he could use to make some of the components. But Mythcrafter batted those thoughts away and instead showed him a step-by-step process on how he could make them with hard work.

It was a painful exercise where he was constantly bombarded with new information. Only the loading bay area of the machine was simplistic, and Sal barely had half a second to breathe before his mind latched onto the next part of the puzzle. Every iteration in his head was broken apart, analyzed, determined, and reconstructed with new parts. It was like he was doing visual deductions with his mind, seeing the problems and fixing them at speed.

This continued for what seemed like an eternity. Finally, Sal was hit with the programming aspect—an area he knew nothing about. He was praying for this moment because it would finally be a reprieve from the onslaught of high-performance ideation. To Sal's dismay, his brain remembered the manuals bought from the Credit Store. In the blink of an eye, his tablet was in his hand, going through the video tutorials at ten times the speed he could conceivably consume it. Yet, all the information was flooding into his head and the Kakushin was navigating through the noise and highlighting what was useful. It was like how his tracker worked.

By Sal's best guess, it had been hours and the Kakushin was finally starting to wear off. As his eyes regained their focus, he could see dozens of sheets of paper all stacked professionally to one side, their entire surface area used to showcase how certain components were constructed. It was barely the foundations of the project, as there was so much more to go through. Sal was grateful for the break and was about to get to his feet when he paused. It was a stupid idea.

A really stupid idea. Sal groaned inwardly as his curiosity beat his judgment. Reaching to his waist, Sal unclipped his visor and secured it over his face. With Perfect still active, Sal took a steadying breath as he picked up the bottle of Kakushin.

"It'll be over soon," Sal lied to himself as he took another swig from the bottle.

CHAPTER 14: ALIAS

Sal's hands shook as he took the visor from his face. It had been another three hours of straight work, but none of it was in the flow state. He was conscious for every moment of it, watching as his tracker and his brain worked together to fix problems he didn't realize existed. There were so many problems, but Mythcrafter refused to let it fail. It meant that there was a possibility of building the vending machine, but it required a ridiculous amount of knowledge and planning to pull off. None of the items he had made in the past were this meticulous, nor did they require this much initial mental capacity. Yet, when it was all said and done, Sal was feeling accomplished.

His tracker had been guiding him through the fundamentals of essence programming and automation techniques. Fabi's guide on the Credit Store hadn't been sufficient enough beyond the basics, so Sal had found himself buying additional courses, which he flew through in record time. All told, he had spent close to two thousand Q-Cred on courses on the Credit Store. Although that should have been a massive sting, he felt it was worth it. Why? Because the knowledge from those courses were now in his tracker, and it was feeding the best points back to him so he could understand.

The best example he could give was the sheet of paper he was working on in that very moment. It was a programming sequence of commands that made absolutely no sense from a logic perspective. It was like a completely different language that used letters, numbers, and brackets. Yet, with the tracker helping him, he was able to create a set of protocols that would be implanted onto an essence chip, which was a big component of the machine's brain. When he first started doing it, Sal's mind had wandered slightly at the possibilities, which resulted in a half page being dedicated to the behaviors of a drone using the same brain-chip. The visor seemingly calculated that it was worthwhile storing the drone protocols before Sal had an opportunity to delete it.

Sal learned his lesson from that and focused on the vending machine concept. With the two sessions of Kakushin now completed, he had a rough roadmap of what he needed to do for the machine to be constructed. There were thirty-one things that needed to be Crafted from scratch. If he counted the machines that needed to be reconstructed and upgraded? That number went up to the fifties. The most astounding thing for him was the fact that it hadn't incorporated any runes or even essence types. This machine had zero reliance on a core or anything like that.

When Sal tried to investigate a power source, it was shown to be an external requirement. Not only did it need to be fed materials, but also cores. Sal wasn't sure that was the smartest path, but Mythcrafter had been insistent, showing how many paths to failure existed if it changed direction and incorporated a power source. Sal was also perplexed by the sheer scale of the machine. It was going to take up the entire carriage when it was done, and there was no way to reduce the scale without compromising the quality.

One of the key takeaways Sal did have was how horribly inefficient the whole design was. It would work, and Sal was immensely grateful to realize that his time was well-spent on all that sketching. But it was over-engineered to ensure that it would work. There were countless fail-safes in place. And the brain, for example, should have been small enough to fit in the palm of his hand, but because of his lack of proficiency, it was twenty times the size. The whole thing was made with Sal's current capabilities, and there were no shortcuts taken.

Shaking his head, Sal blinked a few times before getting back to work on the protocol function. By the tracker's calculation, he had another six thousand lines of text to complete before it would be finished. A single mistake in those lines would break the functionality, so Sal had to be content with writing them all out by hand. It was confusing him why it wasn't asking him to just load everything onto the tracker or make a new tracker and use it as the brain.

And so, Sal sat there until the moon was visible through the skylights. It was a painstaking process, but he managed to finish the segment of code he was working on. Rather than moving onto the next fifty-something tasks remaining, he got to his feet, unclipped the visor, and made his way to the bed on the other side of the secret wall. There wasn't a single shred of guilt or doubt in his mind as he launched himself onto the mattress, burying his face within the pillows. He had somehow signed himself up for the most torturous project known to man. He deserved the sleep that awaited him.

"Are you going to make us regret putting a bed in there?" Sophia set a fresh cup of coffee down in front of Sal. Her disapproval was obvious as she cast a glance around the mezzanine. Scattered papers covered the walls, with some designs perfectly matched up among the haphazard placement. It looked like they had been drawn up on the wall so a timeline could be made across the entire space.

Sal accepted the coffee with a sigh. "Sorry. I'll be home in a few days. I'm making progress and don't want to waste the time that I've got." He looked up at his mother, but saw her staring at the stack of empty food containers. He cleared his throat. "I'll also clean this place up. Sorry about that."

Sophia just made a sound of affirmation. "And don't forget to shower…you're cultivating a whole new odor from yesterday."

Sal blinked at that and smelled at his armpit before recoiling with a wince. "Ah, didn't know you stopped by yesterday. Was just kinda in the flow of things."

"I noticed." Sophia shook her head again. "I'll leave you to it. Just make sure to clean up and get some rest. If you're not home tomorrow, I'll bring in some home-cooked food. You can't keep eating takeout like this."

"Is Dad going to cook?" Sal asked hopefully. His eyes dropped immediately back to the table when he caught sight of his mother's expression. It was like she was daring for him to ask again.

Sophia laughed as she made her way to the stairs. "You're as bad as him. Don't overwork yourself, okay?"

"Promise." Sal watched her leave. When she was gone from view, Sal got to his feet and stretched his back with an aggravated sigh. He was going to turn into a pretzel at this rate. The previous evening it had gotten so bad that he moved to a standing position and started drawing on the walls. It had been a solid five days of just planning out the weapon vending machine, with much of his time having been spent on researching materials and methods to create mechanisms.

"Why do we do this to ourselves?" Sal asked himself with a sigh as he looked at all the pages around the room. It was ridiculous that so much preparation had to go into this, especially when it had taken a couple of days to make the Legendary sniper rifle. For something that wasn't going to be powered by essence, it was a nightmare to manufacture…and even worse to plan out from scratch. Without Mythcrafter, he would have been screwed. From the drawings he'd looked at, he understood that he was being guided to make the base components, which he'd then upgrade. That was without the absolute fortune it was going to cost to just get the materials required.

Sal moved back into position and continued onto the next batch of programming that needed to be done. The patterns were slowly starting to make sense, and he found himself anticipating the format of the code. He knew that there was always going to be a bracket to close, and even some of the functions were starting to make sense. Obviously, none of this was intuition as the tracker was bludgeoning it into his head at every opportunity, explaining the logic whenever Sal hesitated or let his mind wander.

He wasn't sure how it was going to be translated from page to the machine itself, but that was a step down the line. The more he looked at the functions, the more he wished that Perfect would take over and make him a super-genius at programming, but it was unfortunately not happening. And although he had already seen an improvement in his handwriting and blueprint drawings, it was all coming close to the end, and Sal was filled with an excitement that he had never experienced before. If he was considered a prodigy at Crafting, his aptitude for programming was rock bottom. Without the visor, he'd have been royally fucked.

Sal finished the last line of the sequence and let out a relieved sigh as he raised both of his arms over his head in celebration. A burst of pain emanated in his tired joints, reminding him that he hadn't stretched enough recently. With a wince, he brought his arms down and frowned. The workbench had words written on it, beneath the paper.

Run file?

"Yes?" Sal tapped on the screen, noting that the tracker hadn't advised against it. A loading bar started to work on the workbench, and Sal was immediately confused. It had never loaded before.

UnnamedOS Version 0.0.1
Verifying Core Modules…
- Design Interface: Missing Dependencies
- Crafting Directory: Missing Dependencies
- Material Load Order: File Not Found
- Crafting Algorithm: Loaded Successfully
- Security Protocols: Loaded Successfully

A ream of messages populated on the workbench screen, far too fast for Sal to make sense of it all. The tracker started to pick apart the information and didn't throw up any error messages in response, like all of this was expected.

Verifying System Integrity…
- o   Validating Crafting Blueprints: File Not Found
- o   Scanning for Hardware Compatibility: No Devices Recognized
- o   Running Diagnostics Check: Searching…

His tracker told him that he was looking at an operating system for the machine he was building. Sal just stared at it in shock. He couldn't for the life of him understand how the hundreds of lines of text were able to create something like this. When he looked up at the wall of parchment, one of them was highlighted by the tracker. Sal groaned as he moved around the table and plucked the page from the wall. Bringing it back to the workbench, he placed it on the surface and held his breath.

Updating Design Interface…

"Ah." Sal groaned as he looked around at the dozens of pages lining the walls. It was going to be a long evening, but he was hopefully done with the thousands of lines. His hand wasn't going to be able to take it. Blinking a few times, Sal picked up the coffee and took a drink, wincing slightly at the lukewarm temperature. He should have drunk it sooner.

The next while was spent with Sal moving around the room, taking down the pages and scanning them into the workbench to be added to the codebase. The diagnostics continued to run and eventually turned a number of errors into successes as it was patched with new content. Sal could only marvel at the technological capability of the workbench, as it just accepted his handwriting, parsed it into code, and implemented it within seconds.

When he was finally done, Sal was met with a loading screen on the workbench. It took longer than the others, but only barely. A few seconds later, he was greeted with a new set of messages, and a lot more successes. It couldn't detect any hardware, and Sal was fine with that considering he had yet to build any. From a System perspective, it looked to be complete. A few errors were thrown up, with prompts asking if he meant something else. All he had to do was confirm yes or no, or adjust it by rewriting it on the screen.

After a painstaking few hours of correcting his own handwriting, most of which was from the very beginning of the process, Sal was finished. The file was complete and did a fresh install.

UnnamedOS Version 0.0.17
Verification Complete.

Sal didn't care that his shoulders would hate it—he raised his arms in celebration. It was a triumphant moment and he had absolutely nothing to show for it. Painstaking, grueling code…that he essentially copied from Mythcrafter, the tracker, and countless Credit Store manuals. It wasn't really even his own code, but he was proud that it was done and it worked.

As his arms came down, Sal let out a relieved sigh…before the tracker highlighted the next step of the process.

He had more modules to create.

"Why are we doing this?" Sal repeated to himself as he rested his head against the workbench. Taking out his phone, he checked the comment section of the most recent manual he had bought. He wanted to see whether other people had struggled with it as much as he did. A little solidarity would go a long way. A single comment appeared at the bottom of the product page.

Jessajess: Essence deviation fix found! Here's the link!

Sal frowned as he clicked on the link, and was redirected away from the Credit Store. Instead, he was prompted with a login page for the Crafting Corner. "A forum for Crafters looking to help one another?" Sal read the tagline in disbelief.

There were thousands of entries, with multiple sections. He scrolled through the first few topics and didn't see anything worth reading. A search bar at the top was probably his best bet, and he tried searching for a query that was eating him alive for the last few days.

Crafting ability won't incorporate essence.

No results found.

Sal gave up on the search and instead looked for the essence programming section. When he navigated back to the home screen, there was a pinned thread at the top of the page with frequently asked questions. Sal navigated to it and searched through it. One of the entries caught his attention.

Who is Myth? Everything we know about the supposed Mythcrafter at Quest Academy.

Sal just stared at the entry for a few seconds before a single word left his lips. "Fuck."

CHAPTER 15: TUTOR

If Sal wanted something to wake him up more than a cup of lukewarm coffee, the topic of a Mythcrafter on a public forum was just what he needed. He was jolted by it and actually hesitated for a few seconds before clicking into the page. Anderson Royce had pretty much asked him if he was Myth a few months ago, and there was a growing group of people who knew about him. How many of them were Crafters, though?

Sal scanned through the article to find anything that would potentially identify him, but he was shocked after just the first few lines of the comments.

She walks around in a blood-red suit, and can make things with just a wave of her hands.

You should have seen her Savior video—she made a spear out of a prowler bone and some metal.

Battle Support! She has my vote. Did you see how she cut up that prowler in the scavenger run?

You all saw the pictures of the base she made in that camping trip.

Arbiter's Judgment: Proof that Blathnaid Clean, Upgrade's Protege, is Quest Academy's Mythcrafter!

Move over, Fabi…Upgrade has a new favorite! Click to see Forge's Reaction!

Sal just stared at the comments in complete bewilderment. They were all so certain that Blathnaid was a Mythcrafter. When he scrolled up to the body of the main post, he could see a few observations of Blathnaid working with Upgrade on the Arbiter's Judgment coat…and a list of eyewitnesses from the first-year cohorts that said Blathnaid's Savior reel was filled with impressive Crafting.

Looking into the reports, Sal's jaw clenched when he read the initial leak of the Mythcrafter title. It was nothing to do with any of his friends, or even the faculty. It was a single picture of the Legendary sniper rifle, with his Appraisal documents uploaded alongside it. The accompanied text had it all wrong.

One of the Supports in the Reavers Guild just sent a picture of this magnum opus! Look at it…all the names are there. Sal is the Appraiser who is constantly sticking to the Mythcrafter's side; they're in the same cohort and were on a team together in the tournament. Blathnaid is there as Myth, and then you have Upgrade and two people called Martin and Gosia, who are just Crafters in the Quest Academy workshop. This is huge! She's able to make up to the Mythic grade, and did you see those stats?! Tether…at that distance? We have a new Crafting Queen!

Sal just stared at the comments and sighed to himself. In a way, it was nice that none of the focus or attention was on him, but he wondered how Blathnaid was going to react when she saw this. He scrolled through all the comments until another caught his eye.

If there really was a Mythcrafter, do you really think that they would be at Quest Academy? The Hunter Bureau would have them locked up in a small room, forced to make weapons and barriers. There's no way they'd let her just run around the place, making whatever she wanted.

Sal smiled at that one before navigating away from the thread. There was nothing really to gain from scrolling through all the messages. All he'd get was some secondhand anxiety for Blathnaid. He did try a few more searches and even consulted the Frequently Asked Questions out of curiosity. It didn't give him the answers he was looking for, but he was able to go to a request board, where he could ask for the expertise of others. He guessed he didn't have anything to lose, so he tried to put in a few questions as a few posts…but the forum blocked his attempt after his first post. Apparently, he needed to wait for an answer, but could speed up his time by answering someone else's questions?

Sal turned off the screen of the tablet and placed it on the side of the workbench. He'd check in on it later. There was very little chance that there would be a hive mind of Crafters awake in the middle of the night. He was just about to launch into the next part of the project when the screen lit up with a message.

Question answered by F. Maccles:

- <u>Essence Programming</u> - Check the link for details. You'll see that it's not actually programming essence with behavioral patterns, but rather making programs to guide the essence behaviors. You're building protocols that act like instructions to the essence. For most Crafters with essence-based abilities, this will be a monumental task because you can't cheat your way to the finish line by flooding it with essence. You'll need to painstakingly create the protocols the old-fashioned way, and you'll find a basic tutorial <u>Here</u>.

- My advice, if you're just a first-year, is to bring up your problem in class with Upgrade. She'll walk you through it. If you're a second-year, you should be able to afford <u>This Course</u>. And if you're a third-year? You clearly didn't listen in class. Shame on you. :)

- Lastly, it seems really daunting at first…but it's just logic. If you keep going with it, and use the fundamentals in those courses, you'll do great! Any questions or breaks with your code, send them over to me and I'll happily have a look at it.

It took a few minutes for Sal to actually read the text as he was so caught up with the name at the top of the entry. *Fabi sent him a message.* His potential future wife, who he had created a new ability weave for, had just messaged him. It took a bit of time before he was able to read through the text and check out the links. The courses she had listed were ones she had recorded herself, and Sal couldn't help but smile at the fact that she was upselling her own work.

Question marked as Answered by S. Argento:
- Thank you, F. Maccles. This was incredibly useful. I'm a first-year, but I was able to afford that course. I'll listen to it tonight and contact you if I end up having questions. Really appreciate you taking the time to respond.

Sal chuckled to himself as he turned off the screen again and put it to the side of the workbench, when it suddenly illuminated in his hand. There was no way that she was that fast at responding. *Was it someone else answering the question?* He'd need to pause the notifications if that was the case, as it was only going to be a distraction.

Private Message Received from F. Maccles:
- You also bought my engraving course a few months ago, didn't you? Here's a refund for those courses. Use the Q-Cred for materials or outings with the guilds. You need to make sure you get into Second Year! :)

Sal could only stare at the screen as he received a second notification. His Q-Cred had been refunded, just like she said. A part of him wanted to send the money straight back to her, but he didn't want to refuse a gift. Instead, he went with a different angle.

Private Message Sent to F. Maccles:
- There was no need for that, but thank you. I don't like to owe people, so if you ever need an Appraiser, feel free to reach out. I can Appraise anything up to the Legendary grade.

Sal frowned as he removed the last line about Legendary grade from the message. He didn't want to sound like he was being boastful. He also added a smiley face, like she had done in her own messages. A few moments passed before he also deleted the face and hit Send.

Instead of just placing the tablet back on the bench, he turned it off and put it back in his pocket. If he let himself get distracted with messaging Fabi back and forth, he'd get nothing done. The next time he'd message her would be when he had a question that she could help him with. With his willpower in overdrive, Sal sat down and looked at the UnnamedOS in front of him on the workbench. Fabi had managed to clear up his doubts about the essence programming thing.

Mythcrafter had set him on the right path, and although there probably was another way to do it, it was done now. Which left him with a lot of components and mechanisms to build. Sal had to discount all the ones that had particular material requirements, and instead focus on the ones that he could cheat with essence.

He smirked as he recalled Fabi's message. Essence Crafters were cheaters in her eyes, that just flooded equipment with essence to do Crafting. He wondered whether she had a purist mentality, like what Upgrade had warned him about a few months ago. That they'd likely react negatively to how Sal used Mythcrafter to skip dozens of steps.

Mythcrafter moved through all the different phases of the project and eventually landed on the laser engraver. It needed to be disassembled, but there were enough materials in the carriage to upgrade it perfectly. Sal smiled as he looked through the pages and found the design document that dealt with the engraver. Just as he was about to head down to the carriage, he paused and looked at the other phases that he had skipped over. A gnawing part of him was hesitating.

He had already poured days of hard work into the creation of that operating system. Yes, the tracker had helped him and guided him through the whole process, but he had made the tracker, and that was a very easy justification to make. The idea in the back of Sal's head was immature, and he tried to trample it into oblivion, but it wouldn't die…

Would he be able to create this whole thing without cheating with essence? If he followed the directions of the tracker, and only used essence for the upgrades, would he be able to make it work? Mythcrafter took the hypothetical scenario and shattered in front of his eyes. Which was a little offensive, but he understood. He didn't have that level of capability yet.

With a sigh, Sal shook his head and took his tablet out of his pocket, turning it on in the process. He was a little disappointed there was no message from Fabi waiting for him. Navigating to the courses he had bought from her, he clicked into them and played them on normal speed. Rather than having his tracker doing all the heavy lifting for him, he wanted to understand the principles behind essence programming. He didn't want to be a cheater. Upgrade was able to Craft without her ability, and so could Fabi. Sal wanted to hold himself to that same standard.

Fabi's voice filled the room, echoing slightly as the sound reverberated in the surrounding tunnels. It was melodic, calming and filled with an excited energy. She clearly loved the topic, and Sal found himself smiling as he walked, not to the carriage, but to his own bed. Lying down, he placed the tablet on the side table and stared up at the ceiling, listening to Fabi's voice explaining the fundamentals of essence programming.

Maybe it was because Mythcrafter made it clear that he didn't have the skills to do it, or maybe it was the conversations with Upgrade over the last while. Sal wasn't sure, but he was certain that if he wanted to continue to call himself a Crafter, he needed to understand how it all worked. Just because he had an easy method to success didn't mean he had to take it all the time. He was on a break between semesters and now was a good time to experiment.

Fabi's voice continued as she explained how different categories of essence reacted to essence programming. There were apparently whole studies done on the topic, explaining the use-cases of different essence types. Sal blinked in surprise and turned to look at his phone after a certain segment. He went back by a minute to hear it again.

The most primal form of essence programming are runes. Their design instructs atmospheric or internal essence to conform to a certain outcome. This could be an absorption instruction, or even a barrier activation. They're really interesting, and simple to replicate, but are very limited in how much they can reasonably execute.

The most complex rune that we're aware of is the evolutionary rune, but even that is limited by design constraints and surface area. With essence programming, we can create codes and instructions that could reasonably result in hundreds of outcomes, rather than just a handful…but that's a topic we'll come to later.

Sal could only marvel at the realization that runes were essentially a primitive form of essence programming. He hadn't really had much interest in the topic before, and saw it only as an obstacle to overcome…but now? His head buzzed with the possibilities it could potentially open for him.

Sal lay there on the bed and listened to Fabi's voice for the rest of the night. Despite the fatigue of all the code he had written throughout the day, he didn't dare close his eyes in case he missed something. It was only when Fabi's voice faded at the end of the course that Sal finally closed his eyes and let sleep take him. There was a lot of work to do, and he was genuinely excited to get to it.

CHAPTER 16: LISTINGS

"He lives!" Sophia announced in mock surprise as Sal walked into the kitchen of their family home. She tapped a button on the coffee machine and smiled at him from across the granite countertop. "So, should I even ask what you've been cooking up in that workshop, or am I better off not knowing?"

Sal smiled at his mother as he took a seat on one of the barstools beside the countertop. He combed through his coarse black hair with his fingers, slicking it back and out of his eyes. "Bits of studying, some sketching, and a few side projects to keep me busy."

"Keep you busy? You're joking, right? You've been squirreled away in that workshop since we showed it to you." Sophia practically scoffed as she pulled a fresh coffee from the machine and placed it down in front of Sal. "I noticed that the fridge was raided last night, so I guessed you were home." She looked at him carefully before a smile blossomed on her face. "And you even showered. I'm very proud of you."

Sal shot her a withering look before shaking his head with a sigh. "I've been taking days off, I promise. After the auction, I slept for a few days and did pretty much nothing but meditate!"

Sophia shook her head with a smile. "Nope. Doesn't count because that was weeks ago, and we've got no way to prove that you're living like a healthy human. Meditation is that thing you're doing with your essence gates, isn't it? Sounds more like training than relaxing to me." She busied herself around the kitchen and placed a hand on the fridge door. "Breakfast?"

Sal shook his head. "No thanks, not really hungry at the moment." He paused for a second as he looked at his coffee. "Dad said that both of you talked through the argument. Is everything really okay?"

Sophia smiled as she sat at the counter across from him. "I made him work for it, but we're all good. Everything has been moving so fast, and I didn't feel comfortable with him making decisions without consulting me. We're on the same page, though, and you'll be happy to know that I've been brought on to help with the property listings."

"Listings?" Sal repeated in confusion.

"Your father mentioned that you were looking for places around Silver Sanctuary, and I wasn't going to let him recommend the crap he had picked out. I was thinking we could maybe go as a family and inspect a few of the properties they have for sale." She winked at him. "And maybe a few of the places that aren't up for sale…yet."

Sal laughed as he looked at her for a few seconds. "Really? You think that we'd be able to uproot a few families who have lived here for decades?"

Sophia shrugged. "There are a few places in the commerce district that aren't performing well. A nice offer might be all the encouragement they need to settle down in one of the other projects." She thought about it for a second before smiling. "Also, a few of the business owners want to be closer to some dungeons, to really boost trade. I can think of three off the top of my head. Dalton, for example, would probably jump at a decent offer."

"And what sort of price range are you thinking?" Sal asked out of curiosity. He wasn't really sure how much the buildings in Silver Sanctuary would cost, but he was sure it would be a premium. Having the protection of a private gated community, far removed from the dangers of demons, had to come at an inflated cost. Added to that, Silver Sanctuary had a train station that led to Quest Academy and farther into the city. There was no way he'd be able to get something for cheap.

Sophia considered it momentarily before looking back at Sal. "I'd estimate that the Argento Auction House is worth around fifty-five million, just for the amount of storage space and land. We didn't want to make a high-rise building, which many would call an inefficient use of the space, but it suits our needs. You know how much we love that clock tower and the courtyard." She tapped her hand against the countertop as she thought about it. "You probably wouldn't need something this extreme, but it's not a bad idea to get something you can grow into over time."

Sal whistled at the figure, not really sure whether he should be looking at something that drastic right out of the gate. "I'd probably try for something a little more humble than that to begin with. Don't think I'd need something with that much space."

Sophia's brow creased as she looked at Sal in confusion. "If you're going to be operating a guild, then you're going to need training rooms, equipment lockers, a workshop for your Crafting…dormitories, a war room for planning out strategy. There are so many things that go into a guild. The Argento Auction House would probably be too small for what you need. When I said you wouldn't need something this extreme, I meant the limitation of verticality. There should be nothing stopping you from making a high-rise."

Sal frowned as he thought about it. "I like the Argento Auction House, though. The style of it and the fact that it has so much history. I'm not sure how I'd feel if the guild was just some bland tower, if you get me?"

Sophia's smile grew wider. "Well then, I think you've found your topic of conversation for the Arc Guild. Big places like Arc are likely dying to get a real challenge, and I know that Eric dies a little on the inside every time he's asked to make another basic skyscraper like the Paradox Guild Headquarters."

Sal thought about it for a few moments before nodding. "Do you think I'm making a mistake with all of this? The whole guild thing?"

Sophia didn't hesitate for even a second as she shook her head. "No, Salvatore. I think you've come to a very mature conclusion. I would have maybe seen it as a dream a year ago, but after seeing your works in that auction…and seeing the possibilities of how you can help people with their powers? I'm fully behind your decision. The calls we had when you were at Quest Academy were one thing, and I tried to understand what Quest was telling us about this whole Mythic Guild thing…but honestly, all of it was just words until I saw the reality of it."

She reached across the countertop and placed her hand on top of Sal's. "We've had all sorts of conversations about how we should try to help you in your journey. Personally, I was worried you'd get whisked off to the Hunter Bureau or that a guild would take you away from Quest Academy. I'm your mother, and it's my job to worry about you. If anyone was going to tell you that you're making a mistake, I'd be the first in line."

Removing her hand, Sophia stood up from her seat and placed both hands on the countertop, looking at Sal intently. "So, now that we've talked about your future as a property mogul and as a guildmaster, you need to tell me all about the friends you've made. How are things going with that Hannah girl?"

Sal blinked at the sudden change of topic. "We had something going, but then she was mind-controlled by a group of kids from Bastion families, and we had an explosive argument. We've not spoken since. I'm sure we'll clear the air when we're back, though."

Sophia's mouth opened and closed at that. "And what about Divinity? Have you two…?" She looked at Sal meaningfully.

Sal shook his head. "We're just friends. I thought about it, and she's an amazing person…but I don't know if we'd actually be suited for each other. Her power of being able to see into the future means she already knows what I'm going to say, and it constantly feels like a losing battle when arguing with her."

Sophia grinned. "Okay, I like the sound of that one. Beginning as friends is a really good start. Just see what happens in the future. I do want some grandchildren eventually." She winked as though she had just made the greatest joke of all time.

Sal sighed as he folded his arms. "Want to hear something funny, though?"

Sophia sat back down immediately and cupped her face with her hands. "Always!"

"Divinity told me the name of the person I'm supposed to marry. We were all just messing about in the canteen, and Barry was giving her a hard time about not telling us the future…I can't even remember what we were asking about," Sal started explaining.

"Who? Who are you supposed to marry?" Sophia interjected in excitement, her eyes lighting up as she eagerly waited for the answer.

Sal chuckled as he raised a hand. "I'm getting to that! So, Divinity said that one of the statements was true and one was a lie. She said that Barry ends up with Victoria Chase, who is…not a good match for Barry. Then, the other one was Fabi Maccles. That's who Divinity said I'd end up marrying. I haven't even met the girl!" He laughed as though it were the most ridiculous thing ever.

Sophia stared at him in shock. "You're joking…"

Sal shook his head. "Nope, that's the name of the girl Divinity said I marry. But it's hard to know if she was telling the truth or not."

Sophia tilted her head and paused before speaking. "Sal…is this Fabi girl a couple of years older than you?"

Sal froze at those words. "Yeah…she's a third-year. How did you know that?" His mind was in overdrive as he tried to piece together what he might have missed. *How did his mother, of all people, know something like that?*

Sophia bit her lip as she looked at Sal, as though she were trying to stop herself from laughing. "You've absolutely met Fabi before, when you were kids."

Sal's heart dropped into his chest. He didn't remember her at all, and the name wasn't familiar to him either. His mother had to be playing a prank on him, and it was absolutely working.

Sophia chuckled as she shook her head in surprise. "Who do you think got you that prowler blood delivery? Maurice Macaluso. His daughter, who you used to play with as a kid, is Fabrizia Macaluso…" She watched Sal's face intently, as though trying to see whether he had any recollection of her.

Sal was completely floored by the revelation. He searched in the back of his mind but couldn't for the life of him remember her. Sure, they had gone over to Maurice's place a few times when he was younger, for deliveries and things like that…but he didn't remember Fabi being there.

Sophia couldn't help but laugh at Sal's expression. "The Macaluso family thought it would be easier to do business with an easier to write surname, so they changed it to Maccles. Probably why Fabrizia goes by Fabi…Maurizio changed his own to Maurice for simplicity. Personally, I'm grateful your father didn't try the same crap. I would not have married a man called Peter Silver."

It wasn't that Sal didn't want to answer; he just couldn't find the words. Not only was Fabi from Silver Sanctuary, she was Maurice's daughter and he had met her in the past? He looked at his mother desperately. "Please tell me that this is some elaborate joke?"

Rather than answering, Sophia gave him a sympathetic smile. "Maurice was the one who told us what equipment we should get for a Crafter, since he had gone through all the same steps with Fabrizia. A lot of the equipment in the workshop is her old stuff."

Sal couldn't help but laugh. "I can't remember her at all. That's probably a really bad sign, isn't it?" He thought about it, racking his brain for a memory of her, but it just wasn't coming up with anything.

Sophia shrugged. "You were very young at the time. She was whisked off to countless places as a kid, practically bankrupting Maurice. They tried everything for the poor girl, but she was born without an ability, by the looks of it."

Sal bit his lip as he looked at his mother. "About that…"

CHAPTER 17: PROFIT

"Could you two fill me in on what's going on?" Petro asked as he locked the front doors to the Argento Auction House and followed his family out to the street. "I'm only catching the tail end of everything you're saying and missing too much context."

Sophia glared at Petro for a second and raised her hand. "Shush, I'll fill you in later. I don't want him to restart the whole thing." She looked back to Sal, and an excited smile crossed her face. "And she has absolutely no idea?"

Sal sighed inwardly and regretted that he started telling his mother about the whole weave simulation for Fabi. She was reacting in the exact same way Upgrade had, and it was like she was picking out the dress and hat she'd wear at the fictional upcoming wedding.

"Who had no idea?" Petro insisted as he pocketed his keys and followed them out onto the street. Confusion was written all over his face as he looked at Sal for some context.

"Fabrizia Macaluso," Sophia said in an exasperated voice before she rounded on Sal again. "Come on, don't leave me in suspense."

Sal just gestured with his hands. "No, she doesn't know about it…or at least she didn't know about it a few weeks ago. Quest wanted to keep it a secret until he was sure it could be administered properly."

Petro frowned as he looked at Sophia. "Maurice's girl? Is it something about the equipment in the new workshop?"

Sophia let out an aggravated sigh as she turned on her husband. "Sal made an ability weave for her, as part of that skill simulation thing. Divinity told him that Fabrizia might be his future wife."

Petro practically bolted forward to join them. "Whoa! She's an absolute knockout. Well done!" He playfully punched Sal on the shoulder and gave Sophia a wide smile, which was not reciprocated. His smile faded slightly before he laughed. "I mean, they're good people. You could do a lot worse than the Macaluso family!"

"Inspiring as ever, Petro," Sophia said dryly before she tapped Sal on the back. "Now, don't just stop there. What was her ability? You lost me a bit when you started talking about the four different parts of it."

Sal thought about it for a second before picking an example that his mother would understand. It wasn't that she wasn't smart; she just had no interest in it. "Remember that girl you had on the Restoration team, Lori?"

Sophia nodded, but her frown showed her confusion at the sudden change of topic.

Sal continued with a smile. "So, Lori's ability was Repair. It can evolve over time and become Upgrade, which can then become Invent, and finally, Evolve. The thing is, most people won't get an evolution of their ability because of the knots that form in their weave over time. Similar to how Dad's All Sight ability was getting harder to use as he got older."

Sophia's eyes widened as she looked at Petro. "Lori could have had the same power as Upgrade? She was pretty useless, though…"

Petro snorted at that and shook his head. "By useless, you mean she couldn't do Restoration the way you wanted her to do it?"

"It's called standards, Petro," Sophia snapped back, a guilty smile on her face. "How difficult is it to Repair something without having left over parts? That girl…"

Sal cleared his throat. "Anyway! Fabi's weave was a jumbled mess and it prevented her from activating even the most basic version of her ability. I fixed her weave in a way that would allow her to not only activate it, but give it the potential to evolve over time. If she works hard, her weave could end up becoming insanely powerful."

Petro paused. "Who is Fabi? Are you talking about Fabrizia?" He looked over at Sophia, who gave him a quick nod of affirmation.

Sophia tilted her head slightly. "So, you've essentially given her access to four different ability weaves…that she can access as she gets stronger?"

Petro shook his head. "Sounds like the new weave overwrites the previous one." He caught sight of his wife's expression, and he course corrected. "I mean, that's just what I think of when he says evolving weaves. I could be wrong."

Sal shrugged. "Everything is hypothetical at the moment. I don't know how it will all work, or if she'll even go through with the Skill Implant. She's a Savior, though, so I'm pretty sure that she's eligible for it. Grant, the Hero I met with Quest, he's able to copy weaves and implant them into others…so I'm guessing he'll be the best judge of its feasibility."

Petro pointed them to the right. "Okay, we've got a few properties to look at. Dalton's first, Soph?"

The street was incredibly calm as it was afternoon. Everything was pedestrianized, with narrow streets that weren't designed for cars. Ornate stone slabs were constructed at various points along the street, each showing a historical figure of note, usually with ties to Silver Sanctuary. All the buildings in this area were commercial, with no residential apartments in sight. Boutique clothing stores, luxury car dealerships, fancy restaurants: it was the upmarket center of Silver Sanctuary.

"Dalton is the likeliest to sell, so it's probably better to get a few others under our belt first. Have a few that Sal likes so we can work Dalton down to be competitive." Sophia smiled as she hiked her thumb over her shoulder to point to the left side of the street.

Petro smiled as he followed Sophia's direction. "Even if Dalton doubled the price, Sal would probably manage to afford it. Just a few more auctions like that last one and he could probably buy the whole strip." He looked at Sal thoughtfully. "What's your budget for this whole venture? I'd suggest that we look for potential rather than something finished. Developers these days can pretty much pluck the vision you have for something out of your head and make it a reality."

Sal just shrugged. "Browsing for the moment… I don't even know how much money we have to play with. Someone hasn't given me my commission slip yet." He looked at his father pointedly.

Sophia chuckled as she plucked an envelope from Petro's breast pocket. "I don't know why he makes you do a song and dance for a big reveal every…single…time." She smiled at Petro and handed the envelope to Sal. "Here you are."

Petro gave her a mock sigh. "Why can't you let me have a little bit of fun?" He looked at Sal and then at the envelope in his hands. "But yes, go on…have a look and see what you think."

Sal didn't waste any time in breaking the seal on the envelope and pulling out the card nestled within. He desperately hoped that they hadn't shortchanged themselves to give him a bigger payout. After their performance together in that auction, he didn't want them suffering a loss because of their feelings as parents.

"Oh, and we doubled our rates. You can afford it." Sophia smiled as she dug her elbow into Petro's side, as if trying to get him to confirm her blatant lie.

Petro just smiled as he watched for Sal's reaction.

When Sal looked at the number, he froze. He had seen the profit margins after the auction, and he had made his own calculations, but it hadn't prepared him for the reality.

Salvatore Argento: Commission Slip (Evolutionary Collection)
- o   Breastplate of the Unyielding
    - Sale Price: $540,000.00
    - Listing Fees: $27,000.00
    - Argento Artisan: $216,000.00
    - Argento Auction: $54,000.00
    - Restoration: In-House
    - Materials: In-House
    - Total Commission: $459,000.00

Sal smiled when he saw that they had listed the Argento Artisan as a forty percent rate, but that it was added to his total earnings. All he had to adhere to were the listing fees and the flat cut that the auction house took. Essentially, he was taking eighty-five percent of the total amount.

- o   Storm Strike (Total)
    - Sale Price: $8,450,000.00
    - Listing Fees: $422,500.00
    - Argento Artisan: $3,380,000.00
    - Argento Auction: $845,000.00
    - Restoration: Unnecessary
    - Materials: In-House
    - Total Commission: $7,182,500.00

Sal couldn't believe his eyes as he looked at the obsidian daggers payout. He was sure that the big entry was going to be the Wraith Walker set, but the cumulative value of the daggers had managed to blow him away. The first one had gone for more than six hundred thousand, and the prices just went up after that.

"We didn't want to show it to you too soon, in case you started locking yourself in the workshop trying to make even more of those daggers." Petro laughed guiltily before looking over at Sophia. "But then your mother told me that you were locking yourself in there anyway, so we had nothing to lose by handing it over to you now."

Sal just smiled as he moved onto the last entry on the docket.

- o Wraith Walker Set
    - Sale Price: $7,200,000.00
    - Listing Fees: $360,000.00
    - Argento Artisan: $2,880,000.00
    - Argento Auction: $720,000.00
    - Restoration: Completed
    - Materials: In-House
    - Total Commission: $6,120,000.00

Sal looked at the final total at the bottom of the page.

- o Total Commission for Evolutionary Collection
    - $13,761,500.00

Petro grinned as he looked at Sal's stupefied expression. "Now, both of us had talked about this, and we'd like to guarantee the money for whatever you decide on. Be that today, or in the future, we'll help you secure the property."

Sophia nodded, smiling. "Although a few more auctions like that one and you won't need the help. We'd just like to help you as much as we can, before you become super famous and forget about us."

Sal gave his mother a sideways glance. "As if I'd get away with that. You'd hunt me down and slap me sideways if I pretended to forget about you."

"That's my boy," Sophia practically cooed.

Petro stepped beside Sal and clapped him on the shoulder. "And don't feel offended with the fifteen percent. You know the rules." The smile on his face told Sal that he definitely didn't expect Sal to feel any remorse about the loss of fifteen percent.

Sal breathed a sigh of disbelief as he pocketed the envelope. "I'm tempted to hand that Silver token back to the Reavers. I don't think I could ever justify working for them when I could be making stuff for the auction."

Petro chuckled as he started to walk, urging Sal to follow along with his hand still on Sal's back. "Now, don't be like that. Relationships are incredibly valuable, too. Villa is a good person to have in your corner…for whatever situation that may arise. A few quick Appraisals will get you a strong reputation with them, and you'll eventually get to name your own prices."

"So, are we finished with the Fabrizia conversation? I want to know more details." Sophia laughed from up ahead. "If she's going to be my daughter-in-law, I need as much notice as possible for the wedding. Since it's two Silver Sanctuary families, we could use the courtyard at the auction?"

Sal shot her a disdainful look as they continued walking along the street. It wasn't long before Sophia stopped and turned around.

"So, what do you think of this one?" She had a wide smile on her face, and her hands clasped behind her back.

Sal frowned as he looked to his left. It was a partially ruined building, that had previously been three stories. Only the ground floor looked to be in use, with just two walls remaining on the upper floors. It looked like the basic level of care had been applied in keeping the crumbling mess of walls from falling. Sal had to walk to the side to look at it properly. The owner clearly wanted to preserve the architecture of the building before the demonic war, but it was battered beyond belief. Shoddy repairs existed in certain places, with scaffolding holding up an entire segment of the second floor. The only reason Sal could tell that it was previously a three-story building was because a single wall pointed upward where a roof was supposed to be.

"I think…it's…" Sal couldn't find the words as he looked back at his mother's smiling face. "Not really what I was thinking of?"

"Good," Sophia remarked as she pointed in the opposite direction, across the street. "Because that building is part of a set. The seller apparently ran out of money before being able to complete the next phase of the project. All their funds went into this one."

Sal followed her gesture to a beautiful black pergola, covered in grape vines. Grey pavement stones were intricately placed around the wooden structure, offering a stark contrast to the collection of tables and chairs underneath a stylized canopy. Glass windows stretched up along one wall, covering at least four floors. Sal could see a busy kitchen on the ground floor, an elevator shaft nestled on one side that led all the way up to…

"The train station." Petro finished Sal's thought for him as he pointed at the station platform high above ground level. "The thought was that people would be willing to brave a few Red Zones to visit a luxury restaurant. Unfortunately, it didn't really work out for them."

"Wait, so that's included?" Sal turned back to the lot he had confused it with. "All those big windows are facing that…thing." He gestured at the wreckage, as though his point were obvious.

Sophia nodded. "Yeah, there was apparently a whole plan to make a wide corridor that connected the buildings, but elevated high above street-level. Likely a victim of the redevelopment initiative. So many small businesses cashed in on it and couldn't afford the repayments."

Petro nodded somberly. "Hunter Bureau signs a blank check, all in the name of redevelopment of the area, and everyone swarms…without reading the fine print. I'd feel bad for them, but most of them did it out of greed rather than actual need."

Sophia clapped her hands together. "So, are you ready to see the first potential location for the new guild headquarters?"

Sal grinned as he walked forward toward the doorway. "Absolutely."

CHAPTER 18: SUAVE

"By the way…" Sal said as they walked through the door. "I didn't want to give you this when you were angry, because you'd think it was a bribe." He reached down to his holster and unclipped a visor with a black lens. "And I forgot about it when you brought me coffee, but…yeah, I remember you said you'd want one like mine."

He presented the new tracker to his mother. It was a more delicate-looking version of his own. There was no fancy moonsilver or scarlet screen on this one, but it had the basic functionality that she was looking for. Obsidian glass was apparently suitable for the screen, but putting a curve in that material had graced the top three of his least favorite Crafting experiences. Coding was top of the list, with wood refining coming second. One of the fun experiments he had played with was making the runes with the engraver machine. It was so much more efficient than doing it by hand.

"What?" Sophia started as her eyes locked onto the tracker. "You didn't…"

She carefully took it from his hand and cradled it in her own, staring at it in wonder as she turned it over to examine all the details. "It's beautiful. The black and…what's this green?"

"Matches your eyes. I used the prowler blood within the runes for a special effect." Sal encouraged her to put it on.

Petro's smile faltered slightly. "Prowler blood gives off the Stealth attribute?" He was looking at the tracker carefully when his eyes widened. "Oh my. That's…incredible."

Sophia looked at him quizzically as she placed the tracker over her eye. "How does it look?" Her eyes widened as the information started loading up from everything she was seeing, causing her to stumble ever so slightly as she reached out into the air in front of her. "Whoa…this is…incredible. Thank you so much, Salvatore. Honestly, I'd love to play around with it, but I don't want to look like a weirdo in front of the building owners."

Petro grinned. "That shouldn't be an issue." He reached to Sophia's tracker and tapped the side of it. "Perfect. Nobody can see it now."

Sophia stared at him as if he were crazy, but then frowned. The edges of the visor were completely gone. She couldn't see it in front of her, but all the information remained.

Sal smiled as he gestured at his own belt that turned invisible with a touch. "The stealth attribute is very useful for concealing it from view. Now people won't know that you're wearing it."

Petro placed his hands on his hips as he looked at Sal with a slight shake of his head. "So, I take it this is you picking your favorite parent. I should be happy with the power upgrade, but I can't help but feel hard done by." He grinned as he spoke.

Sal shrugged. "I'm surprised you haven't found your own present. I didn't hide it particularly well."

Petro's smile dropped as he looked between Sophia and Sal in confusion. "Wait, what? You made something for me?" His joke had backfired, and he was genuinely curious if he was being messed with.

Sal nodded as he gestured in the direction of the auction house. "When was the last time you looked at all those suit jackets in your office? I added a suit that puts this outfit to shame." He gestured at his own violet-colored ensemble with a smile. "I'm pretty sure Epic grade was a little ridiculous, and the evolutionary runes were a little over the top…but if you ever did decide on fighting on the front lines, you'd take out a few demons for sure."

Sophia's jaw dropped as she looked at Sal in disbelief. "You made this tracker and a suit for your father? When…did you even have time to do that?"

Sal just laughed. "It doesn't take two weeks to make ten daggers. Oh, and you can do the Appraisal of his suit when we get back. I'm pretty sure your tracker can handle that sort of workload." He practically beamed at his parents, who both looked at him in complete shock.

Petro was the first to recover as he put a hand to his head. "I'm not letting you spend your own money on this. I'll do the Appraisals when we get back to the auction, and I'll send you the money. This is far too much to be considered a gift, Sal."

Sal nodded in agreement. "I'll work out the amount of rent that I should have been paying since I got home, since we're being so fair about things."

Petro faltered as he looked at Sal with a tight smile. "Okay…I see how you're playing this one. We'll accept the gifts this time, but this is the last of it." He sighed and shook his head, as though thinking through the costs of how much the tracker and suit would go for in the auction. "Thank you for such thoughtful gifts."

Sophia chuckled as she embraced Sal with a tight squeeze. "No matter what your father says, I love this and I'm not giving it up…ever. Thank you, thank you." She grinned as she adjusted the invisible tracker on her head. "Is my hair sitting okay?"

Petro gave her a nod with a warm smile. "Now, are we going to continue standing here in the entrance looking like a group of weirdos, or will we go and talk to them?" He gestured at a reception desk that was on the other side of the wide entrance area.

The style of the interior was just as beautiful as outside. Black stained wood paneling decorated the bottom half of the walls, with exposed stonework stretching all the way up to the high-rise ceiling. An elegant chandelier was suspended from above with industrial cables; each of the pointed bulbs were actually small cores encased in decorative glass.

"The marble floor is fake," Sophia whispered as she looked at her feet. A wide smile was on her face as she gave Sal a conspiratorial wink. It was clear that she was trying to act natural, but she couldn't resist looking in every direction to get as much information as possible.

Petro looked over his shoulder at Sophia. "Paneling is a laminate and not even real wood."

Sophia veered off from their group to get a closer look, and by the sound of her chuckle, she had confirmed her husband's words.

"Was it a mistake giving it to her now?" Sal asked his father. He sighed as he looked at her with a bewildered expression.

Petro shook his head. "Nope, you've made her year with that one. Well done, kiddo." He moved forward purposefully toward the front desk, where a young woman stood with a polite smile on her face. "Petro Argento. We're here to meet with the owner."

"Just one moment, Mr. Argento," she responded before accessing the interface at her fingers. A few taps later, she looked back up with the exact same smile. "Thank you for your patience. Mr. Pando will be with you shortly. Can I order you any refreshments while you wait? You can take a seat in our lounge area, and we can bring you some menus?"

Sal followed her outstretched arm with his eyes and saw a beautiful glass double door with a black wood frame. The glass had a rippling effect that obscured what was behind it, likely for privacy. So far, his first impression of the place was that it had a lot of underutilized space, but the decor was quite nice, even if it was fake. It just felt like it lacked substance.

Petro thanked her and led his family through the double doors, which opened into the lounge area. The change was immediate when the booths came into view. It was like the designer of the pergola outside decided to try to emulate the same thing for the seating areas, using wood and leather as the primary materials. The ceiling went up for three entire floors, with a series of balconies that overlooked the lounge on the ground floor. Black wooden walkways connected the balconies in an oddly symmetrical pattern.

Sal wanted to see what they looked like, but the booths above were heavily obscured. On the ground floor, there were a collection of couches and tables, all nestled underneath their very own wooden structures. Each had curtains secured at the sides, allowing privacy if necessary. The light source for all tables were candles, and the plates were stoneware.

"Even if it's fake, they've done an incredible job on the decor," Sophia muttered as she walked to the nearest booth. "Here work for you?" She looked at Petro and Sal, her hand resting on a leather armchair.

Sal nodded in agreement. "Yeah, I kinda want to see what the view looks like from up there." He gestured at the balconies above as he took a seat in an opposite armchair.

Petro followed his gaze as he sat on the couch that was placed between the two armchairs. "Structurally speaking…this is a lot of wasted space. You'd be spending a few million getting it fit for purpose." He turned his attention to the massive glass wall that revealed the street outside. "And that eyesore across the street is going to cost a fortune to get into any sort of usable state."

Sophia waved her hand like it was nothing to worry about. "That can be your material storage place. It doesn't need to look pretty, just hold all the stuff that you need." She looked up at the open air above them. "But this is a definite problem…the space here could be used for dormitories, training areas, armories, and so much more." With a slight shake of her head, she laughed. "Well, at least you wouldn't need to do much to put in a functional kitchen."

Petro nodded. "It would need to be an incredibly good deal to make this one worth consideration. What do you think, Sal?"

Sal couldn't help but agree with his parents. "I really like the fact that it's two buildings, and there's definitely potential for future growth. The train station access is a definite plus, too. Guess it will depend on the rest of the space."

They sat there and chatted for a short while before a man appeared in a long black coat, a white shirt open at the collar and suit trousers, finished with the shiniest shoes that Sal had seen in a long time. Even without Appraising the items, he could tell that this man had an expensive wardrobe. In his hand was a tray containing a few different bottles, and a set of glasses. An immaculate haircut and neatly trimmed beard framed his gentle smile; his dark-brown eyes matched his hair color and his skin had a natural tan.

"Apologies for making you wait. It took me far too long to find this treasure." He spoke smoothly as he placed a vintage bottle of whiskey down on the table in front of Petro, accompanied by an ornate tumbler glass. "For the lady of the house." He placed a bottle of white wine down on one of the stoneware placemats; the condensation on the bottle showcased that it had already been chilled.

"And finally, for the young master of the house." He placed a silver percolator with a stoneware mug beside it. When everything was set, he took another few tumblers from the tray and placed them on the table before masterfully flipping the tray and sending it flying across the room like a discus, where it landed perfectly onto a stack of similar trays.

"My name is Michel Pando, and I'm the owner of this fine establishment. My wonderful wife is unfortunately unable to be here as she's managing our downtown boutique. I apologize on her behalf." His voice was deep and held the traces of an accent. "I also hope you'll forgive the intrusion on your personal lives, but I inquired as to your tastes." He gestured at the selection of drinks in front of them.

Petro picked up the bottle of whiskey and whistled slowly as he turned it around for Sophia to take a good look at it. She didn't pay him any heed as she was already pouring her own wine.

Michel winced ever so slightly when he saw her. "We're operating a reduced staff at the moment. Our chief sommelier would slap me if he saw me allowing you to pour your own glass. I hope you'll forgive the lack of professionalism."

Sal hesitated from pouring his own cup as he looked at Michel. "Is it okay if I pour this myself? I'm curious to try it."

Michel waved at him that it was completely fine. "Yes, of course. I hope you like the aroma. It's a very different coffee bean than you'll be accustomed to, but I hope you'll enjoy it."

Sophia took a sip of her wine and released a contented sigh before reclining back in her seat. "I'd like to personally hire your researcher. This wine is extraordinary."

Michel smiled as he inclined his head in her direction. "We're very lucky that we have a whole collection of whites that are designed to age. Our suppliers have the fiercest Heroes you could imagine protecting the grapes. No essence interference, either. I'm glad that you enjoyed it." He took a seat opposite Petro's couch, leaving Sal and Sophia on either side of him. "So, we have a selection of cheeses that should arrive soon. We'll not be talking business until I hear all about this incredible auction you hosted recently. The evolutionary collection, I believe?"

Sal's eyebrow raised as he lifted the coffee to his lips. If he was just going by taste profile, it was incredible. There were no extra effects like with Alex's concoctions, but for flavor alone, it was a contender for Sal's favorite coffee.

Petro chuckled as he lifted his whiskey and looked at the amber liquid in the glass. "What would you like to know about that auction in particular? I'm guessing you had a few customers who had attended?"

Michel smiled as he poured a glass of whiskey for himself. "More than a few. By all accounts, it sounds like the Argento Auction House is evolving into a more serious institution. If I am being honest with myself, it made me excited. There are too many businesses here that are content with what they have. I could happily continue what I'm doing here and carve out a comfortable living with the profits…but it's not enough."

He looked out the window to the dilapidated building across the street. "Even if I poured all my resources into completing this venue, nothing would change. The customer base isn't interested in spectacle and theater…they're barely interested in cuisine. Silver Sanctuary is a stable and safe place, but it's not the commercial hub that I hoped for it to become."

Michel raised his whiskey and smiled at Petro. "But then I hear about your auction, and I am…ah, how do you say it? Fueled? The passion and possibility that I hoped to curate here…is being achieved by you."

The cheese boards arrived, carried by the lady they had met at the reception area. Michel smiled and encouraged them all to help themselves. It was only after the woman had left that Michel placed his glass down on the table and folded his hands on his crossed knee.

"I'd like to know what your plan is." He spoke with a smile. "My thoughts of selling this place are…contingent on what you say next. I want to be a part of something greater, and if Silver Sanctuary can manage that, then I would be a fool to leave."

CHAPTER 19: PLAYED

"What did you think?" Sophia asked as they left the restaurant. She was firstly looking at Petro, but turned her attention to Sal. "He was suave, but I'm not sure how I felt about the proposal."

Sal couldn't help but agree with his mother. "A discounted sales price for a stake in whatever venture we proceed with? On one hand, I like that it's an investor from Silver Sanctuary. But on the other hand, I don't really want to have partners in this venture…especially from the hospitality sector."

Petro nodded as he walked down the street. "The floor plans for the place were promising, though. I had no idea they had so much more space than that room. As Sal said, the elevator to the train is a very nice feature." He thought about it a bit more before shaking his head. "Personally, I think that it would be better for us to do this without him. He's chasing profitability more than anything else, and I'm not sure what value he'd bring outside of a discount to begin with."

Sal smiled. His father was on the same page as him. If they were strapped for money, then it would be a more appealing prospect to partner up with Michel, but as it stood, they didn't need him. "What sort of stuff do you think he's going to send over?"

Petro shrugged. "I didn't want to give him a flat refusal, primarily because it'll be your decision. I think that he just saw that as a window of opportunity to send over some proposals." Shaking his head with a sigh, Petro dropped the topic. "We'll see what he and his wife come up with, but as it stands, they're not a contender for what we need."

Sophia nodded as she looked at Petro. "Do you think it was wise to say that we're looking at starting a guild, alongside the auction house? We haven't gone through the details or gotten any of the approvals yet."

Petro shrugged. "He'll find out faster than anyone else, so it's a courtesy to at least give him the facts that we know. You saw that wine and whiskey…he spent a few thousand on that meeting alone, so it would just be bad manners to give him a lame excuse." With a snap of his fingers, he pointed down the street. "So, should we have a look at Dalton's or are we looking at the other mystery property you have picked out?"

Sophia smiled as she tapped the tracker on the side of her head. "By the way, this thing is incredible…the body language reading is way better than I was expecting. Like, it's a lie detector, too?"

Petro chuckled without stopping. "That's another reason that I was forthright with Mr. Pando. He didn't lie to us once. Seems like a good guy."

Sal nodded in agreement. "I do want to find out where he gets his coffee. It was really good!"

They walked together for a few more minutes, seeing a few others on the street walking in and out of the shops that were open. There was an antiques store with newspapers, books, and even some elaborate pens with metal blades as the tip. Sal had seen a few of them come through auctions, and most recently came across some of the newspapers in the scavenger runs.

The cozy atmosphere of the smaller shops had a greater appeal to Sal. They were individually unique, and had so much character and love in them. Minimal display cases and just a few countertops to show off equipment and gear. He'd only need a couple of people to operate the whole operation, and it probably wouldn't cost an absolute fortune. When he looked into one of the shops, a balding man, with a bushy white beard, gave him a friendly wave. Sal waved back at him and sighed wistfully.

"As a matter of interest, how much would one of these storefronts cost?" Sal asked. It didn't really fit the needs of the guild they were talking about, but he still wanted to know.

Petro looked at them for a moment before waving his hand back and forth. "Give or take, you could probably secure one of them for about two million…but they're not for sale individually. They're incredibly small, and most of them have a residential unit directly behind them for the shop owners." He looked at Sal's expression before glancing at Sophia with a smile. "Follow me for a second."

Sophia just laughed as she shook her head. "I swear, the two of you are the same person." She gave Petro a knowing look before nudging Sal playfully.

Sal was confused by their behavior but followed his father down the street until he came to an abrupt stop.

Petro held his hands out wide to present a massive loading bay. Unlike the shops around it that hugged the pedestrianized walkways, this gigantic empty space had a clearance the size of the workshop in Quest Academy. In the distance were a series of shuttered gates that opened vertically.

Sal looked at it in confusion. "The warehouses?" He was familiar with the location because it was where big shipments came in from other cities. Cargo would be loaded into the large warehouses and stored for the surrounding businesses. When he was younger, he used to love watching as the giant flying ships would come down to land.

Petro nodded. "It's been up for sale for a few years, and nobody has been interested in it for a very specific reason." He grinned as he looked at Sophia, as though telling her, *I told you so.*

Sophia just sighed as she looked at Sal. "I was sure you'd want something more modern, and your father insisted that you'd lean toward charm."

Sal closed his eyes and took a deep breath. "I need a little help here. What are we looking at exactly? The warehouses probably offer the space we need, but it's…well, they're just two-story flat structures. Is it the land we're looking at?"

Petro clicked his fingers and pointed at the Argento Auction House in the distance. "Guess where the tunnels lead in your workshop…I'll give you one guess." He beamed as he traced a finger underneath the ground before pointing back to the warehouse in front of him. "Now, the tricky part of the sale…is that it's a package deal. The owner of this lot owns the collection of shop fronts that used to receive the shipments."

His finger pointed at all the small storefronts that Sal had just walked past. "So, you'd potentially have a rental income from those…and have a place to set up your guild. Hell, you could even call it a plaza at this rate." He chuckled to himself as he looked at all the outlets attached. "There are at least a dozen of them."

Sal blinked in surprise. "Wait, twelve storefronts and a warehouse…with an underground tunnel system? Why was this not the first thing we looked at?" He spoke excitedly as he started looking at the storefronts more carefully. "This sounds amazing!"

"Poor Mr. Pando," Sophia remarked, smiling as she watched Sal study the closest shop fronts. "Are you ready to burst Sal's bubble, Petro?"

Petro brought his hands together as he looked at Sal seriously. "So, the deal-breaker with this transaction—the property is owned by the Hunter Bureau, and they are very unlikely to part with it for cheap. We looked into it in the past and were quoted north of a hundred and twenty million. You can't see it from here, but this place is on top of a certifiable catacomb of collapsed train tracks. Opening them back up, and putting in protective measures to stop the demons from breaking through…really drives the price up."

"A hundred and twenty…million." Sal's mouth went dry as he heard the number. There was no way in hell that he was going to be in a position to purchase that any time soon. He barely had a tenth of that. And even if he parked himself in the workshop until the day he was sent back to the Academy, he wasn't confident that he'd be able to make that number. There were only a few auctions left on the docket for the summer.

Petro nodded. "That would be before you started doing all your renovation works. If you were serious about this, we could absolutely do it in installments with the bureau. We could back you and get you up to a thirty percent deposit, and then it would be up to you to make the payments."

"It's about five times the size of the Argento Auction House. Even if you decided to avoid building vertically and having a high-rise, you'd still end up with more than enough space to make a state-of-the-art headquarters," Sophia suggested from behind them. "But I warned your father that this wasn't a realistic option right now."

Petro nodded. "It's good to have goals though, and this one could be an excellent purchase." He placed his hands on his hips as he looked at the warehouse thoughtfully. "Should we book a tour? I can get onto the bureau and get something set up."

Sal just stared at the warehouse. He didn't even need to see Dalton's outlet. This was the one that he wanted. The moment his father had said the word "plaza," Sal was reminded of the vision that Divinity had shown him. He looked at the storefronts when one in particular caught his attention.

Maccles Materials

"This is included in the sale?" Sal asked for confirmation as he looked at the buildings along the strip. It was essentially an entire street worth of storefronts. All of them curved around this one central location.

Sophia nodded somberly. "The Hunter Bureau is in charge of the rents for all the storefronts here. They've only been increasing as time goes on. An association started a few years ago where all the business owners tried to pool their money and buy out the warehouse and buildings from the bureau, but they couldn't afford the tunnel reconstruction, which is a hard requirement for the sale."

Petro snorted as he shook his head. "If any of them leave their store to set up elsewhere, then the lost rental income is imposed on the others to make the difference. Mutually assured destruction, and the Hunter Bureau gets its monthly payment." He looked at Sal's horrified expression before laughing. "Oh, this isn't a unique story, Sal. They did this in every city they have a presence in. Governments can't compete with them, as they've got no power… Might makes right and all that."

Sophia raised her finger. "But Heroes get tax breaks. So, send your kids to Quest Academy and the noose loosens ever so slightly." She chuckled humorlessly with a shake of her head. "Anyway, are we really going to stand here all day and look at this one…or are we going to look at some realistic lots?"

Sal bit his lip as he looked at his mother. "This is the one." No matter which ones he looked at, it wouldn't compare to the potential of this place. The storefronts were a huge selling point, and Sal could already visualize the likes of Blathnaid and Upgrade being able to sell their works to people on the street. Any of their big works could be transported in the underground railway to the Argento Auction House. He could even get materials shipped over from Maurice in record time if they were using the same warehouses.

The entire infrastructure it offered was so much better than a proximity to a train station. Sal could create his own network underneath the city and have direct routes to everything he needed. Silver Sanctuary could become a powerhouse of commerce, and it all started with that one warehouse.

Sophia sighed dramatically. "Then I guess it's time to head back to the auction. You might as well start thinking of manufacturing flying cars or something, because a few daggers and armor sets aren't going to get us anywhere near close to what is needed for this project."

Petro nodded in agreement. "My best guess is that you'd be looking at three hundred million to finish it to perfection." He laughed as he thought about it. "Man, if only you had something that could just pump out weapons and equipment with a touch of a button. Something like this could be a reality then." He winked at Sal meaningfully.

Sal realized in that very moment that his father had played him.

CHAPTER 20: TRADE

As Sal walked into Maccles Materials, his mother sidled up to him.

"Are you here to ask for his blessing to marry Fabrizia? It's a little premature if you ask me…" she whispered, a wide grin on her face.

Sal groaned inwardly as he shook his head. "I need some materials for the project I'm working on, and I might as well order them while I'm here." He continued into the shop. There were countless shelves on the wall, and drawers that were clearly labeled with tiny shards of materials, similar to the ones Chatfield presented him with in the past.

Clipping off his tracker from his belt, Sal secured it over his right eye as he took out his tablet. "This could take a while. Are you sure you want to hang around for it?" he asked his parents, who nodded in return.

Petro moved sideways to get through two close cabinets that were covered in various plants and leaves. His back touched against one large container of liquid that was resting on the upper shelves of a cabinet. It didn't fall, but instead caused a jingling noise to emanate throughout the store.

Sal watched with a curious expression as the liquid started to glow a bright pink, as though the movement had activated it somehow. His tracker told him that there was nothing to worry about, but he still thought it was really interesting. After a few more seconds of looking at the liquids, Sal was informed that it was tree sap, but densely packed with essence. It was added to his directory of materials, categorized as an excellent varnish for both metal and wood surfaces.

There were so many odd items in the shop that Sal found himself struggling to keep up with his tracker. Countless options were presented to him, and origin points that didn't leave out any of the gruesome details. One of the vials was orbital fluid from a thumper, which was almost guaranteed to add Perception as an ability to items that used it. There were so many liquids that Sal had to turn his head away from them to stop the tracker from identifying everything.

A bell chimed from the other end of the shop, and Sal looked over to see his father leaning against a countertop, his hand raised over a small metal bell. He shot Sal a smile before looking toward a doorway at the back. Raising his voice, he called out in the direction of the door. "You're going to have to modernize this place someday. Otherwise, someone will come in here and steal everything!"

"Anyone who picked a life of crime wouldn't know what to do with half of this crap," Maurice answered, before he even got through the doorway. His lanky frame was covered in a long brown apron; the splashes of green blood looked fresh on his torso. "I'm slaving away back here because someone cleared me out of prowler blood. Are you back to make my life miserable, or what is it?" A warm smile creased his face as he scratched at his bushy greying beard. Icy-blue eyes locked onto Petro before darting over toward the doorway. "Sophia? And Salvatore?"

Sal raised his hand in greeting. "Hey, thanks so much for the prowler blood last time. It was a great help."

"Look what he made with it!" Sophia announced as she tapped the side of her tracker and took it off her face. She gracefully navigated between the cabinets with barely a twist of her body and presented the tracker to Maurice with a smile on her face.

Sal was immediately embarrassed and tried to stop her. But before he could get a word out, Maurice already had the tracker in his hand, a surprised expression written all over his face.

"You'd think I'd be used to all these contraptions the Quest Academy kids come up with, but I'm constantly humbled by it all. Stealth runes, too!" He chuckled as he looked at the visor for a few seconds before handing it back to Sophia. "You certainly didn't get that obsidian from me. I've put in a few requests for it already and keep hitting a wall. Baron get it for you?" He looked at Petro thoughtfully.

Petro shook his head, and a wide smile crossed his face.

"Don't," Sal warned, but it was no use.

"Sal here…killed an obsidian hulker in the tower test at Quest Academy. All under Robert's nose. They practically sent him a crate of the stuff, and he's been using it for all sorts of projects," Petro announced proudly, motioning for Sal to move up closer to the counter.

Maurice's eyes widened as he looked at Sal. "Congratulations, Salvatore! That's an incredible achievement. You should be proud of yourself!" He smiled almost in wonder as he looked at Petro. "What happened to our kids for them to turn out this way?"

Sophia shot Sal an apologetic look, as though she couldn't help herself. She turned to Maurice and smiled. "How is Fabrizia doing these days? Has there been any progress on her ability?"

Maurice froze at those words. He looked at Sophia carefully before turning to Petro. "Did that Quest guy talk to you two or something?"

Petro shot Sophia a sideways glance before he let out a sigh. "You know how Salvatore had those issues with his ability? The weaves and such?"

Maurice, although still somewhat wary, managed to bark a laugh as he looked directly at Sal. "I still hear his words every time I see him. *He has so many knots!*" He chuckled as he beckoned for Sal to come closer. "Let me get a proper look at you. It's been a few years at this point."

Sal reluctantly made his way toward the counter, being extra careful not to bump into anything. When he cleared the cabinets, he stood in front of Maurice and was surprised to see that they were of a similar height. His memories of the man had always been of him being an absolute tower of human, but now he was able to look him directly in the eye.

"You certainly don't get the height from your mother, but you've really filled out. You also didn't get that from your father," Maurice joked as he looked Sal up and down. "You've really grown up…but to take on a hulker? That's not something you hear around these parts very often."

"Thank you, sir." Sal responded with a slight bow of the head.

"Maurice." He looked at Petro with a shake of the head. "How badly did you drill manners into the boy? It's just Maurice." He smiled before gesturing at Petro. "Now, your father was going to tell me why he's suddenly talking about weaves and my little Fabrizia."

Sophia interjected with an apologetic smile. "Ah, that's on me, I'm afraid. Salvatore got into the Savior class at Quest Academy and there was all this talk of Skill Imprints and whatnot. You said before that Fabrizia got into the Saviors, too. I was just wondering if you heard anything was all."

Maurice's wariness vanished in an instant. "Ahh, that makes sense… I'm sorry about being so jumpy with you there. It's just that they've told me it's an experimental thing, that nobody is to know about it. Fabi has been doing all sorts of tests with them, and it's sounding very positive. Poor girl doesn't know if she's allowed to hope at this point, but Upgrade, her teacher, said that the people behind the design of the implant are incredible."

Even though Sal knew that the simulations were beneficial to people, it wasn't until he heard Maurice speaking that he truly appreciated how impactful the work was. He felt bad that his parents were asking him about it, because there was no way that Maurice would feel reassured if he knew that Sal was the person behind the design of the weave.

Petro tapped the countertop a couple of times before looking at Maurice with a smile. "We genuinely wish her all the best. Salvatore here has been making use of all the equipment you sold to us, and he already has another shopping list for materials. We're wondering if we'd get a good deal or if we need to put in a call with Baron."

Maurice's jaw set into a straight line as he stared at Petro. "You always push the buttons, don't you? Someday, I'm going to tell you to fuck off and ask Baron…"

"But that day isn't today, is it?" Petro laughed.

Maurice just sighed as he waved at the shelves. "Have at it. What can I get for you today?"

Sal lifted his tablet and slid it across the countertop. "These are all the materials I'm missing for my current project. I've added in the volumes beside them. The ones with an asterisk are optional…but would be ideal if you had them."

Maurice raised an eyebrow as he lifted the tablet and inspected the list. He read over it for a few minutes, scrolling through the options in a state of deep concentration. "Today might be the day I tell you to go to Baron…" he muttered as he placed the tablet down with a sigh. "A lot of this is heavy-duty stuff, and I don't know that I'll be able to get it for you."

Sal frowned as he bit his lip. He needed those materials if he was going to be able to do the next steps of the vending machine design.

Petro laughed as he looked at Maurice. "You're taking advantage of the poor boy's desperation. What premium would it take to ensure the delivery of all those materials?"

Maurice huffed as he put his hands on his hips, shaking his head slowly. "I'd need to personally go to my supplier, which is through the Red Zones…because this stuff, you need to ensure you're getting the right equipment. I wouldn't be able to live with myself otherwise. Expedited delivery?" He inhaled sharply and looked reluctant to continue.

Sal couldn't help but laugh. He was so lost in thought about the materials, that he forgot who he was dealing with. The game of back-and-forth was what these men lived for, Petro firmly among them.

"Let me tally it up…but it's not going to be pleasant," Maurice warned as he took out a notepad and pen, adding up the numbers with various noises of discontent.

Petro winked at Sal as he leaned over the counter, watching Maurice work. "Looks like you put the decimal point in the wrong place there, Maurice. We're not made of money."

Maurice just chuckled as he continued. "Really? I heard about that recent auction. I'm pretty sure you can afford whatever number I throw at you."

Sal smiled as he also leaned toward the counter. "I might be able to part with some of the obsidian, if we had a good partnership…Maurice."

Maurice's pen stopped writing for a moment. He looked up with a devious smile and tilted his head to the side. "Sounds like a compelling argument." Looking back at the notepad, he shook his head. "Guess that decimal point was in the wrong place."

Sal looked at the numbers being added up, and although he was pretty good at maintaining a poker face, he was a little out of his depth when it came to material purchases. "By the way, what cores do you have? High grade specifically."

Maurice didn't even need to lift his head as he pulled a catalogue out from under the counter. "You can have a look in there. Demonic cores go for more, but you'd save a lot on the ones in need of Restoration."

Sal flicked through it and could see that there were hundreds of variants. Some were manufactured, while others had been pulled from the corpses of demons. There was a whole system for categorizing them, based on outputs, replenishment, capacity, essence category, and size.

Sal reviewed the options, thinking about which ones would be the best to have for future Crafting projects. He was fresh out of them after making the suit for his father and the tracker for his mother. If he wanted good cores for the cane project, or even the future drone project…then he'd need to replenish the stock. His eyes landed on the price of an Epic-grade core. It had a self-replenishment rune embedded into it and reminded him of the one he had Restored on his first day.

Epic-Grade Core
- Essence Category: Generalist
- Origin: Manufactured
- Output: 7/10
- Replenishment: 8/10
- Capacity: 8/10
- Size: 3 inches
- Price: $18,000.00

Sal stared at the price tag in absolute disbelief. How many similar-sized cores had he used in his Crafting? He was instantly reminded of the lackluster spoils he had received from completing his first dungeon. The leecher core that he received would have been worth a lot less than this one, which told him that if he wanted to make money, dungeons might not necessarily be as efficient as scavenger runs.

"Okay," Maurice finally said as he rose, sighing. "Here's the tally." He turned his notepad around and looked at Sal. "Cashing in on your inheritance early, I take it?"

Sal looked down at the notepad with a passive expression.

Total—$184,400.00

Maurice looked at Petro with a relaxed smile. "I can round down to one eighty, but anything after that would be me taking a loss. Now, with some obsidian, I could maybe work something out…"

Sal looked at the paper for a second before nodding. "I'll pay the full amount. No need to round down. And when you deliver them to the Argento Auction House, I'll have some obsidian waiting for you as a bonus."

Maurice blinked in surprise as he looked at Petro in confusion.

Sal shook his head. "No need to look at him. I'm the one paying for all of this. You came through for us when I needed the prowler blood…and I'd like to establish a healthy working relationship from the outset. I'll be Crafting a lot."

"Then I look forward to working with you." Maurice laughed as he offered his hand, which Sal took immediately.

Petro whistled as he leaned against the counter. "They grow up so fast, don't they?"

CHAPTER 21: PRESENT

"Why are you rushing?" Sophia asked with a laugh as they opened the doors of the Argento Auction House. She watched as Petro made his way to the base of the stairs with an exasperated expression on his face.

"You already have your tracker. You don't get to judge me for this." Petro chuckled as he took the steps two at a time until he reached the top of the stairway.

Sophia grinned as she motioned for Sal to follow her up the stairs. She clearly wanted to see Petro's reaction, too. "He's like a child, isn't he?"

Sal smiled as he called up the stairs after his father. "Is now a bad time to tell you to manage your expectations?"

Petro didn't even answer him as he hastily opened the glass door of his office and entered with an expectant look on his face.

It didn't take long for Sophia and Sal to catch up to him, and by the time they entered the office, there were countless suits thrown on the ground.

Petro stood in front of the suit rack with a single hanger raised high above his head. A wide grin was on his face as he looked at it in disbelief. "Should I let you do the honors?" he asked Sal without looking away from the fabric in front of him.

Sophia cooed as she moved closer to get a better look. "Herringbone? How did you manage to get that pattern?"

Sal smiled and offered them a shrug as he moved over to the couch to take a seat. "I was experimenting with the refiner to see if it could make different textiles if I combined materials. Rather than just using the dreadcloth, I wanted to see what would happen if I added the obsidian dust. It takes forever to combine them as the refiner needed to fold the obsidian into the fabric about five times, but a nice pattern came out of it."

Sophia lifted a single sleeve and stared at the gleaming black buttons on the cuff. "Hellfire titanium…for buttons?" She shook her head in surprise. "First time for everything. But I have to say, it really works with the grey."

Petro was quiet as he took the interior hanger out of the suit, letting the jacket remain in Sophia's hands. He took the waistcoat and trousers a few paces away and held them up with a delighted smile. It was only when he turned it around to look at the back that his expression faltered.

"That would be the evolutionary rune," Sal noted as he pointed at the silver stitching on the black satin fabric. "Try it on and see how it fits."

"Close your eyes." Petro chuckled as he undid his belt and started unbuttoning his waistcoat. It was like he couldn't decide on how to undress as quickly as possible.

Sophia rushed to intercept the space between Sal and Petro, holding up the suit jacket to shield Sal from seeing anything he shouldn't. She laughed as she held it. "Perfect solution…we won't have to pay for therapy this way." She winked at him as Petro clearly struggled in the background.

A shoe went flying to the other side of the office, followed by a curse from Petro. It took less than a minute, but when his hands took the jacket from Sophia, he looked excited.

Sal raised an eyebrow at the transformation. He had used the measurements of the existing suits that were on the rack, the very same ones that now littered the floor. It was a wise choice, because the suit was a perfect fit. Tailored to perfection and fit Petro like a glove. "Is it comfortable?"

"It's an absolute dream, Sal," Petro breathed as he put his arms through the jacket sleeves before tugging down on the sides to remove the creases in his shoulders.

The color palette was somewhat removed from his usual greys and silvers that he wore. Obsidian and dreadcloth had combined to create a dark purple, and if the lighting was poor, it would look closer to black. Hellfire titanium was used for each and every button, giving flecks of red to contrast against the purple hues. The waistcoat from the front had the same material as the jacket and pants, but was double breasted to add more buttons. A black chain linked to one of the pockets.

Petro reached into the pocket in confusion, withdrawing a black-rimmed monocle with a perfectly circular cutting of obsidian glass. His eyes bore into it for a few moments before his jaw dropped. "Salvatore…how can you make something like this?"

Sophia moved closer to have a look at the monocle. "Deduction…Insight…" She started to Appraise some of the information with the help of her new tracker, but judging by the frown on her face, it was going to take some time to get used to it. With a slight shake of her head, she laughed and looked over at Sal. "I can tell you without the tracker that it looks really pretty."

Petro continued to stare at the monocle for a few moments before shaking his head in wonder. "Analysis, Appraisal, Deduction, Insight, and Perception. How did you get five abilities into a single piece of equipment?"

Sal smiled as he stood up. "I didn't. I put just one ability into it." He pointed at his father. "Yours. What you're reading is All Sight. If I can't bring your power to its full potential in a safe way, then at least you'll have this. Come on, try it on."

Petro just stared at the monocle in his hands. "It doesn't make sense, Sal. You said yourself that you didn't know what All Sight could do, but now you've managed to Craft something with it? How is that even possible?"

Sal sighed as he shrugged. "When I replicate an ability with Skill Master, the weave becomes available for my Crafting, and I can recreate the ability with essence or by combining materials I'm familiar with. For this one, I used essence." He smiled as he gestured at the monocle. "I should thank you, though—this is something I had no idea would happen. Mythcrafter was made with Skill Master, Restoration, All Sight, and Upgrade. If All Sight is actually a combination of five different abilities, then it explains why Mythcrafter is able to do so many amazing things. I could mass-produce these and make a fortune." Sal laughed as he thought about it. All Sight glasses or monocles would be a massive hit with the students.

Petro's hand shook slightly as he held the monocle. He tentatively brought it to his face, raising an eyebrow to give it enough space to rest against his skin. When he brought his hand away, his brow kept the monocle in place. A flash of white illuminated the obsidian glass, before dying down, leaving a glowing white iris behind the lens. It looked positively menacing.

"Oh my…" he breathed as he looked around the room. "This is a lot." He quickly removed the monocle and blinked a few times.

"Everything okay?" Sal asked in concern as he took a step closer.

But Petro's hand shot out and held him at a distance. "Absolutely. I just need to get used to it…it's very potent." He took a steadying breath before a chuckle left his lips. "Threat profiles are one thing, but to have countermeasures against the two of you, just from seeing how you move? It's oddly terrifying."

Sophia barked a laugh as she looked at him. "Really, you're going to blame the monocle? Take a swing and see what happens," she goaded him playfully before looking at the suit again. "It really looks good on you. So, are you happy with everything your son made for you?"

Petro nodded as he raised the monocle. "Should I expect something else?" He looked at Sal inquisitively, as though he'd be disappointed if there was more. "It's saying this is part of a set, Sal."

Sal waved his hand up and down in Petro's general direction. "Your suit and monocle are a set. Essence absorption runes would have taken up too much space on the monocle, so I just put them on the jacket instead. All of it is Epic grade, but I wanted you to do the honors of conducting your own Appraisal."

Petro faltered as he looked at the monocle again. "So, if it's a set…and the waistcoat is evolutionary…"

Sal nodded, grinning. "Your monocle can evolve, too." He sighed as he pointed at the waistcoat. "Honestly, you're spending way too much time fawning over the monocle. Your suit has the Attune ability, which should help you break open more essence gates and give you more juice with All Sight before getting tired. There's Reflect in there too, which is the same defensive ability that took out the hulker. Cultivate will increase the potency of absorbed essence, and there are quite a few absorption runes on the pants."

"And now repeated in a way I'll understand?" Sophia remarked with a gentle smile.

Sal blinked for a second before nodding. "His suit will naturally absorb a lot of atmospheric essence. Some of it will go toward the evolution of the equipment, but most of it will go to Dad. It'll make his ability stronger and increase his internal reserves of essence." He watched as his mother nodded in understanding before he continued with a sigh. "I wanted to add a new weave called Perfect, but it wouldn't take to the materials. It would have made him a very quick learner."

Sophia snorted at that. "Well, I could have told you that was impossible."

Petro didn't even react to the remark as he tested out the suit by raising his arms and lifting a knee, one at a time. "This is unbelievable."

Sal brought his hands together. "Excellent, you've both been successfully bribed. I hope you're aware of that. I need to get back to the workshop to continue on my project. That okay with you?"

Sophia hesitated as she looked at Petro for backup. "Sal…while all of this is incredible, you've essentially just shown us that you didn't take a break at all in the last few weeks. We want to be encouraging and enable you to do what makes you happy, but we don't want you to exhaust yourself in the process."

Petro shook his head. "Fuck that. Make more stuff. You have my full approval to lock yourself in that workshop until the end of the break. I'll knock on your door when it's time to go back to Quest Academy."

Sophia went to slap Petro on the shoulder, but Sal dove forward to stop her. He thankfully made it in time, and she looked at him in shock.

"Sorry! That might have activated the Reflect ability…which would have thrown you across the room," Sal apologized hastily, releasing his mother's hand after a few seconds.

Petro stared at Sophia's hand before a wide smile crossed his face. "Best. Present. Ever."

Sophia grumbled before giving Sal a thoughtful look. "Face should be fair game, right?"

Before Sal could answer, Sophia reached out and flicked her husband's ear, causing him to flinch back in surprise with a laugh.

Sal shook his head as he watched the two of them squabbling. "I'll be in the workshop if you need me. If the delivery comes from Maurice in the next couple of days, let me know."

Petro nodded. "Will do, kiddo. You just let me know if there's anything I can help with, and I'll be there."

Sal smiled. "Thanks for the offer, but I think I'll be fine for now." He looked at his mother and gestured at Petro's suit. "This didn't really feel like your style, so I'll be coming up with a few ideas for your battle-suit. You know, if Shade decides to bring the roof down in the future."

"Not necessary," Sophia warned as she pointed her finger at him. "No more Crafting for us, got it?"

"See you later!" Sal called as he exited the office with a laugh. He had expected his father to like the surprise, but Petro's reaction was so much better than anything Sal could have imagined. Seeing how much fun both of them had with their new presents was heartwarming, and Sal was proud of himself for being able to give back to them.

As he made his way back to the workshop, he thought about the earlier bartering with Maurice. He didn't appreciate how his parents had started up a conversation about Fabi, but he knew they were just teasing him…and that they were genuinely curious about her condition. It was positive news that she was going to take the Skill Implant, and Sal hoped that it would perfectly adapt to her like the simulation orb suggested it would.

When Sal got back to his workspace, he smiled. There were two train tracks in the tunnel area, which meant that if he got that warehouse facility, he'd be able to have two lines operating at the same time. He was very aware that he was getting ahead of himself, as there was no way he was in a position to make an offer for that group of buildings, but it was fun to dream.

With a performance that closely mimicked his father, Sal took the steps two at a time to get to the top of the mezzanine that overlooked the tunnel and carriage below. He had a lot of work to do if he wanted to create this machine. Getting comfortable in his seat, Sal took out his visor and clipped it over his right eye before picking up the pen.

"Let's do this."

CHAPTER 22: MYTHOS

"Are you sure this is a workshop and not a warehouse at this point?" Petro joked as he helped George place another box of materials down on the stack of other boxes. Looking down at the label on the top of it, he called up to Sal. "Laser modules and crystals! Putting it to the left side."

"Thanks, Dad!" Sal called down from the mezzanine as he continued to sort the boxes into some form of order that would work for him. Maurice had really come through, and in less than a week, he had every component that he had asked for. There were even a few variants thrown in for good measure, like when Doc Ameye had sent moonsilver and scarlet screen rather than lords crystal, because it would work better. Maurice had apparently made the same judgment call.

Sal moved to the railing to look down at the stack of boxes. Some of them were small and ornate, and they were placed in the carriage. The heavy-duty materials were occupying space on the platform near the stairs. Fragile materials were stacked against the wall on the far side of the door. Most of the items Sal didn't recognize by appearance, but Mythcrafter did. He had only seen them as small pieces when Chatfield showed them to him, but many of the items from his tracker's database were in their original forms, just waiting to be manufactured.

"That should be the last of it, but I'll do a double-check with George down at the loading bays. Let me know if anything is missing and I'll get on to Maurice," Petro called up before giving Sal a thumbs-up gesture. "And good luck! I'll keep your mother out of here. Otherwise, she'll have a heart attack."

"Appreciate it!" Sal shouted back. "If I die doing this, I want you to know it's your fault for putting the idea in my head."

"La, la, la…" Petro sang loudly, as though he couldn't hear his son. He left the workshop with George smiling beside him. He closed the doors behind him, leaving Sal to his own devices.

There was a lot to get through, but Sal was elated. With the arrival of the materials, he wouldn't be limited to working on only essence programming and coding. Creating modules wasn't fun at all, and improving the operating system was thankless. No matter how much he accomplished with it, he couldn't see any visual improvements. It was just a few lines of text that told him a new module had been successfully created. He wasn't a fan of it constantly being called UnnamedOS, so he instead renamed it to MythOS. It had a nice ring to it.

When the boxes up at the mezzanine were stacked in a way that allowed Sal to move around, it was time to get to work. The gala was two weeks away, and he didn't have anything else to occupy his time before that. His new dorm was already selected on the tablet, and they were designing it for him over the break. His visit to Ameye Locomotives would be happening after the break, and he would message Barry and Divinity at some point to invite them over after the gala.

Sal's calendar was completely free, and it was an exciting prospect. All the annoying coding stuff was pretty much done…well, until he manufactured and assembled the machine. There was more coding at the end, but that wasn't important. He was finally able to start using his hands for something other than writing.

Sal had his tracker on his face, and a bottle of Kakushin at the ready on the table. His drawings were arranged in the order of components that needed to be made first. It was finally time. Turning off his tablet, Sal unscrewed the lid of the Kakushin and did a quick check to see that Perfect was still in play. When he was certain everything was prepared, he took a quick swig of the elixir, closed the bottle, and placed it on the table before swallowing.

His eyes locked onto the first drawing. The laser engraver.

Images burned into Sal's eyes of all the ways the engraver could be upgraded from its base state. Each of the materials that he had looked at were presented to him as options, but Sal moved down the stairs to the box his father had just delivered. He opened it up and saw a collection of needle-like points, colorful crystals of all shapes and sizes, and a few test-mount plates. There were even some attachments for different widths of crystals.

At just the sight of them, combined with Mythcrafter, Sal was able to determine countless uses for them. His mind started creating a rotary device that utilized all the crystals, turning and locking into place for whatever job was required. With the thought in mind, Sal brought the box back up to the mezzanine and looked at the drawing on the table. It needed to be changed, and Sal followed his instincts and re-designed the laser engraver from scratch, incorporating the new breakthrough.

This happened countless times over the next number of hours. Sal would open a box, see all the materials, and then he would have an epiphany about how they could be utilized better. Mythcrafter adapted to his new concepts and the result didn't break the overall project. He was slowly making it better with each and every new addition. The first actual Crafting he managed to do was when he refined down all the crystals into a uniform shape.

To his surprise, the rotary system was made with non-conductive materials…so there would be no essence irregularities. It made sense, but Sal struggled a bit to find metal without any essence. Thankfully, he was able to use the refiner and two legs of a chair. He never would have thought of that, but Kakushin was there to provide the inspiration.

With his sixty essence gates, Sal had a lot of reserves in the tank. He was able to make the more difficult parts of the mechanism by blending materials together. Because he hadn't gotten around to repairing his Epic-grade uniform that Upgrade made for him, he had to resort to the tools that his parents bought for him. If he was honest with himself, he actually just wanted the excuse to use their gifts.

The plate for the laser engraver was a tricky blend of metals and glass, but they came together perfectly. Sal was actually able to steal the plate from the existing laser engraver in the carriage, and he then upgraded it to accommodate the new sizings. By the end of its creation, it was far more robust and even had a Reinforcement rune on it. The engraver itself had a Refinement rune, which made a lot of sense considering it was being used for precision engineering. It was only when Sal was loading the crystal cylinders into the rotation device that he remembered the original design. There weren't any runes present, but he had already created two…

Looking at the updated design on the table in curiosity, Sal saw that the incorporation of runes were clearly listed on the page. The overall stability of the vending machine wasn't impacted, which was a massive relief. Kakushin reminded him of a specific moment in one of the courses he had watched in the last week, that explained how runes weren't a method to bridge gaps in a broken product. Best practice was to use them as a value-add to a project that could function without them. It was a moment of clarity, where Sal realized that his design for the vending machine could work without any runes. Almost like a light switch going off in his head, Sal recognized he was only able to add runes because the construction was viable.

It hadn't worked that way before, and Sal guessed that the guidance he received from the tracker and Mythcrafter was influenced by the best practice he learned from the courses he watched. In the past, he overwrote what Mythcrafter suggested and got it to adapt to what he was trying to do. This project was the opposite, where Sal let Mythcrafter call the shots. The tracker offered improvements through Analysis; Perfect honed his motor skills in executing those improvements; Mythcrafter acted as the blueprint he worked off; and lastly, Kakushin provided bursts of inspiration to help the process, creating easier methods and ingenious workarounds when he faced an issue.

When Sal combined all those factors with the flow state, he felt unstoppable. Moving from task to task was automatic, and there was no time to waste. The laser engraver took a solid six hours to create, and the only doubt Sal had throughout the whole process, other than the addition of runes, was timing when he needed to drink more Kakushin. The effects were great, but he didn't want to use it as a crutch. Inspiration was fantastic, but he also brought on the risk of over-engineering. Kakushin was the primary culprit of scope creep, and if he let it have its way, the laser engraver would be a state-of-the-art stand-alone device rather than a component of a larger project.

Sal continued his work well into the night, taking short breaks to use the bathroom and reassess where he was with the construction. Even though he had thought he'd be setting up the machine in the carriage, it turned out that it was going to be up on the mezzanine. It was easier for him to quote his drawings and reach everything he needed.

When he reached the end of his stack of paper, Sal knew that he was on the home stretch. The moon was high in the sky and all that remained was putting the parts together. It was a key component of the whole thing, and Sal was delighted with how it was looking. There was a tray that operated like a conveyor belt, feeding the products to the engraving tray. Grips extended from underneath the tray to lock the products in place while they were engraved, and the laser head was on a rotating wheel. Sal reached out and idly spun the wheel, enjoying the assortment of colored crystals moving smoothly in a circle, clicking slightly as it locked into the final position.

A few more tweaks to the overall construction were completed, and when Sal finally stepped back, he was content. The Kakushin in his system was long gone, and he was looking at the component with full control of his senses. "That will do."

Sal took off the tracker and placed it on the table. He stumbled past the countless opened boxes and scattered materials, making his way to the bedroom. With a contented sigh, he let himself fall into bed. The beauty of having two weeks to work on this project was that he didn't have to rush toward the finish line. Closing his eyes, he pushed all thoughts of the vending machine out of his head and let himself fall into a relaxing sleep.

If you'd count three hours as a relaxing sleep.

Sal found himself staring at the ceiling, a thoughtful expression on his face. "Maybe slow down on the coffee…" He reprimanded himself with a chuckle before getting out of the bed with a groan. Rather than doing his exercises—he promised himself that he'd do it before going to bed later—he went straight to the coffee machine. Squinting, he saw that the sun had risen in the last few hours and it was definitely morning. It was a rare sight for him as during the break, he was only rising in the afternoons.

The laser engraver sat proudly on the surface of the workbench. Sal smiled as he looked at it from different angles. He continued to admire his handiwork while he waited for his coffee to pour. When it was done, he brought the mug to his lips and immediately wished he had asked Mr. Pando for his supplier. It wasn't that it was bad—he just knew what he was missing out on.

With coffee in hand, Sal moved over to the workbench and picked up the stack of completed papers with his left hand. He carried them to the countertop of his small kitchenette and left them there. Walking back into the main area, he stumbled slightly over one of the boxes before exhaling slowly.

"Time for the refiner," he told himself before downing the entirety of the coffee. Placing the mug back under the dispenser, he cracked his knuckles and stretched his back with a contented sigh. Moving over to the next stack of papers, Sal took out all the ones for the refiner and laid them out in front of him. He had to move the laser engraver to an empty space near him. That was no easy feat as the materials had seemingly spread out in the middle of the night, limiting the available floor area.

When he got back to his desk, Sal smiled as he clipped on his tracker. "Time for round two."

CHAPTER 23: FATIGUE

Sal learned he had made a mistake, or rather a glaring oversight. It wasn't technical, which was a relief, but rather a practical element. The machine components he was making were heavy. Really heavy. Despite his best intentions, he had to make a compromise…which came in the form of making the enclosure for the vending machine. It was only then that he truly appreciated the scale of what was being asked of him. Those gigantic panes of glass that were waiting down at the door weren't just for show; they were a part of the wall of glass that would show each and every component at work. They were also going to operate as the host for the interface that used MythOS. Sal was having trouble visualizing what it would look like when it finished, but the drawings looked great.

So, that epiphany was what led to Petro and George cursing each other out as they lifted massive panels of glass and sheet metal all the way up the stairs under Sal's careful gaze. All his attempts to help just caused more cursing from Petro. George, who was one of the most attentive and caring people Sal had ever met, seemed to despise the term "lift with your back."

Yet Petro continued to repeat the sentence again and again as he encouraged the Argento employee up the stairs.

Sal had done his best to clear the empty boxes to one side, but there were still so many components that he needed access to. It was an impractical space to do all of this, but Sal wasn't concerned by it, up until he saw the red color on his father's face. All suggestions of getting a specialist in to do it, or even Crafting gloves with the Feather ability, fell on deaf ears. Sal even offered his own, but his dad was hearing none of it. Petro evidently wanted to prove it to himself that he could help, even if that was in the most illogical manner known to man.

With a final grunt from Petro and an agonized sigh from George, the last pane of metal was brought up to the mezzanine.

"Told you it wouldn't take long," Petro breathed hoarsely as he grinned at Sal. "Bet you didn't think your old man had it in him, huh?" He smiled as he moved over to the railing to lean against it heavily. "I could even do that again. Sure there isn't any more?" He looked down at the platform, knowing for sure that there wasn't.

George shot him a withering look before a smile crossed his tired face. "Sure looks like you're up to something great. Haven't seen anything of the like before." He gestured at both the completed engraver and the refiner. His eyes landed on the half-completed 3D printer and he just shook his head. "Where did you learn all of this…it's amazing!"

Petro dusted his wrist against his waistcoat. "Apple doesn't fall far from the tree, George." He looked off to one side, as if to make the implication that he was somehow responsible for Sal's sudden ability to Craft.

"Ha." George snorted as he looked at Petro in disbelief. "I'd more believe that he gets it from Sophia. Pretty sure that's the first time your hands have done a hard day's work in years." He gave Sal a conspiratorial wink before making his way back down the stairs.

Petro shook his head as he crossed his arms. "I'll remember that for your performance review!" he called after George with a laugh. When he was gone from view, Petro turned back to Sal with an exhausted sigh. "That fucking killed me, Sal." He slumped against the railing and looked directly up at the skylights. "I'm never doing that again."

Sal wriggled his fingers. "These gloves literally make things lighter. Why didn't you take them, or let me help?"

Petro chuckled. "It's a two-man job, and George would never let me hear the end of it." His eyes flitted over the machinery scattered around the room. "Whoa…you've really been going at it. How are you faring?"

Sal smiled and pointed at a few sheets of paper on the table. "Just a few more hours and the printer will be done. Then I can start working on the enclosure and put everything into place. I just needed help in getting those massive pieces up here, so thanks for that."

Petro nodded. "I'll leave you to it. Are you running low on coffee beans? I'll bring a few bags over when I next pop my head in." With a wave, he navigated carefully around the boxes on the floor. "Don't let your mother see the place like this." He gave the warning with a chuckle as he moved down the stairs.

Sal looked at the next page and clipped his tracker back on. With a quick swig of Kakushin, Sal got straight back into the flow of things. The 3D printer was similar to the laser engraver because they both had a tray and needle points. At least, that's what Sal figured they looked like when looking at them. The moment he started to work on the mechanisms, he abandoned that comparison immediately. They were nothing alike and it was once again an exercise of incremental gains. Small details that he needed to join the dots with essence and will the pieces to work as intended. The cabling was something he relied on the tracker for help with. Thankfully, he was able to use almost all the inner workings of the existing 3D printer in the carriage. Gutting the older models to create something better felt less like cheating when Sal framed it that way in his head.

He continued working on it for a few more hours, testing and tweaking the cables and the feeder system. There was an entire mechanism designed to move the materials from one stage to the next. One of the already identified problems with Kakushin was that it added complexity where it wasn't needed. A perfect example of this was the old printer head from the carriage being salvaged, upgraded, and incorporated into the design of the new 3D printer.

Thankfully, there were enough materials to make a new head, and Sal wondered whether it was going to do the same justification for the laser engraver that he had already completed. Unfortunately, that very thought made Kakushin connect the dots on how to best execute it as a vision. Sal would have cursed himself if it didn't feel like such a great idea. Two heads were better than one…well, at least that's what he told himself to make it sting a little less.

All in all, that little thought bubble added an additional seven hours of workload. But by the end of it, Sal was left with a laser engraver that held two identical heads—the same for the 3D printer. He didn't even look at the refiner for fear that it would lead to another epiphany.

With all of them done, it was time to focus on the enclosure. There were still so many components that needed to be created to make everything work together, but Sal would complete them when the enclosure was done. He wanted to be able to put the big machines into the casing for the vending machine, just to have some space to breathe again.

Of everything Sal had made in his entire time at Quest Academy, the enclosure was by far the easiest. It was a box. He had all the paneling that he needed, and all that had to happen was cutting and folding the metal. The front screen would be made with glass, and would likely be a pain, but the metal enclosure was almost suspiciously straightforward. With his essence and the Crafting tools, the enclosure looked like it had been professionally produced. There were no awkward areas or rough patches. It was just a simple box. Now, it *was* heavy; ridiculously so. But with the help of his gloves, he was able to get it propped up against the wall, and was delighted that it didn't wobble.

Sal added in the brackets and braces that would hold all the various machines. They were locked in tight to the left. He'd be working on the load components later, that would allow people to feed the machine materials. There were sensors and weighing devices and all sorts of stuff he wasn't looking forward to making.

The payment system was also going to be a hell of a challenge, but Sal wasn't going to be defeated by it. It was a module he had written for MythOS, but he had no way to know if it would work, other than the keyword that said it had been successfully installed.

Stepping back from the freshly installed brackets, Sal admired his handiwork. It was monstrously big, taking up an entire wall. It had to be ten feet in length and roughly eight feet in height. The depth was roughly three feet. The confusing part for Sal was that the machinery really was only taking up about half of the available space. The rest was being used for material storage. Sal looked at it for a while longer before getting back to work. He wanted to finish the evening with all the assembled machinery locked into position in the enclosure.

The feat was completed in a mere hour, a speed that surprised Sal. It was more like assembly than manufacturing, so it was fast. Locking everything into place was made easier by melding the machines into the brackets with essence. There was no fiddling with screws or bolts. Next came the installation of all the conveyor belts that stretched the entire width of the enclosure. Each of the belts had small trap doors that could release materials down to the lower belts. They were sturdy as hell, so there was no risk of something heavy causing damage if it was dropped from one belt to the other.

The engraving was the final stage of the process, so it was at the bottom of the load order. The refiner was in the center, with the 3D printer at the top. Even if one of the higher machines came last in the order, there were elevating plates that could move pieces back up for more work.

Without anything powering the machine, Sal had to push the plates up manually to see how it all worked. He played with the trap doors for a little too long as they made a very entertaining crank sound. After "testing" all the different mechanisms in the enclosure, Sal took some time to tidy up his workspace. A new stack of used papers were deposited into the kitchenette with the others, and the used boxes were folded and stacked behind the full ones still in use. There was a lot more floor space for him to work with, but the imposing glass panels were still taking up a massive section of the mezzanine. There were roughly another two dozen boxes that still needed to be opened, too.

Sal wasn't sure whether he should call it a night or continue for a little longer. He paced around the room for a little bit, looking at the next stack of papers on the table. He was about to reach for them when he remembered the promise he made to himself that morning. With an aggravated sigh, he unclipped the tracker and placed it on the table next to the next batch of papers. He reluctantly went through the secret wall and undressed before getting into position beside his bed. Those damned exercises from Lars. Ever since he had Perfect active, it had drastically improved his form and he felt each and every muscle activation with the routine.

Push-ups, sit-ups, crunches, lunges, and a whole array of stretches—Sal was panting by the end of it but felt better for having gone through with it. He could already tell that he had more mobility from the movements, and the back exercises were improving his posture. It only caused him pain when he was Crafting for long periods of time, so the stretching section was pretty much torturous.

Sal glanced at the containers of liquid on the side of his bed. He wasn't going to try using Kaizen until he had his chat with Prestige about the breathing technique for it. Which left him with nothing he could work on. He debated whether he should listen to some more of the courses, but wasn't ready to risk a chance epiphany, even without Kakushin in his system. If that happened, he'd be working on the vending machine again. His body was tired, but his mind wasn't ready to embrace sleep.

Thinking about it for a few moments, Sal suddenly remembered another thing that he had forgotten to do in the last few weeks: Barry's illusion training. He hadn't been suffering from nightmares in a while, but it was a good practice to keep it going.

Lying back against the pillows, Sal brought Barry's weave to the forefront of his mind and activated it. Even though it wasn't Crafting related, Sal started to visualize the cane-sword that he was going to make for Lawrence Baron. He kept things purely aesthetic and created an illusion of a cane made of obsidian. It was when he was customizing the grip of the cane that he finally drifted off to sleep.

CHAPTER 24: SEQUENCE

If there was one conclusion Sal took from the vending machine project, it was that he would never replicate it. This would be the only version of this machine, and he was content with that thought. Why? Because of the commands that needed to be written out in painstaking detail, that ensured the right materials were selected. He had to create an assessment tool that scanned and evaluated everything that was placed into the materials tray, and it was a nightmare. There was a whole sequence of essence programming that needed to be done, and Sal hated every moment of it. It got to the point where he checked every single box for moonsilver, to see if he could recreate the monocle that used the Calm ability. Something that could knock out all his emotions and get him to the finish line.

But no, there was no moonsilver. There was only disappointment and a few thousand lines of code that needed to be written. He had put it off for so long that there was nothing else he could do without it. The last part of the whole build was going to be the glass screen that would have an interface on it. He was looking forward to that even less than this.

Looking up from his workbench, Sal stared at the monstrosity of technology before him. It was as if it were mocking him for attempting something so beyond his reach, and Sal desperately wanted to throw in the towel and admit defeat. With a sigh, Sal stared at an empty space on the workbench in front of him, counting down from ten. It was the amount of time he allocated to feeling sorry for himself. When he reached the end of his mental timer, he got back to working on the code.

What probably should have taken a couple of days ended up taking close to five. Sal was avoiding it so much that he threw himself into exercise routines and training with Barry's illusion ability. As an experiment for himself, Sal took off the tracker and continued to write the code, using everything he learned. When he reequipped the tracker, he was surprised to see that he only got eighty percent of it wrong. Little games like that kept his mind alive, but he never once felt like he was mastering the subject matter.

When he finally finished the code and compiled it, he was met with several errors. All of them synced up perfectly to his lapses in concentration, and the areas he had tried himself. It took twenty-three attempts to get the code working properly, and Sal was ready to throw the workbench out the window by that point. Not that he'd be able to, but the thought crossed his mind a few times.

The sensor was programmed, and Sal was finally able to install the damn thing. It had a strip that was attached above each of the conveyor belts and the tray areas. Likely so it could inspect everything, no matter what phase it was at. There were so many fiddly little parts that Sal lost patience with, and it even got to the point where he had to step away for a breather because he was at risk of breaking it out of frustration. That little tirade resulted in yet another fruitless search for moonsilver.

When Sal finally came out of the other side of the sensor fiasco, he felt vindicated. There were no error reports from the workbench, and it actually synced with the sensor in the enclosure. It was the first time that the workbench had ever recognized a device, and that alone was enough to bring a tear of joy to Sal's eyes.

It was much needed, because he had long passed his wit's end, and had arrived at the point of cursing vehemently at the enclosure.

Next, Sal synched up all the other machines to the workbench. His luck had seemingly run out as he was faced with dozens of errors, with no solutions offered by MythOS. His tracker seemed to be stumped, too. Mythcrafter said everything was proceeding perfectly, and that scared Sal to some degree.

That blockage took an entire day to overcome, which was eventually solved by Sal reluctantly removing the refiner from the brackets and trying again. The tracker picked up the issue this time, and it was such a stupid thing of the sensor not facing the right direction, which had been obscured from view because it was at the back of the enclosure. A silver lining was that the issue on the 3D printer was the exact same, and he didn't need to take it out to fix it. Just twist a sensor into the right position.

With the refiner back in place and the brackets melded back together, Sal ran MythOS and only got a handful of bugs, which he was able to fix with simple adjustments to the conveyor belt and the loading tray.

Sal sat in a fugue state, working on the monotonous task of creating the interface system. Most of the foundations had been done with MythOS, but he needed to create a custom blueprint reader…just like how the workbench operated. Just as his pen was about to touch the surface, he paused and looked at the workbench carefully. *Would it be so bad to just implant the screen from the workbench and avoid the hassle of using the glass doors? It would look like a janky mess, but would it work?*

Sal seriously considered it for a few minutes before sighing and getting back to work. It would be a monumental disservice to all the work he had done so far, if he just skipped to the end like that. Upgrade would have killed him if he suggested something like it back at the workshop. Actually, she would have killed him for even attempting something like this. He could easily imagine her dragging him to Sergeant Head and making him do more therapy.

One of the pleasant things he experienced from the whole ordeal was the growing stack of paper that accumulated in the kitchenette. It was thick enough that the papers wouldn't bend if you tried folding them, and that was enough to put a weary smile on Sal's face. He had a lot less to work through to finish the project. With the sensors done, all he needed to focus on now were the screen doors and interface.

Even though he knew it was time for rest, Sal persisted through the night. He expertly carved out the runes on the glass panels, following the design guide from both Mythcrafter and the tracker. He didn't deviate from the design he made weeks ago, and he stayed away from Kakushin. This was not the time for an epiphany.

The runes incorporated both Interface and System abilities; that would allow it to communicate with the workbench until the MythOS file was uploaded. When that was done, he'd activate the security protocols to stop any future uploads outside of the approved channels, like his workbench for example. He needed it to receive blueprints from trusted devices. Sal's enthusiasm for the project reignited when he thought of conceptualizing a design with his tracker and sending it over to the machine. Maybe it was because of the file name, but Sal started calling the machine Mythos. It seemed appropriate.

When the runes were complete, Sal checked over them a few times to ensure the quality was perfect. With his Feather ability on the gloves, Sal brought each pane over to the enclosure and slid them into the custom brackets that he would close off afterward. The panels all rested perfectly together, which told Sal that he was a genius in ordering them pre-cut. The last thing he needed was shards of invisible glass around the mezzanine, especially considering how often he walked around barefoot.

The final segment of glass had already been cut to accommodate the materials tray that pulled out like a drawer. It was maybe four foot wide, and three foot deep. *Not enough space for a dead prowler*, Sal thought as he looked at it. Shrugging it off, he moved back to the areas where the glass panes met.

Placing his palm on the new surface, Sal sent a wave of essence into the panes. A slight shimmer of light fused them together, and when it faded, it looked like it was one giant piece of glass that covered the entire front of the enclosure. To anyone else, it might have looked like a display case for stacked machinery.

Sal stared at the construct with a heavy sigh. "Please don't break," he whispered almost to himself, because there was no way he was able to get through that glass in an efficient way. He closed off the brackets at the top and bottom of the enclosure, wisely choosing the non-massacred chair to stand on for the tall parts. Worst-case scenario, he could undo the brackets and pull the entire frame of glass out…but now that it was fused, he'd need about three or four people to do it.

"Positive thoughts." Sal reprimanded himself as he went back to the workbench. He loaded up the transfer window and started the upload of MythOS. It would need a lot of time to do checks on all the devices, but he was okay with that. The final steps would be the interface module, and that could definitely wait until he woke up.

Sal looked at the loading bar for a few more minutes before he started to laugh. It was absolutely going to fail. He was sure of it.

His gaze landed on the two remaining pages on the side of the workbench. Picking them up, he looked at them thoughtfully, wondering just how bad the interface work was going to be. He closed his eyes and kept them like that for a moment, before opening them and looking at the pages carefully. His tracker told him that the code was obsolete. With a quick check of Mythcrafter, it was the exact same. There was no need to update the interface module.

Sal went to the next page and got the exact same result from both the tracker and Mythcrafter. It was only when he looked at Mythos that he understood what had happened. The rune on the pane of glass, for Interface and System, was overwriting the need for the code to be written. Sal frowned at that because he thought he followed the instructions perfectly. He dropped the pages and returned to the kitchenette to find the most recently turned-over pages, and sure enough, there it was…a page written out of sequence, created in a Kakushin-fueled state.

"Shit," Sal muttered as he looked at it. *Had he subconsciously created a shortcut?*

Moving back to the workbench, he looked at the loading bar that seemed to be halted at a certain segment of the code. It earned a humorless laugh from him. He had accidentally played with fate, and it definitely was going to punish him for it. "We'll fix it in the morning," he promised himself, knowing that he had no idea how he was going to get that panel of glass off by himself. He shouldn't have done so much while he was tired, because he didn't test everything enough.

Sal moped his way back into the room and collapsed on his bed. There was no elation for a job well done, nor any of the excitement to see how the progress bar would complete. Every part of the process had bugs and problems, and he was guaranteed the same outcome tomorrow. With that single thought, Sal fell asleep.

Had he stayed awake for another hour, he likely would have heard the entertaining crank of the conveyor belt trays going through their initializing sequence.

CHAPTER 25: UPGRADES

Sal was wrong on two counts. Firstly, Mythos didn't shit itself in the middle of the night. On the contrary, it performed all the initializing checks and was error-free. The second thing he was incorrect about was that he still needed to create a module for the interface. Mythos had an interface that could function as a visual menu, but it didn't have the code that interpreted blueprint designs. That functionality was written into the operating system; he just needed to bridge the gap and do some tests.

Sal had never been happier to code. It was the final hurdle on a project that looked like it was a few inches from the finish line. He was so close. He threw himself into the task and was diligent in following the tracker's instructions to a T. It was so exciting that he did it even before having his first coffee of the day. So exciting that he spent a solid four hours writing the code. He didn't feel that time pass, as each and every line of code brought him closer to his goal.

When he finally reached the last line, he froze. It was the moment of truth. He ran the file, and was immediately hit with a loading screen. It would have been frustrating if it wasn't for the fact that the loading screen was mirrored on the glass wall in front of him. Sal opened his mouth in surprise as he watched the ridiculously long bar load across Mythos.

MythOS Version 1.0.0
Verifying Core Modules...
- o Design Interface: Installation Complete
- o System Interface: Installation Complete
- o Sensor Array: Installation Complete
- o Crafting Directory: Awaiting Input...
- o Material Load Order: Awaiting Input...
- o Crafting Algorithm: Installation Complete
- o Security Protocols: Installation Complete

Verifying System Integrity...
- o Validating Blueprints: Awaiting Input...
- o Scanning for Hardware Compatibility:
    - ▪ Unnamed Device 01: Installed
    - ▪ Unnamed Device 02: Installed
    - ▪ Unnamed Device 03: Installed
    - ▪ Scarlet Moon Visor: Synchronization Available
    - ▪ Storm Lens: Synchronization Available
    - ▪ Argento Workbench: Synced

- o Running Diagnostics Check:
    - ▪ Material Loading Bay: Load Not Specified
    - ▪ Crafting Directory: File Not Found

Sal stared as the messages appeared on the glass panel in sequence. The words were large enough to be read from the other side of the mezzanine, and probably from the tracks below. He'd need to adjust that in the settings, but that wasn't a big deal. What he was more interested in was the fact that it picked up both his own tracker and the monocle he had created for his father as potential synchronizations. Sal picked up his tracker and clipped it onto his face and was delighted when he got a pop-up immediately.

Synchronize with MythOS?

Sal accepted the prompt and was met with a loading screen on the lens of the tracker. It was once again mirrored on the massive machine in front of him. As soon as it finished, Sal was going to load up the tray with some basic materials to see whether it worked as intended. He tried to keep his expectations low, but he couldn't help but be elated by the fact that it was working…at least as far as he could see. The menu screens were encouraging, and assuming the unnamed devices were the refiner, 3D printer, and engraver, he was off to a great start.

All the doom and gloom from before ebbed away as he watched the loading bar finish its progress. When it finally connected, Sal expected something flashy or incredible, but the tracker just went back to normal. He stood there for a few moments waiting for something to happen, but nothing did.

After a few more seconds of being unsure what to do, Sal decided that he'd fill up the loading tray with some materials. He wasn't being particular about them either. A few drawers of stuff from the carriage downstairs would do it, as well as some obsidian glass. A part of him, the negative thoughts side, was warning him to keep his expectations at rock bottom. The likeliest result was going to be a series of errors telling him that the materials weren't compatible or recognized. Sal's rush back up the stairs slowed at that thought, but he wasn't deterred. He had crafted something that utilized programming, and that was one hell of an accomplishment.

With a wry smile on his face, Sal carefully deposited everything from the drawers he brought upstairs. He stacked them neatly into the tray, unsure how it would even process the materials.

Materials Identified!

The message appeared on the screen, which caused Sal to smile. He guessed it would take some time for it to get through it all, so he walked over to the coffee machine and pressed the button on it. When he turned around to see whether the conveyor belts were working, his jaw dropped.

Obsidian Glass: Small x 8
Obsidian Glass: Medium x 14
Obsidian Glass: Large x 5
Dreadcloth Bolt: Standard x 4
Void Metal: Standard Ingot x 2

The conveyor belt was not only operating, but it was stacking the units in a visible manner as though sorting them for later. Because of the glass, Sal could see the inner workings of the machine and saw it creating what looked like cubby holes in the available space around the belts.

Insufficient Upgrade Materials

Sal stared at the words and completely forgot about the coffee as he moved over to the glass screen. He tapped on the Insufficient Upgrade Materials section, and it opened a new menu to show what was missing.

MythOS v1.3.0 Requirements
- o   Core: Small x 4
- o   Cloth: Bolt x 4
- o   Crystal: Small x 4
- o   Metal: Standard Ingot x 2

To say that Sal was speechless would have been an understatement. It finally dawned on him why he had been designing it from the basics, and without evolutionary runes. The machine was capable of upgrading itself with the right materials. It was going to grow over time. Not because of an evolutionary rune, but instead by upgrading each of the individual components.

Logically, it didn't make sense. The machine itself didn't have the Mythcrafter ability. He wasn't exactly sure how it would upgrade over time. The likeliest option was that it would just throw up a series of errors when that time came about. That's what the logic in Sal's head was saying, but he desperately wanted to know what would happen if he got the other components.

Which led to Sal pulling the cores out of the already dismantled refiner, 3D printer, and engraver from the carriage. As much as it killed him, he also took the core out of his coffee machine, but not before making several cups. One of the cores was medium, but Sal guessed that it should be okay. He put them into the tray and was rewarded with an instantaneous notification that they had been accepted. It was only when he saw the cores moving behind the glass pane that he realized he probably could have kept the small core for his coffee machine, and tried to use the medium core to bridge the gap. That opportunity was now gone as he watched the conveyor belt playfully put the cores out of reach.

Sal spent the next thirty minutes sitting cross-legged with the remnants of his dismantled chair and a few other hunks of irrelevant metal he pulled from the machines in the carriage. He didn't have the strength to shape them like Darren did, but he could still refine them with his essence. It was tougher than when he had done it with the wood during the excursion, but it was still doable. He blended them together, massaging the impurities out of them and creating sturdy ingots that were the size of his outstretched palm. There was a reassuring weight to them, but he wasn't sure they'd be classified as standard measurements.

When he double-checked them to make sure they were of decent quality, Sal got to his feet with the ingots in tow and made his way back up to Mythos. He went to the drawer with bated breath and placed them into the tray, closing it up carefully and slowly as though that might alter the chances of success.

A few seconds passed before the requirement for ingots was crossed out. Sal forgot how to breathe in those moments as he watched the materials being brought up to the refiner. It was actually mesmerizing how it all worked. For some reason, Sal thought that everything would start at the top and work its way down, but all the components went to different machines. He was about to sit down and watch it work when an estimated time of completion appeared on the screen in front of him.

Time Remaining: 15 hours, 13 minutes

Sal stared at it in surprise. His eagerness to put in all the requirements for an upgrade had completely backfired. He wouldn't know whether Mythos could actually create weapons or armor for two-thirds of a day. And if the estimate was anything to go by, even if he gave all the ingredients for a weapon, it would probably take another day to see whether it worked.

It wasn't the worst situation to be in, but Sal was still somewhat frustrated with himself for not doing a test run on something simpler. He needed to buy more cores, and stock up on some ingots for whatever he decided to make next. Moving over to get one of the lukewarm coffees, Sal thought about what he should do next, when an option appeared on screen.

Allow use of Stored Materials?

Sal glanced at the obsidian glass and the bolts of dreadcloth that were stored behind the conveyor belt. He wasn't going to be heartbroken if he lost them to an experiment, but the only thing that gave him pause was the chance that it would make the timer extend to a few days. It was that moment of judgment where Sal cursed himself. He selected the Yes option on the screen and held his coffee, waiting for the verdict.

Time Remaining: 36hrs 52mins

"Why am I like this?" Sal breathed the question as he looked up at the skylight, as though the sun would give him some of the answers he was looking for.

MythOS v1.0.0 will be upgraded to MythOS v2.1.0
Construction of Low Uncommon-Grade Equipment will be unlocked

Sal stared at the machine for a few seconds, processing the words that he had just read. The machine that he had poured his life and soul into for the last ten days…was originally capable of creating Common-grade equipment. The upgrade, that would take close to two days, was going to bring its proficiency up to the Uncommon grade? Four cores and a whole chunk of obsidian was going to get him to Uncommon grade.

Sal took a drink of his coffee before he shook his head with a sigh. "Fuck you, Mythos."

The next couple of days went by painfully slow. Sal accompanied his father to buy a tuxedo for the gala. He wasn't in the mood to do any Crafting, and he wanted to stay away from the workshop while Mythos did its thing. Although it was nice to look at the process happening, Sal couldn't help but feel like he had made a horribly inefficient device…that really didn't warrant the level of work that went into it.

Sure, he could consider it from another perspective, that with more investment of materials, it might break into the Rare-grade equipment. But honestly, he wasn't hopeful. The wait times for products and the material costs were likely going to make it a barely profitable machine. Right now, it was operating at a massive loss and would take a lot of production to break even.

If Uncommon grade was the best it could get to, then Sal estimated it would take about nine months to two years before it was able to cover the cost of construction. Assuming that the products it made were in perfect condition. He couldn't help but think of it like an Appraiser.

Despite those sentiments, Sal treated Mythos like an investment. He had a lot of money, and that would allow him to feed the machine whatever it needed to upgrade to the higher tiers. He'd be a lot more forgiving of the machine if it got to Rare grade or Epic grade. Hell, he'd be delighted. It would be a permanent fixture in the Argento Auction House and give his parents a whole range of items that they could sell on his behalf at the auctions. The lie of their secret artisan would be preserved, and all he'd need to do would be to send them blueprints from time to time. That was the goal of the Mythos machine.

One of the primary reasons he couldn't put Mythos out of his mind was his parents. They had cornered him more than a few times. His mother at first thought that he had wrecked the place and was ashamed to show them. His father guessed correctly that it didn't go to plan and Sal was gloomy because of it.

"I don't care if it's a failure, I want to see it!" Sophia announced with an impatient expression as she stood in front of the locked door to the workshop. "You said that it was working, so it can't be that bad." She looked at Petro for support, who nodded in agreement.

"I want to see what all my hard work went into, Sal." Petro flexed his arm for dramatic effect. "I suffered aches and pains for days because of those panels. Only fair that I get to see what it was for."

Sal sighed as he unlocked the door and led them inside. "Voilà," he said dryly as he gestured at Mythos up on the mezzanine. "It still has a few hours of counting down, so you're not going to see much."

Petro moved up the stairs before stopping abruptly when Mythos came into view. He leaned against the railing of the stairs as he tried to comprehend what he was looking at. "I thought we said a vending machine, Sal…why did you build a factory?"

Sal chuckled at the joke as he waited for his mother to head up the stairs ahead of him. "Don't get too excited. It's either hitting errors or still counting down."

Petro shook his head in wonder. "I think you're wrong there, Sal. It's asking for more materials."

Sal frowned as he climbed the stairs. He was sure that it still had a good few hours left on the timer.

MythOS has been upgraded to v3.1.0
Construction of Low Rare-Grade Equipment has been unlocked
Construction of Upper Uncommon-Grade Equipment has been unlocked
Construction of Uncommon-Grade Equipment has been unlocked
Construction of Low Uncommon-Grade Equipment has been unlocked

"Oh." Sal looked at it in disbelief. "That's new."

CHAPTER 26: DISCOVERY

Sophia held a hand to her face as she looked at Mythos in complete shock. "Sal, you didn't make this. This is a joke the two of you did, isn't it?" She frowned at Petro, as though hoping that he'd confirm her suspicions, but Petro was of no help to her. He was just as stupefied by what he was seeing.

Sal pointed at the coffee machine. "I had to take out the core from it, just to get it working on the upgrading cycle." He spoke remorsefully, as though it were the greatest sacrifice known to man. "I haven't actually tried making any equipment with it…I just gave it what it wanted, and it said it would start upgrading toward the Uncommon-grade stuff. I've got no idea why it's skipped up to the Low Rare grade."

Petro shook his head as he combed a hand through his hair. "Why is it so big?"

Sal pointed at the refiner at the top of the enclosure. "Built an upgraded refiner, an upgraded engraver and printer…the design needed massive plates and trays, so I just made those separately by hand. The conveyor belts matched up with the measurements, so my guess is that it was ready for some heavy-duty stuff. I don't know yet, though. Still need to properly test it out."

"And you just put things in that tray?" Sophia pointed at the visible drawer on the right of Mythos. "And it pops them out, fully made?"

Sal nodded. "That's the idea. Pretty much a vending machine…but I haven't even started on the payment system. I'll need to add that to the operating system at some point." He moved to the screen and tapped the open status screen, wondering whether it would give him more context.

Unnamed Device 01: Assessment Complete. Compatible with v1.0.0 to v2.3.0
Unnamed Device 02:Assessment Complete. Compatible with v1.0.0 to v.3.6.0
Unnamed Device 03: Assessment Complete. Compatible with v1.0.0 to v5.1.0

Sal looked at them carefully for a few moments before a thought popped into his head. He quickly navigated back to look at the versions. It looked like the first digit corresponded with the grade category, like Common, Uncommon, and Rare…while the second digit represented where it was placed within that grade: Low, Mid, and Upper. He wasn't certain this was actually the case, but if it was, then it meant his upgrades to the machines before installing them had given them a massive boost.

Looking at the recent log report, Sal could see that the engraver was apparently capable of working on Low Epic-grade equipment. The 3D printer, on the other hand, which was in the center of Mythos, was able to handle Rare grade, and the refiner was initially set as suitable for Low Uncommon grade.

If that was the case, did that mean that the current version of Mythos was capped at whatever its lowest component was? Sal peered in to see whether there were any major differences, but realized his error almost immediately. It would be the top one that would have changed, and he no longer had any chairs to see up that high. Sal chuckled to himself as he settled for what was in front of him.

His opinion of Mythos was changing for the better. He was able to finally see a path forward toward profitability.

"Do you think he's lost his mind?" Sophia asked quietly behind a cupped hand.

"No idea. He's just looking at it and laughing…" Petro whispered back, loud enough for Sal to hear.

Sal sighed as he looked at them. "Sorry, I was just trying to figure a few things out." He turned toward Mythos and cleared the log updates. It opened into a menu screen with basic text at the center.

MythOS v3.1.0
Select Blueprint
Create Blueprint
Production Log
Settings

Sal tapped the Select Blueprint option, curious as to what would come up. A brief loading bar appeared on the screen before snapping to a new open window.

Scarlet Moon Visor (Blueprint Database)
- o Elixir Machine Concept (Requires Assembly Station)
- o Drone Dock Concept (Requires Assembly Station)
- o Argento Drone Concept (Requires Assembly Station)

The list continued with so many of the items requiring an assembly station. Sal frowned as he reviewed the list, flicking faster and faster through the entries.

"Sal, did you create all of those blueprints?" Sophia asked, a note of concern in her voice. "There has to be at least a hundred in there."

Sal shrugged as he tried to cover the list with his torso, even if only to obscure her view of the many iterations he had gone through in the design stage. He didn't have the heart to tell her that these were the only ones recorded by the tracker. After a few more scrolls, Sal finally found something that he was happy to try out.

- o Storm Strike Concept

"Perfect—we'll try this one. We already have obsidian and some small pieces of hellfire titanium down in the carriage, so this should be a good tester." Sal hit Select, expecting that to be the end of it, but he was faced with an entirely new menu. He stared at it for a few seconds, not exactly sure how to react.

Please Select Grade:
- o Common
- o Uncommon
- o Rare

Sal slowly clicked on Rare, not sure whether this was just an extra step that the MythOS had been programmed with. He had constructed that entire program by doing what he was told, with the tracker guiding him. He didn't actually understand what had gone into the operating system.

Please Select 3 Attributes:
- Attune (Obsidian Glass)
- Counter (Hellfire Titanium)
- Jagged (Fey Ether)
- Nullify (Obsidian Glass)
- Overcharge (Fey Ether)
- Recall (Hellfire Titanium)
- Recharge (Fey Ether)
- Shock (Obsidian Glass)
- Siphon (Leecher Blood)
- Thunder (Obsidian Glass)

Sal stared at the screen for a few seconds. He recognized all the abilities. Three of them were from the original Storm Strike design, but for some reason it was prompting him to select whichever three he wanted for it. It was just a test, so Sal picked Rust's ability of Absolute Counter, and guessed that Counter was a lesser version of it. Recall was another excellent one that brought the dagger right back to the user's hand after being thrown. Lastly, he quite liked the Thunder description, where it caused a thunderous noise when thrown, scaring anyone who heard it. With his three selections complete, Sal moved to the next screen.

Materials Required:
Obsidian Glass: Medium x 2
Hellfire Titanium: Fragment x 3
Dreadcloth: Bolt x 0.5

Sal turned around to go and get the materials, when he found his father holding an assortment of stuff from downstairs.

"When you picked the obsidian dagger, I went downstairs to get the stuff you might need." Petro chuckled sheepishly. "So, what are you waiting for? Let's see what this baby can do!" He lifted his packed arms slightly to encourage Sal to take his pick.

Sal laughed as he opened the drawer for the materials. Motioning his father to come a little closer, he took the obsidian glass first, then the hellfire titanium, and lastly the dreadcloth. Rather than getting his father to take back all the other bits he had brought up, Sal put them into the drawer, too. "It takes surplus stuff and stacks it neatly. You'll see what I mean in a second."

Petro just nodded as he dusted himself off, his eyes not leaving the glass in front of him.

Sal closed the drawer and watched as each of the requirements was crossed off the list. When the last part loaded, it started making its projections again. Well, it almost got there; a different screen popped up with what Sal guessed was a warning.

Deviation from Original Blueprint:
- o Continue
- o Make Changes
- o Revert

Sal hit the Continue option, curious what would come out of it. He expected the same loading screen to appear like before, with an estimated countdown…but that didn't happen. Instead, it started describing the process as the materials started to move across the conveyor belts. Small trays elevated them up to the highest part of Mythos, where they were loaded into the refiner.

Refining Obsidian Glass: Completion 0%
Estimated time to next stage: 3 hours, 3 minutes

"Well, there you have it!" Sal announced with a clap of his hands. "It's going to take roughly a day for a single dagger, so it's a lot less efficient than we'd hoped, but what can you do?"

Petro just stared at his son in astonishment. "You're joking, right?" He pointed at Mythos behind Sal. "This is quite literally the greatest machine I've ever seen in my life, Sal. It's creating a Rare-grade weapon…with customized stats…in exchange for a few material scraps."

Sophia nodded emphatically. "If you're disappointed by this, I think we need to get your head checked." She laughed at the ridiculousness of the situation. "This is what you were hiding from? Because it's only making Rare grades? Not one of those obsidian daggers sold for less than six hundred thousand, Sal…and it's going to take a day to make one?"

Sal's words died in his throat. He was currently battling a war of his own personal expectations versus what others were content with. It wasn't right for him to tell his parents that he was disappointed, and in truth, he wasn't anymore. Seeing that the machine had managed to upgrade itself opened a lot more possibilities…but it wasn't the extraordinary thing he thought he had been building. Like, at no point had he inputted any choices when it came to the runes. He thought that would be an option, but it didn't seem to be the case.

"Whoa, that dropped fast," Petro remarked as he stepped to the side of Sal to get a better look. "It really had us fooled there. You're up, Sal."

Sal turned around in confusion, only to see that the refinement process was complete. It had just said that it would take three hours…but it was already done? It hadn't even been a couple of minutes. He looked at the screen to see what his father was talking about, when the words came into view.

Please Select Primary Rune:
- o Evolutionary Rune (Weapon)

Please Select Secondary Rune:
- o Reinforcement Rune
- o Essence Replenishment Rune

Sal tapped the evolutionary rune for the primary slot and chose self-replenishment for the secondary. Those were the ones that were on the Storm Strike series of blades, so he knew that it would be possible to replicate them. Once his selections were underway, the loading screen came back up with another estimated time.

This time, Sal didn't turn around; he watched it intently as it started off with a two hour and something estimate. The refiner slowly powered up again to work on the handles, which was when he realized what was happening. The estimate was being calculated before the machines were fully activated, and then when it got to full power…Sal watched as the two hours became four minutes.

"Okay, I apologize," Sal admitted finally as he looked at Mythos in a whole new light.

"For what?" Petro asked in confusion.

Sal chuckled. "Oh, I was just apologizing to the machine for thinking it was a failure." He thought of how long it was standing idle when he had left it for essentially two days. It was an awful use of the cores he had sacrificed to the machine, as it probably used them to stay alive for all that time. He wanted to investigate alternative power sources…or just fill it so full of cores that it wouldn't ever die. Sal also wanted to know what the assembly station was…it would allow him to create stuff like the elixir machine as well as the combat drone. Definitely something he should be investing in.

Sophia shook her head in disbelief. "I'd swear he's not my son… In what world could this ever be considered a failure? Do you know how many guilds would kill for something like this?"

"I could think of a few." Sal smiled at his mother. "Honestly, I didn't mean to sound ungrateful…you didn't see the pain and torture I had to put myself through to get the programming part of it done. When you go from a sniper rifle in two days that can turn into a Mythic, to a monstrosity of complications that spits out Uncommon grades every two to three days, it's demoralizing as hell."

Petro chuckled as he clasped Sal into a bear hug. "Well, now you're a few days later…and it's making Rare grades every day. How long until we see Unique grades every eight hours, or Epics in twenty minutes?" When he let go of Sal, he was beaming. "Even if it fails, you'll find a way to fix it. If it doesn't meet expectations, you'll find a way to improve it. Quitting isn't in you, Sal…unless it's sports."

Sophia let out an aggravated sigh. "How many times do I have to apologize for that? I thought sports would be a good way for him to make friends!"

Petro grinned at her. "He's made loads of friends, and we're going to meet them at the gala tomorrow, right?"

Sophia perked up at that. "Divinity will be there, I take it?"

Sal sighed as he nodded. "And a few of the others. There's something important you both need to know before you meet them."

Both Sophia and Petro looked at each other in confusion before turning back to Sal.

Petro gave him a small nod. "Of course. What is it?"

Sal stared him dead in the eye. "Anything Barry Francis tells you is a complete lie."

CHAPTER 27: APPREHENSION

"Don't worry about it, Sal. You can fix the machine tomorrow, well…depending on how hungover you are," Petro joked as he put a hand on his son's shoulder. He was dressed in an elegant grey tuxedo with black shirt and a slate-grey bowtie. His shoes were two-toned, with a grey felt material against a shimmering black leather. It was as if he chose the entire palette based on his greying hair.

Sal's ensemble was the inverse of his father. His tuxedo was a regal purple with a high collar and cravat. A black cummerbund was snugly draped around his waist, disguising the fold of his elegant silver shirt. It was surprisingly comfortable, and far too stylish for him. He brought his father along for the tuxedo shopping, thinking that it would be a simple affair…but who could have guessed that Petro had an eye for fashion? The tuxedo jacket was more like a long coat because of the length of the tails that draped behind him. His mother assured him that the suit accentuated his figure and made him look dashing, but he was pretty sure he saw her laughing.

Either way, he fully expected to be outshone by the style of the others at the event. Looking down at his own feet, he wondered how many customers requested purple dress shoes. The material was a blend of purple felt and a shiny black leather.

When Sal's eyes came up, they locked onto the error report on Mythos. There was no obsidian dagger to show for all the efforts, but instead, he had received an incredibly detailed report…written entirely in the codebase he wrote it in. The tracker didn't know what to do with it, and Sal was stumped.

"The car will be here any minute. We should go and wait out front with your mother. If we leave her any longer, I can't promise that she won't start on the wine," Petro warned, as though it were a matter of life-and-death.

Sal snorted at that as he downloaded the report onto his tablet. "With the amount of alcohol you guys ordered in for the after-party, I'll take the bet that she doesn't even make a dent in it."

Petro chuckled as he watched Sal pocket his tablet. "Okay, so you're all ready…no other surprises in store for us?"

Sal looked at him strangely. "What are you talking about?"

Petro shrugged. "You had a whole day of waiting for that result…which is a dangerous amount of time in your hands." He plucked his obsidian monocle from his breast pocket and placed it over his eye. "I almost feel bad for upstaging you like this… Almost."

Sal sighed as he made his way down the stairs. "There's no need to be petty, Dad. When would I ever try to upstage you?"

Petro faltered for a second before following him. It was only when he got to the base of the stairs that he frowned. "Where are you going?"

Sal walked backward into the carriage with a wide grin on his face. "Oh, just forgot a little something."

Petro's smile came back with a vengeance. "You little shit, what did you do?"

Sal brought his hand out from behind the door with a flourish, revealing the most extravagant cane imaginable. It was clearly a sword-cane, but rather than disguising that fact, the black sword was completely visible from the base of the cane all the way to the hilt. What made it truly enchanting was the obsidian snake that was coiled around the black blade, with its head acting as the hilt. Sal tapped it against the ground, causing a ripple of lightning to skewer from the base of the snake's tail, all the way up to its eyes…where they glowed for a few seconds longer.

Petro stared at it for a few seconds, his monocle and eyes doing a rapid Appraisal. "You just happened to make a Rare-grade cane-sword…or was it just lying around? Oh, I see what you've done." Realization crossed his features as he saw the true nature of the sword.

Sal shrugged as he started walking with it. "Wanted to be able to show Lawrence Baron a prototype. This thing would be atrocious for battle, but you have to admit that it looks good!"

Petro sighed as he looked at the cane with a shake of his head. "It's certainly…something! I knew you'd make something to overshadow my new monocle…you couldn't let me have this one thing, could you?" He pretended to be upset, but the smile on his face told Sal that he was enjoying the back-and-forth. "Your mother is going to hate it."

A few moments later, they arrived to see Sophia at the door with a glass of wine. "Car is outside. Are you both ready—" She caught sight of Sal's cane. "Sal, you know I love you…but there's no way in hell you're taking that to the gala. Robert won't look too fondly on us if we arrive armed for battle." She shot Petro a pleading look, but he just shrugged and kept walking.

Sal chuckled as he cut off the trickle of essence he was sending into the cane. The illusion evaporated to reveal a sleek black cane with red cracks offering a comforting glow. "Hellfire titanium for the sheath, and for the guard. What do you think? Oh, and I left the revolver in the workshop, I'm just bringing my visor."

Sophia held her hand over her chest the moment she realized that the snake thing wasn't real. Her relief turned into confusion as she looked at the black cane with a raised eyebrow. "Sheath and guard? Is it a sword?"

Sal smiled as he twisted the top of the cane and pulled it sharply upward, revealing a flash of light that illuminated the entire room. When it cleared, it revealed a gorgeous obsidian blade that thrummed with electrical essence. "Made the entire sheath work as an attuning focus, so the blade is constantly at full power. Hopefully Mr. Baron likes it."

Sophia shook her head as she placed her wine glass down on the countertop. "I'm sure he'll love it, but make sure you don't do that flashing thing when we're inside…it'll blind everyone!"

Sal smiled as he gave his mother a quick nod. "After you!"

Sophia gave him a pointed look as she held up the keys to the front door. "Chivalry is well and good, Salvatore, but not when I'm the one waiting on you so I can lock up. Get your ass in the car, so we can get there on time!"

Sal laughed as he quickly followed his father, who stood outside, buffing up his monocle with a pocket square.

"What did she think of the illusion?" Petro grinned. "You'll be proud to know that my eyes picked it up faster than the monocle this time around. I've been practicing!"

Sal raised an eyebrow in surprise. "You were able to see through the illusion with just your eyes? That's actually really cool. I'll keep you close when Barry is around. He's constantly throwing up illusions."

Petro smiled as he looked past Sal. "Looking radiant as ever, my love."

Sophia shot him a look over her shoulder as she turned the key and tapped her keycard against the terminal at the side of the building. "You knew it was an illusion, didn't you?"

"Our car is here." Petro changed the subject quickly as he gestured at the long black car that rested on the side of the street in front of the auction. "Spared no expense since we're arriving with the top Savior in Quest Academy."

Sal rolled his eyes as he approached the car door. Much to his surprise, double doors opened outward as he got into range of its sensors. More than that, it elevated slightly off the ground, hovering in place to make it easier for Sal to step straight into the interior. He hesitated for only a moment before ducking his head and raising his cane to ensure he didn't bump into anything while getting into the car. Two rows of seats faced each other around a small white table. The chairs themselves were spaced out and looked like luxury recliners, with a range of options on the control panel at the side.

"Very nice," Sophia remarked as she casually moved to the area behind the driver seat, smoothing her white and black dress before sitting down. Her white hat and fur shoulder-warmer were placed on the small table, along with her purse.

Sal couldn't help but think that the puffy white collar of her outfit looked like Darren Lenihan's prowler coat. It was an uncanny resemblance.

Petro stepped in after Sophia and took the seat next to her. He tapped the black-tinted glass behind him before noticing the control panel embedded into the table in front of him. "Ah, old habits die hard." He chuckled before pressing the departure option. The double black doors didn't make so much as a click when they joined together. A soft set of lights illuminated the interior and showcased the rich designs. Placards were mounted to the side of the car, on the inside of the doorway.

Hunter Bureau: Private Service

Sophia cocked her eyebrow. "Oh, so you went all out for your son, yeah?" She pointed at the placard. "And it just so happens to be one of Robert's cars?"

Petro chuckled as he offered a guilty shrug. "Can you blame a guy for trying? It's going to be quite a trek to get there. I'd say we've got about an hour in this thing, so we might as well get comfortable." He looked down at the table console for a moment before pressing another button. Petro's gaze turned to an area in the center of the table, where he waited for a few seconds.

Sal was going to ask what he was expecting to happen when a circular segment of wood rose from the surface of the table. It was a secret compartment that revealed a bottle of chilled champagne with four flutes.

"Now we're talking." Sophia grinned as she reached for the bottle. Placing her palm over the cork, she gave it a quick twist to control the explosive pop...and when she removed her hand, a small plume of white vapor emanated from the top of the bottle. "Petro, get the glasses."

He was already moving and setting them out in front of everyone. "I doubt it'll be enough to fog the senses, but might take the edge off whatever nerves you're feeling."

Sophia chuckled as she looked at Petro in disbelief. "Nerves? He's top of his entire year, and he's going to be seeing all his friends. What's there to be worried about?"

Sal raised his hand and started to count off his fingers. "Meeting Doc Ameye for the first time. Meeting Fabi…and probably having everyone's attention on me. Oh, and the fact that Robert knows I'm a Mythcrafter?" He thought about it. "What am I forgetting? Oh! He's apparently got a surprise gift for us after the tower trial, and that's probably going to involve going up on stage. What if there's a speech part?"

Sophia took the spare glass that was left over and placed it beside Sal's first glass. "Yeah, you get a double dose of the champagne. Drink up and put all those thoughts to one side. All you should be focused on is having fun. By the end of the night, we'll be waltzing around the dance floor."

"No dancing," Sal answered immediately. He caught the shocked expression on his mother's face and tried to clarify. "Upgrade and the other Crafters were giving me shit about it, in a good-natured way, but yeah…it'll just give her more ammunition."

"You wouldn't even dance with your own mother?" Petro asked while shaking his head in mock disappointment. "In front of all your friends, peers, lecturers, and Heroes of the city? What's wrong with you, Sal?"

Sophia slapped Petro's arm. "Come on, they'll be too trashed to even notice. You're both wearing tailcoats, and they're designed for a good ballroom dance! There's a floor dedicated to it, and it's made to be used." She stared at Petro for a second. "If he doesn't dance with me, you're taking his place."

Petro changed tack immediately and rested his elbows on the table to regard Sal seriously. "I think you should dance with your mother, Sal." His face broke into a smile as he brought the champagne flute to his lips. "Besides, we've always done our own thing…this one won't be any different."

Sal smiled as he raised his own drink. "To doing things the Argento way."

"Hear, hear." Sophia laughed as she raised her own glass. "I want to see how many fun people we can steal back to the Argento Auction House for the after-party. We started hosting them when we realized how stuffy the Hunter Bureau late-bar was."

"Can't wait." Sal smiled in return.

CHAPTER 28: MEMORIES

"Where is this?" Sal asked breathlessly as he pressed his hands against the window of the private car. He could scarcely believe his eyes as he looked at the urban redevelopment that flowed across the landscape below. It had taken them over an hour of uninterrupted airspace to get to their destination, and they hadn't needed to punch through a single Red Zone barrier.

Petro frowned as he looked out the window. "Looks like the Hunter Bureau has been keeping a few secrets over the last while." He gestured for Sophia to lean over him to have a look. "It's Grafton Borough…I never thought they'd take it back." Shaking his head with an almost dazed expression on his face, he waited for Sophia's verdict.

Sophia clicked her tongue as she only spared the view a single glance before sitting back properly in her chair. Crossing her arms, she bit her lip. "Why would Robert want to host the gala here, of all places? There's definitely an angle."

Sal squinted as he tried to capture as many details as possible of his surroundings. Old three-story buildings were fully restored on both sides of a single strip of main street. Following the path of the straight road, Sal could see the buildings getting progressively more elaborate and taller, until the street finished into a circular garden-like plot of land at the end. From his vantage point in the sky, it looked similar to a spoon: a long stem of rebuilt offices and apartments, leading to a massive greenery at the head. The garden was surrounded by enormous buildings, and in the very center of the greenery, sticking out like a protest to the sky, was a skyscraper that even dwarfed Quest Academy.

Petro drummed his fingers against the table in the private car, looking out the window thoughtfully. "Is it a show of force, that the Reclamation guilds are doing their jobs? Or is he looking to rejuvenate Grafton by inviting people to move here?"

Sophia let out an aggravated sigh. "As long as he doesn't pull that same stunt as last time, and increase the residence taxes of everyone who doesn't move. It's barely been four years since the last hike." She frowned at Sal. "If Robert offers to set up your guild in Grafton, tell us immediately, okay?"

Petro chuckled as he shook his head. "No. There's no way he'd risk Sal like that. There's always something like a forty percent chance of a newly acquired territory being retaken by the demons, and it would be the height of foolishness to even consider it." He looked out the window again to see the approaching strip of the main street. "My best guess is that there's an announcement coming…probably a few Tier 1 guilds migrating to Grafton to get it set up. They'll never be able to hold Grafton." There was a certainty in his voice as he stared at the mass of destruction in every direction.

Sophia bit her lip as she looked at Petro. "Still, Robert is unpredictable. I don't want Sal being put into any sort of situation like that. If he tries anything, we need to be there."

Sal tore his gaze away from the window and stared at his mother. "I told you before, Silver Sanctuary is my home. That's where I want to set up my guild. I've never even heard of Grafton before…and outside of a few buildings and a park, it doesn't really have much going for it."

Petro smiled as he tilted his head slightly. "We'll see how you feel after you see the Arc presentation. Best guess is that Robert has Eric managing this project, and it'll be something extraordinary."

Sophia nodded as she looked at Sal. "As long as you're not the one who lives here, I don't mind at all. You might even be able to pick up a few buildings for future development, but I'd wait to see what plans they've come up with for expansion. Grafton was massive, and this isn't even a sliver of its former glory."

"Agreed. This is more like nostalgia bait for all the oldies at the gala…and it wouldn't be good to start a pissing match with their wallets." Petro chuckled as he looked back out the window. "Can't help but feel a little hopeful, though. If they can connect up the train line to Grafton, it would be a massive step forward for society and could lead to rehoming close to a hundred thousand refugees."

"That many?" Sal asked in disbelief as he pointed out the window. "Just how big was Grafton?"

Petro pointed behind Sal. "All the way from over there, to about…" He brought his hand across the horizon to aim his finger at another point in the distance behind his own seat. "To around there. You have to remember, Silver Sanctuary is a district with the population of a small town. Grafton was a bustling metropolis and one of the best cities on the coast. If it wasn't for eight calamities in a row, it would have likely endured the invasion and become the central hub of the resistance."

"Eight calamities?" Sal repeated in wonder as he stared at the wide-scale wreckage across the horizon. There were hundreds of demonic towers visible in the distance, their ethereal glows betraying them as otherworldly. Sal was certain that he'd be able to see the demons themselves roaming around if he had his tracker equipped. There were no man-made skyscrapers as far as the eye could see, with the only notable exception being the one at the center of the garden area they were moving toward.

Petro nodded. "Yeah, the problem was that the city was far too big to defend. During the portal outbreak, everyone fled the area and it was far too much space to properly mount a counterattack. The Hunter Bureau—well…they weren't known by that name back then—they consolidated their forces and opted to protect key strategic locations, but the subsequent calamities made holding those locations next to impossible." His tone became somber as he sighed. "It's a genuine miracle that our families managed to hold anything before the creation of the barriers."

"Looks like we're descending," Sophia remarked as she poured the last of the champagne into her glass. "I feel like we should take another bottle for the red carpet." It was clear she wanted to change the topic of conversation as she smiled at Sal.

Sal laughed as he looked at his father, but the smile died when he saw the expression on Petro's face. The jovial attitude was nowhere to be seen. "Are you okay, Dad?"

Petro blinked before forcing a smile to his face. "Yeah, just thinking about useless stuff." He clapped his hands as though it would banish the gloom in the car. "Let's get this over with."

Sal continued to look at his father. Long enough to make it clear that he wasn't convinced.

Petro just shook his head wistfully. "It's something I hope you never see in your lifetime, Sal. Losing territory is one of the most painful realities of this war. More refugees, less resources, and an entire culture of finger-pointing that blossoms from it. Worse than that, it's the crippling feeling of helplessness." He gestured at the partially rebuilt street outside as their car started to land. "I never thought I'd see Grafton again in my lifetime. It's hard to process all of it."

Sophia gave Petro's arm a gentle squeeze. She looked at Sal with a slight smile. "We've seen countless attempts to retake the areas we grew up in, and then had to deal with the disappointments of the bureau losing them immediately afterward. Hell, we lost a small fortune in trying to build a branch of the Argento Auction House at the Shard. Now it's just a desolate wasteland overrun by the demons. You'll get used to it in time, but it doesn't stop you from holding a sliver of hope."

Sal nodded quietly as he looked at his father with concern. "I heard that the Reclamation guilds only prioritized the Bastion properties. Is that just rumors, or is there any truth to it?"

Petro snorted as he looked at Sal in surprise. "You've got some interesting sources. It's a running joke that the Reclamation guilds are useless, but the failures of the past aren't attributable to them. It's the greed of everyone in between the stages that's the problem. Arc is a great guild, but there simply aren't enough groups like them." He gestured at the street out the window.

"You're going to get dozens of contractors all bidding downward to get the reconstruction project from the bureau, and they then try to sell the vision of the future, and it's a coin toss if it actually happens. Crowdfunding from honest people, mismanaging funds, and then disbanding. There aren't nearly enough controls to stop them, and they all return with a different label and the same promises. The bureau washes its hands of them, moves onto new territories. The Guilds Association mediates and gives a fractional settlement to those with losses, and the Scabs pick the places clean to line their pockets. It's a farce."

Taking a deep breath, Petro was about to continue when he caught the warning look from his wife. With a slow exhalation, he tapped the table in front of him. "You're right, sorry." He put on his game face and held the handle to the car door. As the car settled on the restored pavement, he looked at Sal with a genuine smile. "I'm going to do everything in my power to get you the guild headquarters that you want. So, let's get this show started." With that, he pulled the door handle and slid it open.

Sal exited next from his side of the car seat, opening his own door that slid in the opposite direction to his father's. What was waiting for him was definitely a surprise. A red carpet began a few steps in front of him, with velvet rope suspended from golden podiums raised to the height of his waist. Dozens of similar black cars were parked to either side of the carpet; when he turned around, Sal could see even more descending from the sky.

"Argento family?" a voice asked from out of nowhere, causing all of them to turn around in surprise.

When Sal turned to see the source of the voice, he was met with a familiar face, but he couldn't pinpoint where he had seen her before. She was medium height, wearing a golden blouse and black pencil skirt. Her brown hair was pinned up, and her golden lipstick was a stark contrast to her pale complexion. In her hands was a small black box that seemed to be glowing ever so slightly from the cracks.

"That's us. Good to see you again." Petro smiled as he moved over to shake her hand. "Are you here to protect us again?" he joked as he turned to Sal, laughing.

Sal's eyes widened at the sudden realization. "Ah, the girl from the train? You were escorting us on my first day at Quest Academy?"

She smiled at the recognition as she accepted Petro's handshake. "The pleasure is all mine. Who would have guessed that you'd become the top of the year? Congratulations, Mr. Argento." Her blue eyes were locked on Sal as she spoke. "I have a few gifts from the Hunter Bureau before we make our way to the venue." With that said, she opened the small box to reveal three pins. Two of them were black-rimmed disks with a polished white stone in the center. The third, which sat in the center of the box, was the culprit behind the glowing. It was an intricately carved dragon head that had a brilliant white glow coming from the mouth.

"If you'd be so kind as to take the one in the center, Mr. Argento." She spoke as she stepped closer to Sal, just in case there was any confusion. "Please secure it to your breast pocket on the left. It will act as a reference for our other attendees this evening."

Sophia cocked an eyebrow as she moved over to examine the dragon head more closely. "Not very subtle, is it?" She smiled as she looked at the woman holding the box. "Also, what should we call you?"

The lady nodded as she extended her hand to Sophia. "Apologies for the lack of introduction. I'm Castelle, a member of the Sentinel Squad within the Hunter Bureau."

Sophia didn't react in the slightest as she kept her gaze on Castelle. "Sentinel Squad, not Reconnaissance or Espionage?"

Castelle's eyes narrowed ever so slightly. "Sentinel Squad. We all serve the Hunter Bureau."

Petro leaned between the two women and plucked one of the pins from the box. "Left pocket, yes?" he asked in a clueless voice, as though it would lessen the tension between them.

Castelle's smile returned as she nodded. "Yes, please. If you could all place them on the left, that would be wonderful." She encouraged both Sal and Sophia to take their own pins.

Sophia took the pin while giving Castelle an appraising look. After a moment of quiet deliberation, she shook her head and attached the pin to her dress.

Sal looked at his mother in confusion, not sure what had just happened. Taking the gaudy as hell dragon pin, he reluctantly fastened it to his left breast pocket.

When he was done, he looked up at Castelle in time to see the box in her hands vanish into thin air. Her hands raised to point both index fingers like guns in the direction of the red carpet.

"Now, if you'll follow me, we'll get you to the gala in no time." Castelle's smile was a lot less natural than before, and Sal could have sworn that he saw her staring at his mother.

CHAPTER 29: MINGLE

After a solid twenty minutes of walking, Sal arrived at the base of the stone staircase. Their entire journey had involved very little small talk, and the tension between his mother and Castelle seemed to only grow with every step. There wasn't really much to see on either side of the velvet rope, so all Sal could really do was to stare forward for most of the walk, hoping that they'd arrive soon.

Rather than seeing a wreckage of buildings on each side, there were large signs showing the redevelopment plans for the cleared spaces on the other side of the street. Sal had tried looking at a few of them, but his father just ushered him along, with a comment about it being incredibly unlikely for the projects to ever actually happen.

Castelle walked up to join Sal at the base of the staircase. "You should be fine from here. It was a pleasure seeing you again, Salvatore. I hope you'll continue to surprise us with your progress." She smiled and clapped him on the shoulder. "The Hunter Bureau could do with a few Crafters, too. So, don't rule us out when it comes time to decide on your future, okay?"

Sal gave her a slight nod. "I'm pretty set on starting a guild, but it's nice to know that there are other doors open. Thank you for escorting us here, and for the time on the train."

Castelle nodded. "The train was just a job to keep the private cabins safe. Wouldn't be great if a massive chunk of our future Heroes and Hunters died in a freak train accident, would it?" She laughed at her own joke before turning to Petro and Sophia. "Have a lovely evening. The Sentinel Squad is stationed around the building, so there won't be any surprise attacks while you're partying."

Sophia's nose wrinkled at that, but a warning look from Petro stopped her from making any sort of retort. Instead, Petro gave her a gracious nod and a winning smile before starting up the steps. "Thank you for your service, Castelle."

Sal started to move up the stairs, turning to look over his shoulder to see Castelle depart. She was nowhere to be seen, which made him feel somewhat uneasy.

"She has a Teleportation ability, and she's in the Sentinel Squad?" Sophia scoffed as she followed Sal's gaze. "Picked up her ability with the tracker, along with all sorts of records. That girl is most definitely in one of Robert's assassination squads."

"Keep moving," Petro said in a serious tone. "I'd be amazed if these pins aren't recording everything we say."

Sophia looked at the pin on her dress and pinched it between two fingers, lifting it to her face. "If you're listening, Robert, I think that Castelle is an Assassin. Please confirm."

Petro shot her a look of incredulity, but Sophia just shrugged it off as she overtook him on the stairs.

Sal didn't know whether he should laugh or cry at the situation. His mother was wearing the invisible tracker that he had made for her. He wondered whether that was going to cause any issues for them, or if they'd be okay. The expression on his father's face wasn't exactly filling him with confidence, as it looked like Petro was at his wit's end.

When they all crested the top of the staircase, they were met with enormous wooden doors that were wide open. A marble floor stretched out beneath the red carpet that led into the massive entrance hall. The most elaborate chandelier that Sal had ever laid eyes on was suspended from the ceiling, with small cores acting as light sources, embedded within various shards of otherworldly glass. Sal could see some scarlet screen, obsidian glass, and lords crystal in a few different spots of the chandelier, and it really drove home just how wealthy the Hunter Bureau was to be using such precious materials as decoration.

Droves of waiting staff stood at the edges of the hall, all of them holding trays of food and beverages. Their uniforms were somewhat reminiscent of Castelle's attire, with gold and black being the key colors. They stood unnervingly still as Sal and his parents walked through the entrance hall.

"Welcome to the Hunter Bureau Gala. Can I see your invitations, please?" a voice called out from in front of them.

Sal had been so fixated on the chandelier and the statuesque staff that he hadn't noticed the front of house person who stood in front of them. There was no gold or black with this individual. He was dressed in a blood-red ensemble contrasted with a brilliant white. The red was depicted as a coiling dragon that swept over his right shoulder and settled on the chest. Although his outfit looked like it was a refined fabric, Sal could tell from just a glance that it was a really flexible metal. Before he could determine the actual material, his father's body broke his view of the man.

Petro strode forward and gestured at the pin on his breast pocket. "We were guided here by Castelle of the Sentinel Squad. Petro and Sophia Argento, with our son, Salvatore."

Sal made eye contact with the man as he peered over Petro's shoulder to verify each of their pins. His irises were a bright red, similar to Vanessa's when she had worked on breaking through his gates. It was an unnerving reminder of the pain he had gone through, and Sal pushed that memory straight out of his head.

"Excellent. I see you've received your pins already. We've got some refreshments prepared as we wait for the rest of the attendees to arrive. Please make your way through the door behind me, and you'll be able to join our other guests." He spoke smoothly as he stepped to one side, using both arms to gesture at an equally large wooden door on the opposite wall. "You'll find the seating arrangements on the bulletin board near the cocktail lounge. Just head past the sculptures and you can't miss it."

"Thank you." Sophia moved toward the door. As though anticipating her movement, the well-dressed man waved his right hand, causing the entire door to gradually open inward.

Petro gave Sal a tight smile before jutting his chin toward the door. "Ignore everything from out on the red carpet with Castelle. Your mother tends to overthink things."

Sal snorted as he followed his mother. "Pretty sure I got that from her. How many people do you think will be here?"

Petro shrugged as he caught up to his son. "Probably close to a couple of thousand. When you consider how many Heroes and Hunters there are, and all their families and friends…it can really add up. Students and their parents, as well as the staff and guild folk? It'll be a packed one, for sure."

Sal barely had any time to process the answer as the doors opened to reveal a massive, multi-tiered floor, packed with groups of people as far as the eye could see. The first thing that struck him, other than the sheer magnitude of the space, was the assortment of dress. Any fears he had about his somewhat ostentatious outfit were immediately dismissed as he saw the height of ridiculousness being worn by many a guest.

There was one woman on a staged floor to the right who looked to be floating in midair, with a collection of white shawls rotating around her body like they were caught in some kind of orbit. Her dress was a puffy monstrosity of white that dominated every space she entered, and Sal struggled not to stare at it. Another man on the main floor holding a drink was in full-plate armor, but oversized to the point that it looked like he was impersonating a hulker. The shoulder plates alone were the size of a car door. If Sal was to discount the practicality of the outfits, he'd have no choice but to talk about the color palette of the room, where everyone was wearing the loudest colors known to man.

"Where should we start?" Sophia muttered as she stepped forward to stand on the edge of a marble staircase that led to different platforms around the room.

Sal wondered whether the design of the main hall was the inspiration for the training level in the tower where they needed to ascend the staircases. There were far too many similarities for it to be a coincidence. Shaking his head, Sal tried to focus on the task at hand and looked at the room objectively. He wanted to find Upgrade and show her the error report from the machine he built, but it would also be great to see the other Saviors from Quest Academy. The only problem was that he couldn't see anyone he knew in the dense crowd.

"Drinks first," Petro announced as he moved past Sophia and started to descend the stairs, pointing ahead to a bar area that was quite crowded on one side. "The staff here will likely know where everyone is hanging out."

As Sal followed his father, he caught a few people staring at him in surprise. Well, not at him, but rather at the pin he wore on his chest. It was something he'd need to ask about later, because he wasn't really sure what the pins represented. He returned the gazes with a smile and checked out the pins on the other guests. Some didn't have any equipped, while others held ones of completely different designs. Some of the circles were similar to the pins that his parents wore, while others were in a star shape. There were a few creature-themed pins, like his dragon, but they were bears, snakes, fish, and tigers. None of them really gave him a clue on their meaning.

Petro led them to the less packed area of the bar and made way for Sophia to lean against the countertop. He smiled at the nearest barman, and in only a few seconds, they were being served. Without asking for their thoughts, he ordered a white wine for Sophia and a neat whiskey for Sal and himself. Turning his head to look at Sal, he offered a mischievous wink. "Just to settle the nerves. Don't rush it."

Sal accepted the whiskey tumbler from the barman with a smile as he looked around at the group of people laughing around the bar. It was hard to even hear himself think over the noise, but it wasn't the worst situation. He could hear tidbits of conversation from the Heroes and Hunters. There were remarks about the Darwin Cruises and the Reclamation efforts of Grafton. Better yet, there were some people talking about power levels and breakthroughs for internal gates. Focusing on that conversation, Sal didn't turn around to look, but just listened intently. There wasn't anything really of substance, but instead, just two friends goading each other about performance. With a sigh, Sal looked up from his glass to where his father was grinning at him.

Without saying a word, Petro lifted his monocle and placed it over his right eye. The black shard of glass illuminated to show the covered iris in a brilliant white. It looked positively menacing, but Petro's wink with his left eye was playful. "I'll start scoping things out here. Sophia still has her tracker, too. We'll find some people to talk to, so you can go and find your friends. We'll catch up with you later."

Sal smiled as he lifted his glass toward his parents. "Cheers." He touched his whiskey tumbler against their glasses and looked to his left with a steady breath. "Wish me luck."

"You don't need it. Just show off that fancy pin and everyone will want to talk to you," Petro remarked as he turned at the bar. "If you find your friends, we want to meet them before the night is over."

Sophia looked at Sal with a wry smile. "And try not to invite everyone you meet back to the after-party. We shouldn't upstage Robert on his special night." She laughed to herself at the very thought of it, and then looked at Sal with a shrug. "Actually, feel free to go wild. We'll handle the fallout tomorrow."

Sal just sighed as he gave his mother a humoring look. With a final raise of his glass, he left them at the bar and made his way into the crowd of Heroes and Hunters. It was a little unnerving to be surrounded by so many people. He wasn't stupid enough to activate his Skill Master ability to check on everyone's weaves. It would be the fastest way to put everyone on edge or cause a misunderstanding. Prestige had been able to determine his Skill Master ability just by seeing the essence around him, so there were likely many others like her who would detect his ability being activated.

As Sal waded through the crowd, he looked around himself to see whether there were any familiar faces. But the only looks he got were ones of curiosity from strangers. There was no recognition in their eyes.

Just as Sal was about to make his way to an open space where he could take a breather, a burst of red appeared in front of his eyes. It caused him to falter and almost jump back in fright, but something about it seemed eerily familiar. The red light formed into a large X shape. It hung in the air unmoving, so rather than walk through it, Sal turned to move in a different direction, and was met with an entirely new red X.

A few of the other Heroes watched with smiles on their faces as every attempt Sal made to escape the shapes resulted in a new one appearing in front of him.

Clenching his fists, Sal took a steadying breath as he watched a familiar green arrow materializing over his head and pointing at an angle to a platform above him. With his jaw locked tight, he followed the trajectory of the arrow that flew through the air and saw a grinning face watching his every move. As though rewarding him for the discovery, a few congratulatory fireworks were set off, showcasing the culprit in all his smug glory.

Barry waved at Sal to come and join him, before he disappeared from the balcony and melted back into the crowd.

CHAPTER 30: ILLUSIONS

As Sal crested the top of the staircase, he placed his empty whiskey glass on a nearby table. The cane-sword at his side tapped rhythmically along with his stride as he moved toward the area where he last saw Barry. Sal couldn't believe that he would blatantly use his abilities in such a crowded area. *Had the man no fear of the Hunter Bureau?*

It was a lot less crowded on this particular balcony, but the style of the surrounding people was a lot darker in hue. Many of them were dressed in elaborate leather armors that were at least Rare or Unique grade. Without spending too much time on Appraisal, Sal was able to determine that all of them were suited for infiltration and stealth. Navigating through them, Sal apologized to a few of the people he stepped too close to. His gaze was trained on the familiar figure of Barry, who was talking animatedly to a couple of people lounging on a couch.

Sal didn't recognize either of them, but they looked strong. The woman gave off similar vibes to Villa, primarily because she had daggers attached to practically every limb and was dressed in a risqué manner. What really stood out was her stark-white hair that flowed over her left shoulder.

As Sal approached them, her attention snapped to him, and he saw her yellow irises lock onto him. A flicker of light tracked around them, and Sal knew that she was doing some sort of inspection on him. He couldn't tell whether it was Analysis or some type of threat detection, but it was unnerving to be on the receiving end without knowing what was being revealed to her.

"Ah, this is Sal. He's the one I was telling you about. Came first in our year as the top-ranked Savior…and he's a Support class." Barry smiled as he leaned closer to the man on the couch. His voice took on an almost conspiratorial whisper. "Between ourselves, he hasn't a clue about his own self-worth. Wait until you see the highlight reels of how he single-handedly took down the obsidian hulker."

Sal got to watch in real time as the woman's jaw dropped. Her yellow gaze stopped being subtle and instead flared to life as she intently stared at him.

Barry wasn't finished as he crossed his arms and shook his head. "It would have been better if you saw the evolutionary equipment he created." He gave Sal the most subtle of smiles as he continued his barrage of upselling.

Before he could get another word in, the man raised his hand and got to his feet. With a brief clasp of Barry's shoulder, the man excused himself from the conversation as he fluidly walked around the table to extend a hand in Sal's direction.

"You're the infamous Sal?" His chiseled jaw shifted to reveal a charismatic smile that didn't reach his eyes. With a barely imperceptible glance to the side, he was immediately joined by the white-haired woman, who fell into step behind him. "Are you as miraculous as your friend says?" The question wasn't addressed to Sal as he looked at his companion instead, curiosity written all over his face.

"His gates are maxed out, just like the other one." She responded in a respectful tone, her yellow eyes still boring a hole into Sal's soul. "I can't verify the Crafting claims, but he's definitely a Replicator."

With a chuckle, the man looked down at his outstretched hand. "Should I be offended?" He looked at Sal curiously, as though waiting for his reaction.

Sal smiled and gripped his cane a little tighter. "You could be a Body Manipulator looking to do a sense check on my weaknesses." He turned his gaze to meet the yellow stare over the man's shoulder. "And you've already shown that you've got no regard for privacy, so I hope you won't be offended by me declining."

Barry whistled in the background. "If I made him sound like a pushover, that's on me. You give him enough time and the right materials, and he could take down anyone in your guild."

Blinking in confusion, the man turned around to give Barry a look of incredulity. "What did you just say?"

Barry doubled down as he crossed his arms. "What part of evolutionary equipment went over your head? Time and materials. That's all he needs to become a powerhouse."

Sal gave Barry a warning look. "We're not here to pick fights, Barry. Just apologize and we can go somewhere else."

"No, I'd like to hear him out." The man spoke as he looked at Barry carefully. "You approached us specifically and now you're goading me. What is your angle?" He raised a hand to signal for his white-haired companion to stop using her ability.

Barry's face split into a grin as he stared at his opponent. "Masterclass. You've never once done a Masterclass for Quest Academy, and I'd like that to change." He turned around to see the people near them, a look of exasperation on his face. "I have no idea how you're doing it, and it's the most exciting thing I've come across in a very long time."

The white-haired woman tilted her head ever so slightly as everything stopped moving, as though time had frozen.

Sal looked around in confusion as the packed balcony suddenly became empty. Dozens of people vanished into thin air; all the conversations that were happening simultaneously around him evaporated. It was just Barry, the woman, and himself standing there.

Barry just shook his head in amazement. "My illusions are good…but yours are incredible. I want to learn the strategy, placement, the background noise…everything! What would it take to get you to come to Quest Academy and give a Masterclass?" The excitement on his face was genuine as he emphatically spoke about the craft. "How did you manage to make collisions? I intentionally bumped into two or three people. You just touched my shoulder and that was real! The voice modulation, too? There were so many distinct voices in the crowd, and none of their conversation topics looped at any point."

"So, this is the caliber of the Saviors in Quest Academy?" she asked in wonder, looking between Barry and Sal with a grin. "I might need to change my stance on those Masterclasses after all. I presume the goading about your Crafter friend was bait?"

Barry paused as he looked at her in confusion. "Oh, no. He's genuinely that good. I've been teaching him some of my ability, so he'd probably get a lot of value from your Masterclass, too."

"Okay then, final question," she asked with a good-natured chuckle. "Who am I?"

Barry didn't hesitate. "Veil, Hunter Rank 182."

A flicker of disappointment crossed her face and she began to shake her head, but Barry wasn't done.

"You're also Trickster, Hunter Rank 14." Barry grinned as he raised a hand. "And I'm pretty sure you're posing as another Hunter in the six hundreds, as well as operating the Veil Guild."

Rather than answering, she just stared at Barry for a few moments. "Show me your Q-Card, now." Her tone was firm, and a lot of the jovial humor evaporated at the mention of the Trickster name.

Barry produced his Q-Card and moved off to the right, where he held it up in front of an empty space of air. "As I said, I'd really like to learn from you."

Sal jumped as the image of the woman disappeared from in front of him. A distortion of light appeared from the area in front of Barry, with a mechanical arm extending out to take the card from him. Sal immediately started to Appraise it and was astounded to see that the arm was Legendary grade with only three abilities. There was nowhere near enough time for him to properly look at it, but he was certain it was a powerful piece of equipment.

"Barry Francis." Her voice was distorted this time as she spoke. "I'll remember that." The card was handed back as though satisfied.

In a snap of light, the distortion disappeared, leaving both Barry and Sal standing alone on the balcony. Trickster didn't seem to be anywhere near them, but Sal gave Barry a questioning glance as though asking if she were really gone.

"Yeah, she left." He looked crestfallen as he moved to the couch and slumped into it with a sigh. "I came on way too hard, didn't I? She's not going to do the Masterclass." He crossed his arms and frowned, as though running through the conversation in his own head again to see what he could have done better.

"So, first of all…what the fuck just happened?" Sal gestured at the entire room. "You called me up here to be a stand-in for a grand illusion? I thought you were trying to get us killed!"

Barry looked up in confusion. "What?" He stared at Sal for a few seconds before it dawned on him. "Oh, yeah…sorry about that. I needed an alibi to get her to reveal herself, and recruiting the top Savior was a good angle. I couldn't really tip you off in advance because you would have been awkward or suspicious. It's notoriously difficult to find Trickster when she doesn't want to be found."

Sal let out an exasperated sigh. "Why couldn't you just be straightforward with her and ask her outright? She seemed nice."

Barry's brow furrowed as he looked at Sal as if he were an idiot. "She's an Illusionist, Sal. Would you respect a Crafter just because they were a nice person? No, you need to see what they can do, to see if they're worthy of that respect. This whole facade was to show her that I've got some potential, but I don't know if it worked."

Sal moved over to the couch and sat beside Barry. "Man, it's really weird seeing you motivated. Can you not just revert back to the carefree attitude? You're starting to scare me." He looked at his friend and gestured at his own outfit. "So, what do you think of the purple ensemble?" It was a lame attempt at cheering him up, but Sal wanted to at least try.

Barry looked at it for a few moments before he got to his feet. "You tell anyone and I'll deny it." He stretched his arms out and let the illusion fall, revealing a shockingly similar tuxedo in a baby-blue color. It had the same high collar, long pant leg, and the cummerbund at the waist. "I swear that my parents have never even seen a suit, but I'm glad I wasn't the only one." He pointed at his head and let another illusion drop. "There's even a top hat. I've been avoiding my parents because of this."

Sal burst out laughing as he saw the entire outfit in all its cheesy glory. "That is so much worse than the purple...I actually feel bad for you." He was about to make another quip when he thought about what Barry just said. "Wait, your parents are here? What are they like?"

Barry shrugged it off. "Yeah, my father is currently recounting war stories with some of his old buddies down at the bar... He was a Vanguard back in the day, but a smart one. My mother is probably down there telling him to settle down. She has a Healing ability but it's nothing to scream about."

Sal was a little surprised at that. "I kinda guessed they'd be spies or something...you know, with your power being fuckery incarnate."

Barry snorted at that and shook his head. "Nah, they were very concerned when I told them I was going to be a Controller. Because my power is deceptive and I might lead people to their deaths. That was a conversation I wouldn't particularly like to repeat any time soon." He flicked at his baby-blue top hat. "Pretty sure this outfit was retaliation because they couldn't win that argument with me." With his showcase done, he dropped back into the couch with a sigh of relief.

Sal looked at the staircase that led back down to the pandemonium. "Don't suppose you've seen Divinity or the others by any chance?"

Barry shook his head. "Nah, she'd likely seek us out if she wanted to talk. I think the best method with Divinity is to just wait for her to come and find us...and I haven't seen the others. Well, Blathnaid doesn't really count. She's rocking a very...different style. Not really doing much to dispel the image of her being in a band."

"Yeah?" Sal stood. "Might as well go and mingle to see if we can find the others."

Barry reluctantly got to his feet as he recast the illusion on his outfit, appearing to wear a much more classic black tuxedo. "I'd appreciate if you didn't mention anything about Trickster, by the way. I don't want to screw up any of my chances if she does decide to come to Quest Academy."

"Deal," Sal said instantly. "Just don't cause a scene with Doc Ameye and we're golden. I want to make a good impression on the guy, but everything Upgrade has told me makes me think it'll be an impossible task."

With a smile on his face, Barry started walking lazily toward the stairs. "Oh, and by the way...I wholeheartedly approve."

"Of what, me trying to get an in with Doc Ameye?" Sal asked in confusion as he followed Barry.

"Ha, no." Barry chuckled. "You'll know what I'm talking about when you meet her."

"You're starting to sound like Divinity," Sal replied dryly.

Barry shook his head as he placed a hand on Sal's chest. "Okay then, how about this?" He reached over the balcony and pointed at a group of people huddled around a table.

Sal followed his gesture and saw Upgrade laughing in the middle of the group. She wore a dark-green dress with a prowler fur collar draped around her neck. Her hair was pinned up similar to how Castelle wore hers. It was the first time he had seen her wearing makeup and she looked great. As Sal's gaze moved around the group, his throat suddenly went dry.

Barry grinned. "Looks like I don't end up with Victoria."

Sal couldn't even hear what Barry said as he saw Fabi Maccles for the first time. If there was one thing he was certain of, it was that he had zero recollection of her from his childhood. This was a woman he would most definitely have remembered. She was a picture of elegance as she stood beside Upgrade.

Shimmering black hair cascaded down her right shoulder, contrasting sharply with her incredibly pale skin tone. Black lipstick framed a beautiful smile that lit up her entire face when she laughed. A smokey eye shadow gave her a mysterious vibe, and her high cheekbones were a picture of regality. Her black dress was conservative but couldn't hide the hard work she had put into conditioning her body. With just a simple turn, Sal could see the strength in her movements, a quiet confidence as she leaned back in laughter at something Upgrade had said.

"Don't forget to breathe," Barry reminded him, laughing.

CHAPTER 31: FABRIZIA

"What's there to be nervous about?" Barry laughed as he led the way over to the table with Upgrade and Fabi. "She's only your future wife according to Divinity, and one wrong move could completely destroy your entire future. Relax!" He was clearly having a lot of fun with Sal's discomfort.

Sal made another lame attempt to go to the bar, but Barry stopped him by turning around and placing his hands on Sal's shoulders.

"Trust me. Just talk to her like you talk to Upgrade and everything will be fine. She's just another Crafter like Blathnaid, okay? Don't go treating her like some mythical creature that will vanish if you make eye contact," Barry stated as though it were the most obvious thing in the world. "Be yourself, and if you can't do that…be better. It'll all be fine."

"You think that Divinity was messing with us, and that the whole Victoria and Fabi thing was just a lie?" Sal asked hopefully, wondering whether Barry had seen through it somehow.

Barry shook his head. "Nah. If anything, Divinity was trying to get you to focus on someone else and just picked a future where you found happiness with someone who wasn't her." He shrugged it off. "Or she's lying about you and Fabi, but why would she do that? She's not the malicious type, like me. You could end up having a great friendship with her like you have with Upgrade. Just don't overthink it and you'll be fine."

"How can I not overthink it when she might be my future wife?" Sal repeated in a harsh whisper, stopping himself from gesturing wildly at the table on the other side of the room. He looked around to make sure that they hadn't caused too much of a scene.

Barry sighed as he moved behind Sal and started to gently push him. "It'll be weird if you avoid her the whole night. You're friends with Upgrade and it's a group of Crafters. That's literally your ideal group of people to talk to. You can brainstorm solutions and stuff…I don't know."

Sal blinked in surprise and reached into his pocket and produced his tablet. He turned around to Barry with a wide grin on his face. "You're a genius, thank you!"

Barry faltered at the sudden behavioral change and looked at Sal quizzically. "You're not just fobbing me off so you can disappear somewhere else, are you? I want to see you go up to that table."

Sal smiled at him. "I will. Thank you, Barry." He held up his tablet. "I actually need their help, so this is perfect."

Barry kept his grip on Sal's shoulder as he looked at him curiously. "Really? It was that easy? A Crafting problem is enough to make you drop all the anxiety and nerves?"

Sal shrugged as though it were obvious. "Well, originally, I didn't even know what to talk about…but at least now I have something I need their help with. Upgrade is really good at the programming stuff, so she'll hopefully be able to help with this." As Sal started to move off in the direction of the table, he remembered something. "Ah, by the way, do you have plans for after the gala?"

Barry shook his head slowly. "Dad will probably arrange something with the other Vanguard team, so it's going to be a night of babysitting drunk veterans. If you have anything better planned, I'll happily go."

"We're having an after-party at the Argento Auction House if you'd like to come along?" Sal offered, smiling.

Barry nodded. "I'll look forward to it. Good luck with your Crafting problems. I'm going to go and annoy a few other guilds while I'm here. We'll probably see each other at the Savior table for the big announcements." He excused himself with a wave, giving Sal a playful flash of the baby-blue top hat for half a second. With a laugh, he vanished into the crowd of Hunters and Heroes.

Sal just shook his head, smiling, before turning back to the Crafting table across the room. He could see Upgrade looking at him and waving him over to their table. With a steadying breath, he clutched the tablet in his left hand and the cane-sword in his right. Returning the smile, he made his way over to the table, navigating past a few Hunters who were more than a little drunk. When his eyes landed on his destination, he was both relieved and disappointed to see that Fabi was no longer beside Upgrade. It made his task that much easier, but he was looking forward to seeing her up close and hearing her speak.

"When did you arrive? I was asking around and someone said you arrived earlier." Upgrade raised an empty glass. "You've got some serious catching up to do. The trick is to be completely trashed before the presentation. It makes it so much more tolerable."

Sal winced ever so slightly. "I don't think that's exactly true. Shouldn't we be on our best behavior?"

Upgrade laughed as she waved her hand from side to side. "Oh, no. They're going to go through every Hero and Hunter who died…it's harrowing. You don't want to be sober for it."

"And then they harp on about all the budgetary cuts, which is just like another kick when you're down." A familiar melodic voice spoke from behind Sal.

Of course he'd recognize it; he had been listening to her guides for weeks.

Sal turned in time to see Fabi step beside him. Her brilliant white smile was accompanied by a wink as she placed a neat whiskey in front of him.

"Petro told me your drink of choice. I thought it would be funny to get you a juice, but Upgrade wouldn't let me." She laughed as she moved over to Upgrade and placed a glass of wine down in front of her, which Upgrade happily accepted.

Sal was not prepared. He was definitely not prepared for Fabi to sneak up on him and give him a drink. There was a playful vibe with her, and he was immediately out of his depth. With a look to Upgrade, he could see the wide smile on her face, and it was like the doom clock of his life had started to count down. He tried to think of something to say, but his brain had already short-circuited.

"What's this?" Upgrade asked as she spied the cane in Sal's hand. "You cosplaying as Prestige or something?" She chuckled at her own joke as she put out her hand, as though asking for him to show her the cane-sword.

Sal was in autopilot mode, and just handed it to her. It was only when she unclicked the cane that he came back to his senses. "Oh shit, wait!"

Upgrade withdrew the sword from the hellfire titanium sheath with a look of pure joy. The obsidian glass sword shone like a beacon, illuminating the entire hall with a burst of vibrant light. It not only caused a momentary panic among a few of the Hunters, but had the added effect of drawing everyone's attention to Upgrade and Sal.

"You made a cane-sword!" Upgrade announced a little too loudly, holding the sword aloft for literally everyone to see.

Fabi frowned as she looked at the sword carefully. "That's a lot of materials for a Rare grade. How long did it take you to make this?" She looked like she was calculating the cost in her own head.

Sal was filled with a sense of dread because he didn't want to give her the wrong answer. *Was she going to be annoyed by the fact that he used so many expensive materials for a luxury product, or would she be discouraged by how quickly he had been able to make a Rare-grade piece of equipment?* No matter what answer he gave her, he felt like he was setting himself up for failure. The conversations with Chatfield about how he didn't respect the effort involved in procuring materials echoed in his mind.

Fabi looked at Sal in confusion. "Is everything okay?"

Upgrade slid the sword back into the cane sheath and smiled. "Look carefully, Fabi. He's going through multiple answers to see which one will offend you the least. It probably took him a few hours." She gestured at Sal's face. "His poker face is terrible when he's not negotiating."

Fabi's eyebrow shot up as she looked at Sal in surprise. "Hours? Is that true?" She leaned forward, placing both of her palms on the table.

Sal couldn't help but notice how defined her shoulders were. Pushing that observation to one side, he coughed awkwardly before answering. "There were a few iterations, but it might have taken longer than that." He looked at Upgrade with his hands up defensively. "I swear I drew out the blueprint, and iterated a few times. I've got proof." He lifted his tablet as though it were a bulletproof defense.

Upgrade raised her glass and smiled at Fabi. "Wait, it gets so much better." She turned to Sal. "So, what did you do while you've been unsupervised for the last month?"

Sal bit his lip as he thought of what to tell her. Lying seemed to be the best bet. "Nothing. I relaxed and spent some time with my family." He really didn't like how predictable he was in Upgrade's eyes.

Upgrade nodded. "So, if I was to go and ask your parents what you've been working on…would they say that you've relaxed?" She was smiling, but there was a clear challenge in her tone. With a gesture to Fabi, she continued. "She already knows what your parents look like, so they'd absolutely tell her…so, I'll ask again, what have you been working on?"

Fabi looked to be entertained by the topic of conversation and planted her elbows on the table, cradling her chin on interlocked fingers. Her smile was wide as she looked directly at Sal. "Come on, tell us."

"A…machine of sorts," Sal said reluctantly as he tapped at his tablet and held it out to her. "I screwed something up though, because it's not working properly. Brought the tablet so I could get your advice on it."

Upgrade moved closer to examine the tablet. "I won't really be able to tell from pictures, but I'll have a look. What was it supposed to—" She stared at the error report on Sal's screen. Closing her eyes, she exhaled slowly before shaking her head slightly. When she opened her eyes, she looked at Sal. "Please tell me that you didn't learn essence programming in a month."

Sal looked her dead in the eye and shook his head. "If it makes you feel any better, I have absolutely no idea what I'm doing. It makes no sense without the tracker."

Upgrade took the tablet from him and scrolled through the code, frowning. "Fabi, come have a look at this."

Fabi moved over and tilted her head so she could see it better. "What's Mythos? I don't understand that term and it's referenced a few times here." She looked up at Sal in confusion.

"It's an operating system I made. I named it MythOS," he replied lamely, as though that might help them discover the error.

Fabi just continued to stare at him, unblinking, to the point that Sal became unnerved.

Upgrade, on the other hand, was on the move. She tapped a couple of people on the shoulder and pulled them away from their conversations. "Need your brain," was the typical comment she made as she herded them all to a single table.

Maybe it was a testament to how well-regarded Upgrade was among her peers, but not a single person voiced a complaint as they followed her without question. When she glanced up from the tablet, she frowned and looked around the table at the half dozen people assembled.

"Okay, so to clue you in very quickly…we have what looks like a fabricator of some description, with a custom operating system, that can improve itself with the right materials," Upgrade announced as she held Sal's tablet in the air. "It looks like it's not fabricating and we need to figure out why. Who is in?" She looked around at the group and two of the recently acquired Heroes shook their heads with a laugh and started to move away.

Sal didn't want Upgrade to be working off the wrong information, so he decided it was best to correct her before she got started. "It's a 3D printer, refiner, and engraver…all combined with a workbench-like interface. It crafts whatever blueprints you upload to it, kind of like an assembly line."

The two Heroes froze on the spot as they turned to look at Sal in shock. When their attention went back to Upgrade, she just smiled at them.

Upgrade eventually cast her gaze in Fabi's direction, who was still staring at Sal in disbelief. "This is why you can't leave him unsupervised."

Fabi just looked at Upgrade as though the whole thing was some elaborate joke. "A first-year, without formal training…created an operating system for a multifunctional fabricator? How am I supposed to believe that's possible?"

Sal wasn't sure it was going to help his case at all, but he did want to thank Fabi for the tutorials she sold on the Credit Store. "Your guides were a massive help, by the way. I bought all the ones that you recommended on the forums, and reviewed them a few times. I had a few breakthroughs with the Kakushin elixir, which really sped things up."

Fabi's face paled as she looked between Sal and Upgrade. "This is a joke, right?"

Upgrade shook her head, smiling. "Trust me, you get used to it."

CHAPTER 32: DEBUT

After a lot of smooth-talking and promises that they wouldn't be disruptive, Upgrade managed to commandeer one of the display screens at the center of the bar area. It had previously shown the Hunter Bureau logo on a rotating loop, but was now displaying the full error report in large letters on a static image. Similar to how the screens worked in the amphitheater at Quest Academy, the image was visible no matter which way you walked around it.

Sal wasn't sure how he felt about his mistakes being advertised to the entire room, but if it resulted in him getting the answers he needed, then it would be fine. His first instinct was that it would be an easy solution for someone experienced like Upgrade, but it had already been thirty minutes and they were still asking him qualifying questions about the project.

"Best advice would be to scrap the project and lower expectations," one of the Crafters said with a sigh as he gestured at the screen vaguely. "There are so many variables at play here and solving one issue will likely lead to a dozen more being discovered." He turned to look at Sal with a pained expression on his face. "This happens regularly at the prototyping stage, and although I commend you for creating an entirely new operating system yourself…you could always use some of the ones that have been created by others."

Upgrade perked up at that with a chuckle. "Kenzo, this is Salvatore Argento we're talking about. He probably already built the machine." She looked over at Sal with a slight shake of her head. "Go on then…did you build it?"

Fabi's expression was unreadable as she stared at Sal. "You didn't…"

Sal chose to look at Kenzo because it was easier on his heart rate. "I upgraded the engraver, 3D printer, and refiner…wait, let me check." He wasn't sure of the exact materials he had used as he was in a flow state when doing the Crafting. Sal went into his tablet and moved to the blueprints section.

Even though he drew them by hand, they were completed on the workbench and had files saved for each page. The only issue was that they weren't named, so he needed to open them quickly to see which one he was looking for. He didn't want to delay any of the Crafters as they were spending their time helping him, so he flew through each of the blueprints as fast as he could.

"Sal…" Upgrade started with a laugh. "Could you maybe go a little slower?"

When Sal looked up at her, his attention was pulled to the massive display they were using to look at the error report. It was synced with his own tablet, and he had unwittingly been broadcasting all his drawings to the entire gala. He froze on the spot as the realization set in. "Oh…shit." He tried to cut off the synchronization between his tablet, but a voice stopped him.

"Keep going." Fabi stared at the screen, her fist clenched on the table. "I need to see the other blueprints." She looked at him intently, as though daring him to object.

"Ooooh, how long has it been since we've seen that competitive drive?" Upgrade cooed as she plucked her wine glass from the table, smirking. "Sal, I ask this as your lecturer. Please continue the little slideshow. It'll help us better understand the machine itself."

Fabi ignored Upgrade's goading and looked at Sal carefully. "A month. That's what you said, right? You ideated all of this, created the blueprints…and manufactured it, with a completely custom operating system?"

Sal's mouth went dry as he nodded lamely. "Most of the equipment was your old stuff that my parents bought from Maurice. I purchased the additional materials from him and wouldn't have been able to get this far without his help."

Fabi's expression softened slightly at the mention of her father. "Could you show me the other blueprints, please?"

Kenzo stood with his arms folded as he stared at the image of the engraver blueprint on the screen. "Have we considered the power draw? The base cores wouldn't have nearly enough output to handle the upgrades he's proposing in these drawings. They likely wouldn't even start."

"Not to mention the evolutionary runes…you can see them in that picture on the base plate." A tired-looking man approached their table with a pint glass in his hand. He wore an immaculate three-piece suit, and looked incredibly professional. It was his lidded eyes and weary gaze that signaled him as one of their peers. "My best guess would be that there was a misfire when the machine tried to evolve all the pieces at once, and had insufficient power."

Sal shook his head. "No, the first evolution was a success. The machine jumped from being able to produce Uncommon grade to Rare grade after I fed it the required materials. The issue only happened when I selected the ability options for a dagger design."

Kenzo's arms fell to his side. "Selected the ability options? Wait…are you saying that this operating system is making calculations?" He looked at Upgrade in disbelief. "What on earth are you teaching your students?"

Upgrade put up her hand, laughing. "Oh, hell no. Don't pin this on me. If it's anyone's fault, it's Fabi. She's the one who fed him all the courses on essence programming."

Fabi's eyes widened at the implication. She looked between Sal and Upgrade in shock. "But they're just the basics…like, principles and guides. They're not a step-by-step process on how to build a machine like this!"

Upgrade tilted her glass in Sal's direction as she looked at Fabi. "He had your engraving guide for one day and created a coat that nearly killed him. It knocked me across the room and gave him the dregs." She shook her head with a wistful smile. "Those were the days, before evolutionary runes and Legendary grades."

Sal shot Upgrade a look of warning, but she just smiled at him. He didn't want people to know about the Legendary-grade sniper rifle that he had made for the Reavers Guild. Although there were a lot of people who knew he was a Mythcrafter, it wasn't smart to advertise it to a bunch of strangers, especially at the gala where there was an unspeakable amount of powerful people.

"The coat, Sal. What else could I be talking about?" Upgrade placed her wine glass on the table and gave him a wink. "My finest work, if you ask me."

With an insistent, almost pleading look from Fabi, Sal resumed his slideshow of the different blueprints that he had created for the MythOS project. As he went through them, giving about twenty or thirty seconds per page, he noticed that more and more people were moving over to their table. It was like there was an unspoken rule of not speaking during the presentation, and Sal felt a little unnerved by the attention. He kept stealing glances at Fabi, trying to gauge her reaction to the blueprints, but it was only when he got to the enclosure that he saw a smile appear on her face. Unfortunately, the next blueprint was his agonizing time with the sensor programming.

"Whoa!" Kenzo remarked as he stepped forward. "Can you hold on for a minute—I want to look at this!" He moved closer to the screen, a wide smile on his face. "It's like you've created a massive vending machine!" He laughed as though the thought was hilarious.

"That was the intention," Sal answered, smiling. "It was my father's idea. I wanted to have something that could imitate artisanal Crafting for the Argento Auction House." He realized the moment he said it how that sentence could have been misunderstood, so he quickly clarified. "Since he's an Appraiser, he'll be able to separate the duds from the quality goods. So, even if it only has one or two successes out of ten, it'll be worth the costs."

"Come on, next slide." Fabi tapped her hand on the table, laughing. "You can't do this to me. I need to see the interface!" She turned to look at Sal with a bright smile. "You're sitting beside me at the dinner. I have a thousand questions for you about all of this, so don't even think about going anywhere!"

Sal's chest tightened as he moved onto the next slide. He glanced up to see Upgrade stifling a laugh, and he wanted to strangle her. There was no telling how much she had told Fabi about everything, but from the flow of conversation so far, it looked like she didn't know about his work on the Skill Weaves. If he was this awkward around her, then adding that into the pile was going to be much harder to deal with.

The rest of the slideshow went by with a few pauses for closer inspections. Sal realized that he was just feeding their curiosity as there wasn't going to be much insight from the design itself. He was convinced that the error report had something to do with the operating system because that was the area he was least confident in. By the end of it, Fabi practically vibrated with excitement as she whirled on Sal, smiling.

"Okay, you mentioned earlier that the interface allowed you to customize the existing blueprints? How did you factor in the synergies of each material? Did you create a database of effects, and if you did, can you show me?" She spoke excitedly as she peppered him with questions. "How did you manage to bypass the calculation cost? We can know the effects, but the machine would need to solve that logic itself. Did you just create a set of commands to overwrite the calculation?"

Sal was about to answer…well, he was going to say that he had no idea what she was talking about. He felt incredibly out of his depth with even the first question about synergies, and every subsequent question hammered home the fact that he was a fraud when it came to Crafting. Thankfully another voice came to the rescue. Unfortunately, it also came with the worst set of words possible.

"He's a Mythcrafter and hasn't a clue what he's doing. It's all instinct," a grizzled voice answered for Sal.

Sal whirled around in surprise and saw a slender man in a wide-brimmed hat, wearing a set of red spectacles. His white beard made him seem older than he was, and his attire was like a slap in the face to the dress code of the gala. He wore a thick leather coat, a vintage T-shirt, and a pair of shorts, accompanied with a set of thoroughly worn sandals.

Upgrade scoffed at the new arrival. "Guessing your train was running late? I could have a look at it for you, if you want?"

Doc Ameye stared at Upgrade for a short moment before turning and smiling at Fabi. "Good to see you, Fabrizia." He looked around at the others, but didn't offer any sort of greetings to them. He barely acknowledged their existence, Upgrade included. When his eyes landed on Sal, his smile returned. "You've started automation quite early. I'm impressed. It took me a few years to come to the realization, but I can see you've got good instincts."

Sal pointed at Upgrade. "She told me about your talk on automation. That was the inspiration for Mythos."

"Terrible name. You shouldn't have your operating system and machine called the same thing. Work on that." Doc Ameye stated it like it was a fact as he moved over to the table to take the tablet from Sal. "Let's see this error report." He raised the tablet up to eye level and held it out from his face.

"Old age finally getting to you?" Upgrade quipped from the opposite side of the table, her eyes boring a hole into Doc Ameye's head.

Doc Ameye raised his left hand and tapped the side of his glasses. "Protocol, run a simulation for me." He spoke to his glasses in a bored tone, placing the tablet back on the table. "Use the synced display so we can show the kid why his machine isn't working." A moment of silence passed before a wry grin appeared on Doc Ameye's face. "Taking more than a few seconds is good." He glanced at Sal, the smile becoming wider. "Very good."

Right before Sal was going to ask what he meant, the entire display changed to a 3D visual representation of the enclosure. It started to rapidly iterate by including each of the upgraded components, installing them in the visual depiction. Sal was able to watch the machine come to life in real time, with a scarily accurate model. Better yet, the simulation showed the tracks moving with the levers and pulley system.

"Very interesting design choices. I'm guessing you've got access to a small workshop? Stacking the components looks to be necessity rather than stylistic." Doc Ameye made a few observations as he watched the simulation taking shape. "The drawer looks more like an afterthought, but it's serviceable. Using the workbench technology to create an interface…and you used some of the runes for the scarlet screen. Bold choice, but a good one."

Sal watched as Fabi approached Upgrade on the other side of the table. She whispered in Upgrade's ear, who glanced at him for a half second before giving Fabi a nod. He didn't need a tracker to know what happened, as Fabi stared at him and mouthed a single word, her expression conflicted. *Mythcrafter.*

He guessed that she had made some sort of verdict on his ability. It definitely outed him as someone who could just cheat his way through Crafting with essence, and that he wasn't going to be earning her respect any time soon. So much for sitting beside her during the meal, and getting inundated with questions. She now knew he wouldn't have any answers to give her.

A bell chimed from far across the room, cutting off all the displays and plunging the entire room into darkness. A single beam of light illuminated one of the top balconies where Robert stood in a jet-black suit. His silver hair was swept back in a stylized wave, and he sported a wide smile. ***Welcome Heroes, Hunters, Saviors, and the great people of Haven! We hope you've enjoyed this little soiree of refreshments, but it's time for us to break bread before we start the presentations.*** His voice was amplified, much like Quest's during any announcement in the amphitheater. ***I'd kindly request for you all to make your way through the doors to the left and find your seats.***

The display that was synced to Sal's tablet suddenly illuminated, which normally wouldn't have been a big deal…but when the entirety of the room was shrouded in darkness, it was a second beacon that drew the eye. Worse still, it was showing his machine being rendered in real time by Protocol, Doc Ameye's train. Sal panicked and tried to shut it off, but Doc Ameye's hand shot out to grasp at his wrist. Even in the darkness, he knew the older man was smiling.

I'll be out here working with the Mythcrafter. Bring the food to us. Doc Ameye spoke in his normal voice, but it too was amplified like Robert's.

Just that sentence sent ripples through the entire crowd. First, it literally told everyone that there was a Mythcrafter in attendance. Secondly, it told them that Doc Ameye was working with them. Lastly, it sent a signal that the Mythcrafter and Doc Ameye were above the orders of the Hunter Bureau. It was an absolute clusterfuck, and all Sal could do was stare into the darkness at the man who had single-handedly put a target on his back.

Robert laughed from the podium and clapped. ***Ladies and gentlemen, we could very well be on the verge of a technological breakthrough with these great minds working together. Let's leave them to it, and we'll hopefully get more insight from Doc Ameye when he joins us on the stage later in the evening. To everyone not involved in the Mythcrafter project, please make your way to the main hall!***

As the lights came back on, Doc Ameye looked at Sal with a wry smile. "So, where were we?"

CHAPTER 33: NERVES

"You okay, son?" Petro walked over to their impromptu Crafting table. Placing a whiskey down in front of Sal, he looked at him with concern written all over his face. "Thought you could do with a fresh one after that." His gaze flicked past to where Doc Ameye stood with his hands in his pockets. "You had no right to out Salvatore like that. You're lucky that it's me here and not Sophia. She's ready to rip your head off."

Doc Ameye gave Petro a sideways glance before letting out a soft chuckle. "You think this is my first rodeo? Hiding his abilities won't work. You need him front and center, with the backing of an angry bastard who the bureau and guilds won't fuck with." He offered his hand to Petro. "Hi, I'm the angry bastard who just gave your son the mother of all meal tickets."

Petro just looked at the outstretched hand, but didn't take it. "I don't trust you, and all I've seen from you is unnecessary risk. Salvatore is still in his first year, and while he has extraordinary capabilities, he's not ready for the politicking and fuckery that you deal with on the daily."

Doc Ameye withdrew his hand and smiled. "Strange. I usually get along with Appraisers." He looked over at Sal and sighed. "Just being acknowledged by me gives him a lot of breathing room. Robert already knows he's a Mythcrafter, and it's only a matter of time before he gets whisked away to work on the projects I refused to make. Weaponry that no single entity should ever have access to. Do you really think that he'd play nice because your son is a first-year?" Doc Ameye looked at Petro quizzically. "The only way to keep him safe is to keep him in the public eye."

Petro stepped to one side as Sophia launched herself at Doc Ameye. The Crafting expert didn't have the reaction speed to stop the slap that cracked viciously across his face. His red-tinted glasses landed on the table with a clatter. Doc Ameye's face turned with the force of the impact.

"Awesome," Upgrade breathed aloud on the other side of the table. Fabi was stunned by the outburst, while many of the other Crafters had flinched.

Sal took a step forward to intervene but could see that his father was at the ready. His mother was fierce, and he was starting to appreciate how she might have bullied Prestige in the past.

"That was expected." Doc Ameye spoke as though he was tired. With a sigh, he retrieved his glasses and placed them on his face, his brow furrowing as he made eye contact with Sophia. "But that tracker is a surprise. It's invisible?"

Sophia lifted her hand to strike him again, but Petro stepped in to stop her. Although the room was now mostly empty, there were still some waitstaff in attendance.

"Salvatore didn't deserve this. Do you realize how many twisted bastards there are in the Hunter Bureau? All of them consumed with self-interest. All the people you've fucked over because of your stupid list…all of them are going to try to take him from you," Sophia snarled at him. "You haven't supported him at all, and you've just jumped in here like you're some generous protector and benefactor? What sort of future can he possibly have now? They think he's yours, and you've got more enemies than anyone else!"

"Ah," Doc Ameye said finally as he looked to one side. "I can see how you'd see it that way." He pondered for a few more moments before shrugging it off. "He can come work with me in Ameye Locomotive. That should solve everything."

Petro didn't stop Sophia this time as she swung her hand again to hit Doc Ameye.

Sal had anticipated it, though, and stepped between the two of them, frowning. "Mom, stop."

Sophia paused her attack and looked at Sal desperately. "Sal, this fucker is trying to monopolize or ruin your entire future!"

"I won't ever go to Ameye Locomotive," Sal said slowly as he stared at his mother, pulling her outstretched hand down to her side. "He said it himself. A lot of people were bound to find out about it eventually. Robert probably would have said something if the Trainee Guild was approved." He smiled at her as he took her hands in his own. "We'll deal with any problems when they come up, but the Hunter Bureau needs me because of the Skill Master project. They won't get new or improved weaves without me, so I'm safe…trust me."

The sound of shattering glass drew everyone's attention to where Fabi Maccles stood. Her wine glass was no longer in her hand as she stared at Sal in disbelief.

Doc Ameye didn't read the room, or simply didn't care to. He moved around Sal and looked at him with a bright smile. "That's what this is! You didn't inherit the Mythcrafter ability, but created it…didn't you? I knew it was improbable for there to be a realm beyond Legendary, but to find out that it was completely synthetic? Quite remarkable."

Sal immediately understood why his mother so desperately wanted to hit the man. He could even understand why Upgrade didn't vibe with him, either. It took him a few moments to formulate a response, as he pushed down the immediate anger at his ability being called artificial. "There are actually another two realms above Mythic. Guessing that didn't come up in your calculations?"

Doc Ameye's brow furrowed as he stared at Sal. "You believe what you're saying. So, in your mind it's not a lie…but it's impossible. How are you so resolute that there are two grades after Mythic?"

Rather than answering, Sal just moved to stand beside his parents. He looked at them with a gentle smile. "Trust me, I'm going to be fine. Thanks for worrying, but you can both head in to the meal."

Upgrade moved around the table and stood awkwardly beside Petro. "I can see where he gets his temper," she offered with a smile.

Petro looked at her for a moment before realization kicked in. "Upgrade?" He tapped Sophia on the shoulder and pointed at Upgrade, smiling. If it was a calming tactic, it worked wonders.

Sophia's expression softened as she smiled warmly at Upgrade. "Thanks for looking after Sal at Quest Academy. He speaks so highly of you." Her gaze moved over to where Fabi still stood. "Maurice told us how integral you've been to Fabi's development, so it's wonderful that you've also taken Sal under your wing."

Upgrade smiled as she gestured at Sal. "He's one of the good ones. If I could just make him stop overworking himself, he'd be unstoppable."

"Ha," Sophia barked as she hiked a thumb at Petro. "Not my genetics." She smiled at Upgrade before looking at Sal quizzically. "Did you invite your friends to the after-party at the auction?"

Sal looked over at Doc Ameye, who was pacing off to one side, talking to his glasses. No matter what way you looked at it, he seemed crazy. He turned his gaze back to his mother. "I mentioned it to Barry, but didn't get a chance to say anything to Upgrade yet."

Sophia nodded as she glanced at the assembly of Crafters who were pretending to look at the visualization of the Mythos machine. "I hope you'll forgive me, but we'll be keeping it an intimate affair with the people we know. Fabi and Upgrade, we'd be delighted to have you over if you'd like to join us."

Upgrade smiled. "That okay with you, Sal?"

Sal bit his lip as he turned to look at Doc Ameye once again. "Upgrade, do you think you can fix the problem with my machine?"

Upgrade followed his gaze and sighed. "Not as fast as him." She glanced at Sophia and Petro, and added a little more context. "He's a cantankerous old bastard and hasn't a lick of social aptitude, but I've been assured by my brother that he's actually well-intentioned. None of what he said was likely designed to put Sal in danger." She laughed as she glanced at Sophia. "You literally became my new favorite person when you hit him, though, as I've wanted to do it for years."

Sophia shook her head, smiling, and was about to say something when Sal stopped her.

"I'd like to invite him," Sal stated resolutely. "If he can fix the machine, then the Argento Auction House will have new merchandise even when I'm back at Quest Academy."

Upgrade paused as she noticed Fabi still standing rigidly on the other side of the table. "Ah, give me a second." She moved off to stand with Fabi, talking in hushed tones as they made their way over to the bar.

Sal watched them leave and sighed inwardly. That was not the way he wanted her to find out about the weave improvements. He could only imagine how she was feeling about him right now. Both Mythcrafter and Skill Master were ridiculously unfair advantages that he held. To someone who couldn't use their own weave, and couldn't use essence for Crafting…Sal was the exact opposite of her, and could coast to overwhelming success without the effort she had to put in. He guessed that she wouldn't be coming to their after-party after all.

"Are you actually okay?" Petro asked quietly as he moved to the side, to shield Sal from the gazes of the other Crafters. "You can tell us, and we'll leave right now."

Sophia nodded in agreement. "Say the word and we're out of here."

"I'm good," Sal insisted as he looked at them earnestly. "It was a surprise, but it's a little bit of a relief that it's not some big secret anymore. If we're being honest, the Skill Master thing is what we should probably keep under wraps. Mythcrafter is a lot easier to manage and will throw people off the scent when they start looking for the person behind it." Sal laughed as he heard himself speak. "We're being cautious, which is the important thing, but honestly…I think we just need to establish the guild as soon as possible and become a force that can't be ignored."

Petro sighed as he looked at Sophia. "What do you think?"

Sophia studied Sal's face for a few moments before nodding. "That's what you want…that's what we'll do." She smiled at Petro. "I think you should talk to Doc Ameye about our difficulty in securing a suitable guild headquarters. You could even show him the ideal site when he comes to our after-party."

A smile blossomed on Petro's face. "There's the woman I married."

Sal watched as his father moved over to speak with Doc Ameye. He didn't have high hopes of his father getting the support of the old Crafter, but there was no better man to try.

Glancing at his mother, Sal sighed in defeat. "I'm pretty sure I ruined any chances of being close with Fabi."

"How so?" Sophia countered as she looked over to where Upgrade and Fabi were speaking at the bar. "Looked like you two were getting along from where I was standing."

Sal paused as he looked at her suspiciously. "Wait, were you watching us? I thought you and Dad were off schmoozing with the other guests?"

Sophia snorted as she waved her hand like it was no big deal. "Sal, you can't just draw everyone's attention to that cane-sword and expect us not to stare. Lawrence Baron was over like a shot, asking us a million questions about the materials you used. He's going to grill you at the after-party. We had to stop him from going over and interrupting your chat with Fabi."

Sal just stared at her in disbelief. "You really can't help but meddle, can you?"

Sophia shrugged with a smile. "You're the one who gave me this tracker that lets me read body language." She jutted her chin in Fabi's direction. "I'm pretty sure you earned her respect in a significant way. Not with the Mythcrafter or Skill Master stuff, but with the blueprints. Poor girl was shocked beyond belief by the other two, but my guess is that she saw the hard work that you put into that machine."

Sal bit his lip before shaking his head. "It's silly…honestly, I don't know why I'm overthinking all of this. Divinity telling me about a vision from the future has me second-guessing everything. I barely even know the girl, so I don't know why I'm so invested in her liking me."

Sophia chuckled as she gripped her son's hand. "I don't need the tracker for that one, Sal. I saw how you looked at her, and I can tell you without a shred of doubt…it has nothing to do with Divinity's vision."

Sal looked at her in surprise, but Sophia wasn't done.

She gently reached up and cupped his chin. "Don't overthink it. This isn't something to be solved, but rather something to be experienced. Get to know her, and see how you feel. Maybe she's your person, or maybe she'll just become a great friend. Time will tell."

Sal sighed as he looked at his mother with a hopeful smile. "I really hope she comes to the party."

CHAPTER 34: CONDITIONS

Both Petro and Doc Ameye walked over to where Sal stood with his mother. There was a slight smile on Petro's face, as he stepped off to one side. Doc Ameye walked up to Sophia and removed his glasses, sighing.

"I apologize for announcing Salvatore as a Mythcrafter to the entire room." Doc Ameye spoke slowly, as though it were rehearsed. He glanced over to Petro, who gave him a slight nod. Taking a breath, Doc Ameye smiled and continued. "I'd be happy to stop by the auction house later to see the machine he's made. Since I'm in an apologetic mood, I might throw in a few upgrades for good measure."

Sophia looked at Doc Ameye with a raised eyebrow. "That's it? You're not going to pledge to keep him safe?"

"Sure. That too," Doc Ameye added with a shrug. "Since I'll be seeing the machine in person, I won't need to go through all the exploratory steps out here." He looked off in the direction of the main hall. "I want to see how much more tax I'll have to pay toward our woefully inefficient Reclamation guilds…and I could definitely eat."

Sophia just shook her head and looked at Petro to see whether this was all okay with him.

Petro nodded as he gestured toward the main hall. "We'll go on ahead and find our seats." Looking over at Sal, he gave him a quick wink. "I think the Saviors are going to be sitting somewhere separately, so you and Fabi should go together."

Sal's stomach knotted at the thought, but he pushed through the discomfort. He wasn't sure he was ready to have a conversation with Fabi about the Skill Weaves project. Despite his mother's assurances, he wasn't so certain that she had a good opinion of him.

After a quick repeat of telling his parents that he was fine, they moved toward the main hall with Doc Ameye. All the straggling Crafters moved along with them, following Doc Ameye and trying to make small talk with him.

Sal turned to look at the bar where Upgrade and Fabi were still in deep conversation. He didn't want to stand by himself in the middle of the reception area, so he quickly moved over to the table and retrieved his tablet. After it was pocketed, he took the cane-sword that was leaning against the table. Upgrade must have left it there after she showcased it to the entire room. With a slight shake of his head, he gripped the top of the cane and made his way over to the bar where Upgrade stood. He moved slowly, trying to give himself time to think of what to say. *Was Upgrade consoling Fabi, or was she trying to defuse the situation?* There was no way for him to know.

Fabi turned mid-sentence and noticed Sal. She raised a hand to stop Upgrade from continuing, and gave Sal the most beautiful smile he had ever seen. "You have a lot of explaining to do." She laughed as she crossed her arms. "How come you didn't tell me you were the one who worked on my weave?"

Sal was momentarily stunned by the question. There wasn't a hint of betrayal or envy in her voice. She was genuinely curious as to why he didn't bring it up. Sal had been fully prepared for an onslaught of accusations or even contempt from her, but it looked like he was very much mistaken.

"Told you he'd misunderstand." Upgrade raised her wine glass and leaned back against the bar. "He's constantly worried that people will hate him for being competent. Not that you'd know anything about that, would you, Fabi?"

Fabi shot Upgrade a grin. "Not my fault if they can't keep up." When she turned to Sal, she gestured at him from head to toe. "But it looks like I might actually have some decent competition this time. Shame it took two and a half years to find him, though."

The relief that Sal felt was like an immense weight had lifted from his shoulders. There was no knot in his stomach, and he could breathe properly. With a genuine smile on his face, he answered Fabi. "We just met, and I didn't want it to be the first thing out of my mouth. I thought it would be better to start off with the Crafting problems I was having, since you and Upgrade are way better at essence programming than me."

"Good instincts," Fabi said with a thoughtful expression. "I would have thought you wanted something from me had you led with it…but honestly, you absolutely deserve something. If Doc Ameye is going to help with your Mythos machine, that's going to be a bust. What would be an equivalent gift to you giving me a whole new lease on life, and gifting me the Repair ability?"

Sal smiled as he shrugged. "What about helping me rename the machine? Apparently it's stupid to have Mythos as the name of the operating system and the machine. Could do with some help there?"

Fabi rested the nail of her index finger on her chin as she thought about it. "Hephaestus is hard to say and a little too on the nose, but we could probably pick something with a little more style. Let me think about it and I'll get back to you." Her smile returned as she looked at Sal. "I mean it, though…even giving you the entire catalogue of courses on the Credit Store wouldn't make a dent on the debt that I owe you."

Upgrade slid her back off the countertop of the bar. "Well, you could always tie your future to him?"

Sal nearly buckled as he stared at Upgrade. "What the hell are you suggesting?"

Upgrade smiled sweetly. "That she join your new Crafting guild. Doc Ameye will still take her under his wing, even if she spends a year or two getting your guild off the ground. You already have that Sakura girl on the roster."

"Anna Sakura is joining your guild?" Fabi's eyes widened as she clicked her fingers. "You're the one who made the corset for her?"

"That was Blathnaid. She's much better at the fashion stuff. I wouldn't even know where to start with a corset, because there are so many variables with size and—" Sal stopped himself from elaborating further and switched topics. "Yes, Sakura said she'd be interested in joining. I just need to supply good equipment and help with Skill Weaves to keep my end of the deal."

Fabi looked over at Upgrade with a thoughtful expression. "You'd be joining as a mentor, I take it?"

Upgrade spread her hands wide. "Who knows? He might pick Doc Ameye instead of me…Petro was talking to him for an awfully long time over there." She made a forlorn expression, with the back of her hand resting against her forehead.

"Sal didn't even invite me to his after-party. His parents offered me a pity invite because I was there."

Sal and Fabi rolled their eyes at the exact same time. When they caught themselves doing the same thing, they both laughed.

Upgrade placed her wine glass on the countertop of the bar and shook her head. "Of course I'd be there as a mentor. I built the simulation orb, and I won't let it out of my sight." She pointed at the two of them. "And I don't trust either of you to work in a Crafting space unsupervised. If you two worked together, we'd end up with an army of drones or something taking over the city."

Fabi's smile grew wider. "That sounds kinda awesome. Did you show him my drones?"

Upgrade shook her head. "Nah. He bought one of the little hover bots you made in first year. I don't think he's seen any of the combat versions."

Fabi's brow furrowed. "I could have sworn they were sold out by now, but I'm glad it went to a good home." She looked at Sal with a raised eyebrow. "If I find out that you killed my little buddy for spare parts, I'll break your legs."

"If you come to the after-party later, you'll see him safe and sound in my workshop. I promise," Sal answered. "It's a great little invention, and I drew up some plans of how I'd add evolutionary runes."

Upgrade chuckled as she shook her head. "This is what I'm talking about. An army of drones." With a gesture at Fabi, Upgrade continued. "Sal, you remember the combat drone blueprint I showed you? Fabi started iterating on that concept and made it her final year project." She looked at Fabi with a confused expression. "What version are you on at the moment?"

"Eighty-one," Fabi muttered guiltily before looking at Sal in a bit of a panic. "Most were scrapped at ideation stage or at prototyping stage. I didn't make eighty-one drones. That would be insane."

"I guarantee you that he thinks it's perfectly normal to make that many in a year," Upgrade muttered as she shot Sal a look. "Go on, tell me I'm wrong."

Upgrade was right, and Sal had thought it was genuinely possible to make that many drones in a year. Rather than proving Upgrade's point, he pivoted again and gestured to the door to the main hall. "Everyone is heading in to eat. I was told that the Saviors sit somewhere else, and was wondering if you could show me the way?" He looked at Fabi hopefully, and she didn't disappoint.

Stepping to one side, she placed her hand on her hip and angled her elbow outward. "We're at a gala, so we need to act accordingly." She couldn't help but laugh as she wiggled her elbow, just in case Sal wasn't aware that she wanted to link up.

Upgrade grinned as she moved to the other side and mirrored Fabi's gesture. "You can take the two of us in with you, surely?"

"Do you want me to dance with you again?" Sal challenged Upgrade, who immediately withdrew her offered arm.

"Oh, hell no. You can have him, Fabi!" Upgrade jokingly gave him a wide berth as she started to move toward the main hall.

Fabi's eyes practically sparkled. "You dance?"

Upgrade whirled around on the spot. "He's a monster…don't do this to yourself. You won't feel your legs for days." She pointed at Sal's legs. "They're made of some unknown metal, I'm sure of it."

Fabi continued to wiggle her elbow at Sal as she smiled at him. "I think I'll take my chances."

Sal's heart thundered in his chest as he stepped close to Fabi and placed his arm through the offered space. With his cane in the other hand, he suddenly realized just how terrible the ensemble looked. "Hey Upgrade, any chance you could take this cane-sword into the hall with you?"

Upgrade grinned as she turned her back. "Nope, you've committed to looking like a pimp…so who would I be to bail you out now?"

Sal was completely lost for words as he looked at Fabi apologetically.

She held out her hand with a smile. "Give it to me if you don't want to use it. The hellfire titanium makes it look awesome!"

When Sal handed it over to her, she practically beamed as she started to walk forward with it, testing it along with her gait. Even without the Perfect ability, she was an incredibly quick study and looked like a natural after just a few steps. Sal continued to walk alongside her as they made their way to the hall.

"Are you sure you're a dancer? You seem a little stiff," Fabi asked playfully as she looked at him.

Upgrade cackled from up ahead, and Sal did his best to keep his composure. It was just a poor choice of words.

"Still just a little shell-shocked from people finding out about the Mythcrafter thing," Sal lied as he continued to walk with her. "When will you get your weave remapped, if you don't mind me asking?"

Fabi looked a little disappointed as she offered a helpless shrug. "We've signed all the paperwork and done the tests. Hopefully, we'll hear soon."

Sal smiled at her. "Well, if they take too long, let me know and I'll personally remap the whole thing for you."

Fabi gave Sal a sideways glance. "Hey, were you not listening when I said I don't like being in someone's debt? If you're that hell-bent on me joining your guild, just ask."

Sal chuckled as they reached the double doors where Upgrade waited for them. "Fabi, would you like to join my guild?"

She gave him an appraising look, as though weighing up his request. Eventually, her bright smile returned as she faced the double doors. "I'll think about it."

Upgrade grinned at them as she pushed open the doors to reveal an enormous hall comprised of tiered floors. There were dozens of rectangular tables on each tier, with tablecloths of varying colors to denote organization and rank. Ignoring the hundreds of people who looked her way, Upgrade pointed at a large table on the second highest tier. "Dragon crests get to sit in the special seats. I'll be down here with the rest of the plebs if you need me." She set off toward her table, sparing a few moments to wave at the people who looked at her for a little too long.

Sal was not a fan of the stares he and Fabi received as they slowly made their way up to the table. All his instincts told him that he was being disruptive, and that he should crouch down and rush toward his destination, but Fabi controlled his pace by walking casually.

"Don't give them the satisfaction. We may be Crafters, but we're the backbone of this economy," Fabi said in an uncharacteristically serious tone. "If you're going to be a guildmaster, then you're going to need to stand proud and tall among these people. Show me what you've got." That last part was spoken with a smile as she squeezed his arm a little tighter.

Sal raised his head and pulled his shoulders back to improve his posture. Despite his uneasiness, he knew Fabi was right. If he was going to be taken seriously, then he needed to ignore the timid instincts he grew up with. He didn't want to be as rude as Doc Ameye, but he should absolutely be confident in his own self-worth. His own father would walk proudly, so why couldn't he?

"And with that little change, you're now someone to be remembered." Fabi gave his arm another reassuring squeeze. "Walk proudly, Salvatore. You're someone who can change the world."

Sal smiled as all the tension and uncertainty left his body.

CHAPTER 35: INVITE

"Took you long enough. Did someone tie your shoelaces together or something?" Barry mocked as he stared at Sal from across the table.

"Leave him alone, Barry. I thought it was lovely. You both looked amazing." Blathnaid spoke excitedly as she looked at Fabi. "I'm Blathnaid, by the way. I'm in the same cohort as Sal."

Sal didn't initially recognize Blathnaid as her wardrobe had done a complete change from their time in Quest Academy. The blood-red suit had been replaced with an elegant blue sequin dress, with each of the small plates offering a shimmering hue of purple with every movement. The same fur collar that Upgrade wore, which was made from prowler hide, was instead a brilliant white and draped around her shoulders.

"Void metal sequins?" Fabi leaned over Sal to get a better look. "I made a breastplate with scales that didn't come out nearly as good as this!"

Blathnaid's eyes lit up. "That was my inspiration for the dress! I loved how you added individual runes to the scales. I wasn't able to do that level of refinement with my ability, so I just settled for the color effects."

Fabi smiled as she offered her hand to Blathnaid. "It's a pleasure to meet you. I'm Fabrizia Maccles, but everyone calls me Fabi."

Barry's fork clattered against his plate as he stared at Fabi in shock. When he looked up at Sal, his eyes narrowed. "Did you plan this, or is she literally your clone?"

Fabi raised an eyebrow at Barry. "Plan what?" She leaned back into her own seat and glanced at Sal. "Am I missing something?"

Blathnaid couldn't help but giggle at the exchange. "That's literally how Sal introduces himself to everyone, even with the handshake and the nickname." She put up her hands in a panic when she saw the conflicted expression on Fabi's face. "Oh, it's not an insult. I personally like it…it's just a little old-fashioned and Sal was the only one I knew who did it that way."

Fabi shrugged as she looked at Sal. "Guess it must be a Silver Sanctuary thing?"

"Or being the kids of charismatic salesmen," Sal countered. "Dad would literally make me introduce myself to everyone in the auction house when I first started working there."

Fabi chuckled. "Did you also get the whole *handshakes mean something* speech?"

Sal couldn't help but laugh. "Yes! Wow, I thought I was the only person with that ridiculously specific childhood trauma." He lifted a glass of water and took a drink. The starters were being cleared from everyone's table, and the mains would be arriving soon. Both Sal and Fabi had elected to skip the starter and go straight to the meal to catch up with everyone else.

Barry stared between them with his jaw wide open. "Really? How did you go from being terrified of speaking to her, to being best friends?"

Before Sal could even choke on the water, Fabi burst out laughing. "He was terrified? Tell me everything!" She placed both elbows on the table and looked at Barry sweetly. "Don't leave a single detail out...because I'll know."

Barry hesitated as he looked at Sal, but Fabi ran interference.

"Oh no, you've opened this can of worms. You're going to have to deal with the fallout." She kept her eyes locked on him as her smile grew wider. "Was it when you were on the balcony earlier, looking down at our table?"

Sal gave Barry a warning look, and quickly made a cutting motion with his fingers, indicating that he should stop talking.

Fabi nudged Sal in the side with her elbow, not breaking eye contact with Barry the whole time. "Come on, give me all the juicy details. I'll tell you how I spied you on the balcony if you tell me what Sal was so terrified about."

"Okay, I'm going to tell you...I promise," Barry started with an awkward laugh. "But, I just want to clarify with Sal first...how much you know, because that changes my answers."

Fabi sighed as she leaned back in her seat with crossed arms. "You're a Controller, aren't you? Can never get a straight answer from you guys." Glancing over to Sal, she shook her head. "I know you said he was secretive, but this is a little extreme, don't you think?"

Sal was completely lost for words. He hadn't told Fabi anything about Barry, and then there was the fact that she knew they were up on the balcony. Sal was absolutely certain that she hadn't looked up at any point, and he knew with absolute certainty that she didn't have some special ability. He felt like a passenger, along for the ride.

Barry blinked as he tilted his head. "I am a Controller, but I'd consider myself more curious than secretive...how did you know we were on the balcony?"

Fabi smiled as she held Barry's gaze for a few moments before breaking into a laugh. "Come on, how would you react if you saw a little blue hat appearing and disappearing suddenly? Upgrade had us in stitches earlier and when I wiped the tears from my eyes, I saw a little hat popping in and out of existence. Wouldn't you be curious?"

Barry placed his face in his hands and let out an aggravated sigh. "So much for a grand conspiracy. I honestly thought you were posing as someone else to get in my head."

Sal finally realized what Barry was talking about. He was worried that Trickster was pretending to be Fabi to find out more about him, which aligned with the knowledge that they were up on the balcony, talking about Fabi.

Fabi chuckled as she looked at Sal. "Your friends are weird. I like them." She brushed a stray lock of black hair over her ear as she raised an eyebrow at Sal. "But don't think we're done with the whole 'terrified' topic. I still want some answers."

"Join my guild and I'll tell you," Sal playfully countered, but Fabi shook her head.

"Nope, that's tied to the dance performance. You're going to have to make a different wager." She smiled sweetly at him as she moved her cutlery to one side to make room for the main course.

Barry pulled his hands away from his face and sat up just in time to see a pair of steaks being placed in front of both Fabi and Sal. Nearly everyone else at the table had opted for the lobster or the duck. He stared at Fabi in disbelief.

Fabi stared back at him. "What? I'd kill for a good steak. If you're one of those vegetable people, I don't know what to tell you." She chuckled to herself as she cut into it eagerly.

Right when Sal was about to do the same, a side dish of vegetables was placed beside him, which he stared at in confusion. "I didn't order these." He looked up at the waiter, who gestured at a seat farther down the table.

Sal followed his hand to see Rochelle laughing from the far end of the table. He gave her a friendly wave and lifted the vegetables to indicate he had successfully received them. It was too far down the line to see what she was wearing, but it wasn't the Arbiter's Judgment coat that Upgrade and Blathnaid had created. His best guess was that it was something red.

"An in-joke, I take it?" Fabi raised a napkin to her black lips. She didn't look particularly impressed by the vegetables as she smiled. "Don't worry, I'm not going to steal them from you."

"I got a few bad leg cramps during the excursion. Rochelle was our Healer and prescribed vegetables to fix the problem," Sal explained as he reluctantly added a few heads of broccoli and some sticks of carrots onto his plate. "Can't really go against the Healer's orders."

Fabi grinned as she placed a hand on her chest. "Well, I operate as our team's Defense, Healer, and Controller. I could veto her orders if you want...use my seniority as a third-year?"

"How is that possible?" Barry asked in confusion. "There's no feasible way to fill all three roles on a team."

Fabi cocked an eyebrow. "Want to make a bet?" She placed her cutlery down on the plate and smiled at Barry. "It's slim pickings among the third-year groups. Most of our peers have been in teams for the last couple of years, and they're pretty much impossible to poach. Our Healer and Controller didn't make it into the Savior class, so we've been running raids and expeditions as a three-man team. Sakura is an extraordinary Offense, and O'Brien is a world-class Support. It's on me to fill in for the other roles." She picked up her cutlery and resumed cutting into her steak. "All I need to do is craft solutions to our problems, and we operate as effectively as the five-man teams."

"No wonder you're one of the Savior class. I feel like such a fraud because I wouldn't be able to do anything witho—" Blathnaid stopped herself from finishing the sentence as she gave Sal a panicked look. "I mean, it just doesn't feel like I'm on par with everyone else. If that makes sense?"

Fabi looked at Blathnaid carefully. "Shitty weave?"

Blathnaid started to nod before she hesitated. "I had a...breakthrough. It's now a million times better than before."

Fabi nodded in understanding. "I haven't been able to use my ability yet. It's a jumbled mess at the moment, but it looks like someone came up with a solution to my problem." She smiled warmly at Blathnaid. "I don't know about a million times better, but I'd settle for just being able to activate it."

Blathnaid looked at Sal, who gave her a slight nod. Her face burst into a wide smile. "Your ability sounds awesome, by the way. I can't wait to see what you do with it. If you want the blueprint for this dress, I'll happily send it over to you."

Fabi pointed at Blathnaid with her fork. "I'm one hundred percent holding you to that."

As everyone continued with their meal, Sal managed to spy Divinity farther down the table, sitting with a few other students. He thought it was a little odd that she was so far away from their group but decided not to overthink it. As long as he got the chance to invite her to the after-party, it would be fine. He'd get to catch up with her properly then.

Blathnaid and Fabi were talking to each other animatedly, while Barry threw in the occasional quip here and there. Sal sat and listened for a short while before he finally fished his tablet out of his pocket. He didn't have a great track record of keeping in touch with people, and even his best intentions would go straight out the window the moment they started talking about Crafting. While he was conscious of it, he thought it would be best to send Divinity a quick message.

Salvatore: Hey, we're having an after-party at the Argento Auction House later. Would be great if you could make it.

Salvatore: Also, what did you think of Doc Ameye outing me as a Mythcrafter?

He waited for a few moments to see if she'd reply, then looked over at her at the end of the table and saw that she was deep in conversation with someone. Smiling, he pocketed his tablet and returned to the conversation, trying to pick up what everyone was talking about. A few of the other Saviors beside them had joined in on the conversation, and they were mostly learning bits and pieces about one another, with the majority of questions being aimed at Fabi. It was clear that the first-years wanted to know everything they should expect with being Saviors.

"It's a complete change of pace. The whole Savior class thing was only rolled out this semester, so I can't really talk too much about what that will look like for first-years," Fabi explained as she pushed her empty plate away from her. "One of the things that is really cool is the Masterclasses that open up. There are Savior-specific specializations that allow you to get one-on-one training from an established Hero. I got to work at Ameye Locomotive for a short while, which was amazing…I learned so much from him. If you get the chance to get a private trainer, absolutely jump at it!"

Sal felt a vibration in his pocket. He pulled it out and opened his messages to see a new one from Divinity.

Divinity: Absolutely! Thanks for asking me.

Divinity: I knew that Barry was super invested in meeting Trickster, but I wasn't sure about the timing, so I distracted myself by talking to a few of the other clairvoyant Heroes.

Divinity: Oh, and there was such a small chance of the Doc Ameye thing happening. I was so shocked when it actually happened. I hope you're okay!

Divinity: Super happy that you got to hang out with Fabi though. Will I get to meet her at the party later?

Sal smiled as he quickly typed out a response. He was relieved that she seemed to be in good spirits.

Salvatore: I've invited her too, so hopefully you'll get to meet her.

Salvatore: Yeah, it was a shock, but I'm doing okay now. My dad made Doc Ameye apologize to my mother. It was wild.

Salvatore: Trickster thing went well, I think…it's super hard to know if she's going to do a Masterclass at Quest Academy. Barry's worried he came on too hard.

Salvatore: Anyways, I'll catch up with you later. Hope you're meeting cool people!

Fabi subtly tapped Sal's thigh under the table. "Someone's asking you a question." She somehow managed to whisper to him without her lips moving all that much.

"Likely, but do you think they'll keep prioritizing rank for the first-years?" a blond first-year asked him.

Sal tried to recall which of the Savior class he was, but all the videos had very much faded from memory.

"Everything has been performance-based at Quest Academy, so my best guess would be another test for the Savior class whenever we get back. What do you think, Barry?" Sal had no real idea what the start of the question was, but decided to pass the buck to the only other Savior not listening intently.

Barry shot him a sly grin as he launched into an elaborate monologue about his thoughts on the current grading system at Quest Academy.

"Good save." Fabi smiled at him as she raised a glass of red wine to her lips. "Pretending you know what you're talking about is an excellent trait for a guildmaster."

CHAPTER 36: HONOR

After the main meal and desserts were cleared from the last of the tables, a few rounds of drink orders were taken. It was only then that the lights dimmed, with Robert appearing once again in an illuminated space. There were no fancy stages, but instead an elevated tier that looked down on the surrounding Heroes and Hunters.

Now that we've broken bread, it's time for us to talk about the state of the city. You'll have all seen on your way here that we've been hard at work in securing new territory. Grafton has long been an area of great contention, but I'm delighted to announce that we've created a defensible foothold. We're here right now, thanks to the brave efforts of the United Guilds Association, and the assistance of the Hunter Bureau.

If Robert was expecting applause, he would have been disappointed by the lackluster reaction from the crowd. Maybe it was because of the dimmed lights, but Sal wasn't able to see any of the faces around him. Sal wondered whether that was a tactic on Robert's part.

Our plan for this evening will be to update the registry of all our fallen Heroes. We will offer moments of silence, to reflect on their sacrifice in the line of duty. I'd ask you to remember them, and let their passing fuel you in this ongoing conflict. Don't let their sacrifices be in vain.

We will go through the territory map and show our progress from last year's report. Pushing the barriers into new areas will come with a great cost, but also a great opportunity. As we've done in years past, we'll be allocating the acquired territory to the guilds and Hunters that have shown exceptional merit in the previous year.

Doc Ameye will be speaking to all of us on the technological advancements relating to the barriers and the train network. He's best equipped to go over the final details, but we're happy to announce that two new stations have been constructed and added into the Ameye Locomotive family. This comes off the back of last year's update of one new station created in Hope, more specifically in the Aspire District. We're very proud to announce that with the completion of the Aspire District, and the already complete districts of Fortitude, Prosperity, and Serenity...Hope Borough has been fully claimed. It's taken eight years of hard work, but we now have a third borough that is completely reclaimed. Hope, Valor, and Haven now stand as examples of what we can do when we work together.

Robert clapped, and the audience joined him, albeit half-heartedly.

As we've done in the past, we're going to look to the future and not at the past. Grafton Borough...is going to be officially renamed Salvation. The three key districts will be Providence, Ascension, and Redemption. We'll be discussing our Reclamation strategy later in the evening, but I can tell you that our first target will be Providence District, where we currently find ourselves. We will be working hard in the coming months to secure more of the surrounding district. You'll all have noticed on your walk on the red carpet that we've enlisted a number of Support guilds to assist in our reconstruction efforts.

Sal wasn't sure how he felt about that. As much as he wanted to believe in Robert's words, there were too many people who expressed their distrust of the system. There had been no mention of anyone from the Darwin Cruises being rehomed. It was just parts of the new districts being parceled off to individual Hunters and Heroes as a reward. He wasn't sure whether he was missing a key point in the presentation, but it didn't actually sound like they were making much of an impact outside of gaining new territory.

"Pretty sure he ripped off your name for the city." Barry chuckled in the darkness from across the table. "Guess we know where you'll be setting up your guild."

"No chance," Sal answered immediately, not wanting to be a test subject for the new territory. "I want to set up shop in Silver Sanctuary."

"Good luck getting land," Fabi quipped from beside him, laughing. "The Hunter Bureau will pretty much block any chance of you getting into Silver Sanctuary if they want you somewhere else."

Sal frowned as he looked at Fabi's silhouette in the darkness. "Are they trying to send you somewhere you don't want to go?"

Fabi placed her hand on his forearm, startling him slightly. "I absolutely dominated at the evals, so I'm almost certain to have a whole range of offers from the Tier 2 and Tier 3 guilds. Ameye Locomotive is also interested, so I won't really have to make any drastic choices. I still have another semester to go, and I'll be taking as many Masterclasses as humanly possible. If I increase my worth enough and do well in the eyes of the scouts during the portal expedition, then I'll pretty much have my pick of the guilds."

"No desire to be a Hunter? Just do it all solo?" Barry asked out of curiosity.

Fabi shook her head. "Too much risk. I need materials, and the guilds would be more than happy to have an in-house Crafter working with their spoils. You'd be amazed at how many places just lump all their stuff into the Credit Store and hope for a profit. If you have an in-house Appraiser and an in-house Crafter, you're at a massive advantage over the other guilds."

Sal half listened to Robert, who was still talking about the benefits of investing in Salvation as a territory. He was likening it to Haven, and spinning Providence as if it could be the next big commercial hub, comparable to Beacon District. No matter how many assurances he gave, Sal couldn't help but feel it was contrived. If he was a first-year and he felt this wary, there was no way that the rest of the Hunters or Heroes were convinced. At least, that's what Sal hoped.

The smattering of applause that followed Robert's words told Sal that there were a few people in the crowd who wanted to believe what he was saying. He was immediately reminded of his father on their journey to the gala. His dad wanted to believe, but had been disappointed too many times to hold onto hope.

Now, before we turn the lights back up and start the notices on our fallen comrades, I wanted to announce that there will be a shuffle in the Hunter Bureau rankings. We have a few key changes to the top ten that you won't want to miss. We're also going to be showcasing some of our newest Heroes to the world. The Savior class of Quest Academy is in attendance, and we've procured a few highlight reels of their exploits to show you that investment in the future is paying off.

"Ha! I hope they show your video again. I need to see that hulker body slam again." Barry laughed as he slapped the table in front of him. "It's going to be a very different story if they try to showcase your work ethic to a group of grizzled veterans," he teased before taking a drink of water.

"Hulker body slam?" Fabi repeated the words in confusion, tapping Sal's forearm as though it would unlock the context she was missing.

"You didn't tell her how you took down a hulker? I probably would have led with that," Barry said in mock disbelief.

Sal didn't get to see Fabi's reaction because of the dim lights, so he instead just tried to focus on what Robert was saying.

Lastly, we will be announcing the creation of a few new guilds as well as tier changes of the existing ones. So, without unnecessarily drawing things out, let's get started. Could we get the lights back, please? I also want the screens for this next part.

Robert spoke off to one side, not addressing the audience this time. As soon as he said the words, the lights came back gradually to illuminate the room. Multiple screens popped up at each table, with none being more than a few feet away from any single guest.

One of the screens flashed into life in front of Sal and Fabi, and he could vaguely see Barry through the holographic image. Text appeared on the image, writing out a name, followed immediately by a headshot picture.

We honor Henry Walters. Known to the public as Aegis, the 281st Rank in the Hunter Bureau.

Aegis was an excellent Vanguard of the Paradox Guild. Died aged forty-eight and is survived by his wife, Meredith, and his son, Dominic.

Aegis held off a horde of demons during the Pinnacle portal outbreak last month. His sacrifice ensured the survival of his teammates. He was and always will be a Hero.

We will never forget you, Henry. Your sacrifice will not be in vain. The Hero name of Aegis will be reserved for Dominic Walters if he chooses to inherit his father's mantle.

Sal's chest tightened as he looked at an older version of Dominic Walters on the screen. He looked like a friendly bear of a man, with an enormous shield that was close to eight feet tall, and half as wide. His smile was almost drowned by a bushy beard, but the resemblance to Dominic was uncanny.

Sal looked away from the screen and saw that both Blathnaid and Barry were somewhat shaken by the reveal. All the other tables were filled with somber expressions, with many of the Heroes silently raising their glasses in salute. Sal couldn't even fathom what it must have been like for Dominic to lose his father. He couldn't imagine a future without his own.

We honor Archie Lyle. Known to the public as Schemer, the 587th Rank in the Hunter Bureau.

Schemer was a gifted Tactician of the Delvers Guild. Died aged twenty-nine and is survived by his mother, Abigail.

He was and always will be a Hero. The Hero name of Schemer will be available for selection after a cooldown period of one year.

Sal was curious as to why the eulogy was so short for Archie, when it was a much more elaborate affair for Henry. *Was it because he was a lower rank?* The next few deceased Heroes had similar vibes to the first one, and it was only when Robert spoke of another person in the Delvers Guild that Sal saw the pattern emerging.

We will remember Bert Flores. Known to the public as Skulk, the 2,298th Rank in the Hunter Bureau.

Bert was a member of the Delvers Guild. Died aged thirty-seven.

An investigation is ongoing as to the circumstances of their tragic portal run, but we will still mourn the loss of another life.

There was zero sentiment in that last one, with the tone changing completely. There was no fondness for the person, or any sort of platitude. Robert had merely stated that someone was dead, and didn't waste any time in moving onto the next one. It continued for more than two hours, which brought the mood of the entire hall down to rock bottom. The Delvers Guild had eight casualties in the last year, which was five more than the closest competitor. Only one or two of them had a nice send-off from Robert, while the others had the same sort of brevity as Bert's. The key difference was the people Robert claimed to honor, versus the ones he said would be remembered.

Sal was partly relieved that the only name he recognized on the whole list was Dominic Walters's father. It was still incredibly sad, but he wasn't prepared for another shock revelation. He could only imagine how tough it was for the veteran Hunters who knew a lot more of the names on the list. He even felt sorry for the Delvers Guild. It was unlikely they were all as bad as Shade, but nobody deserved to have eight of their friends and teammates killed in a single year. It had to be one of the most traumatic things anyone could ever go through.

"Pretty rough, isn't it?" Fabi asked Sal as she gave him a sad smile. "I could tell you that you get used to it, but it would be a lie. The list was shorter than last year, but not by a lot."

Sal just shook his head and sighed. "Dominic Walters is in our cohort. He ranked high at the start, but then had a bad string of luck with the subsequent rankings…I feel horrible for him."

Blathnaid reached over and pinched Sal.

He jerked his arm away in surprise, looking at her like she was crazy. "What was that for?!"

Blathnaid smiled at him. "You're thinking of how you could help him increase his rank, aren't you?" She gave him a pointed look. "Dominic is strong and has a great ability. He just needs to work on his own confidence and he'll be fine. If you're going to agonize about people being left behind, then focus on the ones who are actually close to failing. Okay?"

Barry just stared at her with a raised eyebrow. "Nope. I don't like this. Bring back the timid Blathnaid who was filled with self-doubt. She was much more fun."

Blathnaid rolled her eyes as she turned her attention back to Sal. "Sorry, Sal. I didn't mean to lecture you…I just think you should be a little more selfish with the time and resources you have available." She laughed and waved her hand. "Or you know, ignore me, and try to recruit every failing student into your guild. That would work, too."

Fabi smiled as she looked between Sal and Blathnaid. "It goes without saying, but that's a terrible idea."

Sal chuckled as he leaned back in his chair. "Hey, we don't even know if I'm going to get approval to start a guild. With my luck, they'll grant it and station me out in the middle of Grafton…Salvation? Whatever it's called now."

Fabi hummed for a second as though she were deep in thought. "I don't know…it wouldn't be the worst thing in the world if you started your guild out of the Quest Academy workshop."

Sal stared at her. "Upgrade got to you, didn't she?"

Fabi's smile turned into a grin. "Literally the first thing she told me at the bar."

CHAPTER 37: REMEMBRANCE

After the death notices, there was a definite lull in the entire hall. People had started to leave halfway through the announcements and retired to the previous reception room to hang out at the bar. By the time that Robert had finished all the obituaries, the room was a lot less full, with many of the Heroes having changed seats to console their friends. It was tough seeing them grieve for their fallen comrades, and Sal felt hollow after hearing the total death count. Just under two hundred Heroes and Hunters had died in a single year. Sal thought it was a ridiculously high number, but Robert praised the efforts of the Hunter Bureau and Guilds Association for reducing the casualties so drastically. Apparently, it was one of the lowest death rates on record.

"It's still way too many people. Hell, just a single person dying is one too many," Sal breathed as he stared at Robert on the balcony in disbelief. "What sort of numbers was it in the past?" He looked at the others at the table to see whether they had any insights. A part of him expected Blathnaid to know the answer. Ever since the scavenger run, he came to appreciate that she lived much closer to the danger than anyone else he knew at Quest Academy.

"Depends on if you're asking about Heroes or if you're asking about people dying in the war," Fabi answered for him, sighing. "Robert is only announcing those with Hero names, and none of the thousands of people who died without having taken up an alias."

She turned in her seat to look at him pointedly. "Don't confuse it with casualties. This whole thing is designed to grieve for the loss of firepower in the war, not show remorse for those caught in the crossfire. If we only had a couple of hundred deaths in a year, we'd be absolutely thriving as a society. Yet, there's overcrowding on the Darwin Cruises, the reconstruction projects are constantly reset, and the bureau is obsessed with securing territory rather than consolidating what they already have."

Sal thought about that for a few moments. It made sense. There would be no way that they were losing the war if Robert's report was accurate. Even if he went with the top ten thousand Hunters in the rankings, a loss of two hundred wouldn't have been enough to tip the scales in the demons' favor. The real question was what else was happening in the city for them to be struggling so much?

Thank you for joining me in the remembrance of our fallen Heroes. Securing a foothold into Salvation has been one of the key milestones of the last year. We had a series of calamities that needed to be mitigated, and through the hard work and perseverance of our Hunters with the Foresight ability, we were able to stop many of them from developing into large-scale disasters.

Maximillian Volta, known publicly as Chronos, is still alive. His timeless war is ongoing, and his power continues to hold the Stage Ten calamity at bay. We're continuing to construct defenses at the Shard, where Chronos has trapped the Stage Ten. As with other years, we don't have a definitive timeline of when we'll be ready to free Chronos from his time-lock. Our Seers are still holding out for an ideal future where we can take down the Stage Ten and keep Chronos alive.

"Did you understand any of that?" Sal whispered, not wanting to be overheard by the others at the table.

Fabi turned in her seat to give him a look of incredulity. "You don't know Chronos? The epitome of what it means to be a Hero?" She shook her head in wonder. "The Stage Ten is a massive fuck-off dragon that makes the entire Quest Academy campus look like a toy. It took up nest in Pinnacle Borough, beside the Shard. Chronos used his time dilation ability to lock both himself and the dragon in a form of stasis. There's a whole unit of Heroes dedicated to healing him and keeping him alive for the last two years."

She stared at Sal. "Literally every Seer has seen a calamity with that Stage Ten wiping out humanity. Quest is literally counting down the days until it breaks free, which is why the Saviors program was created. The Hunter Bureau has been ramping up in preparation of a massive raid to take it down and free Chronos."

Barry leaned forward and looked at both of them with an uncharacteristically serious expression. Raising a finger to his lips, as though telling them to be quiet, he slowly tilted his head farther down the table.

Sal followed his gesture to see a black-haired girl staring intently at the screen in front of her. Realization clicked in his head almost immediately.

Barry glanced at Fabi and pretty much whispered his next words. "Maxine Volta. She's one of the first-year's Savior class, and has a time fuckery sort of ability."

Fabi's next words hitched in her throat as she looked at Maxine carefully. After a few moments, she shook her head and looked back at Barry, frowning. "If she was the key to freeing him, then she would have been taken away from Quest Academy and trained by the top Hunters." Her eyes returned to Maxine before she let out a sigh. "Looks like being a Savior runs in the family."

Sal activated his Skill Master ability and looked at Maxine's internal weave. If she was dead set on taking on the Stage Ten and freeing her own father, he wanted to see what sort of power she was going to do it with. It took a little bit of concentration to remove the visual noise from his line of sight. Moving people with their weaves glowing brightly were quite the distraction, but after a few seconds of concentration, he was finally able to see her power.

"How does it look?" Barry whispered, catching on immediately to what Sal was doing.

Sal's brow furrowed as he tilted his head slightly in confusion. "It's…an absolute mess. It looks like she's somehow brute-forced her way through the stages, and the weaves are practically falling apart." Sal blinked as he deactivated Skill Master. "I'd need to see it in more detail, ideally with the simulation orb, to get a better understanding of it."

Fabi looked between Sal and Barry in confusion. "Wait, did you just look at her ability?" She put her hand on Sal's forearm. "That only took a few seconds?"

A wide smile crossed Barry's face. "That's our Salvatore. Fastest guy you'll ever come across. Done in seconds."

Blathnaid snorted before covering her mouth in embarrassment.

Fabi raised an eyebrow at Barry. "And you've got firsthand experience? Or…just hand experience?" She smiled sweetly at him, as though inviting him to continue.

Barry opened his mouth to reply, when Robert's voice reverberated through the hall once more.

I appreciate you all joining me in a moment of silence for the remembrance of our fallen Heroes. Refreshments will be brought to each of your tables, so please don't be shy in raising glasses in their honor. We will hear from the Arc Guild on new construction efforts across Haven, Hope, and Valor. There will also be some early-stage concept work presented on what Salvation may look like in the next three years, assuming we can count on all of your hard work and support.

Nemesis will provide us an update on the latest deciphering of demonic runes and communication patterns. She will be accompanied by Harlan Geist to help us understand the newest demonic behaviors. After Nemesis, we'll hear from Quest on the latest news from Quest Academy. He'll be accompanied by Grant, who will be sharing progress on our last major advancement, Skill Implanting. We're incredibly excited to share our newest breakthroughs.

We're very excited to have Vector joining us today. Without his stratagems forty years ago, we wouldn't have been able to hold the demon hordes back. He's here today as more than an honored guest. Vector will be presenting his newest research on predictive analysis, and how we can outmaneuver the demons when retaking Salvation. He will be joined by his Tactics protégé, Alastair Maxwell. It's definitely not one to miss!

Doc Ameye will be giving us a talk about the latest technological advancements at Ameye Locomotive. The Hunter Bureau has commissioned a range of new countermeasures from Ameye Locomotive, including improved barrier technology and additional teleportation gates between boroughs. We'll also hear more from him regarding the recently rolled out Protocol System that has been an extraordinary resource in preventing casualties.

Then, after all the talks have concluded, we'll be announcing the individual awards, followed by the advancements of our guilds. There are a few exceptional ones that are moving up the tiers, and we'll be allocating territories and resources to each of them in accordance with their new status. So, there's a lot to look forward to! Get your refreshments, enjoy dessert, and give us your full attention. We have the makings of the greatest Hunter Bureau Gala of all time. You won't want to miss it!

The applause this time was a lot more enthusiastic, likely from the promise of rewards being given out by the Hunter Bureau. Throughout Robert's speech, many of the Hunters who abandoned the hall had returned with drinks in hand. The room was filling back up as the waitstaff pushed dozens of trolleys packed with alcohol to nearby tables. Sal watched in fascination as cocktails were created on the spot at each trolley, as each Hunter and Hero got a custom order. It took a little longer for their table's trolley to ascend all the way up to where they were seated, but when it arrived it was fully stacked with luxury drinks.

"Whoa." Barry leaned across the table to look at the trolley in surprise. "We're able to have any of it?"

"Three old-fashioneds for me, please," Fabi announced as she made room in front of her, stacking her own plate with Sal's before placing it in the center of the table. It had barely touched the white cloth before another member of waitstaff cleared it from view. She smiled at the bartender, who prepared them without complaint.

"Just one old-fashioned for me, please." Sal looked at the trolley. "Is this like the only free round or something?"

The bartender just shook his head. "Not at all, but as time goes on…demand increases and lines become inevitable." He tipped his head toward Fabi. "Your friend has the right idea with stocking up. Would you like to reconsider?"

Fabi posed to look modest, which got a laugh from Sal.

"No, I'll stick with the one. I'll join the line later if I'm feeling thirsty." He looked at Fabi and gave her a shrug. "I'll need to be sober for the dancing later."

Fabi just stared at him as though he were crazy. "Wait, you want to be sober when dancing in front of people? It's usually the opposite, isn't it?"

Sal's smile grew wider. "You're the one who asked for this. Don't blame me when you throw up."

Fabi's eyes narrowed as she accepted the glasses and placed them in front of her. "If I'm going to throw up, it'll be on your fancy new machine…oh, and what about Athena?"

"Athena?" Sal repeated slowly, not following.

Fabi turned in her chair so she faced him. "The name of your machine. Athena was the goddess of Crafting…and war, but I guess if it's going to be making weapons, that fits too?" She gave him an expectant look, clearly curious on what he thought of the suggestion.

"Don't you think it's a little too conceited to name a machine after a goddess?" Sal asked a little awkwardly. "Personally, I'd rather go with something that was a little more rooted in reality."

"You named it Mythos. You can't get any loftier than that," Fabi countered with a laugh, before furrowing her brow. "But I get what you're saying…let's see, someone more human? What about Arkwright? Pretty much the father of automation. You can't have Archibald, by the way…I used that for my drone dock."

Sal perked up at the mention of the drone dock. "That's actually something that I want to create at some point. The machine told me I can't make any of the drone concepts without the docking station."

Fabi stared at him for a moment, frowning. "The machine told you it needed a drone dock?" She started to shake her head. "Unless you somehow managed to get a calculation ability embedded into the interface, it's impossible."

Sal desperately wished he had the level of understanding that Fabi had when it came to Crafting. He felt out of his depth already and it had only been a couple of sentences. Floundering around in his own head for something to say, he focused on the calculation aspect. "When you say calculating ability, do you mean like Deduction or Analysis?"

Fabi nodded, a smile blossoming on her face. "Exactly. There aren't any runes that can grant calculating abilities, so they're a lot harder to integrate into equipment. You'd need access to ridiculously expensive materials, and even then it's not a guarantee that they'll be enough to grant the ability to the finished product." She turned back in her seat, away from Sal, but still looked at him slyly. "This is the part where you're going to tell me that you've got access to some ridiculous materials that got you a calculating ability?" She lifted one of her old-fashioneds to her lips and took a drink.

Sal returned the smile and shook his head. "Nope, a lot more boring than that. I used my tracker to synchronize everything to the interface. It has Analysis, Deduction, and Insight."

Fabi practically choked on her drink.

CHAPTER 38: NEMESIS

The hall lights dimmed, with the exception of a main stage at the center of the room. It was almost reminiscent of the amphitheater, but it was a completely different environment in the hall. The Hunters and Heroes were quite uproarious by comparison. A number of the Hunters seemed to already be drunk, with a few earsplitting songs breaking out in the crowd. It held the promise of a very interesting evening. When a blonde woman appeared in the center of the room, it did nothing to quell the conversations happening between the tables.

Settle down.

The raucousness ceased immediately. With just two words, Nemesis had quieted the entire hall. It wasn't due to some terrifying presence. And even if she had attempted to threaten them, there were some incredibly heavy hitters in attendance who wouldn't be cowed. Yet, with just those two words, she had the absolute quiet of the entire room.

We have a lot of new faces this year. I'm Steph Parker, but many of you know me as the third-ranking Hunter at the bureau, Nemesis.

There was no applause. Just an eerie quiet around the entire hall. No matter which way Sal looked, everyone had their attention focused squarely on Nemesis.

Since the last gala, I've become proficient in the language of three new commander dialects. My Influence ability is now effective on the lord class entities, and I've instructed more than twenty-one of them to eradicate their personal armies and kill themselves. As a result of my research, I've personally closed four portals and taken down eleven towers. It's a marked decrease from last year, but the additional dialects as well as the runic research has been a worthy compromise.

"Whoa," Barry whispered in an almost reverential voice. "That's incredible..."

Sal couldn't help but agree with him. Her Influence ability was similar to Victoria's, but she went so far as to learn how to speak the same language of the demons? *Had she any offensive capability, or did she simply get those results by commanding the demons to kill themselves?* He had so many questions, but was somewhat starstruck by the sheer determination of the woman.

Just as I did before, I will be taking the next month to work through the recordings we have of demons, adding my translations to see if we can gain more insights. The Invention Guild has teamed up with the Hunter Bureau and created a robust translator for all our discovered demonic languages. Since much of their language is non-verbal, I will be working with them to fine-tune the device. Our hope is that in the future, understanding the demons and their behaviors will be second nature to our Heroes.

Before I bring Harlan up here to talk about the evolving behavioral patterns and the newly discovered enemy types, I'd like to highlight a few resources that are now fit to share.

With a wave of her hand, a series of hand-drawn runes appeared above her head. They were large enough to be seen by anyone in the room, but there were very few people who would be able to understand them. Sal stared at them and could tell very quickly that they were similar to the runes that he used in Crafting.

Fabi was much faster than him. "Haste?" She spoke cautiously, as though second-guessing her hypothesis.

One of the most barbaric acts I've witnessed in my travels across the country were the mutilations of the lower-grade demons. The commander variants that I've encountered have taken to carving runes in the bodies of prowlers. This particular rune allowed the prowlers to move up to forty percent faster in short bursts of time. Now, I'd like to draw your attention to this.

Another image appeared alongside the first rune. It was a series of sharp and angular symbols, like a letter from a forgotten alphabet. Straight lines and geometric shapes stood side by side, carved in a way that gave different thickness to each of the lines. Sal stared at them for a few seconds, wondering what the relevance was. Beside him, Fabi practically stood up as she got a closer look at the runes.

"It's a deconstruction! Perception and Flow…but I've never seen them presented like this," Fabi breathed as she looked back toward Sal, as though her words would make perfect sense to him.

The picture on my left is the completed rune that we know gave the prowlers an increase in speed. The picture on my right is a deconstruction of the same rune, using the words I discovered over five years ago: Perception and Flow. These words, written in a demonic alphabet, have been combined to create an entirely new rune. If this discovery is indeed a breakthrough, then we will be reporting on it at the next gala. Right now, we've attempted to create a logic flow of how certain words can combine to create real runes.

Nemesis smiled wide as she placed her hands on her hips, her blue eyes almost twinkling in the light.

Imagine my disappointment when I reported this to the Hunter Bureau and I'm told that someone has already been creating entirely new runes using my old research? If it was a peer I respected, that would be one thing…but Quest, I'm going to have to have a word with you about your students. A dangerous little Runesmith is hiding among your first-years.

She put her hands up as though holding back imaginary outrage from the Hunters and Heroes, even though there was none.

I won't overstep on Quest and Grant's announcement, but imagine finding out that we have all the tools we need to create new runes. How exciting of a prospect is this? We could essentially use the abundance of atmospheric essence to dramatically overhaul our defenses! Imagine going to Robert with this information, sure of the fact that we've just taken a pivotal step forward in reclaiming the homes of our parents and grandparents…and imagine your discovery is second to what they've been cooking up at Quest Academy.

Nemesis laughed as she looked over at Robert's table. Specifically to where Quest was seated beside Neuro.

I'll be seeing those students for myself, Quest. I already rejected the Influence Masterclass, so let me teach the Supports about runes. I want to meet…

Sal turned around slowly to where Blathnaid was sitting. "Are you thinking what I'm thinking?" There was no way it could be anyone else. Sal had seen Jack's equipment as they went into the tower, and he couldn't properly Appraise half of the runes he wore.

Blathnaid just smiled as she gave him a slight nod. "He's been working hard on the sidelines. You should have seen him in the tower!"

Fabi looked between them with wide eyes. "Wait, you know who it is?"

Blathnaid chuckled as she shrugged. "He's part of the original dream team and a good friend of ours, so yeah…there's a high chance you'll meet him if you watch the inter-cohort fights."

Barry stared at her in confusion. "There's no way they're going to continue with that competition now that Chatfield is around. Now that we've been killing demons, they're going to just keep pushing us into dungeons and towers." He considered it briefly before a chuckle escaped his lips. "But man, if they do make us go back to it…poor Anthony. It'll be three Saviors, a Runesmith, and him. That's going to sting."

"But the three of you are Supports," Fabi said in confusion. "How did Rust let you get away with that composition? Is Anthony a Controller?"

Sal smiled as he shook his head. "Five Supports. We had the second last pick of teammates, but managed to win top of the Silver cohort."

"Undefeated," Barry added, as though it was a very important distinction. "Wait until you see Blathnaid's highlight reel of throwing Victoria over her shoulder. It's magic."

Fabi smiled brightly as she looked past Sal to where Blathnaid sat. "That sounds awesome. I can't wait to see!"

Rather than being embarrassed like every other occasion it came up, Blathnaid returned the smile and thanked Fabi for the kind words.

On the main stage, Nemesis spoke back and forth with Robert and Quest in a joking manner about her conducting a Masterclass at Quest Academy. There was a lighthearted tone to the whole thing, and it got more than a few laughs from the crowd when Nemesis pretended to negotiate her rate by asking for more rations for her next outing into the wilds. When she fully returned her attention to the crowd, she started going through all the different runes that had been discovered so far, and highlighting the gaps in their collective knowledge.

One of the key things we want to understand is how the higher stages communicate. With the disturbing advent of the Psionic commander variant, we are assuming that the highest variants use Psionics to communicate and control their armies. Of the high-level entities that I've observed, very few of them use vocal commands and instead use signals. I'll be retiring my efforts of understanding the voiders. Harlan agrees that they are typically soldiers and never in a position of command. Their evolved forms are dangerous, but fiercely individualistic. My focus will be on learning more about the switchers. Since I travel alone, they can only assume my appearance…which I'd consider flattering in any other circumstance.

Since they can emulate human speech, I want to capture a switcher and use my Influence to interrogate it. If we can successfully learn more about the demons, their origin, and their goals…then we'll be in a much better position to counteract. Thank you for your continued support. Next year will have even better results, I'm sure. I'd like to now invite Harlan to the stage, to walk us through the newly discovered behavioral patterns.

"If he starts talking about the spiders again, Divinity is going to throw up." Barry chuckled as he looked down the table to where she sat. "Why do you think she's all the way down there?"

Fabi raised a hand with a laugh. "That's my fault. She offered me her seat when we were out at the reception. If you'd prefer her company, I can switch back? I think she wanted to talk to O'Brien about something, though."

"He's one of your team, along with Sakura, right?" Sal asked to move the conversation along. He didn't want Barry poking into why Divinity might have switched seats, nor did he want Fabi to feel uncomfortable about sitting beside him.

Fabi nodded. "Yeah, he's the best. He pretty much controls an entire battle-field with smoke. If he's charged up enough and has the essence to spare, he can even spark some of the smoke to create small explosions." Her smile widened. "He has a few issues with his ability, so he's hopeful that it can be improved in the future with some hard work."

"I'll put him top of the list," Sal answered with a smile. "If you join my guild."

Fabi put her hand on her heart and pretended to be fatally wounded. "Ah, I was hoping to just help you make a docking station…"

Sal sighed in defeat as he shook his head. "Okay, that's a good compromise. I'll just have to figure out a deal that will get you into the guild at some point. We have to make an army of drones, remember?"

"It'll be the best army," Fabi agreed as she lifted her glass. Before taking a drink, she looked at the whiskey cautiously. "Are you about to say something completely outlandish again, or am I safe to take a drink?"

"You're absolutely safe," Sal reassured her as he put his own hand over his mouth. "I won't say a word."

Harlan and Nemesis spoke for close to an hour on the newest discovered behavioral patterns, which were very high level. Sal tried his best to pay attention to them, but it wasn't content that was designed for him. Commander variants and above were unlikely to be his opponents for quite some time. Sure, Anna Sakura had managed to kill one of them during the raid in his first month, but that was an exception. She was an Offense and had a ridiculously good ability for nullifying opponents. She was also training to be an Assassin. Sal doubted that he would be put into the same situations in the near future.

When Sal looked over at Barry, he was surprised to see his friend listening intently. He had made a few remarks in the past about doing some of the Assassi-nation modules, but he didn't have the best track record of telling the truth. Sal looked at him in a different light. Even without the formidable equipment, Barry was a scary opponent. If he got a Masterclass with Trickster and learned how to use his ability to an even higher standard, would he eventually follow in Sakura's footsteps?

Barry turned and smiled at Sal. "You've gotta admit, Nemesis is looking pretty damn good for her age."

Sal immediately deleted all the positive sentiment aimed at Barry over the last few minutes. "I thought you were actually paying attention."

Barry's smile grew wider. "Of course I am. Demons using sign language to communicate? What happens when they see an illusion giving them the wrong commands?"

"You really are a scary bastard." Sal laughed as he picked up his drink.

CHAPTER 39: BATTLE-SUIT

Shortly after Nemesis and Harlan exited the center stage, the desserts and drinks trolleys appeared once again. There was a lot of chatter and debate about the runes, with a few Heroes coming over to the Savior table to ask about Jack Allen. They didn't know him by name, but they wanted to. It was clear from their questions that they were interested in some early scouting for their guilds, but none of them really seemed to be Support oriented.

At the sight of Fabi at the table, some of the guilds even offered to open up a specialized Crafting facility just for her, but she turned them down with courteous smiles and promises to think about it. When they politely took a few of the names, they paid closer attention to the little badges on each Savior's jacket. That fact wasn't lost on Sal, and he tried to keep his own from view as much as possible. Until he knew what they really meant, he didn't want to be flaunting it around.

They wouldn't even let me finish the pie. Can you believe it?

The artificially enhanced voice rang out, causing everyone to look around in surprise to the center stage, where an older man stood with a wide smile. If he was to be judged by appearance alone, he looked like an incredibly warm-hearted man who lit up the room just by being there. In his hand was a plate with a half-eaten piece of pie. He held it aloft for everyone to see.

We all know that Robert likes to keep a schedule, so there's no helping it. Most of you will know me as Vector, but if that's a little too pretentious, you can just call me Ron. I'm not going to go through the resume, because I'd like to get back to my seat sooner rather than later.

He chuckled along with the crowd as he bent on one knee to place his plate on the ground beside him. With a groan, he got back up and dusted himself off with a sigh.

So, let's get this show on the road, shall we? Throw up the screens and we can start talking about the Reclamation efforts.

In a flash, a huge map appeared all around the room. All the screens on each table reflected the same image for people to inspect it closer. Vector wasted no time in getting into the information, and his cheerful persona was pushed to one side as he stared at the images with clear disdain.

Our attempts at securing Grafton in the past were flawed. Fundamentally. We looked at it from the wrong perspective. Rebuilding shouldn't be a case of reconstructing what was there before. We need structures that are resilient against future threats. Each and every building should be a part of the city's defense network—natural barriers, evacuation routes, and resource flows. We need to create bottlenecks for any future conflict and have a comprehensive plan for reclaiming or surrendering territory.

How will we do it? By building a self-sustaining defensive stronghold that we can gradually expand. I've mapped thousands of scenarios and created the best reconstruction framework, peer-reviewed by Specs at every point. My findings have been very positive. We're going to implement a predictive defensive grid in Grafton. We won't be reacting to incoming attacks, but rather, we'll be predicting them before they happen. With the data provided by Doc Ameye and

Protocol, we've managed to create a state-of-the-art algorithm for this project. Additional data has been provided by our clairvoyant Heroes, which has stress-tested and helped refine the predictive defense grid by incorporating so many variables that would otherwise have been unknown.

Our attempts to use the satellite arrays have been predictably blocked by Bastion, but Doc Ameye has constructed a solution for us. We will be using his Tower Turrets as our eyes in the sky. Normally, I wouldn't need to explain all of this to you, but there comes a lot of risk when creating the array. We will need to secure pockets of territory in Grafton...sorry, Salvation. It will sound insane, with teams being deployed into the heart of enemy territory to capture structures cut off from the rest of the safe zones. These tasks will not be on the Reclamation guilds, but rather on our trusted Offense guilds.

Vector paused as he looked around the room. There was nothing but silence in the room. Taking a napkin from his breast pocket, he dabbed at his forehead a few times before tucking it away with a deep breath.

I'll be honest, I expected a bit of screaming with that one. Thank you for not causing a riot.

"Send the Reavers!" Villa called out from one of the tables on the main floor. Her feet were on the table, and at her words, more than a dozen of Heroes at her table started to drum their hands on the table in support of the motion.

"Send Goliath!" another voice shouted from a different table, which resulted in more voices piling on top of one another.

"Pick Paradox, Vector!"

"Tempest is ready for action...what do you say, would Eclipse join us?" A bearded man challenged another table as he got to his feet. He was close to seven feet tall, with the widest frame Sal had ever seen in his life. A single pauldron on his shoulder was enough to obscure three people who sat next to him.

Before the guildmaster of Tempest could get his answer, Villa was on her feet and pointing at him. "I knew you liked Eclipse, but isn't this a little too obvious, Thunder?"

A roar of laughter echoed throughout the hall, made funnier by the shocked look on the giant bear of man, who couldn't physically shrink away from the embarrassment. His size was far too much for him to do anything other than stand there and take it.

A lithe woman got to her feet and crossed her arms with a smile on her face. "Thank you, Thunder...but Eclipse can handle this ourselves." She held out a hand and gestured at Vector. "We trust you, Vector. You tell us what we need to do and where we need to go, and we'll get it done."

You all have my thanks. I wish I could do more than crunch the numbers, but I'll do everything in my power to ensure that there are no casualties with this project.

"We love you, Vector!" a female voice practically sang from the back of the room. "Just tell us what to fucking kill so we can get you some pie."

Vector smiled sheepishly as he brought his hands together.

Doc Ameye has offered to provide assistance, pro bono. Having Ameye Locomotive involved will drastically increase the survivability of whichever guilds take on this project. When we have our predictive defensive grid in place, by using essence readings, we'll be able to detect portals before they open. We'll be able to pinpoint accurate head counts within dungeons and towers, and will be able to identify all registered demonic entities. With the work of Nemesis and her research, we may be able to factor in commands to disorganize the demonic forces. We will gradually rebuild Salvation, and preemptively strike the enemy when they least expect it.

Vector hesitated for a moment before continuing.

On my way here, I saw some provisional advertising for apartment buildings or guild headquarters. I can say that from my own research on this topic, it would be ill-advised to prioritize the construction of such buildings. I know that the Hunter Bureau needs to secure funding from our esteemed guests in this room…but I would ask those very people to invest in the long-term revitalization of Grafton…sorry, Salvation. Whatever you want to call it. This city can be re-built—not in the image of what was once Grafton, but something better. We can create a fortress city that becomes the precedent for expansion across the country.

Help us with this project. Before vanity projects that ask us to reclaim old ground for the sake of more land, we need a command center, medical facilities, reconnaissance tools, offensive strike teams, the adaptive defense systems, re-source extraction units, and barrier perimeters. All of those will cost a fortune, especially when you consider the scale of the project. We have all the data and systems required to make this a reality, and we have all the manpower we could want to see it done properly. If you want this gala to go down in history, let it be the one where you funded the future of humanity.

Now, I'm sure that Robert will want to have some words with me…so, I'll be taking my pie back to my seat. Thank you for listening to this old man's request.

Vector left the stage to thunderous applause from the crowd, with quite a lot of the guilds shouting their support for his proposal. He stayed true to his word and got down on one knee to retrieve his plate with the pie. The side of ice cream had long since melted, but he didn't seem too bothered as he moved back toward his own table.

Sal watched him move across the room. When he spoke about the simulations and models that he had run through for the project, Sal became very curious about what sort of ability he had. It sounded like a calculation ability, on par with the Analysis ability that Beck Syme used. But when Sal activated Skill Master to have a look at the internal weave, he saw nothing. Vector didn't have a weave.

"He doesn't have an ability…" Sal said aloud in surprise, which caused Fabi to smile.

"He's old-school, which is why so many people love him." She laughed as she raised her glass. "We love you, Vector!" She shouted those words across the room in time with all the other Hunters who were giving him a Hero's welcome. When she looked over at Sal, she gave him a playful wink. "He's been trying to change the Hunter Bureau for the last forty years, and every procedural change he's made has resulted in massive casualty reductions. You'll get to see how awesome he is in second year."

"Does he do a Masterclass or something?" Sal asked in surprise.

Fabi shook her head, pausing to pull a lock of hair behind her right ear. "No, nothing like that. His research is adapted into course materials for the Ethics module. Who do you think came up with the retrofit of the Darwin Cruises to make them habitable for refugees, or convinced Quest to create an academy? His work has saved so many lives that he was made an honorary Hero."

"So…he's done thousands of modeling scenarios without an ability?" Barry asked suspiciously. "Is that why they got Professor Syme to check his work?"

Fabi turned around in her chair to look at Barry with a raised eyebrow. "Are you going to tell me that you don't trust people without an ability? Tread carefully."

Barry's lips almost melted together into a grimace, as he realized in real time how he had just put his foot into it. "Ah. I didn't mean that."

Fabi chuckled as she glanced at Sal. "Is he usually this easy to tease?" She smiled at Barry. "He's done so many research papers on predictive analysis with Professor Syme as the coauthor. If you tried to read them all, you'd graduate before you were done with them. They've been at this nonstop for decades, and each new advancement or ability changes everything. It's really interesting going through them all, even if only to see the progression of our own advancements since the war started."

"You seem to really keep up to date on all sorts of research. Where do you find the time?" Sal asked with a nervous laugh. He wasn't sure whether it was a feeling of inadequacy or whether he was finally becoming aware of how little time he was spending on learning from an academic perspective.

"Audio." Fabi tapped her ear. "Crafting without essence means a lot of mind-numbing assembly and waiting on fabrications. I listen to research papers when I'm in my workshop."

"You've got your own personal workshop?" Barry asked in surprise. "How did you manage that?"

Fabi shrugged. "The course materials I sold on the Credit Store earned enough for me to get a room with a custom workshop. Not having to share a space was one thing, but also not having the scrutiny of every other Crafter telling me that I was being too ambitious was the main reason." She drummed her fingers against her chin as though thinking about the question a little more deeply. "It was also perfect for keeping certain projects a secret. My first battle-suit took a lot of time to put together, and I needed to commission a few others to help me on the essence front."

Barry perked up at that, at the exact same time as Sal. Both of them asked the same question in unison. "Battle-suit?"

Fabi laughed as she looked between them, as though trying to pick who to answer. Eventually she settled on Sal as she held her glass on the table, rotating it slightly. "Yeah, we had a girl who was an Epicrafter. She was the year ahead of me. We made all sorts of stuff together, and she was very happy to take my Q-Cred in exchange for putting parts together and following a blueprint. My first battle-suit carried me through all of first year, but the one I have now eclipses it in pretty much every way."

Lifting her drink, she finished it off and then reached down for one of her spares. "I kept the pants and boots, but threw the rest up for sale. Got it restored to good as new but it still took a year to sell it off. That said, someone is now a proud owner of the Vengeful Vambraces!"

Barry's jaw dropped as Sal burst out laughing.

CHAPTER 40: MISCOMMUNICATION

"What am I missing here?" Fabi asked, laughing as she patted Sal's arm to get him to answer her.

Barry just shook his head in disbelief. "You made the Vengeful Vambraces? You're serious? Sal didn't tell you to say that to mess with me?"

Fabi's expression brightened. "Oh, were you the one who bought it? They anonymize the buyers, so I didn't know who picked it up. I never would have thought it would go to a first-year, if I'm honest."

Barry sighed as he pointed at the still-laughing form of Sal. "He bought it and gave it to me, as a trade to get me to join his guild in the future. He's rolling in Q-Cred from all the Appraisals, Crafting, and secret projects."

"Oh, well, I'm happy that it went to someone I know. What do you think of it?" Fabi pulled her seat in closer to the table so she could rest her elbows on the surface. She looked at Barry intently. "What way do you use it in battle?"

Sal finally regained his breath as he crossed his arms with a smile on his face. He couldn't believe it. Even when he had been hearing her name everywhere, he managed to buy not one, but two things she had personally made: the little hover bot and the Vengeful Vambraces. It was wild to think that of all the things he saw in that bazaar, those were the two things that he decided to get. He didn't believe in things like fate, but it was far too much of a coincidence.

Barry listed out how he was using it alongside his illusion ability, and Fabi's face transformed throughout the explanation. Shock and awe were the two most recurring reactions as she listened to him.

"Tell her about how you learned to fly," Sal interjected, laughing.

Barry tilted his head to one side. "Come on, if they show the highlight reels, it would have been a much better reveal." He looked at Fabi's expectant expression before giving a resigned sigh. "Fine…I created two flat blades and stepped on them. Then pretty much lifted them into the air while I controlled the others. Made all of them invisible just to fuck with the rest of the team. The Hunter Bureau pretty much stopped the tower trial three times to check that things were working properly."

Fabi burst out laughing. "That's fantastic. I never thought of doing that with the blades. Have you tried reinforcing your limbs with them? Just coat yourself with a layer of essence and you can jump higher, punch harder, and take more hits without worry." She turned to look at Sal. "And if you decide to use it at some point, you can make all sorts of tools with essence. It's great for Crafting, but way too uncomfortable for long sessions."

"Wait, forget about the Crafting stuff and go back to the reinforcing. How can it make you jump higher? Are you talking about making springs at the bottom of your feet or something?" Barry's curiosity was piqued, and he became absorbed in the conversation.

Fabi looked at him strangely. "Springs? No…you just need to create a layer of essence and use intent. Just like how you control the trajectory of the essence blades, you will the essence around your body to move in certain directions. It takes a lot of control, but if you've already fine-tuned how to use multiple blades, you're far more of a natural than I was."

Barry looked at her intently. "Hypothetically, if you were to use blades with the Vengeful Vambraces, how many would you be able to control now?"

Fabi held up two fingers. "Blades this size?" She held her fingers a few inches apart.

Barry just stared at her fingers and seemed to come to some sort of horrifying conclusion.

Fabi's smile widened. "You've just realized you were making dagger-length blades, when tiny ones would do the job for less essence?" She widened her fingers out. "If it was dagger length, then probably around twelve. Smaller blades, that number would double…but keeping them to independent trajectories would be a challenge. I don't want to even think about how difficult it would be to put an illusion over them, too."

Barry wiped at his face with his hands. "Why was I making them that big?"

Fabi shrugged as she winked at Sal. "I can't answer why you feel the need to overcompensate." She smiled sweetly at Barry. "But I could hazard a guess, if you want?"

Barry shook his head as he stood. "I'm going to the bar. Do you want anything?" He looked at Blathnaid, then at Sal and Fabi. When all answered in the negative, he excused himself and made the trek down past the tables. There were quite a few Hunters still walking around and talking, and it looked like it was going to be awhile before the next speakers got onto the stage.

Sal was surprised at how relaxed the atmosphere was at the gala. He had been worried that it would be a pompous and high-society kind of arrangement, especially with how many powerful people were in the room. Yet, as he sat there and looked around, he could see people laughing and joking with each other, Hunters catching up with one another and generally letting off steam. It took him quite a while to spot his parents in the crowd, and when he saw them, he was surprised to see his father locked in a conversation with Villa from the Reavers Guild. He hoped she wasn't giving him a hard time about him being Myth.

"Who are you keeping an eye on?" Fabi turned around in her seat to scan the faces. "Anything interesting happening?"

"Villa from the Reavers Guild is over talking to my dad, and I've got no idea why. Where is Maurice sitting?" Sal looked at the other people at his parents' table. "I thought they might have put our parents together?"

Fabi pointed to the table that Vector had returned to. "Dad is sitting over there, right next to Lawrence Baron. My best guess is that they want all the material suppliers to play nice around Vector, and that Vector is going to try to sway them with a master plan for the future of resource depots."

"You got all that with a glance?" Sal asked in disbelief.

"Naturally." She held a serious expression before finally breaking with a laugh. "No, Dad said it the minute he saw the seating plan." She continued to look at Sal for another few seconds before leaning in close. "So, you made that cane-sword for Lawrence Baron. I wouldn't be a Maccles if I didn't ask what your intentions were. Are you trying to drop my dad as a supplier?"

Sal jerked back from the sudden invasion of space, not prepared for Fabi to move that close. He wanted to reassure her that he'd continue to work with Maurice, but his intention had been to get in with Lawrence to have access to rare materials and ingredients. That said, Sal didn't want to lie to her. It was their first time meeting, and he didn't want to start things off with misunderstandings or anything like that.

"Honestly, I made the cane-sword to impress him. I was hoping he'd be able to get me access to high-level materials, the sort of stuff that your father wouldn't really stock. I promise it wasn't anything personal. Your dad really came through for me with the materials for the machine." Sal spoke quickly and tried to read her expression to see whether she was annoyed with him.

With a slight smile, Fabi nodded. "I get it. I've already told him that I'm going to outgrow the store if he can't get better contracts. It's a business, at the end of the day, and I'll always give him first refusal…but he'll be straight with both of us and tell us what he can and can't get." Her smile grew wider. "Thanks for being honest with me. And yeah, just promise that you'll check with him first before you go to Lawrence on special orders. I want Dad to get a little more ambitious, and if there are two Saviors in Silver Sanctuary and both of us are Crafters? Well, I think he's going to have his work cut out for him."

Fabi turned her head to look at the crowd. "Oh, and a freebie tip…people are going to ply you with drink at this thing and offer you incredible contracts. Don't believe a word they say…until you see it in writing, and you're handed it by someone sober. Shade is likely going to try to pick you up because he's short of Appraisers."

"He's tried already and failed," Sal responded with a dry laugh. "At our last auction, we pretty much ridiculed him until he left." He blinked as he realized that Fabi knew he was a Mythcrafter. "Oh, I can actually tell you what happened." He laughed again before sitting up in his chair and describing the auction. When he spoke about creating the obsidian daggers really quickly, Fabi needed a moment to process, but she soon got back into the story, cackling in laughter at Shade being outbid on the items he refused to pay for.

"And they were all evolutionary? That's incredible…for you to be able to make them that quickly." She looked at her own hands for a moment before shaking her head. "It's so hard to process the fact that I'll have an ability soon. I'm trying to keep my expectations low so I don't get disappointed, but it's really hard." Looking up at Sal, she shrugged. "I don't even know what to expect when I get the Assemble ability. Will it even make that much of a difference to how I Craft? I mean, you'd only really need to use it when you're putting things together, so at best it's just going to be a time-saving thing."

Sal frowned. "What have you been told about your ability?"

Fabi looked at him strangely. "It's called Assembly and it's the first stage of a four-part evolution. With how mangled my internal weave is, you've had to rewire it to access the Assembly ability. It'll have room to grow and can get stronger with time." She smiled and put up her hands. "Don't get me wrong, I'm incredibly grateful for the work that you've done. It's just when I hear about you making obsidian daggers in less than an hour, it's hard not to feel a little…ugh, I don't know."

"Who told you all this?" Sal asked carefully, not sure how to proceed from here. If someone was giving her a lowball on the outputs of her ability, then it might have been for a good reason. The only problem was that Sal was an expert on Fabi's weave and knew it inside and out. There were no problems with his weave design. And even with Grant's programmed margin of error, he was still able to get it to a hundred percent. It was a safe weave that was custom-built for Fabi.

Fabi gestured across the room to where her father sat. "Quest sat me down and told me that they were going to look at imprinting my existing weave in a different format. He said they ran multiple simulations and there were four options available. Each of them was safe, but they'd be capped in terms of potential until I opened more gates. My father asked for the least risky one, and Quest said to start with Assembly and work up from there." Fabi sighed as she shook her head. "He said the best it can get to is a Grade 2."

Sal stared at her in disbelief. "Okay…so all of that is wrong."

Fabi's eyes widened in shock.

"Yeah, so that Grade 2 is correct, but it's for the fourth stage of Assembly." Sal closed his eyes and groaned inwardly. He could tell where the miscommunication was, but it was still frustrating when it had been playing on Fabi's mind all this time. "Your ability starts at Assembly, then it becomes Innovate, then Fabricate, and finally Customize. The Grade 2 that they talked about is for Customize, not Assembly. I know this because I built your weave from scratch, in a way that would allow you to start with Assembly and, depending on how much essence you push into the ability, it'll allow you to use all the later stages. Giving you four abilities in total."

Fabi just stared at Sal, with eyes wide, but Sal wasn't done.

"Hell, if Grade 2 was the best they could do, I could literally do it right now." Sal exhaled in exasperation as he gestured at her chest. "Seriously, it's like three…" He tilted his head slightly. "Okay, it's more like seven adjustments…but still? How could they tell you that and ruin all your excitement for this?" He shook his head and looked over to where Quest sat. "And obsidian daggers in less than an hour? You'll be able to wave your hand and make things in a flash. Then, when they're done, you can use Customize and pretty much swap out whatever attributes you're familiar with."

Sal looked at Fabi with a laugh. "Seriously, there's nothing to be jealous of with me. You're amazing without an ability, but when you finally get it…you're going to be unstoppable."

Fabi put her hand on Sal's shoulder and smiled at him. "Is this the part where I tell you I desperately want to join your guild?" She gave him a playful wink. "But I do have a conspiracy theory…"

Sal was flummoxed. "A conspiracy theory?"

Fabi nodded sagely. "If you're right and you've made the perfect weave for me…then there's a reason they're not giving me that power. If I was able to wave things into existence as you've said, it means they're likely scared."

"Scared of what?" Sal asked nervously.

Fabi turned around and stared at Sal before biting her lip to hold back her own laughter. "Our drone army."

CHAPTER 41: SHOWCASE

As Quest and Grant stepped onto the center stage, Sal looked over his shoulder to see whether Barry was on his way back to the table. Judging by how long he had been gone, the lines at the bar must have been insane. He wasn't sure how much of the updates from Quest would be relevant to the Saviors or whether it was going to be tailored for the Hunter Bureau. Considering Nemesis already alluded to Quest having a massive update, Sal guessed they were going to give some information around the simulation orb and the research they were conducting in the workshop.

It's been a year since we stood here on behalf of Quest Academy. When we last spoke to you, we explained the advancements of our Skill research, and introduced the concept of Skill Implanting and Imprinting. We fully expected that this year we would be giving you an update on the successful implants in students who reached the Savior class. But an entirely new development was borne from our research.

Before we get to that, I'd like to highlight that the Skill Registration was an absolute success. We've managed to catalogue the internal Skill Weaves of all incoming students, and gave them a minor imprint for their trouble. Professor Lombardi has highlighted that the Skill classes in first year are progressing faster than previous years, with many of the students already surpassing their counterparts in second and third year. We have some first-years with access to more than a hundred essence gates. The imprint has resulted in the first-years having a greater control of their innate abilities, and their access to so many gates makes them the most powerful set of cohorts we've seen at Quest Academy thus far.

I'm confident that this future generation of Heroes and Hunters will be the best we've ever seen.

Quest spoke with his hands clasped together in front of him. He was smiling throughout his presentation, which was a very nice change from the usually tense atmosphere from the last few months. There was no Chatfield or Robert throwing a wrench into his plans, and he looked to be quite relaxed. Beside him was Grant, who practically buzzed with excitement.

Now, the update that we're excited to share with you. I'll need to hand it over to Grant for this as I wouldn't do the research justice.

Quest stepped back with a smile and gestured for Grant to step forward and address the room. Grant didn't so much as hesitate, the wide smile on his face showing his excitement.

As a Replicator, I can temporarily grant abilities to others. We've developed the Skill Implant device with my powers in mind, where I can hold the weave in place in the target, and the device will map an artificial essence weave into their body. Our imprinting technology uses the same principles, but instead of creating a new weave in the target, we reinforce the existing weave with our artificial one. The cost of creating that thread is huge, and our efforts in the last year have been dedicated to improving our process before we carry out the implant.

Our focus had been to reduce the cost of implanting. We relied on the Skill Registration to catalog the abilities of the first-years coming into Quest Academy. Their abilities were added to the existing database of Heroes and Hunters who opted in for the minor imprint, as well as the other students.

Just like you've heard from Nemesis, there is a student at Quest Academy who has been creating runes from the demonic language. All through instinct. Well, there's definitely something special about the first-years at Quest Academy, because we also have a Replicator who has been able to create new Skill Weaves.

While the room had settled down for Quest and Grant going up to the stage, there had still been a few conversations that remained ongoing. Although it hadn't really been disruptive, it was clear that a lot of the Hunters were only giving half of their attention to the headmaster, with some just ignoring the words completely. When Grant dropped the bombshell that there was a Replicator who could create new Skill Weaves, the entire room became deathly quiet. It was an ominous atmosphere as everyone stopped what they were doing and looked at Grant in disbelief.

Yes, you heard that correctly. We have a Replicator who has been able to create new Skill Weaves. Have a look at this.

Grant raised his hand and a series of images appeared around the room. They showed the simulation orb with a weave fixed in place. The glowing lights showing the movement of the weave looked impressive in the dim lighting, and Sal was relieved to see that the pictures they chose didn't have him present.

Hunters literally got to their feet to get a better look at the images floating in the center of the room, despite them being readily available on each table. It was clear that they had questions, but all of them kept quiet for fear of missing something. Many of the faces in the crowd were simply stunned. Sal's personal favorite was Villa, who had been throwing a dagger up into the air and catching it. At the mention of new weaves being possible, the sound of her dagger clattering to the ground was blended into the noise of glasses shattering in the hands of shocked Heroes.

You're looking at a revolutionary new weave with a very high synchronization rate. Our Replicator can not only create these new weaves, but understands how to refine them through the simulation orb we've created. The results have been simply extraordinary, with many catalogued abilities being improved dramatically. Our understanding of weaves has changed, with the simulation orb finding commonalities between the abilities and assigning them to different families. In simple terms, we've discovered how weaves can evolve to a higher form, all within a controlled environment.

All of this has been possible because of the simulation orb. Without it, our Replicator wouldn't have been able to do any of this. We'll be supporting them over their time at Quest Academy to improve the simulation orb and to continue making breakthroughs. I'd ask you all for your continued support in protecting Quest Academy and keeping our research alive.

Should we tell them about Perfect? Grant turned to Quest with a grin on his face.

The headmaster chuckled as he stepped forward once again.

The ability weave that was created with the simulation orb is called Perfect. To do the research justice, we'll give you the description from the simulation orb itself.

'Perfect grants the user an evolutionary proficiency focused on internal and external development. Offers heightened capability for learning new skills and techniques and continuously refines them.'

As you've just heard, it's a Body Manipulation ability that restructures the body and ability in the most optimal way. If a Hero had Perfect as an ability, they would learn new techniques at a monstrous rate while cultivating their internal essence subconsciously. Not only that, we have reason to believe that Perfect works on elixirs, upgrading their potency by utilizing internal essence once they're consumed. I think you can all appreciate how incredible this discovery is, but it's still at only sixty-two percent stabilization. We need to continue refining the weave with improvements to the simulation orb and hopefully next year we will be above eighty percent, and ready to offer it as a Skill Implant to those with a suitable synchronization rate.

You would have been able to hear a pin drop with the stunned silence in the crowd. There wasn't a single person in the room who looked composed at the revelation, and all the stragglers who came through the doors from the bar were hushed immediately.

Sal wondered why Grant chose to reference the initial stability of the Perfect weave. He had personally improved it up to a hundred percent in the board room.

Grant stepped forward with a finger raised and an easygoing smile. He delivered his caveat to the research with a practiced humility.

Hopefully we'll have also driven down the cost by that time, too. This is expensive research, and we wouldn't have been able to get this far without the support of the Hunter Bureau. Most of the funding available goes straight to the Reclamation efforts, so we can't guarantee that this will be ready by next year. While this is still incredibly exciting, we'd humbly ask you all to be patient with us as we try to navigate these new advancements. As a Hero, I understand the desire to rebuild Grafton into the city of Salvation, and I'd never want to take away from that project. We stand behind the Hunter Bureau and their priorities for retaking territory, but we would happily look at private funding for this research if there were any interested parties.

Quest tapped Grant on the shoulder, which stopped the Hero from continuing. The headmaster looked around the room with a smile on his face.

We're not here to play the game of funding. I hope you'll forgive Grant for trying to bait you into donating to the project. The truth of it is, we want to see this succeed more than anyone else, to give the next generation of Heroes everything they'll need to win the war. I've spoken with Robert at length about how to navigate this new research, and we've decided that the best course of action is to create a specialized research group for these revolutionary advancements. Quest Academy will be upgrading our entire workshop facility, with the help of the Hunter Bureau, to create a center of excellence. Over the next few months, we'll be publishing research materials to the Hunter Bureau and the United Guilds Association. You'll all have access to our discoveries and improvements.

If you can afford the cost, the weave is stable, and your synchronization is high enough, you'll get the implant. It's as simple as that. There won't be any gatekeeping or playing favorites. We don't want this technology to be given to the highest bidder, or to be locked away to create an unfair monopoly. We're in this war together, and we're going to win it together.

Vector got to his feet with a bright smile on his face and started to clap. That was what started it all, with every seated Hunter getting up out of their chairs and giving Quest a standing ovation. Sal noticed that all the students at their table were on their feet too, and he stood up alongside Fabi and joined in with the applause.

Sal was grateful that the focus was placed on the simulation orb, rather than on himself. From Grant and Quest's description, it sounded like Sal had just been a tool in the greater scheme of things. Every Hunter and Hero would be focused on supporting the simulation orb project, rather than trying to steal Sal for themselves. Announcing Perfect as the first weave was an excellent method to garner goodwill, as it would provide a marked improvement to every single person in the room. It didn't prioritize a certain class or power set.

"He's rarely this smooth in the academy announcements. Must be in a good mood," Fabi remarked with a chuckle as she continued to clap. "They really played down your contribution, though. Not sure how I feel about that." She gave Sal a meaningful look, as though she were disappointed on his behalf.

Sal just smiled and shrugged it off. "Safer for me this way. Less people who know about my abilities, the better."

Fabi returned the smile and gave him a playful nudge with her elbow. "Well, I'll consider myself lucky for knowing your little secret."

Thank you all for your support. We're absolutely delighted with the outcome of the research. Now, before we finish up, it would be unfair to talk about all the amazing work that has gone into this project without referencing a certain person.

Quest drew everyone's attention back to himself, and the applause ceased pretty quickly, with everyone curious as to what was coming next.

Sal held his breath, wondering whether Quest was going to try to spin a certain narrative that gave him praise without painting a target onto his back. He couldn't fathom how he'd manage to do it, and hoped he just didn't say anything at all. *Maybe he was going to talk about Upgrade?*

Fabrizia Maccles is going to be the first student at Quest Academy to receive a Skill Implant.

The crowd of Hunters applauded the announcement, likely out of politeness. Some of them knew who Fabi was, but many of the others didn't really care about an unknown Support.

Sal frowned as he looked at Fabi, who raised her arm in thanks to Quest. "It's not an implant, though. It should only be an imprint since it's your actual ability." He wondered whether it was just an error on Quest's part, or whether they were going to try to implant her own ability into her.

Through the incredible work of our Replicator and the simulation orb, we have a perfectly constructed weave that will give Fabrizia the capability to activate up to four different stages of her Crafting ability, depending on her essence output. Better yet, it's her own weave, that has been restructured to be a picture of efficiency. All of this was possible through the simulation orb's refinement.

Fabrizia, as a Savior, will have her existing weave imprinted with the new design…and she will then be receiving an implant of the Perfect skill. Our logic was that the Perfect ability would help her acclimatize to her newly constructed weave, and give her the opportunity to learn, develop, and grow over time.

For those of you who aren't aware of who Fabrizia is, she is the pinnacle of what it means to be a Hero. She came to Quest Academy without having access to an ability. Academically, she's top of the third-years, and has placed first in nearly every category at the evaluations. Even without access to an innate ability, she has proved herself to be an extraordinary Hero. We believe that she deserves this more than anyone else.

I'd ask you to give a round of applause for Fabrizia Maccles, who will undoubtedly go down in history as the pioneer of Skill Weave research.

Sal enthusiastically applauded while Divinity let off a loud whistle from farther down the table. Barry and Blathnaid were both applauding, and even Sakura grinned as she joined in with them. No matter where you looked, there were smiling faces and cheers of encouragement. Sal looked at Fabi to gauge her reaction, and was surprised to see her biting her lip and trembling. "Are you okay?" he asked in concern.

Fabi just nodded quietly. "It's not real yet." She shook her head and gave him a slight smile. "Ask me again after the imprint."

Now, if it was up to me…we'd be doing this in a controlled environment, but this is the Hunter Bureau Gala. Robert can be quite insistent when he wants something, so I'd like to ask Fabrizia to come down to the stage.

Fabi suddenly straightened in shock as she stared at Quest in disbelief. The crowd faltered in their applause before it dawned on them what was happening; the resurgence of cheering came loud and fast, with many of them banging on the tables and chanting Fabi's name. It was the epitome of peer pressure, but Sal was certain that Fabi could rise above it.

Upgrade was out of her seat in a flash, moving swiftly around all the tables and over to where Fabi stood in a stunned silence. "You can say no if you want. You don't have to do this now. Robert apparently strong-armed Quest to make a big song and dance about it, but Quest will shut it down if you're uncomfortable."

Fabi just blinked as she looked at Upgrade. "Now? I could have the ability now?"

Upgrade grinned as she gripped Fabi's shoulders. "Right now. We can go onto to that stage, and you'll leave it with loads of new abilities. Four of your own and a fancy new implant!"

Fabi just nodded before her face went white. "I had like five whiskeys." She looked around at all the people chanting her name, and then at Quest, who stood expectantly on the stage with a warm smile on his face.

"I'd be more worried if Grant had five whiskeys… Look on the bright side—you definitely won't feel any pain." Upgrade laughed as she looked at Fabi carefully. "But are you sober enough to tell me straight if this is something you want?"

Fabi smiled brightly as a tear rolled down her right cheek. "Let's just get it over with."

Upgrade looped Fabi's arm with her own and guided her down the steps—not because Fabi couldn't do it herself, but because the shock was clearly too much for her. Looking back over her shoulder, Upgrade grinned at Sal. "What are you waiting for? They're going to know you're the Replicator sooner or later."

Sal knocked back his whiskey before following Upgrade and Fabi to the center stage.

CHAPTER 42: PROMISES

Sal genuinely wished he had opted for a few more of the whiskeys. Having just the one at his table was doing absolutely nothing for his nerves as he strode behind Upgrade and Fabi up to the center stage. It felt like the entire hall was watching him, and it took everything in his power to maintain the posture Fabi had reminded him of. He was so self-conscious of the fact that he was going up to the stage that he didn't even feel embarrassed about his ridiculous outfit. Thankfully he had opted to leave the cane-sword at the table, which was a small victory at least.

Excellent. I'd like to also welcome to the stage the people who helped make all of this possible. You heard us talking about a first-year Replicator who created the weave with the help of the simulation orb? He's our top Savior from first-year, and one of our most promising Crafters. Salvatore Argento!

Quest spoke like a proud parent as he gestured at Sal walking a step or two behind Fabi and Upgrade. His announcement caused pretty much every person to switch their attention to him from Fabi.

If Sal had been self-conscious before, it was nothing to how he currently felt. It was like the amphitheater fiasco all over again, but this time, instead of the students finding out about his exploits, it was the most powerful Hunters and Heroes the guilds and bureau had to offer.

Joining Fabrizia to the stage is Upgrade, who constructed the simulation orb to Grant's specifications. She was the one who encouraged Salvatore to try to work with the weaves. Without their work, we wouldn't have a solution for Fabrizia today. Please give them a warm welcome to the stage.

The moment Fabi got to center stage, Grant was over in a heartbeat. His voice was no longer amplified as he looked at Upgrade with a panicked expression. "I'm so sorry. We tried to stop Robert but he really put his foot down. Threatened to pull all funding if we didn't give them a showcase here and now." He looked over his shoulder at Quest, giving a smile for the audience. When he turned back, his face was almost sickly with worry. "I'm confident that we can do it, but I feel horrible for springing this on you. Are you okay to go ahead with this?" He was looking at Fabi, a desperate edge to his voice.

"Whoa now, settle down." Upgrade patted Grant on the shoulder. "Fabi is fine…just a little surprised is all. Just give her a bit of space to breathe, and you can do the same." She gave Grant a pointed look. "You'd be a lot more reassuring if you weren't in such a tizzy. Do you have the implanting setup here?"

Grant shook his head and gestured at an area at the back of the stage. "Robert wants us to warp it in."

Upgrade straightened as she stared at him in disbelief. "He wants to teleport highly sensitive equipment? What the fuck is his problem?" She shook her head before glancing over at Quest in surprise. "He's really okay with this?"

"Not at all…nothing like an audience of every fucking guild to set up an implant procedure." Grant fussed as a bright light flashed from behind them.

Sal blinked repeatedly to regain his sight, but it took close to ten seconds for his vision to clear properly. What he eventually saw was one of the Skill Registration machines from when he first arrived at Quest Academy. But just from a quick look, he could tell that it had been heavily modified. They had a bit of time, so he did a rough Appraisal on the machine to see how different it was from the Skill Registration machine.

His ability detected the ridiculously large essence core that took up almost a third of the entire construct. Rather than having a singular hole for the arm to be placed into, a makeshift bed was constructed on the top of the rectangular device. It was only when Sal moved forward that he realized there was a lid that was suspended from a set of hinges on the other side of the bed. *Was it going to be clamped over Fabi's body?*

I'd suggest you all get your drinks orders in because the setup of this will take a little while. We're going to run a few initializing tests to ensure everything is working properly before we proceed. The machines weren't designed to be transported to the middle of a hostile area.

Quest said those last words with a smile on his face, but he intentionally turned to look at Robert point-blank as he finished the sentence.

Upgrade wasted no time in moving over to the implant device. Positioning herself at the back of the machine, she lined up to the center before lifting the lid up with controlled strength. The lid gradually moved with her effort and slowly started to close, encasing the bed area with a soft thud. A suction noise echoed out as the lid sealed itself against the main body of the machine. "Heaviest damn tanning bed you're ever going to lay down in," she joked at Fabi before moving to the interface that was on top of the lid. It had been hidden from view until now, but it was flashing with all sorts of options.

Sal stared at the machine in a mixture of shock and respect. They had somehow created two rectangular cores that were perfectly fitted above and below the bed area. Fabi would be able to lay down on the bed and the core would still take up more space than her body. It was like they were going to sandwich her between two massive essence batteries.

He moved closer to get a better look at the interface that Upgrade was working on. The first thing he noticed was how premium the whole thing looked. It had a metallic body, but the interior was all made from custom brand-new pieces of technology. Just like the simulation orb, there was a whole processing center that Sal couldn't even begin to understand. A part of him had expected something more haphazard, similar to the mountains of cabling with the orb. His reverie was broken the moment he saw Fabi's weave being loaded up on the display.

"Whoa, you've got it loaded onto the main—" Sal looked at the weave more carefully. "That's the wrong weave." He looked at Upgrade in confusion. "That's not the evolutionary one that we worked on." It was one of the earlier weaves that he had submitted to the machine. Specifically, one of the ones he had wanted to delete.

Upgrade looked between the weave and Sal in bewilderment. "This is the preloaded one on the machine. Grant?" She looked over at Grant expectantly, waiting for him to explain himself.

He looked between them with a raised eyebrow. "It's the one with the highest recorded stability and synchronization. The algorithm believes that with time and effort, Fabrizia will be able to access all levels of the weave." He smiled as though it would somehow reassure them both. "It's the best course of action, trust me. In this sort of environment, it's best to go with the surest method of success…and it'll actually work out a little cheaper in terms of core output."

Upgrade tilted her head and looked like she was about to say something unsavory, when she suddenly stopped herself and gave Grant a radiant smile. "Okay, sounds good. How about you help me talk Fabi through the process? She's going to be really nervous about all of this…especially with so many eyes on us.

"Sal, you can finish this up, right? It's already finalized, so just export it with this button when I give you the go-ahead," Upgrade said, pulling Sal's attention to the interface.

It wasn't finalized. Sal immediately read between the lines, and was instantly reminded of how Upgrade had begged him to help Blathnaid. There was no way Upgrade was going to be fine with Fabi having a half-baked weave after everything she had gone through. But Sal was conflicted…this single action would likely remove all of Quest's trust in him in relation to the Skill Master ability. He'd never be allowed to use his ability in Quest Academy if things went wrong here.

Looking at the weave in front of him, he tried to reason with himself that it was good enough, and that it would give Fabi everything she had been looking for. He even tried to justify it with himself that he could rewire it in the future if she hit a wall.

Sal glanced up and locked eyes with Fabi. She was smiling at him, as though telling him that everything was going to be okay. Clenching his fists at his side, he threw away all the agonizing thoughts and focused on what was in front of him. Fabi was going to have a subpar weave because the Hunter Bureau wanted to parade the new technology around. There was no way he'd let that happen, even if it meant he'd be forbidden to use his ability for the rest of his time at Quest Academy.

Without wasting any time, he took off the purple jacket and let it drop to one side. Unbuttoning the sleeves, he rolled them up and looked at Fabi more carefully. He knew her weave inside and out, but this wasn't a time to be complacent. He had a few minutes to rewire her entire weave without making it look obvious to the entirety of the Hunter Bureau and United Guilds Association. Every eye was on them, and Quest's request that they go get drinks had fallen on deaf ears. They were watching every movement intently.

Before Sal started to pull at the weave, he tried going through the other folders to see whether there were other preloaded weaves with the optimal one. Unfortunately, after going through them, he was met with even more mediocrity. Grant had apparently prioritized the weaves that had the highest chance of success, which were only superior by a few percentage points. It shouldn't have mattered, considering he had a stability and synchronization rate of over a hundred percent. *Was their logic that the Perfect ability would somehow improve her ability weave over time? If they were being so damn risk averse, why would they be doing an implant of a weave with a sixty-two percent stabilization?*

Sal was fuming as he reached to his invisible belt, unclipping the visor and securing it over his right eye. When it flashed in recognition, he got to work as fast as he could. The first time he had worked on Fabi's weave, he didn't have the assistance of the tracker. He also didn't have Perfect activated. There was a lot of visual noise in his peripheral vision because of the abundance of terrifyingly powerful Hunters, so Sal had to focus his visor on the task at hand, making sure that all its processing power was aimed at improving Fabi's weave. He already knew instinctively how it needed to be corrected.

Quest's voice echoed in the background, but Sal ignored it as he rearranged the threads on the interface. There was a percentage bar in the top corner of the screen, trying to calculate the stability of the weave, but Sal ignored that too. He restructured the foundation of the weave, and created the necessary space to allow a healthy evolution. Assembly was done in a flash, with Innovate coming next. It was a little jarring trying to use his Skill Master ability on an interface rather than using the cables of the simulation orb, but after a few minutes of working on the screen with his fingers, Perfect kicked in and turned his janky finger swishes into flawless strokes.

By the time he got to Fabricate, the weave was looking really healthy. His visor offered minor suggestions, but Sal wanted to wait until he had Customize added into the weave. That took him another forty seconds, with a lot of looping and frantic tapping of the interface. It was like drawing a picture he had already sketched out a hundred times. He knew the shortcuts to get the whole thing done quickly. When all four of the abilities were represented, Sal tweaked the weave with his own intuition to get it back to the state he had presented it to Quest.

"Fabi's going to be getting in now. Are things done?" Upgrade whispered at him in a strained voice. "I can't really stall them any longer. If you're not happy, we can pull the plug on this and I'll take the blame."

Sal didn't react to her sudden appearance as he remained crouched over the interface. "Give me another two minutes. Do whatever you need to do." He was angry that this was happening, but it wasn't Upgrade's fault. It was the Hunter Bureau, Robert, Quest, and Grant that had made this fucked-up situation happen.

With his visor locked onto the interface, he looked at the weave intently. Deduction, Insight, Analysis, and Perfect were all focused on the single weave, and unsurprisingly, there were suggestions. Skill Master was working through the visor, making all sorts of calculations on rotation flow and the spacing. Sal had to ensure that it was paired to Fabi's internal gates, and thankfully all it took was a glance at Fabi to confirm he had it mapped out correctly.

The tweaks took more than the two minutes he had quoted Upgrade, but he didn't care; he needed it to be done right. Massive loops of space were condensed and pulled closer to the main weave. Sal had originally created too much space to allow room for growth. He reworked the weave against the suggestions his visor showed him, and his intuition told him that each change was an improvement. There was so much more threading available after he made his changes, which Sal assumed would result in more room for growth in time.

"Sorry, Sal, but it's time," Upgrade whispered as she appeared at his side with Fabi.

Sal ignored her as he stared at the interface one last time, double- and triple-checking everything. A small tweak here and there happened with each check, but at the final glance, there was absolutely nothing that he could see wrong with it. He pressed the Finalize option and uploaded the weave for the imprinting process.

"All good on my side." He forced a smile to his face as he wiped the sweat from his brow. "Sorry it took me so long to figure out the new machine." He spoke loud enough that the Hunters in the first row would hear. If he was going to play the part of the incompetent Replicator, then this was the best approach.

Upgrade smiled warmly at him as she opened the lid of the Skill Imprinter. "Thank you, Sal."

Fabi looked at him strangely as she sat on the center of the bed. "We're going to have a very long talk about what just happened, okay?"

"Just trust me," Sal answered with a smile as he stepped back from the stage to stand alongside Grant.

Fabi winked at him as she pulled her dress up from the ground, and lay back on the bed with a smile. "How awkward will it be if this thing kills me in front of everyone?" She looked at Upgrade, laughing. "If you bury me in this dress, I'll haunt you forever."

Upgrade just shook her head as she closed the lid over Fabi's body, leaving only a sliver of her dress visible from the side of the device. With a glance at the interface, she froze on the spot. She stood there for a few moments, staring at the screen until Grant moved forward to escort her away from it.

Sal wasn't going to stand around with his hands in his pockets. There was another phase to all of this, and he wasn't going to let them fuck that up either. To everyone else, it probably looked like Sal was standing numbly and staring off into dead space. In reality, he was pushing his visor to the absolute limits of its processing power. He was trying to map the Perfect weave to Fabi's new profile.

Thank you all so much for your patience. The setup and checks have all been completed, and it's time to start the imprinting. The next time you see Fabrizia, she will have access to the ability she was born with, but never able to activate. You're about to witness the cumulative results of our research. As always, we'd like to extend a massive thank you to the Hunter Bureau for giving us this platform and allowing us to push the boundaries of what these abilities have to offer.

Quest tapped an area of his lapel, ceasing the announcement voice. He moved over to where Sal stood with Upgrade, leaning forward to whisper to them both. "Did you have enough time to fix the weave?"

Sal stared at him for a few moments, not completely registering what was going on. *Quest not only approved of him fixing Fabi's weave, but was encouraging it?* With a smile appearing on his face, he nodded. "It's fixed. Please don't ever do that to me again."

Quest let out a sigh of relief. "Thank you, Salvatore. This is one of the many reasons I don't want the Hunter Bureau anywhere near your guild." He shook his head before muttering darkly, "They were prepared to sacrifice Fabrizia's potential for a cheap morale boost."

Upgrade was still in shock as she looked numbly between Sal and Quest. "We can undo the damage, right? If it all fucks up?"

"It won't," Sal stated resolutely as he smiled at Upgrade. "I promise."

"No offense, Sal…but you have a horrible track record with imprinting machines," Upgrade responded dryly.

CHAPTER 43: SURPRISES

It was the Hunters with Foresight who reacted first. They had clearly been curious as to the results and looked into the future. Shouts of alarm rang out in the crowd as they rushed forward to warn Quest about what was about to happen. The first to get there was Scry, one of the members of the Doom Society. He waved his hands as he bolted toward the center stage, his face a mask of panic.

Sal looked at him curiously, not sure what was happening at first, but a tightness developed in his chest. His breath hitched as he turned his attention toward Fabi. There was nothing wrong with the weave; he was positive of that. A looming sense of dread started gnawing at Sal. *Had he somehow doomed Fabi?* It had to be the machine. He was certain of his own abilities with the weave, so it had to be something else. Doubts hammered on his mind as he took a tentative step forward, not knowing what he could even do if there was something wrong.

"The cores are faulty!" Scry shouted as he pointed at the imprint machine on the stage. "It's going to try to pull the essence from the girl to complete the process!"

Divinity was behind him, her eyes white as she looked at the machine in a panic. "It's not that they're faulty—there's not enough essence stored in them. Whatever is happening needs a massive amount of power, and the machine can't handle it."

Eclipse, the master of the guild bearing her name, blinked into existence on the stage beside Quest. With her right hand, she sent an ethereal whip of light that adhered to the machine. Her left stretched out to the crowd. There was zero hesitation in her movements as she smiled at the assembled Heroes. "Transference link is active. Anybody want to spare some essence for the girl?"

Thunder was over like a shot, his massive frame knocking two tables over as he set himself down on one knee in the center of the room. "Four hundred gates." He raised a hand, which Eclipse latched onto with another thread of light. His actions caused a chunk of the Thunder Guild to follow his lead, to the point that Eclipse couldn't tether enough of them.

It was chaos in the entire hall, with dozens of Hunters getting to their feet and moving closer to the stage. Some of them looked cautious, while others were simply curious. Many of the new arrivals weren't rushing forward to help, but instead looked up to the balcony that housed Robert and the top ten. As though waiting for his verdict on what they should do.

The answer came from the top balcony, not in words, but in the actions of a single Hunter. With her cane gripped in her right hand and the train of her dress secured in her left, Prestige floated down from the balcony above. Her black hair rippled behind her as her body seemed to almost sink in the air, as though she were descending through water.

When Prestige's heels landed on the surface of the imprinting device, her hair fell down naturally at her shoulders. "That won't be necessary, Eclipse." She spoke confidently as she tapped her cane against the metal surface between her heels. "I can handle this with the Catalyst ability. She needs Invention essence, right?" Prestige looked over at Sal with a knowing smile.

Sal could only nod, wondering what sort of shitstorm he had created. His conviction of his weave being perfect had evaporated as he watched Prestige's cane come down to rest on the lid of the machine.

"Then let's give it all the essence it can handle," Prestige remarked with a smile as she activated her ability.

A swirling vortex of glittering light appeared on the stage around Prestige. It was like a swarm of fireflies were sparked into existence, each of them holding a distinct color as they bounced off each other and dispersed. The movement of the swarm started to slowly adapt to go in the same direction, with the colors flickering to match each other. More than that, the sheer number of lights multiplied at a dramatic pace.

Sal turned to look at the Hunters who had offered to help Eclipse. Their own essence was being pulled to fuel the growing swarm around Prestige. Multiple colors of red, green, blue, and yellow were all pulled into the haze that was now giving off a purple hue. A massive flash of white in the center of the swarm highlighted Prestige's smile as the cloud of essence grew more aggressive.

Wanting to understand what was happening, Sal stared at Prestige with his visor. He already knew that her weave was the Catalyst ability, but he wanted to understand how she was using it. Because it was currently in use, he was able to see not only how the weave was mapped out, but how the different rotations worked in her body. The tracker pointed out minor inefficiencies, that were negligible due to the sheer power of her essence gates. Her output of power overwhelmed the weaknesses in the weave. He stored the information in an updated profile for Prestige.

Turning to look at Eclipse, Sal repeated the process of cataloguing her weave. Rochelle had the same Transference ability as the guildmaster. If Sal was able to see how the power worked properly, he'd be able to hopefully create a new solution for Rochelle. His visor flickered as it locked onto Eclipse. Because there were so many Heroes in the background, Sal had to stop it from making partial profiles for all of them. In just the turn of his head, he already had six new partial records for people he hadn't even registered in his vision.

Strangely enough, rather than documenting the Transference weave for Rochelle…the visor started to update an existing file. It was much slower than when he had looked at Prestige's weave, and when it popped up in front of Sal, he was reminded of the time he had sat with Rochelle in the canteen. Her essence flow rework—it was being updated with Eclipse as an evolution of the same ability.

Transference (R:8) Essence Structure and Calibration Method is being updated…

Transference (R:20) Essence Structure and Calibration Method has been recorded.

Transference (R:1) Essence Fortification and Enhancement Method has been recorded.

Transference (R:10) Essence Fortification and Enhancement Method has been recorded.

Would you like to initiate Essence Remapping?
Template to Use: Essence Fortification and Enhancement Method
Profile: Salvatore Argento (Incompatible)
Chance of Successful Remap: 14%
Estimated Completion: 3 days, 18 hours, 13 minutes, 42 seconds
Ability Weaves
Skill Master Grade Improvement: (9) - 12
Mythcrafter Grade Improvement: (15) - 16
Perfect Grade Improvement: (25) - No Improvement
Essence Gates: (60) - No Improvement
Essence Absorption Rate: (62%) 86.2%
Essence Control: (98%) - 100%
Essence Refinement: (72%) - 85.1%
Essence Calibration: (94%) - 97.3%
Essence Fortification: (0%) - 20%

Sal refused the remapping process. To his surprise, while he was busy reading the information, the visor hadn't stopped with the profiling of Eclipse. Her weave was dramatically more powerful than Rochelle's, and the fact that her essence circulation was so powerful told him that she was probably one of the best essence specialist Hunters in the entire bureau. Sal turned his attention to where Prestige was still standing on the machine that contained Fabi. There was no doubt in his mind that Prestige was the pinnacle of essence refinement.

In the minute that he had been looking away, Prestige had managed to create a veritable maelstrom of essence that weaved around her. She still didn't look satisfied with the amount as she manipulated the atmospheric essence into a condensed blanket of purple light.

Robert appeared in a puff of black smoke beside Quest and started pointing at the machine and asking him questions. He didn't look annoyed, but rather curious as to what was happening.

Sal couldn't hear them over the shouts of the Hunters in the room. Many were asking how they could help, while others asked for updates on what was going on. Prestige seemingly didn't hear them or was ignoring them.

Sal wondered whether he should tell Robert that he had altered the weave. It was a hard thing to factor in, because he knew that the weave was good. Hell, he just looked at Eclipse's weave and managed to create an entire upgrade schematic for his essence channels. His visor and his Skill Master ability were clearly up to the task. Divinity had said it herself that the essence was insufficient. She didn't say anything about the weave being tampered with.

When Sal looked in her direction, for some sort of guidance, their eyes met. Rather than looking anxious or nervous, there was a smile on her face. *Did that mean that this was something that needed to happen?*

A thundering crack echoed out from the stage, and Sal's head whipped around to see a massive fissure appearing on the lid of the imprinting machine. His visor started to give him all sorts of error reports that the machine wasn't going to make it through Prestige's onslaught of essence.

Sal looked at the machine, powerless to do anything. Upgrade was holding one side of the lid, while Doc Ameye was on the other side. They were shouting at each other, with Doc Ameye wanting to pull Fabi out, and Upgrade telling him to wait. Their words were drowned out by the constant barrage of essence that moved in the air like a swarm of fireflies.

A flicker of annoyance crossed Prestige's face as she gripped the cane tighter in her hand. "Just how much essence does she need?" she asked in almost wonder before sending the entire wave of purple essence into the machine. The swirling blanket of light was sucked straight into the cracks to fuel the custom cores. She frowned, as though she had just made some quick calculation. With a glance into the crowd, she shouted a single name.

"Andrew!"

All the Hunters bolted to the side to clear the way as one man leapt high into the air. His body floated upward in an arc, as both of his arms were imbued with an ethereal green glow. Andrew's hands shot out and created an intricate rune of glowing light that suspended in the air in front of him. Another rune was created in seconds, followed by another, all layered on top of one another. Then, with a practiced movement, he brought his right hand back, clenched his fist, and punched the layer of runes as hard as he could.

A flash of light erupted throughout the room, creating a blindingly bright tunnel that led from Andrew's position all the way down to where Prestige stood.

Sal's panic abated the moment he heard Prestige's musical laughter over the sound of the chaos.

"Incredible, Andrew! You've gotten even stronger. Keep buffing me, and we'll be able to save this girl before the machine explodes." Prestige's voice called out before she let out a groan of annoyance. "If there are any Heroes with the Repair ability, now would be a very good time to get onto this stage!"

"It's SIGILS!" Andrew shouted back at her. "You have to use my Hero name!" He drew his fist back again and launched it forcibly at a set of ten new runes that were layered in front of him. The effect was both immediate and dramatic as the tunnel of blinding light redoubled and caused even Prestige to take a knee.

Andrew didn't waste time in creating new runes of light. His hands, still glowing otherworldly green, moved swiftly in the air, forming new markings that rotated around his body. Pulling his arms together, it looked like he was struggling to make his palms meet, with the runes surrounding him vibrating in protest. With a laugh-like roar, Andrew's hands slapped together in front of him, causing an explosion that rocketed around the whole hall.

Sal's breath caught in his throat as a sudden surge welled up within him. He felt near invincible, like he could easily take on another obsidian hulker. His visor was going crazy trying to deduce what was going on, but the conclusion that Sal got was from Prestige.

"Andrew has done his part. Anyone with the Repair ability needs to come onto this stage immediately!" Prestige shouted. "The machine isn't going to last long enough to complete whatever it's doing. We need someone to repair it."

Sal watched in horror as the machine continued cracking along the lid. It wasn't built to withstand the force of so much essence being pumped into it. He was reminded of what happened at his own Skill Registration. If Upgrade hadn't pulled him out of the machine, then he likely would have lost his arm. It was no longer a case of the weave failing or succeeding. Fabi's entire body was trapped in the machine, and she was in danger.

Sal rushed forward, pulling his mother's weave into his mind and activating it with Skill Master. All his instincts told him that he needed to get to the machine and use Restoration before it broke down. He needed to make sure Fabi was safe.

When his foot reached the first layer of barriers, a surge of essence erupted through his body. It was as though he had just run through a wall of searing flame. His skin tingled like pins and needles were being stabbed into every inch of his body. It took all he had just to continue breathing, and Sal pushed forward to the next layer of barrier.

Those pins and needles were now made of liquid flame, and Sal wanted nothing more than to curl up into a ball and die. All the faux bravado he had gained with Andrew's runes had evaporated, and all that was left was a maelstrom of essence that ripped away at him. His gates were already maxed out, so there was nowhere for the excess essence to travel. With a grunt of effort, he threw himself forward under the weight of the dense essence and managed to grasp the side of the machine with both hands.

Sal let go of Perfect as he activated Restoration and threw everything he had at it. The fierce concentration required to keep the weave stable distracted him from the excruciating pain on the side of his face. Blinking rapidly, Sal couldn't see with his right eye; he realized his mistake instantly. He had brought an evolutionary visor into a condensed barrier of Invention essence—it was evolving while latched to his face. The searing heat split his cheek, cauterizing the wound instantly, but spreading the burns across his face. His ear was practically aflame, with his matted hair burning freely. Gritting his teeth, Sal couldn't even find the strength to rip the visor off his face. All he could do was keep his hands on the lid of the imprint machine. He'd happily trade an eye to save a life.

Sal opened his left eye and watched through tears as the machine started to repair itself. Despite the swell of power he was putting into it, it wasn't enough. Restoration in its highest form wasn't enough to offset the wave of essence threatening to break the machine. Sal looked up at Prestige with his one good eye, hoping she had a plan to protect Fabi.

She wasn't looking at him, though, but someone behind him. It was one of the rare occasions that Prestige looked genuinely surprised.

CHAPTER 44: DISCOVERY

Sal flinched as the visor was carefully pulled from his face and dropped to the ground. He tried to see who it was through the essence maelstrom, but it was all he could do to continue blinking through the pain. A palm pressed against the wounds on his face and he could feel…something happening. Essence coursed through his face, but it was different from Healing. He knew what that felt like, and this was very different. The pain evaporated gradually as he slowly opened his eyes to see his savior.

"Bold move, using that sort of essence in this environment." Prestige spoke quietly, her entire attention focused on Sophia Argento.

Sal looked at his mother in a panic. "What are you doing here? You need to get out of the barrier!" He pulled her palm from his face in shock, not even registering what had happened. If his mother was subjected to all this essence, then she was going to be in unbearable pain as her essence gates opened. He never wanted her to experience that sort of agony.

Sophia gave him a reassuring smile as she placed her right palm on the lid of the machine. "I'm just here to save Fabrizia." She gave Prestige a meaningful look. "Nothing more than that. You called for Repair, right? Restoration works just as well."

Prestige nodded curtly then smiled. She turned to look at Sal and raised her cane in one hand. "Mr. Argento, I think it might be time to teach you that breathing method to give you access to some more gates."

Sophia's expression darkened. "We're here for Fabrizia, Elaine. Just do your part and create some void essence."

Sal blinked as he looked between his mother and Prestige. "That's not one of the essence categories though? What are you talking about?"

"Void essence!" Doc Ameye laughed as his hands sparked on the other side of the lid. "What are they even teaching you in Quest Academy? It's integral for subspace Crafting and Reversion abilities. You can refine down void metal to get a taste of it."

Upgrade slapped her palms down on the lid and looked at Doc Ameye with wide eyes. "Are you trying to improve the damn machine while we're trying to save her?"

Doc Ameye shrugged. "What better time than now? You won't let me take her out of it, and I didn't build this thing. Only way I know she'll be safe is if I improve it." He jutted his chin over to the back of the stage. "Make yourself useful and carry over the materials I warp in."

Sophia looked at Doc Ameye cooly. "We need to be aligned on this. I'm going to revert the machine to its optimal state. I can't do that if you're upgrading it."

Doc Ameye gave her a sideways glance. "Reversion, not Restoration?" He paused for a few moments before his eyes widened. "Void essence and Reversion…you've got to be kidding me."

"Work with me on this, not against me. There's a girl's life at risk." Sophia took her left palm from Sal's face and placed it against her right. "If we go the other way, I'll need even more essence than this. How confident are you in your upgrades?"

Doc Ameye's face brightened. "Holy shit…this is really happening." He looked at the machine and shook his head a few times, as though making a whole set of new calculations. "I'm extremely confident. I'll need five minutes from when the materials are brought in."

Sal stood awkwardly, looking at his mother and Doc Ameye. "Can I help?"

Doc Ameye shook his head as he turned to speak quickly with Upgrade.

Prestige looked at Sophia with a knowing smile. "He could help if he Replicated your weave."

"Absolutely not," Sophia snapped with a glare aimed at Prestige. "Stop treating this like a game. Why do you desperately want him to open more gates? What's your angle here?" All while she spoke, her hands started to spark and send tendrils of electricity across the surface of the machine lid.

Sal couldn't understand what was happening. His mother was a Restorer. He knew she was a Restorer and had seen her weave countless times when he was younger. Just to prove it to himself, he looked at her weave and saw exactly what he expected. Restoration was sitting there in her chest, active and waiting to be utilized. It was practically lit up and…

Sal froze as he stared at his mother. If it hadn't been for the research he had been doing with Skill Master, he would have missed it. His mother's gates practically glittered all over her body. Far too many to count, but well above what he had expected. It was a category that he couldn't figure out when he tried adapting it in the private lab. *Body Manipulation.*

His mother was a Body Manipulator…and had a Restoration weave? It didn't make sense, no matter how many ways he looked at it. He stared at her in shock, and he watched numbly as her weave shifted into an entirely new shape, adapting to the multiple essence gates around her body. It moved differently than Replication, because rather than a weave moving, she was moving the gates to contort her existing weave into a different shape.

Sophia's smile faded as she looked at Sal. "I promise we'll talk about this later. Right now, I need you to go to where your father is standing, okay? We'll take care of this."

"Oh, I haven't seen this sort of output from you in years. Should we expect you to come back to the Hunter Bureau?" Prestige asked, smiling as she watched Sophia's hands intently. "I could do with a bit of competition, if I'm honest."

"Shut up, Elaine," Sophia snapped at Prestige, before looking at Sal. "Please, just go to where your father is. I'll make sure Fabi is safe. You can trust me."

Sal had no idea how to process what he was seeing and hearing. He was numb, both physically and emotionally. He loved his parents and knew they would never do anything to put him into danger, but this…was one hell of a secret to keep from him. All those years of feeling like he was a danger to everyone around him…because his ability was so powerful, all of it was instilled into him by his parents. His cautious approach, the overthinking…all of it stemmed from how he was raised. And he finally understood why his mother was so scared of him using his ability.

She was able to create weaves, too.

Prestige, a Hunter in the top ten of the entire bureau, respected his mother. Sophia had even stepped up to the stage when many Heroes stood by and watched. Now, she was willing to risk a secret she kept for her entire life, just to save Fabi.

Sal brought his hand up to his face and touched the completely healed skin around his eye. *No, she had come up to the stage to protect him.* All those thoughts swirled in Sal's head as he watched his mother barking instructions to Doc Ameye and Upgrade. He didn't know what they were going to attempt to do, but he wanted to help her. If she was ready to show the world that she was a Hero, then he could do the same.

Looking up at Prestige, Sal was a little surprised to see that she stared at him, smiling.

"I told you that you were definitely her son. What are you going to do, Mr. Argento?" Prestige asked carefully.

"Help me open my essence gates," Sal answered resolutely as he stared at his mother's back. If it was pain, he could handle it. He wanted to be strong enough that she wouldn't need to lie to him anymore. "I want to help her."

Prestige gave him a warm smile as she brought her voice down to a whisper. "The breathing method is a little bit of a misnomer…there's no real meditative way to build up your gates beyond what you've been born with." She directed the butt of the cane in his direction. "Grab on to this, and try to continue breathing. That's the method."

Sal looked around himself and was surprised to see that he couldn't see through the barrier. The essence had condensed into a blanket so much that it obscured everything within the space.

Prestige tapped the cane against his chest. "Don't worry. I've been holding back on sending waves of essence into the machine. Fabrizia is stable and will emerge from it like a butterfly escaping the cocoon. I'll just need to give your mother enough void essence to do her part." She looked past Sal, with the smile appearing again. "You're safe from prying eyes, too."

"Why are you helping me to this extent?" Sal asked Prestige as he gripped the cane in his fist and stepped forward so that his chest was pressed against it.

Prestige raised an eyebrow. "I could tell you that I just want to repay an old debt to your mother, but that would be a lie." She chuckled as she looked over to where Sophia stood. "It's great seeing her come out of hiding, but that isn't enough of a reason, either." Prestige's piercing gaze moved back to Sal. "The stronger you become, the better chance Gallant has of recovering. Every Seer I've met with tells me that Gallant's chance of a good life is tied to your survival…so, I'm going to do everything in my power to make that a reality."

Prestige's hands started to glow. "This will hurt like a bitch, Salvatore Argento. Resolve yourself and come out of it stronger. The more essence gates you possess, the greater potential your abilities have to grow. Take slow and shallow breaths, but most importantly…try not to scream. We can't have any of the Hunters coming through the barrier and seeing this."

"What the fuck are you doing, Elaine?" Sophia shouted as she turned to see Prestige's cane pressed against Sal's chest. She looked like she wanted to move over to them, but she couldn't lift her hands from the lid of the machine.

Doc Ameye glared at her in disbelief. "The moment you lift those hands, she's dead. Keep your head in the game!"

Prestige smiled back at Sophia. "I'm only doing what Salvatore asked of me. Why would your son want to be stronger in this instance? Maybe you should be asking yourself."

Doc Ameye shouted at Sophia to get her attention. "The essence is condensing to a ridiculous degree. It's not being wasted, but rather being refined at an ungodly speed. Fabi is absorbing not just the atmospheric essence, but the material essence of the machine. Leave Prestige to handle the atmospheric, while we keep this machine from disintegrating."

Upgrade just stared at him in disbelief. "That's far too much essence! There's no way she's able to absorb that much."

"If it's an ability like Fabricate, it's likely trying to stockpile a lifetime's worth of essence accumulation to activate. You can't just turn a key and expect it to work—her body is creating the reserves it thinks the ability needs," Doc Ameye snapped back. "She's skipping an entire lifetime of natural evolution! Just how aspirational was this damned weave?"

"Probably Mythic grade," Upgrade responded flatly as she jutted her head in Sal's direction. "He doesn't do things in half-measures."

"By the gods…" Doc Ameye whispered as he looked at the machine in disbelief. "Materials aren't going to cut it. Protocol, warp in the commander cores!" He practically roared the last part.

"Andrew, if you can hear me…give me all that you've got! We're so close!" Prestige thundered from inside the bubble of essence. She raised her left hand aloft as though it would conduct the essence from the environment. Her right hand held the cane tightly. "Good luck, Salvatore."

A thunderous roar came from outside the barrier as Prestige's entire body glowed magnificently. Her overcoat rippled behind her and her hair rose high.

Just as Sal was about to speak, a surge of essence crashed through his chest to the point that he was certain there was a gaping hole where his torso should have been. Everything he had experienced with Vanessa's Body Manipulation was child's play compared to this. His eyes glazed over as he lost the ability to breathe.

"Salvatore, withstand it. We have an after-party to get to after this fiasco. You better not fall unconscious!" Sophia shouted at him with a forced laugh. It was obvious she just wanted to keep him conscious.

Only his mother's voice gave him a sense that he still had a pulse. She was his anchor, and the grip he held on Prestige's cane was the only thing keeping him upright. A wry smile crossed his face, before his eyes shot open in shock.

In devastating sequence, each of his gates started to explode. A single essence gate shattering should have been enough to put him into a state of paralysis, but sixty…one after another…made him want to die. Tears flowed down his cheeks unabashedly. The only silver lining to the experience was that he couldn't hear the bickering of the Crafters around the machine.

"Excellent work, Salvatore. You're doing extraordinary…I need you to try to hold off on absorbing essence into the fragments. I just need a moment," Prestige encouraged him as she lifted her free hand into the air, smiling.

Even in Sal's hollow state, he was able to see the swirling blanket of colors around them change. It felt strange, but familiar.

"Now, Sal, this essence is just for you. Replication essence, custom-made just for your gates," Prestige instructed him. "Take it into the fragments and let them gradually reform."

Sal was in a complete haze. He tried to look within himself, but it was so hard to maintain concentration. Everything was blurry and chaotic, but he managed to somehow see a weave in front of him. *It was his own...but it was in the shape of the Restoration weave?*

With his mind, he sluggishly waved it away and brought back the weave he had been keeping active for the last few months. Perfect. It would know what to do. Sal wanted to laugh at the delirious state he had fallen into, but the barrage of exploding gates made it hard to focus on anything other than misery. He couldn't push any essence into the weave with exploded cores, so Perfect just floated there in front of him. With the gates that were last in the line of fire, Sal tapped into their sliver of power and tried to activate Perfect. He doubted it would have made much of a difference, but it was all he could do to try.

Explosive.

It was the only way Sal could describe what happened in his own body. Perfect was active for barely half a second before his first gates were stabilized. Sal frowned as he tried to determine what he just saw. It was clearly a single gate, but Perfect was treating it like four gates. When Prestige had said double, he had assumed that his new maximum count of gates would be a hundred and twenty. If the first gate was split into four parts...

"You're eventually going to have two hundred and forty gates." Prestige chuckled at the expression of disbelief on Sal's face. "You're doing a remarkable job of staying conscious. I can already sense the new gates forming with the Replication essence."

Sal gritted his teeth and blinked through the pain as his essence gates fragmented and healed immediately. With Vanessa, most of the pain was derived from his essence being sucked away from every part of his body...but in this case, there was an ocean of essence waiting for him to utilize. His internal state was constantly reforming, and massive surges of power welled up within him.

Perfect allocated the excess essence to his weaves, and the threads of Skill Master grew thicker and more robust. *Was that why Prestige was giving him Replication essence? She wanted his Skill Master ability to grow stronger?*

As he crossed the threshold of a hundred essence gates, Sal felt incredible. All his original gates had been shattered, but with every passing second, a fragment was converted into an independent gate and forged with Replication essence.

"Looks like we're about to finish up," Prestige remarked as she glanced behind her at the Crafters.

Sal blinked through tears and saw Doc Ameye in a completely different light. Both of his arms were bathed in a golden light, his spectacles were shattered, and his hat had long since blown away. His white beard fluttered in the storm of essence as he channeled the commander cores directly into the imprinting machine.

Upgrade stood behind him with both of her hands on his back, a fierce determination on her face.

Sophia had both of her hands on the lid of the machine, her own hair flowing like she, too, was at the center of the storm. Where Doc Ameye emitted a golden light from his arms, Sal's mother was the inverse, with black lightning shooting out from her palms and restructuring the entire machine. It warped and changed shape countless times, as though struggling to find the optimal state.

If Sal wasn't already breathless from the ordeal of his gates shattering, he would have lost all remaining air at the sight of his mother forcing the machine to reconstruct itself under the waves of essence channeled by Doc Ameye.

"And…here we go!" Prestige announced as she brought her cane up high into the air before slamming the butt of it straight down on the center of the lid. The surrounding storm of essence converged on her cane and funneled straight down into the machine, seeping into every crack, causing Fabi's enclosure to crackle and shift with the pressure.

Doc Ameye staggered backward with his hands raised in front of him, squinting through the remains of his shattered glasses as he inspected the machine.

Sophia pushed herself from the lid and let her shoulders slump in exhaustion. She smiled at Sal as she walked over to embrace him. "I'm sorry, Salvatore."

Sal didn't hesitate as he wrapped his arms around his mother. "Is Fabi going to be okay?" He looked over his mother's shoulder to where the machine vibrated on the stage floor. He had a thousand questions for his mother, but none of them were as important as Fabi's safety.

"More than okay." Prestige answered for Sophia as she smiled down at the lid she was standing on. "I think we may have gone a little overboard…"

Doc Ameye sighed as he placed his hand on the machine. "How long before she wakes up?"

Prestige floated gracefully to the ground as she ruffled her wild mane of hair to get situated properly. "A couple of minutes at best. I'm sure she was aware something happened throughout the process, but I don't think it would be wise to scare her when she emerges. There's no telling what way her abilities will manifest." She stumbled slightly against her cane before catching herself with a sharp intake of breath. "How many cores did you go through?"

Doc Ameye glanced at the area beside him. "Eight in total. A single one can power my train for a week, and she went through them like they were nothing."

Upgrade let out an aggravated sigh as she emerged from behind Doc Ameye. "Screw the cores. Let's get her out of this damned casket thing." She looked up at everyone and shook her head. "You're going to scare her if you crowd around like that, looking all horrified. Get back and give her some space."

Prestige nodded as she moved away from the machine, gesturing with her cane for the others to follow suit. With her free hand, she raised her fingers to her lips and let out a shrill whistle. "Andrew! You can stop the barrier now."

A half second later, the hall came back into view, revealing a very different scene than before.

Robert stood in a full suit of armor with his arms crossed. Behind him was Quest and Grant, with Maurice Maccles looking positively panicked at their side.

Practically all the Eclipse and Thunder guildmembers were on high alert, with their Defense classes front and center, ready to protect from whatever came out.

On the other side of the stage, the Reavers were ready with Villa at the front, daggers in hand.

It wasn't the warm welcome that Sal had hoped for. The merriment and revelry of before had evaporated into a tense environment of anxiety and uncertainty.

"Status report," Robert asked of Prestige as he stepped forward onto the stage to examine the machine carefully.

Prestige stood up straight, and positioned her cane between her feet. "As the Seer said, the imprinting device wasn't able to handle the essence required, so Doc Ameye upgraded it to handle more. Sophia Argento worked on Restoration of the device with Salvatore Argento. Upgrade assisted Doc Ameye, while I pulled essence from the Heroes to make up the difference."

Robert raised an eyebrow as he looked over at Sophia. "Restoration?" It was clear that he didn't believe what he was hearing.

Sophia stared right back. "Restoration."

"With your current state, it was reckless of you to risk your life going into that environment." Robert spoke more for the benefit of the crowd. "But I thank you for your bravery in stepping up to help the girl."

"Her name is Fabrizia," Sophia answered curtly. Her eyes cast around the room, where all the Hunters were watching her. With a resigned sigh, she smiled warmly as she put a hand on Sal's shoulder. "What sort of parent would I be if I couldn't follow my own son's example?"

Robert smiled as he brought his hands together to applaud the decision. "An excellent point. The Argento Auction House really stepped up today." He turned to look at the other Hunters, the smile still fixed to his face. "Give them a round of applause. We've just witnessed an extraordinary act of Heroism!" He clapped even louder as the others joined in. "And for Fabrizia…doesn't she deserve a Hero's welcome!"

The Hunters moved out of their readied stances and looked at their guildmasters and officers in confusion. A quick consensus was to follow along with whatever Robert was doing, so it didn't take long for the hall to break into a halfhearted applause, led by the president of the Hunter Bureau.

Upgrade ignored the proceedings as she pried open the lid of Fabi's cocoon.

Sal wanted to move over to help, but his mother kept her grip on his arm. When he looked at her in confusion, she just shook her head. "There's a good chance that the essence destroyed her dress, so better leave it to Upgrade for now." She squeezed his arm reassuringly. "You were so brave to run forward like that to help your friend…but I just wish you took a little better care of yourself."

Sal smiled down at his mother. "I was half hoping for an argument or a lecture."

Sophia grinned up at him. "Nah, I'd lose that fight. I only pick the ones I can win…you should know that."

"Are we going to talk about it though?" Sal asked cautiously, trying to keep his voice down while looking around to see whether anyone was paying attention to them.

"Of course," Sophia answered as she finally let go of his arm. "All that you need to know right now is that I love you. We'll talk about it properly when we're home, I promise."

"And Dad knew, too?" Sal asked quietly, knowing the answer already, but wanting to hear it from her.

Sophia didn't answer immediately as she looked beyond Sal. "You can probably ask him yourself."

Sal turned to look, but before he could so much as brace himself for the impact, his father wrapped him in a bear hug and held him tightly. No matter what feelings of betrayal Sal felt from the lies, he couldn't help but feel reassured that their love for him was real. He brought his hands up to hold his father's back and tightened the embrace.

"Are you okay?" Petro stepped back from the embrace and looked at Sal carefully, as though checking for injuries. His hand moved to Sal's face where the burns once were.

"I'm good, I promise." Sal cupped his father's hand on his face. "Who knew that Restoration worked on wounds?" He smiled at his father's conflicted expression.

Petro sighed as he moved his hands to grip Sal's shoulders. "We're going to have a very long chat about all of this. Right now, we need to focus on damage control." He looked past Sal to where Sophia stood. Whatever signal she gave him was clearly reassuring, as Petro sighed in relief. "Good…that could have been problematic.

"Are you okay to put on a game face until we get back to the auction house?" Petro asked Sal seriously.

"Fine by me." Sal smiled, and he genuinely meant it. He knew that he should be feeling confused or betrayed, but there was an excitement building in him. It was hard to explain, but the moment he saw his mother with an ability similar to his own, he felt a sense of belonging that he hadn't experienced before.

"I don't think I'll be much of a dancing partner tonight, Petro," Sophia admitted from beside Sal as she moved closer to join them. "I'm sure you're devastated." Her smile was warm as she squeezed both of their arms. "Should we just cancel the after-party and head home?"

"Nope," Sal said as he looked at their surprised faces. "Robert still owes me a reward, and I want to see that Fabi is okay."

"And you promised me a dance," Fabi spoke with a laugh. "You're not going anywhere, mister."

Sal whirled around in shock to see Fabi standing beside Upgrade. The latter was holding up the former as they slowly made their way over to them. Maurice was being held back by Quest, clearly for his own safety. There was no way to know if she was going to be a danger to the other Hunters. Robert had already stepped forward to verify for himself.

Fabi's bright smile was infectious as she placed a hand on her chest. "I don't know how to describe it…but I can feel it. Dancing lights whenever I look around, seeing how it can all be molded. It's simply breathtaking!"

"You can see essence?" Prestige asked incredulously as she stared at Fabi in shock.

Fabi was about to answer when her face contorted slightly. In a flash, her legs gave out and she stumbled forward. Before Upgrade could catch her, the floor of the stage shot up in a malformed curve to catch her. Tendrils of cold white marble coiled around her like snakes to prop her up.

Upgrade fell back in surprise, staring at the construct that had appeared in the blink of an eye. "What the fuck is that?"

Fabi looked down at the marble that nestled against her waist, holding her upright. Her hand slid across the surface of it, causing it to melt away and give her room to continue moving forward. The marble, once she had moved forward, froze into a solidified shape.

Sal was stupefied. There was no concentration required, or planning…she had unconsciously caused the floor to transform into a shape that she needed in a split second.

Fabi grinned as she placed a hand on the marble structure in wonder. "Well, that's new."

CHAPTER 45: DEBRIEF

As the massive double doors closed behind Robert, he let out an exasperated sigh. Raising his fingers to stop anyone from speaking, he looked up toward one of the balconies in the reception area. His brow furrowed as he stared at the space for a few moments. Finally, he blinked and looked at the assembled group who had occupied the center stage of the main hall.

"Sorry about that. You can never be too careful when Trickster is in attendance." Robert spoke with a sigh as he gestured for them to move over to the main bar area. The staff had already vacated the area by his instruction, so he took it upon himself to move behind the bar, pulling at bottles and glasses. "We've got quite a situation on our hands…but no need to rush things. Things were getting a little tense in there, and I thought we could all do with a breather to get to the bottom of this."

Sal cautiously followed his father's lead of taking a seat at the bar. It was only when his mother sat on the other side of his father that he wondered whether his mother was avoiding him.

"We're going to have to stop meeting like this." Fabi laughed as she took the vacant seat beside Sal. Her eyes practically sparkled as she sat excitedly, with both hands tapping the bar counter in front of her. "Why is everyone so glum?"

Robert smiled as he placed a bottle of whiskey down in front of Petro, with a few glasses. "That's a very good question…would you like a vague or nuanced answer?"

Sophia reached out and grabbed one of the free glasses, while Petro was already twisting the cap off the whiskey. He stared at Robert quietly, his All Sight monocle pocketed since they entered the space.

Upgrade and Doc Ameye sat on the other side of the bar, leaving Robert in the center between them all. As though he wasn't trying to pick sides, Grant sat to the smaller side of the bar, sitting with a very confused Maurice Maccles. Prestige decided to remain standing off to one side, as though she wasn't in the mood for any of this.

Robert placed glasses and an array of bottles down in front of everyone seated before leaning heavily on the bar, looking directly at Fabi.

"I owe you an apology, Miss Maccles." He gave her a tired smile as he planted the bottle back on the counter and lifted the glass to his lips. In a swift movement, he knocked the drink back and let out a satisfied sigh. "The nuanced answer in all of this…was that I was worried about the Skill Implanting technology. I gave Grant and Quest a serious ultimatum, in the hopes that they would give you the bare minimum that was possible."

Fabi stared at Robert in shock. "Why were you worried about it? Was there something wrong with it?" She looked around the group to see whether there was something she was missing, but all she found were confused faces aimed at Robert.

Robert stretched his index finger out from his whiskey tumbler and pointed directly upward. "We have an entire society floating over our heads, waiting for an opportunity to rip power away from us. They would love nothing more than for us to provide a key. That's what I feared with Skill Implanting. If they could empower themselves and skip the natural evolution we've endured, they'd destroy us from within."

Robert moved his hand to point at the double doors they had just exited from. "As much as I'd love to say that I trust every person in that room to be faithful to our cause, the Bastion families are a parasite that has spread its influence far and wide."

He looked at Quest meaningfully. "How many of the second-year Saviors are actually on our side?"

Fabi blinked in shock. "There's no way that they'd be swayed in Quest Academy!" She looked at Sal, as though he would back her up.

Robert smiled as he nudged the bottle toward Sal. "Go on, tell her how you managed to uncover the Bastion plot at Quest Academy. You and Miss Khan proved quite capable in helping us root out those issues."

He glanced over to where Quest sat. "I'm not bringing this up to twist a knife. You're doing a sufficient job at the academy. The Doom Council have told me to back off on interfering too much, but I think we've managed to help the first-years get back on track."

Quest reached out and took one of the glasses, giving Robert a curt nod. "Thanks for the vote of confidence. Would you like to get to the point of why you've asked us out here?"

Robert smiled as he shook his head. "I wanted to ensure that you all understand the position that you've put me in. We're going to have to find a spin for this whole debacle, one that doesn't spiral out of control. The story we decide on now is what I will announce to the Hunters and Heroes in that room. It is the story that all of you will back up."

"Cores were fucked. We un-fucked them," Upgrade suggested lamely, which resulted in a laugh from Robert.

"Ah, but that doesn't do much for our main agenda. We need to dissuade guilds from attempting to build their own Skill Implant machine. If it's as simple as getting some high-quality cores, then half of them out there will try to imitate it." Robert shook his head as he tapped the countertop. "We need to give them an angle where they won't look at Mr. Argento, or try to kidnap either you or Grant to recreate this for them."

"Let them try." Upgrade started to laugh before her smile vanished abruptly.

Robert's stare had that effect.

Petro rotated his whiskey glass in circular motions on the granite counter. He looked at Robert carefully before speaking. "Put Prestige on recovery leave, citing that the essence required for the activation of the machine was far too vast for her to handle." He pointed across the bar. "Doc Ameye can quote the most expensive materials that were needed, which should dissuade people from trying to replicate it."

Finally, he placed his hand on Sal's shoulder. "Salvatore's weave was insufficient for the job, and it caused massive problems that could have cost Fabrizia her life. It was only due to Prestige, with Sigil's assistance, who managed to course-correct this whole thing…making the outcome a costly fluke that would be impossible to replicate."

Fabi looked frustrated by what was being said. She looked at her father with an eyebrow raised. "Before you all start making up a series of events, could someone tell me what actually happened? I have a right to know."

Robert nodded and gestured at Prestige to give the report.

Prestige stood exactly where she was and looked at Sal. "I can explain the damage control, but not the inciting incident. I would need to hear from Mr. Argento on that part before I could continue." Her tone was professional, but there was a hint of a smile on her face.

Robert nodded and waved his hand in a circular motion. "Yes, okay…Salvatore. Would you mind enlightening us as to what caused all of this?"

Sal hesitated for a moment, which wasn't what Robert was waiting for. The president of the Hunter Bureau reached a hand across at lightning speed, but not to attack. It just rested on Sal's hand, before giving it a reassuring pat.

"There's no reprimand here. This isn't a cloak-and-dagger exercise where we're trying to suss out who to blame. I know everything about you, and your family. Just be as honest as possible." Robert's casual tone sounded a little forced, as though he were frustrated.

Sal nodded. "I understand." He straightened his back and looked Robert dead in the eye. If he was going to be interrogated like this, he might as well have a bit of pride in his work. "I created a new Skill Weave for Fabi. The one I constructed would give her access to all the ability evolutions of her innate ability." Sal gestured over to where Grant sat. "When I saw the interface with the proposed weave, it was nowhere near the efficacy of the one I had designed for Fabi. I made a judgment call to correct it, as I didn't want her to have her potential capped."

Robert shook his head. "If you corrected it, then it shouldn't have had such a dramatic effect like what we saw. There was something else that happened."

Sal nodded again. "I didn't revert it to the version I created before. I corrected it with the knowledge, equipment, and abilities I had at my disposal. My tracker uses Analysis, Insight, and Deduction. Coupled with Skill Master and the Perfect weave that was being kept active, I was able to reconstruct Fabi's weave in a way that would gradually grow with her over time."

Sal unconsciously reached for the tracker on his belt, but didn't find it there. His mother had pulled it off him, and he felt a pang of dread as he realized it could be laying on the center stage. Robert was looking at him strangely, so Sal tried to put it out of his head for the moment. He wasn't leaving the gala without it.

"Grow over time?" Robert asked in confusion. His frustrated tone had been replaced with curiosity as he looked at Sal, as though seeing him properly for the first time.

Sal looked across the bar at Upgrade and smiled. "When I created Mythcrafter with Skill Master, I was in a similar panicked state, with not much time to think. I combined the weaves of my parents and Upgrade to create Mythcrafter."

Turning to Fabi, Sal was a little startled to see her staring at him with wide eyes. He pushed past the momentary surprise and continued. "I did the same with Fabi's weave, blending in Perfect with her existing evolutionary weave. I fixed everything up with the tracker and triple-checked it would work."

Sal looked at Robert and held the stare. "You can ask Upgrade, Grant, or Quest about how extensively I've worked on the Skill Weaves. I still have a lot to learn, and I've been working on them practically nonstop for months, to the detriment of my training and Crafting. I want to help people with my ability, and I couldn't stand by just to watch Fabi's wings getting clipped…because it was bad optics for the Hunter Bureau."

"Fuck me." Doc Ameye chuckled from across the bar. "I'm starting to think every Crafter is anti-establishment. What do you say to that, Robert?"

Sal could see from the corner of his eye that his father was smiling broadly. Just the confirmation that he was of the same mind as his father was enough to sooth his soul and steel his resolve.

Robert's face twitched to reveal a wry smile. "From everything I've heard about weaves from Grant, shouldn't the inclusion of Perfect into Fabi's existing weave cause it to turn into something completely new?"

Upgrade held up a hand and waved it, as though waiting for Robert to give her permission to speak. With a dig in her ribs from Doc Ameye, Upgrade flinched before finally speaking. "The description of Fabricate matches up pretty well with what we saw in there. She should be able to use atmospheric essence to construct things. Oh, and with unconventional materials. That was the description, wasn't it, Grant?"

Grant nodded, his eyes still somewhat downcast as he looked at the empty glass in front of him. Of all the people there, he looked to be the most haunted by Robert's presence. "That's the description of Fabricate…but the speed is too fast. Not even Chatfield's Concept can work that fast. Ideation shouldn't be instinctive."

Doc Ameye coughed on his drink. "What did you just say? Ideation shouldn't be instinctive? You're sitting with three bona fide Crafters. We can instinctively look at anything and see how it can be better."

Upgrade started visually counting Sal, Fabi, and Doc Ameye before she launched a slap at the latter. "Four Crafters!"

Robert sighed as he poured himself another drink. "Okay then, we have Mr. Argento creating an entirely new weave…which recreates the fiasco from his own Skill Registration?" He looked at Upgrade to see whether there were any corrections to be made. When there were none, he continued. "Then we realize that the machine is in no way suited for the imprint of an entirely new skill, and it starts sucking itself dry." Robert gestured over at Prestige. "Which results in the timely intervention of Prestige and Sigils, creating a fortified essence cannon to make up the difference."

He nodded as though he were getting the facts straight in his head. "Then we have the Argento family stepping in to provide the necessary Restoration work on the machine, while Doc Ameye and Upgrade provide it with commander cores from the warp gate. Am I missing anything?" He looked around the group to see whether there was anything else to be added.

Doc Ameye looked at Sophia for a moment before he shook his head. "That's it."

"Whoa," Maurice let out before catching himself and apologizing.

Fabi smiled at him before turning to look at the group. "Seems I'm doing nothing but getting myself indebted tonight. Thank you all so much for everything you've done for me. I hope that my new ability, whatever it may be, will be useful in the fights to come."

Robert smiled at that. "Now that you're up to date on what happened, we just need to decide on the cover story. Then we can relax a bit and I can give you and Salvatore your rewards from the Hunter Bureau. Though, I think they may need to be revised somewhat after this."

"Punishment for acting like a Hero? Sounds about right." Sophia smiled as she raised her glass in Robert's direction. "There's nothing you can give Sal that we can't do for him already."

Robert cocked an eyebrow. "If it was anyone else, I'd have guessed you were goading me, Sophia. When it's you, I am always wholeheartedly assured it's criticism."

"Petro, let's call a car and get back to the auction house. I've had enough Hunter Bureau for the year." Sophia got to her feet and smiled at everyone else. "You're all more than welcome to come back to the Argento Auction House for our after-party. It's a little more humble than this, and far more tasteful."

Prestige chuckled from where she stood, smiling at Sophia and then looking at Robert for his reaction.

Sophia's announcement was clearly a curveball for Robert. His fist clenched for the briefest of moments before he outstretched his palm with a sigh. He stared at Sophia and seemed to chew on his words for a moment before speaking. "You understand the position I'm in. We need to get this story straight."

Sophia nodded as she looked at him. "And why do you feel the need to antagonize my son and make him feel like a villain for doing the right thing? His reward might be changed because he acted like a Hero stepping into that barrier to save his friend? Is doing your best against the Hunter code?"

She threw her arm out to where Fabi was seated. "This is possibly one of the greatest moments of Fabrizia's life, and you're content to stand there and lecture her on how she needs to keep this all a secret, because you're scared of those fuckers orbiting our skies?"

Sophia laughed as she stared at Robert. "Your answer is simple. You tell the Hunters in there that the machine exploded and the only man in the world who can make one fit for purpose is Doc Ameye. Put the target on his back—he's used to it. And you can protect him…you're used to it."

Doc Ameye grinned. "Simple and effective. It fucked up because I didn't build it. The one I make will be better…but my commission slots are full, so it'll take a while."

Upgrade sighed as she crossed her arms. "Do we really have to say it fucked up because he didn't build it?" There was a smile on her face, but she didn't want to concede so easily.

Doc Ameye gave her a sideways glance. "I'll need the original architect to show me the designs so I can improve them. Makes sense for the first test subject and the Replicator to be on board, too." He pointed across the countertop at Fabi and Sal. "That way, they're under the care of Ameye Locomotive."

Robert nodded as he jutted his chin in Grant's direction. "Want to take him, too?"

Quest raised a hand. "I believe that Grant should move his research to Quest Academy. We'll be able set up a lab in the upgraded workshop for him, and he'll be able to work alongside Salvatore."

Robert mulled over everything before nodding in agreement. "Okay, that's how we're going to play it." He looked at Sophia and gestured at the seat she had just vacated. "Can we now talk about how the Hunter Bureau would like to reward the top Saviors in Quest Academy?"

Sophia smiled as she remained standing. "I'll sit the moment you apologize to Salvatore and Fabi."

Upgrade's grin was the widest that Sal had ever seen.

CHAPTER 46: FIGMENT

Robert smiled at Sophia before turning his attention to Fabi and Sal. "I'm a firm believer that actions speak louder than words. I don't want you to feel that there is a glaring disparity between your rewards, but we do need to respect the accomplishments that have been achieved." He looked over at Sophia meaningfully.

"Now that we have approval from the Argento matriarch, I can continue." He laughed in a jovial tone that didn't suit him. "Taking on an obsidian hulker was an extraordinary feat, but the true value you've brought to us was in the evolutionary equipment blueprints. Grant and Quest can gush about the Skill Weaves, and while they're an incredible advancement for us, they also come with a massive risk."

Robert took a breath and smiled. "Yet, you shouldn't be penalized for the risk. That should be on the shoulders of the Hunter Bureau. We take enough tax that it's the least we can do." Leaning down so he was eye level with Sal, Robert continued to smile before speaking. "You wanted to create a guild. That's something that could happen without our intervention at the Hunter Bureau, so I won't dangle that in front of you like a reward."

Robert's eyes flickered over to Petro. "Your father has made no secret that you'd like to establish a guild headquarters in Silver Sanctuary. Which brings us to the big question…are your contributions enough to warrant the Hunter Bureau approving the request? You're not just asking for land in prime real estate, but an entire array of storefronts and an underground railway network. There have been countless bidders on that land, with none of them offering us a reasonable use case for it."

Robert stopped leaning over the counter and stood back up, looking at Sal thoughtfully as he did so. "How can we possibly justify giving that resource to a Trainee Guild, when we're keeping the power of the guildmaster a secret?"

"You can secure it against the Argento Auction House," Petro answered. "Classify it as our first foray into expansion with plans to rejuvenate Silver Sanctuary's commerce center."

Robert chuckled with a shake of his head. "Unfortunately, that wouldn't fly. The Scavenger Network proposed the exact same thing, and their bids are relentless. As mighty as the Argento Auction House may be, you cannot compete with the Scavenger Network."

"Are you talking about the depot?" Fabi's eyes lit up as she looked between Petro and Robert. "What if we went joint on it? It's a lot of space, and we'd save a fortune if we're using all the same equipment. We could treat it like a Crafting incubator or something?" She was clearly excited by the prospect. "We could have Dad's materials across the road, Argento Auction House is down the street…and the storefronts could sell what we make."

Sal was floored by the sudden suggestion. He hadn't really expected to get the land from Robert, but now that Fabi was sliding into the negotiation, it was like a sudden ray of hope had appeared.

Robert paused as he looked at Fabi curiously. "You'd want that as your reward? We have much more suitable land in Haven, Hope, and soon enough, we'll have it in Salvation."

Fabi grinned as she hiked her thumb at Sal. "This is perfect. I don't like being indebted to people, and I owe Salvatore quite a bit at this point. We go halfsies on the depot, and that should make us square. I want this as my reward."

Robert folded his arms as he looked between them. "We can work something out with this, if it's the two of you together. The Maccles and Argento families are well-respected in Silver Sanctuary, so there'll be no resistance from the district. I'll need a use case for the storefronts, warehouses, and railway line, but that's something that can be ironed out later."

Petro smiled as he raised his hand. "Ah, and we can talk about the new business incentives and how the Hunter Bureau can best support them. I wonder if Ameye Locomotive would have any expertise on clearing out railway tunnels?"

Doc Ameye smiled from across the bar and raised his own glass. "Don't push your luck. I've got no desire to expand the network to Silver Sanctuary."

Fabi shrugged it off, the beaming smile not leaving her face. "Even without Ameye Locomotive being a part of all this, we'll make something amazing." She looked at Upgrade meaningfully. "And you're absolutely coming along, right? If it's the headquarters for his guild and it's my workshop, you're going to have to stop us from making terrible decisions."

Upgrade nodded sagely. "Only if you promise to knock this old bastard off his pedestal." She jutted her thumb at Doc Ameye, who just chuckled and shook his head.

"Really? It's been barely a minute since I offered to paint a target on my own back, just for their benefit," he asked with a hand on his hip. "And you're asking them to take me down…unbelievable." A smile creased through his white beard.

Robert clapped his hands together and looked at them all. "Excellent. I think we're done here. Alibi is secured, and we're all aligned on it. Right?"

When everyone gave him a nod, he smiled. "Perfect. Then we can get back to the festivities. We just need to know what ability we're announcing." Reaching into his pocket, he withdrew a smokey black visor with red etchings on the screen. "I believe this belongs to you."

Sal stared at the Scarlet Moon Visor placed down in front of him. It looked nothing like it had before, and Sal wasn't even sure it would activate when he put it on. Just as he was thinking of using Restore to bring it back to normal, his father let out a low whistle.

Robert chuckled as he looked at Sal. "I'd be a little more careful with leaving Legendary-grade pieces of equipment lying on the floor."

Sal smiled as he held it in his hands, turning it over to examine the sleek grooves along the earpiece. The scarlet screen had eroded into a smokey black color, with flecks of red representing the runes he had layered into the glass. No matter what way he looked at it, it felt like a downgrade aesthetically. Sal thought back to Doc Ameye's glasses shattering in the essence storm, and guessed that his visor hadn't fared much better.

Name	Scarlet Strategist's Visor
Origin	Crafted
Age	Relatively New
Grade	Legendary (Upper)
Materials	Infused Moonsilver | Scarlet Screen | Refined Mythcraft Essence | Refined Replication Essence | Refined Invention Essence | Refined Catalyst Essence
Attributes	Judgment: Ability to rapidly make calculated deductions based on a complex array of visible information sources. • Judgment derived from following Attributes: ○ Insight ○ Deduction ○ Analysis Cypher: Optimizes all stored information on the device, allowing for background calculation and creation of predictive models. • Cypher derived from following Attributes: ○ Network ○ System ○ Interface Zenith: Ability to activate a peak flow state, harmonizing abilities and amplifying their efficacy at the cost of internal essence. • Zenith derived from following Attributes: ○ Lock ○ Calm ○ Focus ○ Synergy ○ Amplify Calibrated: Device has been bound to user. Listed abilities will benefit from an increased proficiency when using the device. • Synched Abilities: ○ Skill Master (10% Grade Improvement) ○ Mythcrafter (10% Grade Improvement) • Calibrated derived from following Attributes: ○ Attune

	○ Cultivate
Abilities	Judgment | Cypher | Zenith | Calibrated
Power Source	Internal Essence
Evolution	No
Quality	Good
Condition	68%
Value	Est. $1,250,000.00 – $2,200,000.00

Sal felt like he couldn't breathe as he looked over the Legendary piece of equipment in his hands. It was no longer a set item, and he guessed that was the price to pay for leaving the revolver at home. His mother had advised him against taking it, and even though it would have been invisible in his belt, people like Doc Ameye would have seen it immediately.

The name of the item had changed to be more in line with the new abilities, and Sal was happy to keep the new moniker. Scarlet Strategist had a really nice sound to it. Previously, the set items of the visor and revolver had an evolutionary trajectory that would hit Mythic over time. Sal was a little disappointed that the set bonus had disappeared, but it was a wonderful trade-off to have a Legendary visor. By his count, the visor had accumulated a total of thirteen abilities, which it absorbed to create higher-tier abilities.

Just as he was looking at the options for Zenith, he heard Robert clearing his throat. Sal glanced up in surprise and realized that everyone was waiting on him to review Fabi's weave.

"Sorry, the attributes are all different and I was just making sure that it was safe to wear," Sal explained as he held it up to his face. "But, I think we're all good. It doesn't synchronize with the revolver anymore, but I'm fairly sure I've got enough essence to do a quick Analysis of the weave."

Turning in his seat, he was met with the expectant smile of Fabi Maccles.

She looked at the visor on his face before tilting her head slightly. "I want to see your blueprint for that, by the way. Do you have it back at the auction house?"

Sal shook his head. "No, they're all on my workbench in the workshop."

"Whenever you're ready, Salvatore." Robert chided him again, as though asking him to get a move on.

Sal sighed inwardly as he started to look at Fabi's weave. His visor hesitated only slightly as it powered up for the first time. The draw of essence was a lot more than Sal had anticipated, but it wasn't drastic. It felt strange for the essence within him to be drawn out from the side of his face, but he was able to ignore it. Although his view was obscured by the sooty black glass, he watched as the flickers of red started to blossom and glow into a full rune-like circle. It flashed a couple of times and seemed to target lock on Fabi in front of him.

"Yeah, I definitely want that blueprint," Fabi admitted, laughing as she leaned in closer to get a better look at the transforming visor. "Might need someone to get me some scarlet screen though, by the looks of things." She turned to look at Doc Ameye meaningfully.

Sal was about to speak when the familiar Analysis window leapt into view.

Name	Fabrizia "Fabi" Maccles
Alias	To Be Determined
Class	Support
Profession	Current: Student, Quest Academy Current: Hunter, Independent Previous: Intern, Ameye Locomotive
Rank (Hero)	Quest Academy: Third-Year Rank | 2 Guild Association: No Affiliations Hunter Bureau: Current Rank | 3,981
Accreditations	Challenge Crests: 23 Completed Masterclasses: 7 Completed Advancements: 13 Licenses Acquired: 5
Ability	Skill Name: Figment | Rating: 39 Skill Category: Psionic, Invention Skill Mastery: 91% Skill Efficiency: 87% Progress to Next Rating: 71% Evolutionary Capability: No Potential Cap: 50 Natural Synergy: Cultivate | Catalyst | Domain
Essence	Essence Type: All Essence Gates: 320 Essence Absorption Rate: 100% Essence Control: 100%

	Essence Refinement: 100% Essence Calibration: 100%
Wealth	Q-Credit: 26,904

Sal's jaw dropped as he stared at the words on the screen. There were far too many surprises for him to really process the information. Sure, the visor was literally pointing out things to him that were prudent, but it was still one hell of a shock. Domain, the ability he had made for himself that created an area of death with Concept-style weapons? Turned out Fabi had a natural synergy for that now. Gates, over three hundred of them…and that was before the insanity that was her ability. It wasn't Fabricate, or even Customize, but a whole new thing called Figment?

"Should I be worried, flattered, or relieved?" Fabi tapped Sal's knee, laughing. "Your face isn't really giving me much to go off of, but I can tell that it's something!"

Sal jerked at the sudden motion and blinked a couple of times, bringing Fabi into focus with his non-covered eye. "Your ability is called Figment." He looked over at Grant to see whether there was any reaction from him, but it seemed the researcher had no idea about that ability either.

Robert frowned as he looked at Fabi, as though trying to parse what the ability might mean.

Sal realized he needed to give them a lot more information, so he started with the most ridiculous aspects. "In our ideal weave for Fabi, we got Customize to go up to Grade 2, I think. It might have been Grade 6. Anyway, the typical rule for most of those weaves is that they have a cap, usually in the twenties for lower-grade abilities, and into the thirties and forties for stuff like Mythcrafter." He pointed at himself to set the stage as he explained.

Turning his hand to point at Fabi, Sal continued. "Figment's ability cap is fifty…and there's no evolutionary capability, so it's the ultimate version of whatever ability family it's in."

Upgrade frowned as she looked at Sal worriedly. "Is she going to have the same issue as Gallant, with the mastery stuff?"

Sal shook his head. "No, she's at eighty-seven percent in efficiency, and over ninety percent in mastery. Her current grade is nearly forty." He looked at the shocked faces around the room. "Oh, and she also has like three hundred and twenty gates."

Prestige whistled as she finally moved from her standing position. In a fluid movement, the bottle of whiskey that was resting on the table snapped across the room to land in her hand. "Not sure how I feel about a student having more essence gates than me."

Grant looked to be on the verge of hyperventilating. He stared at Quest and spoke in a strained voice. "We've never seen an ability go that high before…it's completely unprecedented!"

Quest smiled warmly as he raised his glass and nodded in Sal's direction. "Excellent work, Mr. Argento."

Doc Ameye, on the other hand, seemed to be mulling over what he had just heard. "Perhaps I was a little hasty before. Silver Sanctuary might not be the worst place to extend the rail network." He chuckled before waving a hand. "And consider the scarlet screen a congratulatory gift, for unlocking such a wonderful ability."

"We don't even know what it does yet," Robert remarked as he looked at Grant expectantly. "Can't you put your machines to work to figure out what it does?"

Fabi ignored the conversations happening around her. All her focus was on Sal as she leaned in uncomfortably close. "I want to hear absolutely everything!"

CHAPTER 47: STIPULATION

When Sal got back to his seat with Fabi walking beside him, they were immediately bombarded with a million questions by Barry, Blathnaid, and a whole slew of other Saviors at the table. Rochelle and Divinity had strong-armed their way into shifting seats, with O'Brien and Sakura joining Fabi. It had instantly become chaotic, but in a relieved and good-natured kind of way.

"And you're certain you don't need Healing?" Rochelle looked at Fabi with clear concern written all over her face. "That thing pretty much exploded with you in it. How the hell can you be sure you're okay after that?"

Barry, who would normally be the first to poke fun at the whole thing, looked to be somewhat shaken. "It's probably better to be on the safe side. There was a ridiculous amount of essence being pumped through by Sigils and Prestige…there could be all sorts of side effects."

Fabi just smiled as she lifted the restraining locket that rested around her neck. "Eclipse gave me a quick check-up when we came in, and Quest gave me this for my own protection. Just so I don't accidentally turn the table into an art piece like the marble floor." She laughed at her own joke before shaking her head. "But honestly, I'm fine. Thank you for the concern."

Divinity didn't raise her voice over the sounds of everyone else, and instead opted to send Sal messages to his tablet.

When he saw her holding her own, and felt a vibration in his pocket, he fished it out to see what she had said.

Divinity: Are you sure you're okay? I saw your mother going in straight after you.

Sal paused at that. He wasn't sure whether it was a loaded question. *Did Divinity already know about his mother's ability, or was she asking about how he was feeling?* There was no need to lie to her, and he didn't want to stall for too long as he stared at her message. She was sitting nearby and would see his hesitation.

Salvatore: Yeah, it was a massive shock. She and Prestige were bickering the whole time, which was wild to watch. Really happy that Fabi got the right ability, and that she's okay. Thanks for warning us about the cores!

Divinity's response came through almost immediately, showing Sal that he was the only one overthinking things.

Divinity: Of course! I already showed you that ideal future, and Fabi getting the Fabricate ability was a pretty important factor for it to happen. I'm delighted I was able to help in some way.

Sal froze at those words. Divinity was under the impression that Fabi had the Fabricate ability. But in reality, she had the Figment ability that was a few tiers higher than Fabricate. Customize, which was the evolved form of Fabricate, only went up to grade thirty, yet Fabi had Figment at thirty-nine.

Salvatore: I think Grant is going to be running some tests on the weave to find out what it does properly, but from the analysis so far, Fabi is probably somewhere on par with Prestige in terms of power levels. That's definitely a win.
Divinity: You can say that again. We should probably be social. Catch up at the after-party later?
Salvatore: Sounds great. Looking forward to you meeting my family.

Sal placed his tablet back in his pocket and mulled over what had just happened. He didn't want to correct Divinity about the Figment ability, just in case she started obsessing over whatever deviations had been caused in the future. The stress of the night was past them, and Sal wanted to enjoy the last of the gala before they retired back to the auction house.

"I wouldn't exactly say a knight in shining armor, but he did apparently jump in to help." Fabi answered one of Barry's questions. She was looking at Sal with a smile. "But, since I was unconscious in that machine, and there was a whole big barrier of essence…it could just be bullshit." She gave him a playful wink before turning her attention back to Barry. "I think we can upgrade Salvatore to the somewhat-dependable category. Might not be a fully-fledged guildmaster just yet, but we'll whip him into shape."

"You're going to join his guild?" Barry asked in disbelief. "Even now that you have your powers?"

Fabi shook her head. "I prefer to think of it as a potential business partnership. We're potentially going to be working together a bit in the next semester, so we'll see how we get along."

Sakura frowned at those words and was about to speak when Fabi interrupted her with a raised hand.

"Ah ah, you don't get to have second thoughts. You already accepted the bribe of that corset." Fabi laughed as she pointed at Blathnaid. "Also, I've been told she's the culprit who actually made it."

Sakura's eyes lit up, and she appeared beside Blathnaid in a flash, startling Blathnaid tremendously. "What other things can you make with the Stealth effects?" Sakura looked at Blathnaid intently.

Fabi looked at Sakura meaningfully. "Oh, and as for the other promise that was made…I can personally attest to the effectiveness. Very safe pair of hands." It was vague enough that nobody would have understood the meaning behind it, except for Sal and Sakura.

Fabi had just given him her endorsement for reworking Sakura's weave. If it worked out as planned, she'd have access to the Void ability. The only issue was they had no idea whether the Skill Implant or Skill Imprint program would be scrapped after the fiasco that happened with Fabi.

Sal wondered whether Quest would get Doc Ameye to create a new Skill machine in the upgraded workshop. That would allow them to carry out the weave improvements on the students in a controlled environment. Had Sal not rewired Fabi's weave, the machine would have been able to handle the imprint with no issues. Grant being posted at Quest Academy would speed things up, too. If he brought all his simulation equipment into the workshop, there would be far less calculating time for the new weaves.

"What's going through that head of yours?" Fabi asked suddenly, pulling Sal out of his thoughts.

"Nothing, just thinking about the workshop upgrades," Sal admitted as he looked around the table, checking to see whether people were listening to them. Everyone seemed to be chatting to each other and in the midst of conversation.

"Which one? Quest Academy, or the one in Silver Sanctuary?" Fabi asked curiously. She leaned an elbow on the table and propped her chin on her palm. "Because I can't stop thinking about how we could change the entire layout of the place. I know I've joked about the whole drone army thing, but we could create an automated workflow and start selling gear through the shopfronts."

Sal smiled as he thought about it. "Honestly, I'm more curious about how your ability will work. There's a solid chance we wouldn't even need the Hunter Bureau to clear out the tunnels if you're able to just melt rock with your thoughts." He laughed at the mental image that popped into his head. "If you're able to Refine materials yourself, then that would massively reduce production costs. I learned how to do it when I was out on the excursion and during the scavenger run, making dead trees into workable materials and turning scrap metal into essence-infused ingots."

Fabi raised an eyebrow but didn't say anything for a few moments. When she did, she approached the topic from a very different angle. "What if I was to Refine materials, but in a dungeon instead? Between the two of us, we could probably do a few runs a day before the end of the break."

Sal's mouth dried up at the thought of spending the rest of his break running through dungeons. There was something about how offhand Fabi was when she spoke about them. She didn't have an ability until a few hours ago, but she was confident when it came to killing demons. The sticking point for Sal was that they had a very similar upbringing…so she should have been just as sheltered as him. More so, since she didn't even have an ability to activate.

"There's that thinking face again." Fabi smiled. "You don't want to do dungeons with me?"

There it was. Fabi was asking him to join her on a dungeon run. Just the two of them. All of Sal's anxiety was thrown to the side as he found himself nodding.

"I think I'd like that," he finally answered, smiling. "Despite taking down an obsidian hulker, I still overthink everything and get anxious when it comes to fighting the demons. Pretty terrible mindset in a world at war." He tried to play it off with a laugh, but Fabi's expression didn't change at all.

"Overconfidence is a terrible trait in a guildmaster. While cautious ones can sometimes be frustrating, I like that you know yourself enough to warn me about it." Fabi took her elbow off the table and sat up properly, stretching out her back with a contented sigh, with both arms raised over her head. "I was scared shitless of leechers for my first year. I still get a little unnerved when they float into view. Now, my battle-suit pretty much takes them out without me even noticing their approach."

Sal nodded appreciatively. "Thanks for not making fun of me for it." He couldn't explain why he felt so relaxed around her. She just gave off an air of competence that he felt drawn to. Not that he was actively seeking her approval, but he wanted to have her respect.

Fabi chuckled as she looked at Sal. "Did Upgrade drag you to a dungeon, too?"

"No way," Sal said in disbelief. "She took you, too?"

Fabi nodded with a laugh. "Yeah, for my sins. I was in a bit of a rut when it came to material costs, and how imbalanced the whole damn system was for Supports. Gave her a whole speech about how we were being punished for not being able to go to dungeons and get our own materials."

"Oh no," Sal practically whispered, already knowing where this was going. It was an almost carbon copy of the circumstances that led to Upgrade and Chatfield bringing him to a dungeon.

"Oh yes," Fabi corrected, smiling. "She pretty much dragged me there and crippled everything to the point that I could make the killing blow. We had to do it like…a dozen times before I was confident enough to take on the leechers alone. The haul from that single day was enough to give me a nice Hunter Bureau rank. Started getting a few bonuses, and it helped the Crafting, so I just became obsessed. I'm probably the only Support in Quest Academy with a higher dungeon and tower clearance than scavenger run participation."

"That's genuinely so impressive. I kinda did the opposite and suffered with nightmares for ages after the first dungeon experience. You'll laugh, but I had a revolver that I made…so there really wasn't anywhere near as much danger as you experienced," Sal admitted with a shake of his head. "Going into the tower was a lot more straightforward. Having a team really calmed the nerves a bit, and having Prestige looking out for us."

Fabi didn't answer immediately as she continued looking at Sal. She eventually nodded before turning in her chair to face him. "Okay then, how about we make a deal." She pointed at Sal's pocket that held his tablet. "We'll first sort out your Arkwright machine, and get it up and running. Then you're going to help me with my drone project…and then, we'll bring that drone to a dungeon to test it out. If it works the way I want it to, then it'll be able to handle anything that comes at us."

"You really do have a thing for drones, don't you?" Sal asked with genuine bafflement.

Fabi shrugged. "My goal is to be able to clear dungeons and towers without risking a single life. Doc Ameye has an entire carriage of drones that carve up the demon bodies and retrieve materials. I want to take it a step further than that."

"A step further?" Sal inquired, but Fabi just tapped her nose as though it were a secret.

"You need to accept my deal first that you'll run dungeons with me. Then I'll tell you more about my master plan." Fabi crossed her arms. "And be warned—if we're going to be sharing a workshop and a business, then you'd better be on my good side. I can be a nightmare to work with."

Sal very much doubted she could ever be a nightmare. He was already committed to saying yes when she first asked him to go with her to a dungeon, so it really wasn't a stretch to agree to her terms. The only little thing that stopped him caused him to laugh.

"I'm sorry, but as a matter of principle…I can never accept the first offer," Sal admitted with a guilty shrug.

A grin appeared on Fabi's face. "Okay then, any caveats you'd like to add?"

Sal thought about it for a moment before an idea came to him. "Help me make a drone dock for Arkwright, and then you've got yourself a deal."

Fabi nodded as she offered her hand. "Material costs are on you, though. I'll help with the manpower, design, and programming."

"Perfect." Sal shook her hand, happy that he'd be spending more time with her and getting her help on the docking station as well as Arkwright. It was still a little strange calling the Mythos machine Arkwright, but the name was growing on him.

Fabi's smile grew predatory. "Okay, now that we have a deal…your first mistake was not stipulating how many dungeon runs I intended on taking you on. You, sir…have just agreed to however many I wish, and I personally think we need to do at least a thousand of them."

Sal just stared at her numbly before a nervous laugh escaped his lips. "A…thousand?"

Fabi pointed a finger at him jokingly. "Don't push your luck, or I'll double that number."

CHAPTER 48: REWARDS

All the Hunters in attendance were clearly waiting for some sort of explanation from Robert about what had happened with Fabi during the Skill Imprinting showcase, but he kept them waiting until the end of the presentations.

Doc Ameye had gone up to the stage and spoke about his latest developments, keeping the details vague. He just stated that "Project Leviathan" was underway and to expect updates in the coming year. Barrier technology had been improved, as well as the commitment to help Vector with the predictive defense grid, should the funding come through.

Eric from the Arc Guild did a very brief presentation on three megastructures that were in ongoing development. Two would be private entities designed for the United Guilds Association and the Hunter Bureau, while the third would be a long-term solution to reduce overcrowding on the Darwin Cruises. He went on to speak about the property development side projects that were being completed ahead of schedule, and how investment in those projects helped fund the megastructure development.

To the surprise of a few of the Hunters in attendance, Eric finished his talk by asking Quest Academy to create an Advancement Module that specialized in construction. Apparently, the training time to get people up to speed was negatively impacting their timelines.

Finally, Robert took to the stage and lay a hand on the marble art piece that Fabi had unintentionally made. He waved at the audience and gave his trademark charismatic smile.

I know many of you have burning questions about our little spectacle earlier. I'm delighted to announce that Fabrizia was able to successfully activate her ability. We've had the Eclipse and Harmony Guilds check her out, but there were no wounds. She's perfectly safe.

Robert paused to allow the Hunters and Heroes to give a round of applause for Fabi. He waited for a few more moments before using both palms to quiet down the cheers.

Due to some faulty cores, and an overly ambitious weave design…the machine wasn't able to handle the workload. We've decided to place a pause on our Skill Implanting and Imprinting projects while Doc Ameye works on an improved model of the machine. We can't always guarantee that we'll have Sigils and Prestige on hand, nor would we have the accumulated essence of our gala attendees to ensure success.

While this research had a positive outcome this time, our calculations have told us it was a fluke. Replicating this sort of outcome would be next to impossible, so I'd like to personally thank our Hunters with Foresight who warned us well in advance.

When we next announce the Skill Implant and Imprint research on stage, we'll be much more confident in what we're offering. So, watch this space.

There were no cheers for that announcement, but rather a few exchanged glances between the guilds. It was clear that they had been hoping for a different verdict. Robert's concerns regarding imitations being created looked to be correct, with some of the Hunters in attendance looking pissed off with the update.

Now, we can finally move on to the changes of ranks, and we can retire to the bar. I hope you'll forgive me for extending the suspense, but we're going to start with the rewards for our students in Quest Academy.

All the screens started to showcase highlight reels from the tower exercise. It was an amalgamation of the different students, with the most eye-catching parts being featured.

Sal stared at the screen and saw Barry, Blathnaid, Kyndra, and Darren's reels go past in twenty seconds, snippets of their performance being shown to excite the guests. Sal guessed it would take far too long to go through each one, and was relieved that Robert wasn't going to go through them individually. His own parents hadn't even seen the footage, and he didn't want to risk his mother attacking Neuro or Erika for what happened in the excursion.

Starting with the first-years, we've got fifteen Saviors in attendance. Each will be gifted a one-year accommodation guarantee in Haven, with access to the Hunter Bureau's training and research facilities. This will start from the moment you graduate from Quest Academy, or decide to end your studies.

The screens showcased Barry again, followed by Divinity and Thorsten. Maxine Volta came next, and it was the first time that Sal was able to see her blinking to different areas of the tower floor before appearing beside enemies for the killing blow. Robert continued to speak to the crowd, ignoring the screens around him.

This guarantee can be extended by increasing your Hunter Bureau rank to certain thresholds. More support and bonuses will become available to you as you climb the ranks, such as permanent accommodation in our newest facilities.

In addition, we wish to respect Quest Academy's private economy, so rather than a monetary reward, we would like to provide each of the Saviors with one-on-one coaching from a list of eligible Hunters ranked in the top thousand.

Lastly, for our top-ranked Savior in the first-year cohort, Salvatore Argento. The Hunter Bureau will be assisting you in the creation of your Trainee Guild, by providing a suitable headquarters and some resources to get you started.

As much as I'd love to offer you a place in Haven or Hope, we must respect that you're just a first-year right now…so, we're going to give you a more moderate location in a smaller district, Silver Sanctuary. With the right guidance, we believe your guild will become a wonderful institution over time.

A number of the Hunters nodded their approval at Robert's words, but many looked unconvinced about such a massive reward being handed out. In just a few sentences, Robert had managed to somewhat make the depot in Silver Sanctuary sound more like a punishment than a reward. Few people in the crowd seemed to be aware of how incredible the location actually was.

Then, just as it looked like Robert was finishing up, a massive screen illuminated over his head to show Sal launching the desperate haymaker punch at the obsidian hulker. What made it that much worse was the audio, that blended Sal's scream with the shattering impact of the attack.

Well done, Salvatore, on being the top-ranked Savior of the first-years.

A thunderous applause exploded from the crowd. If anything, the scene of Sal taking on the hulker had managed to sway the dubious Hunters. A first-year Support had taken down an obsidian hulker, and that wasn't something to be ignored.

"What was that about you relying on a revolver?" Fabi asked with a laugh as she stared at Sal. "Because that looks pretty damn fearless to me."

Sal just smiled, grateful that it didn't go through any of the other parts of the reel. The body slam would have been mortifying to watch in front of everyone.

The second-years were given a more robust set of rewards, with a three-year guarantee on accommodation and access to the training facilities at the Hunter Bureau Headquarters in Haven. Mentorship was also offered with Hunters in the top hundred of the rankings. The key differentiator was that each of them would be receiving a set of gear that would be tied to their time at the Hunter Bureau. When Robert announced that it was going to be an evolutionary set of equipment, the student table practically exploded with excitement. They had just been given a shot at getting equipment that would someday get to Epic grade.

Sal just stared at the reactions around him. The Hunters looked to be shocked by the level of reward, and the students were positively ecstatic. It really put things into perspective when he saw how everyone was losing their mind over the Epic grades. With a glance at Blathnaid, he saw that she was having the exact same thought as him. Both of them were capable of making Epic grade equipment, and had done so already.

Lastly, for our top-ranked Savior in the second-year cohort, Victor Buchanan. The Hunter Bureau would like to offer you an exclusive cadet traineeship to become a captain in our ranks. If you decide that you'd prefer to avail of the guild offers that you're no doubt swimming in, we'll respect that, but the door is always open.

In addition to this, you'll be receiving a custom evolutionary set of equipment that is yours to keep if you decide to work with the bureau. We've been assured by Doc Ameye that it will be capable of reaching the Legendary grade over time.

Much like what happened for Sal, the screens highlighted Victor's accomplishments in all their glory. And glory would have been an understatement.

"You've got to be shitting me," Barry breathed as he looked at the screen in front of him in disbelief. "How is that a second-year?"

Sal just numbly watched the footage of Victor flying through a tower at insane speed. Vertically.

Victor punched through floor after floor in his ascent, utilizing speed and strength as he dispatched an entire horde of demons. A few of his kills were featured, including a vicious front-kick that knocked a voider out of the tower window…a backhand swipe that splattered a prowler and even a head-butt to a hulker, reducing it to rubble.

"Hype is such an overpowered ability," Fabi remarked dryly before catching herself and laughing. "Guess I can't really say that anymore." She wiggled her fingers in front of her, as though half expecting something to happen.

"That's Hype?" Sal pointed at the screen in wonder. "The same ability that Gallant had?"

Fabi nodded, smiling. "Yeah, that's why they're coddling Victor. They're terrified that he'll burn out like Gallant did, so they're constantly watching him and giving him a lot of breaks. He's nowhere near the same level that Gallant achieved, but if you give him another few years, he might be able to catch up."

Now, on to the last of the Quest Academy section. We'll be doing this on a more individual basis this time as the evaluations have come to an end and we have some incredible results to share.

Robert actually looked excited as he spoke. The screens all changed to feature different student profiles. There were pictures and statistics on each one, with observational quotes from professors at the academy, as well as some Hunter feedback.

The evaluations have been a massive success since we introduced the system ten years ago. We want to give each of the guilds a chance to procure the best talent on offer, assuming that their chosen Hero accepts their terms.

We invited fifty eligible guilds with comprehensive recruitment programs to apply to take part in the evals. They needed to make themselves available throughout the term, providing Masterclasses, guild outings, and licensing exams for the students. In addition to these terms, they needed to commit to the protection of Quest Academy throughout the year.

Participation was very high this year, and we saw some new guilds climbing up the ranks…clearly hoping to secure the next generation of talented Heroes. Our Tier 1's are listed on each of the screens.

As with years past, the top guilds will have the option to make a bid on a student and offer them a guild contract. There can be stipulations on what the student needs to achieve before the end of their third year, but those negotiations should have already taken place after the evals.

Robert's smile grew wider as he pointed above his head with a flourish, showing a list of names from the third-year cohort.

This is the list of students who have opted out of the evaluations cycle for this year, for their own personal reasons.

Sal looked at the list and was surprised to see that he recognized three of the names on display. Vanessa had already highlighted them as the dream team that were the rising stars of the third-year classes.

- Anna Sakura, Rank 1
- Fabrizia Maccles, Rank 2
- Emir Alper, Rank 4
- John O'Brien, Rank 5

Fabi looked at the list with a smile on her face. "This is the part where he does the rug-pull on everyone who's snubbed the bureau and the Guilds Association. Wait for it…" She expectantly glanced over at where Robert stood on the stage. "He hates losing."

In previous years, we made the decision to withdraw fiscal support from the students who opted out of our evaluations program. We felt that with the resources that were being poured into each individual, there should be a penalty for them when they opt out of repaying society.

We've since learned that not only was this short-sighted, it was unfair. With the introduction of the Saviors class in Quest Academy, these students are not holding out their hands and looking for a payout…they're pushing themselves to the limits to be Heroes. That is something that should be rewarded.

All the people on this list will be receiving the same rewards as their peers in the third-year Savior class.

"Oh, thank fuck." A man cupped his face in his hands as though incredibly relieved by the statement. His brown hair was tight cropped and his beard neatly trimmed.

Sakura just shook her head while Fabi laughed at his reaction. "Come on, John, I've already told you it's bullshit selling your soul and future for an apartment and some gear."

O'Brien looked at Fabi through his fingers and exhaled slowly. A plume of greyish smoke left his lips as he did so. "Yeah, but this really does lessen the sting if we can get both."

Speaking of which, the rewards for the third-years will be gear that can evolve to Epic grade. This will be gifted to those who have decided to leave the evaluations program. For those who opt in, they will have gear capable of reaching Legendary grade.

Custom weapons will also be designed for each Savior, with the help of our skilled Artisan team in the Hunter Bureau. We will guarantee up to Epic grade, depending on the options you select for the weapon.

Each of you will receive a Hunter Bureau Gold Card, allowing you to receive preferential treatment when you stay in any Hunter Bureau safe zones across the country. This is also great for discounts on all suppliers within our network.

Sal smiled at that. "Doesn't sound bad. You can bankrupt Lawrence Baron with that thing before you give it up."

Fabi chuckled as she shrugged. "Might just give it to my father so he can stockpile materials for us at a hefty discount."

Lastly, for one of our top-ranked Saviors in the third-year cohort, and the star of today, Fabrizia Maccles. The Hunter Bureau understands that you've decided not to join us or the participating guilds in the evaluations program. We know that you've set yourself on becoming an independent enterprise, and while we can't offer you a commensurate reward based on your achievements and contributions, we've decided to use an opportunity that has presented itself to us today.

The headquarters location for Salvatore Argento, in Silver Sanctuary, will be shared with Fabrizia Maccles in joint ownership. It's a much easier justification for us to allocate this between the two of you, and it will allow us to spend more resources in building it up as a premises.

Well done, Fabrizia. I hope that the rewards are to your liking.

"Smooth," Sal muttered as he crossed his arms.

Fabi nodded in return. "Yeah, we're going to squeeze every bit of assistance we can out of him. Hope you know that?"

Sal chuckled. "Naturally. He's going to have to deal with our parents… He doesn't stand a chance."

Fabi turned in her chair to look at Sal. "I'd be willing to forgo the dancing if it meant hitting that after-party a little early. I don't particularly want to hear about the granular movements of the Hunter Bureau ranks."

Sal looked across the table and received a nod of agreement from Barry.

"We're going to a party?" Sakura asked in confusion, looking over at O'Brien for confirmation, as if to ask whether he knew anything about it.

Fabi looked a little conflicted at the question, so Sal jumped in to avoid any awkwardness. "Yes, just a small thing back at the Argento Auction House. Would you and O'Brien like to join us? There's wine."

"Sold," O'Brien stated, rising to his feet. "I take it we're leaving now?"

Sal blinked in surprise as Fabi and Barry started getting to their feet. He shook his head slightly as he picked up his cane-sword and turned to look in the direction of his parents. Petro stared at the ceiling as though wanting a lightning bolt to finish him off, while Sophia cradled her head in her crossed arms against the table.

"Yeah, it's definitely time to leave." Sal laughed as he made his way over to his parents.

CHAPTER 49: AFTER-PARTY

"Did you see Robert's face though, when we all started leaving?" Sophia practically cackled as she unlocked the doors to the Argento Auction House. "It started like a mass exodus, before his big finale of the Hunter Bureau and the rankings."

Petro smiled as he looked over his shoulder at the rest of the cars coming in to land. "We need to keep him sweet until the deal goes through on the depot. But just having him announcing it was incredible, as he isn't the type who will want to lose face by going back on his word."

Sal listened to his parents as he eagerly waited for his mother to open the doors. Fabi was getting out of the car with her father, and all Sal could think about was the fact that she was going to be seeing his workspace. He couldn't for the life of him remember whether he made his bed or even tidied around the place. The first thing he wanted to do after he got inside was bolt to his workspace and make it presentable.

"We can talk about…everything else, tomorrow. If that's okay with you?" Sophia pushed the door forward. "Petro, turn off the alarms."

Petro slipped past her and made his way to the terminal in the main hall.

Sal nodded, smiling. "Unless you end up telling me after a few wines. I won't say no."

Sophia gave him a conspiratorial wink as she opened the double doors to make way for their guests. "I think we'll probably end up having around thirty people at least. Did you invite all your friends?"

"Yeah, and a few surprise guests. Nothing to worry about, though. They're friends with Fabi, and one of them is going to join the Trainee Guild." Sal waved back at Fabi, who gestured that they were stopping off at their shop before coming inside.

"Is your workshop presentable?" Sophia's motherly tone came out in force. There was a challenge there, and all it took was a look at Sal's face before she sighed. "You can't have it looking like a pigsty, so get your arse up there and tidy it up. I'll make sure your friends get the Argento tour while you're at it."

"Thank you," Sal practically breathed in relief as he jogged toward the workshop. He took the steps two at a time as he descended, feeling the rush of the earlier whiskeys. Slowing down, Sal's heart thundered and he took it a little easier as he pulled the doors open and flicked on the lights.

The carriage looked fine and wasn't in a rough state. He quickly moved loose materials into their respective drawers: buttons from the uniforms, and threading that was uncoiled from their spools. Sal practically slapped the drawers back into place, and slid everything that was lying on the surface area into a spare drawer that he hid to one side. When it was done, he left the carriage and pulled the door over.

Going up the stairs was a little more of a labor, especially with how restrictive his purple suit was. He wondered whether it would be bad form to change into his more casual clothing. Everyone else would be dressed up, so he reluctantly decided that it would be best to keep the tuxedo on. When Sal reached the top of the stairs, he groaned inwardly. It was cluttered. Not a mess, per se, but not tidy by any means.

Sal closed up the back of the coffee machine from when he took out the internal core. He straightened it out and moved all the strewn mugs from the workspace into his little kitchenette. There were so many sketches lying around that he just ignored them and focused on picking up pieces of debris—material residue, metal cuts, small pieces of crystal. There was far too much to properly clean away, so he just focused on the big stuff.

Finally, after a few moments of indecision as he stood around, Sal decided it was time to straighten out the bed. It was then that he heard his mother's voice from down below.

"Where he got off to. He's usually in here until all hours," Sophia explained to someone as she opened the door to the workshop. "You better not be getting changed. There are ladies present!"

Sal pulled the corners of the duvet and roughly smoothed it out with his hands before leaving the secret room in the wall that led to the mezzanine. When he stepped out of the bedroom, he closed the door and made his way to look over the balcony. Gripping the railing with both hands, he took a relieved breath. It didn't look half as bad as before.

Sophia's lips were pursed as she looked around her at the base of the stairs. "I hope you'll excuse the mess. He gets that from his father."

Upgrade just chuckled as she shook her head. "I don't think we're ever going to get him back to Quest Academy if this is what he has at home." She lifted her glass of wine and took a sip. "Before that cantankerous old bastard gets here, I just want to compliment what you've done with the place. It's an amazing workshop, despite what he may say later."

"I can hear you!" Doc Ameye's voice shouted from the stairs that led down to the old train track. "Don't give the woman a worse impression of me."

Upgrade pulled her long dress up with one hand and started ascending the stairs, with Sophia remaining at their base.

"I'll send your other friends down here when they arrive," she called up to Sal, who gave her a thankful wave in return.

"Don't bother. Just send Fabi when she gets in," Doc Ameye muttered as he entered the workshop with a wince. "Is this a joke?" He pointed at the train carriage that was directly in front of him.

Upgrade rolled her eyes as she turned on the stairs to look at him. "Seriously, not everything is about Ameye Locomotive." A grin appeared on her face as she tilted her head to one side. "Are you expecting it to talk back to you like Vulcan? Has your age finally gotten to you?"

Doc Ameye barked a laugh, which seemed to surprise Upgrade more than anyone else. Instead of moving up the stairs like Upgrade, Doc Ameye opened the carriage door and started looking around.

"That's rude!" Upgrade shouted at him, turning on the spot and moving down the stairs to apprehend the older Crafter.

"He's fine. You can leave him to it. I want you to see the Arkwright machine," Sal insisted as he gestured for her to come up. "You made really good time, by the way. I didn't think you'd get here before the others."

Upgrade smiled as she shrugged. "Your parents said it was fine, but I thought I'd tell you. Raven is here. He's already won over your father, and it's only a matter of time before he gets everyone else."

"Your brother?" Sal perked up at those words. He genuinely wanted to meet the man to see how similar he was to Upgrade.

"You're not allowed to like him. You were my friend first, got it?" Upgrade insisted with crossed arms. "And I'll know if you're—" Her words died in her throat as she saw the Arkwright behind Sal.

"Whoa," she breathed as she moved forward, placing her glass on the workbench before getting closer to take a proper look. "It's beautiful." Her hand traced across the interface and it responded instantly to her touch.

The same error message that Sal had been met with earlier in the night was on display, and Upgrade scrolled through it, not taking her eyes off the text.

"So, this is the fabled fabricator?" Doc Ameye grunted as he got to the top of the stairs. He had a small hip flask in his hand, already unscrewed. Taking a swig of it, he cast a glance around the room as though looking for anything of note. When nothing else caught his attention, he moved over to Upgrade and started to read the error report over her shoulder. "Step back so I can take a proper look at it."

Upgrade didn't protest as she moved to one side, giving Doc Ameye more room to inspect the machine.

Barely a few seconds passed before Doc Ameye let out another barking laugh. "Let me know when you've figured it out. I want to see how long it takes you." Doc Ameye moved away from the machine and leaned against the balcony, a roguish smile on his face.

Upgrade tore her eyes from the machine to look at him in disbelief. "Fuck off. You didn't figure it out already? It took you ages to run those simulations back at the gala."

Doc Ameye shrugged as he gestured at the machine with his hip flask. "I just needed to see it in person to know what was wrong with it. I thought it would be a hardware problem for sure, but it's not. Your little protégé has managed to create quite the vending machine."

"So, you know how to fix it?" Sal asked eagerly, stepping forward unconsciously as he looked at the Arkwright. It was high praise from Doc Ameye, and it put Sal's mind at ease that he had built it correctly.

"Yes, but this is a learning opportunity. Let's wait for Fabrizia to get here, and we can walk through it," Doc Ameye muttered as he shook his hip flask from side to side. "You'll get your answers faster if you fetch Fabrizia and a bottle of whiskey." He looked at Upgrade pointedly.

Upgrade bit her lip and was about to retrieve her glass of wine when Sal interjected. He looked at his mentor with a warm smile before gesturing at the Arkwright.

"Since we're waiting on Fabi, why don't you keep looking at it, and see if you can figure it out? I'll go get some more drinks for us." He took off his purple jacket and draped it over the railing.

Before Sal moved down the stairs, he smiled at Doc Ameye. "You're at the Argento Auction House, so I hope you'll treat all our guests with respect."

Doc Ameye flicked the brim of his hat. "Understood, Mr. Argento. I'll treat Upgrade with the utmost respect."

Upgrade smiled as she moved back to review the error report. "You know, it wouldn't kill you to give me a hint."

"It actually would," Doc Ameye countered instantly.

Sal left them for a few minutes as he got some drinks for the workshop area. He could see that the auction house was starting to fill up with people. There were quite a few of them he didn't recognize, and guessed that they were invited by his parents, or people who had invited others along. Maurice and Lawrence were laughing with each other, Vector standing between them and telling a funny story.

Sal was surprised to see that Vector was at the party. *Had the linchpin of society bailed on the gala just to hang out with them?* He wondered whether Maurice had invited him, or potentially Lawrence? Sal gave them a wide berth as he moved through the lobby. He didn't want to get caught in a conversation about the cane-sword.

As Sal walked along the side of the room, he saw Sakura and O'Brien talking to a tall and handsome individual. Sandy-blond hair and a perfect smile, he was laughing while making elaborate gestures. It was clear that both Sakura and O'Brien were hanging on each of his words, and when he finally hit a punch line, both of them started to laugh uncontrollably. It was the first time he had seen Sakura so relaxed and carefree.

Barry and Divinity looked to be deep in conversation. Well, Divinity looked to be in deep conversation, while Barry nodded along with whatever she was saying. He was going to go over to them to say hello, when Barry caught his eye. It was the most imperceptible of headshakes, but Sal caught it immediately.

Sal desperately wanted to know why Barry was warning him against approaching, when he saw Divinity's hand reach for her wine glass. It sloshed around in her hand, and he just stared at the scene in amazement. Looking at Barry for validation, he received a weak nod from the illusionist.

Divinity was drunk.

"That's a good friend right there," Fabi said quietly as she appeared beside Sal. She had changed into more comfortable clothes, and wore a pair of black jeans with knee-high boots. Her dress had been replaced by a deep-blue turtleneck sweater, and her hair was pulled back into a high-tail. She gave him a wink. "Couldn't resist getting out of those heels, but don't worry. I'm pretty sure I can still dance in these bad boys." She lifted her leg forward and rotated her foot right and left.

"What makes you say he's a good friend?" Sal looked back at Barry. It was clear, now that Sal had context, Barry was simply humoring everything Divinity was saying.

"O'Brien mentioned that she was really knocking back the drinks after the Skill Implant thing happened. Poor girl must have been worried because of the futures she saw." Fabi sighed. "She pretty much horrified O'Brien with a story about a first-year who nearly became a calamity. A zombie army or something?"

"Ah, Melanie." Sal nodded. "That was stopped though, so we're all good. Don't worry." He looked over at Divinity, who was oblivious to the wine that was spilling over her hand and her dress. "Should we get her home or something? I don't want to leave her like this."

Fabi shook her head with a smile. "Nope, it looks like help has arrived."

Sal watched as Rochelle appeared on the couch beside Divinity and placed a hand on her shoulder. The glowing green eyes was a signal that she was using Transference to heal Divinity.

"Healing works on hangovers?" Sal asked in disbelief.

Fabi just stared at him. "Man, you haven't lived! We're going to have to rectify that."

Sal grinned as he moved over to one of the display tables. Rather than showcasing an item for auction, the display tables were stacked with an array of drinks. Picking up a couple bottles of whiskey, Sal laughed when he saw Fabi tucking a bottle of wine under her arm and picking up a few glasses.

She gave him a conspiratorial look. "Fixing this Arkwright machine is going to be thirsty work!"

CHAPTER 50: ARKWRIGHT

"Is it the timing difference between the different hardware components?" Upgrade asked as she leaned heavily against the Arkwright machine. Her hands were pressed against the glass, her face inches from the error text.

"Nope," Doc Ameye answered glibly as he finished off the remainder of his hip flask.

"Is it the fault from the unmatched load order that was put in for the build?" Upgrade tried again, her voice showing clear signs of her frustration.

"Nope," Doc Ameye repeated as he continued to lounge against the railing of the balcony.

Upgrade let out an aggravated sigh. "Okay…simpler question. Is it a problem with the operating system?"

"Yes, but also, no." Doc Ameye lurched off the railing and moved to greet Sal and Fabi, who had arrived just a few moments before. He took one of the bottles of whiskey from Sal and smiled at Fabi.

"Since Fabrizia is here, and the whiskey…I'll put you out of your misery." Doc Ameye chuckled as he ignored the glasses and instead started refilling his hip flask with his new bottle.

"Please." Upgrade responded in a monotone voice as she pushed herself off the Arkwright with a pained groan. "It's annoying me how you figured it out with just a look. It means it's something simple that I'm overlooking."

Doc Ameye frowned as he looked up from the hip flask. "Why in the world would you think that? I had Protocol running diagnostics since the gala, and all I was missing was a look at the actual machine. It had nothing to do with that snippet of code you had on the screen."

Upgrade whirled around and glared at the old Crafter. "That's cheating!"

"I made the train, so I can absolutely take credit for their discoveries." Doc Ameye shrugged it off like it was nothing. "Besides…the solution wouldn't have come to you any time soon. It's a nuanced issue that comes from Mr. Argento being a Mythcrafter."

Upgrade grumbled a little but still accepted the fresh glass of wine from Fabi, who smiled brightly as she looked at the Arkwright.

"Enlighten us." Upgrade's voice was devoid of any enthusiasm as she stood beside Sal, gesturing at Doc Ameye to continue.

Doc Ameye took a swig from his hip flask before speaking. He sighed and wiped at his face, smoothing out his beard while looking at the Arkwright. "Application of will. That's the problem we have here."

"Eureka," Upgrade muttered in a deadpan tone.

Ignoring her, Doc Ameye continued. "Mythcrafting, if it's the same as Legendcrafting…allows the wielder to apply their will to whatever they're Crafting. We can make substitutions with essence, bending materials to whatever outcome we desire. The entire operating system is built with the Mythcrafter ability in mind, but it doesn't have any capability to apply the will of a Crafter. Your machine here is unable to replicate the influence of an actual Mythcrafter."

"So, he can only make straightforward designs then, that don't require deviations?" Upgrade asked suddenly. Her cutting tone had been replaced with curiosity.

"I didn't say that." Doc Ameye corrected her, earning him a glare in return. "You just need to give it an artificial will. Best chances you have right now are with that visor you made. Wear it and guide the machine into doing what you want, and you'll be able to correct the issues with your Mythcrafter ability as they arise."

Sal frowned as he thought about it. He had hoped it would be a more simplistic fix, but having to wear the visor and guide the machine through each Crafting session sounded arduous.

Fabi tilted her head slightly. "Hypothetically, what makes this different from Vulcan?" She looked at Doc Ameye as she spoke.

Doc Ameye's eyebrows rose. "Alphabetically or categorically? The list is endless! Vulcan is an artificial mind that has decades' worth of robust calculations and detailed processes. This…thing…is a husk that has shit itself on its first attempt at crawling."

Sal grimaced at the glowing praise he'd just received on Arkwright. "Don't suppose a dungeon heart would solve the problem of will?"

Doc Ameye halted his tirade and stared at Sal. "If you think I'm going to sell you a dungeon heart, you have another think coming. I maintain my monopoly on them for a reason, and I can't in good conscience give you one for this project. I need them for Project Leviathan."

"I already have one. Won it for coming first in the cohort tournament," Sal admitted with a laugh. "Doubt it even had time to be listed on the market. Sakura and the professors took down a Psionic commander in a dungeon raid, and a lot of the loot was gifted to the students."

Doc Ameye looked at Arkwright for a moment before shaking his head. "Tell you what." He turned to Sal. "Trade me the dungeon heart, and I'll get Vulcan to make whatever it is you designed this to do."

"Not happening," Fabi answered, surprising everyone else in the room.

Sal looked at her, wondering what angle she was going with. He wasn't going to take the deal, but he wanted to know her reasons for objecting.

"I beg your pardon?" Doc Ameye chuckled as he lifted his hip flask. "I don't think you've got the authority to make decisions for Mr. Argento."

Fabi crossed her arms as she looked at Arkwright for a few more seconds. "You said it yourself…it needs a will. When I took that internship at Ameye Locomotive, it was to learn about Vulcan and how I could replicate that model for my drones." She uncrossed her arms and waved her right hand as though she were brushing something away. "I'm pretty sure I can harness a dungeon heart like you did." With a smile blossoming on her face, she gestured at Upgrade and Sal. "And between the three of us, my guess is that we'd do a pretty good job."

Doc Ameye screwed the lid of his hip flask shut before pocketing it. He took his leather jacket off and slung it over the railing beside Sal's purple jacket. With a reluctant sigh, he interlocked his fingers and cracked his knuckles. "Okay then, let's just get this over with. Bring me the dungeon heart."

"I'm not trading it," Sal insisted, but Doc Ameye just shook his head.

"You're going to fuck it up if you try harnessing it yourselves. I don't want to see a dungeon heart shattering because of incompetence." His voice was stern as he looked at Fabi, but when he turned to Sal, he offered a begrudging smile. "So, I might as well do it right. Hell, you get this thing operating properly, it might give me a break from the endless commission requests."

Sal didn't need to be told twice as he moved over to the secret door in the wall. Pushing it open, he stepped through to his room that housed a couple of the material chests he brought from Quest Academy. The dungeon heart lay to one side in the box, and Sal quickly retrieved it. Turning around to go back out, he was surprised to see both Fabi and Upgrade standing beside his bed.

"Oh." Sal jumped slightly.

"You have a secret room!" Fabi said, her eyes wide. "This is awesome!" Her gaze landed on the stack of drawings on the countertop. She made an immediate beeline toward them and rifled through the pages with a wide grin on her face. "I think this is my new favorite place…we need to have secret rooms in the warehouse."

Upgrade chuckled as she looked around the room. "I should have guessed you'd have a bed in your workshop. Tell me, though, have you ever used it?" She laughed at her own joke before following a very distracted Fabi back to the main area of the workshop.

Sal followed them out, with the dungeon heart in his hand.

"That? That's not a dungeon heart…it's only a fragment." Doc Ameye gave it a dubious look. "You should have said that was all you had. I've got no problem squandering something at that level for your machine."

"So, what do we need to do?" Sal handed the dungeon fragment over to Doc Ameye. "Do we need to come up with some form of housing unit?"

Doc Ameye laughed as he shook his head. "You just need to give me some space to work. I'll even let you watch if you promise to stay quiet."

Sal headed for the workbench and poured himself a drink. He was curious about how Doc Ameye used his ability, and even though it would be his second time seeing it, Sal wasn't really in a position to appreciate it a few hours ago.

"Protocol." Doc Ameye spoke as he glanced off to the side. "Show me the Vulcan schematic. Adapt the dungeon fragment I'm holding and simulate the optimal integration for the MythOS machine you analyzed earlier."

Doc Ameye waited for a few moments before his brow furrowed. "What do you mean you can't see it?" He reached up to his face and groaned when he realized his glasses were no longer there. They had been shattered earlier during the essence storm.

Upgrade opened her mouth to say something, but Fabi jabbed her in the ribs, causing her to flinch back in pain.

Sal wanted to laugh, but Fabi also gave him a playful look of warning.

Doc Ameye pulled at his jacket and rummaged through the pockets until he found what he was looking for. A set of hunting glasses appeared, with one of the eyes completely blacked out. The other was a vibrant yellow with black runes etched into the surface.

"Give me a damn minute," Doc Ameye muttered to Protocol as he put on the glasses and held up the dungeon fragment. "There you go…yes, adapt to the size…no, there's no need. I can work around that…okay, that's bigger than I anticipated." His one-sided conversation with Protocol continued with Doc Ameye making random responses that sounded funny to Sal and the others.

Upgrade gave Fabi a pleading look, as though asking for permission to call Doc Ameye senile, but Fabi extended her fingers and quietly threatened her with another poke.

"Okay, let's get started." Doc Ameye took off his glasses and slid a single stem into the neck of his T-shirt, letting them dangle against his chest. With both fists at his side, he raised his shoulders slightly before jutting his arms down in a flash of golden light. Each arm emanated a warm glow as he moved over to the Arkwright. "Since you didn't give me a shit whiskey, I'm feeling in a charitable mood."

His golden palm plunged into the side of the enclosure, melting through the metal casing and causing the refiner, 3D printer, and engraver to illuminate in the same golden light. By holding his hand there, the golden light flowed inside the Arkwright like ink blossoming in water. "We're first going to properly calibrate and synchronize this setup. You won't be having any more issues with the estimations."

"Thank you." Sal blew out a breath, relieved. He honestly had no idea how he was supposed to fix that, and Doc Ameye just shoving a hand into the machine was giving him hope that he'd someday be able to Craft in that sort of manner. He was starting to wonder whether the amazement he felt right now was how people had looked at him using Mythcrafter.

"You're worse," Upgrade remarked, as though reading his thoughts. "Like, a thousand times more dramatic." She pointedly looked at him, smiling.

Doc Ameye sighed as he watched the golden light grow stronger within the enclosure. "I'm going to use the loaded materials to create the docking area for the dungeon fragment. Cores and obsidian glass wouldn't normally cut it, but I can shave off some of the materials that are redundant."

That caught Sal by surprise. "Redundant? I made it with Mythcrafter, so I thought it was quite efficient with the materials I had available."

Doc Ameye looked at Sal and shook his head. "You'll learn in time that the ability isn't always right. There are more efficient methods and shortcuts that can be taken to reduce material cost. You've over-engineered massive parts of this, like the conveyor belts. If you used the right materials, you could have created a subspace that the machine sources from." He waved his free hand as though struggling for an example.

When he clicked his fingers, he gave Sal a smile. "Like how I warped in the materials earlier from Vulcan when we needed them. Imagine having something like that in this. You could transport materials from your warehouse directly into the storage hold and have it working nonstop. Your ability will never suggest something like that, because while it's practical, it's also a blatant waste of essence."

Before Sal could reply, Doc Ameye winced. "Okay, that's a lot of the fine-tuning done." He withdrew his hand from the still glowing machine and retrieved the dungeon fragment from the workbench. "Now for the difficult part. Come over here."

Sal blinked in surprise as he looked at the others for a moment, curious whether it was him being summoned.

"You. Salvatore. Get over here. We need your Mythcrafter essence for this part," Doc Ameye insisted as he gestured for Sal to come quickly.

Sal walked over to him and stood awkwardly, not sure what he was supposed to do.

Doc Ameye held out his hand. "Handshake, and hold it there."

Sal complied and gripped his hand, still quite baffled at what was supposed to happen.

Doc Ameye, with his right hand clasped with Sal's and his left hand holding the dungeon fragment, started to push the fragment into the side of the enclosure. Once it entered, the golden light started to get sucked into the fragment at a rapid pace. "Okay, now I'm going to pull on your essence. Prepare yourself."

Sal wondered whether this was going to be as painful as his ordeal with Prestige earlier. But, to his surprise, the draw on his essence was barely noticeable.

"Can you handle more?" Doc Ameye's brow furrowed. "The more we can give it, the higher chance of it stabilizing and adapting the will of a Mythcrafter."

Sal nodded, still confused. "I can handle a lot more than this." *Had he really progressed that much from getting access to those other essence gates?*

Doc Ameye nodded as he pulled more essence from Sal. The golden light pulled Sal's essence through Doc Ameye's arms and straight into the dungeon fragment. This continued for a few minutes, with Doc Ameye looking like he was concentrating quite a bit.

When Sal's hand was finally released, he flexed his fingers a few times and tried to sense his own internal essence reserves. By his own rough estimate, he was down to roughly sixty percent after all of that. In comparison, Doc Ameye looked to be positively exhausted by the ordeal.

"How is it looking, Doc?" Upgrade stepped away from Fabi, just in case the question was construed as mockery and resulted in another poke.

"It'll take a bit to stabilize, but we've flooded the little bastard with Mythcrafter essence. The housing unit is like a thing of beauty, if I do say so myself." Doc Ameye smiled as he rolled his shoulders, laughing. "If I had just taken it easy and done a quick install, I wouldn't be this damn exhausted."

"What did you do instead?" Upgrade took a step closer to Arkwright to have a look.

Doc Ameye grinned. "Well, you said it yourself that it's going to compete with Vulcan someday. I need to make it a fair race…and crippling you at the starting line wasn't going to work."

Upgrade's mouth opened as she caught sight of the glowing purple crystal that rotated inside the Arkwright. "You've put evolutionary runes on the dungeon fragment? Using obsidian glass?"

Fabi was over like a shot, staring at the rotating crystal with wide eyes. "How is that even possible? A dungeon heart can evolve?"

Doc Ameye chuckled as he wiped at his face. "Of course. That's what Project Leviathan is all about. That little fragment will grow, along with the rest of the Arkwright. Let me sit down for a few minutes and we can run some diagnostics."

Sal barely heard what Doc Ameye had said. His full attention was transfixed on the Arkwright. The internal changes weren't as drastic as he had assumed. Each of the conveyor belts had been shortened in length to make room for the crystal mount. It gave the whole thing a more mystical appearance, and the purple glow was somewhat villainous.

"Thank you so much for your help. I really appreciate it," Sal said to Doc Ameye as he turned around with a wide smile on his face. "I was so worried that I'd never get this working properly, but it looks even better than before."

Doc Ameye faltered as he looked at Sal for a few seconds. His eyes narrowed for the briefest of seconds before he looked down at the ground with a rueful grin. "You're very welcome."

CHAPTER 51: RAVEN

With the Arkwright running a full diagnostic, it was time for Sal and the others to rejoin the party. Sal felt like he could finally relax now that the machine was fully operational. The upgrades from Doc Ameye would remain to be seen, and he was incredibly curious as to how the dungeon fragment might improve Crafting. It was some well-needed excitement after the ordeal of the gala. If he was honest with himself, he was trying to distract his mind from dwelling on the revelations about his mother's ability.

"What are you going to make first?" Fabi asked as she fell into step beside him as they collectively started moving up the stairs. "You know, since you now have the world's most expensive and extravagant Crafting assistant."

Sal grinned as he shrugged. "Honestly, I was thinking of just stockpiling weapons and equipment for the Argento Auction House to sell while I'm off at Quest Academy. Build up some financial reserves since I don't know how much all the guild stuff is going to cost." He thought for a few more seconds before letting out a sigh. "But there are a few commissions that I need to get started on. I've got an idea for a completely different vending machine that I want to put together."

Fabi looked at him in disbelief. "Wait, you want to make a second Arkwright? What could you possibly want to build that needs two of them?" Her brow scrunched as she clearly put thought into what he might be talking about.

Sal laughed as he shook his head. "It's a promise I made to Alex in the workshop. Looking to create a type of coffee machine that uses Refine and Alchemize." He waved his hand as though it wasn't something to worry about for now. "If I can add in Perfect to that, then it'll be able to make the best elixirs imaginable."

"And bankrupt yourself with ingredient costs," Doc Ameye monotoned before he paused, looking at Fabi carefully. "Unless the heiress to Maccles Materials decides to help you out?"

Sal raised a hand to stop Doc Ameye. "No need for that. I already have my own solution in mind, and I think the Arkwright will make the production a lot easier." He smiled at Fabi. "Not that I wouldn't be grateful for your perspective, but this is a project that I want to take on by myself."

Fabi grinned. "I can respect that, and look forward to seeing what you come up with." She gestured back at the workshop housing Arkwright. "If that's what you come up with when you're left to your own devices, you can be sure I'll stay out of your way."

Upgrade sighed. "I've already seen the crazy design he's made up for the project." She looked at Fabi and almost gave her a look of warning. "If you're able to break in here to stop him from overworking, please do so."

Fabi shot Sal a guilty smile. "If I'm being honest, I did want to pop by from time to time and play with the Arkwright…if that's okay? I've got no idea how long it will take me to get used to my ability, and there are so many designs that I don't trust other Crafters with."

Sal's curiosity was definitely piqued. "What sort of designs?"

Doc Ameye snorted. "It's Fabrizia, so it's either a drone or a battle-suit. Seeing as you don't have a drone dock synched up with the Arkwright, she wants to make a new battle-suit." He raised his hip flask and gave her a pointed look. "Tell me I'm wrong."

Fabi's face went a slight shade of red before she rolled her eyes. "I have more range than that, but it just so happens that I was going to build the Macclemark III...since it looks like I'll be doing a few dungeon runs and need to boost up the protective functions." She shot Sal a wink at that last part. "You're not a charity, though. I'll be paying for the use of the Arkwright, since I'd be spending it on commissions anyway."

"It'll depend on how long the Arkwright needs to make each thing. If it ends up being weeks to finish your stuff, then I might need to ration your time with it." Sal came to a stop at the top of the stairs. Looking out at the party, he let out a reluctant sigh. A part of him wanted to stay in the workshop with the other Crafters to wait until the Arkwright was finished with the diagnostics. He was having fun talking to Fabi, Upgrade, and even Doc Ameye. Their expertise was excellent, and he felt comfortable when he was around them.

Doc Ameye stood beside him and seemed to have the same thought. Pocketing the hip flask, the older Crafter gave Sal a sideways glance. "Forget about the elixirs for a few weeks. You should focus on building yourself a uniform that will help you harness your abilities." He tapped his arms as though the meaning were obvious. "Sleeves that turbo-charge my essence and control." Reaching out to Sal, he tapped against Sal's shirt. "Now that you've got some more gates unlocked, you should start thinking about how to best utilize them."

"Like a battle-suit?" Fabi asked with a hopeful smile. "All of them are attuned to the wearer, so he'd get a proficiency boost to his abilities."

Doc Ameye rolled his eyes before setting off into the party. "Sure, something like that." He dismissed them with a wave before pausing his departure. Looking back at them for a moment, his eyes found Fabi and locked onto her. "That Controller spec that you designed at Ameye Locomotive...it wasn't bad. I'd probably start with that." Doc Ameye's hand moved to point at Sal. "Let him finesse the design himself, though. His eyes will find ways to improve it." With that said, he made his exit from their group.

"Macclemark IV," Fabi explained to Sal, grinning. "That's the spec he's talking about." She let out a satisfied sigh before glancing back at Upgrade. "So, now that the babysitter is gone...do you want to go back and have a look at the Arkwright? We can wait out the diagnostics and see it in action!"

A wide grin appeared on Upgrade's face. "Oh no, you've made your bed and now you're going to sleep in it."

Fabi blinked in confusion. "I don't follow."

Upgrade pointed out to the party area. "I believe Sal promised you a dance. I'm not going to miss this for the world..."

Sal smiled as he stepped through the archway that led to the party. He could see to his left that Barry and Divinity were still seated in the lounge area. Divinity's head was in her hands, and Rochelle was no longer with them. Judging by the grin on Barry's face, he was clearly having a great time in recounting everything Divinity had said to him. On the right side of the room, Doc Ameye had started up a conversation with the handsome sandy-blond haired man who was casually leaning against one of the stonework pillars with a glass of red wine in hand.

The main showcase was in the center of the room, where all the tables had been cleared to make space on the polished wooden floor. Over thirty guests loosely encircled the space, all in something of a hushed silence as the surrounding music bounced against the walls.

"Oh, they've started." Sal took a few steps closer, smiling. "If you think I was bad, don't dance with my parents." He spoke to Upgrade with a wink.

"You've really started to hype up—" Fabi's words came to a stop as Sophia's body was swung in a wide, graceful arc through the air.

Her entire being looked to be suspended in midair, with her only tether to the floor being Petro's arm. Petro wasn't holding back either, with his body flowing like water, his legs tracing half circles on the floor as he pivoted and shifted his weight to throw Sophia in a series of elaborate movements. They moved in rhythmic phases, with Petro pulling Sophia close against his chest, his arm clutched at her waist, before he sent her flying again.

"Whoa…" Fabi breathed as she looked at Sal. "And you dance like that?"

Sal smiled as he nodded. "Depends on the partner."

Upgrade laughed as she clapped both of them on the shoulder, leaning forward to place her face between them. "Ooooh, Fabi…I think he's challenging you. That was definitely a challenge."

Sal chuckled as he shrugged. "I've only danced with one Crafter, and she was incredibly lacking. I'm not sure if it's a trend or something."

Upgrade's laughter died off as she pouted playfully. "I will admit, it wasn't my best showing…but I think Fabi will definitely redeem the Crafting department. No pressure, Fabi."

Fabi continued to stare at the dancing. Petro had somehow managed to throw Sophia upward, launching her almost his full height off the ground in a spiral motion, her dress fluttering in the air.

"Your parents are awesome," she breathed as she turned to Sal in disbelief. "I don't remember them being like this when I was younger."

Sal looked at Fabi curiously. "They told me that we met when we were younger. Do you remember?"

Fabi nodded slowly, still distracted by the dancing. "Yeah, Dad went to a couple of the auctions years ago, but they were far too pricey for him, so he stopped." She glanced over at Sal, smiling. "You were an excellent cloak attendant, though. I remember you had a little stool that you stood up on at the door, beside the racks."

Sal laughed at the sudden memory. Although he didn't recall meeting Fabi, he definitely remembered that horrible job when he was a kid. "My parents thought it would make me less shy if I started talking to people as they came in. It was a nightmare."

"You were shy?" Upgrade scoffed as she unclasped her hands from their shoulders and walked around them. "I guess that their tactic worked wonders."

Smiling, Sal held out his hand to Upgrade. "Want to dance in front of all these people? I'll go easy on you, I swear." He had zero intention of going easy on her, and both of them knew it.

Before Upgrade could say anything, Fabi reached out and grasped Sal's hand. "Promise to go easy on me? I've apparently got a whole Crafting department to redeem…"

Sal chuckled as he started walking with Fabi toward the dance floor. "That really depends…how many dungeon runs were you thinking of taking me on?"

"A man who plays the long game? I can appreciate that." Fabi laughed as she slowed down at the end. "We should let them finish their dance, though. It's intimidating as hell joining when they're there." She looked meaningfully at Petro, who was rotating with Sophia at rapid speeds, before he halted suddenly and continued twirling Sophia with his right hand.

"It'll only get more elaborate if you leave them like this." Sal laughed as he stepped onto the dance floor. "Just have fun, that's all that matters. Okay?"

Fabi smiled in response. "I think I can manage that."

Sal made eye contact with his father, who shot him a massive grin. In a split second, a whole swath of space was cleared on the floor as Petro repositioned Sophia, who laughed in delight throughout the whole experience.

"So, do we just—" Fabi started before Sal pulled her forward onto the dance floor.

Sal's hand pressed against Fabi's lower back as he guided her other hand to rest on his shoulder. Interlocking their fingers with his remaining hand, he gave her a reassuring smile. "Let your body relax and move with the momentum. When I lift, tense your core. When you're landing, soften your knees. I will catch you if you lose balance."

Fabi just laughed as she looked at his arm holding her back. There was the barest of space between them when she finally made eye contact. "I'm calling bullshit on you ever being shy."

Sal laughed as he waited for the music to reach a certain beat. Just so he didn't catch her off guard again, he gave a gradual countdown. A small part of him expected her to be nervous, but to his surprise, she looked quite excited. "Two, one." Sal finished the count just as the song hit the right beat.

With a surprising amount of grace, Fabi glided with his arms in a full circle. She wasn't looking at him, but rather at something over his shoulder.

Sal turned the dance to see what she was looking at and saw his mother in yet another elaborate twist of the torso, mirroring Petro's stance. Both of them had a single hand clasped, with their entire bodies at a forty-five-degree angle, leaning outward. Their feet practically touched at the bottom as they continued to flow in a spiral. It was by far the most unnecessary maneuver and a definite sign that they had continued drinking after arriving at the auction house.

"I want to try that," Fabi said excitedly as she caught Sal's exasperated expression.

"Wait for it," Sal said dryly as he continued twirling with Fabi, giving her plenty of chances to glimpse what was to come.

Petro's right foot slammed into the floor with a massive clap as he lifted Sophia with just a single arm, using their accumulated momentum to swing her slender body in the air like gravity didn't exist. His entire body was the anchor as he utilized everything physics had to offer. Sophia's feet were higher than her head, but it didn't stop her from switching hands to make wide kick rotations. Sal was grateful that she wasn't at risk of flashing anyone; she wore a dress that would maintain modesty even if she started to cartwheel around the room. Sophia's infectious laughter wasn't drowned out by the music, and the entire crowd of guests burst into cheers of applause at the dramatic showcase.

Fabi's movements deteriorated as she gaped at the dancing. "How is that even possible? Was your mother a gymnast or something?" Her eyes practically sparkled as her grip on Sal's fingers grew tighter. "You'd tell me if you could do that. Wait, did you do that to Upgrade?"

Sal laughed as he continued to go through a set of basic sets with Fabi. There were a few spins and lifts, and by the third rotation, Fabi was clearly getting more comfortable as she started doing a few kicks. Her jeans and turtleneck were a far cry from his mother's dress, but in Sal's eyes, she still looked radiant. He smiled at her as he leaned a little closer. "So, do you want to increase the tempo?"

Fabi nodded. "If you throw me into a wall, I'll kill you."

"Noted," Sal answered as he flung Fabi away from him, before pulling her back in a spin. A Latin-style track came on and Sal thought it could be fun to move away from the eccentric ballroom style. Before changing, he wanted to see whether Fabi was comfortable with the change. "How are you with moving your hips?" Sal asked the question before the implication registered in his own head.

Fabi's laughter was explosive and immediate. So much so that it not only drowned out the music, but also the cheering of the crowd. She had to disengage from Sal's arms, mid-dance, to excuse herself because she couldn't breathe.

Chuckling, Sal left the dance floor with a shrug. The crowd wasn't bothered at all as Petro and Sophia weren't slowing down.

"You took it easy on her!" Upgrade declared accusingly as both Sal and Fabi returned. She looked at Fabi in bewilderment. "Do I even want to know what happened?"

Fabi leaned her back against the wall and pointed at Sal with a grin as she wiped a tear from her eye. Just as she was about to speak, Sal ran interference.

"I asked if she was comfortable with movements for Latin-style dancing. That was it, and she overreacted," Sal explained, laughing as he stepped in front of Fabi and looked at Upgrade earnestly. "Anything she says to the contrary is a barefaced lie. You shouldn't believe her—she's been through a terrible ordeal today and anything she says is probably the exhaustion speaking."

Fabi's laughter doubled as she leaned back against the pillar, struggling to breathe. Her pitch increased until it was almost a shriek. "How good am I at moving my hips?"

Upgrade's lips disappeared as she tried not to laugh. "Oh…honey."

Sal sighed as he placed his hands on his hips and bowed his head. "I'm not going to hear the end of this, am I?"

Upgrade shook her head. "It's firmly in the top three of my favorite Sal moments. My perfect guess at Divinity's prediction is still winning, by far."

Fabi finally started to breathe as she moved away from the wall with a satisfied sigh. "What's this? There's a list? What's the prediction?"

Upgrade tapped her nose. "Where's the fun in that? It's a secret!"

Sal gave Upgrade a deadpan look before turning to Fabi. "Divinity predicted that we end up together." He gestured at Fabi and then at himself. "Upgrade guessed your name, but I wouldn't worry about it. I've accidentally changed the future half a dozen times since I arrived at Quest Academy."

Upgrade's jaw dropped as she stared at Sal in disbelief. "What? You just…told her, like that?"

Sal shrugged, smiling. "Honestly, I'd rather be in control of my future rather than leaving it to fate. I've used Divinity's power before and there are so many branches of possibilities, and it's impossible to say that one is certain. At least, that's how I looked at it." He gave a warm smile to Fabi. "Also, I have enough secrets to keep, and not many people who know all of them. I'd prefer to keep Fabi in the group who knows everything."

Fabi couldn't stop herself from smiling as she looked at Upgrade with crossed arms. "Since we're being honest…Upgrade? Is there something you'd like to tell Salvatore?"

Upgrade smiled ruefully. "I already told her. Like, immediately after our conversation." She spread her hands. "I was really vague though."

Fabi scoffed as she looked at Sal, mimicking Upgrade's voice. "Hey Fabi, guess what? I know who your future husband is!"

Upgrade winced and waved her hands. "Way more nuanced than that, Sal. I promise."

Sal looked between them, laughing. "And you're okay with it? It didn't freak you out or anything?"

Fabi smiled as she shrugged. "As you said, it's one of many possibilities. By the time you graduate, I could be dead on the battlefield or have met someone."

"Let's hope it's the latter." Upgrade frowned, before catching herself and looking at Sal. "I mean, of those two options." She looked back at Fabi before sighing. "Vote for dropping this topic and getting drinks?"

"Yes!" Both Sal and Fabi agreed immediately.

When they turned to move in the direction of the drinks table, Sal was surprised to see the handsome sandy-blond haired man standing a few feet away from them awkwardly. In his left hand were three wine glasses, each of the stems between his fingers. In his right, a freshly opened bottle. He looked at Sal with an easygoing smile. "I didn't want to interrupt. Upgrade had her serious face."

Upgrade's entire body tensed up at the sight of the man, but Fabi's face broke into a wide grin. "Raven!"

"The one and only…until I die and someone takes the name! But right now, the only one!" Raven answered, laughing, and raised both his arms in celebration. "Want to see my new bow? Doc Ameye made it and it's awesome!"

Upgrade turned toward Sal, staring him dead in the eye. "You're not allowed to like him…got it?" It was clearly a threat.

Raven noticed Sal and smiled brightly. "Oh, and I brought a gift for you. I hope you like it! Crafters love rare materials…well, the ones I've met anyway, so I brought some evolved falcon feathers with me. They're in the car, so remind me to give them to you before we leave."

Sal grinned as he extended his hand. "Upgrade told me I'm not allowed to like you, but I've got a feeling that won't be possible."

Raven shook his head like it was nothing. "Oh no, that's completely my fault. Don't judge her too harshly. I endanger myself constantly and it drives her nuts! I gave her some of the feathers, too. And some other stuff. So she has to be nice to me today."

Upgrade grumbled as she took the wine bottle from him. "Show us the damn bow."

CHAPTER 52: GROWTH

Sal had to reassess everything he thought he knew about design. The Legendary-grade bow in front of him was not only a master class of design, but it was also a thing of beauty. It was one of the first times in his life where he didn't even think of appraising the item, because he was just so lost in the appearance of it.

Raven had pulled out what looked like a knuckle-duster from his pocket, which he slotted over his fingers and gripped tightly. With a single flick of his wrist, the bow flashed into existence in all its glory. Golden light, almost like a flowing river of molten metal, seemed to live within the ivory wood. It pulsated as it coursed through the bow, with little trickles of gold fraying off at the sides to create a series of small runes.

Sal moved his attention to the grip, which was a polished leather, expertly wrapped. It gave off an almost rustic look to the bow, and rested perfectly in Raven's hand.

"You'll notice that there's no string," Raven started excitedly as he waved his hand in the space between the curved edges. "All I need to do—"

"Don't you dare!" Doc Ameye was over in a flash, holding onto Raven's elbow as though he had just prevented a catastrophe. "What did I tell you about drawing it in public?"

Raven looked sullen as he let the bow disappear. "Not to."

Doc Ameye nodded slowly. "There are times I can tell that the two of you are definitely related." He glanced at Upgrade before he gave Raven a look of exasperation. "You could just explain to them rather than giving a demonstration. Also, I didn't give you that so you can parade it around. Do you have any idea how many people you skipped in the commission line?"

Raven nodded quietly. "Sorry, I just got excited and wanted to show them. My sister hadn't seen it yet, and the way the golden light makes the string is amazing." He held up his hand with the knuckle-duster-like grip. "What if I showed them outside? Would that be okay?"

Doc Ameye stared at Raven as if he were insane. "What possible justification do you have for that? It's a residential and commercial district. If they want to see it in action, then take them to a dungeon like everyone else and do it there."

Raven's entire demeanor lit up at the suggestion, but before he could say anything, Upgrade interjected.

"Absolutely not. While I've got every confidence in Fabi taking care of herself, you're not letting Sal anywhere near a dungeon," Upgrade stated firmly as she crossed her arms. She raised her palm at Raven's insistence. "No buts!"

Fabi gave Sal a sideways glance. "Could be fun? Dungeons are a great way to test new equipment!"

Sal was curious about Upgrade's insistence. She was the one who had dragged him into a dungeon first, so how was it any different if her brother was to do the same? When he looked at her quizzically, she seemed to read his mind.

"That was different. It was a controlled environment with Chatfield and me. Raven would get all excited and bring you into a high-level dungeon." Upgrade stared at Raven. "Tell me I'm wrong."

Raven let out an exasperated sigh as he wiped a hand through his hair. "Come on, they're not *that* hard. They give the best materials and loot, like…I'll have the birds with me, so we'd be even safer." When he saw that his tactic wasn't working, he shifted to a different angle. "Look, just a single run with me and their Hunter Bureau ranks would skyrocket!"

Upgrade shook her head slowly, and it was clear that she was very close to killing her brother. "Bring the birds? Which means it's not a dungeon at all…but a portal? You'd take them to a different fucking world, just to get materials?"

Raven looked at her and nodded slowly. "Yeah, but…the birds would be there. Nothing bad can happen when they're around."

"This is what I'm talking about. Can't you hear how insane he is?" Upgrade asked Sal, almost pleading him to see her side.

It really wasn't a difficult choice. Raven was suggesting they go into a portal. Sal, a first-year at Quest Academy…going into a portal, and protected by a Hero who could *talk to birds*.

With a single glance at Sal's expression, Raven clearly understood he was on the losing side of the argument. He grinned as he tapped his chest. "Trust me, the birds are amazing. The falcon feathers came from one of my friends, and she is fiercely protective of me. You make something good with her feathers, and she will see you as one of her own. I guarantee it."

Sal tried to choose his words carefully, at the risk of insulting the Hero. "As much as I'd love to see the bow in action, I think I might have to pass for now. Portals are a little outside my capabilities at the moment. I've only done a single dungeon and a fake tower with the Hunter Bureau."

Raven waved it off like it was nothing. "You said you were starting a guild, right? Do one of those runs with me and you'll shoot up to like the sixth tier. Your finances and administration can be atrocious and they'll still promote you if you have those sorts of outputs." His enthusiasm was apparent, but his logic was awful. "And, you'll gain a ton of rep with the Falconers Guild. It's good to have friendly relations with guilds, especially when it comes to collabs for the big expeditions."

Fabi perked up at those words. "Oooh, can you get me and my friends on one of those expeditions?" She was clearly excited by the prospect, and not even Upgrade's urging could discourage her. Fabi pointed across the room to where Sakura and O'Brien were watching the dance floor in a state of astonishment. "Those two are my team, and we're all third-years. We've already done simulated expeditions and excursions. The waiting list for a portal outing is massive, and I missed the last one because I was at Ameye Locomotive." She glanced over at Doc Ameye and gave him a guilty smile. "Which was amazing—I've got no regrets! Doing a portal is like the next logical step before I graduate."

Raven grinned as he nodded. "Already got them places for the next one! I don't really understand all the logistics that goes into it, but people just tell me where to be and they're typically cool when I bring others along." He gestured at Sal. "And it's an open invitation, man. You're more than welcome to come with, and I'll make sure to protect you."

Fabi faltered as she looked at Sal in confusion and then back at Raven. "He's a first-year, though. If it was a dungeon, that's different…but not a portal."

Sal nodded in agreement. "We've only done simulations of excursions and the tower, so I wouldn't even know what to do in a portal. I'd just be a liability." He couldn't believe he was even having this conversation. "Like, it's only been a few weeks since I've learned about the different types of demonic entities. We only really covered prowlers and leechers in a tower environment…"

Raven frowned as he placed a hand on his hip. "Chatty said you guys would be ready, though. The first-year class is apparently way better than the previous years…" He looked at Fabi and gave her a disarming smile. "No offense intended! I can tell you're one of the massive exceptions."

"None taken," Fabi responded as she looked at Upgrade in concern. "Do you know anything about this?"

Upgrade bit her lip as she stared at Raven. "I know the curriculum was up in the air. They moved the excursion from the end of second year to the end of the first semester, so the timelines are completely out of whack." She looked at her brother and sighed. "I take it that Chatty is Captain Chatfield?"

Raven nodded. "He gave a presentation to the Hunter Bureau about the proposed changes to the curriculum. Looks like the first-years are going to be doing a portal expedition in the next year or so. Or at least the ones in the Savior class." He gave a shrug as though it wasn't a big deal. "That's why they made the Savior class, isn't it? So they could be the best Heroes who can lead on the battlefield? Doesn't really make sense for them to graduate and need further training."

Upgrade's face paled as she looked past Raven to where Quest was speaking with Vector. "Quest signed off on this?"

Raven's eyes widened before a massive laugh left his lips. "Fuck no. He's been fighting it nonstop, and Robert had to be called in to stop him from attacking Chatty."

Doc Ameye shook his head as he stared at Raven. "This is a complete farce."

Raven faltered at those words, looking down at the older Crafter in shock. "What do you mean? Getting them ready for the realities of being a Hero…that's kinda what Quest Academy was built to do?"

"By whose definition?" Doc Ameye snapped as he gestured at Sal and Fabrizia. "You've got two exceptional Crafters here. What sort of Heroes do you expect them to be on the other side of the portal? Would Upgrade here have been able to foster their growth if she died on one of those portal runs?"

Upgrade froze as she looked at Doc Ameye in surprise. He wasn't done, though.

"Robert's insistence that anyone with an ability needs to hold a weapon is ridiculous. We've grown far past the reliance on Offense and Defense, but somehow we've now entered the era of Controllers? Healers stand to the sideline and fix us up as we bludgeon our heads against the facts. When will he finally get it through his thick skull that Crafters shouldn't be on the front lines?" Doc Ameye's voice was a growl as he stared at Raven, as though waiting for an answer.

Raven's expression softened as he spread his hands. "Doc, I didn't mean it like that…you know I wouldn't have been able to do half the shit I can do without equipment. Actually, a lot more than half." He laughed as he scratched at the back of his head. "The guilds and the bureau are tasked with keeping people safe, but the Crafters need to understand the war if they're going to have any chance of making us the right tools for the job!"

Before Doc Ameye could continue, Raven spoke quickly, as though he had just found the perfect solution.

"Like, think about it…if we ensure they're protected, and they understand what's really needed on the battlefront, wouldn't that improve them as Crafters?" He looked between Doc Ameye and his sister. "You guys both fought, so you know what it's like! When you see people making stupid shit or doing useless research, doesn't it make you angry? If we align the next generation of Heroes with the actual problems we're facing, they'll be more motivated to work on solutions to those problems."

Upgrade snorted as she shook her head. "Incredible save."

Doc Ameye folded his arms. "Raven, you're on the wrong side of this if you think it's wise." He lifted a single hand to gesture at Sal. "If I was a first-year at Quest Academy, would you send me through a portal and risk traumatizing me? None of the technology I've built would exist because I wouldn't have had the time to Craft. I'd have to spend all my time training for fighting and tactics, and being your definition of a Hero."

Raven scoffed as he shook his head. "That's not fair. You're different, though."

Doc Ameye clicked his fingers. "Exactly. But there's nothing in place right now for the people who are different. By my estimation, Salvatore Argento and Fabrizia Maccles have the potential to catch up to me." He gave them both a steady look. "In a good few years."

Fabi looked conflicted as she glanced between them. "I agree with Doc Ameye when it comes to Salvatore, but for the direction I want to build my career…I need to go into portals. I've trained for them and know the risks, so I should be allowed to enter them rather than being forced to shelter because of my capabilities."

Doc Ameye nodded. "And that should be your choice. It's a foolish one, but it's still your choice."

Sal wasn't sure how he should feel about everything that was going on. Raven was essentially telling them that the curriculum had been revised to include a portal expedition at some stage in the future? Having only done the excursion with Prestige and the tower trial, there was no way that Sal felt equipped to take on something like a portal. He agreed wholeheartedly with Doc Ameye that they shouldn't be sending Crafters into portals just for research purposes. Fabi seemed to be different in how motivated she was for battle, but she was an exception. Sal couldn't imagine Blathnaid or Jack jumping at the opportunity to run into a portal. Hell, even Barry and Divinity would advise against it. Gallant was the only first-year who came to mind when he thought about capability.

"When do you think it's going to happen?" Sal asked suddenly. He wanted to know whether it was something he truly needed to prepare for.

Upgrade looked at Sal seriously. "This isn't something you're ready for. Even if you make a full Legendary-grade set, you don't have the experience to take on a portal. It's a whole new world on the other side of those things, and it's near impossible to determine the power levels of the demons you'll face." She looked incredibly stressed as she spoke. "Put it out of your mind until I have a chat with Quest. We need to know what our options are, and they can't be as black-and-white as Raven is telling us."

Raven lifted a finger. "There's a whole department at the bureau dedicated to the assessment of the portals. They've got dozens of specialized Hunters with the Foresight ability working on calamity prevention and strategy stuff. They've already given the green light on the expedition, before the portal even opens up!" He paused when he saw the incredulity on his sister's face. Coughing nervously, he apologized. "Sorry, just when you said it was impossible to determine the power levels…"

Sal raised his hand. "I'm only asking when it's happening so I have time to prepare, if we end up getting forced to do it." He explained his reasonings to Upgrade. "I've got no desire to step into a portal. Divinity had a vision that I walk into a portal at some point in the future and never return. I can't just ignore that when I'm being told a portal is part of the curriculum."

Upgrade's eyes widened as she focused on Sal. "What? When did she predict that?"

Fabi stared at Sal with concern. "When were you going to bring this up?"

Sal laughed awkwardly and tried to defuse the tension. "Hey, I thought that I wouldn't need to worry about it. Seemed pretty preventable, you know…by not setting foot in a portal!"

"We could tell Robert," Upgrade said as she looked between Raven and Doc Ameye. "If there's a genuine threat to Sal when portals are considered, then we can use that to get him a free pass on doing that part."

"Why are you looking at me?" Doc Ameye asked in exasperation. "He should just drop out of Quest Academy. Fabrizia, too."

Fabi shook her head. "No way. Not when I'm this close to the finishing line. I have my ability now, and I'll need that Skill class more than ever." She looked at Doc Ameye and sighed. "I've created my own path and it's not going to be spent hiding away in a workshop for the rest of my life. My people are safer when I'm there, and I'd never be able to live with myself if something was to happen to them."

Sal nodded in agreement. "Despite all the crap I've had to endure, I'm enjoying my time at Quest Academy. I want to see how much more I can grow there. When my Trainee Guild starts off, I intend to continue learning by surrounding myself with people who are smarter than me." He grinned. "And with Upgrade there, too."

Upgrade shot him a smile and raised her hand in warning. "There's no need for them to leave Quest Academy, Doc. We just need to ensure it's a safe and stable environment. I'll be having a chat with Quest about all this portal stuff." She gave Doc Ameye a straight look. "I don't know how effective I'll be, but I know that the other faculty won't sit idly by when the bureau is making moves like this."

Raven turned around to look at the dance floor, his face conflicted. "I get what you're worried about." He looked back at Upgrade with a serious expression. "Just know that if any of your people do have to go through a portal, I'll take care of them." He pointed at Sal meaningfully. "And I'll absolutely make sure he comes back. My birds will rip through every demonic realm to get him if needs be."

His entire demeanor had shifted when he spoke, and it was only when Upgrade smiled that Sal felt reassured.

"Let's hope it doesn't come to that." Upgrade sighed as she looked around the room. "We're not going to be able to solve the academy's problems tonight, and Quest looks like he's in no shape to handle any sort of accusations." She jutted her chin to where Quest was leaning heavily against a stone pillar, his eyes focused on the glass of whiskey in his hand. "So, let's keep an eye on this and wait until we know more."

With that said, Upgrade indicated that she wanted to have a chat with Raven in private. They walked off to one side, while Doc Ameye excused himself to meander off in the direction of Quest. It looked like he wasn't going to adhere to Upgrade's suggestion and wanted to have a word with the headmaster, regardless of how drunk he was. It left Fabi and Sal standing side by side.

"So…that was intense," Fabi muttered under her breath with raised eyebrows. "How are you feeling?"

Sal exhaled slowly before offering her a shrug. "I've gotten to the point where I'm no longer really all that surprised when this shit happens. The excursion caught me by surprise, then the tower…even the dungeon with Chatfield and Upgrade. It's like every single time I have a moment to breathe, something comes up and I need to give it my full attention." He raised a hand to his face to stifle a yawn, before apologizing. "Sorry, apparently I'm also tired of all the bullshit, too." He chuckled as he looked at her carefully. "What about you? What has you so interested in the portals?"

Fabi frowned at him. "It's not okay for you to be strung along like that, though. First and second year were super straightforward for me and the others, but you seem to be pulled in every direction. Why don't you just take a break from all of it and decide what you want to do when you get back in the second semester?"

Sal blinked in surprise. "What about all those dungeon runs? I didn't think you'd let me off the hook that easily."

Fabi shook her head, her smile nowhere to be found. "We can go on them if you want, but there's no obligation. I was just teasing you at the gala." She tilted her head in the direction of the Arkwright. "I'll clear out the dungeons with Sakura and O'Brien, and we'll trade the materials for a shot at using that fancy machine of yours. If that's okay with you? I don't want to be yet another person deciding your future."

Sal faltered ever so slightly. "Like, I really do appreciate the offer of help, and I do think I need to get better at standing on my own two feet." He laughed nervously. "And the idea of running dungeons with you isn't all that bad, but maybe just simple ones to start so I can get into the groove with them. Having Sakura and O'Brien there really does add another layer of safety. I saw footage of her taking out a commander variant."

"Groove?" Fabi repeated with a smile. "A Latin-style groove, perhaps?"

Sal groaned as he looked at his feet. "I'm adding that into my list of mortifying comments. Thanks for reminding me."

Fabi glanced around the room as though looking for someone. When her eyes landed on Sakura and O'Brien, she nodded. "Okay, I'm going to catch up with the guys for a bit. Have a think about what it is you'd like to do going forward and we can start discussing the warehouse and the depot. We need to draw some lines in the sand so we're not taking advantage of each other, or getting in each other's way."

Sal nodded. "I'm fully convinced my father and yours have already decided our next five years."

Fabi barked a laugh as she shook her head. "Good luck to them. If my father thinks he's getting a shopfront rent-free, he's got another thing coming."

CHAPTER 53: APPREHENSION

"Portal expedition?" Barry repeated slowly as though he hadn't heard Sal properly. Without prompting, he took Sal's glass from him and gave it a sniff. "What are you drinking for that to sound normal?" His frown increased as he stared at the clear liquid in shock.

Sal smiled as he retrieved his glass of water. "Sounds like it's going to be factored into the curriculum at some point, if Raven is to be believed." He grimaced. "It's actually nice having a bit of a heads-up this time rather than finding out when we get back to Quest Academy."

Barry stared at him as if he were going insane. "Did you already have your freak-out before coming over to talk to me? Because this is something that warrants freaking out." Looking over Sal's shoulder, his eyes narrowed before he refocused his attention on Sal. "You should check in on Divinity, by the way. She's had a pretty rough night."

Sal nodded in agreement. "Did she just drink too much, or was it something she saw in the future?" He was still thinking about Divinity's message about Fabi's power. There was the looming question of whether his actions at the gala had thrown yet another obstacle into her planned future. While Sal cared for Divinity and really valued her as a friend, he was getting a little wary of how she was so bought into certain futures happening.

Barry twisted his palm from side to side. "Both, but nothing really to worry about." He let out a pained sigh as he gestured around the room. "Alcohol and overwhelm got to her all at once, coupled with the Saviors pestering her for visions after she predicted the thing with the implant."

Sal paused at that. "Wait, so there's no looming calamity on the horizon or something?"

Barry just shook his head. "Nope, she was mostly just keeping people pacified with visions. She was playing nice, but she burned herself out and spiraled from there." He put his hands on his hips and sighed in exasperation. "She went from being all happy and giddy to melancholy in a flash. Everything went all doom and gloom, with her fears that we were all drifting apart."

"Drifting apart? Is it because I spent most of the night talking to Fabi?" Sal was ready with his defense. Divinity had changed seats with Fabi in advance, so he wasn't going to feel guilty for getting along with her.

Barry stared at him before slowly shaking his head. "No, man…the whole excursion thing and then straight into the tower. She misses the days where we all hung out and worked together in the training hall." He smiled faintly before offering a shrug. "I had no idea she enjoyed all that stuff, either."

Sal exhaled slowly as he let his shoulders drop. Looking off to one side, he thought about Barry's words and felt a growing sense of shame. He had been prepared to accuse Divinity of meddling, and although she was probably still doing it, tonight was just a series of poor judgments on her own part.

Barry clapped Sal on the shoulder and smiled at him. "She's a little sensitive at the moment. Even with Rochelle sobering her up, she's absolutely mortified…so maybe hold off on asking for the future for a while."

"Concern, from Barry Francis?" Sal returned the smile. "I wasn't intending to ask her anything about the future, to be honest. The less I know about when the portal expedition is, the better."

Barry laughed and shook his head. "Okay, no…that one request should be an exception to the rule. There's no way I'm going back to Quest Academy blind if there's a chance of learning more about it now." He looked across the room to where Fabi was speaking with Sakura and O'Brien. "Looks like things went well with Fabi?" His smile was wide as he looked at Sal meaningfully. "I really hope you two click."

Sal was surprised at the sudden vote of confidence from Barry. "Thanks. She's honestly pretty amazing…but I've only just met her. I'd like to meet her when I haven't been on whiskey the whole night."

Barry nodded encouragingly. "Perfect. If you two work out, then I won't need to worry about Victoria." He grimaced at the mention of her name. "Honestly, since Divinity threw that prediction at us, I've been second-guessing all the teasing messages. Like, can you actually imagine? Two Controllers in a relationship…it would be a disaster."

"Divinity is a Controller, though," Sal countered with a smirk, giving Barry a meaningful nudge.

"Completely different," Barry answered with a wave of his hand. "Victoria actually controls people, like Erika. I make random shit appear, and Divinity sees random shit in the future. We wouldn't be that bad of a match, so it's like an exception to the rule." He brushed the comment off casually, as though it wasn't a big deal.

"Right…and two Supports?" Sal gestured at himself and then over his shoulder to where Barry had just looked. "Would we be doomed as a pairing?"

Barry snorted with a quick shake of his head. "Eh…no. Have you met your own parents? Two Supports absolutely works."

Sal smiled along with Barry, but it opened the door to Sal's own thoughts about his mother. There was a high chance that she wasn't a Support class at all. Although it was all a bit of fun to talk about the different class types in relationships, and wasn't worth any real analysis, Sal couldn't shake the thought that his mother had been lying to him for years.

"Blathnaid is doing the babysitting at the moment, but you should head over to talk to her. Just don't give her shit." Barry pointed over to where Divinity stood with Blathnaid near the edge of the drinks tables.

When Sal turned around, he could see Divinity looking a little worse for wear. Her eyes were downcast as she held her glass of water. Blathnaid looked to be reassuring her in some way, but Divinity just kept shaking her head from side to side.

"Let's go." Sal moved over to where Divinity and Blathnaid stood. He smiled warmly, which was only returned by Blathnaid, who noticed his approach. Barry was only a step behind Sal and soon all four of them were reunited.

"She's saying that she wants to go home," Blathnaid said gently as she looked at Sal. "I've been telling her that she didn't make a scene, and that nobody really noticed."

"Notice what?" Sal asked with a perfect poker face. "You're more than welcome to stay. We've barely spoken all night."

Divinity sighed as she gave Sal a conflicted expression. "I know you're just being nice…everyone noticed. I drank way too much and got a little emotional."

"A little?" Barry folded his arms, giving her a look of disbelief. "You pretty much poured out your entire heart and soul, to the point that I was worried you weren't long for this world."

Divinity's jaw dropped in horror, and Sal had to elbow Barry, laughing. "What happened to not giving her a hard time?"

Barry grinned. "Hey, I said that *you* shouldn't give her a hard time. I've had her drooling on my shoulder for the last few hours—I get a free pass!" He put his hand over his own heart as though he were the most upstanding and honest citizen in existence. "I did that out of the goodness of my heart, and she just kept repeating that I'm the absolute worst…talk about a one-sided friendship!"

Divinity's face flushed as she looked at Blathnaid for context, like she was genuinely terrified that it was true. Unfortunately, Blathnaid could only smile guiltily. "There were a few accusations like that…but really, it wasn't that bad!"

"Truce?" Sal threw into the group. He pointed at himself and smiled at their confused faces. "Nobody gives me shit about the hulker body slam." His finger went to Barry. "We forget about him confessing his undying love for Divinity at the end of the tournament."

"That didn't happen," Barry said adamantly through a wry smile.

Sal then pointed at Divinity. "And we forget that Divinity had a few too many drinks at the gala?" He smiled at them. "Sound good?"

Divinity nodded instantly. "I very much like this truce. Can we put it in place immediately?" She gave Barry a sideways glance, as though hoping that it would prevent him from torturing her further.

Blathnaid raised a hand. "Er, I don't really get anything out of this truce…" She laughed before offering a shrug. "But I'm not really the type who would want to make anyone feel bad, so I'm happy to go along with it."

Barry looked at Blathnaid quizzically. "We'll stop suggesting that Darren likes you?" He waved his hand as though the trade were obvious.

Blathnaid's face went beet red as she nodded instantly. "Yep, I agree to the truce."

Divinity smiled gently as she looked around at them. "Thank you. I feel like such an idiot…and I didn't mean to cause such a scene." With a shake of her head, she looked around the room. "I'm so thankful your parents were dancing though, because I feel like everyone would have had their eyes on me otherwise."

Sal shook his head. "What happens at the auction house, stays at the auction house. We pride ourselves on our confidentiality." He gave her a reassuring smile. "Except for pretty much everything to do with Mythcrafter and Skill Master. That shit seems to spread like wildfire anytime I meet someone," he finished with a laugh. "Do you guys want to see the Arkwright and my workshop?"

"Arkwright?" Barry repeated in confusion. "That thing you were talking about with Fabi?"

Divinity shook her head slightly. "If it's okay with you, I'll have a look at it another time. I don't want to risk all those stairs right now." She gestured vaguely at herself. "Rochelle may have sobered up my brain, but everything else feels like crap right now."

Blathnaid looked conflicted before shaking her head, too. "Yeah, we can look at it another time. Gives us an excuse to hang out again during the break!" She perked up at that last part as she looked around at them hopefully. "If you guys aren't too busy running the tower trial?"

Barry grinned as he offered her a shrug. "It's been a lucrative little business. We've helped so many people get up to the fifth floor, and I genuinely feel like I'm getting the hang of being a Controller."

Divinity shot him a look. "Really? Shouting at people that they're doing things wrong is your idea of a good Controller?"

Barry nodded. "Naturally. It works wonders. Throwing up illusions to show them what to do is pretty effective, too. I personally enjoy the shouting, though."

"I'd love if you guys came over to hang out sometime." Sal gestured around the room. "Maybe when it's a little less crazy. I'm going to be working on some gear for myself before the semester starts back up."

Blathnaid's eyes brightened. "Oooh, what are you thinking of making? I want to see the designs when you've finished the blueprints."

Sal laughed as he shook his head. "I've got no idea just yet. Fabi was talking about battle-suits, and I want to get her input on what they're supposed to do. There's a whole lot of guild stuff going to be happening, too." He paused as he looked at them. "I know that I've spoken to all of you about it, but I'd love to have you in the guild. If not now, then in the future."

Barry sighed as he tapped against his chest. "I've already been bribed, so I'm pretty much signed up."

Blathnaid nodded slowly. "If Upgrade is in, then I'd be interested. I still have a lot to learn, and there were a lot of guilds talking to me at the gala. It's nice having all the options, but I have a feeling we'd make better stuff than whatever their Crafting programs have to offer."

Sal smiled at the responses before he looked at Divinity. "I know you said that you were going to do your own thing when I asked you before. Just know that the option is always going to be open for you." He wanted Divinity to know that she was always welcome in whatever guild he set up. In the past, she had made a joke about Fabi becoming his vice-captain of the guild, instead of her. Although Sal was of the mind that the future changed based on his actions, Divinity seemed to place a higher focus on them…probably because of how regularly she looked at them. Sal wanted to make his stance crystal clear. Whatever guild he started, he wanted her in it.

Divinity gave Sal a warm smile as she nodded in thanks. "It's not the right time for me, but I really appreciate the offer."

Barry frowned as he stared at Divinity. "Why not?"

Divinity hesitated instead of answering, so Sal put up his hand to stop her from continuing.

"You don't have to tell us. Just know that you're welcome whenever you decide, okay?" He meant every word, and didn't want her feeling uncomfortable about it. If she was being cagey, there was probably a reason. Forcing her to admit that would just result in an argument, and he didn't want to aggravate her when she was already feeling fragile. "We're a team, and we work well together."

"Thanks, Sal." Divinity smiled as she gave him a grateful nod. "I'll let you know if things change."

Barry folded his arms and just shook his head. "This stuff would be a hundred times easier if you both just spoke your mind." With a sigh, he gestured at Sal and then to Divinity. "Are you going to tell her about the portal expedition?"

"The what now?" Blathnaid said in a panicked voice as she looked between Sal and Barry in shock.

Divinity grimaced. "Ah."

Barry groaned as he looked at the ceiling. "If you're about to say that you knew about this, just keep it to yourself."

CHAPTER 54: ENDORSEMENT

Sal waited until the private car with Divinity finally departed. Despite their collective reassurances that she was fine, she had insisted on going home early. Well, early wasn't the right word…as it was close to three in the morning when the car came to collect her. When he finished waving her off, he became conscious of how cold it was outside and walked back toward the auction house. The sounds of merriment emanating from the building were a stark contrast to the deathly quiet of the outdoors. Before stepping back inside, Sal waited outside for a few more moments. His body was heating up to counteract the sudden cold, but it wasn't an unpleasant feeling.

He could see, through the glass doorway, a few people on the dance floor bumping into one another and laughing, which brought a smile to his face. All the tension surrounding the gala had evaporated and he had left the venue a much richer man than before. Getting the depot was a massive win, and sharing it with Fabi was a great move for Silver Sanctuary. A materials supplier on the doorstep, as well as her being there while he was at Quest Academy…it was a definite recipe for success. Although it would have been nice to get it fully for himself, sharing it felt like a weight had been lifted from his shoulders. It was clear that the bureau would be watching their development carefully, so Sal wanted to give it every chance for success. Fabi Maccles being a part of the new enterprise increased those odds dramatically.

With a contented sigh, he reached for the door handle and let himself back into the party.

Sal smiled and waved at a few of the people who raised their glasses in his direction as he passed them. He could see his father talking to Lawrence Baron and Maurice Maccles over by the buffet table. Sal hadn't even noticed when it had been set up beside the drinks area, but it was a glowing testament to how efficient his parents operated as hosts.

"Salvatore!" Lawrence announced as he moved forward in a flash. "I've been hoping to catch you before we wrapped up. That cane-sword is truly remarkable, and I have to say that you boys in Silver Sanctuary are quite good at keeping secrets." He laughed as he looked at both Maurice and Petro. "I asked high and low about a skilled artisan who works with obsidian, and would you believe what my sources came back with?"

Sal smiled as he nodded. "That there are hundreds of skilled artisans who use it?"

Lawrence grinned. "Barely a dozen. But…a shipping company that we use had a lot to say about a shipment of obsidian glass being delivered to Silver Sanctuary. With your name on it." He waved his hand around in the air like it was mere coincidence. "Then we factor in the murmurings of a Mythcrafter project, announced by none other than Doc Ameye…who disappears to your private workshop?" Lawrence clapped Maurice on the shoulder. "So, imagine my surprise when Maurice here tells me that you've bought all of young Fabrizia's old Crafting equipment."

Petro rolled his eyes from behind Lawrence before offering Sal a shrug.

"So many coincidences, Mr. Baron," Sal agreed with another nod. "But I guess the question still stands…is the obsidian cane-sword good enough to secure you as a materials supplier?" He gestured at Maurice. "Because I've got a feeling that Mr. Maccles here is going to be stepping up to help Fabi with her upcoming projects. I could avail of a local seller and keep that cane-sword."

Petro slid into the conversation with a knowing wink. "Ah now, Salvatore. We don't need to antagonize the poor man. While you were off chatting with Doc Ameye, I had a very frank conversation with Maurice, Lawrence, and Vector." He nodded to where Vector was talking with Quest near one of the pillars. "Obviously, it would be your decision, but Vector took a keen interest in the rejuvenation project at the depot. He believed a consortium approach would be the best method to ensure all suppliers played nice. Giving both Maurice and Lawrence an ample opportunity to compete on certain materials, and providing the best value to you and Fabrizia, both."

Sal stared at his father. He tried not to show his shock, but there was no way that Lawrence Baron was going to take that deal. It was like a luxury goods store aligning with a corner shop. It didn't make any sense for Baron's Material Exchange to cooperate with Maccles Materials.

Maurice smiled as he gave Sal a playful nudge. "I will say, those coincidences that Lawrence put together sure made him very keen on working with us. Coupled with the stellar showing of Fabrizia's new ability." He practically beamed with pride, and it was the first time Sal had seen the man not looking tired.

"So, they're going to negotiate down out of the goodness of their hearts?" Sal asked his father, his eyebrow raised. "What sort of deal comes from our side?"

Petro shook his head and gave the two men an apologetic glance. "Sorry, I don't know who raised this suspicious child. I blame his mother."

Both Lawrence and Maurice gave a good-natured chuckle before Petro filled Sal in. "It's nothing set in stone, but moving Maccles Materials into one of the storefronts would be a massive cost saving in terms of rent. Now, we're not talking about waiving the fee completely, but a reduced rate that would allow him to price his goods more competitively and put him right next door to the depot." He turned and gestured at Lawrence. "As for Mr. Baron, he has factored in that a material supplier on your doorstep would likely cut him out of the equation completely…so rather than letting that happen, he's suggested a partnership with Maurice, giving Maccles Materials an exclusive contract on certain goods, like high-quality cores and rare ingredients."

Lawrence nodded. "Exactly that. I'd rather lose a few dollars if it meant having a good relationship with the artisan of Silver Sanctuary." He then caught himself and gestured at Maurice. "And there's opportunity here for Maccles Materials to level up their product offering. Everyone wins."

Sal's eyes narrowed. "And are you expecting commission slots?" He aimed the question at Lawrence.

"Naturally, but that can be discussed at a later date." He responded with a shooing gesture, as though waving it off. "Right now, I just wanted to congratulate you on the creation of such an exemplary cane-sword. I stood outside like a buffoon, illuminating the entire street by waving it around!" He laughed at himself before pointing at Maurice. "You can ask him. It was a sight to behold!"

"I'll pass on your regards to the artisan, but I'm glad you liked it." Sal smiled. Even if Lawrence already knew he was a Mythcrafter, he didn't want to be the one to confirm it for him.

Petro snapped his fingers before looking at Sal. "By the way, Quest spoke with us earlier and was very complimentary about your first semester. You should thank him for coming along after the gala." He gestured at Lawrence and Maurice. "I'll keep these two honest while you're gone. I'm pretty sure we can squeeze a little more out of Mr. Baron." He gave Lawrence a sideways smile.

"At this rate, I doubt I'll be leaving with my own car," Lawrence complained.

Sal nodded as he looked to where Quest stood. Turning back to his father, he smiled. "Have fun with the negotiations, but don't make any handshake deals until both Fabi and I have a look." He pointed at all of them, laughing. "I want to get Blathnaid into one of those storefronts, so try not to promise them all away."

Lawrence paused at that and looked at Sal seriously. "The girl who was able to Craft a spear out of the prowler leg? She's associated with you?" All airs were completely abandoned as Lawrence Baron went into hard business mode.

"Yes, and she also needs materials. She's the highest rank in the scavenger runs out of the first-years." Sal pointed to where Blathnaid was talking to Barry. "And she's standing right over there. Don't mention the thing about the storefront though, because I'm hoping to keep it as a surprise."

"And charging her rent for the privilege?" Petro suggested with a raised eyebrow.

Sal chuckled as he nodded. "When she starts earning, yes. I'd rather see the storefronts active as personal workshops rather than sitting empty. Having it as a bonus for the guild's Crafters would be a great hook! But, I'd need to run all of that past Fabi. I've got no idea what she'd think of that plan."

"She'd love it." Maurice smiled. "She'd absolutely love it."

"Glad to hear it," Sal replied earnestly before excusing himself. "I'll go and say hello to Quest. Hope you both enjoy the rest of the party." He gave Lawrence and Maurice a polite nod before smiling at his father and setting off to Quest, whiskey in hand.

"Salvatore." Quest raised his glass in greeting. "We've certainly come a long way from that first Doom Society meeting." He looked around the room at everyone having fun before sighing and shaking his head slightly. "I'd like to apologize for the events earlier today."

Sal shook his head. "That wasn't your fault, though. You were strong-armed by Robert into doing that."

Quest chuckled wryly. "I'm the headmaster of Quest Academy, with my name on the damn building." He looked at Sal and smiled. "I should have been able to do more for Fabrizia." He looked into his whiskey glass, frowning, and sighed. "I also should have stopped drinking a while ago."

"It all worked out, and Fabi has an incredible new ability." Sal tried to cheer Quest up, but it looked like there was nothing that could be said to change the headmaster's mood.

"You've done incredible things in your first semester." Quest smiled faintly as he gestured around the room. "And when I see how many people come together to support you, I can't help but hope for a bright future." He paused for a moment as though debating his next words. With a glance to see that Sal was still beside him, he continued. "Robert Locke is a very principled man. He is a powerhouse on the battlefield and that is unfortunately reason enough to give him absolute authority."

Quest let his hand drop to one side, sighing as he forced a smile. "I genuinely hope that you don't follow Doc Ameye's footsteps too closely, Salvatore. You have the potential to be a very different leader than Robert, if you keep on the path of becoming a guildmaster."

Sal wasn't exactly sure how to respond to that. In just a single sentence, Quest had managed to criticize both Doc Ameye and the president of the Hunter Bureau. Even the insinuation that Sal could somehow usurp Robert was laughable, but Quest didn't seem like he was joking.

"Doc Ameye approached me earlier." Quest placed his empty glass on the nearby table. "He's not too impressed by the machinations of the Hunter Bureau, and I can't say that I blame him. They pivot endlessly between new strategies without giving anything time to come to fruition."

Sal remained quiet, not really sure how he could speak about the Hunter Bureau. He was certain that Quest's tongue had been severely loosened by the alcohol. Although the man did confide in him quite a bit, this was on a whole different level and Sal wasn't sure how to proceed.

"I've tried my best to prolong the sense of normalcy for the students, but it doesn't match up to their damned timeline." Quest chuckled humorlessly. "Portal expeditions seem to be in the cards a year from now, which is the height of ridiculousness. Even if we started training you all for the next two semesters, it wouldn't be enough time." He shook his head with a pained sigh. "We need to get that workshop upgraded, and indenture every Support enrolled at the academy. If it keeps them off the front lines, I'll chain them to the workbenches if needs be…" He looked at Sal and paused, as though realizing that he was talking to a student.

"Ah, forgive me for the ramblings." Quest waved his hand. "You'll be informed with the other students when a decision is made regarding the amendments to the curriculum." He tried to move back into an authoritative tone, but the slight slurring in his voice was a key sign that he wasn't sober.

Sal felt conflicted as he realized how tough it was for Quest to keep Quest Academy moving in the right direction. By all reports, the Hunter Bureau was constantly meddling with how things were done, and it resulted in their excursion and tower run in just the first semester. It sounded like it was only going to continue down that path, with the current first-years being tasked with more difficult trials in the years to come. Sal was annoyed, and it was validating to see that Quest was in agreement with him. Still, it was going to be tough to navigate such a heavy conversation.

"What do we need to achieve for Robert to leave us alone? The Supports, I mean?" Sal carefully asked; wondering whether Quest was going to stonewall him and disregard the question. The conversation he had with the headmaster after the infirmary, post excursion, was still in his mind. Quest wanted him to change the landscape for the Support classes, and create a path for them to be Heroes worth reckoning with.

Quest looked at him for a moment, his eyes coming into focus long enough for him to properly register the question. "Nothing." He smiled as he said it. "You've already done such amazing things since you've stepped into the academy, Salvatore. The weight of responsibility isn't on your shoulders, and you don't need to do anything."

He placed a hand on his chest as he pushed off the wall and staggered slightly. "Me, on the other hand…I have a lot of work to do." He clapped Sal on the shoulder and let out a satisfied sigh. "It's been a while since I've gotten to relax like this. Please thank your parents on my behalf for a wonderful end to a horrible evening."

Sal realized he wasn't going to get anything more out of the headmaster and conceded. "Do you want me to call a car for you?"

Quest just shook his head. "No, I want to walk for a while and collect my thoughts. I'll need to have a sit-down with Robert to hash all of this out, and buy as much time as possible." He looked around the room and smiled wistfully. "Focus on setting up your guild and showing the world what Support classes are capable of. Your success will take you up the ranks until you're in a strong position to effect change."

"Like leading the Hunter Bureau?" Sal joked, still wondering what Quest meant by that statement.

Quest snorted as he shook his head. "Heavens no. You're destined for things far greater than that, Mr. Argento. I just hope I'm still around to see it."

With a halfhearted salute and a wry smile, Quest excused himself from the party and made his way to the doorway with his hands tucked into the pockets of his tuxedo jacket.

Sal watched him leave, wondering how things were going to play out for Quest Academy in the coming semester.

CHAPTER 55: TRUTH

"That's the last of them?" Sophia asked wearily as she leaned back in a chair and pulled off her shoes with a relieved sigh. "I honest to God thought we'd be serving them breakfast." She laughed with a shake of her head before reclining back in the chair to release a reluctant yawn.

Petro smiled as he locked up the front door. "That's it. I thought it would be the kids who lingered. But Lawrence Baron?" He laughed in near disbelief. "You could tell there was a lot of excitement, though. I can hardly blame him."

Sal trudged across the makeshift dance floor with a tub of used glasses. He was finding them everywhere, and wondered whether the guests had started hiding them, like some sort of game. The party had been great, but it ended up dragging on for far too long. It was close to seven in the morning, and the cleanup had officially started. Ever since he was a child, they had performed this ritual of making the auction house presentable before leaving.

"Did you have a good time with your friends?" Sophia asked from her seat. She had taken to rubbing her soles as she looked at Sal with a smile.

Sal readjusted the tub in his hands and gave her a nod. "Yeah, but I won't lie…the whole portal thing kind of put a damper on everything. The excursion and tower was one thing, but they want us to go into a portal while we're students?"

Petro let out a sigh as he folded his jacket and draped it across the back of one of the chairs. He rolled up his sleeves and gave Sal a reassuring smile. "You doing all that work on the weaves will certainly give you a free pass from the portal. There's no way they'd risk your contributions by throwing you into danger like that."

Sal blinked as he stared at his father. "Not going to lie, I was kinda expecting a little bit of outrage or disbelief from you guys."

Sophia laughed as she gestured around the room. "We're tired, so all you get is logic and practicality tonight. I'm emotionally spent after all that small talk."

Petro nodded in agreement as he lifted one of the buckets and set off toward the lounge area to find more discarded glasses and empty wine bottles. "We'll make quick work of this and get back to the house. I don't want George and the others coming in and thinking this is their responsibility."

Sal placed his tub on the ground before stretching out his back, wincing slightly. "Since we're in a logical and practical mood, would you like to tell me the truth?" He gave his mother a level stare, but forced a smile to his face. "It's technically tomorrow. I won't be able to sleep if we don't do this now."

Sophia hesitated and looked off to the area that Petro had disappeared to. In just a few seconds, he returned without the tub, but with a bottle of whiskey and three glasses. "You can't be serious, Petro?" She looked at him with wide eyes. "Coffee. I've only just sobered up!"

Petro shrugged as he placed the bottle on the table and gestured for Sal to join them. "I need more than coffee for this conversation." He gave his son a smile and pointed to a free seat at the small table.

Sal tentatively walked over to the table and took a seat, eyeing the whiskey suspiciously. His head was already throbbing and the last thing he wanted to do was continue drinking. If anything, he wanted to keep his head clear to properly understand why his parents had been lying to him for so many years.

Petro poured a whiskey for himself before placing the bottle between Sophia and Sal. "So, where should we start?"

Sal ignored the bottle in front of him. "From the beginning, and don't leave anything out." He realized that his tone had become cold and he tried to stop it from coming out that way, but his father just waved him off.

"Salvatore, you've got every right to feel pissed off and betrayed. Don't apologize for taking a tone with us. We're the ones who owe you an apology." Petro smiled at his son as he swirled the whiskey in his hand. "You might be feeling betrayed by your mother, but I'm equally to blame in all of this. Probably even more so."

Sophia's lips went tight as she stared at her discarded shoes on the floor. "We had intended on telling you when you went to Quest Academy, but…a part of us was convinced that you'd drop out and join us back here at the auction. If that happened, then we'd be able to continue as normal and wouldn't ever have to bring this up."

Petro grimaced. "Okay, it sounds bad when you say it like that." He placed his whiskey down and looked at Sal. "We didn't want you growing up in an environment where the weight of society pressed you down. Both your mother and I worked hard to build a life away from the Hunter Bureau and the Guilds Association. We've got countless agreements in place with them so they stay out of our way, and that we're never enlisted into their schemes. We pay our taxes and do our own thing. It's worked for just over two decades."

Sal shook his head. "Start with your abilities." He didn't want this to devolve into a conversation about them wanting to protect him. If his mother had the same ability as him, then he wanted to know what it was.

Sophia nodded as she reached for the bottle of whiskey. "My ability falls into the Body Manipulation category. It's called Shaper, and I used it to imitate the abilities of other Heroes." She poured a whiskey for herself without looking at either Petro or Sal. "Your father has All Sight, and he used to map out the weaves of other people that I could use with Shaper."

Sal's jaw dropped as he stared at his father. Yes, both of them had been lying to him…but his father was able to see weaves? Not only that, but he had experience of mapping them out? Although a lot of the revelations were horrifying and a massive betrayal, Sal couldn't help but feel excited by the fact that he had basically inherited the hybrid of his parents' abilities. Pushing the positive emotions to one side, he needed more answers and he didn't want to get distracted from getting them. "Were you a Hero?" he asked his mother bluntly.

"Yes," Sophia answered before downing her whiskey. "So was your father."

Petro smiled as he offered Sal a shrug. "If it helps, I was nowhere near as badass as your mother!"

Sophia shot him a warning look, but Petro wasn't abated in the slightest. He leaned across the table and grinned at Sal.

"I meant what I said about your mother bullying Prestige." He pointed at Sophia with a look of admiration. "She joined the Silverson Group as a cadet while I was still in basic training. Had I not tried my luck with an officer, you probably wouldn't exist." He laughed at his own joke before tapping the table. "She was fierce on the battlefield. You should have seen her. Nobody knew what her power was, because of the sheer versatility of Shaper. She was an extraordinary Healer who saved countless lives, but was no slouch when it came to the front lines."

"That's enough, Petro," Sophia said quietly as she cast a worried glance in Sal's direction. "Your father tends to exaggerate. It wasn't anything that great."

Sal just stared at them in total disbelief. "Both of you were Heroes…and you were on the battlefield?" Everything he had known growing up was a complete lie, and Sal had no idea how to compartmentalize that information. All the days where they had cautioned him about his power…they had created an environment where Sal felt safe and welcome. Being the son of two Supports—it had shaped his entire identity. "You're…not Supports?"

Just before Petro could answer, Sal put up his hand. "Wait…what's Silverson?"

Sophia's face broke into a smile. "You're up." She looked at Petro with a smug smile on her face. "I'll correct you if you try playing it down."

Petro grimaced before shaking his head with a chuckle. "That would be my grandfather's guild." He looked at Sal with an awkward smile. "We went our separate ways a number of years ago and decided it was better to keep it that way." He waved his hand like it was no big deal. "You have him to thank for the silver eyes."

Sophia cocked an eyebrow as she stared at Petro. "Who was it that founded Silver Sanctuary?"

Petro's smile tightened. "Silverson Group has close to five thousand members, spread across the entire country…Silver Sanctuary is a common naming convention."

Sal just continued to stare at his father. "I have a grandfather? You said we lost our family in the war." He couldn't keep the accusation out of his voice, but this was a massive deal.

Petro shook his head with a sad sigh. "The truth of it, Sal…is that we lost our family because of the war. I have brothers and sisters, but we don't talk to that side of the family anymore. I gave up the right to the Silverson name when I left the group. That's why we're the Argento family."

Sophia snorted. "Gave up the name? We were kicked out." She reached for the bottle again but stopped when she saw Sal's face. Her expression softened as she reached out to grip his hand. "None of this changes how much we love you. Please understand that, Salvatore. We wanted to reinvent ourselves after the Silverson shit-show, and we raised you in the life that we wanted for ourselves and for you."

Petro nodded. "Had we stayed, you'd have been enlisted in a military academy with Gallant from an early age." He tilted his head to one side and gave Sophia a meaningful look.

Sophia laughed at Petro as she shook her head. "You can say it if you want, but we both know that's not how it would have happened. No amount of money or status was going to make that a reality."

Sal looked between them in confusion, but Petro came to the rescue with an explanation. "Your mother was being paired off with a…different son of the Silverson Group. As I said, she was an extraordinary force on the battlefield. The Silverson Group didn't really believe in things like love. They matched people with synergistic powers, and…well, let's just say they didn't approve of us as a match. Arranged marriages became a very common trend in the guilds as they tried to guarantee the next generation of Heroes."

"Too shifty and analytic?" Sophia said, as though remembering something funny. "Wasn't that how they described you?"

Petro ignored her comment and smiled at Sal. "We had already secured a piece of land in Silver Sanctuary, and moved across the country to get away from the Silverson Group. They thankfully don't have a presence in this state, and we've been left to our own devices for the last twenty years."

Sal frowned as he looked between them. Their explanation was only creating more questions, and he didn't even know where to start. "Wait, so Shaper is your ability? It's Body Manipulation, but it works like Skill Master?" He was confused about the definition of the ability and wanted some clarification before he moved onto the next questions.

Sophia nodded. "Shaper lets me move my internal weave. I'm not able to move the threads like you, but I can reposition the gates in my body that hold the threads." She sighed as she placed a hand on her chest. "I'm woefully out of practice though." She smiled and reached out to squeeze Sal's hand again. "But I was thankfully able to remember the sequence for Reversion, and got to you before you lost your eye."

Sal blinked in surprise. He hadn't come across the Reversion ability before, but it sounded incredibly powerful. "And what was the thing about void essence that you said to Doc Ameye? Is that the essence that powers Reversion?"

Sophia smiled as she nodded again. "It works for abilities like Teleport, Nullify, and Reversion…but since Doc Ameye was already working on the machine, I was going to try using Realization, instead." She rolled her eyes. "I can't believe I thought I'd be up for it. My body was far too knotted to even get close."

"What does Realization do?" Sal asked, hating the fact that every explanation seemed to conjure more questions that moved away from his parents' past.

"If you think of Reversion as bringing something from its past state to the present, Realization is temporarily bringing something from a future state to the present. Void essence allows for that, but it's a pain to accumulate," Sophia explained with a dismissive wave of her hand. "Before you ask, the cost of essence required to bring a weapon or armor piece from the future would cost more than the essence required to evolve it permanently. That essence storm from Prestige provided the only conditions where it would have been possible."

Sal's jaw had long since dropped as he stared at his mother in shock. "How could you keep all of this from me? You're able to use a power just like mine." He whirled around to look at his father. "And you actually mapped out ability weaves, exactly like what I've been doing with my visor for the whole first semester. You could have been teaching me, rather than letting me flounder around from failure to failure!"

Petro grimaced as he looked at Sophia.

Sophia sighed as she looked at Sal with a sad expression. "You can blame me for this. Your father wanted to tell you when your powers first started to manifest, but I stopped him." She sat up in her seat and leaned her elbows on the table, looking at the empty glass in front of her for a few seconds in silence. When she continued, she gave Sal a serious look. "You have a very gentle nature, Salvatore. If we trained you to fight, or to use an array of abilities, we feared that you would want to join the war. It was a selfish reason, but we wanted to protect you and give you the life that we weren't able to have."

Petro reached out and placed his hand over Sophia's. "We both made the decision to protect you as much as we could. Your mother never once complained about the pain her ability causes her, and for years she used Reversion on the accumulated injuries from her time in the war. If she didn't keep those Reversions active, she'd have collapsed a long time ago. Shaper has a massive cost on the body, and your mother has been paying the price for years. We didn't want that for you."

"I complain all the time. You just don't listen," Sophia muttered, smiling. She glanced at Sal's horrified expression and quickly continued. "Don't worry, Sal. I've seen countless specialists over the years, and I'm pretty much fine as long as I don't try using Shaper. Body Manipulators with Configure have helped readjust my internal state, and Healers have restored a lot of the damage over the years. Now all I'm battling is age and a reduced output. It would be devastating for a Hero, but I'm just an Auctioneer, so it's trivial at best."

Petro smiled at Sophia before turning his attention to Sal. "We didn't want you to go through the same pain as your mother. So, I hope you'll forgive us for keeping this secret from you."

Sal just shook his head. "You should have told me. I got headaches when I looked at my own weave, and the solution was to wear sunglasses?" He laughed at how stupid it sounded. His mother's ability was tearing her up from the inside, and instead of telling him why, they just made him cover his eyes.

Petro pointed at his own eyes. "That was my suggestion. I used to wear an eye patch to ease the burden of All Sight. I was starting to go blind in my thirties. You're unlucky in terms of genetics, because both of us had abilities that were far stronger than our bodies. Now, don't get me wrong, the Silverson Group had a specialized Healer unit, but they only ever fixed you up to get you back on the field. They never gave a full Restoration."

"I think I'll take that whiskey now," Sal said in disbelief as he looked at his parents, as though waiting for them to object. When he got no resistance, he poured himself a glass. "So, putting all of this aside for a second…is there anything I can do with Skill Master that can help, or make your lives easier? Like, do I need to make a Healing weave or something?"

Sophia blinked in surprise. "That's your first question? Not why we've kept this from you all your life?"

Sal nodded as he raised his tumbler to look at the amber liquid within. "I'm going to need time to process all of this, and I have a thousand other questions…but the most important thing is making sure you guys are okay." He looked at them expectantly. "Since we're all on the same page, I expect you to tell me the whole truth from now on."

Petro smiled as he looked at Sophia. "Guess we didn't do such a shit job in raising him?"

Sal grinned as he raised his glass, as though in celebration. "You managed to raise the top Savior in Quest Academy, so I think you deserve a bit of praise."

Sophia's lips twitched into a smile. "We're going to have to work on that budding ego, though." She looked at Petro, her eyebrow cocked. "He's getting a little too full of himself, I think."

Petro nodded sagely. "I find that cleaning up after a party is an excellent method for humbling a child." With that, he got to his feet, grinning. "Let's get this finished so we can go home."

Sal reluctantly got to his feet and sighed. "Joking aside, this is an awful lot to process. I'm going to have a lot more questions."

Sophia joined him as she got up, groaning. "And we'll answer them, Salvatore. Every single one you have." She smiled as she reached out a hand to cup the side of his face. "We're so proud of you. I want you to know that."

Sal faltered at the unexpected tenderness, which only grew when his mother lovingly embraced him.

She looked up at him with a warm smile. "I was worried you'd hate us for keeping it from you. I still am, if I'm honest."

Petro walked around the table and embraced Sal from behind, his arms wrapping around Sophia's small frame. "Just to make it that little bit more awkward."

Sal laughed as he tried to move, but his parents' arms had him locked in place. "Come on, this place isn't going to clean itself!" he complained as he playfully tried to get away from them. He wasn't sure of his feelings about everything he had learned, but it didn't change the love he felt for them both.

CHAPTER 56: RESEARCH

Sal stared at the ceiling of his workshop bedroom, thankful that the hangover hadn't followed him into the next day. By his best guess, it was already late in the afternoon, giving him roughly six hours of sleep. Cleaning with his parents had taken close to an hour, but they had talked throughout, about the Silverson Group and his parents' contributions in the war. It had initially been hard for him to wrap his head around everything, but both of his parents were incredibly forthright about their past. It seemed that once the topic had become open for discussion, the doors were thrown wide open. They held nothing back.

Sal groaned as he got out of the bed. His body ached, and he wondered whether it was due to Prestige's breathing technique. Placing a hand on his chest, Sal grimaced as he tried to sense his internal state. Closing his eyes, he focused on his weave to see how it was looking, and he was surprised at how quickly it came into view. When he had opened gates in the past, the threading had become thicker in his weave…but for some reason, it actually looked thinner this time.

Sal focused on the weave to look at it, and he could see his essence darting along the thread at a ridiculously fast pace. So fast that it was impossible for him to follow it with his own eyes as it pinged around his chest. Prestige had broken up his sixty gates into four parts, giving him a new full capacity of two hundred and forty gates…which were stable, but not fully accessed.

Rather than counting the accessed gates manually, he'd use the tracker on a reflective surface to see how much his body improved. He was also curious about how the circulation of essence would change if he used the fortification pattern from Eclipse. According to the visor, it wasn't suitable for his body before, but now that he had more gates…it might be possible? As exciting as it was for him to be constantly improving, he didn't much care about the gates or his essence control for the moment. All he could think about was in the next room.

Sal threw on his Argento uniform, and made a mental note to pick up some extra clothing for himself for the workshop. He was in the mood for jeans and a T-shirt, but all he had available was the pressed uniform from the recent auction. Well, that and a purple tuxedo, but that wasn't going to be worn anytime soon. Sal quickly did up the buttons of his shirt and then his waistcoat before moving toward the secret door that led out to the workshop. When he pushed past it, he saw his butchered coffee machine and frowned. Getting a new core for the machine moved to the top of his list. He placed a hand on it as though saying goodbye to an old friend.

The Arkwright, at the edge of the mezzanine, gave off that villainous purple glow as it waited for instruction. The dungeon fragment within rotated constantly, causing flickers of light to shine across the room like a beacon. Even in the brightly lit workshop, the purple veil managed to cast itself across multiple surfaces as it moved.

Sal moved up to the interface, tapping at it cautiously to bring it to life. He was rewarded with a notification instantly.

MythOS v5.1.0

Registered Upgrades:

- Scarlet Strategist's Visor: Synchronization Successful
  - Judgment has been successfully shared through proximity
  - Cypher has been successfully shared through proximity
- Dungeon Heart Fragment: Installation Successful
- Protocol Array v6.3 has been installed
- Vulcan Interface v6.3 has been installed
- Mythcrafter Algorithm v1.0 has been installed
  - Cypher Build Progress: 8.3%

Diagnostic Report:

- Compatibility Issues have been Resolved:
  - Argento Workbench has been removed
  - MythOS Design Interface has been removed
  - MythOS System Interface has been removed
  - MythOS Sensor Array has been removed
  - MythOS Crafting Algorithm has been removed
- Core Modules:
  - No Errors
- System Integrity:
  - No Errors

Sal stared at the report in surprise, re-reading it to make sure that he understood what was happening. Not only had Doc Ameye installed the dungeon fragment, but he had also given him some of Vulcan and Protocol's systems? It looked like he had a new sensor array and interface from Doc Ameye's train. Adding to that, the Crafting algorithm had been upgraded to the Mythcrafter algorithm.

Sal smiled broadly as he shook his head in wonder. Even his visor was synchronized to the Arkwright, and it was sharing the computational abilities of Judgment and Cypher. It was a surprise, but he was happy about it. The only downside was that it looked like he would need to keep the visor beside the Arkwright if it was working on a specific build.

Speaking of build…Sal stared at the Mythcrafter algorithm section. Cypher, the ability that he got with his Legendary-grade visor, was working in the background to create a new build for his Crafting algorithm. Assuming that it had been working overnight on it, and it was only at eight percent, Sal guessed that it would be a long-term investment having the visor permanently situated in the workshop. He'd need to take it out and use it for the upcoming dungeon runs with Fabi, but the excitement of having it constantly working on the Arkwright was massive.

Sal tapped on the interface again to dismiss the report and move back to the Crafting section. When he had last looked at it, the Arkwright was able to make up to the Rare grade. He wanted to see whether that had increased.

Please enter a name for Placeholder.Vulcan.Interface

Sal entered the name "Arkwright" into the machine and was happy to see that the temporary naming convention at the top of the interface vanished. There were only a few seconds of loading before Sal was met with the Arkwright Design screen. It was a much more polished version than what he had in place before, with an entire side-bar menu that he could navigate to different sections. Unlike before, Sal was met with an entirely new set of options.

Arkwright Design
- o   Recommended Components
- o   Recommended Upgrades
- o   Recommended Material Synthesis
- o   Recommended Research

Sal faltered at the new options that had appeared. There was still an entire section dedicated to the free designs and the blueprint upload, but the recommended section was completely new. Curiosity got the better of him, and he selected each of the options, one at a time. The first one, labeled Components, was a list of small mechanisms that were needed for a larger build. Sal went into the top one, and was surprised to see that it was for the assembly station that was quoted to him before by the machine. There were over twenty components that needed to be made for it to become a reality, but the resource cost wasn't massive. Sal frowned as he looked at the list of requirements. None of the materials looked to be expensive, either.

Pausing his curiosity about the Components section, Sal moved on to the Upgrades section to see what the Arkwright was recommending. The reason Sal was confused going into this section was because the Arkwright had just been improved and refined by Doc Ameye. If the Arkwright still required upgrades, then they were likely going to be astronomically outside of Sal's capability.

Tapping into the section, Sal was met with a series of blueprints that were rendered into a 3D image, rotating on the screen with pieces of information being tagged at the sides. They were from his time at Quest Academy, with Divinity's circlet appearing first on the menu. It started with a prompt that obsidian glass could be bent into a circular shape, which was the exact thing Sal had avoided because it was a pain in the ass. He had ignored his Mythcrafter instincts and shaped it in a way that was comfortable, but the Arkwright saw that as an inefficiency?

Next on the list was his father's new monocle, followed by his mother's visor. Sophia's invisible visor was the most interesting, because the Stealth factor was determined by Arkwright to be a mistake rather than a design feature. It showed a series of improvements that could be made to the design to substitute the prowler blood from the infused runes…with obsidian dust?

Sal scratched at the back of his head as he looked at the Arkwright in confusion. Was it just using the materials it had in supply to create upgrade proposals? If that was the case, it was going to try to add obsidian glass to everything. Sal made a mental note to add more materials to the machine before rechecking the Upgrades section.

Moving on to the Synthesis section, Sal selected it with far less enthusiasm than before. He guessed that there was going to be a prompt about obsidian glass being refined into dust or something.

Material Synthesis
- o Create Stormweave Bolt
  - ▪ Dreadcloth will be synthesized with Obsidian Glass
  - ▪ Estimated Completion: 15 minutes, 13 seconds per Stormweave Bolt

Sal stared at the words for a few seconds before he tapped on the screen that he wanted the Arkwright to make the new material. He hadn't ever heard of it before, but he knew that storm steel was incredibly valuable. Stormweave might be something worthwhile, so it was definitely worth the risk. It wasn't like he had intended on using the dreadcloth stored in the Arkwright for anything else, and the amount of obsidian glass he had was…significant. Sal watched as the dungeon fragment rotated a little faster than before.

Material Synthesis
- o Stormweave Bolt is being created
- o Estimated Completion: 15 minutes, 8 seconds
- o Chance of Breakthrough: 11%

"Breakthrough?" Sal wondered in confusion. He tapped on the section that included the words, to see whether it would give him any further context. A new line above pushed the text downward, causing him to press his finger against the words *Stormweave Bolt*.

Stormweave Bolt:
- ▪ Synthetic Combination
  - ▪ Dreadcloth, Obsidian Glass
- o Estimated Quality
  - ▪ 60% Chance to produce Rare Grade
  - ▪ 25% Chance to produce Unique Grade
  - ▪ 15% Chance to produce Epic Grade
- o Ability Synthesis
  - ▪ Feather (Dreadcloth), Uncommon Grade
  - ▪ Attune (Obsidian Glass), Epic Grade
  - ▪ Reflect (Dreadcloth), Rare Grade
  - ▪ Cultivate (Obsidian Glass), Epic Grade

Sal stared at the options that populated the interface. *It had calculated the probability of the quality, before it even started?* He had already combined dreadcloth and obsidian glass when he created the suit for his father, and it came out as an Epic-grade set, with all the abilities listed for stormweave. With Mythcrafter, he had managed to create the optimal quality while there was only a fifteen per-cent chance of the Arkwright replicating that same effect. It wasn't disappointing, but it wasn't that exciting either.

The text that had pushed down the options was simply a loading bar that indicated the completion time for the stormweave bolt. Sal ignored that and returned to the Breakthrough section. He was able to press it properly this time, and was met with a whole new tab of information. Whatever he had expected was wrong, because the Stormweave Breakthrough was listed simply as a chance to develop a new ability through the synthesis. Sal looked at it for a few seconds before shrugging and exiting out of the tab. The last one that he wanted to check was the Research section.

Sal tapped into it with zero expectations, but was surprised to find a list of all the known material effects that was picked up by his visor. All the material fragments that he had looked at with Chatfield were displayed on the screen. Sal guessed that it was going to try to do the breakthrough thing and combine the materials, but the prompt at the top of the list was quite different.

Research Available
- o Scarlet Moon Series
    - Scarlet Moon Sniper Rifle
    - Enhanced Scarlet Moon Revolver
    - Enhanced Scarlet Moon Visor
- o Argento Set Series
    - Enhanced Argento Slacks
    - Enhanced Argento Shirt
    - Enhanced Argento Gloves
    - Argento Mask
    - Argento Boots
- o Storm Suit Series
    - Enhanced Storm Lens
    - Enhanced Storm Suit Jacket
    - Enhanced Storm Suit Vest
    - Enhanced Storm Suit Slacks

Sal stared in disbelief at the options that appeared in front of him. The Research section had apparently categorized the items he had made as sets, and was offering research into further enhancing them. He could see the set he had made for his father, and the set that was made for him by Upgrade, Martin, and Gosia. Most surprising was the Scarlet Moon Series, which was suggesting he research a sniper rifle variant. Was that because of his work on Watcher's sniper rifle? He had so many questions, but top of his list was the suggestion that his own uniform set was incomplete. *He could add a mask and boots to the set?*

Sal's smile grew wide as he tapped on the Argento Set Series. Although the sniper rifle sounded really cool, there was no way he was going to secure more scarlet screen which would absolutely be required for something like that. A few options became available when he went into the series menu, with everything themed around research. He wondered whether this was the power of Judgment and Cypher, or if it was down to the new Mythcrafter algorithm. Either way, he wanted to see how it worked and how much it could handle. If it was able to conjure up some new idea that was alien to him, then it would absolutely be a success.

Research Options for Argento Set Series:
- o   Research Variant Set
- o   Research Enhanced Set
- o   Research Combination Set

Sal glanced through the options and quickly learned that a variant set would keep each component static, but rework the abilities. The enhanced set would make an improved version of the existing set, while the combination would try to formulate a completely new set. There was no hesitation as Sal tapped for Arkwright to research the combination set. Considering it was just research, it wasn't going to cause any issues, and he was curious to see how the Arkwright would handle a rework of the entire set.

Combination Set
- o   Scarlet Moon Series
- o   Argento Set Series

"Oh." Sal looked at the new option that appeared. It looked as though he had misunderstood the meaning of combination, but that was fine. It didn't really matter if it turned out crap. He tapped on the Continue button and was met with yet another pop-up screen. A part of Sal thought the menu options were becoming a little overkill.

Cypher is currently in use.
Please select Priority:
- o   Mythcrafter Algorithm Build: Progress 8.4%
- o   Combination Research Set: Not Started

Sal was shown a sliding scale that represented Cypher's capacity, which he dismissed with a laugh. "Let's go all the way." He moved the slider to put the full capacity of Cypher on the new research and stepped back, smiling as the screen changed.

Stormweave Bolt is being created...
Combination Set is being researched...

When he glanced down at the timer, Sal's smile faded.

Estimated Completion: 9 hours, 52 minutes, 48 seconds

CHAPTER 57: GENEROSITY

"Dad said I shouldn't turn up empty-handed." Fabi laughed as she climbed the stairs in the workshop toward the mezzanine. "But this is a little excessive, don't you think?" She jostled the crate in her hands as she looked toward Sal, who was carrying the second behind her. She had only just arrived, but was already making a beeline straight to the Arkwright machine. Both of Sal's parents were at home, so it was just him and Fabi…and the rest of the Argento Auction House staff. But they knew better than to just barge into the workshop, which left the task of carrying Maurice's presents to Fabi and Sal.

"Are you sure he's not just trying to bribe his way into one of those storefronts?" Sal chuckled as he followed Fabi up the stairs. "I don't know how to break it to you, but there's still like another few hours left on the cooldown. I don't think we're going to be getting much out of the Arkwright today."

Fabi shrugged it off as she reached the top of the stairs and deposited her crate on the workbench. "Ah, you make it sound like I'm only after one thing." She looked over her shoulder at Sal, who crested the stairs. "And you're making it sound like my father only wants one thing, too." She winked at him before pulling out a small core from her crate.

Sal's eyes lit up at the sight of it. "Ooooh, I can finally have coffee!"

Fabi just laughed as she moved over to the coffee machine, core in hand. "Great minds think alike, Sal. I noticed it was busted the other night, so I made sure to have one of the small cores with me when I popped over today." She twisted the machine around and slotted the core against the tiny sensors. A few twists of her hand later, she snapped the back of the machine closed. She smiled. "And now we have coffee! We can craft solutions to all the world's problems now."

"You're honestly such a lifesaver!" Sal said enthusiastically as he deposited the second crate beside the first. He dusted off his waistcoat before moving to the small kitchenette to get two cups. "I don't have cream or sugar, by the way…hope that's okay?"

"Perfect," Fabi answered. "Wouldn't want you polluting it." Her voice faded for a few seconds before sounding out again. "What's stormweave?"

Sal emerged from the kitchenette with two cups and saw Fabi standing beside the Arkwright, looking in at the dungeon fragment as it rotated smoothly within the enclosure. He set them down at the coffee machine before answering. "It's material synthesis, combining obsidian glass with dreadcloth."

"Oh, that's pretty damn cool." Fabi nodded as she bent over to look at the refiner in action. "Does it have any special effects?"

Sal grinned as the coffee machine burst into action. "Oh, how I've missed you." He patted the side of the machine affectionately.

"I'll take that as a compliment, but it's only been a few hours." Fabi straightened, shooting him a grin.

Sal returned it as he jokingly caressed the side of the machine. "Sorry, I try not to pick favorites, but you're currently third." He gestured at the coffee machine and then at the Arkwright, before his hand finally rested in front of Fabi.

Fabi nodded in understanding. "That's fair…but we'll see what you think after we start designing the battle-suit." She turned her attention back to the Arkwright. "Were you intending on using the stormweave as a material? I can't really guarantee how effective it will be since I'm not familiar with it."

"Ah, they were materials that were already loaded into the machine, so I just wanted to test out the new functions," Sal admitted as he moved across the room to hand Fabi the first cup of coffee. "As for the synthesis, the item grade had a few percentage simulations. There's a fifteen percent chance that it'll be an Epic-grade material, and that would give the effects of Attune and Cultivate. Lower grades will give Feather or Reflect."

Fabi smiled appreciatively as she took the coffee. "That's pretty damn good. It's nice to know it can create materials, but I wonder if adding cores will increase those percentages?" She looked over her shoulder at the crates on the workbench. "There's enough here to keep it running for the next month…"

Sal faltered as he looked at the crates in surprise. "That's a lot more than a few presents, Fabi…like, a *lot* more. I can't accept that."

Fabi just shrugged as she lifted the cup to her lips. "It wasn't my call. He was rambling about you saving his only daughter." She smiled around the cup as she took a drink. With a satisfied sigh, she placed the cup down on the workbench, interlocked her fingers, and cracked her knuckles. "So, are you ready to get started?"

Sal shook his head as he held the handle of his own cup, waiting for it to fill at the machine. "Nope, I can't accept that amount of generosity…seriously, it's far too much."

Fabi stared at him for a second. "But a first-year Healer can walk around in a Legendary-grade coat? A first-year Controller can wear the Vengeful Vambraces?" She shook her head. "That's without considering the Unique-grade corset for Sakura. You seem to give very elaborate gifts, but it's different when they're for you?"

Sal frowned as he thought about it. "The Legendary-grade coat wasn't a present. More of a loan, or a bribe…I don't know. Those times were different."

"Sure they were." Fabi nodded. "And this is different, too." She smiled brightly as she lifted a larger core from the crate. "Do you think loading up the Arkwright will interrupt your current progress?"

Sal sighed in defeat. He wasn't going to win any sort of argument with her, so he decided it was easier to concede. He'd thank Maurice for the materials in person; it was the least he could do.

When Sal moved over to check on the progress of the Arkwright, he thought about Fabi's question. He couldn't see how it would impact the machine negatively. The last time there was a conflict of priority, the Arkwright gave him a prompt to allocate resources. It would probably do the same if they started loading it up.

"Let's do it," Sal answered finally as he gestured with his cup in hand to the area that accepted the matterials. "Oh, and there was a whole section dedicated to recommended components. There's a whole build list for making an assembly station. Pretty cool, huh?"

Fabi's hand halted as she looked around at Sal in confusion. "Wait, like a whole build list? How does it know how to make an assembly station? Did you give it a blueprint for that?"

Sal shook his head as he gestured again with his cup at the interface. "It loaded up a proposed version. The original version of MythOS already identified that it needed an assembly station for some of the Crafting, so my best guess is that it's prioritizing that with a build list."

Fabi stared at Sal for a few seconds. "But you didn't give it the design?"

Sal realized it would be faster to just show her, so he went over to the screen panel of the Arkwright and navigated to the Components section. After selecting the assembly station, he stepped back to let Fabi have a proper look. Countless pieces of equipment appeared on the screen, with various material costs and time estimates for completion. They were seemingly organized in build order, with the first twelve pieces completing the first phase. Sal couldn't see how many phases were involved, but he knew that it wouldn't be a quick build with how many parts were called for.

Fabi scrolled through the list quickly and quietly, before she moved out of the tab for the assembly station and navigated to the drone docking station.

Sal could only guesstimate from the amount she scrolled, but it looked like the drone dock had less phases than the assembly station. The banner of information that stayed constant at the top of the screen indicated that the assembly station was required before the drone dock could be started. Even though it was an extraordinary machine, it looked like the limitations of time and materials would make it a financial burden for the first few weeks and months.

"This is wild," Fabi said excitedly as she turned around to look at Sal. "It's pretty much creating everything like a jigsaw, and custom-making each piece." She shook her head in wonder before looking back at the Arkwright. "It's good that the materials don't cost a lot, but it's going to take a chunk of time to assemble it all…" Her gaze moved around the mezzanine, her eyes narrowing. "And you're going to run out of space."

"We could assemble it down by the tracks, or in the carriage," Sal suggested as he pointed over the railing at the platform below.

Fabi shook her head as she looked at the secret wall leading to the kitchenette. "The two options I can think of…would mean using the entire space up here, or moving the Arkwright." She looked at Sal's stupefied expression before a guilty smile crept onto her face. "Sorry, I'm a bit of a stickler for efficient workspaces. You can absolutely have it up here, but it'll get a little cramped."

"Don't worry about it. I've got no intention of taking it with me to Quest Academy, so there's no real point in moving it." Sal shrugged. "And even if we did get the deed to the depot, I wouldn't feel comfortable moving it there just yet. Both of us will be going back soon enough, and there'd be nobody there to look after it."

Fabi nodded in agreement. "It'll just be a pain feeding it materials with all the stairs…we might need to get you an elevator for this balcony."

Sal chuckled as he tried to visualize something like that. It would completely remove the functionality of the tracks if they adopted that approach, which was something he didn't want to give up. Although he didn't want to become like Doc Ameye and start operating a train, it was nice to think that someday the train network could be restored.

Fabi leaned over the railing and looked at the tracks below. "We could probably do something that could lift directly off a carriage, but the cost of that would be far more than just moving the Arkwright." She stared at the tracks for a few seconds, deep in thought before shrugging and smiling. "But that's a problem for the future. Right now, we need to feed this guy."

With that said, she lifted the core in her hand and placed it into the drawer. She looked over at Sal as though to verify that she was doing it correctly. When she received a nod of approval, she started to push the drawer closed before stopping midway. Looking back over to the crate, she smiled broadly. "A single core would just be a taste…"

Sal laughed as he put down his own cup and lifted the crate he had carried up the stairs. He brought it to where Fabi was crouched and deposited it in front of her. "Do you want the two crates?"

Fabi nodded enthusiastically as she stacked the various ingots into the drawer. "Sounds like a plan." There were bolts of cloth, bundles of wood, multicolored crystals, and an assortment of vials that were placed neatly into the drawer. Fabi paused as she looked at the vials. "I've got no idea if it'll be able to identify these guys, so let's leave them out for now."

Both the crates were promptly emptied, excluding the vials of liquid. Sal was only able to identify the green one as prowler blood, but the others were a complete mystery to him. The auction house didn't deal with raw materials or ingredients, so he couldn't really guess their value from experience. Although he could have used Appraisal on them, he wanted to see how Arkwright did with them instead.

"Put them in and we'll see what happens," Sal suggested as Fabi faltered with the vials in hand.

"You sure? You're not going to kill me if they explode and leak everywhere?" She slowly lowered a vial into the drawer, not breaking eye contact with him.

"I won't blame you if it happens." Sal laughed as he gestured for her to continue. "Something tells me that it's advanced enough to determine what's in those bottles."

Fabi smiled as she finished loading the two crates into the drawer. It was packed to the brim but Fabi didn't struggle with sliding it back into place.

Materials Detected in Loading Bay
Updating Inventory...

Sal and Fabi watched as each of the materials started being highlighted on the screen, with their amounts registered. Each of the cores flashed into view as the refined conveyor system moved them to a separate area within the enclosure. The Arkwright sorted through them quickly, allocating them to areas by some unknown logic. The moment of truth flashed past in seconds, with each of the liquids being categorized instantly and secured on a shelf behind the conveyor system.

Soon there were feathers and crystals nestled around a stack of cores. The bottles shone brightly as the purple dungeon fragment highlighted them with each rotation. The metal ingots were stacked by color, although it was hard to tell. But the sheer amount of materials brought the entire Arkwright to life and looked like a menagerie of materials and vibrant colors.

Fabi read through the list with a look of wonder. "This is so exciting…are you seeing this?" She pointed at the notifications in the top right corner of the interface. "Looks like the cores woke it up!"

Stormweave Bolt has been added to Inventory
Combination Set is being Researched...
Estimated Completion: 18 minutes, 39 seconds

CHAPTER 58: MACCLEMARK

"So, did you bring the design blueprints for the Macclemark suit?" Sal asked hopefully as he tore his attention away from the countdown displayed on the interface. "Have to admit, I'm excited to see what they're like."

Fabi chuckled as she plucked her Quest Academy tablet from her pocket, waving it in front of him. "Everything I need is right here, but you're going to be disappointed."

"How so?" Sal asked cautiously, not trusting the smile on her face.

Fabi placed her tablet on the workbench and navigated through the different folders on the device. "Before I get to that, let me ask you a question." She glanced up from her tablet to look at Sal. "You're aware that there is a massive skills gap among the Crafters in Quest Academy, right? Like, not everyone can flood a machine with essence and produce an Epic grade out of raw materials?"

"Yeah?" Sal nodded in agreement, immediately thinking of Anthony, who was in the same Crafting class as him.

Fabi returned her attention to the tablet in front of her. "When you get to the advanced classes, output isn't the most important factor…it's process. That's why you won't find many essence-based Crafters in the advanced classes, because they can't wrap their heads around the required minutiae and logic." She laughed, shaking her head. "The Macclemark series aren't just a collection of abilities and raw materials—they're custom-made with specific essence programming designed by function."

Sal frowned as he looked between Fabi and the tablet on the workbench. "So, it's kinda similar to the visor? You've given it a calculation-type ability?"

Fabi shook her head, grinning. "My scripts *are* the calculation ability. You saw how the Vengeful Vambraces create those essence blades? Macclemark IV will take your essence and convert it into offensive and defensive measures. You'll be shielded by essence-based constructs, and you'll have projectiles that target any approaching enemy." She raised a hand and pointed at the ceiling before moving her outstretched arm in a sweeping arc. "From any direction, even if you can't see it, the sensors in Macclemark IV will detect the demons and counterattack."

Sal stared at her in disbelief. "You can do that with essence programming?" He now understood why she was so confident about her designs. If he could walk through a battlefield wearing a battle-suit that did the fighting for him, he wouldn't need to worry at all. "What's the catch? Why isn't everyone wearing one of these?"

Fabi smiled as she offered a lame shrug. "Might be because of the cost, or it might be because everyone is so focused on those fancy evolutionary sets?" She gave him a wink before continuing. "But, for real…the programming is custom-built around the user, so it takes a lot of tweaking and adjusting. The people who can afford a Macclemark likely aren't going to stand around for a few days to get it properly calibrated."

"How much are we talking?" Sal laughed. He had a good idea of how much the Vengeful Vambraces cost, so he was curious about how much her prices had increased since she Crafted it.

"Roughly about eight thousand Q-Cred. Can spiral to a lot more depending on the material choices," Fabi answered with a grin. "And they typically take about three months to make, with another month for calibration."

Sal blinked a few times before answering. "Okay, the cost aside…four months for a total build? I guess we won't have it ready for the dungeon runs."

Fabi lifted her hand to the amulet strung around her neck. "Well, my hope is that when I can get used to my power, I'll be able to bring that time down drastically." She let go of the amulet and hiked her thumb over her shoulder. "And your Arkwright could do a lot of the heavy lifting with precision engineering. A lot of the time goes into Crafting tiny components." Finally, Fabi pointed at Sal. "And then we have a Mythcrafter. So as long as you're following my blueprints to the letter, then we'll be able to speed things up dramatically."

"But to go from four months…to what? A month?" Sal glanced at the Arkwright. "I've never worked on one project that took that long. What grade does it end up?"

Fabi shrugged, like it didn't matter. "Well, I only ever build them to hold two abilities…so, Uncommon grade? Maybe Rare grade if I add in another one. It really depends on the spec we go with."

Sal's jaw practically dropped as he stared at Fabi. "Eight thousand and four months, for a Rare grade…at best? I feel like I'm missing something." He knew that she was responsible for the Rare-grade breastplate he saw on the Credit Store a few months ago. Each of the scales on the armor had individual runes inscribed on them, and it looked like a lot of precise work to get to that result. But, even if she didn't have an essence-based Crafting ability, it was too much of a chasm to cross. There was no way that he could justify paying eight thousand on a Rare grade.

"Go on." Fabi smiled. "Say that it sounds ridiculous and overpriced. You've arrived at the crux of why people aren't lining up for the Macclemark battle-suits."

Sal faltered before continuing. He was definitely missing something. There was no way that Doc Ameye would recommend one of Fabi's suits if they weren't the real deal. If he excluded the costs and the resulting grade…it still didn't sound like a great value proposition. Biting his lip, Sal wondered about the effects of Fabi's programming.

"Tell me more about the programming features. What are the actual effects in a dungeon?" Sal asked finally.

Fabi's smile grew wider as she stood up straight and looked him in the eye. "With the Controller specification, nothing within twenty feet will be able to approach you. That's the death zone, and the Macclemark can dispatch leechers, prowlers, and voiders without draining the internal cores." She raised her hands to illustrate the distance. "That's the standby mode, where you don't need to consciously control the battle-suit. If you were to move into offense mode, you can send essence-based projectiles up to around fifty feet, depending on the size of the projectile. Sending it in a straight line is best so it can increase the maximum range and keep the essence reserves in a healthy state."

"There's no way something with that potential could be classified as Uncommon or Rare grade." Sal crossed his arms. "It sounds like it's closer to Unique or Epic grade."

Fabi nodded as she looked at him expectantly. "Do you want to hear about the other features? It can sync up with other Macclemark suits. Healer spec has the Transference ability, which is kind of like a tether between teammates. It allows for the exchange of essence or healing, depending on the need."

As they were talking, the Arkwright interface suddenly illuminated with a completion notice. Fabi turned around to have a look at it. "We can talk about Macclemark in a bit. I'm really curious how it handled your research requirements." She moved closer to the interface and reached out a hand to see the results, before stopping short and smiling. "Ah, you should be the one checking, since it's the maiden voyage of the Arkwright."

Sal smiled as he moved over to the space Fabi had just vacated. "It's just a research report. It's not like we've asked it to do something insane." He tapped the report button on the machine. "My best guess is that it'll be a failure. The sets that it tried to combine don't really have any synergies."

"How so?" Fabi asked as she stood beside him, looking at the research topic closely.

"Well, the Argento set was made by Upgrade, Martin, and Gosia. It has the Transform and Synergy abilities, with Reflect and Feather for good measure. I don't really know how that's going to play nice with the Scarlet Moon Set. That's a visor and a revolver," Sal explained as he waited for the report to compile and load on the interface.

"Ten Q-Cred it makes a stupid name like Scarlet Argento." Fabi extended her hand to confirm the wager.

"No bet." Sal laughed as he ignored her hand. "I have zero faith in the naming conventions."

The Arkwright interface took its time in creating the report, but when it started, the text flowed seamlessly to explain the results of the research.

Research Complete: Combination Set Successful
- o   Transformative Sets can now be created
  - ▪   Unnamed Set has been added to blueprints

"That's kinda underwhelming." Sal laughed, looking to Fabi to see whether she found it as funny. He faltered when he saw her wide eyes locked onto the screen. "Everything okay?"

Fabi wordlessly tapped on the Transformative option, causing the Arkwright to clarify the meaning.

Results from Cypher:
- ▪   Mythcrafter Crafter Algorithm has created the Transformative function
- ▪   Transformative function occurs through the management of the Synergy and Transform abilities

- Transformative function allows for set items to exist within subspace and be summoned at no cost of internal essence
- Attune ability is used to offset the essence draw of the Transformative function

"How can this be possible?" Fabi finally breathed out as she looked at Sal with a horrified expression. "How can it use essence programming?"

Sal was a little slower in reading the words but ended up coming to the same conclusion. "Are you going to be angry if I say I've got no idea?"

Fabi laughed as she stared between Sal and the Arkwright. "Do you have any idea how amazing this is? Even if it can't create something with the Transformative function, it can give us the blueprints for it." She took a few steps back from the Arkwright and shook her head in wonder. Eventually she found her way back to the coffee cup on the table, and downed the remainder of it in one swig.

When she finally placed the cup back on the bench, she grinned at Sal. "This pretty much changes everything…the calibration period for Macclemark was to work out those exact functions to minimize essence consumption!" She pointed at the Arkwright meaningfully. "This is so much better than what I was expecting. That Mythcrafter algorithm is the real deal!"

Sal smiled as he pointed at Fabi's discarded tablet. "Do you want to see what happens when we add your blueprints? We could probably run another combination research to see what happens?"

Fabi stared at Sal, her wide smile growing. "That sounds pretty damn exciting." She snatched up her tablet and stood in front of the Arkwright. "Do I just send it to your tablet, or is there a method to synchronize it? I don't want to screw up any of your folders."

Sal gestured at the Legendary-grade visor perched on the countertop. "I'll use that to do the synchronization. Just get the blueprints ready." He smiled as he saw Fabi rifling through the folders on her tablet, swiping at the screen like a woman possessed. It only took him a few seconds to get the visor equipped and primed for the task ahead.

"Take whatever you want from that folder. It's all dedicated to the Macclemark research," Fabi insisted as she presented the screen to him, grabbing both sides of the tablet and holding it with outstretched arms in front of her face, as though it would improve his view of it.

Sal directed his visor to start processing the information. Just when he thought that he'd need to swipe through the different sections on the screen, his visor surprised him with a notification.

Macclemark Research Folder 004 has been successfully copied
Folder has been uploaded to Arkwright Crafting Directory
New Research has become available

"Oh," Sal said in confusion as he took off his visor. "That was…much faster than I expected."

Fabi lowered the outstretched screen. "You got all of them?" She turned the tablet to see it was still on the first page.

Sal, on the other hand, moved over to the Arkwright and was rewarded with a notification on the interface that new research had become available. He navigated to the Combination Research like he had done before. "Did you say that it was the Macclemark IV?"

Fabi appeared beside him, frowning. "Yeah, but there are hundreds of blueprints in there. There's no way that it copied all of them."

Sal decided to trust the Arkwright as he selected the research conditions.

Combination Set
- o   Unnamed Transformative Set Series
- o   Macclemark 004 Set Series

Without hesitating, Sal initiated the research and waited for the prompt to signal the estimation. It was going to be tough to determine a timeframe, as the last one had been drastically reduced after they introduced cores to the Arkwright's inventory. His hope was that it wouldn't be something ridiculous.

Combination Set is being researched...
Estimated Completion: 2 hours, 33 minutes, 51 seconds

"Oh, that's not bad!" Sal said with a bright smile, looking back at Fabi in excitement. "What do you think will happen?"

Fabi just stared at the Arkwright in wonder. "I've got absolutely no idea." She turned her attention to Sal, a wide smile appearing on her face. "None of the Macclemark sets have ever used Transform. I'm curious to know how it will work with that revolver of yours."

Sal chuckled as he pointed at the interface. "Afraid not...I just picked the Transformative research with Macclemark."

Fabi also pointed at the interface, raising her hand a little higher. "Are you sure you've had enough coffee? You picked the Unnamed Transformative Set." She grinned at him. "You've just added the combination of your Scarlet Moon and Argento sets to the Macclemark research. It's going to be a pretty insane fusion or an absolute failure!"

Sal stared at the screen to see that Fabi was right. He had picked the wrong option.

"Oh," he replied numbly. "So, what would you like to do for the next two hours?"

Fabi shrugged as she gestured at the coffee machine. "Coffee and chat?" She smiled brightly before hiking her thumb over her shoulder. "Or we can go and raid Maccles Materials for more cores. It might speed up the timer!"

Sal chuckled as he moved over to the coffee machine. "Chats it is."

CHAPTER 59: CONFIDANT

"So, they've been lying to you…for pretty much your whole life?" Fabi asked incredulously as she gripped her coffee cup with both hands. Her expression was conflicted as she looked at Sal. "Like, I can kinda understand why they did it…but that's rough. How are you handling it so well?"

Sal offered a slight shrug as he gave her a tired smile. "Honestly, I'm still just processing everything. I know I should be angry with them, but all I could think about were the changes I made to my father's weave." Sal slumped as he looked over Fabi's shoulder, not wanting to look her directly in the eye. "His All Sight ability was making him blind, but he had it in a manageable state. Then I just swoop in and fix his weave a bit, which will probably speed up the degradation. What if I had done that on my mother…the pain she'd be in…just because I wanted to help?"

Fabi's brow tightened. "No." She reached out a hand and gripped Sal's. "You can't start thinking like that, otherwise you'll worry yourself to death. Anything you've done can be undone with the knotting, right?" she asked rhetorically before continuing. "You said it yourself—you gave him a suit that will help him acclimatize to his essence, and that monocle can use All Sight…so he doesn't need to put his body under any sort of stress."

Sal nodded, sighing. "I know, but I just feel like an idiot." He gave her a weak smile. "I genuinely thought I was raised by two Auctioneers…but instead, they were secretly a part of some massive militia? There were so many signs over the years and I just ignored all of them, or didn't connect the dots."

Fabi tilted her head. "Why aren't you angry? If this happened to me, I probably would have torn down Maccles Materials in a rage."

Sal looked at Fabi before shaking his head. "If they stayed with the Silverson Group, then I would have been trained as a Hero from an early age and pushed into dungeons. If they had told me, I probably would have been paralyzed in fear that I'd need to go and fight demons someday. Hell, I pretty much grew up fearing my own power…and it's only now that I realize why my mother never wanted me to use it." He grimaced before forcing a smile to his face. "Sorry, I feel bad for putting all of this on your shoulders."

Fabi let out an exasperated sigh as she looked at the ceiling. "First rule of coffee and chats. You're not allowed to apologize for talking through what's troubling you." She lowered her gaze to meet Sal's and raised her other hand to point at him meaningfully. "Second rule, you're not allowed to speak negatively about yourself. Understood?"

Sal smiled as he nodded. "Understood, boss."

Fabi stared at him. "Now, are you going to tell me what's really going on in your head? If you're not angry, what is causing the jumble of thoughts in your mind?"

"Why I'm not angry?" Sal started as he pushed his empty coffee cup farther away from him. "It's because I think I would have had the same life as Gallant, if they had been honest with me. If they stayed at the Silverson Group, there's no way that a Skill Steal ability wouldn't be utilized for warfare. They protected me from that, and I know I had a great life because of that decision." He frowned as he vocalized his thoughts. He was conflicted about everything, but it was hard to put those feelings into words.

Sal paused for a few moments. "I just feel disappointed that they didn't trust me enough to be honest with me. Protecting me was one thing, but they could have gently worked in the truth over time. Like, it was only a few weeks ago that my father admitted to seeing lights in people when he was younger, and I was delighted." He laughed humorlessly as he looked at Fabi. "It was the first time I felt like I was truly my father's son, and that our abilities had some semblance of connection. He was lying to me then, too. Even being the top-ranked Savior in Quest Academy wasn't enough for him to be honest with me."

"You are your father's son," Fabi said earnestly. "If that was something you were worried about, you now have the proof that you've got a blend of your parents' powers. And sure, while it's not the greatest way to find out…you should be able to put those thoughts to rest at least." She sounded a bit flustered as she tried to explain her point. "And there's a massive silver lining here…your parents will be able to teach you how to control your powers now that the secret is out!" She paused for a second as though revising her advice, when another question popped up.

"Why did you call it Skill Steal?" Fabi asked in confusion. "You never take away anyone's power, but instead make them better? If anything, you're actually gifting skills."

Sal shook his head. "You don't get it…I can utilize anyone's power better than they can. I can see their weave and activate it without any of the knots, and bring out their full potential. That's not really something that makes you friends, and it's also caused so much shit for me when people learn what I can do. They expect me to be stepping up to the front lines to take care of the demons single-handedly."

Fabi nodded with a smile slowly forming. "So, you used your powers unfairly? Your team victory in the cohort battles, the excursion, and the tower…you used your Skill Master ability to make it easier?"

Sal frowned. "No, I didn't use it for anything like that. I've only really adjusted Upgrade, Blathnaid, and Divinity…and a couple of the Crafters." He looked at Fabi's raised eyebrow before adding the last one. "And Sakura, but that's it."

Fabi tapped her fingernail against the surface of the workbench. "This is just an observation, so it might not even be true." She stopped tapping as she smiled at Sal. "But everything you've achieved has been due to the hard work you've put in at the workshop. Sure, you created your own ability with Mythcrafter, but you've had to learn how to use it."

Sal chuckled as he shook his head. "I'm not questioning the work that I've put in, or Mythcrafter really…it's more to do with my parents and the choices they've made up until now."

"Let me finish," Fabi insisted as she continued to look at him. "If you were raised by two Heroes of the Silverson Group, would you have had the same respect for Supports and Crafters? Would you have spent countless hours in a workshop making things like the Arkwright? Or would you be throwing yourself into dungeons to increase your rank with the bureau?"

Sal didn't know how to answer that. He had been raised by two Supports and a lot of his personality was geared around fairness and equity for those at the bottom of the food chain. Blinking a few times, he frowned. "You're saying that my parents raised me this way so I'd help Supports? Seems a little convoluted, don't you think?"

"You said it yourself—they moved away from the Silverson Group to settle down and have a family." Fabi smiled as she looked at Sal meaningfully. "They had already created the whole Argento Auction thing before you were born, so the real question is why two powerful people decided to join hands with the lowest rung of society's Heroes."

Despite knowing that, it hit different when Fabi said it to him. His parents hadn't fled the Silverson Group after having him. He was born into the life they wanted for themselves.

Fabi continued with a reassuring smile. "I'm not saying that you shouldn't be angry, or that you should just get over it. What they've done has obviously hurt you, and I think you need to have another conversation with them about all of this." She took a breath before tapping her fingernails against the workbench again. "They're not the malicious type, and they did a great job of raising you. Maybe you're a little too sheltered, but you're a hard worker and you don't look down on people. Personally, I'm happy you turned out to be a Crafter, rather than another Gallant."

Sal smiled as he stood up, slipping away from Fabi's right hand that rested on his wrist. "Thank you for listening to me. It's genuinely so nice having someone who knows all the secrets. I really appreciate it."

Fabi placed her hands on the workbench and got to her feet. "I mean what I've said, though. You need to talk to them about this. Otherwise, you'll end up building resentment over time."

"I will, I promise," Sal said resolutely as he looked past Fabi to where the Arkwright was counting down toward the finish line. There were only a few minutes to go, and Sal was surprised at how much time had passed when he was talking to Fabi. Their conversation had started out lightly, with him telling her about his first semester…everything about creating the Mythcrafter ability, up until the revelation with his parents. It had been a lot to cover, but Fabi had patiently listened to everything he threw at her.

"Also, I'm not sure if you need to hear this," Fabi started suddenly as she lifted an empty cup from the workbench. "But you're doing a great job. Anyone who says otherwise is full of shit." She grinned as she moved over to the coffee machine. "We're going to run out of coffee beans at this rate. Don't suppose you could create a self-replenishing coffee machine?" She chuckled at her own joke as she pressed the button on the front of the machine.

"Do you want to see the blueprint?"

Fabi looked at him in confusion. "What blueprint?"

Sal pointed at the coffee machine. "For the self-replenishing coffee. I've designed it as an elixir production station."

Fabi held his gaze for a few seconds before shaking her head. "Of course you have…but, no. I want to see the result of this research first…and then we can build out a plan of how to upgrade your workshop." She waved a hand around Sal's private workshop. "All of this is amazing, but it won't scale enough to support a guild in the long-term. I think we need to start discussing the facilities for the depot."

Sal shrugged as he moved toward the Arkwright. "Sounds like a good plan. I can't wait to see the storefronts in use again."

"Same," Fabi agreed as she handed him a coffee.

Sal looked over at the workbench in surprise and saw that she had taken his cup and refilled it first. "Thank you."

Fabi winked at him as she retrieved her own from the workbench and moved back to the machine. "I'm just buttering you up so I can use the Arkwright when you're not looking."

Research Complete: Combination Set Successful
- o   Dominion Sets can now be created
  - ▪   Dominion Set has been added to blueprints

"What's a Dominion set?" Fabi asked as she squinted at the screen in confusion. "I've never heard of that ability."

Sal's mouth went dry as he stared at the Arkwright in shock. "I created the Dominion ability." He breathed the answer as he raised a shaky hand to press the report.

"Is it good?" Fabi paused when she saw Sal's reaction. "I'm going to take that as a yes."

When Sal's finger touched the option on the interface, the drop-down appeared with the context he was looking for.

Results from Cypher:
- ▪   Macclemark 004 has been successfully combined with Unnamed Transformative Set
- ▪   Mythcrafter Crafter Algorithm has created Essence Fortification as a function
  - ▪   Essence Fortification occurs through the management of the Transference, Attune, and Cultivation abilities
  - ▪   Essence Fortification is used to offset the essence draw of the Dominion function
  - ▪   Transformative function has been combined with Dominion function
  - ▪   Enhanced Scarlet Moon Set has been converted to respective essence signatures within Dominion
  - ▪   Enhanced Unnamed Set has been converted to respective essence signatures within Dominion

"Essence Fortification?" Fabi read it aloud. "That's another one I'm not familiar with as a function, but if it's using Transference, Attune, and Cultivation, it must be pretty powerful." She sounded excited by the prospect as she looked at Sal with bright eyes. "The Arkwright is able to make abilities?"

"No," Sal said finally as he read through the report. "It's using the things the visor has already discovered. I picked up the Essence Fortification pattern when I was at the gala. It was from looking at Eclipse as she used her ability." He pointed at the area of the report that read *Dominion*. "And this one is a Skill Weave I tried to create using Chatfield's Concept ability. It wasn't compatible with any Hero, and had a very low synchronization rate."

"What does it do?" Fabi looked between Sal and the report. "The Arkwright isn't exactly spelling it out for me."

Sal didn't even need to think about the answer; he had obsessed over the ability for a while. "It's a combination of Conquest, Absolute Counter, and Concept." He smiled at Fabi. "It creates a zone of death, like the Macclemark…but it uses essence constructs that can be summoned at will."

Fabi frowned at hearing the description. "So, it's like an ability that imitates the Macclemark functions? It sounded a lot stronger."

Sal smiled as he tapped the screen a few times, navigating to the Crafting menu. "Well, let's see how woefully unprepared we are for the materials."

When Sal went to the Crafting section, he saw the Dominion set that had been added into the Blueprints section. "Ten Q-Cred says we don't have enough materials."

"No bet." Fabi smiled. "But go on, put me out of my misery."

Dominion Set cannot be Crafted
Please resolve the following errors…

"Here we go." Sal chuckled as the interface loaded the issues. "Guess it was too good to be true?"

Please add measurements of the following blueprints: Dominion Set
Use measurements of Argento Set?

Sal accepted the suggestion and waited to see the next error, but it never came. Instead, a very unexpected message appeared on the screen.

Dominion Set (1/1) is being Crafted...

"It's just one piece?" Fabi asked incredulously before a smile appeared on her face. "I thought you said it would ask for the desired grades and abilities?"

Sal frowned as he stared at the estimated timer. "It did before…I don't know what's going on." He tapped at the blueprint to see what was being created, hoping that the actual design would make more sense. When it appeared as a three-dimensional image, rotating on the screen, he felt a little underwhelmed.

"A jumpsuit?" Fabi looked at it carefully. "It's…quite basic in appearance. I was kinda expecting something a little more flashy."

Sal activated Mythcrafter to see the design in more detail. "Oh," he breathed as he looked at it in surprise. "Yeah, there's no way the Arkwright is going to succeed at this one." He laughed as he pointed at the visor on the workbench. "Put that on and have a look for yourself."

Fabi picked up the visor and equipped it, frowning. "Ugh, hair is getting in the way. How do you deal with everything being thrown at you all at once?" She blinked a few times before focusing on the Arkwright. "It's showing me the structural information on the…oh, there it is." She moved closer to the image. "Ah, this is amazing. I definitely need to get a visor like—" Fabi's jaw dropped.

Sal nodded in agreement. "Yeah, looks can be deceiving. No evolutionary capacity, no visible runes, and nothing that would make it stand out."

"How can this only be Rare grade?" Fabi asked in disbelief as she stared at it in shock. "It's saying there are plenty of abilities based on the essence signatures? But they're all under the Dominion label?"

Sal grinned as he gave her a gentle nudge with his elbow. "Essence Fortification and Transformative are functions, not abilities. This set only has a single ability, which is why Arkwright wouldn't let us customize it."

Fabi reluctantly took off the visor and stared at Sal. "I've got no idea where my designs contributed to this, but…that isn't a Macclemark."

Sal nodded, the smile not leaving his face. "What about calling this new version the Mythmark?"

CHAPTER 60: SILVERSON

The Arkwright continued production well into the night. Fabi went home for a while, but made Sal promise that he would contact her the minute that the Mythmark was complete. The estimated time kept jumping around as it continued work on the Mythmark. Even though Doc Ameye had aligned all the sensors to accurately determine time, the Arkwright was completing dozens of tasks all at once.

Sal had been correct about the materials not being sufficient for the Mythmark, but he hadn't counted on the material synthesis being able to help out. All of Fabi's donated materials were currently being broken down and reformed alongside other reagents to create new fibers. Stormweave was one of the products that needed to be synthesized another three times to get to the desired materials for the Mythmark.

Sal was transfixed on the Arkwright, and had sat contentedly for hours just watching the new materials being created. A flowchart was displayed on the interface, showing the combinations that resulted in new materials being registered and stored. It was slow progress, but the additional cores that Fabi brought were doing an incredible job of keeping everything moving smoothly. The rhythmic rotations of the purple dungeon fragment were oddly calming, and Sal didn't feel frustrated by how long it was going to take. He was happy to continue watching it until he fell asleep.

"You're awake?" Petro asked as he crested the stairs, a few bags of coffee beans under his arm. He looked at the Arkwright before moving his gaze to Sal.

Sal smiled at him and gave a nod. "Thanks for the coffee. I'd have likely run out by tomorrow."

"Of course." Petro moved over to the machine to start filling up the tray. "How was your afternoon with Fabrizia?" He didn't turn around as he spoke.

Sal exhaled as he put his palms on his knees. "Good. We were working on some Crafting stuff…but I also got to talk to her about everything. The Silverson stuff." He left the sentence hanging in the air, as though waiting to see whether his father would pick it up.

Petro nodded again. "Would you like to talk to me about it?"

"Honestly, I don't know," Sal answered with a forced chuckle. "I feel emotionally drained by all of it. I'm not angry…but just, really disappointed that you both couldn't trust me with all of this."

He leaned back in his seat, but didn't look over to see his father. It was easier for him to continue staring at the Arkwright as he spoke his mind. "I'm worried that I've sped up the degradation of your eyes. Worried if I'll be able to properly trust you in the future, and worried that there's still so much more you're refusing to tell me."

Petro pulled the chair from the workbench and set it down between the Arkwright and Sal. When he sat, he stared directly into Sal's eyes. "You have every right to be angry. Let's get that clear first." He folded his hands and kept his gaze trained on Sal. "Don't worry about my eyes. I can always visit the clinic to get them checked out." He gestured at his own irises as though it were no big deal. "You've Crafted a monocle that allows me to use All Sight, even if I lose my natural ability. Please, under no circumstances, ever feel guilty about how much you've helped me."

Sal frowned and thought about how to respond, when his father suddenly grasped his hand. "Listen to me for a second, kiddo."

Petro smiled warmly at Sal before continuing. "I'll give you any answer you want. It'll be the truth. I swear on my life."

Sal glanced up at his father and nodded slowly. "Okay then. Why didn't you trust me with this?"

"Because we had so much to lose, Sal," Petro responded seriously before letting out a resigned sigh. "Your mother broke herself to participate in the war. She sacrificed so much that we never thought we'd be able to have a child…and yet, you came into our lives, and we never wanted to risk losing you." His grip tightened around Sal's hand. "If that meant protecting you with everything we had, and having you live in an isolated bubble, it was worth it to ensure you were safe. We kept you away from the training schools, and doubled down on you being a Support who couldn't use his power. It protected you from the eyes of the Hunter Bureau and the Silverson Group."

Petro paused for a moment, his silver eyes locked onto Sal's. "Your first ever registration highlighted your Replication ability, and we genuinely thought we could rest easy. It wasn't a Body Manipulation ability like your mother, which is what we were scared of. Had you been a Body Manipulator, then we wouldn't have been able to prevent you from entering a training school and being on the Hunter Bureau watch list."

Sal blinked in surprise. "There's a watch list?"

Petro nodded somberly. "Your invitation to Quest Academy was all but guaranteed the moment you were categorized as a Replicator." He let out another sigh. "If we continued to block their advances, then it would have led to all types of scrutiny from the Guilds Association and the Bureau. By not playing nice with their systems, you'd have been subject to the mandatory draft and would have been enlisted in the military. That's why we had to send you to Quest Academy, with the hopes that you'd drop out with the other Supports. An Appraiser is a valuable profession, so we trained you to be the best Appraiser possible, and had you standing at the auction house from a young age. Hiding in plain sight."

Sal couldn't believe what he was hearing. "You're making it sound like I would have been murdered if they knew the truth."

Petro stared at Sal, his expression unflinching. "We knew you could adjust the weaves of other people, Sal." He took a steadying breath before continuing. "I could see with All Sight that your ability was getting stronger with every passing year. How do you think I taught you how to use Appraisal? I could see your weave as you were making the pattern, and guided you into doing it properly." Petro grimaced, shaking his head. "You pointed at one of my knots and undid it in front of me, when you were seven years old."

Sal's jaw dropped. "When I was seven?"

Petro smiled grimly. "Yeah…it was a definite rough point in the marriage. You can probably imagine your mother's reaction? It wouldn't have happened if I hadn't taught you Appraisal." He shrugged it off as though it were no big deal. "But that event scared us. Like, really scared us. If you were able to adjust the internal weaves of Heroes, then you were going to be invaluable to every organization in the country. By keeping the secret from you, we knew you wouldn't be able to tell anyone or feel conflicted about the morality of not using your power to help others.

"We know it was selfish, but we wanted to protect you more than anything else." Petro gave Sal's hand another reassuring squeeze. "We practically grew up in the Silverson Group, and we knew exactly how the big organizations treated those with talent. They were never used for the betterment of mankind, but instead harnessed like a secret weapon or trump card. You deserved a different life than that, Salvatore. Your powers came from the union of your mother and me, and our only saving grace was the fact that the Silverson Group saw me as a failure. Thankfully, they thought my son would be one, too."

Sal tried to smile as he looked at his father. "I don't know how anyone could see you as a failure."

"If you're unlucky enough to meet your aunts and uncles, you'll get the idea." Petro chuckled. The laughter and mirth in his voice faded as he continued. "When Quest informed us that you had pioneered a new ability, we were terrified. I had to talk your mother down, but she was going to pull you straight out of the Academy and have us move to a different safe zone. But imagine our luck when the ability you created turned out to be even more eye-catching than Skill Master? All of a sudden, we're being offered support to protect you, with the guarantee that the Silverson Group will never know about it?"

"Quest did that?" Sal asked in surprise. "With the Trainee Guild sponsorship?"

Petro nodded, smiling. "Yeah, it was Quest. We were wary of him at first, but we believe that he's a good guy who's just looking out for his students. The whole Fabrizia debacle aside, of course. That was a shit-show at the gala. Your mother knew that stepping in would cause a scene, but she couldn't let anything happen to Fabrizia."

Sal frowned again at those words. "So, even though you've kept this massive lie for my whole life…you risked it all to ensure Fabi got a better power?"

Petro barked a laugh with a shake of his head. "You were getting hurt because of that visor, and your mother was beside you before I had time to blink. You can hate us for lying to you, but I'd ask you to never doubt how much we love you and want to protect you. Just to add a sprinkle of levity, she did make the joke that she was also saving your future wife." He gave a halfhearted smile before the frown reappeared on his face. "We know we fucked up, Sal…and I don't want us to simply brush all of this under the rug. We want to be honest with you and build back our relationship on trust."

"You're sounding like an Auctioneer." Sal smiled.

Petro let go of Sal's hand and pressed his palm to his chest. "That wounds me, Sal." He gestured at the coffee machine. "I could always try to buy back your love with coffee?"

Sal sighed as he looked at his father carefully. "Why is it just you who's here?"

"Because she said she'd cry, and she didn't want you to feel bad when you've got every right to be angry," Petro said. "She wanted me to say my piece before she offered her own apology, so it wouldn't feel like we were ganging up on you."

Sal's shoulders dropped as he put his face in his palms. "Thanks for that, I guess." With an aggravated sigh, he pulled his hands away from his face and sat up straight. "Even though I feel betrayed, I love you both. Nothing will change that, okay?"

Petro nodded in understanding, but waited for the continuation.

Sal clapped his palms against his knees before giving his father a tired smile. "But I can't keep living like this...I went to Quest Academy scared of my own shadow. I nearly fainted when I fought against leechers, and now I'm signed up to do dungeon runs, and I feel like the biggest fraud of all time. I'm the top Savior in Quest Academy, and I'm genuinely scared of portals, towers, and dungeons. You see where I'm going with this?"

Petro nodded solemnly. "We didn't teach you how to survive in a war against demons."

"Every day I feel like I'm constantly hit with something that should be common sense, and I don't know anything about it," Sal said in a strained voice, his frustration coming through. "Like, I was sitting at the canteen table and literally asked Divinity what the Bastion was." He looked at his father with wide eyes.

"Ah." Petro grimaced. "They're the bad guys, by the way."

"I know that, now!" Sal said with a laugh of disbelief. "I'm going on dungeon runs with Fabi, and it'll only be my third time fighting demons. See what I mean about being a fraud?"

Petro thought about it for a few minutes before clapping his hands. "Okay then, how about we start with that?"

"Start with what?" Sal asked in genuine confusion.

"Training you to be a Hero," Petro said without even a sliver of mockery. "You have awhile before you go back to Quest Academy, so we have some time."

Sal just stared at his father in complete disbelief. "You? You're going to teach me how to be a Hero?"

Petro grinned as he rose. "Yes, and your mother is going to kill me for it."

"No, I mean...you're an Auctioneer. You've not been a Hero for like...twenty years!" Sal floundered to explain how ridiculous this whole plan was to his father. "I'm going to learn with Fabi anyway, so there's no real need for you to put yourself at risk."

"You said that Perfect ability allows you to master movements, right?" Petro smiled at Sal.

"Yeah..." Sal answered tentatively, not liking the direction this had turned.

Petro clapped again. "Good. Then it's about time you learned your family legacy."

"Lying?" Sal guessed with an awkward smile.

"Silverson Arts." Petro grinned. "A martial style developed for anti-demon combat."

Sal just stared at his father. "You?" He pointed at Petro. "Are going to teach me martial arts?" He gestured at himself, just to be doubly sure that he was hearing this correctly.

Petro's smile grew wider. "The top-ranked Savior at Quest Academy should be able to take out a half-blind Auctioneer, surely?"

"You're insane." Sal laughed as he shook his head in disbelief.

"And you're stalling." Petro moved toward the stairs. "Come on. I'm curious to see how that fancy Perfect weave works."

CHAPTER 61: KICK

"I'm telling you, my leg doesn't go that high!" Sal insisted with a grimace as his father continued to push.

"Take a deep breath," Petro insisted, imitating the motion as he inhaled deeply. When Petro exhaled alongside Sal, he pushed Sal's leg forward.

"Ugh!" Sal groaned as he tapped at the floor with his hand before pulling it to his head to tug at his own hair. The instruction hadn't even started, and he was already trying to tap out of the stretching routine.

"You told me you started doing all these fancy stretches to get yourself into shape, but your mobility is shocking," Petro said in disbelief. "How do you expect to land a kick if you can't even raise your leg?"

Sal felt a slight reprieve from the pain and shot up to try to swipe at his father, but it was no use. "When the hell will I try to kick a demon? I shouldn't be any-where near them—I'm a Support!"

"You need to approach this from the mindset of making your body a weapon, Sal. You should be able to kick a prowler to death," Petro said with a weary smile. "So just shut up and focus on your breathing, okay? We're just going to loosen up these muscles."

Sal groaned again as he felt his hamstrings burning. The only solace he had was that Perfect was constantly adjusting his internal state to adapt to the move-ments. As much as he didn't want to admit it to his father, the stretches were increasing his mobility at a staggering rate. However, judging by the smile on Petro's face, he had already come to the exact same conclusion…which meant zero reprieve for Sal over the last twenty minutes.

"No, no…you already did that leg," Sal insisted as he tried to shoo off his father from grabbing his barely recovered leg.

"Then you should have no issue with repeating the same stretches." Petro smiled. "We've got a whole lifetime to catch up on, so just bear with it."

Sal stared at his father in shock. "This is the worst apology ever! You're liter-ally torturing me."

Petro chuckled as he pushed Sal's leg into the air, securing his shoulder behind it and gradually pushing it higher between breaths. "Hey, I'm doing you a favor here, Sal. You were going to feel all guilty about hating us…at least I'm giving you a reason."

"You're the absolute worst at apologies," Sal barked between stretches, strug-gling to regulate his own breathing.

"Yeah, yeah…focus on managing the pain and let your weave do its work," Petro shot back as he watched Sal's chest intently. "I can see your body adjusting to the movements, so you might as well stop your complaining and just follow along. You'll be far nimbler for it."

Sal ignored his father as he tried to think of positive thoughts. The sooner he was done with this weird charade, the sooner he'd be able to get back to the Ark-wright. He'd get his Dominion set in a few days…maybe, and then he wouldn't need to worry about these silly martial arts. His mind wandered to the chest of elixirs that he had. There was Kakushin and Kaizen, but he wondered whether he had any basic health potions. They'd be able to numb the pain and put him to sleep. Sal smiled at the thought of an instant cure for this torture. Even though he knew he didn't have a health potion, it was nice to dream.

"There we go," Petro insisted as he pushed Sal's leg to the point that Sal could see his own foot directly overhead.

"Whoa…" Sal said in disbelief. He was lying flat on his back, and his own foot just came into view. He didn't really remember a time where he could willingly lift his leg above waist level, so to see it coming up all the way to his head was insane.

"We're just getting started." Petro grinned as he stepped back and let Sal's leg move back to the floor. "Let's work on those shoulders. If you're anything like your mother, they're likely going to be like granite."

Sal sat up with his father's assistance. "Granite?"

"Rock hard," Petro clarified. "Overthinkers tend to have the most tense shoulders…it's not science, but I feel like it's true." He positioned himself behind Sal and massaged his shoulder blades. "Lay on your front. We're going to start working on the arms now."

Sal stifled a groan as he reluctantly lay down on the floor again, this time with his cheek resting against the polished wood. "You know, we could have gotten training mats or something."

"Probably," Petro answered as he started pulling at Sal's arm, rotating it in different directions…that it seemingly didn't want to move in. "Well, this is even worse than the legs. Have you not been able to scratch your back all these years?"

Sal ignored his father's jests as he grumbled through the pain. As much as he hated to admit it, his legs were feeling much better after the stretches. Sal wasn't sure whether it was due to the Perfect ability making adjustments, or whether it was his mind playing tricks on him now that he was experiencing pain somewhere else. Either way, he had come to terms with the fact that this was good for his body, even if he had to endure his father's personality throughout it.

"Okay, now we're making progress. You're going to need this sort of flexibility to really get everything out of the Silverson Arts…and you're practically cheating with that Perfect ability. It would take Heroes years to get their body into the sort of condition that you'll be starting with," Petro said, a proud smile on his face. "Just having the flexibility will change how you move, run, and jump. It'll take a little getting used to, but I'm sure your weave will take care of that."

Sal grumbled something, but his face continually slapped against the floor every time his father changed his grip on the arm.

"I agree, I think this is a wonderful father-and-son bonding experience." Petro laughed as he started to rotate Sal's wrist. "So, while I have your undivided attention…let me explain a little more about the Silverson Arts."

"Mmph," Sal muttered, either in agreement or dissent. It didn't matter, as Petro was seemingly set on delivering his speech.

"So, you've fought against leechers, prowlers, and an obsidian hulker, is that right?" Petro moved onto Sal's other arm, repeating the process of massaging the muscle before slowly rotating the arm.

"Yeah, and…some voiders in the tower," Sal managed to breathe out between gasps.

"Good. The Silverson Arts are only really effective on those variants. I can't really say much about the higher tiers as we didn't teach styles to combat those," Petro explained as he rubbed Sal's shoulders. "Essentially, it starts with a set of stances that allow you to counteract their movements and exploit weaknesses. Leechers can be taken out if you joint-lock their tentacles, or even just stabbed with two fingers in their central mass. Prowlers can be fooled with deceptive movements, so heightened agility is key and opens a window of opportunity to take out their sensory organs."

"Sensory organs?" Sal repeated with a wheeze. "What…like, smacking their ears?" He tried laughing, but the awkward position of his arms made it difficult to catch his breath.

"Stabbing their eyes with your fingers." Petro corrected him as though it were a perfectly normal sentence. "You can also slap your hands to throw off their heightened sense of hearing. Being quiet only plays to their advantage, so you need to disrupt their flow."

"Who even are you?" Sal laughed as he tried turning on the floor to look up at his father. "Seriously, after a lifetime of sheltering me…you're now telling me to run up to a prowler and poke its eyes out with my fingers? You're hearing yourself, right? This is insane!"

"Do you really want me to say it? Because I'll say it," Petro threatened as he continued to rub Sal's shoulder. "Back in my day…we didn't have the budget for all this fancy equipment. There was a stigma around using what we claimed from the dungeons and portals, as they practically sucked our minimal essence reserves dry."

Sal couldn't help but laugh. "You're joking, right?"

Petro lifted Sal by the armpits so he could get to his feet. He brushed off the back of Sal's waistcoat before turning him around by the shoulders. "Good thing you made your outfit nice and stretchy." He smiled broadly.

Sal sighed as he looked at his dad. "For a second, I really thought you were going insane…there's no reason for me to learn martial arts. I don't really care about that Silverson stuff, and I do forgive you both for keeping the secret from me. I just needed a bit of time to think through it."

Petro placed his hands on Sal's shoulders and looked at him. "You looked like you needed to loosen up, and it was a good excuse. I'm not actually expecting you to run up to a prowler and poke its eyes out, but I also don't expect you to throw punches at obsidian hulkers."

"Ah." Sal grimaced.

"You might never need the Silverson Arts, and that's totally fine with me," Petro continued. "But if you're going to find yourself in situations where you need to throw a punch or launch a kick…then I might as well show you how to do it properly. Just a couple of little combinations that will make your life easier. Sound good?"

Sal nodded in agreement. "Sounds good."

Petro smiled as he took a few steps back. "Okay, so I want you to watch me carefully. When we were back in the Silverson Group, we had these silver-tipped shoes…and they made every kick deadly. Imagine that a leecher has entered into my combat area."

"Your combat area?" Sal raised his eyebrow. "What's that?"

Petro sighed as he pointed in front of him. "Ten-foot radius, Sal. What are they even teaching you at Quest Academy?" He shook his head as he moved into a crouched position. "So, tell me where the leecher is appearing."

Sal shrugged as he pointed at an area in front of his father. "Right there. It's floating in from the ceiling, about two feet above your head." He picked the ambush of the leecher that attacked him in the dungeon when he went with Chatfield and Upgrade. As much as he wanted to humor his father, he wasn't sure that this was truly the best method. *Maybe he should suggest that they Appraise stuff together or something?*

Right before Sal was about to speak, Petro lazily leaned back on his left leg and launched his right leg in a vicious arc that swept through the empty air. His toe sliced into the vacant space that Sal had pointed to. What was more impressive was that Petro's foot was suspended in midair, in a controlled stance.

"Okay, where's the next one?" Petro grinned.

Sal couldn't find words to speak as he watched his father in action. He quietly pointed to another area and watched in a sort of mute horror as his father's foot swept through that area, once again, toe-first.

"If we incorporated the Silverson Sweep…" Petro crouched into a squat and turned his entire body before launching his right leg out in a wide arc. "We can clear away as much as three leechers that have gotten too close." He lifted his arms, waving his fingers. "And with our hands, we can increase our speed and use them to joint-lock any that are out of reach. Pretty simple."

"What…part of that is simple?" Sal breathed as he gestured vaguely at the empty space his father had pulverized with kicks. "How can you even do that? It's been like twenty-years!"

Petro grinned. "All that dancing isn't just for show. We adapted some of the stances and footwork into playful dances, just so we wouldn't lose our edge in case of an emergency." He shrugged as he gestured at Sal's feet. "So, are you going to ask me a million questions, or are you going to learn how to kick properly?"

"And you know how to punch, too?" Sal asked quizzically, still not sure how to process everything that was happening.

Petro shook his head. "Nah, that's your mother's department. You Craft yourself something that can pack power into a punch, and she'll show you how to take down even the scariest of opponents."

"I've changed my mind…can we just go back to keeping secrets?" Sal laughed as he looked at his father's readied stance. "We'll just pretend this never happened, and I can get back to Crafting."

Petro smiled as he nodded. "If you give it an honest effort just a single time, I'll drop the topic and we'll leave it at that. I'm sure you'll do excellently in front of Fabrizia in your dungeon run."

Sal stared at him quietly. "You're goading me, aren't you?" A wry smile tugged at his lips.

"And it's working." Petro smiled back.

CHAPTER 62: ITERATION

Just having the Perfect weave in place was a godsend. Sal's labored breathing only ever lasted a few seconds before his body controlled itself. His movements were becoming more fluid with every iteration of the kick, and although Perfect was attempting to assign the muscle memory of the kick, Sal was actively trying to improve it. The only problem was that he reached the natural plateau of his body, and no amount of Perfect was going to help him overcome it.

"Great work, Salvatore." Petro congratulated him as he held his own leg out. "Try to activate the muscle groups in your leg rather than using momentum to swing it. You need to be controlling the movement so that you can be precise when it's an attack. It'll allow you to regulate the strength of the attack and avoid exhaustion in a prolonged battle."

As he spoke, his foot hovered in the air and made slow sweeping movements from side to side. "Holding this stance will strengthen your leg that's acting like an anchor. The burning in your thighs is a sign that you're activating the right muscles."

Sal sighed as he repeated the action, maintaining his outstretched foot in the same position his father was holding. The burning in his left leg had subsided a long time ago, but he knew there was fatigue accumulating that he'd pay for tomorrow. He wondered whether Perfect was subduing the pain so he could continue practicing. Either way, he had made progress, and despite his expectations…his father was actually a pretty great teacher.

Petro moved over to where Sal stood and grasped his foot gently with his right hand. His left hand moved to Sal's bent knee that was wobbling slightly as Sal tried to maintain balance. "Okay, so you're not looking to bludgeon a leecher with the side of your foot, so you'll need to bend here." Petro moved Sal's foot while keeping his knee balanced.

"Turning your foot mid-strike loses all the power, and opens up the chance of injury. Trust me, you do not want a shattered ankle on the battlefield." He smiled reassuringly as he gently simulated the movements of the kick using Sal's leg. When that was done, he moved to adjust Sal's torso. "Now, try it again as slow as you can."

This was the hardest part. Doing the kick slowly eroded Sal's previous tactic of using momentum to reach a greater height. With a grimace, Sal began the painstaking process of starting the kick as slowly as he could. When he tried to speed up earlier, his father had asked him to repeat it, again and again, until Sal finally started doing it as he was told.

"Great work…nice and slow. Let your body learn the movement. If we get it right, we'll add more speed to it over time…form is the most important part of the technique and you need to make sure it's perfect," Petro instructed as he watched Sal's body gradually move through the motions. When Sal's torso started to vibrate, Petro steadied it with his hands and bade him to continue.

Sweat trickled down Sal's forehead as he brought his foot up, knowing that it was going to falter in the exact same place as every other attempt. The stretching from earlier had been a lie…his body couldn't bend that way in reality, and his muscle groups seemed to be retaliating against his resolve. When his foot moved upward, Sal frowned as he looked at it.

"And this is why we move slowly through the motions. My guess is that Perfect is trying to master a novice-level kick, but we need it to recognize the Silverson Arts before it starts committing it to muscle memory." Petro smiled as he watched Sal's foot rise to the highest point they had achieved so far.

"Whoa…" Sal said in disbelief as his foot completed the ascent. Despite a few wobbles, he managed to hold the position like his father had shown him. "I didn't know I could bring it up that far."

Petro nodded as he gently let go of Sal's shoulders. "Now, you've brought your leg into the combat position…but it's time to attack. You're going to complete the movement in a slow snap, utilizing your knee and focusing the toe of your foot like the tip of a sword." Petro pointed at Sal's thigh. "Your body shouldn't move from here. Only the area below your right knee is allowed to move. Give it a try and do it slowly."

Sal followed his father's instruction and was surprised at how easily his body adjusted to the movement. His body was rigid and he slowly but surely managed to bring his toe forward in a straight line, tensing his calf and imagining that his shin was a shield designed to bludgeon the imaginary leecher. His lower leg was a sword and shield, with his toe piercing and his shin following through with the impact. It was a good analogy for what he needed to do, and Sal kept his composure as he finally brought his foot to the point where his leg was almost fully outstretched. Apparently, it was important to keep a small bend in the knee and never to let it lock into place.

"Fantastic progress, Sal. Now reverse the whole process and bring yourself back into a standing position," Petro said with a clap of his hands as he moved around Sal to watch his progress.

"So, that's it?" Sal asked hopefully as he slowly brought himself out of the kicking stance, delighted to have both feet back on the ground.

Petro looked at him in surprise. "Oh, not even close. I want you to repeat that ten times, gradually building up your speed until it's perfect. Then you're able to throw in the towel and head back to the workshop."

Sal groaned inwardly as he grit his teeth. "Why do you have to say it like I'd be giving up?"

"A single kick does not a martial artist make," Petro said sagely as he stood in front of Sal. "The Silverson Arts are most deadly when used in combination and adapted to muscle memory so you can react faster than anyone. Even now, after all these years, I feel confident and capable. That's a feeling that money will never be able to buy." He pointed at Sal, who was still going through the motions of his slow kicks. "If you want to feel confident in a dungeon, then the best way is to train your body to protect you and the people around you. If all your weapons, equipment, and abilities fail you…your body will protect you. That's the goal of the Silverson Arts."

Sal waited until he had raised his leg to the highest point, happy to see that it had managed to rise a little higher than the last time, before speaking. "You know an awful lot about the Silverson Arts. Did everyone in the group get trained like this?"

Petro nodded. "I was one of the instructors for it. All Sight made it very easy for correcting mistakes and helping the troops break through bottlenecks." He gestured vaguely at Sal's leg. "What you can learn in minutes is something that took many of them days, sometimes weeks. We alternated training different muscle groups to avoid injury, but it was a grueling regimen."

"Kinda hard to imagine you ordering soldiers around." Sal chuckled as his foot wobbled. He immediately trained his attention back on his foot and stabilized his balance, cursing himself inwardly for losing focus. If he was going to get this done, he'd need to do it right. Despite his father's goading, the increase in height from the kick felt like massive progress and it had happened because of the slow training…and not the Perfect weave. Sal wanted to at least learn this competently before he decided on learning the combinations.

Petro smiled at him as he gently adjusted the foot that had wobbled. "Ah, it was easier than you'd think. All the troops in the Silverson Group were there because they had people to protect or avenge. We had a method of making them stronger, and I had an ability that guaranteed their progress and improvement. Your mother had it much worse than me, and was out fighting on the front lines. I trained soldiers and worked on strategy reports for Command."

"Didn't you teach them how to use their abilities? Like how Quest Academy does it?" Sal asked curiously.

Petro shook his head. "Like I said, we taught—" He caught himself in his own sentence and smiled ruefully. "Sorry, the Silverson Group taught people how to use their bodies as weapons, rather than relying on gear. Anyone who had strong abilities back then was fast-tracked into officer positions, which included your mother." He grinned as he thought of something funny. "And Elaine, who you know as Prestige. She was one of the officers in the Silverson Group, a lifetime ago."

"So the story about Mom bullying Prestige?" Sal asked between breaths. He was only just finishing the second iteration of the kick, and his Perfect weave had seemingly given up on suppressing the fatigue. His body was screaming at him to stop this stupid training method.

"That's from your mother's hometown. It was a place called Barrier, and it was…like it sounds, on the edge of a Red Zone." Petro sighed. "There were all sorts of theories back then, that the proximity to Red Zones gave children a stronger ability. And that led to some very problematic practices, that I'd rather not get into." He waved his hand as though dismissing the topic. "Elaine and your mother had a very competitive relationship over the years, and that had its own share of problems while we were at the Silverson Group. Elaine held onto her place after we left, and I believe that Gallant likely occurred from an arranged marriage."

Sal's foot froze in midair as he looked at his father in surprise. "Wait…the Silverson Group…does that mean I'm related to Gallant in some way?"

Petro brought his hand back to Sal's foot and started to guide it slowly in the pattern that was etched into Sal's memory. "No. We have a very good idea of who Gallant's father is, based on the powers he's able to draw on. He's not from our family." With a furrowed brow, he looked at Sal before sighing. "I told you that I wouldn't keep any more secrets from you, but you can likely appreciate that I'd rather not discuss their personal lives. I'll finish on that topic with a single point, so you can truly appreciate the type of people who make up the Silverson Group. After Gallant's birth, Prestige was tasked with having another child."

"And that's why she left the Silverson Group?" Sal asked lamely, not sure whether his father would confirm or deny the guess.

Petro smiled as he let go of Sal's foot and watched him move it through the air in a complete cycle. "She reached out to your mother, and arrived in Haven a few weeks later with Gallant." He looked at Sal for a few seconds, as though weighing up his next words. "Prestige is a proud woman, and while she has the unique ability to get under your mother's skin, she's a good person. I'm glad you were able to help Gallant with your ability."

Sal wasn't satisfied with dropping the topic there. He knew he was likely pushing his luck, but he wanted to know the answer. "Gallant is ridiculously strong." He left those words hanging in the air as he moved to the next phase of the kick with a grimace. "So, why would the Silverson Group willingly let him leave? If their whole thing is about curating the best group of Heroes?"

Petro held Sal's gaze for a few moments. "Robert Locke is one of the few people who the Silverson Group is wary of. He was the leader of Phantom, which was an absolute powerhouse when it came to political maneuvering. They hid in plain sight, with each of their members belonging to different guilds. When Robert made his move on the government buildings, there was nothing that could be done to stop it. Various guildmasters and vice-captains revealed themselves to be members of Phantom and followed Robert to what he called his newly formed government, the Hunter Bureau. It destroyed the guilds of that time, and led to the formation of the United Guilds Association. By the time they had organized themselves, Robert had created an entirely new ecosystem that introduced Reclamation projects." Petro chuckled humorlessly. "He won over the people, destabilized the guilds, and established the Hunter Bureau as the only institution that could lead humanity forward."

Sal's eyes widened. "So the Hunter Bureau is less than twenty years old?"

Petro nodded. "Yeah, and they've done a pretty good job. The Silverson Group had established Sanctuary as a foothold, but it was Robert who paid them lip service by renaming it Silver Sanctuary. He went on to establish Haven as an economic hub, and built out the other boroughs over the years. The stalemate of progress has only been in the last ten years, and I'm certain that he's pushing to retake Salvation to maintain his hold."

Sal finished his third iteration of the kick, but paused when he brought his foot back to the floor. "Are the Bastion really the bad guys? You're making it sound like Robert is the villain for staging a coup on the government."

Petro shrugged as he gestured for Sal to move onto the fourth kick. "You'll lose progress if you hang around—get back into stance."

Sal shook his head as he tried to sort through everything he had heard. The upside of it all was that he had a direct source for a wealth of information he'd never heard of. The downside was the thousand questions that popped up every time he received a new piece of context. "How many safe zones are there? I thought Haven was the biggest one," Sal asked finally, wanting to at least know where they stood in comparison to the rest of the world. Sure, his father's information might be twenty years out of date, but he still knew far more than Sal did.

"Get into the kicking stance and I'll tell you. Keep gradually increasing your speed with each iteration." Petro was adamant and didn't resume talking until Sal obliged with the kicking maneuver.

When Sal started to go through the motions, Petro walked around him and started to answer. "It really depends on who you ask, Sal. The Bastion would have you believe we exist alone in a desolate wasteland, surrounded by demonic hordes…and reaching out a hand to them will guarantee our salvation." He chuckled at his own words as he continued to monitor Sal's stance. "If you ask Robert, he'll tell you that we've secured countless strategic zones across the coast, just waiting for redevelopment funds from our social elite. With the right investment, we'll be back to normal and have the demons eradicated in the next decade."

Sal looked at his father, and asked his next question tentatively. "And what does Petro Argento think?"

Petro smiled as he stepped in front of Sal. "Petro? Well…he's not as cynical as Bastion, nor as hopeful as Robert. He's somewhere in between." He thought about the question for a few seconds, looking off to one side. "There are a lot of strong people out there, Sal. If they were aligned on what truly mattered, then the war wouldn't have lasted this long. Sure, the demons are evolving and becoming harder to kill…but so are we." He reached out to reposition Sal's foot ever so slightly. "Each generation of humanity is stronger than the last, and our understanding of our capabilities grows by the minute. I think that your generation could be the one that sees the end of this war, and I genuinely hope I'm around to see it."

"What happened to not being as hopeful as Robert?" Sal asked dryly, trying not to laugh as he wobbled.

Petro grinned as he pushed Sal's foot, causing him to lose balance and stumble backward. "I take it back," Petro teased as he watched Sal spread out on the floor like a starfish. "It's probably the generation after this one."

Sal groaned as he stared up at the ceiling. "Can I go back to the workshop now?"

CHAPTER 63: SACRIFICE

Sal numbly stared at the Arkwright. He had just spent the last four hours peppering his father with questions, while subjecting his entire body to the worst punishment he had endured. That was a lie—shattering his arms in the excursion was far worse, and the gates being opened by Vanessa and Prestige were competing for the top spot, too. Sal was in pain and an overall sense of discomfort, and he just wanted to complain. The last thing he needed right now was the message on the interface of the Arkwright.

Deposit Scarlet Moon Revolver into Arkwright Inventory Tray

Sal just stared at the message, his brain not fully comprehending what was being asked or why. He would have happily paid a hundred Q-Cred just for one of Alex's coffees, if it gave him the sweet release from fatigue…but there was no way for that to happen. Sal didn't have an easy reprieve this time, and was forced to use what remaining brainpower he had to solve this problem.

Tapping at the interface, he could see that the message was recent. The dropdown didn't really give him any additional information other than the fact that the Scarlet Moon Revolver was required to complete the Dominion set. What it did tell him was that he needed to deposit the ammo cartridges he had created, too. Sal was tired, but he wasn't an idiot. There was no way that he was going to give away his only weapon—days before he went into a dungeon with Fabi—and trade an evolutionary gun with rare materials like scarlet screen…just for a black jumpsuit with a single ability.

Sal groaned as he looked at the ceiling. The revolver was great, but it couldn't take out the obsidian hulker. Switching the cartridges was a pain, and the only reason he had made it was because Barry and Quest had suggested it. The materials weren't actually at his own expense, as Chatfield and Doc Ameye had supplied them. He wasn't going to trade in the Legendary-grade visor, that was for sure…but he wasn't completely against trading in the revolver, particularly now that the set had been broken. The more he thought about it, the more reasons he came up with for getting rid of it. It was no longer synched with his visor, so the evolutionary rune was likely defunct. Synergy was also going to be useless on the weapon.

"Why am I like this?" Sal groaned as he made his way over to the carry case he created for the revolver and the cartridges. Opening the lid, he looked at it warily, as though weighing his options. It had only managed to serve him for a couple of months, and was a great weapon…but was it really the best weapon for him? If he used Perfect, he could become adept with whatever weapon he held.

Sal grimaced as he reached for his belt, unclipping it and pulling it away from his waist. If he got rid of the revolver, then his belt would become an overpriced accessory. He looked at the belt before a frown bloomed on his face. "What the hell?" Sal brought the belt up close to his face, inspecting the burn damage across the surface.

He didn't even need Appraisal to tell him that the evolutionary rune had been broken. Four of the cores were also out of action. Sal turned it over in his hands, using his Appraisal to determine what had happened. He stood there for a few moments in silence until the answer eventually found its way to him. He was wearing the belt at the gala, and it didn't react to the surge of essence as well as his visor had. That was an understatement. *Had Prestige's essence effectively overloaded the rune and the backlash caused the cores to explode?*

The best conclusion Sal was able to come up with was around the materials he used for the design. Although the cores were sufficient, the prowler components had been the weakness. Sal made up his mind as he looked at the dimly lit cores that remained on the belt. He was going to frame it as an investment of materials, rather than a sacrifice. That's what it was…an investment. Sal placed his belt into the case that contained the revolver and cartridges. *It was an investment*, he told himself again as he brought them over to the tray of the Arkwright.

Pulling out the tray, Sal sighed as he lifted the Scarlet Moon Revolver out of the case. He looked at it fondly as he felt the reassuring weight of it in his hand. "Thanks for everything." He spoke in an almost dream-like state as he placed the revolver into the tray. Next went the essence cartridges and the bullets made from material shards. "I wouldn't have made it through the tower or the dungeon without your help," Sal muttered as he looked at the deposited goods. With a sigh, he chucked in the belt, not having the same emotional attachment to it like he did with the revolver.

Just as he was about to push the tray shut, he paused. This was a new chapter for him, after all…and he had already committed to making himself a better weapon for the dungeon runs. The Arkwright was making a battle-suit for him, so he wasn't going to need his old uniform. Upgrade had made it for him, but she was also in support of him making a better suit for himself. Nostalgia was one thing, but practicality was another.

Besides, he also had the Legendary-grade coat that she had made, with grappling hooks. Sal made up his mind as he got to his feet, moving into the bedroom area to collect the outfit he wore throughout his first semester—the Epic-grade Argento set. Sal hadn't gotten around to restoring them, and it felt wrong to place them in the Arkwright in their current state.

Closing his eyes, he focused on creating his mother's weave. The Restoration ability that he had memorized as a kid quickly came to him and activated. Using Perfect alongside Restoration was…interesting, but the draw wasn't nearly as drastic as Sal had feared. His accessible gates practically vibrated as his essence flooded into the shirt draped over his right arm, and his slacks draped over his left. In his hands, he gripped the gloves as they reformed between his fingertips. Perfect kept trying to interfere with the basic Restoration, and Sal was too exhausted to put up any sort of fight. He stood there for a few minutes, groaning all the while, knowing that it would have been faster and more efficient if he had just flooded the damn things with essence.

"Finally." Sal let out an exasperated sigh as he felt the draw on his essence evaporate. In his hands, the Argento set looked brand-new. He smiled to himself as he placed them into the drawer along with the Revolver. Although he was somewhat reluctant to let go of them, he knew it was for the best. He was a part of the Savior class now, and he needed a new suite of equipment that could keep up with his growing abilities. Just like his first shirt had been made out of fear, his revolver was made from a reluctance to be near the enemy.

Sal slid the tray closed and moved to the interface with a slightly heavier heart. The message on the screen disappeared, only to be replaced with a new one.

Research Status…(2/26)
- o   Scarlet Strategist's Visor: Essence Signature Verified
- o   Scarlet Moon Revolver: Essence Signature Verified
- o   Enhanced Scarlet Moon Revolver: Research Pending
- o   Scarlet Moon Rifle: Research Pending
- o   Enhanced Scarlet Moon Rifle: Research Pending

Sal stared at the message for a few more seconds before he dropped his gaze to an option he hadn't noticed earlier.

Accept All?

Sal didn't want to be monitoring the Arkwright all night, nor did he want it to be wasting essence from the cores by waiting for his answers. He had already given the machine what he wanted, so it was best to just let it do its work. Sal selected the option for accepting all prompts, and stood back with a relieved smile. A few loading screens moved faster than his eyes could track, and it looked like a few dozen prompts had been waiting for his approval. But all of them disappeared as quickly as they had appeared.

"Goodnight, Arkwright," Sal said with a stifled yawn. If there were any problems with it the next morning, Sal was content with blaming his father. That stupid Silverson kick was the cause of all this anguish.

Just as he got to the doorway to his bedroom, Sal paused and looked at the area of empty space on the mezzanine. He visualized a leecher floating about five feet off the ground and, with a fluid extension of his right leg, he leaned back and flawlessly struck at it with pinpoint accuracy. When he was done, he returned to a normal stance and let out a dry chuckle. He hated how good of a teacher his father was.

The last of Sal's athletic prowess was spent getting undressed before he launched himself at the pillows. Fishing his tablet from the blankets, he opened it up and sent a quick message to Fabi.

Salvatore: Going to sleep. Suit isn't done yet, I'll keep you posted.
Salvatore: Had a talk with my dad. I feel a lot better about everything, but still need to talk with my mother.
Salvatore: Thanks for listening and the advice, I really needed it.

Sal could only keep one eye open to verify that the message had been sent, and when it was done, he finally relinquished himself to the sweet embrace of sleep…for all of four hours.

Because that's when the Arkwright kicked into overdrive.

Sal blearily staggered out of his bed, tripping over his blanket and collapsing to the ground as his legs seized up simultaneously. With the fusion of a gasp and a groan, Sal clawed his way back up to the bed and flopped back into a half-seated position. He was still trying to process what was going on, but he couldn't for the life of him determine the sounds that were coming from his workshop. *Had Fabi come over with a buzz saw? Or had a hulker decided to swan dive through the skylights?*

Sal practically crawled from the bed toward the open door leading to the workshop. He pulled at his discarded shirt and pants, somehow managing to make his legs comply with getting dressed. He'd happily risk Fabi seeing him looking like shit if it meant getting the noise to stop.

After the arduous task of using his jelly-like legs to get to the doorway, Sal leaned heavily against the frame and looked at the Arkwright in confusion. The first thing he was able to determine was that nobody was present. The second factor he discovered was that the noise was coming from the Arkwright…but it was impossible to tell what was causing it.

Sal paused as he looked at the coffee machine. Shaking his head, he continued his journey on malfunctioning legs to get to the interface. He was going to stop whatever was happening and get some more sleep. No coffee, no noise…just sleep. Sal rubbed at his eyes and squinted at the interface, noticing that there were more than ten windows open, layered over each other.

Research Complete: Essence Signature Verified
Research Complete: Essence Signature Verified

Sal reviewed them and saw the same words on each of them. He dismissed them one by one, until he could see the main menu appear again. The culprit behind the noise was finally revealed, but it didn't make a single bit of sense.

Scarlet Strategist's Sniper: Researching...
- Material Synthesis: Complete
- Optimal Configuration: Complete
- Viability Prototype: Constructing (18%)
- Essence Signature Registration: Not Started

Sal stared at the words, not really taking any of them in. He tapped one of the buttons to change the transparency of the glass, revealing all the mechanisms at work. Directly in front of him, he could see a series of lasers working on what looked like the barrel of a rifle. He was instantly reminded of the Legendary sniper rifle, and that was enough to wake him up. Sal tapped the glass again to re-read the message, and it was only then that he finally appreciated what was happening.

"Why is the Arkwright making a sniper rifle?" Sal asked as he took a tentative step backward. "And why does it have the same name as the Scarlet Strategist's Visor?"

Sal frantically looked at the list of reports that had come through. There was no way that the Arkwright was capable of making a Legendary grade. It had only been upgraded a few days ago. And even with the addition of a dungeon fragment, there was no way that the Arkwright was on par with Vulcan and Protocol.

Sal turned away from the Arkwright and tried to collect his thoughts. His eyes landed on the coffee machine, and he decided that his fractional amount of sleep was going to have to do for the day. With a resigned sigh, he placed his unwashed cup under the spout and tapped the button.

"What's a viability prototype?" Sal muttered as he glanced back at the interface. Leaving his coffee to fill itself, Sal moved over to the report and tapped on that specific wording choice.

Results from Cypher:
- o   Viability Prototypes are a computational function that is made possible by Judgment, Cypher, and the Mythcrafter Crafting Algorithm
- o   Viability Prototypes determine the viability of an overall project by constructing problematic components that can't be simulated
- o   A completed Viability Prototype will result in a Blueprint being added to the Design Folder
- o   An Essence Signature can be registered with a completed Viability Prototype

Sal blinked again as he tapped on Essence Signature.

Results from Cypher:
- o   Relating to project of Dominion Set:
  - ▪   Essence Signatures are key components of the Dominion ability
  - ▪   Registered Essence Signatures can be summoned to the battlefield through the Dominion ability
  - ▪   Only Essence Signatures tied to the Dominion Set are compatible
    - ▪   Scarlet Strategist Set (Compatible)
    - ▪   Ultimate Argento Set (Compatible)
    - ▪   Vendetta Macclemark Set (Compatible)

Sal turned around and went over to his freshly poured coffee. His hand shook as he picked up the cup, but it had nothing to do with the exhaustion. No matter how calm he tried to act, his mind had received enough of a shock to fully wake up. He brought the cup to his lips as he looked back at the Arkwright. Sal was almost scared to look away lest the words disappeared.

Vendetta Macclemark…Ultimate Argento…Scarlet Strategist.

Sal replayed the words in his mind as he continued to drink his coffee. His eyes were locked on the words, and he had no idea how to process it all. The Arkwright wasn't able to make equipment at the higher grades, but it was somehow able to simulate their creation? These viability prototypes were enough to create essence signatures, which, in turn, would let him summon parts of those sets on the battlefield?

As Sal drained his coffee, he took a deep breath before facing the Arkwright. "Be as loud as you want." He had to laugh as he watched the progress bar ticking upward to the sound of screaming metal being drowned in a sea of sparks. There was no way he was going to be able to sleep after all this, so instead, he doubled down and pressed the coffee button again. He'd sit through the chaos with a smile on his face.

Mythmark was surely something worth waiting for.

<u>CHAPTER 64: EXPECTATIONS</u>

"Did I miss it?" Fabi asked in an almost panic as she reached the top of the stairs. She looked between the Arkwright and Sal, with her gaze lingering on Sal for a few moments. "What happened to your shirt?"

Sal looked down at himself and saw that all his buttons were mismatched. He hadn't fixed himself up since getting out of bed, and his haphazard method of dressing wasn't the best advertisement of his sanity. With a chuckle, he turned away from Fabi and started to undo the buttons and align them correctly. "Sorry about that. I only got a few hours' sleep before this thing woke me up."

Fabi walked into view as she approached the Arkwright. She wore fitted blue jeans and a black tank top. Her hands were adorned with black fingerless gloves, similar to the ones that Upgrade had made for him. She peered through the interface into the mechanisms at work. "I could watch this all day."

"I'm at roughly three hours," Sal agreed as he tucked in his shirt and straightened out his own appearance. "Watching it, I mean," he clarified as he stepped forward to stand beside Fabi. "You didn't miss anything. It's still working away on the Dominion set…but the timer seems to be recalculating every few minutes. It's been on a loop for the last while, but every time it resets, the number is lower."

Fabi nodded quietly before finally pulling her attention away from the Arkwright. "Want to see something cool?"

"Always," Sal answered instantly.

Fabi smiled as she pointed over the rail. "I dropped them off at the door as I was coming up, but I made a few bits and pieces last night that I wanted your opinion on."

Sal leaned over the railing to see what looked like a haphazard pile of metal instruments bundled together in a frayed blanket. "You made all of them?"

Fabi nodded proudly. "With my ability." She moved toward the stairs excitedly. "I felt like I was getting better at it, but then I thought to myself…why not ask the Appraiser? You'll be able to tell me if I'm just making a load of crap."

Sal followed her, not sure what to expect. The fabric that covered them looked rough, and he didn't recognize it at first glance. It was like a grayish cloth that stretched unnaturally around the metal, with matted sections of what looked like fur. It was only when he got to the bottom of the stairs that he saw the blood stains on the material.

"Where did you get the materials?" Sal asked tentatively, wondering how Fabi's ability had manifested at home.

Fabi took a knee beside the stack and pulled at the layers of grayish material, revealing a series of discolored, misshapen weapons. There were at least five spear-like weapons, with a few swords and a collection of daggers tied with more of the gray cloth. Fabi sorted through them, laying them all out on the cloth as though she were displaying them for sale. "I went to a dungeon last night to try Figment. I killed everything like I would normally, and then tried out the power."

Frowning, Sal looked at the weapons. "Did you just will them into existence?"

Fabi nodded, grinning. "Yep, but it was a challenge. It was my first time making things without a blueprint. I tried picking basic weapons, but even then, it was difficult to make the materials conform."

Sal took a knee beside one of the spears and looked at it carefully, letting Appraisal do its work. "Okay, this one is Uncommon grade…but it's a difficult one to describe." He frowned as he rotated the spear to get a better look at it. "The materials are excellent, but the design is lacking."

"You're faster than most Appraisers." Fabi moved her hand to the next one, as though asking him if it were better.

Sal shook his head. "No, there's more to this one." He brought Fabi's attention back to the first spear. "How did you manage to infuse voider heart into a spear?" He looked at the spear in confusion. It was a jagged mess of rust-like metal, with so many imperfections that it looked like junk. Yet, it was undeniable—there was a collection of incredible materials locked behind the dull appearance.

"Gloomhusk!" Sal said in shock as he broke off the Appraisal to stare at Fabi in utter disbelief. "How the hell did you combine a gloomhusk and a voider heart?"

Fabi grinned at him before offering a small shrug. "I killed a voider, and a gloomhusk…then fused them with the fragments of metal I could find." She moved toward the next one and tapped it. "What about this one?"

Sal wasn't sure he was getting through to Fabi. "The gloomhusk fang and voider heart could make you a Siphon blade or an ethos blade. They're really good materials…and both would be in the Epic grade range. We should break this down and reform it into something else."

Fabi's smile grew wider as she looked at Sal. "Trust me. You'll want to look at the next ones."

Sal faltered as he moved to the spear that Fabi was touching with her palm. In terms of appearance, it looked pretty much the same as the one before, but Appraisal saw through it in an instant. Sal fell silent as he looked up at Fabi in disbelief. "Why does this one have a voider core?"

She laughed as she pointed at the varying weapons. "Okay, I'll put you out of your misery. There were roughly about sixty demons in the dungeon. Prowlers were the weakest, and you'll see a few of their components littered among the earlier versions. The voiders were much more plentiful, and I used their stuff alongside the prowler materials and the gloomhusks." She moved her hand over to the left, where the materials looked a little more visually impressive. They were still rusted and ugly, but flecks of brilliance peeked through.

"The main prize of the dungeon was an elite scuttler. There were a few evolved voiders and they were controlling the gloomhusks from the shadows, blending them in with the prowlers in the hopes of ambushing. It was a lot of fun."

Sal just stared at her as if she were insane. "How many people did you go with?"

Fabi smiled at him innocently. "I went in with the Macclemark, so I was fine. The best part of going on outings with guilds is that you learn effective countermeasures for the elites and evolved. Scuttlers are slow, with high defense. All you have to do is get an essence blade through the chitin and you're all set." She held out her two hands and widened the gap between them. "Enlarge the blade once it's inside, aim for the head, and it goes down instantly."

"I've never even seen a gloomhusk, or a scuttler," Sal admitted as he shook his head. "You make it sound so easy."

Fabi tapped the weapons that lay in front of her. "Hey, do you have any idea how much I struggled to make these? I had all the materials I could want and these were the best I could do." She laughed while tilting her head to one side. "You make Crafting seem easy, so I think it's a fair trade."

Sal practically scoffed at that remark as he looked at her in disbelief. "Seriously, you're going to catch up in no time. You'll be willing Epic grades and Legendary grades into existence before long."

Fabi nodded in agreement. "And soon you'll be taking down commander variants, too."

Sal faltered as he looked at her, but could see that she was deadly serious. "Should we talk about managing expectations?" He laughed, suddenly eager to switch topics and focus on the Appraisal.

Fabi shook her head. "Nope, because as far as I'm concerned, you have everything you need to be successful. All you're missing is experience."

"Don't expect me to take down an elite scuttler for a while, and we'll be fine." Sal laughed it off as he reached for the next weapon in line.

Fabi pulled the spear out of reach, and leaned down to make eye contact with Sal from across the weapons. "Hey, look at me."

Sal looked up to meet her gaze, not sure how he should navigate this conversation.

Fabi smiled reassuringly at him. "I don't know how much you've been agonizing over these dungeon runs, but we're not going to take risks. We clear the low-ranked ones as much as necessary, and only when you feel comfortable moving to the next stage…we move to the next stage. Okay?"

She pointed at herself. "I'll give you every piece of information on each and every dungeon. You'll have strategies for every little thing, so even if you make a mistake or a surprise attack happens…we'll be fine."

Sal exhaled slowly as a smile tugged at his lips. "Why are you so convincing?"

Fabi grinned as she slid the spear back into reach for Sal. "Because I want you to succeed. If we're going to be working alongside each other in the future, I want to be able to trust you with my back. Right now, there's too much of an imbalance…so, we need to correct that."

"Speaking of balance," Sal started as he lifted the spear, his eyebrow raised. "Did you do this one with your eyes closed, or was it an accidental Craft?"

Fabi's face reddened as she looked at the crooked spear defensively. "It's not that bad!"

Sal winced playfully as he rotated the spear, showing a massive curve in the shaft. "At least tell me that the scuttler chitin is hard to work with…"

Fabi crossed her arms for half a second before moving onto the next one. "Okay, look at this one instead." She tapped at the next spear, the last of the long and slender weapons.

"Just so we're on the same page here." Sal pointed over at the first three. "You've got a Low Uncommon, a Mid Uncommon, and…an Upper Uncommon." His hand glided over the spears to land on the fourth one that Fabi insisted he look at. "What do you think that this one will be?"

"Low Rare grade?" Fabi asked hopefully, her eyes seemingly searching for any clues as to what differentiated them.

Sal shook his head. "Nope. You're back to the Mid Uncommon grade with this one." He quietly inspected the rest of the weapons with passing glances, not looking at the materials or the abilities they held. His only focus was looking at the grades of each piece.

"Fuck." Fabi groaned as she looked at them, grimacing. "I really thought I was getting the hang of them, too. The last ones I was making in seconds."

Sal paused as he looked at her in surprise. "You were trying to cut down your time?"

Fabi nodded, waving her hand. "Yeah. You know, to activate it properly? That marble thing I made at the gala was done in a split second, and I want to get to that speed of activation."

Sal looked at her. "You can't Craft that fast."

It was Fabi's turn to laugh. "What, so only Mr. Argento is allowed to make things at the speed of light?" She waved at his body as though it explained everything. "You and Doc Ameye are able to just put your hands on things and then they get Crafted perfectly. I thought with how everyone was speaking about Figment, that it was something as strong as the ones you guys have."

Sal shook his head slowly. "Most of my Crafting takes hours, though." He looked at Fabi. "I can flood things with essence, but that's only because Mythcrafter has blueprints."

Fabi frowned as she crossed her arms. "Anyway, you're saying that none of them are higher than the Uncommon grade?" She clearly wanted to switch to a different topic, her eyes already lingering on a few of the swords and daggers at the end of the row.

Sal sighed as he got to his feet. "One of them is a Rare grade. See if you can identify which one it is, but you only get one guess." He pointed at the selection of weapons, smiling. "I need to go back upstairs for a second, but I'll be right back. Don't pick one at random."

Fabi grumbled as she readjusted her kneeling position to sit on her heels. "I knew that one of them would be Rare grade!" she shot back, as though it invalidated everything Sal had said.

Sal just smiled as he moved up the stairs, taking two at a time. When he reached the top, the Arkwright was still working on the Dominion set. There were no changes, and he was happy that he had a small distraction to occupy his mind.

Sal moved across the room to pick up the Legendary-grade visor. Out of curiosity, he leaned over the railing to glance down at Fabi, who was plucking at the weapons and discarding them, looking increasingly frustrated as time went on. He chuckled before moving back down the stairs to join her. It was time to put her out of her misery.

"You lied about the Rare grade, didn't you?" Fabi accused as she looked up from the weapons. "They all look the same."

Sal humored her with a smile as he placed the visor over his face. "So, what you're missing is the blueprint aspect." He pointed at his face. "I'm going to create a blueprint with Mythcrafter, and save it to the visor. Then I'll give it to you, to see if you can use your power to refine these into something a little better."

"What makes you think it will work?" Fabi asked dubiously as she stared at the visor. "Just because there's a blueprint in front of me, I don't have any sort of fine-tuning ability with my essence." She held up her fingers and wiggled them. "I literally just bombard it with essence until it achieves the shape I want."

"I don't even know where to start on how ridiculous that is." Sal laughed as he looked at the first spear at the edge of the blanket. "We'll start with this one. Since it has voider heart and gloomhusk, let's make it a Siphon spear. Any objections?"

Fabi sighed as she threw her hands in defeat. "Sure, you can go for it. What do you want me to do in the meantime as you're ideating? Will I go get coffees?"

"No need," Sal said as he utilized both the visor and Mythcrafter to create a visualization of the new spear. Rather than tailoring it, he simply allowed for Mythcrafter to run wild with it, making sure that the abilities he was looking for were represented. Just like he had expected, the supposed grade was a minimum of Epic grade, and there was an abundance of excess materials that could be used in the Crafting. Sal saved the blueprints to the visor and kept them up on the screen. "Here you go." He offered his visor to her.

"This is what I'm talking about," Fabi said with an exasperated sigh. "That was only a few seconds!" She took the visor from him and threw her hair to one side so she could clip it over her ear.

"Now, you have the blueprint and all the materials you need." Sal pointed at the visor and then at the spear on the ground. "Do you need anything else?"

Fabi picked up the spear from the ground and looked off in the direction of the train tracks. "I need space."

"Space?" Sal repeated in confusion.

"Lots of space," Fabi agreed with a smile as she hopped down from the platform and walked over to the blocked tunnel. "I'm still learning how to control my outputs, so it's a little chaotic."

Sal was about to ask her what she meant by chaotic, but the moment she activated Figment, he understood.

CHAPTER 65: EVASION

"A purple cloud?" Fabi asked breathlessly as she handed Sal the spear before vaulting up to join him on the platform. "It kinda felt like a hazy distortion when I'm doing it, but it looks like a cloud to you?" She sounded curious, but also slightly worried.

"Yeah, it pretty much enveloped you when you started working. Like it was pulsating around your body before funneling into the spear." Sal described the scene as he saw it. He had watched her in a sort of mute fascination as she used Figment on the spear. The tracks at her feet had both melted and warped into a disk-like shape, creating a circular blend of steel and wood.

Fabi frowned as she looked back at the mess she had made of the tracks. "When I have this under control, I'll fix that. I'm really sorry." She unclipped the visor and handed it back to Sal. "Also, I want the blueprint for this thing. Even if I have to make it the manual way…it's unbelievable."

"It's stored in the Arkwright, so you'll be able to get it to make you one if you have the right materials." Sal hiked a thumb over his shoulder. He moved the visor to his belt but stopped, frowning when he realized he had sacrificed the broken belt to the Arkwright.

"Lose your belt?" Fabi asked as she noticed his hesitation.

"Donated it to the Arkwright. The evolutionary rune exploded at the gala, and ruined more than half of the cores," Sal admitted, the visor in his hand. "Did you check the specs?" He handed the spear back to Fabi, appreciating just how different it looked in comparison to before.

"Wanted to let the in-house Appraiser do the honors, but I can't say I wasn't curious," Fabi admitted with a smile as she gratefully accepted the sleek black spear. "It certainly looks to be the best of the bunch, and the essence required wasn't nearly as much as I was forcing into them back in the dungeon."

Sal nodded as he activated Appraisal, looking at the spear carefully.

Name	Void Needle
Origin	Crafted
Age	New
Grade	Epic (Low)
Materials	Voider Heart | Gloomhusk Core | Scuttler Chitin | Refined Figment Essence | Refined Invention Essence

Attributes	Unstoppable: Can bypass majority of essence-based defenses. Phase: Utilizing the Void, the weapon will phase through material objects until it strikes an essence-based target. Devour: Weapon will rapidly drain essence from struck targets. Recharge: Weapon uses devoured essence to amplify strike damage.
Abilities	Unstoppable | Phase | Devour | Recharge
Power Source	Internal Core
Evolution	No
Quality	Excellent
Condition	89%
Value	Est. $185,000.00 – $225,000.00

"So, this is a much better version of Siphon than I was expecting," Sal finally said as he looked at the spear from top to bottom. Although the sleek body was very impressive, the tip of the blade was actually a reforged gloomhusk core. It was a brilliant white and seemed to emit a sort of static energy. There were no runes adorning the weapon, but there was a grip at the midpoint that looked to be a part of the design. The same brilliant white crystal appeared at the butt of the spear, too.

"So it's good?" Fabi asked hopefully as she twirled the spear around in a perfect circle.

Sal just looked at her in disbelief. "Surely you're already able to tell that it's good?"

Fabi pouted ever so slightly. "It would be nice to hear it."

Sal smiled warmly. "It's very good. Epic grade, and the options are great. Unstoppable, Phase, Devour, and Recharge. It can be thrown through walls to attack targets, and when it hits, it'll take a chunk of essence from the demon."

"Okay, that does sound pretty damn good," Fabi said proudly as she held out her spear and looked at it fondly. "It's hard to believe that I made this with just essence and a blueprint...how long did it take?"

"About fifteen minutes." Sal grinned. "But if you start telling me you want to cut that number down, then I'll stop you from using the visor."

Fabi chuckled as she clutched her spear defensively. "Hey, I'll have you know that I was intending on donating all of those to the Arkwright." She gestured with one hand to the scattered array of weapons that lay on the blanket.

Sal had to do a double take. "Wait...what?"

Fabi nodded, laughing. "Yeah. It's only the haul from one dungeon, really. I wanted to see what sort of cost-to-revenue ratio we'd have with the dungeons and selling equipment." She looked up at the Arkwright that was still working hard on the Dominion set. "Would it be better to put them in when they're fixed up, or as materials?"

Sal just stared at her. "This is far too much to just lump into the Arkwright." He tried to get her to understand what she was suggesting. "Right now, if we conservatively say that you can bring all of these up to the Epic grade..." He counted the assortment of weapons until he passed a dozen. "Then you're looking at anywhere between one and a half to three million dollars." He let those words settle for a few seconds, trying to gauge Fabi's reaction.

Fabi just stared at him. "And?"

Sal blinked in surprise. "Three million dollars' worth of goods, and you're talking about putting it into the Arkwright?" He couldn't keep the exasperation from his voice as he looked at her. "Seriously, you just said that you were doing a cost-to-revenue ratio. Can't you see how much money you're throwing away by depositing it in the Arkwright?"

Fabi's eyes suddenly widened, and she laughed.

"Ah, you get it now?" Sal asked as he joined in her laughter. "I thought you were going to just sacrifice all of this!"

Fabi shook her head. "No, Sal...I'm laughing at the misunderstanding. The cost-to-revenue concept isn't for this." She gestured at the weapons on the floor. "It's for that." She moved her hand up and pointed at the Arkwright. "If we're able to earn three million from a days' work in the dungeon, then I want to see what sort of revenue the Arkwright can earn with the right materials. It'll help us build out a cost-plan for the upgrades to the machine, and we can then pick and choose the right dungeons for everything we need."

Sal stared at her dumbly, not sure how to process what she just said.

"Besides, I managed to fuse a few dozen cores into these things. My guess is that the Arkwright can break them all down for materials," Fabi continued with a hopeful shrug. "Worst-case scenario, you'll have some extra stock in reserve."

"Fabi, I don't think I can accept this," Sal said in disbelief. "If this is because of some indebtedness, then you can just forget about it. You've already been a great help to me, and I don't need any sort of reward."

Fabi snorted. "No, Sal, it's nothing to do with that." She looked at him curiously. "This haul was from about eight hours in a dungeon. So, it's really not a big deal...besides, if I continue raiding my father's stocks, I'll feel bad. I want to build up as many materials as possible to push the Arkwright to its limits. The more raw materials it can access, the more synthesis options become available, and then we'll have a higher chance of making some cool stuff! It's simple when you think about it."

Sal exhaled slowly. "I'm going to keep a ledger of how much you're investing in the Arkwright, because there's no way that it's fair. You're putting in far too much, and I don't want to take advantage of that." He didn't want their friendship, or at least their beginnings of a friendship, to devolve into a supplier agreement.

A part of him was feeling guilty about how he had practically unloaded all his family history onto her when she came by to Craft, but rather than getting spooked, she had been a great listener. Divinity was a great friend and an excellent listener, but he wanted a more neutral opinion than someone who knew the future. If it was Barry, then it would have been a coin flip on whether everything was turned into a joke, or whether he'd take it seriously. Blathnaid…well, she already thought that he was too sheltered. Telling her the extent of his ignorance wasn't likely to really elevate her opinion of him, or make her more interested in joining his guild.

"Upgrade was right." Fabi chuckled as she started to bundle up the weapons. "You really do think too much." When all the misshapen chunks of metal were assembled, Fabi picked them up effortlessly and made her way toward the Arkwright. She looked back over her shoulder. "Come on. If it makes you feel better…just think of this as a deposit on some cool gear. Or preparation for the drone dock."

Sal sighed as he followed her. "Do you need a hand with those?" He gestured at the weapons.

"Nope. All good," Fabi responded as she casually carried them all the way up the stairs. "I didn't train my body just to look nice." She laughed as she made her way to the Arkwright. "Can it take materials when it's in the middle of Crafting?"

Sal nodded as he crested the stairs. "Yeah, I gave it a whole load of stuff last night. But I think it might be worth waiting until it's done with the Dominion set."

"Cool. Well, it's almost done. Only another few minutes to go." Fabi deposited the sack of weapons down in front of the Arkwright. "Not enough time to fix up another of the spears, though."

Sal's headspace was conflicted. He was still trying to wrap his head around the fact that a single dungeon had somehow earned her close to three million worth of profit. It was a ridiculous number when he thought about it, and she was casually donating all her spoils to the Arkwright. There were no protective feelings from Sal when it came to the Arkwright being utilized, because he knew already that the biggest drain on his own finances would be the materials. Fabi was from Maccles Materials, and she would know all the useful things they'd need to collect from dungeons. But by that same logic, she should know how much the materials cost that she was giving away. He didn't want there to be such a huge imbalance between what they were bringing to the table.

"Go on. What's your next persuasion tactic?" Fabi goaded as she moved over to the coffee machine. "I can see it on your face that you're worrying about something."

Sal chuckled as he crossed his arms. "I'm just thinking that it's far too much of a donation. Even if you want to use the Arkwright, or if you're happy to run in dungeons. It's too much for me to get my head around."

Fabi tapped the button of the coffee machine as she looked at Sal thoughtfully. "Are you aware of why it's better to make things at Quest Academy, rather than out here?"

Sal looked between the bundle of weapons and the spear that Fabi was still proudly holding. "Ah." The answer suddenly dawned on him. "The tax."

A wide grin appeared on Fabi's face. "Look at that, you got it in one." She laughed as she held her spear aloft. "Epic grades have a forty percent taxation rate, that goes straight to the Hunter Bureau. If you make it at Quest Academy, you'll get roughly thirty percent less than the market rate, but you don't pay tax." With a deft movement, Fabi angled her spear to point at the collection of weapons. "Which is why it's better that these materials stay off the books. All I have to do is make the most incompetent designs at the dungeons and pay a minimal fee on Uncommon grade, and walk straight out of there."

"You're saying that you intentionally made them shit?" Sal asked dubiously.

Fabi's face reddened ever so slightly. "No, but the inspector literally waved me off when he saw them. Didn't even do an Appraisal on them. I thought about it as a strategy on my way here, but wasn't really sure how salvageable they were." She shrugged as she looked at Sal. "On the plus side, they were so bad that the dungeon inspectors didn't want a cut."

Sal laughed as he turned to look at the Arkwright's countdown clock. "So, you're telling me that the Arkwright is your tax evasion scheme?"

"I wouldn't exactly say it that way." Fabi grinned as she lifted the coffee to her lips. "It's just a nice little loophole that I aim to exploit until I get a slap on the wrist."

Sal frowned as he looked at her. "How much would you have to pay on the materials tax, if you hadn't tried combining them?"

"It varies from piece to piece, but it depends on the grade and quality of the extraction. Then you have other factors like the territory management fee, the guild licensing fee, and if you're a member of the Scavenger Network," Fabi explained, as though the topic were exhausting. "Most people just accept whatever bill they send, but the Hunter Bureau is notorious for fudging the numbers. I'll show you the ropes when we start doing the runs for real."

"Can't wait," Sal replied humorlessly with a shake of his head. "Who knows, this Dominion set might be a complete failure?"

"Guess we're about to find out," Fabi said excitedly as she watched the timer finally reach zero. "I can't wait to see how it incorporated the Macclemark functionality!"

CHAPTER 66: DOMINION

Sal held his breath as he looked at the interface to once again confirm that he wasn't acting prematurely.

Strategist's Dominion has been Crafted Successfully
There is a new item in the Loading Tray

"Come on, take it out," Fabi insisted as she stood directly behind Sal with an excited smile on her face. "I want to see how it looks."

Sal pulled at the tray and was rewarded with a mass of black fabric. It was, quite literally, the most underwhelming reveal of all time.

"You'd think it would at least fold it properly." Fabi snorted as she looked over Sal's shoulder. "Wait…why is it moving like cloth?"

Sal pulled out the fabric and was a little horrified to see that it was indeed a one-piece jumpsuit. It flowed around his fingers, threatening to slip out of his grip if he wasn't careful. There was no real way to describe it other than a dark piece of cloth, and Sal was at a loss as he looked at Fabi in confusion. "Is this what your Macclemark looks like when it's done?"

Fabi shook her head slowly. "No, the Macclemark is made of equal parts metal and cloth. There's no way that this thing has the mechanisms required for proper functionality." She sighed before her face brightened. "Did you Appraise it? Is it a dud?"

Sal shook his head. "No, not yet." He turned the fabric over in his hands, looking at it without his power to see whether there was anything at all that stood out. He wanted to appreciate how others would see it, because his Argento set had been somewhat flashy by comparison. Sal wasn't sure he wanted to wear a skin-tight black jumpsuit around Quest Academy.

"Then hurry up, I'm dying to know!" Fabi urged, laughing. "There's no way it did that much research and synthesis just to make a piece of crap."

Nodding, Sal smiled. "Let's have a look and see what we're dealing with." His eyes flooded with essence as he stared at the fabric intently, turning it over in his hands to find any secrets it was hiding. The first thing he realized was that the Dominion set was far from a failure. He turned it over in his hands, pulling small parts of the fabric closer to get a better look. Every little piece of the puzzle started clicking together, and Sal was genuinely astonished at what he was seeing. None of it made sense.

"Should I be worried that you're taking longer than the spear Appraisal?" Fabi asked.

Sal's frown transformed into a smile. "It's an Epic grade." He glanced up at Fabi, his smile turning into a wide grin. "And it has two abilities."

Fabi stared at the cloth in disbelief. "Why does an Epic grade only have two options? Isn't it supposed to be four?"

Sal continued to turn the fabric in his hands, shaking his head as he got to the integrated gloves. The feet were included in the jumpsuit, and there was even a face mask that didn't have an area for the mouth or eyes. It covered every available inch of skin, and it looked to be rather unforgiving in terms of fit. It was going to stick to him like paint if he wore it.

"Come on, don't go quiet on me. What's the verdict? If it's Epic grade, then it's not a failure…right?" Fabi insisted hopefully. "Is one of the abilities called Automate?"

Sal's attention snapped up at those words. "Wait, how did you know that?"

Fabi's face lit up in excitement as she grasped Sal's shoulders. "It has Automate?!"

"Give me a second." Sal laughed at her infectious delight. "I'll tell you what it says."

Name	Strategist's Dominion
Origin	Crafted
Age	New
Grade	Epic
Materials	Dungeon Heart Essence | Mythcrafter Essence | Moonsilver | Scarlet Screen | Lux Crystal | Lords Crystal | Blue Fang | Switcher Sinew
Attributes	Dominion: Casts a substantial area of effect around user. Allows for essence-based constructs to be summoned and controlled at will. Registered essence signatures can be summoned at substantially reduced essence cost. • Ultimate Argento Set (Registered) • Scarlet Strategist Set (Registered) • Vendetta Macclemark Set (Registered) Automate: Integrated functionality of Strategist's Dominion will be activated automatically when conditions are met. • Vendetta Protocol • Initiative Protocol

Abilities	Dominion	Automate
Power Source	Target Essence	Internal Essence	External Essence
Evolution	No
Quality	Perfect
Condition	100%
Value	Est. $175,000.00 – $200,000.00

Fabi stared at Sal for a few seconds. "Initiative…and Vendetta?" Before she could get an answer, her coffee was on the workbench and she was flicking through her tablet at incredible speed. "They're from completely different Macclemark battle-suits. They shouldn't both appear in the same one!"

Sal blinked in surprise as he finally heard what Fabi was talking about. He was so preoccupied with the fact that one of the ingredients was switcher sinew. There was no way that they had access to the ingredients of one of those shapeshifting bastards. After a few moments of silence, he ventured a question, hoping for more context. "Do they conflict with each other? Vendetta and Initiative?"

Fabi shook her head. "No, they just…shouldn't be able to fit on the same piece of equipment," she finished lamely as she looked up from her tablet to stare at the limp jumpsuit. "Like, Initiative is activated from having sensors all over the body. The function allows for you to see whenever an attack is incoming and gives a nudge to let you know the direction it's coming from. Kinda like a sixth sense, but…how can it be integrated into cloth?"

"And what about Vendetta?" Sal asked curiously.

"It's the walking death thing I told you about," Fabi answered as she walked over to get a closer look at the cloth. "Similar to the Vengeful Vambraces, where it will automatically send essence projectiles to attack anything that comes into range. I just can't get my head around how the Arkwright integrated them."

Sal smiled as he held up the flimsy-looking fabric. "I don't think I can wear this."

Fabi just stared at him. "No backing out of this, mister. You're absolutely going to wear this, and we'll test it out on a dungeon run." She placed her hands on her hips, as though daring him to argue with her.

Sal stared right back at her. "I'm sorry…but can you see this?" He held up the fabric against his chest, just to show how small it was compared to his frame. "I'd be arrested for indecent exposure if I wore this!"

Fabi snorted, but her stance didn't shift. "Go try it on. You said it yourself—that there's a whole load of sets already registered to it—so it probably lets you summon it as armor."

Sal faltered as he looked at her. "That…actually makes sense." He looked at the cloth in his hands and let out a sigh. "Fine, but I'm trying it on in the other room. If I can't get the armor to appear, then we go back to the drawing board…deal?"

"Absolutely not," Fabi countered. "We'll take it to the dungeon and make it work. Crafters shouldn't give up on their inventions." She smiled at him before jutting her head in the direction of his room. "So, go try it on so we can see how it works."

Sal sighed as he looked at the Arkwright. "Oh, there's a diagnostic report from the Crafting!"

"Nice try." Fabi laughed as she moved forward to intercept him. "You get changed, and I'll have a read of the report." She pointed at the discarded weapons on the floor. "And I'll even load up your Arkwright with all the new goodies, because I'm nice like that."

With a resigned groan, Sal moved off toward his workshop bedroom, tapping the coffee machine as he passed and placing his cup underneath the spout. "I'll be back in a second."

"If I hear you scream, I'll come in and help." Fabi gave a sweet smile.

Sal entered his room and firmly closed the door. Placing the battle-suit on the bed, he quickly took off his shirt and pants. There was a moment of hesitation as he looked at his underwear, and then back at the battle-suit. "Nope." He corrected himself as he picked up the suit. He wanted to keep a little piece of his dignity while wearing it. With careful movements, Sal pulled at the nape of the neck. If it hadn't been for the Appraisal, he wouldn't have known where to even begin with opening the suit up.

"There we go," Sal whispered to himself as the black fabric parted perfectly in a straight line, allowing him access to the waist and legs of the jumpsuit. Despite looking like it was going to be too small, the legs fit perfectly, and Sal's feet slid into place with a reassuring spongey sensation under his soles. The black cloth gripped at his calves and thighs, but didn't offer any resistance as he pulled it up at the waist. Sliding his hands into the gloves, Sal was surprised to feel the back of the fabric stitching together around his torso. All that was left was the face mask that hung at the back of his neck.

"You okay in there?" Fabi's voice called from dangerously close to the door.

"Yes, just give me a second," Sal called back quickly, looking down at himself and groaning. It did cling to him like a second skin. With the thought that he should get it over with, Sal pulled the mask over his face and felt the material knit itself together around his neck. For a brief second, Sal panicked a little now that he was fully cocooned within the jumpsuit, but that passed when he felt a barely imperceptible tingle. It was like his Argento gloves that allowed him to use the

Transform ability, but…it was more like a hair trigger this time around. *Was it because he had access to more gates?*

With a flex of his essence, Sal sent a small surge through the material and was surprised to feel it distribute equally throughout his whole body. Normally he just threw his essence into his hands and then let it spread from there, but this was like a consistent stream that didn't require him to push himself. Sal looked forward in shock as the hazy black material dissipated to reveal a ridiculously clean view of the room. It was more than that, as small details started to highlight in front of him as Analysis activated.

"How the hell?" Sal started as he turned around, but faltered when he felt a crease in his waist. Looking down, he could see he was wearing a black shirt with a silver blazer. His slacks were silver, too. "Fabi?" Sal called out in uncertainty. "I think it works, but I've got no idea what I'm looking at."

"I swear if I open this door and you're naked, you're dead." Fabi laughed from the other side of the door. "Am I safe to come in?"

"Yeah, come on in." Sal pulled at the jacket, surprised that it felt surprisingly normal. "Can you bring the visor with you? I'll need you to take a look at this."

Fabi opened the door with the Legendary-grade visor in hand, and she very nearly dropped it when she caught sight of Sal. "What the hell is that mask?"

"Mask?" Sal repeated in confusion. "I'm wearing a mask?" He lifted his hand to his face, thinking that Fabi was mistaken, but he felt a cool metal surface under his fingertips. Sal moved his finger to his left eye and was amazed to see that it was compressing against an invisible force an inch away from his eye. "Whoa…"

Fabi numbly stared at him, the visor in her hand completely forgotten. "Is that the Ultimate Argento set?"

Sal did a mock twirl. "I have no idea, but it's ridiculously comfortable. What does the mask look like? I don't have a mirror in here."

Fabi's lips curled into a smile. "If I'm honest, you kind of look like a Villain." She pointed at Sal's face. "It doesn't have any facial features…just a smooth silver surface that covers your face, but with a slash across your eyes in a horizontal line." She drew an invisible line across her eyes to mimic his appearance. "There's a glowing red light where your eyes are supposed to be."

"And how does the suit look? Do you see any evolutionary runes?" Sal turned to point at his back. "Or any runes, for that matter?"

Fabi lifted the visor to her face and clipped it over her ear. "At first glance, there's no runes on it. It just looks like a really fancy suit. But I doubt it would really be—" Fabi stared at Sal in disbelief. Her mouth hung open as she pointed at his pants first, then his chest, and then at the mask. "It's…all Legendary grade? How can that be possible? The battle-suit is only Epic grade!"

Sal couldn't help but laugh as he stepped toward Fabi. In a flash of light, Sal felt his waist press against the railing of the mezzanine with so much momentum that he had to grasp at the metal to stop himself from being thrown over it. "What the fuck?" He gasped as he turned around in shock to see Fabi in the doorway of his room, looking at him in astonishment.

"Did you just...teleport?" Fabi asked incredulously as she looked back to where Sal had been, and then back at where he was currently located. "You just teleported straight through me?!"

Sal steadied himself and threw up his hands. "I didn't know it would do that!" The moment his right hand rose, he felt a weight against his shoulder. It was reassuring and familiar, but still felt foreign to him.

Fabi just pointed at him. "Did you just summon that?!"

Sal looked at his right arm and saw a beautiful sniper rifle nestled against his shoulder blade and held up proudly, as though in some form of salute. "I just put up my hand!" he said in amazement as his mask quickly threw up an interface he hadn't seen before. It wasn't an Appraisal or Analysis...but something else entirely.

Scarlet Strategist's Sniper Rifle (Dismiss) (Change)
- o   Mode: Impact (Change)
- o   Bullet: Essence (Change)
- o   Passive Essence Cost: 4%
- o   Essence Expenditure Remaining: 72%

The sniper rifle was gorgeous and had a sleek silver barrel, tipped with the red trim of scarlet screen, but the real beauty was in the stock and sights. It was a polished ivory that had embedded obsidian glass into a beautiful rune. With just a hint of curiosity, the identity of the pattern was revealed to be a Supercharge rune.

Sal remembered that Anthony had a similar ability that temporarily brought equipment to a higher grade in exchange for essence. Looking through the options that appeared, Sal focused on the change option, and was delighted to see the sniper rifle disappear and be replaced with a very familiar friend.

Scarlet Strategist's Revolver (Dismiss) (Change)
- o   Mode: Quick Fire (Change)
- o   Bullet: Shock Lance (Change)
- o   Passive Essence Cost: 2%
- o   Essence Expenditure Remaining: 70%

"Did that just happen, or did you do that intentionally?" Fabi pointed at the revolver in his hand. "Maybe you should take off the suit until we're in a safer location, or until I have my own suit on?" She sounded a little nervous, but it didn't stop her from slowly moving closer to where Sal stood.

"I did that one intentionally. Give me a second." Sal willed the revolver to disappear. In an instant, it was gone, and he was left standing against the balcony, empty-handed. "I don't know how to cycle between the different sets...or how to control the abilities. What is it telling you on the visor?"

Fabi gestured at Sal's empty hand. "Both of those were Legendary grade, but they only had four abilities each. I didn't have long enough to assess them though, so I can't really tell you much more than the grade."

"No worries, I'll be able to check it later," Sal reassured her. "That visor only has four abilities, so I'm guessing the abilities of the guns also improved. Were you able to figure out anything about the suit?"

Fabi nodded carefully. "Yeah, it wasn't Teleport. It's called Ambush…which is why you were able to appear behind me."

Sal laughed. "Well, it's not very good if it threw me so far away from you."

Fabi shook her head. "Automate likely put you at a distance where you could use your guns."

"Oh," Sal said simply as he looked at his empty hand. "That's quite scary."

"Tell me about it." Fabi sighed. "But yeah, there are other abilities…Dominion and Automate are carried over to your Ultimate Argento, and you have Ambush." She squinted at the visor, as though trying to focus its attention on his chest. "And something called Calibrated? Any idea what that does?"

Sal smiled as he placed a hand on his chest, sighing. "It gives me a passive bonus to my inherent abilities. So, Skill Master and Mythcrafter will get a boost." He pointed at his face. "The visor that you're wearing gives me a ten percent bonus to them, so I'm curious what the Ultimate Argento offers."

As though summoned by that very question, a menu appeared in front of Sal's face.

Switch to Vendetta Macclemark Set?
- o   Passive Essence Cost: 47%
- o   Essence Expenditure Change: -25%
- o   Essence Expenditure Remaining: 69%

Currently Equipped: Ultimate Argento Set
- o   Passive Essence Cost: 22%
- o   Essence Expenditure Change: 0%
- o   Essence Expenditure Remaining: 69%

Sal noticed that in the few minutes he had been wearing the suit, his essence reserves had dropped by a few percent. Which meant that keeping everything active was draining him of essence over time. He wondered how much of an impact the switching of weapons had on his essence, or even how much the Ambush ability had cost. Those were things he'd need to look into to ensure he didn't suffer from the dregs at the worst possible moment.

"Wait, sorry, I was wrong," Fabi said suddenly. "Dominion and Automate keep sliding into view because it's trying to identify the battle-suit, but there are other abilities for the thing you're wearing. I just don't think I can see them?" She groaned as she plucked the visor from her face. "How do you use this without getting a headache?"

"Practice, I guess?" Sal shrugged lamely before looking over to the Arkwright, which was already back in action. "What did you start working on?"

"It's just breaking down the materials and storing them," Fabi clarified with a smirk. "So, we'll need to go out and get more."

Sal just stared at her for a few seconds. "What…now?"

"Why not?" She smiled sweetly. "We should see what your suit can do on the battlefield. A small leecher dungeon should be a good start, and we can build up from there."

Sal looked at the silver gloves that covered his hands. They weren't fingerless like the ones Upgrade had made for him, which was a little regretful. "As long as you take responsibility for whatever happens." Sal looked at Fabi, grinning.

"Really, you're up for it?" Fabi asked in surprise.

Sal nodded. "I have to admit, I'm really curious about it myself. So, let's go and test it."

"Awesome," Fabi breathed as she collected her tablet from the workbench. She paused before taking the coffee cup from the machine and handing it to Sal. "You can drink in my car."

Sal smiled as he accepted the coffee, before he perked up in surprise. "Wait, you have a car?"

Fabi grinned. "Yes, and if you say a word about my driving, I'll drop you off in a Red Zone."

CHAPTER 67: OUTING

"I'll be honest, it's not what I was expecting," Sal said tentatively as he walked around Fabi's car. It wasn't one of the self-driving ones, which was strange, but Sal didn't press too much about it. The main aspects that drew his attention were the armored plates that were fused to the roof and doors. "Do you make a habit of driving it through Red Zones?" He gave Fabi a sideways glance, only half-joking.

Fabi smiled as she patted the roof of the car. "Know the way the Crafting classes work on group projects?" She lifted her arms to present the car as though it were a grand reveal. "Well, this was the culminative effort of my second-year group…but none of them were able to afford it outright, so I bought it."

"How did they feel about that?" Sal asked with genuine curiosity. "Can't imagine it made you very popular."

Fabi snorted and shook her head. "I was like the Queen of the Workshop for about twenty minutes. They all got a payout that more than covered the material costs." She smiled at Sal and tapped the roof of the car again. "Seriously though, you should take a look at the storage in Quest Academy. There's so much half-completed crap that they just sell off in chunks, either to break down into materials…or to try to complete them."

"I'll take a look when I'm back," Sal agreed as he looked at the car. It was Uncommon grade at best, with a wildly inconsistent build quality, but it had some charm. The mishmash of components made it seem like it was more than twenty projects in one. Blue upholstery lined the interior, and was clearly put together by a gifted Tailor. The sliding doors looked to be custom-crafted and opened up like gull wings, while the back of the car had a transparent armor, revealing a complicated-looking engine within. "Did you guys rip this out of a classic car?"

"Ah, my beautiful V8." Fabi grinned as she practically bounced over to where Sal stood. "She's beautiful, isn't she? If the cores run out, then she kicks in to save the day."

Sal just stared at it in disbelief. "You have one of the loudest engines possible, that can literally die at any time out in the field?" He just shook his head slowly, laughing nervously. "It's like you want to get the attention of every demon out there."

"Hey, come on…it can fly. I just like having the option of being able to drive it around the streets if necessary." Fabi pulled up the passenger door with a grunt of exertion. The door creaked slightly and offered a bit of resistance before sliding up with a pneumatic hiss.

Sal watched as the door wobbled in midair. "Time to go?"

Fabi grinned as she stepped to one side, offering the passenger seat to Sal. "It's a little low to the ground, but you'll be fine. I need to put in some handlebars on the inside of the door to make it easier for tall people."

Sal smiled as he awkwardly squatted and shuffled into the car. He was only a foot or so off the ground, which was really disconcerting, but it wasn't worth mentioning to the clearly excited Fabi. It was only when he was fully in the car that he appreciated the amount of leg room that was available to him. The car was a two-seater…but not by design. Fabi had apparently converted the rear seats into a storage unit, with a series of drawers and cases stacked in a metal cage. Just as Sal was turning in his chair to get a better look at them, he jumped at the sudden slam of the door beside him. He didn't have long to wait until he heard the creaking lurch of the opposite door being pulled open.

"Miss me?" Fabi laughed as she hopped into the car and pulled the door down after her, slamming it shut. "Don't forget to harness in, just in case I take a shortcut through the Red Zones." She grinned as she reached over Sal's shoulder and pulled a strap that attached to the side of his waist, and pressed against his chest. When she repeated the process for herself, she tapped the yoke steering device in front of her. It was two vertical hand grips on either side of a warped rectangle, and it literally moved forward to get closer to her body.

Sal stared at the interface that flickered to life on the screen, not sure what to expect from it. *Had she somehow made the windshield into a visor?* His hopes of seeing something extraordinary were dashed when an archaic guidance system sputtered into life, asking for directions. It was suggesting a series of streets and roads that no longer existed, and clearly wasn't designed for flight routes. "Very classic."

"Shut up." Fabi laughed as she pressed a button to the right of the steering device. "It's rough around the edges but there's a lot of charm in this thing, I'll have you know."

"Will you upgrade it when you get your ability under control?" Sal asked curiously as he looked around himself, trying to see whether there were any other improvements that Fabi had added to it herself.

Fabi shook her head as she poked a few buttons on the console. "Nope, I'd probably keep it this way for sentimental value." She looked at Sal's face, as though trying to gauge his reaction.

"Ah…that's cool," Sal said eventually as he watched surrounding buildings melt into the ground as they started to levitate.

Fabi chuckled. "I'm joking, Sal. Of course I'm going to upgrade it. It's a piece of crap…but it gets me from point to point." She completed a few safety checks and tapped more buttons before steering the car to face a clear expanse of open space. "Every time I get a dungeon payout, I contemplate just getting a new one. But I'd prefer to make my own, if that makes sense?"

"Absolutely," Sal agreed as he relaxed into his seat. "We'd need a very big assembly station for the Arkwright, though." He chuckled while appreciating the size of the car around him.

Fabi grinned but didn't take her eyes off the route in front of her. "While you were getting changed, I took note of the materials needed to get started. What do you think? Should we make that the first big project of the Arkwright?"

"Building a car?" Sal asked in disbelief.

"The assembly station." Fabi scoffed as she pushed a lever at her waist, causing the car to thrust forward. "I still think it would make more sense to build it at the depot so it can scale over time, but it's ultimately your call."

Sal nodded as he leaned forward to get a better look out the windshield. The sights of Silver Sanctuary were still beautiful even at a great height, and he couldn't help but smile as he saw the very depot they were talking about nestled on the streets below. "How long until we get to the dungeon?" He was conscious of the upkeep cost on his Ultimate Argento set, which continued to eat into his essence reserves as time passed.

Currently Equipped: Ultimate Argento Set
- o   Passive Essence Cost: 22%
- o   Essence Expenditure Change: 0%
- o   Essence Expenditure Remaining: 61%

With just a rough estimate, Sal was starting to understand the per-hour passive essence cost of wearing the suit. Which meant that he would only be able to wear it for five hours in total, without expending any essence for attacks. It was enough of a drain to cause him some anxiety; the last thing he wanted was to get the dregs in a dungeon, wearing a skintight jumpsuit.

"Roughly twenty minutes. You getting cold feet?" Fabi gave him a quick glance to check on him.

Sal shook his head. "No, I just need to find a way to preserve essence. Could you keep your eyes forward for a bit? I'm going to try to dismiss parts of the Ultimate Argento set."

Fabi nodded in agreement. "Sure, but why don't you just meditate while you're in the car? We're up pretty damn high, so the concentration of essence will be better up here."

Sal frowned as he looked over at her. "Isn't meditation just for opening gates?"

"Professor Lombardi didn't teach you that?" Fabi asked. "It's like one of the fundamental things you learn when you get all your gates opened. Restoring them is a big deal, and just leaving it to a passive absorption rate is a recipe for disaster."

"Ah, I kinda skipped out on the last classes because I got all my gates opened and had a perfect grade," Sal admitted ruefully. "Don't suppose you can teach me?"

Fabi just sighed as she shook her head. "Nah, I'm not the best person for that. I learned without being able to activate my ability, so it was likely very different since there was nothing draining my essence. I was able to smash through the gates because I didn't have anything to use it for."

Sal nodded as he focused on his suit jacket. He pulled it away from his chest and stared at it intently, willing for the Dismiss option to appear in front of his eyes. Unfortunately, he was a little too fast in hitting Dismiss when it appeared that he didn't realize that it was his trousers that had been highlighted. Sal stared at himself in absolute horror as his black-painted legs came into view.

"Good thing I don't have any peripheral vision." Fabi diligently stared forward at the open sky with a grin on her face. "Because that right there would have been pretty hilarious if I saw it."

Sal willed the jacket to disappear next, along with the shirt. He just wanted to get this over with, and it would be easier to start from scratch with summoning them one by one. He looked at his gloves and stared at them intently, hitting Dismiss when it appeared in front of his eyes.

"You've gone from distinguished Villain, to a very budget Villain," Fabi remarked, laughing.

"Just how good is that peripheral vision of yours?" Sal asked dryly, wondering how she had such a good view of him when she was staring straightforward.

Fabi just pointed at the windshield that showed Sal's reflection. "That right there makes it a lot easier."

Sal just sighed as he checked the essence drain again.

Currently Equipped: Ultimate Argento Mask
- o   Passive Essence Cost: 6%
- o   Essence Expenditure Change: 0%
- o   Essence Expenditure Remaining: 61%

"Okay, that seems to have stalled it somewhat," Sal muttered as he willed his pants to reappear. He was okay with his torso being covered with just the jumpsuit, but that was his limit. After a few moments, the silvery material reappeared around his legs, and Sal moved onto the next part of his experiment. Reaching to his neck, he pulled at the material to reveal his face. His gaze was still locked on the silver pants, wondering whether his plan would work. When he felt the sudden coolness of air touching his skin, Sal was dismayed to see that the pants immediately reverted to the black jumpsuit. "Fuck."

"What's up?" Fabi asked. "Did you break it?"

Sal shook his head with a sigh. "No, it's just that I have to have the suit completely covering my body if I want to summon anything. The passive cost is too high, and would only allow me to wear it for a few hours at a time. I've barely done anything today and I'm already at sixty percent of total capacity."

Fabi bit her lip and remained quiet for a few seconds. "Okay, then we'll change up our plans. Keep it off for now, and stay in the car while I handle all the administration stuff. I'll come and get you when it's time for the dungeon."

"It's not that bad. You said it'll take twenty minutes to get to the dungeon," Sal disagreed as he gestured at the open space in front of them. "Sixty percent will still give me three hours, and with the two of us, a leecher dungeon shouldn't take that long?"

Fabi shook her head as she sped up the car by pushing the lever all the way forward. "Nope. I want to see the Vendetta Macclemark set, and that one has a much higher cost…so we don't really have that much time at all."

Sal stayed quiet as he closed his eyes. "I'll try meditating to see if that helps at all, but worst-case scenario, we'll just have to test the Vendetta Macclemark another time."

Fabi smiled with a nod. "Look at you, already planning our next dungeon run." Her shoulders tensed as she gripped the steering yoke in front of her. "Buckle up. We'll be there in twelve minutes!"

"Can't wait," Sal muttered as he tried to focus on his internal gates.

CHAPTER 68: DRAIN

"Salvatore Argento?" the dungeon attendant repeated as he tapped at the console in front of him. "I have on my records that your designation has been changed. Are you assisting Fabrizia Maccles, or would you like your ranking points to contribute toward your guild?" He looked between Sal and Fabi with a bored expression. "As you know, Trainee Guilds are not eligible for—"

"That's fine. Put us down as the guild." Fabi interrupted him with a smile. "We're on a bit of a time crunch at the moment, so can we just go in?" She gestured at the dungeon behind the attendant, who looked more than a little irked by the sudden change of pace.

"As this is Mr. Argento's first time participating in a dungeon as a Trainee Guild, there are a certain number of processes and procedures that need to take place," the attendant clarified as he tapped at his console in a painfully slow manner. "We need to create a card for him and conduct a few more pieces of due diligence."

"This card?" Sal asked as he held up the white card that Cooper had given him a few months ago.

The attendant looked up and stared at the card for a few seconds. "Yes, actually. May I?" He reached out to take it from Sal, who obliged with a smile.

"Ah, I see that you've completed the Evergreen Dungeon…by yourself? Excellent. Then there's no need to delay you any further." He smiled as he handed the card back to Sal. "I can tell with just a glance that your equipment far exceeds the requirements, and you're assisted by an accomplished Dungeoneer. Thank you for your patience. You will have free rein of the dungeon for the next two hours. If you complete it earlier, you can exchange your remaining time for a different dungeon."

"Thank you very much." Fabi smiled as she quickly moved toward the dungeon entrance. "Come on, Sal. We'll get this started right away."

Sal gave the attendant a nod before moving after Fabi. He hadn't been able to restore any of his essence in the car, and apparently, he wasn't able to wait for Fabi to jump through the administrative hoops. They needed to talk to him in person and verify that he wasn't entering the dungeon under duress, and that he was aware of the risk and dangers. All in all, it had taken five minutes, but you'd think with Fabi's reaction, they had been detained for half a day.

"Those guys are the worst," Fabi breathed as she looked back at Sal, looking over his shoulder to ensure they were out of earshot. "All they do is create new rules and take the spoils of our work." She gave him a grin as she stood beside the dungeon gate. "So, I don't want to pull you into this thing unwillingly. How are you feeling?"

"Good." Sal steeled himself. He had dealt with a lot worse in the tower exercise, and had already completed a similarly ranked dungeon when he went with Chatfield and Upgrade. "I feel ready, so we can go in."

Fabi's grin grew wider. "That's what I like to hear. Let's go." She turned and started to move forward when Sal suddenly stopped her.

"Eh, Fabi? You're wearing jeans," Sal said awkwardly as he pointed at her in confusion. "Aren't you going to change into your battle-suit?"

Fabi just smiled at him as she continued into the dungeon. "The Macclemark is recharging from last night's run. I'd be good in here with just a blindfold, so don't worry." She caught his stare and laughed. "I have some equipment with me, so trust me. I'll be able to jump in and stop anything if things go wrong."

Sal followed her through the gate with a slight grimace. He was grateful that the Ultimate Argento set covered his face, so there was no way for her to really see his expressions. If there was one thing he was grateful for, it was the practice of dismissing the individual set pieces in the car. Sal had to show his face to the attendant, which was thankfully possible by just dismissing the mask and keeping the rest of the suit equipped. He needed to wear it to see the essence drain, and there was no way he was walking into a dungeon without having some form of Analysis active. The threat detection of the visor was a necessity for his own sanity, even if they were only going to be fighting leechers.

"Okay. You good?" Fabi moved down the steps to the underground tunnels. "You've been to the Evergreen Dungeon, so that makes this a lot easier to explain." She gestured at the slimy walls, smiling. "This was previously a sewer before it became a dungeon. Because of the moisture, there's a good chance that the leechers will have either an aquatic or toxic trait."

"Aquatic trait?" Sal repeated in confusion. "I fought against one that had bonded with metal. Do we need to have antidotes or something for the toxic ones?"

Fabi shook her head. "Nope. The aquatic variants tend not to float from above or clump at the ceilings. They disguise themselves in puddles and will try to ambush you from the ground and walls, so be mindful where you step. As for the toxicity, they can only administer it when they make contact with your skin, so you'll be fine as you're fully covered. Best way to deal with them is at range, and not to inhale any of the vapor that is released from their bodies. If they get close, it's better to take them out with blunt damage rather than piercing."

Sal nodded in understanding. "So using the guns would be a bad idea?"

Fabi waved her hand back and forth. "If it was a small space and there were a huge amount of them, then yeah…that's a good instinct. There are only usually around twenty leechers in this place, and a single guaranteed variant." She sighed as she placed her hand on her hips. "How is your essence drain?"

Sal didn't even need to check as he had been watching the dwindling number constantly.

Currently Equipped: Ultimate Argento Set
- o   Passive Essence Cost: 22%
- o   Essence Expenditure Change: 0%
- o   Essence Expenditure Remaining: 53%

"It's just over fifty percent." Sal read the words aloud, which seemed to disappoint Fabi.

"We're not going to risk you having the dregs by activating the Vendetta Macclemark. So, how about you just try Dominion instead?" She casually gestured at the sewer entrance. "It would be good to see what sort of effect area it offers."

Sal nodded as he stepped forward, looking left and right warily to see whether the mask picked up any leecher signatures. He was relieved to see that the mask worked the same as his visor, and the targets in the distance started locking with a targeting system. It continued counting until all the demons had been registered. "Ah, it's working. It's already highlight—"

Targets Identified: 21
Automating Functions…

Sal barely had time to see the words appear on his visor when a dramatic chunk of essence was forcibly ripped from his body. He had absolutely no idea how the Vendetta protocol, and from the earlier Ambush experience with Fabi, he didn't want to endanger her. "Stay back!" he called in a strained voice as he moved as far from her as his aching body would allow. It wasn't the dregs, but it was enough of a pull to make him nervous about his remaining expenditure.

Sal frantically looked in every direction, searching for an unseen enemy, but his visor wasn't picking up a single reading. It was only when he turned back that he saw Fabi standing guard in front of him with her fingerless gloves clenched into fists.

Targets Defeated: 21
Basic Leecher: 20
Evolved Leecher: 1

"What?" Sal said numbly as he looked at the reading on his mask. "They're all dead?" He breathed those last words as he glanced at Fabi in amazement. He quickly navigated to his remaining essence and was shocked to see how drastically it had reduced in just a few seconds.

Essence Expenditure Remaining: 19%

"Sal, would you like to explain what's going on? What was that surge just now?" Fabi asked cautiously as she turned to look at him with wide eyes. "A blast of essence just pulsed out of you and went down both sides of the tunnel." She looked a little panicked by the whole thing, but there was concern in her eyes as she inspected him for any obvious injuries. "We should leave and get you out of that thing. It's clearly dangerous and this isn't the place to be testing it!"

Sal just held up a hand as he caught his breath. "I'm down to nineteen percent." He dismissed the mask so that Fabi could see his face. "And it's telling me that all twenty-one of the leechers are dead, including an evolved leecher."

Fabi just blinked, not saying a word. Then, very slowly, she moved down the tunnel. "Let's have a look before we leave, then." Glancing back over her shoulder, she gave Sal a conflicted look. "I mean, if you're up for it? You can wait here at the entrance if you want. Or we can just call it a day and head back now?"

Sal shook his head and gestured at the darkness ahead of them. "No, I want to see what happened, too. Let's have a look."

"Stay behind me though." Fabi flexed her right fist, causing the void needle to appear out of nowhere. "I don't want you expending any more essence. I'd even prefer if you changed back to the jumpsuit form, just to be on the safe side."

"If it drops lower, I'll dismiss it, I promise," Sal insisted, not wanting to feel naked in a dungeon. "Lead the way."

Fabi and Sal walked through the murky tunnel, and it was only about twenty feet before they saw the destruction. A dozen or more leechers floated lifelessly in the sloshy mush at their feet. Just like Fabi had said about them hiding in water, Sal was able to see a sickly green residue that coated the tentacle-like tendrils that floated to the surface.

With a flick of her wrist, Fabi's spear disappeared, replaced with a carving knife. "Just give me a second, okay?" she said to Sal as she crouched down on one knee, cutting deftly into the body of each leecher with a single swipe, and clicking her fingers over the corpse with her left hand.

"What are you doing?" Sal asked as he moved to the side to get a better look.

"Cutting out cores and putting them in subspace," Fabi explained as she clicked her fingers again, to reveal a marble-like core that appeared out of thin air. "I have the activation set to certain hand gestures, which makes it easier when doing it at speed. Most of the Macclemark works with gestures, and I thought I'd be teaching you how to use it down here." She laughed at herself as she looked at all the corpses. "This is not what I meant when I said walking death."

Sal smiled awkwardly as he shuffled to the side. "Would you like me to help?"

"You're all good. It's only fair I do this since you killed them all." She shot him a wink as she quickly made her way through the rest of the visible corpses. "If we were being really diligent about this, we'd drain the toxin and store it…but honestly, they're too low level to really be worth the time." Getting back to her feet, she walked forward again. "But the evolved leecher is a different story. Depending on the type, we might get some nice stuff."

Sal nodded as he moved with her down the tunnel. He was still reeling from the fact that Dominion had obliterated all the leechers in seconds. The range was far more than he had envisioned, but the real questions he had were surrounding the Automate ability. It had seemingly used Fabi's functions from the Macclemark and activated it with devastating force.

"Fabi, what are the functions of the Macclemark? My visor said that it was Automating just before everything died," Sal asked as he watched Fabi expertly loot the demon corpses.

Fabi didn't stop what she was doing as she replied. "Well, since it was the Controller specification, I'm guessing that it interpreted the protective field a little differently than I intended." She chuckled to herself as she looked at all the corpses. "Like, a really different interpretation of protecting the wearer. It's supposed to activate countermeasures if something enters into your personal space or comes too close. Usually by taking essence and creating small projectiles." She looked around to meet Sal's gaze. "Definitely not creating a tsunami wave of essence to obliterate everything."

Sal thought about Fabi's words for a few seconds, trying to make sense of the different functions. "Wait, so if the personal space was expanded dramatically…like through Dominion?"

Fabi looked off to one side as a smile appeared on her face. "Oh…like, the whole dungeon is considered your personal space?" She thought about that for a few seconds, before her jaw dropped. "How much essence did it take from you?"

"Over thirty percent," Sal replied glumly. He had been thinking about that exact thing. He'd need to really focus on building up his essence reserves, or at the very least create something with multiple cores, like the coat he gave Rochelle.

Fabi, on the other hand, looked excited by the prospect. "The Dominion set is a definite winner, and I can only imagine how good the Vendetta Macclemark is! I think we should create that next. But let's forget about all the additional sets and summonable stuff."

Sal just shook his head. "Even if we do that, the issue will still be the essence draw."

Fabi grinned at him. "If only we knew someone with over three hundred gates open…"

CHAPTER 69: PRINCIPLES

"Are you disappointed?" Sal asked finally as Fabi started to pull at the different containers in the back of her car. The sound of clinking indicated that she was depositing all the cores from the leechers into one of the storage spaces. When they had reached the evolved leecher, Fabi had cursed and even gave it a kick before they left the dungeon.

"Nah, it's a low drop rate. Evolved cores tend to have better options, and leechers specifically have some good ones," Fabi answered. "In a toxic and aquatic dungeon, you can get a specific core that gives the Purify attribute. It's really good for Healing equipment and sells for a ridiculous amount." She put her hand on the edge of the doorframe and pulled herself out with a relieved sigh. "But getting a few small cores will be a nice little snack for the Arkwright, don't you think? Not bad for roughly thirty minutes of work."

"Agreed." Sal moved around to the passenger door. "So, do you want to go back and do a mock-up of your new Dominion suit?"

Fabi looked back at the plaza thoughtfully. "Well, I could probably clear the rest of the dungeons here in a couple of hours, if you wanted to hang around and wait for me? They're all low-ranked, so it wouldn't be worth much." She turned her attention to the storage containers in her car. "I could pick up some bits and pieces for my dad while I'm here."

Sal shrugged as he rested his folded arms on the roof of the car. "Really up to you. I can't imagine that I'd be much use to you in the dungeons with this suit. I'd likely get the dregs the moment I enter one of them. I could wait for you." He smiled at her and gestured at the car. "But you do run the risk of me getting bored and remodeling your car."

Fabi gave Sal a level stare for a few seconds. "Yeah, I don't trust you. Get in." She broke her act and laughed as she got into the driver's seat, pulling the door down after her. "The dungeons can wait until we figure out a solution to the essence problem."

Sal smiled as he joined her in the car. "Well, let's just say that the first Mythmark is a very successful battle-suit, but far from perfect."

Fabi whirled around in her seat. "You're actually serious about calling it a Mythmark? I should sue!"

Sal was about to put his hands up defensively when he realized what would happen. He didn't want to accidentally summon a sniper rifle in Fabi's car and smash through the windshield. When he pulled his mask off, Sal's clothing shifted to become the skintight black jumpsuit. When that was done, he then put up his hands. "In my defense, it's a great name!"

Fabi just gave him an appraising look, making a point to deliberately stare at his current clothing. "Far from perfect is a good word for it. We'll need to find something that doesn't look like pajamas." She started the car and grinned. "Or at the very least, a suit that leaves something to the imagination."

Sal chuckled as he pulled the harness strap over his shoulder to lock in. "Are you going to make the Vendetta Macclemark as a Dominion suit?"

"That's the plan. What about you?" Fabi looked at him curiously. "I think it would be a waste to sacrifice that suit to the Arkwright. It's definitely something you could grow into over time as you get more essence reserves."

Sal smiled as he shook his head. "I've been blindly following the Arkwright and hoping for the best in the last few weeks. I think it's time to get back to the basics and start Crafting myself."

"Do you have a timeline in mind?" Fabi asked suddenly. "I'm not trying to rush you, but I'd rather book in the next dungeon runs so we have a clear strategy and route forward." She navigated from the parking area of the dungeon plaza while biting her lip and checking each of the mirrors a few times.

"I just need a few days," Sal answered confidently. "Worst-case scenario, I can just create a new weapon and outfit for these dungeons specifically."

Fabi nodded as she pushed the lever forward, accelerating the car in the direction of Silver Sanctuary. "Don't put yourself under pressure, though. We could just make a few pieces of equipment and sell them off to buy essence tonics. For the gates you have open, Kaizen would probably be a good choice…but it's a bit pricey."

Sal blinked in surprise as he stared at Fabi. "I'm an idiot."

"Might need a little more context before making that judgment." Fabi chuckled as she gave him a passing glance.

"I mean, I have Kaizen and Kakushin back at the workshop. I got Vanessa to get them for me before I came back for the break," Sal explained quickly as he calculated the difference of power he felt after Prestige opened more of his gates. *If he was able to get more of them open, would that solve his essence issue?*

Fabi tapped her fingers against the lever as she shook her head. "Okay, wait for a second…let's put a pin in the Kaizen and think this through." She continued tapping her fingers as she stared out the windshield. "What was your solution going to be before you thought of Kaizen?"

Sal shrugged. "Well, I thought of reworking the Mythmark to incorporate more cores into the base design." He gestured vaguely at his body. "It probably sounds stupid, but I was thinking of a breastplate made completely out of cores, with replenishing runes on them…or that Devour trait?"

Fabi nodded. "Okay, let's say that fails and you don't have Kaizen. What would you do then?"

Sal bit his lip as he thought about it. "Eh…I'd probably try to make that elixir machine? Try and make Kaizen myself."

"Like the Arkwright? You just feed it ingredients and it makes elixirs?" Fabi asked curiously.

"No, I was going to make another enclosure kind of thing using Anderson Royce's ability. It allows him to grow plants with essence, so I thought it might be a way to continually harvest ingredients," Sal lamely explained as he gestured with his hands. "Then I could use Alex's Alchemize ability to turn them into the elixirs. Maybe add in Refine, or something like that?"

Fabi just shook her head in wonder. "That's the level of thought and detail you have before starting a project? Really?"

Sal nodded slowly. "Is that bad?"

Fabi chuckled before letting out a resigned sigh. "No, it's not bad. It's just...unorthodox. I have to think of every little detail, and then I tear it apart with a feasibility study or research. It sounds refreshing, just throwing yourself into a project like that."

"Hey, you made a pretty amazing Epic-grade spear! There wasn't a whole lot of research or feasibility thrown into that." Sal tried to reassure her, but felt out of his depth.

"But there was. A fantastic blueprint and map of how to create it with multiple options to suit my tastes," Fabi corrected him. "Which you made with your visor in a few seconds." She looked at him strangely. "With the visor you created."

"Ah." Sal floundered a bit as he tried to switch the topic. "So, what's your thoughts? Should I work on adding the cores to the Mythmark?"

"Smooth." Fabi laughed as she tilted her head to one side and continued to drum her fingers against the acceleration lever. "If I was Salvatore Argento, what would I do?" She asked the question of herself thoughtfully. "I'd focus on building up my Hunter Bureau rank, that's for certain. According to that attendant, you are already listed as a Trainee Guild, so that's a great start."

Sal was content to listen to her. He wasn't sure he had anything of value to add to the topic.

"I'd also focus on building a battle-suit," she said finally, after a few seconds of deliberating. "While the elixir machine sounds great and would be a real money-maker, it would be best to make it at Quest Academy and keep it in your dorm. You'd be able to make a killing by selling it to students and you'd ace your Administration class."

Sal smiled. "That's actually a good point. The royalties I'm earning from the weave research is likely enough to keep me in high grades."

Fabi nodded in agreement. "Having a good battle-suit will help you in your other classes. You should start doing some outings with the guilds, because they are the absolute best places to learn while being protected by the best of the best."

"So, the verdict is to make a new Mythmark?" Sal asked.

Fabi smiled as she looked at him. "This is the hypothetical of me being Salvatore Argento. I'm not telling you what to do, as you're big enough to make those choices yourself." She shrugged it off, chuckling. "Besides, if you just did what people told you to do, wouldn't that make life super boring?"

Sal smiled and let out a sigh. "There's a big difference in taking advice from someone you respect, versus blindly doing what you're told."

"Okay, that was actually smooth." Fabi laughed as she gave him a playful nudge with her elbow. "So go on, feel free to ask your respected senior for her sagely opinions. What else do you want to know?"

Sal thought about something he was genuinely curious about. "If you had Mythcrafter, what would you make?"

Fabi blinked in surprise. "Oh, like is that the same question as before, but just reworded?"

Sal shook his head. "No, I'm not asking what I should be doing now...but rather, what would you use Mythcrafter for if it was your ability? Long-term. Not right now?"

Fabi frowned as she thought about it. "Man, the options are kinda endless, aren't they? There's nothing saying that Figment won't get to that stage, so it's a good question for myself. Let me think for a bit."

Sal guessed that it would take her a few minutes to give him an answer, but it was only when they landed back at Silver Sanctuary that she spoke. Getting out of the car, she plucked a container out from behind the driver seat with a thoughtful expression on her face. "It's a hard one," Fabi said finally as she closed the car door. "The question, I mean."

"How so?" Sal closed his own door and moved toward the Argento Auction House to open the door for her.

Fabi tucked the container under her arm as she walked through the open door. "Because it's like a question of morality versus ambition, isn't it? Do you dedicate your life to the creation of better barriers or support equipment to help people…or do you become Doc Ameye? Create machines of death and build an empire on the back of it?"

Sal let the door close behind him as he moved in step with Fabi to the workshop. More than a few of the auction staff gave him a confused look, and he realized he was still dressed in the jumpsuit. "If I change the parameters of the question, and add the caveat that you'd never be judged for what you decide, would that change your answer?" Sal was genuinely curious to know what way she'd choose.

Fabi nodded thoughtfully. "Then it's easier. I'd make Mythic-grade Macclemark suits."

Sal was confused by the answer. She'd only create Mythic-grade Macclemark suits if the question of morality and judgment was removed?

Fabi looked at Sal, smiling. "I'm just guessing, but the resources required to make a Mythic grade are likely insane…and could be used for much more useful and altruistic goals. I'd never want to be the reason something is defunded, or deprioritized. It's one of the reasons I respect Doc Ameye, because he never wavers when it comes to his principles."

"I never really thought of it that way," Sal said as they descended the steps to the workshop platform.

"You'll see what I'm talking about when you meet the refugees." Fabi sighed. "When you see how they're forced to live, you'll come to understand that we're misaligned when it comes to priorities. It's one of the reasons I can't justify spending stupid money on a car, when I know that same amount would be able to re-home a group of families in a Reclaimed Zone."

"Ah." Sal was at a loss for words, but thankfully Fabi was there to save him from floundering in guilt.

"Best way to justify all of this expense is experience." Fabi pointed up at the Arkwright. "Without investing in yourself, the Arkwright wouldn't exist. Would a nice car or a second property result in a technological breakthrough? No, but investing in your Crafting can. If we build up the depot and get those storefronts operational, then we'll start earning enough to actually make a difference."

Fabi placed the container onto the workbench and moved to the coffee machine. "There's enough cores in there for a necklace or a wrist-guard, but not enough for a breastplate. Feel free to use them all…they were your kills."

Sal stood at the top of the mezzanine with a conflicted expression on his face. "Thank you, Fabi." It was a perspective that he hadn't considered before. Everything that he was learning, everything he was Crafting, was all in the pursuit of becoming a better Mythcrafter. The Arkwright was potentially stunting his own development, and Sal was starting to realize that painful reality. He had an expert of essence programming in front of him, and he had been content to just press a few buttons on an interface and hope for the best, instead of learning from her.

Fabi turned around in confusion. "For what? Answering your question?" She smiled as though it were no big deal. "Or for the cores? I mean it—they're all yours."

"If I asked you that same question about Mythcrafter, but said that the morality and judgment was still in place, what would your answer have been?" Sal asked out of curiosity. "Because I've a feeling I already know the answer."

Fabi crossed her arms as she gave him a look of feigned annoyance. "Oh, he knows me a few days and already has me figured out? Go on, then. What would I have said?"

"Same thing you've said to me nonstop since we've met." Sal chuckled. He could already see the smile tugging at the side of Fabi's lips. "Tell me I'm wrong. You'd make a Mythic-grade drone."

Fabi threw her arms up and let out an exasperated cry. "Come on! It would be incredible! Why am I the only one who thinks that?"

Sal grinned as he pointed at the Arkwright. "Let's finalize the design of the Vendetta Macclemark sets, and get it working on producing them for both of us." Sal moved his hand to point at the workbench. "And then we'll get to work with the blueprints for the Mythic-grade drone."

Fabi's jaw dropped as her eyes widened in disbelief. "Wait…you're aiming for Mythic straight out of the gate?"

Sal chuckled as he retrieved fresh sheets of paper. "You asked me what I wanted to do." He offered her a slight shrug as he passed her and went into the kitchenette. "I want to push Mythcrafter to the limits to see what's possible."

"You're actually insane," Fabi breathed as she followed him. "Didn't you hear me when I said the material costs are going to be astronomical?"

Sal sidestepped her with pages in hand and pointed through the doorway at the Arkwright. "Good thing we have something doing material synthesis, isn't it?"

Fabi just stared between Sal and the Arkwright. "If this is just an elaborate hoax to get my hopes up, I'll actually cry." She stared at him as though daring him to break and tell her the truth.

Sal reached past Fabi to press the button on the coffee machine. "Nope! If anything, it's an elaborate method of avoiding dungeons and keeping you happy." He grinned at her stupefied expression. "Everyone wins!"

CHAPTER 70: FLAW

"Why can't we do this back at the workshop? The train tracks worked fine when you made the spear," Sal asked casually as he looked back at the Argento Auction House in the distance. It was brightly illuminated by the streetlights and stood as a stark contrast to the surrounding buildings that were long closed for the evening. He turned to look at Fabi, who had her arms locked at her sides, holding folds of excess material so it wouldn't cause her to trip over herself. She was wearing the Dominion set that he had taken to the leecher dungeon, and the fabric hung loosely against her frame.

"I don't want to risk the Arkwright or your workshop." Fabi laughed as she continued walking toward the old warehouses they were gifted by the Hunter Bureau. "Besides, we're going to be working in the depot eventually. We might as well take a look at the place."

Sal nodded as they continued in silence down the next street. His grand plan of working on the Mythic-grade drone hadn't exactly worked out like he envisioned. They never got to sit down and work on the designs for it, because the Vendetta Macclemark sets couldn't be loaded into the Arkwright. Even after so many hours, it was still breaking down the Uncommon-grade weapons that Fabi had fed it, and would be doing so for at least another full day. With that plan out the window, they decided to review the diagnostics report for the Dominion set, and it was riddled with issues. The suit contained an internal list of programmed conditions that were managed by Automate, and according to Fabi, they were a complete mess…sorted by performance rather than practicality.

"I wonder if it's going to fit when you pull the mask on?" Sal said as he looked at the baggy black jumpsuit on Fabi. "Or if you're going to have a really baggy version of the Ultimate Argento set?"

Fabi smiled as she offered him a slight shrug. "It won't matter. As long as I can use the mask to check the internal programming, I'll be able to switch things around and make a better load order." She looked at the visor on his face and tapped him on the shoulder. "And we'll leave Appraisal of the suit to the expert this time. It sucks that it won't show us the full specifications of the suit until the components are summoned, but it is what it is."

"I'm curious myself," Sal admitted as they rounded a corner toward the depot in the distance. "Ambush feels like such a weird option to have on something that's apparently an ultimate version of the Argento set. If anything, it should be Reflect that was upgraded."

"What other options did your original outfit have?" Fabi asked in a curious tone.

"Well, the trousers had Steady and Impact." Sal began listing them. "The gloves had Pocket, Overcharge, and Transform, while the shirt had Defiant, which works like a reflective ability. There was Synergy and Chameleon, too." Sal counted them out on his hands. "I think I only used the trousers properly one time, by jumping out of a tree during the excursion." He laughed at the memory. "The gloves were amazing, though."

Fabi whistled in appreciation. "And you just chucked that into the Arkwright? That's a lot of great abilities to just throw away."

"Yeah, and I expected the Ultimate Argento set to have functionality that was closer to those abilities," Sal admitted, sighing. "Dominion was supposed to be a blend between Concept and Conquest, which would allow me to summon weapons and equipment onto the battlefield in an area of effect…but all it did was let me switch between weapons and gear sets for myself."

Fabi jutted her chin in the direction of the depot ahead. "Well, let's find out what's going on. You ready?"

Sal shrugged as he adjusted the visor on his face. "Sure. Want me to hang back here? Just in case you accidentally ambush me?"

Fabi gave him a quick nod before she bundled up the excess fabric in her hands and set off toward the center of the wide loading bay area at the front of the depot. "Yeah, just give me a few minutes to get my bearings, okay?"

"Sounds good!" Sal called after her. He watched as she moved over to the center of the open area, curious what would happen when she pulled on the mask. Fabi had a lot more essence reserves than he did, and nearly three times as many gates open as he did. Although he had access to two hundred and forty, he still needed to break through those gates, and Kaizen was going to help him reach that full potential.

Sal sighed inwardly as he thought about the Kaizen elixir. It had been sitting in his room and he had spent the last few days so focused on the Arkwright and the Silverson stuff that he had completely forgotten about the elixir.

"I'll meditate before I go to bed," Sal said to himself quietly. His sleeping pattern was screwed up anyway, and he was pretty tired after such little sleep the night before. With Perfect and Kaizen, he guessed that he'd be able to break through a substantial number of gates, which might solve the essence requirements for the Dominion set.

Sal thought about how much time he had until it was time to go back to Quest Academy. There were so many things he wanted to get finished before then, and the list seemed to grow longer with every passing day. He watched Fabi in the distance as she adjusted the baggy jumpsuit, kicking her feet out and wiggling her arms to spread the excess material around her body. The sight of it made him chuckle.

Sal saw her leg flash up quickly, and was instantly reminded of the training with his father. That was another thing for the list—learning the Silverson Arts. The whole conversation with his parents about his family history was still very much in the back of his head, and Sal saw the Silverson Arts as a good olive branch to learn more about them while improving his own skills. In just a day, his father had pretty much given him a vicious kicking technique, which made Sal wonder how much he'd be able to learn in the remaining few weeks before it was time to return to Quest Academy.

"Okay. I'm going to start!" Fabi called from farther ahead, snapping Sal back to reality.

He gave her a thumbs-up gesture, and watched as she positioned her body to face him directly. Reaching behind her head, she pulled the mask down over her face…resulting in an immediate transformation of the entire body suit. The Ultimate Argento set appeared into existence, and just like Sal had expected, it was a baggy mess on Fabi. She had been right about the mask looking positively menacing, and Sal actually paused when he caught sight of it. If the ensemble fit her, it would look a lot scarier, but as it stood, the mask was crooked on her head, almost like it was slipping to one side because of the excess space.

The visor flashed into action, and Sal focused his attention on Appraising the set.

Name	Ultimate Argento Set (Mask)
Origin	Crafted
Age	New
Grade	Legendary (Overcharge)
Materials	Dungeon Heart Essence | Mythcrafter Essence | Moonsilver | Scarlet Screen | Lux Crystal | Lords Crystal | Blue Fang | Switcher Sinew
Attributes	Analysis: Ability to interpret visual data and information Network: Allows user access to a network of information databases that improve System. System: Allows user to interpret abstract information from essence signatures. Calm: Wearer enters a calm flow state when activated. Insight: Wearer can analyze patterns and predict outcomes. Overcharge: Grade and Abilities of item are enhanced for a short period of time. Synergy: Abilities are shared among set items.
Abilities	Analysis | Network | Interface | Calm | Insight
Power Source	Essence Reserves
Evolution	No

Quality	Perfect
Condition	Summoned

Sal stared at the reading for the Argento Mask in confusion. It wasn't the Scarlet Strategist's Visor that was being emulated, but an entirely different product? None of the abilities were nearly as impressive as what his own visor offered. He focused on the information that was being relayed to his eye, and it finally struck him what one of the fundamental issues was: the passive essence drain was coming from maintenance of so many abilities on each piece of equipment. Coupled with that, one of them was Overcharge, which explained why the Epic-grade suit was displaying as Legendary grade. Everything in the Ultimate Argento set was being forcibly maintained at a higher level than it was designed for.

Without focusing too much on the details, Sal quickly moved his attention to the gloves, then the trousers, shirt, and jacket. He didn't focus on the words, but rather on the number of abilities. "Five on the shirt, four on the trousers…six on the gloves, and five on the jacket?" Sal counted them all, and with the addition of the mask, it was over twenty-five abilities that were summoned into an active state. None of them were high-tier abilities, and if he were to guess the grades they offered, none would be higher than grade ten on the simulation orb.

"How is it looking?" Fabi called out, causing Sal to look up at the menacing mask that covered her face.

"Kind of shit, if I'm honest." Sal laughed as he walked closer to where she stood. "It's constantly using Overcharge, pulling the grade up from Epic to Legendary." Sal gestured at the ensemble that she wore. "It's got more than twenty low-tier abilities, all primed and active…but there's little to no cohesion with them, other than the mask."

Fabi nodded in understanding, causing the mask to tip to one side, removing one of the glowing red eyes from the horizontal visor. It looked comical, and was only made funnier by Fabi's muffled curses from behind it. "Okay…let's call this one a dud for now. Stay where you are, and I'll switch over to the Vendetta Macclemark set."

Sal wasn't convinced it was going to be any better after he had seen the results of the Ultimate Argento set. It was a sequence of essence signatures that he was definitely going to delete from the Arkwright. His best guess was that the Arkwright created an artificial evolutionary path for the set. Or maybe it was because Overcharge was one of the registered abilities? There were too many questions, and Sal wasn't exactly sure how he felt about it. A part of him had expected something extraordinary after the performance in the dungeon, but the reality left him with more questions than answers.

"Don't worry about any sudden attacks, by the way," Fabi said as she moved her lopsided mask. "I've reset a chunk of the Automate functions, and will only activate the ones that add value. Let's start with Transform."

"Transform?" Sal repeated in confusion.

A shimmering energy rippled across Fabi's entire body, causing the silvery suit to tighten around her form as it reshaped itself. "That's better." Fabi stretched her arms out to test the new fit. "Resized, but it's still a little too masculine." She pointed at the sides of the blazer that hung from her shoulders straight down. "But it's not falling off me, so that's a win."

"I thought you were working on the functions? Did you just activate the Transform ability, instead?" Sal frowned as he looked at the shrunken form of the suit that had pretty much molded itself to Fabi's body.

Fabi nodded slowly. "Yeah, it's an odd one. Each Macclemark is usually created with just a couple of abilities, and all the functions are tied to them." She plucked at the blazer before letting it hang back at her waist. "But this thing has pretty much altered all the programming and stuffed the Automate sequence with a whole range of abilities that are in conflict with each other."

"Ah, so you're able to see what I was seeing?" Sal pointed at the visor. "All the abilities?"

Fabi shook her head slightly. "No, it's a little more nuanced than that. The Arkwright seems to have emulated the functions of the Macclemark, but in a poorly executed way. For every ability on the list, there seems to be close to a dozen useless permutations that are conflicting against one another. Like, that Ambush ability seems to have activated because you moved forward with intent while an entity with essence was in front of you." She pointed at herself. "Me."

Sal let out a pained sigh. "Are you sure we shouldn't just stick it into the Arkwright and try again? Maintaining Overcharge constantly and having so many abilities with poor functions doesn't sound like a great piece of equipment."

Fabi took a tentative step backward. "Give me a few more minutes with it. I want to see if the Vendetta Macclemark has a better set of functions."

"Go for it," Sal agreed as he waved at her to continue. He mirrored her action by taking a few steps back, and kept his visor pointed directly at her.

Fabi didn't move from her new position in the center of the depot delivery area. It took a few moments of silence before the silvery suit evaporated and was replaced by the Vendetta Macclemark. If the Ultimate Argento set was considered villainous, then the Vendetta Macclemark was positively menacing. Before Sal could even properly get a look at it, the jet-black fabric shimmered as it shrunk to tighten around Fabi's body, but it was her face that Sal couldn't tear his eyes from.

"You look like you've seen a demon!" Fabi laughed as she gestured at herself. "Is it really that bad?"

Sal just shook his head as he pointed at her head. "That looks incredible." Unlike the silver mask that covered her entire face, Fabi's new headpiece was a constantly shifting strip of red electricity that suspended itself over her eyes. Small skewers of angry red lightning zapped harmlessly over her ears, as it held itself against her skin. The effect was only made more dramatic by the crackling noise it emitted just from existing, and the flashes of red that surrounded Fabi each time it flared up. Her shoulders had the same red lightning that seemed to flow all the way down to her fingertips, contrasting sharply with the jet-black shine of metal that encased her arms and torso. A dull red glow appeared between the joints, highlighting the areas that allowed for flexibility with the armor.

Fabi smiled as she looked down at herself. "It's making my abs look amazing." She laughed as she touched her stomach carefully. This was followed by her testing the movements in the suit one by one, with a rotation of the arms, and then a few leg raises. "It's like I'm wearing cloth," she admitted with a slight shake of her head. "And the essence drain isn't bad at all."

"Not bad for normal people…or not bad for you?" Sal asked with a laugh, still staring at the incredible armor. His loyalty to suits had evaporated the moment he locked eyes with it.

"In what world is a Mythcrafter considered normal?" Fabi countered, smirking as she looked off to one side. "I'm going to check the functions. You good to give an Appraisal?"

Sal smiled as he started Appraising the Vendetta Macclemark. "Even if the options suck, the style makes it worth keeping."

Fabi grinned. "The functions are pretty great, too. So, we might be on to a winner if we just produce this without the Ultimate Argento set."

"Ah, but I'll need to keep the Scarlet Strategist set to have some form of firepower," Sal reminded her. "Just keep that in mind."

Rather than answering him, Fabi raised her finger and pointed it at an empty space in the distance. With what looked like zero effort, a bolt of red lightning pierced through the darkness and impacted against the ground, leaving an angry red residue that sparked erratically before dissipating into the night.

"I wouldn't be so sure." Fabi smiled as she looked at him. "This thing definitely packs a punch."

Name	Vendetta Macclemark Set
Origin	Crafted
Age	New
Grade	Epic Grade
Materials	Dungeon Heart Essence | Mythcrafter Essence | Moonsilver | Scarlet Screen | Lux Crystal | Lords Crystal | Blue Fang | Switcher Sinew…

Attributes	Automate: Integrated functionality of Vendetta Macclemark Set will be activated automatically when conditions are met. • Vendetta Protocol (Inactive) • Initiative Protocol (Inactive) • Transform (Active) • Scan (Active) Assimilate: Absorbs the target's essence to permanently increase the user's proficiency, ability or base competencies. The gains will depend on the level of the target being assimilated. • Assimilation Count: 0 • Ability Grade Improved: 0% • Essence Reserve Improved: 0% • Acquired Techniques: 0 Ravage: Unleashes a relentless surge of electrified essence at target, increasing in damage power the longer it's active. Dominion: Casts a substantial area of effect around user. Allows for essence-based constructs to be summoned and controlled at will. Registered essence signatures can be summoned at substantially reduced essence cost. • Vendetta Macclemark Set (Active)
Abilities	Automate | Assimilate | Ravage | Dominion
Power Source	Essence Reserves
Evolution	No
Quality	Perfect
Condition	Summoned

"Do I want to know why you're looking so horrified?" Fabi laughed. "Because I'm going to guess that there's a massive drawback to how stylish and destructive this thing is?"

Sal blinked as he looked up at her face. "It's not individual items…the whole thing is just one piece." He gestured vaguely at her whole body. "And…I think we found an ability that's stronger than Devour?"

"Yeah? What does it do?" Fabi asked excitedly. "Does it use the lightning to suck essence out of demons?"

Sal tried to grapple with the interpretation he had from the Appraisal. There had to be a mistake somewhere, but he just couldn't figure it out. When he met Fabi's excited gaze, his shoulders sagged and he decided that they could figure it out together at a later point. "I might be wrong on this, okay?" He pointed at the Vendetta Macclemark set. "But I think you have an ability that lets you get stronger when you kill things?"

"Get stronger?" Fabi scoffed as she stared at him. "What, like…it increases physical strength?"

Sal folded his arms as he continued to stare at the Appraisal reading on his visor. "I think we're going to need to test this out in a dungeon." He desperately wanted to know how it worked, or at least what sort of impact it would have on Fabi's abilities. If it functioned the way it was described, then he'd finally have a method to increase his ability grades of Skill Master and Mythcrafter. "It looks like it can increase all sorts of stats, depending on the demons you kill."

Fabi's smile was as bright as it was beautiful. "We're not setting foot into a dungeon until we both have these suits. Got it?" She laughed as she pointed at the darkness behind Sal. "Let's get back to the workshop so I can change out of this thing. We can meet up tomorrow and put together a plan of action."

"What about the functions?" Sal asked in confusion as he watched Fabi walk past him gracefully in the black and red suit. It looked even better up close, and he could see the metal material bending to accommodate her breathing. It moved like fabric, but he was certain that it was hard as steel when struck.

Fabi just waved her hand like it didn't matter. "This whole thing is screwed up. Each and every function has been overwritten or condensed into something useless." She let out a sigh as she turned to look at him. "I think your Arkwright has picked up a few bad habits already. Streamlining processes is only great when they're actually useful."

Sal nodded in agreement. "Were you able to figure out how I killed all those leechers in a single attack?"

Fabi's body shimmered and reverted to the black jumpsuit that drooped immediately around her smaller frame. "Yeah, that was the Vendetta Protocol with Automate. There's a really long explanation from an essence programming perspective, but the simplest way to describe it…is that your suit decided that enemies needed to die as fast as possible, using all the essence you had to spare." She laughed as she hiked up the excess fabric in her hands so she could walk properly. "You'll be happy to know that you wouldn't have gotten the dregs, though. It locks off about five percent of your essence pool and will deactivate everything when you reach that point."

"Well, that's a bit of a relief," Sal muttered as he followed her to head back to the Argento Auction House. "So, what are your plans when you get home?"

Fabi shrugged. "Eat, shower, and sleep." She smiled as she glanced in his direction. "Or…I'll probably stay up stupidly late working on a custom suite of protocols for the Vendetta Macclemark set. What about you?"

Sal tapped his chest. "Going to meditate and try to open up some of these gates."

Fabi continued to stare at him. "And then you'll actually go to sleep?"
Sal smiled guiltily. "We'll see."

CHAPTER 71: REMAP

Sal was incredibly proud of himself. After Fabi drove back to her own place, he had gone to the workshop and managed to walk straight past the Arkwright. There were notifications waiting for him, but the closest he got to reviewing them was when he placed the visor and the black jumpsuit down on the workbench. With all the determination he could muster, he made a beeline through the fake wall to get to his bedroom, and closed the door behind him for good measure.

"Let's do this," Sal breathed to himself as he tidied the bed, pulling at the covers and propping up the pillows so he could comfortably meditate. When he was satisfied with his progress, he stepped over to the small chest that contained the Kakushin and Kaizen bottles. The Kaizen was completely untouched, so it wasn't hard to differentiate it from the rest. Sal plucked a bottle from it and moved to place it on his bedside locker. When that was done, he moved over to the bundle of clothing that he had haphazardly thrown to the side of the bed at some point. Picking up the waistcoat of the uniform he made for himself, Sal smiled as he pulled it on. It had the Attune ability, which would be perfect for essence control and refinement.

"Probably overkill," Sal muttered as he buttoned the waistcoat over his shirt. When that was done, he kicked off his shoes and sat on the bed, getting into position. He propped himself up against the bed headboard and activated the Perfect weave in his mind. When he was sure it was active and working, he reached over and picked up the bottle of Kaizen. "Cheers," he said to himself with a smile, drinking the entirety of the bottle in one go and letting the empty glass fall to the mattress. Closing his eyes, he tried to activate Attune within the waistcoat, but it didn't seem to be an active ability.

Before Sal could try again, the elixir in his throat reacted violently with the Perfect weave, almost making him throw up. He grimaced as he forced himself to swallow the burning liquid, hoping that it would solve the problem.

It didn't.

An inferno of essence circulated within Sal's chest, causing his entire body to break into a pained sweat. Breathing had become a luxury as every attempt to inhale made him feel like he was stoking an invisible furnace. He was certain that if he opened his eyes, he'd see fire coming from his mouth. Gritting his teeth, Sal clenched his eyes tight and focused all his attention on not throwing up. Seconds turned into minutes, and Sal wasn't even sure anything was happening in his body. All he could feel was the searing heat that pulsated in his body with every heartbeat. When he brought his hand to his chest, he felt the damp shirt that was stuck to him.

Despite all his best instincts, Sal opened his eyes and saw steam rising from his body. His hands, arms, and torso were emitting a cloudy vapor…and it was the first time that Sal thought he might have made a mistake. Kakushin had been taken in small swigs, and Alex had given him a bottlecap's worth of it at Quest Academy. Why the hell did he think it would be fine to drink the entire bottle? Hell, the health elixir that Quest gave him had resulted in a full-grown beard!

Sal recalled Prestige's words about the breathing technique. She said that the technique was to keep breathing, and that's what Sal latched onto. Pushing every emotion out of the way, and ignoring the pain, Sal sat in his crouched position and continually forced himself to breathe in and out. Perfect was still active, and the waistcoat was probably doing its thing. He didn't have the luxury of being able to look within himself to see the progress of the gates, but he guessed that they were working properly. Well, he hoped that they were.

It was impossible to tell how long had passed as Sal sat there, sweating profusely on the bed. Even with his labored breathing, the fire hadn't dulled in the slightest. He reached into his pocket with a trembling hand, pulling out his tablet to check the time, but it slipped through his clammy hands and fell to the floor beside him.

"Fu…ck," Sal said, before his eyes widened in shock. His words were slurring as if he were drunk. He tried reaching for the tablet, but the movement caused the world around him to lurch violently. In the least acrobatic manner possible, Sal collapsed off the side of the bed, headfirst, with neither of his arms coming up to brace his fall.

The last thing he saw was his right hand's pitiful attempt to grasp at the blanket, before darkness consumed him.

Sal awoke with a pained groan. He was contorted on the floor, with his blanket draped over his head. His arm was twisted behind him and had gone numb from the lack of circulation. With a bleary-eyed attempt at getting up, Sal managed to pull the blanket off his bed, causing the empty bottle of Kaizen to hit him in the face. Sal winced at the impact and let himself slump back to the floor. He twisted his numb arm from behind him, ignoring how it flopped uselessly against his chest.

As he opened his mouth to verbally rebuke himself for being an idiot, his lips cracked. The sharp sting caused him to lift his good hand to his face, where he felt a sticky residue. *Had he gotten sick throughout the night?* Sal pulled his hand away and saw blood on his fingertips. "Lovely," he croaked out as he moved his tongue around the inside of his mouth, tasting the metallic tang of blood against his teeth.

Sal closed his eyes and took a steadying breath. The fire in his chest was gone, and the sweat had seemingly dried on his body…leaving him shivering as the cool air swarmed him all at once. He wasn't sure whether he had vomited blood, or whether he had somehow bit his lips. Either way, he wanted to see whether Kaizen had actually done what it was supposed to.

His subconsciousness didn't materialize as quickly as it usually did, which confused Sal for a few moments. It was difficult to concentrate, and he guessed that he was severely dehydrated. After another failed attempt to check his gates, Sal opened his eyes with a pained groan. He reached out feebly to grasp at the bedframe, attempting to pull himself upright.

With a pained sigh, Sal ignored the aching discomfort and managed to somehow get to his shaky feet. He sat on the edge of the mattress and felt the remnants of his shirt and waistcoat fall to the floor. The fabrics were in complete tatters, with a charred burn on the floor beside his bed. Sal looked at his chest and saw that his abdomen was completely bare. Thin strips of material lined his shoulders and forearms, but that was it. *Had Kaizen caused Attune to break, or did his essence somehow destroy his clothing?*

Sal had far too many questions and not enough answers as he dragged himself to his feet and stumbled across to the kitchenette. He had to brace against the countertop as he lifted a shaking hand toward the selection of coffee mugs. Once he had some water, he'd figure out what had gone wrong. The only clear thought in his mind, other than the need for water, was how lucky he had been that he managed to wake up. Drinking an entire elixir with Perfect active had been a terrible idea, and he was paying the price for that mistake.

When the water touched his lips, Sal had to resist the urge to instantly swallow. Instead, he swirled the water in his mouth to catch as much of the blood as possible, before spitting it out into the sink. The murky black mixed with red wasn't very reassuring, so he repeated the process until everything had cleared up. Washing his face cleared his head a little, and the cool water was a thankful reprieve from the pounding headache that had set in.

The most bizarre thing was that his lips hadn't bled. There were no wounds or pain points in his mouth or throat, which meant that…the blood had come up from his stomach? Sal stood there for a few minutes, holding himself against the countertop as he drank cup after cup of water. When he reached the point that it would have been painful to keep drinking, he went back to the bed and pulled the remainder of his fragmented clothing off his body. Rather than getting up and starting his day, he felt like it was best to try to get some more rest.

Sal sighed as he collapsed onto the bed. He pulled the half-charred blanket onto his torso and repositioned the stack of pillows behind him. Just before he let himself drift back off to sleep, he reactivated the Perfect weave. It had ceased the moment he had fallen unconscious, so there was a good chance that it hadn't managed to do what he intended. If more of the gates were open, Sal hoped that Perfect would work on repairing whatever damage caused the blood in his stomach. It had healed him during the tower when Rochelle gave him the Transference essence, so he hoped it would do the same now.

Stifling a yawn, Sal put Perfect in place and closed his eyes again…trying to sense where the essence in his body was being redirected. He barely managed to see a convergence of bright lights in his chest before he fell asleep once more.

Name	Salvatore Argento
Alias	Myth
Class	Support
Profession	Current: Student, Quest Academy Current: Trainee Guildmaster, Unnamed Guild Previous: Appraiser, Argento Auction
Rank (Hero)	Hunter Bureau: Current Rank | 31,214th Guild Association: Current Rank | Not Ranked Quest Academy: Current Rank | 1st Scavenger Network: Current Rank | Scrounger V
Ability	Skill Name: Skill Master | Grade 9 Skill Category: Replication Skill Mastery: 92% Skill Efficiency: 100% Progress to Next Rating: 34% Evolutionary Capability: Yes Potential Cap: Grade 15 Natural Synergy: Amplify | Configure | Enhance Skill Name: Mythcrafter | Grade 16 Skill Category: Invention Skill Mastery: 52% Skill Efficiency: 58% Progress to Next Rating: 21% Evolutionary Capability: Yes Potential Cap: Grade 30 Natural Synergy: Construct | Concept | Refine Skill Name: Perfect | Grade 25 Skill Category: Body Manipulation | Energy Manipulation Skill Mastery: 100% Skill Efficiency: 100% Progress to Next Rating: 0% Evolutionary Capability: No Potential Cap: Grade 25 Natural Synergy: Enhance | Catalyst | Domain
Essence	Essence Type: All Essence Gates: 163 / 240

	Essence Absorption Rate: 70.0% Essence Control: 92.1% Essence Refinement: 80.3% Essence Calibration: 91.8%
Physical	Strength Rating: 4.1 Mobility Rating: 9.1 Speed Rating: 7.3 Fitness Rating: 6.8 Current Status Effects: Injuries: • Internal Bruising Illnesses: • Essence Inversion • Essence Pathway Obstruction
Scout Status	Arc Guild: Inquiring (Tier 1) Ameye Locomotive: Inquiring (Tier 1) Cirque Guild: Interested (Tier 1) Thunder Guild: Interested (Tier 1) Eclipse Guild: Interested (Tier 1) Harmony Guild: Inquiring (Tier 2) Invention Guild: Interested (Tier 2) Reavers Guild: Interested (Tier 2)
Wealth	Q-Credit: 19,250

Sal frowned as he looked at his stats. Although the new gates being open and activated were definitely cause for celebration, he wasn't happy at seeing the illnesses he had somehow picked up overnight. Bruising as an injury didn't seem that bad as it would likely heal over time, but the illnesses looked like a more serious issue. Skill Master hadn't really improved by more than a few percent, but Mythcrafter had gone up a grade point, which was always a welcome sight. He guessed it had to do with his work on the Arkwright.

There were a few other points of note on the stats, and they didn't escape Sal's notice. Some of the guilds he had met at the Hunter Bureau Gala were apparently inquiring about him, even though he was setting up a Trainee Guild. The attention was nice, but he guessed it had more to do with his rank as the number-one Savior out of the first-years.

By his own reckoning, he had slept for close to nine hours in total…but the fatigue in his body felt like he had just come back from the excursion or the tower trial. It wasn't going to be a day for Crafting or doing any sort of research. He thought about getting a health potion and using it with Perfect, but he wasn't even sure that would solve his problem. It might only work on the bruising, rather than the essence inversion and pathway obstructions. Instead, Sal decided to check out the Transference update he got from analyzing Eclipse at the gala. He had been inundated with updated blueprints for essence flow, and the verdict at the time was that he wasn't advanced enough to benefit from it.

With his visor securely attached to his face, Sal moved away from the mirror in the bathroom and returned to the workshop. His body felt tender and he had to take the steps slowly as he made his way up to the balcony. Sighing wearily, he moved into his bedroom and sat on the bed, frowning. On one hand, he felt like it was a good idea to check the new Transference pattern, but on the other, he was conflicted about potentially injuring himself further. Coughing up blood wasn't really something he wanted to experience again, and he genuinely wondered whether he was being foolish.

As he hesitated, he thought of the Vendetta Macclemark set that Fabi had worn the night before. The red lightning that shot out from her extended fingertip, and the menacing visor of pure electricity that rested over her eyes was, by far, one of the most incredible things he had seen. He desperately wanted to have his own version of it. At his previous essence status, the Vendetta Macclemark would have drained half of his available essence reserves for just an hour of functionality. Rather than making armor that enhanced his reserves, he wanted to improve his own body to handle it. Just like his father insisted before, he needed to make himself into a weapon for the moment when all else failed.

Sal perked up on the bed and took a steadying breath. He willed the Transference window to open in front of him, wondering whether the conditions would have changed since he had increased his internal essence gates.

> Would you like to initiate Essence Remapping?
> Template to Use: Essence Fortification and Enhancement Method
> Profile: Salvatore Argento (Compatible)
> - Cypher Analysis: Recommended
> Chance of Successful Remap: 80%
> Estimated Completion: 3 days, 6 hours, 43 minutes, 18 seconds
> Ability Weaves
> Skill Master Grade Improvement: (9) - 12
> Mythcrafter Grade Improvement: (16) - 18
> Perfect Grade Improvement: (25) - No Improvement
> Essence Gates: (163) - 180
> Essence Absorption Rate: (70.2%) 89.7%
> Essence Control: (92.1%) - 100%
> Essence Refinement: (80.3%) - 89.2%
> Essence Calibration: (91.8%) - 97.3%
> Essence Fortification: (0%) - 25%

A wave of relief washed over him as he looked at the option in front of him. The previous screen had something like a fourteen percent chance of success, and this one was dramatically higher. Sal wasn't sure what sort of state he'd be left in with this, so rather than just clicking Accept and falling unconscious again, he decided to do some preparations in advance.

The first was ordering in some food for himself, and stocking the refrigerator. Next, he messaged his parents that he'd be working on something for the next couple of days. And lastly, he sent a message to Fabi, letting her know that he needed extra time for meditation.

It took him close to an hour to wrap everything up, because rather than being satisfied with a text message, his father had called him to ask what he was doing. That conversation ended with a plea to be careful, followed up instantly with a scheduling of their next Silverson Arts session. Apparently, his mother would be joining them for that one.

The food delivery arrived, courtesy of a very confused George, who looked at Sal's shredded clothing with a raised eyebrow. Another instance of being told to be careful checked that off the list, and finally Fabi replied to his messages.

Fabrizia: Why do I feel like your version of meditating is going to be explosive?

Fabrizia: Just don't die. I've got a whole set of protocols written up for the Vendetta Macclemark.

Fabrizia: What are you going to get the Arkwright to work on while you're meditating?

Salvatore: I'll throw on some research just to keep it busy, and I promise I won't die.

Salvatore: Looking forward to seeing what those protocols are!

Salvatore: I'll message when I finish up.

Pocketing his tablet, Sal stocked the fridge with all the pre-made meals that should last him close to a week. When that was done, he looked at the silent Arkwright on the mezzanine. It was in standby mode with nothing to do, and Sal approached it curiously. He had a few days to kill, and rather than just having it sit idle, he wanted to give it something to do.

Navigating through the menus, Sal discarded the Strategist's Dominion set, as well as the Ultimate Argento set. They were available in the blueprints section, but he wasn't going to prioritize adding them to the next iteration of battle-suit. Sal instead brought up the Vendetta Macclemark battle-suit, and looked at the options that were available for research. Sal read through the drop-down list, and wasn't particularly blown away by any of the suggested modifications. He locked the options for both Assimilate and Ravage, ensuring that they would be maintained in the research outcome. Sal also locked in Automate, to allow for Fabi's functionality. The Dominion aspect was where Sal was hesitating. *Was it even that necessary?*

Sal looked through the options of abilities that would fit with the Epic-grade Vendetta Macclemark. After a few moments, he sighed and exited from that menu. Rather than trying to brainstorm something new and revolutionary, he decided that the best bet would be to increase the supply of new materials. Sal navigated into the Material Synthesis section and gave the Arkwright free rein in the creation of new materials they could use for Crafting.

Material Synthesis
Research New Materials for Vendetta Macclemark Custom Preset?

Sal looked at the previously minimized window that showed the Vendetta Macclemark with Automate, Ravage, and Assimilation locked in as guaranteed abilities. Smiling, Sal selected Confirm. It would be great if they could just have the suit without the need for summoning it with essence.

Material Synthesis
Task 1 of 94…

Sal looked at the insane number of permutations that seemed to spider-web out on the screen in front of him. There were so many things that needed to be broken down, infused, combined, and altered to reach the end goal. And they all added up to nearly a hundred processes. Sal hesitated as he held a hand over the Cancel option. It was going to take a lot of resources, and potentially a lot of wasted materials, just to satisfy a moment of curiosity.

Material Synthesis
Task 1 of 94…
Estimated Completion: 4 days

"Oh, that's fine then." Sal chuckled as he moved back to the bedroom. He'd be finished up with his essence remapping a few hours before the Arkwright was done. "Let's see which one fails and which one succeeds." Sal lay down on his bed and activated the remapping process.

CHAPTER 72: WEAK

Sal learned a lot about himself over the course of the following days. It turned out that wearing the visor while projectile vomiting was an excellent method of understanding essence blockages. His plan to sit quietly in his room for the day had been thwarted the instant he started the essence remapping process. Eighty percent of the process was spent in the bathroom, either sitting in the staff shower or hugging the toilet bowl.

Remapping was doing more than just realigning his gates; it was forcibly purifying his body of inefficiencies. His body and nervous system were not taking kindly to the reorganization, and all his senses screamed at him that his life was in danger. Vomiting, shaking, sweating, and crying were on an hourly cycle, with a searing pain coming in spurts as each gate shifted in his body. The self-pity had long since turned to anger, and by the second day, he was cursing Prestige's name every time a gate moved.

If he had just the normal sixty gates, like his body naturally possessed…that would be fine. However, Prestige had fragmented his sixty gates into four parts apiece, giving him access to two hundred and forty in total. They weren't placed strategically, which meant the realigning process had a lot more work to do. That was the cause for Sal's suffering, and the little updates on his visor weren't helping in the slightest.

When he crossed four percent of total progress, he was already collapsed in the bathroom and wishing for death. Thirty percent, he brought his pre-made meal to the bathroom, knowing that he'd be throwing it up almost immediately after ingesting it. At seventy percent, he wrote his last will and testament, gifting the Arkwright to his parents. When he reached ninety percent, the sleep deprivation and exhaustion had culminated in a very dazed state. He lay on his bed in a sort of stupor, staring at the ceiling and waiting for it to be over.

When the progress bar neared a hundred percent, Sal stared at it lifelessly. He was just waiting for a little pop-up to tell him that it had failed and that his pain was all for naught. The inkling was already in the back of his head, that the process only had an eighty percent chance of success. With the pain and misery he had endured, he was certain that this was going to be the moment of karma. His luck had been extraordinary for so long, and this was likely going to be the sobering moment that would deal the most amount of psychological damage.

As the number moved from ninety-nine to a hundred percent, Sal stared at the information, almost willing it to confirm his suspicions. The pain had subsided, and there hadn't been any shakes for a while. The last six percent or so had been calm by comparison, and Sal was very much over the whole thing. His previous conviction about turning his body into a weapon seemed laughable when he considered how weak he was.

Taking a slow breath, Sal waited until the text changed on his visor.

Essence Remapping has been Successfully Completed
Profile: Salvatore Argento
- Essence Fortification (Complete)
- Essence Enhancement (Complete)

Ability Weaves
Skill Master Grade Improvement: 12
Mythcrafter Grade Improvement: 18
Perfect Grade Improvement: 25
Essence Gates: 180 / 240
Essence Categories: Replication, Invention
Essence Absorption Rate: 89.7%
Essence Control: 100%
Essence Refinement: 89.2%
Essence Calibration: 97.3%
Essence Fortification: 25%

"Yay," Sal deadpanned as he plucked the visor off his face and let it drop to the mattress beside him. He had absolutely no capacity for anything other than rest.

With a heavy sigh, Sal closed his eyes and drifted off to sleep. Maybe it was because he hadn't been drinking coffee, or maybe it was because his body was exhausted, but it was one of the best sleeps Sal had in a very long time.

***

"Thirteen hours?" Petro repeated in surprise as he stood opposite Sal on the wooden floor of the lobby.

Sal nodded as he eyed his mother on the other side of the room. "I think my body needed it. I ate like four of the meals the minute I woke up…and I was still hungry."

Petro whistled as he hooked his thumbs into his belt, looking Sal up and down. "Well, you've certainly bolstered your essence. I'd be able to see that a mile away—you're lit up like a Christmas tree!" His smile faded to become more of a grimace. "And you're saying it was from a remapping?"

Sophia moved across the floor, wearing a white tracksuit with rolled-up sleeves. She effortlessly adjusted the sparring gloves on her hands, while giving Sal a conflicted look. "Did you get the idea after hearing about the Shaper ability?" There was an unreadable tone in her voice, and Sal wasn't sure whether she was disappointed or sad.

"Rochelle had circulation issues with her essence." Sal gestured in the direction of his workshop. "The visor picked up the pattern she was designing, and created a method for essence refining. When I saw Eclipse using Transference, it was a lot stronger than Rochelle's ability, and the visor just updated the method with the new information." He tapped his chest with his right hand. "It successfully remapped my internal state, so the gates are working a lot more efficiently now."

Sophia's expression softened as she looked at Sal with concern in her eyes. "Are you okay? Moving gates can be excruciating, especially the first time you do it."

Sal gave her a gentle smile and a nod. "Yeah, I'm better now." He waved his hand as if it were nothing. "I never want to experience it again, though. Unless we install a bathroom in the workshop where nobody can hear me scream."

Sophia's face broke into a smile. "I used to wear a bib for whenever I started spitting up blood. Saved countless outfits that way."

Petro looked between them as though they were crazy. "Okay, I'm not liking this trauma bonding. Can we get back to beating up our son, please?" He stepped to one side and gestured at the open space on the floor. "Soph, I'll leave him in your tender care."

"What have you taught him so far?" Sophia asked Petro as she moved opposite Sal with an easygoing smile. She moved seamlessly into an attacking stance, her arms raised protectively in front of her, guarding her face.

"Just a couple of kicks and the Silverson Sweep." Petro looked over at Sal, as though seeking confirmation that he had actually taught those things.

Sal nodded in agreement. He had spent the entire morning and afternoon with his father, practicing the initial kick, and then moving on to the Silverson Sweep. It was a full-rotation kick that could be executed with a jump, or by standing and pivoting around on a single foot. Compared to the initial kick he learned, the sweep was a far more challenging maneuver. There were so many moving parts, but Perfect was once again an excellent assist in getting it right. Sal had been grateful that his body was still able to execute the leecher kick flawlessly. It gave him a slight hope that he'd be able to build up a catalogue of the Silverson Arts before heading back to Quest Academy.

During the afternoon, Sal had gone out for lunch with both his parents, and it was thankfully nowhere near as tense as he had expected. His mother had been a little on guard with him at first, but slowly eased into their usual banter. Petro had already told him that Sophia would be joining them for the Silverson training, but Sal made a point to ask her for her help. It was definitely the right call, as his mother practically lit up at the suggestion and started fussing about getting her old sparring gear out of storage.

And now, she stood in front of him with an outfit that had been restored to look brand-new. When Sal saw her stance and guard, he had trouble believing that this was his mother.

"You have that Perfect ability thing active, yeah?" Sophia asked suddenly.

"I do, but it only really helps with learn—" Sal was cut off by the sudden disappearance of his mother from view. He barely had time to register that she was beside him, when he saw her fist launch at his face with vicious speed. Before he could even flinch, her gloved hand tapped him gently on the cheek.

"We're going to train your reaction speed, first," Sophia smiled brightly. "I'll keep myself slow enough that you can read my movements."

Sal grinned as he regarded his mother in an entirely new light. "You did that just to show me how fast you are, didn't you?"

Sophia bounced back to her original position, a guilty smile on her face. "Hey, I can't have you thinking that your father is the only fighter in the family." She resumed her stance and gestured for Sal to mirror it. "When I attacked, I went into a position that could be countered by either of the kicks you learned. You should be able to aim for my ankles with the sweep, or take out my ribs with the kick." Her smile was encouraging as she pointed at both areas. "Don't worry about hurting me. Try to connect your attacks."

Sal nodded as he moved into the attacking stance. If he was able to predict her timing, then he'd be able to start his—

Sophia's clenched fist suddenly blocked out Sal's vision as she lightly grazed his nose. "This is what happens when you think too much."

Sal just stared at her in disbelief. "That was even faster…"

"Your mother is a sore loser." Petro chuckled from the side. "There's no way she'd slow down for you to get a hit in."

Sophia grinned as she got back into position. "Come on, am I not allowed to tease my own son a little?" She pressed both her palms together and gave Sal a small bow. "Okay, I promise…I'll go slower this time."

"Bullshit." Petro laughed. "Sal, just throw a punch and hope for the best."

Sal's mind was in overdrive as he carefully watched his mother. He had been paying attention to her, but he couldn't see her move. *What had he missed?* Looking down at her knees and feet, he guessed that they would be the first indicator of an incoming attack. When he saw the heel of her left foot rising, Sal immediately started the Silverson Sweep. It covered a wide area, and was his best chance of catching her.

"An attempt was made." Petro sighed as he gave Sal a thumbs-up gesture.

Sal couldn't process how it had happened. He had reacted as fast as humanly possible…so how was his mother's fist in front of his nose again?

"So, now that I have your attention," Sophia started, smiling as she withdrew her fist. "I can start teaching you."

Sal just stared at her numbly. "How can you move that fast? I saw your foot move but there was nothing I could do."

Sophia shook her head as though he were misunderstanding something. "You're never going to win against a Body Manipulator when it comes to speed and strength. Essence infuses every fiber of our bodies, so we've got a physical advantage from the moment we're born. While I'm not specialized in enhancing my reaction speed or cognitive functions, I can still outpace someone with a non-movement or non-mimicry ability."

Sal frowned as he looked between his mother and father. "So, is this just a lesson to tell me there's no point in attacking someone stronger than me?"

"Nope," Sophia said. "It's a lesson to show you that being reactive won't work against a stronger opponent."

Petro nodded in agreement as he folded his arms. "The Silverson Arts were developed by weak people, so they could fight the strong. Controlling the flow of battle is key, and you'll never do that by standing still."

"So…what? I just run at them and hope for the best?" Sal laughed nervously. "I don't think I'd be able to hit you, even if I attacked."

"Try." Sophia got into stance again. "Take the initiative and make me react. That's how you start the flow of combat, Sal. If I need to counterattack, I'm already prioritizing defense. That singular moment could be all you need to take me down. It's a moment you don't earn by giving your opponent a starting advantage."

Sal got into his stance again and readied himself. Rather than planning his attack, he rushed forward and launched straight into the Silverson Sweep. To his surprise, his mother didn't move from her position and instead hopped up into the air to avoid his leg.

"Now, I'm off-balance. How do you move onto the next phase of attack?" Sophia landed on the wooden floor and gestured at Sal. "Don't move from that position while you're thinking. We're going to slowly go through each phase of attack, then put it all together in a sequence."

Sal kept himself in a lowered crouch, wondering what possible move he could do with his limited experience. *Were they really going to slow-fight, one move at a time?* He looked at his mother's expression and saw that she was resolute.

"Show me what you've got." Sophia grinned as she gestured with her upturned palm and fingers, inviting him to attack her.

CHAPTER 73: ALL SIGHT

Sal's two feet slid backward across the wooden floor, while he fought his instinct to fall over. Directly in front of him was his mother, her leg at full extension. She held it in that pose like an invitation, and Sal was happy to take it. Pushing off against the floor once more, Sal launched himself to her left, twisting his torso to allow him to aim a kick at her head.

"Nice!" Sophia congratulated him as she ducked under the attack before launching the Silverson Sweep at Sal's anchored leg.

Sal put his hand to the ground and tried twisting his body into a sort of cartwheel. The momentum of his kick carried over and his anchored leg was no longer his weak point. All his instincts screamed at him to just fall and admit the loss, but his parents had warned him that he needed to overcome those intrusive thoughts. Demons wouldn't praise his attempts, or give him a participation trophy. If he wanted to survive with his body as a weapon, then he needed to sharpen himself and train until the hesitation was gone.

"Behind you," Petro announced as he launched forward with an incredibly obvious punch. He drew it back far enough to give Sal plenty of time to react.

Sal's cartwheel was more like a flailing tumble of limbs, but he managed to get back into a guarded stance, keeping both of his parents in plain sight in front of him. His father's punch hit the empty space that he had just occupied, and Sal was grateful that they were still going easy on him. It had been like this for hours, with endless sparring and the tempo being increased gradually so that he could adapt to it. Perfect was keeping his muscles and breathing in check, and none of the attacks were actually designed to hurt him. Those two factors had allowed Sal to genuinely try his best to evade and counterattack his parents. Each punch and kick had been perfected by his weave. What he was really training was mindset and intuition.

Sophia suddenly leaped upward, her right leg spinning in the air with a kick aimed at his left shoulder.

Sal brought his guarded arms up to block the attack. He was wary of his father, and didn't want to leave himself open…but when his mother's kick bounced off his arms, he saw an opportunity for a counter. Just like he had done with the obsidian hulker, Sal brought his right fist back while extending his left hand forward to keep the distance between them. With another glance to ensure his father wasn't attacking, Sal threw a fast jab at his mother's face.

Sophia's hand materialized in front of his fist and caught it effortlessly. She grinned at him broadly. "Excellent instinct!" She let go of his hand and took a few steps backward, letting out a small laugh. "I won't deduct points for that punch. Keep using the Silverson Arts so you can blend the movements together. You're doing a fantastic job so far."

Sal exhaled slowly and gave her a slight nod before bringing his hands back up in a guarded position. "Thanks. When are you going to teach me the combination stuff?"

Petro smiled as he stepped into view. "You're already learning it. It'll start making sense when you put it into practice."

Sal let out a sigh and shook his head. "Okay, I'm ready when you are."

Sophia looked at Petro, smiling. "Come on, why don't we show him? We'll do a practice spar. I'm guessing you've already memorized the movements?"

Petro chuckled as he slid across the floor to stand in front of his wife. "I'm not blind yet."

Sophia glanced at Sal and gestured for him to step back a bit. "We'll show you the fight again. First with your movements, and then with the proper combination."

"Watch carefully with this." Petro smiled as he threw something from his pocket in Sal's direction.

Sal caught it and recognized it as the monocle he created for his father. "Why do you want me to watch you with this? Won't All Sight just show me an analysis of your body?" He was confused what his father wanted him to see.

"Cover your other eye and watch the fight through the monocle." Petro turned his attention to Sophia. "Let's show him a proper spar first, and then we can recreate his one."

Sophia gave her husband a dubious look. "What are you up to?"

Petro just smiled as he glanced at Sal, as if checking to see whether he was wearing the monocle. He made a gesture with his hand, imitating the action of putting it onto his eye.

Sal did as he was told and covered his right eye with the monocle. "Are you happy?" Sal started as the black lens flared to life, coating the entire room in darkness, with the exception of his parents, who were bathed in a white light. Sal brought a hand up to cover his left eye, so he could appreciate the sensation that much better. "There's no color?" he asked awkwardly, not sure whether he had activated it wrong.

"Perfect," Petro said with a satisfied sigh. "Now, darling…will you go easy on me?" He smiled at Sophia, who was already cracking her knuckles.

Sal watched as his mother's ethereal form twitched. He could see almost indistinct white vapors streaming from her legs, flowing as if they were part of a current. Then, faster than he could have anticipated, her entire leg swung up from the ground at a dizzying speed, flowing in phases as she initiated her attack. Sal could scarcely believe it. All Sight was showing him more than a dozen stages of his mother's attack, with each movement represented by the vapors that followed her form. It was like an innate understanding of how she moved. Fast, powerful, and precise: those were the best words to describe her fighting pattern…and yet…she wasn't landing a single attack.

Petro's arms snapped up to block the first kick, his body weaving as he evaded the punch, spinning kick, sweep…everything! His poise and form were like an unbreakable fortress, with small movements that disabled each of Sophia's attacks. Sal could see his small changes in stance, predicting his mother's movements, and positioning himself to stop every one of them. It was like he was watching the ultimate counterattacker, fighting against a ridiculously strong opponent.

By the time Sal realized he was holding his breath, there were nearly forty afterimages of his mother's body, all in sequence, showing the full pattern of her attack. All the images showed a comprehensive form of how she linked each attack into the next one. It was like a style guide for the Silverson Arts, and Sal couldn't help but be impressed. Each wide kick created space, the grapples threatened to lock movements, and the punches were for dealing damage. Yet, each one of them looked to be incredibly vicious.

On the other hand, his father's movements were far more frightening. There was only a single body. The afterimages were all of him in a central location…but there were close to a hundred spectral hands and feet. They seemed to blossom out of his body to represent all the negation he had been doing. Every time his mother went for an attack, it was repelled by the slightest of movements from his father. It was like a battle between bloodlust and efficiency…and it was impossible to tell who was winning. You had the quietly confident form of Petro, who was blocking and negating anything that came toward him, and the powerful attacks of Sophia that were delivered like a barrage.

"Changing tempo," Petro announced as he moved forward.

Sophia's hands came up in a guard instantly, her grinning face peeking through her wrapped fists. "Bring it."

Sal's jaw dropped as he watched his father land the sickest kick he had ever seen. He had gone from defending to attacking, and Sal was not prepared. Maybe it was because his father shared his height, or maybe it was because of his posture, but every single kick had terrifying range. Sal watched as the vapors shifted to show Petro's subtle movements, and Sal was amazed to see that they were far more controlled than his mother's. *Was it because he was a part of the Silverson family?* His technique for each of the attacks was perfect, deliberate, and devastating. He had gone from being an unbreakable fortress of defense to being a calculated onslaught.

Each technique that Sal had been taught was on display. The effectiveness was ridiculously high, and they flowed seamlessly into each other like a dance. Petro's feet glided around the wooden battlefield, giving him multiple windows of opportunity to launch attacks. Sal could see how his movements forced his mother to defend two areas at once, and his father always picked the one she couldn't stop. It led to a frantic back-and-forth where his mother needed to prioritize her speed and evasion to make up for the attacks she couldn't block.

Then, just when Sal thought it couldn't get any better, his father slid across the floor, appearing right in front of his mother, catching her in a grapple.

"Ah, you bastard!" Sophia laughed as she was entrapped.

Petro grinned as he pulled her right arm, hooked his shoulder into her armpit, and turned his body to throw her across the room. His height, coupled with her small frame, resulted in Sophia flying through the air with a delighted laugh. She landed on her feet, grinning as though daring him to try that again.

"Whoa…" Sal breathed as he looked at the two of them in utter disbelief. "That was a lot better than I expected."

Petro nodded with a grimace as he sat on the floor. "Hooo…that takes it out of you. I think a small break is in order."

Sophia watched him for a moment before she took a knee on the floor. "I'm only stopping because you're tired," she said before sitting down fully. "Will we call it a draw?"

Petro nodded as he pulled a handkerchief from his pocket to dab at his brow. "We've gotten so out of shape."

Sophia chuckled as she shook her head. "We? I could have kept going." She waved over at Sal, smiling. "So…what do you think?"

Sal was completely lost for words as he looked at the two of them. "Are you sure I'm your son?"

A snort was Sophia's initial response. "You were a big baby. I vividly remember giving birth to you." She gestured over at Petro. "And you have his genetics. You're going to have a monstrous kicking capability when he's done with you."

"Oh, but if only he had someone's stubbornness," Petro countered, with a meaningful look aimed at his wife.

Sal smiled as he looked between them. "If you say so, but I don't really foresee myself getting to your level. Were you using your abilities?" He looked at his father specifically, wondering whether he was damaging his eyes using All Sight for the fight.

Petro shook his head. "Nope. I don't need to when I'm fighting against your mother. We know each other's patterns by heart."

"And he always goes for the throw when he's tired," Sophia added, as though it were a relevant tidbit of context. She let out a pained sigh as she got to her feet, rotating her shoulder as if to alleviate some of the tension in it. "I think I'm done for the day. What about you two?"

Petro nodded as he looked over at Sal. "Sorry, kiddo. No more sparring from us today, but I'll walk you through some of the stances and movements before we wrap up."

Sophia gingerly walked across the floor, flinching slightly as she moved her right leg. "We're getting takeout tonight. You're more than welcome to join us, if you want?"

Sal shook his head, smiling. "As much as I'd love to hear all the stories about you guys fighting demons, I'll be staying in the workshop tonight. I haven't Crafted in a few days and I've got stuff to work on before I go back to Quest Academy."

Petro smiled and offered a shrug. "Of course. And if you make a few too many things, just let us know. We've got an auction coming up in a few days…and I've got a feeling that it'll be packed after our last one."

"Petro." Sophia scolded her husband. She turned her attention to Sal. "Just make whatever you want, and don't worry about the auction."

Petro pointed at Sal and gave Sophia a look of mock disbelief. "Hey, I have an understanding with my son. I teach him how to fight demons, and he gives me nice things to sell at the auction!"

Sophia let out an exasperated sigh. "We're training tomorrow. Same time." She gave Sal a pointed look. "If you want to see continuous improvement, you'll need to put in the effort."

"She means to say, don't stay up all night Crafting," Petro added as he stood up with a pained growl. "Because we'll be dragging you out of that bed if needs be."

Sal laughed as he moved over to his father to hand back the monocle. "I'll see you tomorrow then." He watched as his father pocketed the monocle. "All Sight is a pretty cool ability, by the way."

Petro clapped his two hands onto Sal's shoulders. "And someday, when we're sure that you won't go blind from it, I'll teach you how to use it properly."

CHAPTER 74: REQUEST

"Is that the last of it, George?" Sal asked from the balcony railing. He could see George patting the last of the boxes that had been in storage. Each of them branded with the lettering for Quest Academy.

"All that I could see in there. There's also a nice-looking box that Petro said was yours." George spoke as he lifted a long and slender box into the air. "Look familiar?"

Sal gave him a thumbs-up gesture. "That's some feathers that Upgrade's brother got for me. I put them with the rest of the tower materials. Thanks for reminding me."

"All good. Just give me a call if you need help moving anything else!" George said before he spied some of the empty containers at the side of the platform. "You need me to flatpack these and get them out of the way?"

Sal shook his head. "No need, George. I'll take care of them." They had been the latest sacrifice to the Arkwright. Three entire containers' worth of obsidian glass, and prowler fangs, cores, claws, and bone. All of it offered to the Arkwright in the hopes of furthering the materials research. Sal had spent hours stacking the loading tray, so he was now a bit of an expert when it came to organizing materials.

"Okay then, I'll see you later." George hobbled off toward the stairs, waving as he went.

Sal waved back before turning to look at the Arkwright. After he had returned from the sparring with his parents, he had started to fill the Arkwright with all the materials from storage. It was funny, because only a few days ago he had been nervous about the expense of fueling the Arkwright, but now he was literally throwing in whatever he could find. There was a very good reason for that change in perspective.

New Materials Registered:
- Abyssal Steel (Metal)
- Storm Steel (Metal)
- Starlight Steel (Metal)
- Shadow Glass (Material)
- Siphonstone (Material)
- Veilstone (Material)
- Venomstone (Material)
- Wraithstone (Material)
- Nightshade Leather (Fabric)
- Bloodshade Leather (Fabric)

Material Breakthroughs:
- Fragment Infusions
  - Obsidian Glass = Shadow Glass = Veilstone
  - Leecher Core = Siphonstone = Venomstone
  - Prowler Hide = Nightshade Leather
  - Scuttler Chitin = Abyssal Steel
- Research has become available

- Enhanced Veilstone
- Enhanced Venomstone (Suggested)

Sal couldn't help but smile at the research results. The huge donation from Fabi had seemingly helped the Arkwright create almost a dozen new materials. Loads of materials still hadn't been factored into the results and were in the storage area, waiting to be used. Although there was definitely enough for him to start reworking the design of the Vendetta Macclemark set, Sal's curiosity was piqued by the "Suggested" research of the enhanced venomstone. Apparently, when he had locked in the requirements for the Vendetta Macclemark, the Arkwright had taken that request literally.

Blight Core (Enhanced Venomstone):
- Synthetic Combination
  - Leecher Core, Siphonstone, Venomstone
  - Estimated Quality
    - 30% Chance to produce Epic Grade
    - 70% Chance to produce Legendary Grade
  - Ability Synthesis
    - Subsume (Blight Core), Legendary Grade
    - Assimilation (Venomstone), Epic Grade
    - Devour (Siphonstone), Unique Grade
    - Siphon (Leecher Core), Rare Grade

Right now, the venomstone was enough to ensure that he could get the Assimilate ability onto the next iteration of the Vendetta Macclemark. The fun part was that an even stronger ability had appeared as an option for him to research. Sal wasn't going to fall into the trap of constantly iterating on the same piece of gear. Well, he didn't want to. It might happen, but he was trying his best to keep his head on straight and focus on the main goal.

That said, he was unnaturally happy with their decision to incorporate the dungeon fragment into the Arkwright. Its demonic essence was like a guiding purple light for the materials being researched, and he could see the reports highlighting the influence of the fragment in all the synthesis results.

He doubted he would have been able to do this without all the leecher cores that Fabi had gifted him from their run in the dungeon. If he wanted to get enough cores to fuel the research, then he'd need to do more runs with her. A lot more. The only problem was that he didn't have any equipment, considering he had pretty much donated everything to the Arkwright. He could theoretically just wear the existing Strategist's Dominion suit, but it was woefully unoptimized for what he needed. Even with his new gates, he doubted that it would last him for more than a couple of dungeons, and he didn't want to drag Fabi all the way to the dungeon site just for an hour or so.

Sal frowned as he looked over the railing. They had taken out a lot of leechers in the tower trial. *Was there maybe a few cores mixed in with the rest of the loot?* He was pretty sure that he had used them already; otherwise, he wouldn't have needed to take apart his coffee machine to get the Arkwright operational. With a sigh, Sal plucked his tablet from his pocket and checked his messages.

Salvatore: Hey Fabi, would you be able to take me to a few leecher dungeons? I need a lot of leecher cores for a project.

He stared at his tablet for a few seconds, wondering whether he was being an idiot. A few moments of deliberation passed before he decided there would be no harm in trying.

Salvatore: Barry, want to do a leecher dungeon with me? I need a lot of leecher cores for a project, but I'm lacking the equipment to do it solo.

With the two messages sent, Sal placed it on the workbench and busied himself with stacking the loading bay with the new delivery of obsidian glass and other materials. Sal didn't even bother to look at the feathers. As a material, he guessed they were high value, but it would be worth more for the material research by donating them to the Arkwright. Ever since he donated the revolver and uniform, he had become desensitized to the sacrificing of materials and equipment. A few hours passed with Sal alternating between cleaning, packing up the empty boxes, and loading the Arkwright. In that time, he didn't get a reply from either Fabi or Barry.

Sal sat down at his workbench and looked at his tablet in confusion. He had thought they'd get back to him by now, but there was still nothing. Sal didn't really know what to do with himself. Going to the messages, he selected the call option. A part of him couldn't believe what he was doing, and he guessed that he was going to be ridiculed for even suggesting it.

"Sal?" Petro answered the call immediately. "Is everything okay?"

"Yeah, Dad. Everything is fine," Sal answered as he started to laugh. "Eh…you can totally say no to this. I know you're likely tired from the sparring earlier."

"I'm all good. What's the issue? Need help with moving some stuff again?" Petro ventured a guess.

"Actually…" Sal began, still smiling at how ridiculous this was. "I was wondering if you'd take me to a dungeon? I need leecher cores for a project I'm working on."

The call went silent for a few moments, before Petro's voice came back. "Did your mother put you up to this?"

"What? No," Sal answered in confusion, not sure how his father got that idea.

"Okay, I'll be out front in ten minutes," Petro answered in a matter-of-fact tone. "Also, you don't need to bring any equipment with you. I have that covered."

Sal stared at the tablet in front of him. "You have it covered?" He just shook his head and laughed in disbelief. "Okay, I won't bring anything. See you outside."

"Good man. Be there in a few." Petro signed off before hanging up the call.

Sal sat numbly in his chair, wondering what his father could have possibly meant by having equipment covered. *Was he taking something from the upcoming auction? Or was it some old-school equipment from their time in the Silverson Group?* An involuntary shudder crossed his shoulders as he came to terms with what he had just done. He was not only asking to go to a dungeon, but he was going to go with his father? Sal smiled as he stood, moving over to the Arkwright.

"I'll be back soon with some fresh leecher cores for you," he said jokingly to the machine as he opened the research section for the blight core. "So, you better work hard on making it a damned Legendary-grade material."

Sal moved back to the workbench, where he pocketed his tablet. He then went into the bedroom area to pick up a light jacket from the railing. When he zipped it up, he put his hands in his pockets and made his way to the front of the auction house. He already knew that his father said ten minutes, but he was much likelier to be there in five. The man hated being late.

A few of the staff waved him off and wished him a pleasant evening, and he thanked them before pushing through the glass door that led to the cool evening air. Just as he had predicted, his father stood there with a black duffel bag resting at his feet.

"Is that the equipment?" Sal asked, moving straight to the bag.

Petro's hand came up to stop him. "Ah, not until we get into the dungeon." He smiled as he said it, but was insistent.

Sal looked at him in confusion, and was about to say something when a private car descended from the sky to land on the other side of the street. "Wait…you got a private car?"

Petro grinned. "Not every day that my son asks me to run a dungeon with him. Let's just say I splurged a little?" He picked up the duffel bag and slung it over his shoulder. "Are you okay with that jacket getting covered in leecher ooze? You're going to be getting up close and personal with the little bastards."

Sal blinked as he looked at his jacket. "Yeah, I guess it's fine. I can Restore it later."

"Then let's get a move on." Petro walked toward the private car. "We can't have anyone seeing what's in the bag, so don't reference it when we get in the car, okay?"

Sal nodded in understanding as he jogged around to the other side of the sleek black car. It was a definite improvement from Fabi's car, but it wasn't anywhere near as luxurious as the one that had been sent from the Hunter Bureau. The door opened before he could even reach for the handle, revealing a simplistic, yet pleasant interior. It looked like a faux leather was used for the upholstery, in a beige color that contrasted sharply with the black exterior. Sal slid into the seat and made sure to lean away from the door as it closed automatically beside him. His father slid in beside him and placed the bag under the small table in front of them. It was a two-seater passenger car, with a driver up front behind a black-tinted visor. All sorts of stickers decorated the screen, with many of them being licenses and accreditations for the taxi service.

"How many did you want to do?" Petro asked as he settled into the seat, sitting up to straighten his own jacket. "Do you have a quota for the cores, or are you thinking of just getting as many as possible?"

Sal shrugged. "Honestly, as many as possible would be great. Hadn't really thought about it." He chuckled. "Probably because I thought you'd say no."

Petro grinned as he gave Sal a slight nudge with his elbow. "I was certain your mother put you up to it. I was talking to her last week about taking you to a dungeon, but she told me to wait."

Sal blinked in surprise. "You wanted to take me?"

Petro nodded, smiling warmly. "Of course. Ever since we had our little heart-to-heart, I wanted to teach you how to fight in an actual dungeon. We'd dispel all your fears, and show you that the demons aren't worth shit."

"Ah, so you thought Mom asked me to call you?" Sal asked, finally understanding what he had meant.

"Yeah, and she made me promise that I wouldn't bring it up with you. That you'd come to us when you were ready. Those were her words…but I'll be honest, I didn't expect it to be this quick. I'm proud of you, Sal." Petro smiled as he tapped against the table excitedly. "We're going to make it fun. Trust me."

"I trust you." Sal smiled. "Just as long as we don't have to play catch with the leechers, it's all good."

Petro gave him a look of mock surprise. "Now…that's an excellent idea."

Sal looked out the window, before a frown started to appear on his face. "Wait…this isn't the way, is it?" He had been to the Evergreen Dungeon with Chatfield and Upgrade, and the site he went to with Fabi was in the same direction. A part of him assumed that all the low-level leecher dungeons were in the same location.

"I called in a favor. We're going to have a few dungeons all to ourselves." Petro grinned. "It'll be better because you won't have to line up or answer a thousand questions from the Hunter Bureau."

Sal just stared at him. "You got a private car…and arranged a private dungeon, all in five minutes?"

Petro shrugged, smirking. "A few organizations have been dying to do me a favor for years, and this is one of the first times I've ever asked for their help."

"Wouldn't it be better to hold onto that for something worthwhile?" Sal asked in disbelief, wondering why his father would waste a favor with the guilds for something trivial like this.

Petro smiled warmly at Sal. "You'll understand when you're a father."

CHAPTER 75: DRAGOON

When Sal got out of the car, he had to take a moment to compose himself. The dungeon sites he had gone to before had been small areas that were maintained by the Hunter Bureau. They had vendor areas that were similar to the pop-up stalls that the Scavenger Network used. If Sal had to guess, the previous dungeon sites only ever had about a hundred people milling around, and that was at peak hours.

What was in front of him now, though…was an entirely different scenario. A metal wall, covered in countless scars, stood imposingly in front of them. Automated turrets were mounted at intervals on the top of the wall, and Sal could see the blue shimmer of light that surrounded everything within. It was a safe zone, with additional barriers…but the question remained—were the barriers there to keep things out, or to keep them in?

"We'll get changed inside the dungeon," Petro remarked as he circled the car and overtook Sal, a playful smile on his face. "They keep making these walls higher."

Sal followed him while looking in every direction, trying to take in as much as possible. By his best estimate, they were in Remembrance…an area that had been absolutely ravaged by the demonic outbreak decades ago. Everything looked very militaristic in style, and the guards on the towers all wore a matching uniform. They didn't look like they were a part of the Hunter Bureau, or even the Guilds Association.

"Identification, gentlemen," a voice requested from a sliding grate at the center of the wall. "Pass them through here." A small drawer pushed out from the metal wall.

It looked archaic by design, and now that Sal was close to the metal structure, he could see that it was a mass of patched-up scrap metal, hastily fused together. It was a wonder that the drawer actually moved with how much debris surrounded it. Sal couldn't help but wonder how much essence it would take to refine the entire wall into something more durable, without all the impurities. He was instantly reminded of the fortress he had created in the excursion, and that thought then led to his own curiosity on whether the structure survived the following months.

Petro slid a black card into the drawer, and waited patiently. His eyes were locked onto the grate that emitted the voice.

"Both of them. I need to see your companion's identification, too," the voice requested, this time with a hint of impatience.

Sal reached into his own pocket to retrieve his Hunter Bureau card, but his father stopped him. Sal looked at his dad in confusion.

"I'm here alone," Petro insisted as he pushed the drawer shut. "You can check my details. I was informed that I wouldn't be held up when I arrived." He readjusted the duffel bag over his shoulder and stared at the grate, as though daring them to hold him up any longer.

"A moment, please." The voice spoke, this time without the impatience, but holding a hint of curiosity.

"Take your time." Petro looked at Sal, giving him a playful wink.

Sal was confused as to what was happening. *Why was his father not letting him show his Hunter Bureau card? Were the people here not affiliated with them?* Rather than voicing any of his questions, he just remained quiet and let things play out to see what would happen. Although there was a whole lot of mystery surrounding the Silverson Group, Sal trusted his father. He wasn't the type of person who would walk into a trap.

The door suddenly opened inward with an ear-piercing screech of metal grinding against metal. Sal winced as he turned his head to endure the noise, but in doing so, he noticed something interesting. The thickness of the roughshod wall was revealed, and the entire scrap metal exterior was actually a facade. It was only in the briefest of moments that he could see it, but Sal was certain that the two-foot-thick wall was made entirely of essence-infused metal, save for the flimsy coating that looked desperate.

"Not what you were expecting?" Petro smiled, seemingly reading Sal's mind. "You're in for a few more surprises."

Before Sal could so much as utter a response, a booming voice heralded their arrival into the compound.

"Petro Argento! As I live and breathe!" A uniformed man, who looked more like an officer than a soldier, appeared. His dark-green beret had seen better days, and fragments of trimmed white hair were scarcely visible over his ears. Despite his age, he looked like an absolute monster of a man, with a muscular physique and imposing presence. A litter of small medals had been fused onto a scarred black breastplate, that hung over a set of black combat trousers. At his side was what looked like a ceremonial sword, but Sal could tell, even at a distance, that it was at least Rare grade.

"You get bigger every time I see you." Petro grinned as he moved forward to clasp hands with the burly man. "Sal, this is Luke. He's an old friend of the family." Petro glanced over in Sal's direction to introduce him.

Luke's eyes widened as he looked in Sal's direction. "Salvatore?" He let out a bark of laughter before releasing Petro's grip. "And you're telling me that I'm the one getting big! Look at him!" He was over in an instant, and before Sal could react, Luke's bearlike hands clasped him at the shoulders. "Let me get a good look at you."

"We're here to do some dungeons. The boy has taken a shine to Crafting, and needs to get some leecher cores," Petro explained as he looked around the encampment. "You've been trying to drag me out here for years, so I thought I'd give you a call."

Luke continued to look at Sal with a broad smile on his face. "A Crafter? With that many essence gates?" He chuckled before shooting a glance in Petro's direction. "I won't pry. But if it's leecher cores you're looking for, we could just sell them to you at a reduced price. The place is practically overflowing with them." Luke released his hold on Sal's shoulders and moved a few paces away to give him space to breathe.

Petro shook his head. "I also want to show him around a dungeon."

Luke nodded in understanding. "Don't suppose you'd teach a few of my cadets while you're at it?" He chuckled at his own joke, looking over at the uniformed men standing at attention. "Their discipline is good, but not a lick of initiative in the lot of them. Fairly sure you could beat those instincts into them."

As if to test his theory, Luke's voice thundered across the encampment. "I asked if any of you have initiative?!"

"NO, SIR!" came back instantly in a collective cacophony.

Luke just sighed as he looked at Petro. "See what I'm dealing with?"

"I have full faith that you'll turn them into killing machines in no time," Petro responded encouragingly. "Sal is just back from his first semester at Quest Academy. Wanted to show him the ropes so he doesn't fall behind his friends."

Luke's expression darkened ever so slightly. "You know Robert is pulling the strings there, right?" He glanced at Sal, as though weighing his next words. "A Crafter will get chewed up by the Hero system, and they'll end up indentured to whoever picks up the pieces. If you want to set him up for a career, bring him into the cadets and we'll have him trained up as a Dragoon in no time. Hell, he'd likely have his own mount within a year!"

Luke gave Sal another appraising look, as though to clarify his estimate. With a curt nod and a broad smile, he turned his attention back to Petro. "A single year. I'm telling you, he'll have way more opportunities with us, and he wouldn't be under Robert's thumb."

Petro smiled again, but his voice was firm. "I appreciate the concern, Luke. Sal is fairly hell-bent on being a Crafter, so we're just here to run a few dungeons, and then we'll be out of your hair."

Luke grimaced before letting out a sigh. "I've cleared you for dungeons 1-A to 1-E, but if you need to up the level, just let me know and we can switch around the training teams. I'd have no issues in getting you into 3-A, 3-B, or 3-D. There's a group stuck on 3-C, and I don't want to pull them out prematurely."

Petro nodded in understanding. "Got it. We should be fine with the 1's for now, but if we get a taste for prowler, you'll be the first to know."

Luke smiled as he looked at Sal again. "I worked with your father in another life. Listen to everything he says in that dungeon and you'll do great!"

"I'll do my best, thank you," Sal answered as he looked at his father, wondering whether he would get more context when they entered the dungeon. It was his first time hearing about Dragoons, and he was curious.

Luke turned on his heel and walked toward all the man-made dungeon entrances at the back of the encampment. Close to thirty turrets were mounted at varying heights on the walls, towers, and building roofs, all aimed at the dungeon entrances. Staggered trenches were dug out, with wooden boards creating a maze-like passage to each of the entrances. An incredibly large floodlight constantly bathed a set of dungeons with a bright light, and Sal instinctively knew it contained prowlers.

"Okay, there's no time limit for you guys. You're more than welcome to use our canteen, and we can have beds made up for you if it gets too late." Luke pointed at each building as he spoke. "We've got a medical team on standby, too. You can use the armory if you wish, but unfortunately, we'll only be able to give you the scraps. They're maintained well enough, but I'd recommend using your own gear if possible."

"This will most likely be a flying visit," Petro answered. "We'll probably only have time to finish up a few of them."

Luke looked over his shoulder in confusion. "I thought you said you wanted to teach him about dungeons? You can't just do one or two. Bring him back here until you do the full circuit, and we can give him one of these." He gestured at the beret on his head, smirking. "What do you think, Salvatore? Would you like to try your hand at being a trainee cadet?"

Sal smiled as he shook his head. "I appreciate the offer, but I don't think it's the right path for me."

"Suit yourself." Luke walked across the wooden boards that lined the trenches. "It's all yours." He gestured at the stone steps that seemingly descended into darkness. "There's lamps installed, but the fuckers keep breaking them. Bioluminescence should give you a decent bit of light, but I'd suggest taking your own with you."

Petro unslung his duffel bag and gave it a meaningful shake. "Got everything we need right here. Appreciate you taking us personally, Luke."

"Don't mention it," Luke responded as he stood to one side. "It goes without saying, but take care of yourself in there."

Petro smiled in response. "Thanks. Let's go, Sal."

Sal gave Luke a passing nod as he followed his father down the steps of the man-made entrance. The darkness seemed to coagulate into an ominous pool that not even the surrounding lights could penetrate. Yet, his father moved through it like it was absolutely nothing. The whole experience was far removed from his time at the other dungeon sites. They had barriers and everything set up, but here…things were just in the open. It was like they were inviting the demons to ambush and attack them.

Petro whistled to himself as he reached the base of the stairs, and Sal could hear the zipper of the duffel bag being pulled.

"There we go." As soon as the words came from Petro's mouth, the darkness subsided immediately. A shoulder guard was held in Petro's hand and it emitted a powerful glow that pierced through the surrounding gloom. "Hold this for a second." He passed over the shoulder guard before rooting through the duffel bag. "I'm hoping that it fits you, but I guess we'll find out soon enough."

Sal just waited patiently, holding onto the glowing piece of armor. He was curious as to what his father was talking about, but it didn't take him long to have his answer.

Petro withdrew a simple blue shirt from the bag and handed it to Sal. "Take your jacket off and put on that shirt. I need to send a picture to your mother."

Sal did as he was told, trying not to laugh at the ridiculousness of it all. "We're in a dungeon and we're doing a fashion show?"

Petro chuckled as he pulled out two silver gauntlets. Their shine seemed to react with the glowing shoulder guard, and it caused the entire dungeon to be bathed in light, flickering only when the gauntlets shifted in Petro's hands. "Put these on over the blue shirt, and then we'll secure the shoulder guards and kneepads."

Sal did as he was told, fighting the urge to Appraise the gauntlets he had been given. They looked like they were made by an expert craftsman, but there was no essence signature in them. When he placed them on his hands, he was surprised to feel a reassuring padding underneath the metal. It felt snug, like he was wearing a warm glove. The silver contrasted sharply with the deep blue of the shirt, and the kneepads and shoulder guards were silver, too.

"Now, for the final piece of the puzzle." Petro grinned before pulling out a set of wingtip shoes that were seemingly made of pure reflective silver and deep-blue felt. There was black rubber on the soles and the laces were a silver cord. "Put these on and we can get started." He placed them on the floor in front of Sal, practically beaming with pride as he watched Sal get dressed in the new attire. Petro bundled up Sal's jacket and shoes, placing them into the duffel bag, before he took out a tablet from his pocket. "Smile for your Silverson debut!"

Sal faltered at those words, looking down at himself in surprise. "Wait, this is the Silverson uniform?"

Petro smiled as he zipped up the bag and left it at the base of the stairs. "Correct. Those shoes will obliterate any leecher that gets too close, and the gauntlets aren't just for show."

Sal chuckled nervously. "There's not a single drop of essence in any of them, though?"

Petro nodded. "Of course, but they're made of pure silver, so it's even better. They've been treated for years so they won't get infused by essence." He started to walk into the now illuminated dungeon with a relieved sigh. "So, shall we get started?"

Sal just stared at his father as he followed him. "I don't mean to sound ungrateful, because it looks amazing…but are you saying that a decorative metal is better than essence-based equipment?"

Petro blinked as he looked at Sal in confusion. "You're joking…right? Demons are weak to pure silver."

"What?" Sal asked in disbelief, not sure how he was hearing this for the first time.

Petro just stared at him in equal measures of disbelief. "Salvatore, I don't know what's worse." He started to chuckle as he gestured at the silver gauntlets. "That you think the Argento name comes from a decorative metal…or that you've probably been Appraising silver weapons incorrectly for years."

Sal just stared at the gauntlets and shoes. "Like, how weak are they to it?"

Petro smiled as he pointed at a leecher floating in the distance. "Why don't you go and kick that to find out?"

CHAPTER 76: TUTELAGE

"Also, no using the Perfect weave," Petro added as a condition as he walked alongside Sal. "You'll get complacent if you rely on it too much, so treat this entire instance like you've got zero essence at your disposal." He clapped Sal on the back. "But don't worry, I'm here for you every step of the way, so nothing bad will happen."

Sal let the Perfect weave fizzle away in his subconscious as he approached the leecher that was floating slowly in his direction. "Should I go with the Silverson Sweep?" he asked his father, but not tearing his eyes away from the incoming demon.

"That's completely up to you, Sal. Just keep your emotions in check and you'll be fine." Petro took an extra step to the side, as though ensuring that the leecher would prioritize Sal as the target. "If you fall into a frenzy or start panicking, then you'll make mistakes."

"Got it." Sal clenched his fists with the gauntlets. He had killed so many of these little bastards during the tower exercise, but it was different when you weren't fighting at long range. Going up to a leecher, and getting into the range of their tentacles and teeth was something that Sal was loath to do. But his father was with him, and Sal felt safer just from that alone.

Pushing forward, Sal was somewhat surprised at the flexibility of the shoes. He had expected the silver would make them heavy or, at the very least, uncomfortable. Yet, they were just like the gauntlets…reassuringly spongy, which made him feel like he was ready for anything. Sal moved forward, initially intending on a punch, but when he saw the trajectory of the leecher shift to the side, he pivoted his heel and brought his right leg in a full extension up into the air.

"And now the killing blow!" Petro commented from the sidelines as Sal's foot snapped forward to obliterate the leecher.

Sal looked at his outstretched foot in shock. The residue from the leecher sizzled on the toe of his shoe, and the impact of the attack had caused the leecher to literally explode. It had been a simple movement that they had practiced during the first day, but it had the destructive force to cause a leecher to detonate?

"Don't forget to pick up the core. We're just getting started," Petro reminded him as he gestured at the small leecher core rolling away from the melting remains. "I'll keep hold of them so you don't need to worry about filling your pockets."

Sal brought his foot back down to the ground and looked at his father in a mixture of shock and awe. "That was…really easy?"

Petro simply nodded. "Don't get complacent. Repeat the process, and alternate your attacks so you get to practice all of them equally."

Sal took a breath before moving farther into the cave, his shoulder highlighting all the leechers in the surrounding area. "Should I take them one at a time?"

"Oh? Are you thinking of trying a combination attack this early?" Petro asked curiously. "This is the lowest grade of dungeon they have, so if you want to try out your moves…go for it. We'll be a touch more cautious in the next ones."

Sal nodded as he moved forward in pursuit of the next leecher. Four of them were in front of him, and he could see they were all floating at different elevations.

Thankfully, they were also staggered at different points throughout the tunnel so they weren't likely to gang up on him.

A shrill whistle came from behind Sal, and he instantly recognized the pitch as his father. The effect was immediate, and Sal could see the leechers descending from the ceiling of the cave. *Had the noise somehow disoriented them?* Either way, it was good news for Sal as all his targets were now in reach.

The first one he apprehended was met with a quick jab from his right gauntlet, and the resulting explosion was almost euphoric. Sal rotated his body to launch a sweep kick at the next two, and although his shin did bounce off one of them, the toe of his right shoe impacted the second for another well-earned explosion. Sal lashed out with his left hand, fingers extended, and pierced through the third leecher, impaling it and causing it to explode around his wrist.

None of the explosions seemed to harm Sal in any way, and he was bizarrely excited by how easily the gauntlets and shoes were taking them out. Even when he got up close and could see the detail of their teeth bared at him, he was faster than them by a considerable margin. The mobility he had been training, coupled with the strength from Lars's training routine…Sal felt unstoppable. With a smile blossoming on his face, he rushed to the fourth one in view and decided to add a slight flourish with his attack. The spinning jump kick that he had seen from his mother was a bitch to properly execute, but he had done it close to a dozen times with Perfect, so it was etched firmly into his memory.

Sal's body floated through the air like a mock imitation of his opponent, before his foot slapped into the target with dramatic force, causing the leecher to splatter into the cave wall. When Sal landed, he fought to catch his breath, looking back at his father with a wide grin on his face. "What do you think?"

Petro clapped, smiling warmly. "Excellent, but you'll end up winding yourself if you keep up that sort of pace." He reached down to the ground to pick up two of the leecher cores. "Slow things down, make it methodical, and save the flashy movements for your finishers against the final opponent."

Sal nodded as he sucked in more air, fighting to control his thundering heart. "Perfect usually keeps my breathing in check, so I probably went a little overboard."

Petro nodded as he continued to give Sal advice. "Adrenaline is great, but it typically arrives at the cost of judgment. Keep a cool head and you'll be able to take down any opponent." He pointed farther down the tunnel. "I want to see you perform the combinations, alternating between kicks, jabs, and evasive actions."

Sal smiled as he moved toward the next batch of leechers. With the instruction in place, it felt more like a game than a dungeon run. The reassurance of having his father with him was indescribable, and Sal felt like he was able to do so much more just because he had him there. There was also the small factor of him wanting to impress his father with the Silverson Arts.

Ever since he had heard about the Silverson Group, Sal had felt weak. It was previously justifiable for him to avoid combat, because he was just like his parents. He could be proud in his status as a Support, because the two people he admired most and emulated in life were Supports. But…the moment that reality came crashing down, Sal had to reassess everything he thought he knew about the world and the people he looked up to.

Sal came to a halt in front of two leechers that floated menacingly ahead of him. He took a half step back from them to create the distance he needed, before launching into the Silverson Sweep. It was a well-timed and practiced movement, with no room for errors. Sal's foot collided with the first leecher, impaling it and carrying through to the next one, which he ended up bludgeoning with the body of the first. There was practically no resistance, like he was literally kicking cabbages out of midair.

Before he had fully righted himself from the sweep, Sal pushed off toward the third leecher that was a little higher in the air. There was no whistle from his father this time, so Sal had to adapt to the scenario by jumping up high and sending his outstretched hand like a spear at the leecher. The base of the demon was lined with teeth. Sal didn't like the idea of aiming there, but he resolved himself to the attack, and was instantly rewarded with yet another explosion of demonic lettuce.

"Eyes up," Petro warned.

Sal landed and turned immediately to see a leecher slide into view from a crevice in the wall. Without even thinking, Sal backhanded the leecher and resumed his stance, looking around for another threat.

"I thought you'd try to dodge that one." Petro chuckled as he took a knee to retrieve the dropped cores. "But excellent work on your distancing. You really lined them up nicely, and the execution was flawless."

"Thanks, Dad." Sal answered with genuine appreciation as he took a steady breath.

Petro got back to his feet and pointed farther down the tunnel. "Do you want me to jump in while you catch your breath?"

Sal shook his head. "No, I'm good. Thanks for the offer."

"Good man," he answered, pocketing the small cores. "We'll need you to take off the Silverson gear each time we go into a dungeon. Luke is a good guy, but it wouldn't be wise to flaunt the Silverson Group colors here."

Sal leaned against the wall and looked up at the ceiling, focusing on getting his heart rate back to normal. The exertion of jumping around with attacks was draining, but his recovery rate was surprisingly good, even without Perfect in place. "I thought with the way you spoke to Luke that he knew about the Silverson Group? He said you knew each other in a past life?"

Petro chuckled and offered a shrug. "When we first arrived at Silver Sanctuary, we only knew military life. The guilds felt more like clubs, and the Hunter Bureau was like a cult. Luke was one of the last surviving branches of the military that hadn't been disbanded or absorbed into the Hunter Bureau. They operate like a militia, and their territory maintains a neutral stance with the other organizations. Your mother and I did some work with them, giving them a taste of the Silverson strategies that we found useful against the demons on the west coast."

Sal pushed off from the wall, his heart rate back to normal. "And when you said that you called in a favor with a guild?"

Petro shrugged. "Easier to say that than a paramilitary group that actively rejects the status quo. I can guarantee you that our driver has no idea what's behind the wall to this encampment. Luke is particularly careful about who can get in."

"And do they like, live here?" Sal asked in disbelief. The encampment didn't really look that habitable, and the idea of living beside open dungeons wasn't particularly enticing.

Petro shook his head and pointed down the tunnel. "Those leechers are going to be finding nooks and crevices to hide from the light on your shoulder. The longer you delay taking them out, the harder it is to find them." He smiled as he motioned Sal to continue down the tunnel. "And no, this place is more like a boot camp facility. Luke would love if he could foster some cadets with an eye for strategy, but resources only allow him to give them basic training."

Sal continued down the route with his father. He didn't really have an opportunity to link his attacks into a combination as they were too far spread out, but he did learn how to control his breathing as he went from bout to bout. The novelty of the gauntlets and shoes had started to wear off, but Sal still took great satisfaction from the explosions each time he connected a hit. It felt like a reward each time he got a critical hit, and Sal started to aim for the vitals of the leechers to ensure he got an explosion.

"Seriously, I thought you knew about the silver, because you made that gun out of moonsilver," Petro remarked suddenly as they neared the end of the dungeon. "Was it just a coincidence?"

"Yeah, I really had no idea." Sal laughed as he held up the gauntlets. "I don't think it's common knowledge, either. Why aren't people using silver for all the weapons and equipment?"

Petro shrugged. "There are two answers to that. First would be that the material was massively depleted when it was used for bullets a few decades back, but the other... you saw it yourself at the auction house. People will buy something if it sounds menacing. When you have materials called void metal and hellfire titanium, people stop caring about the commodities that served us well for centuries. Remember that damned Doom Scythe? It wasn't even that good."

Sal smiled at the reminder. "So, how many of these do you think we can get finished before we head back home?"

Petro looked off to one side. "Two more if we keep chatting and you take breaks. Four if you're focused...and ten if I help you."

Sal stared at his dad, not really sure whether he was joking. "Want to help?"

Petro thought about it for a moment. "Depends. Do you want to help make some gear for the auction house?"

"Deal," Sal replied instantly. "But only if we manage to clear ten of them."

Petro didn't even flinch as he looked at Sal carefully. "Counter proposal." He raised a hand with all digits outstretched. "We finish up this one, and do four more." He then raised his other hand with a single finger raised. "And then we do a single prowler dungeon. What do you think?"

Sal faltered at those words. Fighting prowlers bare-handed felt like a terrible idea. Rather than succumbing to his emotional response, he instead turned it around as a question. "Do you think I'm ready for that?"

Petro continued to look at Sal carefully. "I know you are."

CHAPTER 77: COMPETENCE

Sal moved like a man possessed. With his father helping him, it had become much more of a challenge to find opponents. The little wagers created by his father weren't even that enticing, but it was the principle of not wanting to lose against his dad. For every leecher he managed to kill, Petro got three…and the gap seemed to be growing wider as they progressed through the dungeon runs.

With no time for excess thought, Sal couldn't afford to be indecisive. He was operating under pure desperation and instinct, lashing out with controlled movements, kicking at anything within range, and going for the jabs with both hands like his life depended on it.

"Oh, I thought I had that one." Petro laughed as he watched Sal bludgeon a leecher to death with his knee. "Plenty more up ahead, though." He sprinted at a ridiculous pace, and Sal had no choice but to burst after him if he had any hope of taking out more targets.

When Petro slowed down, Sal ran straight past him to go farther into the winding path. His best chance of getting confirmed kills was to overtake his father and take care of them before he arrived. In a blur of movement, Sal's limbs cracked against the leechers with incredible force. The sobering moment was when one floated too close to his face, and by sheer instinct, Sal gripped it at both sides and ripped it in half before it could even so much as twitch a tentacle.

Yet, even then, in that crazed moment, he didn't stop as he continued forward with devastating efficiency. His breathing was both labored and controlled, and he knew exactly how much he could push himself from all the previous runs that evening. They had close to a hundred leecher cores stored in the duffel bag, and Sal didn't even care.

"Incoming." Petro appeared in a flash, twisting his body in midair to take out four leechers at once. "You must really be excited to get to the prowlers," he joked as he dusted off his sleeves. "We're definitely ahead of schedule. I didn't anticipate you getting this stubborn." He was clearly goading Sal, and it was absolutely working.

With an exasperated sigh, and a smile on his face, Sal set off farther down the tunnel. They'd retrace their steps to pick up the leecher cores later, but for now, the focus was on killing as many demons as possible. In the first dungeon, Sal had tentatively taken out an evolved. The second and third, he'd confidently taken out a variant. The fourth, he had a Rochelle moment and didn't realize he had killed the boss leecher until a different-colored core dropped from it. Now, on the fifth, Sal was blitzing his way through the tunnels, with his limbs blurring between the attacks. He was a force of nature, and it was one of the most exhilarating moments of his life. There was something so carnal and addictive about confidently taking on a demon. He genuinely hoped he'd get to feel this way against stronger opponents, but a part of him guessed he'd still be overtaken with nerves when facing against prowlers.

"You're overthinking," Petro announced as he sliced past Sal with his hand, taking out the leecher that was just a step out of Sal's reach. "Keep your composure and move forward. Momentum is everything."

Sal nodded in agreement as he dismissed the thoughts of the prowlers. He'd deal with it later. Both he and his father continued their onslaught of the leecher dungeon until the very end where Petro stepped to one side, just like the previous encounters. It was a bittersweet moment, because it meant that Sal was going to take on the final boss of the dungeon. When it was done, they'd be moving onto the prowler dungeon.

"What did I say about overthinking?" Petro asked casually.

"Not to." Sal sighed as he reluctantly moved forward, drawing back his right leg and kicking the variant leecher with the tip of his shoe. Rather than sending the demon flying with the impact, his shoe burned straight through the mass of rock and slime, causing the horrifying construct to convulse in agony as the burning trail quickly spread throughout. Then, for good measure, Sal slammed his foot back downward, cleaving out another chunk of the leecher. "Oh, it's a white one?" Sal remarked as he saw a fist-sized orb thunk against his foot.

Petro moved closer to see what Sal was talking about. "Hmm, looks like a slightly rarer variant of leecher core. We can take a proper look at it later."

"Time for the prowlers?" Sal forced a smile.

Petro shook his head. "No…first we pick up all your leecher cores, then we get changed."

"And then…" Sal asked, already knowing the answer.

Petro grinned. "And then we hunt some prowlers. You should warm up your throat muscles—you're going to be doing a lot of screaming."

Sal's blood went cold at those words. "I'll be screaming?"

Petro nodded, grinning. "Yeah, I told you…they thrive on darkness and quiet. Take out both of those factors, and you're suddenly kicking very confused cats."

"You make it sound so easy," Sal remarked as he picked up the leecher cores that littered the dungeon floor while retracing his steps back to the entrance.

"And you make leecher killing seem easy, Sal," Petro said in a matter-of-fact tone. "A year ago, you would have shit yourself at the sight of one. Give me two weeks, and you'll be laughing at the current version of yourself."

Sal chuckled. "I highly doubt that."

Petro grinned as he joined Sal in the retrieval of the cores. "Perfect. It'll be that much more satisfying when I prove you wrong." He looked over at Sal, and gave him a slight poke in the side. "You've done an amazing job today. I'm incredibly proud of you."

Sal scoffed at that, but couldn't help but smile at the praise. "Like you said, it's just a few leechers."

"Taken out in seconds, using a martial art that you didn't know existed a few weeks ago," Petro clarified. "I'm delighted that you asked me to take you to a dungeon. Genuinely."

"And I'm glad that you're here," Sal admitted as he got to his feet to go farther down the path. "I'm sure Mom would have caused a fuss if we brought her. Can't imagine she'd be on board with the prowler plan."

Petro laughed out loud. "Oh, Sal…I know it's probably too soon to make this joke, but you really don't know your mother. If she were here with us, she'd be pushing for us to go straight to the voiders. It's hard to believe, but I'm the sensible one in our marriage!"

"Calling bullshit on that," Sal remarked instantly, looking over his shoulder at his dad. "You're the sensible one?"

"Okay, sensible is probably the wrong word…but seriously, that woman is more of a demon than anything you'd find in a dungeon," Petro warned playfully with a good-natured chuckle. "Back in the day, she'd launch herself into fights with impossible odds, just to protect the people around her. She was an absolute force of nature."

"You seemed just fine in your spar earlier," Sal countered thoughtfully. "Were you also incredibly badass in your prime?" He couldn't keep the teasing tone from his voice.

"Hardly." Petro smiled. "If Soph used her powers, then it would have been over in less than a heartbeat."

Sal found himself relaxing as he spoke with his father. It was just idle banter as they picked up the cores, but it helped keep his mind off what was to come. His father thought he was ready to fight against prowlers, and although Sal had a few kills of them during the tower trial, they were under the direct supervision of the Hunter Bureau. Fighting one in a dark cave was very different than fighting something chained to a wall or on an open rooftop. Also, Sal had never fought one up close. Everything had always been at range, with the assistance of his equipment. Right now, all he had were some silver gauntlets and shoes. He was the weapon.

"And before I forget, you can use Perfect when we're in the next dungeon," Petro said in an offhand manner, as though it were no big deal.

"Why now, and not before?" Sal asked in surprise.

Petro vaguely waved at the dead leechers. "By using your body and mind, you took care of all of this. You've already shown that you're able to utilize the Silverson Arts, and this whole evening has been an excellent refresher for you on how to apply them in the real world. If you use Perfect with everything you've learned, it'll hopefully help you make some improvements."

Sal was inwardly grateful that he'd at least have the Perfect weave in place. It wasn't going to drastically change anything, but he felt a little safer knowing that it would be supporting his movements and breathing. They continued with their back-and-forth until all the cores were collected and they were back at the entrance to the dungeon.

"Into the duffel bag," Petro announced as he pulled the heavy black bag into view. The bulging at the sides was a testament to how much they had accumulated, and it was far more than Sal had anticipated.

Sal emptied his pockets before looking at his father carefully. "Your turn."

"This again?" Petro asked in mock indignation. "I swear I didn't kill that many." He proceeded to empty all four of his pockets, depositing nearly three times as many cores as Sal had. "See? It's roughly the same amount!" he insisted with a small smile.

Sal rolled his eyes as he took off the gauntlets, shoes, shoulders, and kneepads. He had gotten proficient at changing quickly, even without the help of the Perfect weave. And in a single minute, he was fully dressed and back on his feet.

"Perfect." Petro shouldered the heavy bag, grimacing. "We might need another bag for the next one." He looked at Sal as though debating whether they had enough space.

"It's totally okay if you want us to go home," Sal offered, smiling.

Petro looked at Sal before a wide smile appeared on his face. "We'll borrow a couple of bags from Luke."

***

The first thing that became apparent to Sal was that the prowler dungeons had a completely different layout and vibe compared to the leecher dungeons. Although the leechers thrived in damp environments where they could nest, like subways or sewer systems…the prowlers had seemingly adapted their environment to suit their fighting style. Claw marks covered the walls, which were thankfully bathed in the light of his glowing shoulder, and they revealed a series of carved-out dens that overlooked their path. There were so many footholds that would allow the prowlers to literally stalk them from a higher elevation as they walked along, making it perfect for ambushes.

Without the visor equipped, Sal was reliant on what he could see with his own two eyes and that was quite terrifying. The faint sound of dripping in the distance was the only thing that echoed throughout the whole space. Not being able to see or hear his opponent, and knowing that they were there, did not fill Sal with confidence in this plan.

"Ah, so shall we get started?" Petro asked in a chipper voice. "You have your Perfect weave active, right?"

Sal nodded as he strained to see whether there was movement on the recently illuminated walls. "I can't see them at all, and I can't hear a thing."

"Don't worry about that," Petro replied nonchalantly before raising two fingers to his lips and letting out an ungodly whistle that made Sal shudder involuntarily. "They'll come to us. You hear that padding?"

Sal's ears were still ringing from the whistle, but the sensation was almost immediately cut off as Perfect regulated his hearing back to normal. It was then that he could hear the faint padding in the distance. "Wait, are they charging us?" he asked in a panic. "How many of them?"

Petro stepped forward and brought his arms out wide while watching the darkness in the distance. "Probably around four. I can take three of them and give you one to face. It'll be similar to our leecher score." He smiled before bringing his hands together to clap loudly. Immediately afterward, he let out another shrill whistle, and the effectiveness of it was dramatic.

The first of the prowlers to run from the darkness flinched in the light before the noise of the whistle took effect. Sal watched in an almost grim fascination as the prowler started grinding its face into the rocky ground, as though trying to stop the sound from reaching its ears. Quiet snarls were replaced by growling as more prowlers stood just outside the cutoff point for the light.

Petro casually moved over to the prowler that was writhing around on the ground, seemingly oblivious to the approach. With a swift jab, Petro's unarmed fingers plunged directly into the prowler's eye, causing the entire mass of black fur to collapse to the ground. "Makes it easier to skin them when they die like this," he admitted before turning his attention to the prowlers lurking in the darkness. "Silver will work wonders on them, by the way. If you run straight at them, screaming and bathing them in light…you'll get a few kicks in, which will probably do the trick."

Sal looked at his father in disbelief. "You want me to run at a group of them?"

Petro held up his bloodied green hand. "Just aim at the head and the silver will do the rest." He continued to stare at Sal. "Want me to show you again?"

Sal took a breath as he looked between his father and the prowlers shrouded in darkness. With a few shallow breaths in quick succession, he crouched low to start himself off…before sprinting straight forward with a bloodcurdling scream. He put as much strength as he could into his legs to keep himself moving forward through the fear. His scream was cathartic, but it didn't distract him fully from the reality of what he was attempting. The light on his shoulder moved the perimeter forward, bathing the prowlers in its glow. Their reaction to the sudden light wasn't pleasant, and coupled with the disarray that his screams caused…they looked like they were ready to bolt away in the opposite direction.

With everything he had learned from the leecher dungeon…Sal burst forward, estimating the distance as well as he could, and launched a kick at the nearest prowler with as much force as he could possibly muster. Every single part of his brain screamed at him that this was a mistake, and that it was going to end terribly. He was sure that the prowler's tough body would somehow shatter his shoes, or break his leg. Images of Sinclair destroying the first-years appeared in Sal's head, and he tried pushing them away as he let out a roar. In that split second, time felt like it stood still, before his foot connected with the head of a prowler.

There was no explosion like the leechers. Instead, it was like he had kicked freshly fallen snow. The key similarity was how the shower of green blood exploded against the wall, with the remains of the prowler's head raining down around him. Shock replaced fear, and before Sal could even so much as blink, a second prowler leapt at his face. Whipping his right gauntlet around in a backhand attack, Sal was certain that his swatting technique wouldn't be sufficient, and yet, he felt a sickening crunch as the snout of the prowler collapsed from the impact. Several fangs dropped to the floor as the prowler yelped helplessly, clawing at the ground as though trying to deal with the pain.

Sal wordlessly ended the prowler's life with a swift kick to the neck. Even with Perfect trying to regulate his emotions, Sal's adrenaline had skyrocketed.

Petro stared at Sal's blood-covered body. "Having fun yet?"

CHAPTER 78: ELITE

Sal looked at his bloodied gauntlet in a mixture of horror and fascination. The green blood of the recently killed prowler sizzled on the surface, only to drip away like it was being repelled by the material. No matter how many times he pressed his father for an explanation, he was hit with the same facts. Demons were vulnerable to silver. Apparently, it became less effective on the stronger demons, but it was ridiculously potent against the lower-tiered ones like leechers and prowlers.

Sal refused to believe that something so simple could have such a devastating effect, and he was angry that they weren't standard issue to everyone. If people knew that it could be this easy to fight demons, maybe less territory would have been taken during the main years of the war.

"You're overthinking again," Petro stated as he plucked a core from a dead prowler. "If you're planning on mass-producing silver equipment, think again." He grunted as he got to his feet, before stifling a yawn. "It's only really useful on the low-level demons, like leechers and prowlers. Its destructive efficacy falls off a cliff when you start fighting against voiders and so on. It will bend or break with just a few punches, and the cost of making armor with pure silver isn't worth the cost...especially after the price skyrocketed."

Sal just stared at the gauntlets before shaking his head. "Then why do you outfit everyone with them? If they don't hold out well against tougher opponents?"

Petro pointed at the dead prowlers at Sal's feet. "Because they teach people how to overcome their fear of demons. When you learn how to fight them, and you see that they're not invincible, you gain the confidence to fight the tougher opponents." He looked at Sal carefully for a few moments before continuing. "There also comes a risk of hubris. Where people gain too much confidence without skill, and they run into scenarios they can't possibly win. Don't fall into that trap, and you'll be fine. This whole exercise is to make you comfortable in your own body, and helping you execute techniques and maneuvers that could save your life in the future. When you can confidently kick a prowler in the head, or gouge its eyes out without hesitation, then you're already in the top ten percent of fighters."

"So...are there materials that can easily take down hulkers?" Sal asked as he continued to examine the gauntlets. "Like, what if you made the Silverson uniform with different materials that have the same sort of devastating effect?"

"There's my boy." Petro grinned as he clapped Sal on the shoulder. "You're now asking the very question that the Silverson Group has been obsessed with for as long as I've been alive. I'll show you the iterations of the uniform that the officers get to wear when we go back to the house. I think you'll be pleasantly surprised."

Sal nodded as he looked at the darkness in the distance. "How many more of them do you think there are?"

Petro blinked in surprise. "Oh, I thought you knew already?" He pointed into the murky gloom, smiling. "We've taken out roughly thirty of them, so all that's left is the boss. Are you feeling up to it?"

Sal rotated his shoulders as he stared into the abyss. "Yeah. I am."

"Excellent. I'll be right beside you, just in case it has a nasty ability set," Petro explained as he started to walk toward the darkness. "How is your throat doing? Your shouting has fairly died down."

Sal smiled as he followed his father, watching as the darkness melted away under the light from his shoulder. "Voice is all good, but I think I need to learn how to whistle. It seems far more effective." With that thought in mind, Sal started to blow air through his lips, which started off roughly, with barely a tone coming through. The second time, there was a little more power as his lips shifted. When he tried a third time, it was almost on par with his father's…and by the sixth, he had a deafening burst of sound that he could do with just a minor lip movement.

"That Perfect ability is ridiculous," Petro admitted with an expression of undisguised jealousy. "I don't even want to think about how long it took me to learn how to whistle like that."

Sal grinned as he looked at his dad. "I could teach you, if you want?"

"Don't push it, or I'll let the prowler maul you." Petro chuckled as they walked into the final den of the prowler dungeon.

It was a large open space with a series of decayed bones lying around the floor. Standing imposingly at the center of the room was a large outcropping of solid rock that jutted out from the ground at a forty-five-degree angle. Perched on that rock was a red prowler that was three times the size of the others. Two fangs protruded from the top of its mouth, curving down menacingly over its lower jaw. A singular paw was draped over the tip of the shard, showing a set of black claws, tipped with a reddish hue.

Sal grimaced as he looked over at his father. "You're definitely helping, right?" Whatever he had been expecting from a variant prowler, this most certainly wasn't it. This thing looked like a solid match for the obsidian hulker.

Petro twisted his head slightly as though thinking about it. "Give me a second," he eventually muttered before his eyes started glowing with All Sight.

"Will the silver work on that thing?" Sal asked as he took a half step backward. It wasn't through cowardice, but rather from instinct. Something was telling him that this wasn't a fight they should attempt.

Petro's eyes returned to normal, and he pinched at the bridge of his nose, sighing audibly. "This is going to be anti-climactic, I'm afraid." He blinked a few times to stop his eyes from watering, before glancing at Sal. "I was hoping we could have you fight this thing and leave all triumphant…but I think this one is a little beyond your capabilities at the moment."

"So we should leave?" Sal clarified, just to ensure they were on the same page.

Petro shook his head slowly and held out his hands. "Nope. Give me those gauntlets for a second."

Sal stared at his father. "You're exhausted!" His voice threatened to raise, but with a quick glance at the lazing prowler, he kept himself quiet. "We've got more than enough of the cores, so there's no point in taking a risk like this!" Sal whispered, as though it were obvious.

Petro just looked at Sal quizzically as he reached for the gauntlets on his hands. "Just so we're clear, I'm not doing this because of bravado, or because I want to impress you. That thing is an anomaly in this sort of dungeon, and it shouldn't have evolved to that state." He pointed at the bones on the ground. "It has a cannibalistic trait that has allowed it to grow too much. If another group came in here to clear this place, they could die."

"Then we can tell Luke," Sal whispered, this time more desperately. "I don't want you to get hurt." He kept stealing glances at the prowler, worried that it was biding its time to strike.

Petro smiled as he slid the gauntlets off Sal's hands. "That's a good motivation, Salvatore. You should keep that." He secured the silver gauntlets onto his own hands, tightening them at the forearms. "When you get stronger, you'll be able to step up and keep your weak father alive." With a gentle chuckle, he shook his head. "I was the one who suggested we do this prowler dungeon, so I'll be the one to clean up the mess."

Sal put his hand on his father's jacket. "Wait…I could use Skill Master to use an ability to take it down."

"Absolutely not." Petro smiled. "Although, if you did that…your mother would be angrier with you than with me." He looked like he was debating the pros and cons of that particular scenario, before eventually shaking his head. "Stay here, okay?"

Sal didn't let go of his father's shirt. "Can you give me ten minutes? Just…don't fight for like ten minutes?"

Petro looked at him strangely. "I know we've been joking around a lot, Sal, but you don't have to worry about me. I'm in decent condition and I'll be able to take it down. It's just a bigger, faster, more resistant prowler."

"Ten minutes…please," Sal practically begged his father.

Petro sighed as he slowly walked back into the tunnel, farther away from the boss. "Okay, you've got ten minutes. What did you want to talk about?"

Sal didn't waste any time as he rolled up the sleeves of his blue shirt. "Pass me a couple of those cores," he instructed his father as he knelt beside the most recent prowler corpse. Ever since he had seen Blathnaid's highlight reel from the tower, Sal was curious about something. He watched her transform a dead prowler's leg into a spear, and he wondered whether he would be able to do the same with the Mythcrafter ability.

Petro placed three cores down beside Sal, before sitting against the wall opposite him. "What are you even planning?"

Sal ignored his father as he used one of the fangs to cut into the thick hide of the prowler. When Brophy taught him how to break down a prowler, he never envisaged that he'd be in this sort of situation. Right now, the only way he could be helpful to his father was to give him gear that would help in a fight against that prowler. He had the benefit of understanding a portion of the Silverson Arts, which helped him adapt a weapon to his father's fighting style. Sal wasn't going to be making some prowler shoes or something stupid like that…he was going to make a set of gauntlets. Looking up at his father for the briefest of moments, he took in the full design of the Silverson gauntlets.

"You're going to Craft…here? With a corpse?" Petro asked in disbelief as he watched Sal's hands start to move.

The design of the gauntlets was quite basic, so Sal decided to add a few reinforcements. They didn't need to be anything extraordinary, but they did need to pack a punch. If he was overthinking all of this, and the silver would already be sufficient for the prowler…then he'd only make one. Sal changed his design to a single gauntlet, and he was reminded of the one he had created for Hannah with just a few ingots of metal and essence. He was sitting with a prowler and all the materials he'd need, coupled with a few cores. Then, there was how much Mythcrafter had increased in grade, as well as his own essence reserves. Sal had no excuses. He'd be able to make something far better than those Barrier gauntlets.

"Give me the left one. You tend to prioritize the right," Sal instructed as he held out his hand.

"You're going to destroy a family heirloom?" Petro asked, chuckling. "Fine by me." He unstrapped the forearm of the left gauntlet and handed it over to Sal. "Are you going to talk me through what you're doing?"

Sal shook his head. "Nope. Let me concentrate on this, okay?"

Rather than going through a series of painful modifications on the blueprint in front of him, Sal decided to go with the brute-force method. He mentally flicked through the different options available to him, and eventually settled on a design that he was happy with. Then, with his right hand, he placed the single gauntlet onto the chest of the dead prowler and started to channel his internal essence into the silver metal. That's when Sal realized something very important. His essence gates had improved dramatically since he had last Crafted something. What used to be a steady stream of essence had turned into a firehose that blasted into the gauntlet with reckless abandon.

On the plus side, it meant that he could speed things up. On the negative side, it meant that he had to make dozens of decisions in a split second. *Did he want to use the fangs or the claws? Did he want to use the heart or the core? Did he want to use the bone or the hide?* All the options shot through his mind, and he had to quickly select them, while Perfect operated in the background, ensuring that the torrent of essence was being directed into the intended places. Had he not had Perfect active, the gauntlet would have undoubtedly shattered from the overflow of essence.

"Fuck…" Sal groaned as he maintained concentration on the Crafting. It was the most volatile process he had ever attempted, and not having the materials carved out of the prowler was making it ten times harder than was necessary. His essence needed to roam through the corpse to find the materials required, and although he had plenty to spare, his mental bandwidth was taking a beating. Each sensation of his exploratory essence sent a report back to him with its findings. Because of that very fact, he had a picture-perfect recreation of the prowler's insides burned into his brain. Sal finally understood how Darren had been able to determine how strong he was. It was an insane amount of information being relayed back to Sal, and he had to stop himself from retching.

"You okay, Sal?" Petro asked in concern.

"I'm doing this because you refuse to back down from that damned prowler." Sal didn't even look up as he grimaced. "And you had the gall to say I get my stubbornness from Mom?!"

"Ah, and here I thought it was just an early entry for the auction." Petro smiled. "I'm going to have a hell of a time telling people a fabricated version of this story."

Sal wanted to sigh in relief when he felt his essence pulling the selected components of the prowler into the silver. Unfortunately, the process involved a lot of blood splashing in every direction, practically coating Sal's torso as he maintained his concentration on the flow of essence. A series of snapping noises were accompanied by squelching and bubbling.

Just the sounds alone would be enough to turn someone's stomach, but the smell that came from the innards of the prowler was almost enough to put Sal over the edge. Yet, he held on and continued, willing every component to fuse with the silver. First came the fangs that took a scenic route through the prowler's skull to reach the gauntlet. Then the claws that flayed the entire hind quarters. Both the heart and the cores were fused without much issue, but the shards of bone almost embedded themselves in Sal's hands as they snapped into the construct. Finally, after all the pieces had melted together in a glowing light of essence…the fur started to peel away from the body.

"That is by far one of the most disgusting things I've ever witnessed," Petro remarked as he got to his feet to get a better look. "And yet, I can't look away."

Sal waited patiently for the rest of the components to fuse, and it took almost a full minute before everything looked to be finished. Because it was being brute-forced with his will alone, Sal decided to avoid any useless runes. He didn't have the luxury of creating patterns, so he instead just relied on the power of the materials and the design. A few little tweaks went into the shaping of the gauntlet, and a bit of mental massaging had to go into the silver to make it play nice with the other materials.

That was something Sal should have anticipated, considering the silver caused the demons to explode. He probably shouldn't have tried combining them, but Mythcrafter didn't seem to have any issues with it, and Sal didn't really care at this point. It just needed to work for a single fight, and it could implode at a later date.

After a few more minutes of gentle refining, the draw on his essence evaporated. With a heavy sigh, he leaned back against the wall and looked at the glowing gauntlet on the ground. "It's not perfect, but it'll definitely help you in the fight. We just need to let it cool down."

When he received no answer, Sal looked up in a panic to see that his father was no longer in front of him. With a surge of dread, Sal scrambled to his feet and bolted toward the den. His father didn't even have a light source, let alone a weapon. As Sal burst into the space, his shoulder dispelled the surrounding shadow to reveal a ridiculous sight.

Petro was seated happily on the edge of the jutted shard where the red prowler had been resting. In his hands was an angry red core the size of his head. Looking at the base of the shard, Sal saw the devastated corpse of the variant prowler. Its entire body had been sliced, and it looked like both its eyes had been gouged out.

"Your mother sent a text to hurry up," Petro said, as though that explained everything. "How did your Crafting project turn out?"

CHAPTER 79: OUTBURST

"I see that the two Argento men have successfully conquered their first dungeon!" Sophia declared from the entrance of the Argento Auction House. She was leaning against the open door with a wide smile on her face, that only faltered when she saw Sal's expression. "What happened—is everything okay?"

"Ask him," Sal shot back as he jutted his chin in his father's direction. He lifted each of the duffel bags out from the trunk of the car, while Petro appeared from the other side with three bags slung over his shoulders.

"What do I need to be asking you?" she asked Petro coolly as her eyes fell across the numerous bags being stacked on the pavement. "Would it have something to do with all those bags?"

Petro put up his hands in a placating gesture. "There was a small miscommunication. Everyone was fine and safe, and there was nothing to it."

Sal lifted the last of the borrowed bags from the car and closed the trunk with an aggravated sigh. "He didn't trust me." He pointed at his father, just so there was no doubt who he was talking about. "He went into a fight without a decent weapon, and he could have been killed."

Sophia's eyebrow rose. "In a leecher dungeon?"

"Prowler...the boss was like five times the size of a normal prowler," Sal answered before Petro could get a word in.

Rather than the reaction he expected, Sal got a delighted smile from his mother. "You went into a prowler dungeon! That's fantastic, Sal. How did you fare with the uniform?"

Petro must have decided that was the perfect time for a quip. "Well, we're down one left gauntlet...but we've got a snazzy new Unique grade in its place." He gestured at Sal. "I was a little tired when we got to the boss room and needed time to think. Sal got concerned and tried to Craft a weapon for me, but I ended up taking care of the prowler anyway."

Sophia's eyes widened as she looked between them. "You Crafted...in a dungeon?" She stopped herself with a shake of her head and turned her attention to Petro. "What sort of boss are we talking about?"

Sal groaned. He had already told her how big it was and yet she went straight over his head to ask his dad. It was just another point of aggravation to add to the list.

"Cannibal trait. It fed on the surrounding prowlers but looked to be in a fairly lethargic state. Best guess was that it couldn't fit through the tunnel with its increased size and was starting to starve," Petro remarked, sighing. "It had Bloodlust, too. I ended it before it could activate it."

"Good work," Sophia said, nodding before glancing at Sal. "Bloodlust isn't something you're ready to fight against, Sal. It's like a frenzied state where the enemy won't retreat...no matter how much damage you inflict on it. Going into something like that with gauntlets is a death sentence."

Sal lifted the bags and strapped them to his shoulders. "I'm annoyed that he risked himself instead of retreating. He didn't need to fight that thing."

"So it would be better to make it someone else's problem?" Sophia asked curiously. "Someone who might not have the strength to take it down?"

Sal closed his eyes for a moment and exhaled slowly. "That's not what I said…I don't want him dying because he needed to protect me. I made him promise that he'd give me ten minutes, but he went ahead and fought it while I was trying to help. That's what I'm annoyed with. He didn't trust me enough to tell me the truth."

Sal stared at them both. "Which seems to be a recurring theme with us, doesn't it?"

Sophia nodded as she stepped to one side, clearing the way for Sal to move into the auction house. "We deserve that. Well done today. You should get some sleep."

Petro sighed as he picked up the bags and followed Sal. When they were in the main lobby, he finally spoke from behind Sal. "You can be annoyed with me as much as you want, but your mother doesn't deserve to be spoken to like that."

Sal dropped the bags and whirled around to stare at his dad. "I thought you were going to die!"

Petro let his own bags drop to the ground, but he didn't say a word.

"Why are you just making jokes about all of this?" Sal asked in a hoarse voice; his throat was already close to breaking. Heat rushed to his face. "You two have been my everything for my entire life, and I've never once expressed any desire for something more than that. But you both lied to me…about who I am, about who you *really* are, and how scary the world truly is."

Sal felt the tears welling, and he hated how his voice was cracking with each word. "You're both probably really relieved that the secret is out. That you can be your true selves with me. But my parents, the people who raised me, are Auctioneers. When we stood in front of that prowler, I wasn't standing with some Silverson officer—I was there with my dad…"

"Salvatore." Petro spoke gently. "I'm truly sorry for how I handled that." He moved across the floor and embraced Sal, bringing him into a bear hug. "I fucked up, and I'm sorry. I shouldn't have left you like that."

Sal dug his head into his father's shoulder. If he had just managed to get back to the workshop, he would have been able to avoid all this. He wouldn't have said that to his mother, and he definitely wouldn't have confronted his father. They were trying their best, and he knew that. They loved him, and he knew that, too. His emotions were jumbled the moment he faced the first prowlers, and all that anxiety and adrenaline had compromised his headspace. Couple that with the panicked Crafting, followed by a betrayal of trust from his dad…it just caused him to break.

Sal felt horrible, both inside and out. He didn't want to fight with his parents over this. He just wanted them to understand that it was tough. Being expected to catch up with their legacy, to suddenly be someone who jumps into dungeons and fights? Then, to feel horrible that he wanted to retreat from that prowler? Sal didn't want it to be someone else's problem, nor did he want to sentence anyone to their death. All he cared about was making sure his father was okay.

As he ruminated on everything up until that moment, his father's grip loosened on his back. Sal took a breath and looked at his father, ready to apologize—not for what he said…but for how he said it.

"If you try apologizing for having feelings, I'll throw you over my shoulder." Petro gave a gentle smile as he patted Sal on the back. "In all seriousness, thank you for opening up and talking about it. We guessed that you were staying in the workshop because you didn't want to come home."

"That's not it at all," Sal insisted as he wiped at his face. "I had a lot of work to do."

Petro continued to smile. "And that's something we're adapting to. You've become a lot more independent in these last few months, and it's an incredible transformation for us to see." His smile faded as he placed his hands on Sal's shoulders. "We're trying to give you some semblance of normalcy while you're back here during the break. I can see, with the gift of hindsight, that running dungeons and teaching you martial arts probably wasn't the best method to ease you into the family history."

Sal laughed weakly as he placed both of his hands on his face, hoping it would cool down his skin. "I actually had fun in the dungeons today." He was surprised by it, too. Sal would have sworn that he'd hate every moment, but fighting the leechers with his father had been an incredibly liberating experience. The prowlers were a little more hectic and scary, where Sal felt like his emotional state was fraying with every encounter.

"I enjoyed it, too," Petro admitted. "I wanted you to see for yourself that you don't need any special weaves to be a Hero. You tore through those demons with just your body, and the martial arts you'd never heard of a couple of weeks ago. I meant it when I said that I was proud of you. I always have been, even before you were a Mythcrafter or a Savior."

Sal brought his hands away from his face and looked at his father earnestly. "Really? Before I was the pension plan?"

"That was just an added bonus," Petro clarified, grinning. "Come on, I'll help you bring these into the workshop, and then I'll head home with your mother."

Sal sighed as he shook his head. "I should apologize to her first, though."

"Good man." Petro clapped his hands against Sal's shoulders. "I'll start bringing the bags up to the Arkwright."

Sal didn't wait around as he moved back toward the doorway of the auction house. When he pulled the door open, he saw her leaning against the archway, looking at the empty street. She turned to look at him, and there was a momentary flash of surprise on her face.

"If he told you to apologize to me, you don't need to," she said with a gentle smile. "We deserved that, and a lot more. I'm sorry for how you found out, for all the lies...and for our stupid method of trying to fix things. I can't look at that damned workshop without thinking it's a bribe for you to stay in our lives."

"What?" Sal said almost as a reflex. He hadn't even considered the notion that they'd have made that workshop to give him a reason to continue visiting them. "This place is my home. You'd never need to bribe me to stay."

Sophia's expression softened as she looked at him. "But you're angry. Aren't you?"

"Yeah...a little bit, but it's okay." Sal smiled. "I got most of it out of my system with Dad."

"Tell me," Sophia insisted. "If he took the most of it, I'll take what's left."

Sal was going to dismiss the topic and laugh it off, but he shut that plan down the moment he saw the desperation on her face. She needed him to be honest with her…even if it was from a place of anger and resentment.

"I hate that I grew up thinking there was something wrong with my power." Sal spoke slowly. He didn't need to dig deep to find what he was looking for. All of it was available on the surface, and had been for quite some time. "My whole life has been in a bubble where you have protected me, and now…I'm out of that bubble and I'm trying not to drown."

He looked past his mother, not wanting to see whether his words were hurting her. "Everyone who learns about Skill Master wants me to be a Hero. It's a Heroic ability and would probably make a hell of an impact on the front lines." He spoke sarcastically, unintentionally mimicking Erika's voice. "Those who understand what Skill Master can really do fill me with all kinds of disastrous scenarios where I'll be kidnapped by Bastion, held by the Hunter Bureau…abducted by the guilds!"

Sal laughed humorlessly as he raised two fingers. "And then we look at Mythcrafter, and it's the same exact story. I've unlocked an incredible power…that could probably end the war, but I need to be careful. Because I could be abducted. Do you see where I'm going?" He shook his head in disbelief. "But it gets better. I'm now a part of a secret legacy that values, you guessed it, people with incredible powers…and what will they do if they find out that one of their own has not one, but two abilities they'd want?"

Letting out an exasperated sigh, Sal waved his right hand like he was dismissing the thought. "I've spent my whole life being scared. That my power could hurt someone, or even myself. I avoided using it, or training it, because of the fear instilled in me by you and Dad. You wanted to protect me, and I understand that…but I've grown up under a blanket of fear. Now, everyone is expecting me to stand up and fight for humanity? In a war that I know next to nothing about. Against demon types I've never heard of. Switchers sound horrifying, by the way. Aligning with factions I didn't know existed, all while being terrified of a *group of people in space*? You can probably appreciate how ridiculous it all sounds, right?

"I just want to do the right thing. But so many people have different ideas of what the right thing actually is." Sal's voice shook, that familiar creak coming back into it. "Do I say fuck it…and become an Offense? Take Prestige's ability and just launch myself onto the battlefield? Do I catalogue every single power I come across and rotate between them, wrecking my body that's not built for them, and hope for the best? Or do I *hide* in a workshop and Craft equipment?" Sal clenched his fists and relaxed them a couple of times before letting out a shaky breath. "Everyone is pushing me toward being a Hero, and that has never once been my dream. You know that."

Sal looked at the Argento Auction House behind him. "This was the *one* place where I could exist, without the pressures of society. Not a single person wished for Salvatore Argento, the Appraiser, to become a Hero. This was my safe place, where I was good at what you trained me to do. I could work the customers, negotiate the prices…it was fun, and we were all in it together." He smiled bitterly as he turned back around to look at his mother. Her tear-streaked face was like a dagger through his heart, but she needed to hear this.

No matter how much it stung, Sal had to keep his resolve. "But now? When I walk through those doors, I'm the top-ranked Savior at Quest Academy. I've lost the chance of being the Appraiser for the auction house. Too many people are focused on what direction I move in, and it's exhausting. Even with the creation of a guild, there's no guarantee that people will leave me alone and let me do my own thing."

Sal spread his hands helplessly. "That's what's annoying me, Mom."

Sophia just stared at Sal in a stunned silence. That quiet grew for an uncomfortable length of time, until Sal finally broke. Although it had been cathartic to get all of that off his chest, he didn't want his mother to leave the auction house thinking that he hated her or blamed her for everything. He had said his piece, but he wanted to finish on a more gentle note.

"So, when I did this earlier with Dad…we hugged it out at the end. Want to give it a try?" He offered his outstretched arms and smiled at her reassuringly.

Sophia nodded quietly as she stepped into his arms, her slender arms gripping the back of his black jacket. "We'll make this right, Salvatore." She pulled her head away to look him dead in the eye. "I promise you, on my life. We'll make this right."

"How did you manage to make that sound like a threat?" Sal laughed as he held his mother.

CHAPTER 80: AUCTIONEER

As much as Sal would have loved to just retire to the workshop for the evening, after the explosive outburst with both of his parents…there was something more pressing that needed to be done.

"I was sure we drained them back at the dungeon," Petro insisted as he threw the last of the washcloths into the pile of green-soaked fabric. He stretched his back as he looked at the polished wooden floor in distaste. There were still some smears of prowler blood visible on the surface, a result of two duffel bags leaking all the way to the workshop.

"You'll likely be receiving an invoice from that car company, too," Sophia muttered as she dragged a refuse bin across the floor. Bending down, she picked up all the washcloths with clear distaste before chucking them into the bin with a shudder. "Did you not think to look down while you were walking around?"

Petro pointed at Sal accusingly. "We were having a familial crisis! I didn't really think to look at my feet when my son needed me." He looked over at Sophia to see how his excuse landed, but just laughed when he saw the scowl on her face.

"Stop weaponizing your son." Sophia gave an exasperated sigh before she looked at Sal meaningfully. "Don't listen to your father. You didn't need to be here to help with all of this."

Sal smiled as he offered a slight shrug. "Honestly, I'm glad that we got to talk and hang out like this after I said my piece." He gestured at the floor. "Besides, it's better we do it now rather than before the sparring tomorrow."

Sophia blinked as she looked at Sal carefully. "You still want to keep up with the sparring?"

"Of course." Sal nodded slowly. "I literally ripped a leecher apart with my almost bare hands, and kicked a prowler to death. That's the result of the training with you two, so I'd be an idiot to ignore it."

Petro dusted off his shoulder as though he was completely responsible for Sal's sudden burst of confidence. He had to stop when a washcloth was flung at him from the bin.

Sophia lifted another cloth and stared at Petro, as though daring him to continue. When Petro smiled and backed off, she turned her attention back to Sal. "Okay, we'll be ready for your sparring tomorrow. We'll need to wind things down, though, with the auction coming up next week. You're also going to be heading back to Quest Academy soon, so you'll probably want to spend some time with your friends?"

Sal nodded. "And get some Crafting done with Fabi. There's a long list of things I need to get done before I go back, but I don't want to sacrifice the training with you two. I'm enjoying the feeling of being more competent, and I'd like to see how far I can go before heading back to school."

"Then we'll give you some killer techniques and combinations before you leave." Petro grinned. "I was watching you move in the dungeon, and I've created a few Silverson combinations that would fit your style perfectly."

Sal blinked in surprise. "When did you have time to do that? We were both rushing throughout the whole thing."

"Speak for yourself." Petro laughed. "I obviously had to lower myself to your level." He gave Sal a wink.

"Ignore your father. He was bitching about his joints when you went looking for more washcloths earlier." Sophia outed her husband without a sliver of hesitation. "He's going to be crying in his sleep later."

Sal laughed as he surveyed the floor at their feet. "Now that we're done, am I okay to head back to the workshop?"

Sophia nodded, smiling. "Yes, and as much as I'd love to tell you to get some sleep…I know you're going to take apart all those materials. Just promise me you'll try to get some rest, okay?"

"I promise." Sal nodded before glancing at his dad. "You can have that Unique-grade glove for the auction, if you want?"

"It already has a price tag." Petro pointed at the glass window of his office upstairs. "Locked it in there just in case you had any second thoughts."

Sal laughed as he moved toward the workshop. Before he left, he wanted to just make his stance very clear with his parents. With a pause, he looked back at them. "I love you both. Even if there are secret organizations and powerful families that have it in for us, I'm happy that I have the two of you in my corner. Thanks for listening to me tonight."

Petro smiled softly. "We're happy to listen anytime you want to talk. Rebuilding your trust in us is our main priority, so please don't hesitate to reach out if you ever need us."

Sophia nodded in agreement. "You have our full support for whatever it is you decide to do going forward. We want you to be happy, and if that means the Argento Auction House backs your guild to the top ranks, then that's what we'll do."

"Whoa, I just said trust. I didn't say anything about turning his guild into a superpower!" Petro jokingly raised his hands as he was hit with another washcloth.

Sal couldn't help but laugh as he shook his head. "Thank you. We'll take baby steps toward something like that. First step is getting the depot fixed up."

Petro shrugged as he looked over at Sophia. "We could manage that, if you wanted? Similar to what we did with your workshop. Get it into a working state that you can add your own personal flair to when you come to visit?"

Sophia nodded in agreement. "As long as we're not at risk of going into the red, then we're happy to help where you need it."

Sal smiled as he looked between his parents. "I think you're both really underestimating the Arkwright. I don't think there's any risk of us going into the red."

"It'll take a lot more obsidian daggers to fix up an entire warehouse." Sophia let out an awkward laugh. "But I'm sure we can lean on the Hunter Bureau for some funding."

"No," Sal answered. "I don't want their help on this, or to be indebted to them." He looked at his mother seriously. "We're going to do this ourselves. Use all the money that I've earned on commissions, and I'll create a system for the Arkwright. It will give you enough goods for the next semester's worth of auctions."

Petro beamed as he stepped forward with arms wide. "My favorite son!" He wrapped his arms around Sal and hugged him tightly. "I always knew you'd grow up to do great things. Didn't I say that, Soph?"

Sal laughed as he wormed his way out of his father's embrace. "Seriously, just let me put a plan together. Send me over the list of upcoming auctions, and I'll make sure there are showcases for all of them."

"You don't need to do that," Sophia insisted, looking at Petro for backup.

Sal spread his hands and smiled at his mother. "It's a partnership, Mom. I can't have the Argento Auction House getting a bad deal just because we're related."

Petro bit his lip as he put his arm around Sal's shoulder. "Told you he was my son." He then proceeded to use Sal as a shield against the incoming washcloth.

"I'll see you tomorrow for training." Sal finally excused himself, laughing as he caught the cloth and threw it back in the direction of the bin. "I'm going to load up the Arkwright with the materials from that red prowler."

"And sleep!" Sophia insisted as Sal left the lobby.

"That too," Sal answered with a wave as he made his way down the steps to the workshop.

He could see the traces of prowler blood that lined the floor and he wondered which unlucky staff member would be assigned the cleanup duty in the morning. A part of him hoped it wouldn't be George. His bad leg would make the cleaning process a lot tougher. Sal wondered whether he'd have time to clean it up himself if he finished up with the Arkwright early.

As he entered his workshop, he closed the door behind him and looked at the staircase leading up to the mezzanine. A pang of relief hit him when he saw that his father had brought each of the duffel bags up to the balcony. It meant a lot less lifting, which was a nice little bonus for Sal's tired state. He walked up the stairs, not paying too much attention to the new green stains that littered the metal. It didn't take a genius to figure out what was causing the leaks. They had decapitated loads of the prowlers and packed the bags with them. The likeliest culprit was the red prowler. His father had helped him carve up that one, and more than five of the bags contained components just from that one creature.

When Sal reached the top of the stairs, he smiled at the sight of the Arkwright. The eerie purple glow bathed the room in villainous light. It was the color that represented Supports, and he'd need to factor that color scheme into whatever outfit he made for his second semester. With the Strategist's Dominion suit being a dud, he needed to create something suitable for himself. An outfit he could wear at all times, that would fit in with the dress code of Quest Academy, but that could be used for battle when necessary.

Sal moved over to the first bag and rummaged through it. He repeated this process with the next seven bags until he came across the Silverson Group outfit. Taking the right-handed silver gauntlet from the bag, Sal placed it into the loading tray of the Arkwright and was very careful in selecting the Analysis option. He wanted the machine to register the design as a blueprint, rather than breaking it down for materials. When the Arkwright started powering up to tackle the task, Sal moved around the different bags, sorting their contents and assessing the blood-soaked damage of the clumped fur.

Create Name

Sal glanced up at the message, frowning. It hadn't been analyzed by his tracker, so there wasn't an assigned name to the silver gauntlet. Sal fought his initial instinct to name it after the Silverson Group, as he didn't want anyone seeing that name in the future if they looked at it. Instead, he selected something that made him laugh.

Auctioneer Set (Gauntlet) has been registered

Sal repeated the process and added the shoes to the Arkwright. He was going to name them after the Argento Auction House, rather than his paternal family. Next in was the shirt.

Auctioneer Set (Shoes) have been registered
Auctioneer Set (Shirt) has been registered
Auctioneer Set (Shoulder) has been registered

When all of them were successfully registered to the Arkwright, Sal removed them from the machine and put them in a safe space near his bed. He didn't want to sacrifice family heirlooms for materials. One of the interesting things that he was able to do with the gauntlet was mirror the pattern to create a left-handed gauntlet design. Had he known that earlier, he would have saved time in registering both shoes.

Sal moved through the different bags and realized that there was no conceivable way the Arkwright would be able to store all of it. He'd need to be choosy about which materials he put into the machine for the next project. The reason he had gone to the dungeon in the first place was to continue the research of the venomstone and blight core. Now that he had an entire duffel bag worth of leecher cores, he decided it was a good place to start.

Placing the bulging duffel bag into the tray, Sal upended it and let the cores bounce to the bottom of the tray, clattering against one another like glass marbles. He was initially worried that they would shatter, but that was seemingly a useless thought as they ricocheted off one another, emitting a pulsating glow at the contact. When the tray was practically half full of leecher cores, Sal had to get down on one knee to push the tray back in, his hands leaving a sweaty print on the door.

Blight Core (Enhanced Venomstone):
- Synthetic Combination
- Leecher Core, Siphonstone, Venomstone

Confirm Research?

The Arkwright seemingly sensed what Sal wanted to achieve. Smiling, he moved in front of the interface and hit Confirm. Rather than using the prowler cores in the same way, he was going to use them for his next design. Because the

Dominion set had such a high demand on his internal essence, Sal planned to create a suit that rivaled the coat Upgrade had made for him. His initial thoughts of making a necklace or a set of rings had been replaced when he counted up the duffel bags filled with cores. He had enough to create an entire chest piece made of cores.

Sal smiled as he moved the duffel bags away from the workbench. Picking up his stylus, he started to map out a new design for a suit. He could get Arkwright to make the intricate pieces if he needed, but this was a project Sal wanted to design himself. Well, almost by himself. He reached across the workbench to pick up his Legendary-grade visor, equipping it with a contented smile. It gave him a boost to his Mythcrafter ability, and Sal wanted to see what he could do with the excess materials before the research was completed.

CHAPTER 81: OUTREACH

As Sal put the finishing touches on the new gauntlet design, he smiled broadly. If he was honest with himself, he had no idea whether this would work…but he wanted to try. Back when he had worked on the sniper rifle for Watcher, they had made a mistake in overlapping the blueprint with Blink's Siphon blade, which had led to the discovery of his first evolutionary rune. Sal was going to try to replicate that process, but he had a different outcome in mind.

Picking up the sheet of parchment, he hesitated only for a few seconds, looking to see whether there were any immediate errors or issues. His tracker wasn't finding anything out of the ordinary, and Perfect had ensured all the lines were smooth. When he was finally happy with the second and third round of checks, he placed the parchment over the previous sketch.

Turning the backlight of the workbench on, Sal illuminated the drawings and watched as they overlapped. Nothing happened for the first few moments, and Sal moved the top blueprint around to see whether it would catch onto his intentions. His eyes were drawn to the ridiculous sheet underneath, and Sal couldn't help but laugh at what he was trying to accomplish. Just when he was certain that he was asking too much of Mythcrafter, a familiar spark of inspiration connected in his head and the Mythcrafter grasped onto it. Both drawings appeared in front of Sal's eyes as a visual, albeit riddled with inconsistencies and errors. That didn't matter, though, because Sal was absolutely elated. He finally had a proof of concept for the stupidest invention yet.

The first drawing he had made was for a drone dock, but not an industrial-sized one like the Arkwright needed. Instead, he had tried to make a smaller one that could comfortably house the little hover bot he had bought at the bazaar—Fabi's little drone, that had been kept on his bedside table. It wasn't suitable for combat at all, but he'd be able to change that with a few tweaks to the design. Like if he made the rotary blade out of silver—that would absolutely give it a fighting chance against leechers.

The small form-factor design had been an easy one to sketch out, and it was little enough that the Arkwright would be able to manufacture it. The diminutive size of the dock gave Sal the silly idea of embedding it into the shoulder of his gauntlet-sleeve-thing. If he was going to be making armor with a ridiculous number of cores, then why not double the functionality and have it operate as a charging station for a small drone? The hover bot was barely the size of his fist, and the dock was about the size of his open palm. At best, it would only be an extra inch or two in thickness at the shoulder.

Placing a fresh sheet of parchment over the two blueprints, Sal started to sketch out the new design that Mythcrafter was highlighting to him. It was a scarily accurate design compared to what he had been visualizing before layering the pages, and it seemed to naturally flow onto the parchment. In principle, the gauntlet was an imitation of both the Vengeful Vambraces and the Silverson gauntlet. He had created an insulated glove, covered with silver and small plates made entirely of essence cores.

As just a rough estimate, Sal thought he'd need roughly three or four prowler cores for a single arm. If essence was going to be his bottleneck in the future, then he wanted to create armor that would allow him to tap into reserves. The only requirement he had of this left arm gauntlet was the Pocket ability, as he wanted to be able to harvest future cores and materials like Fabi did in the dungeon. With that as the only requirement, and everything else being channeled into essence reserves, it became a remarkably easy design to draw.

Of course, there was the issue that the arms might not sync up properly with the rest of the armor. But that would be something Sal could come back to later. He had learned some truly sobering things in those dungeons with his father, the key lesson being that he relied too heavily on his equipment and their abilities. His father had a wealth of experience, but even after twenty years of not fighting, he had been able to take on that red prowler with just a single gauntlet. Now, that said…Sal wasn't an idiot. Having incredible firepower at his disposal was very welcome, and he'd prefer to walk into an environment where he had a lot more utility than just his hands and feet. That's where the right-handed gauntlet would come in. He was still debating the overall design for that one, but he had a good idea of what he wanted it to be.

Sal meticulously drew out the embedded drone dock, which was neatly fixed into the side of the shoulder. It was visually satisfying to see an indent that would house the small body of the drone, and a perfect circle as a groove for the rotary blade to clip into. Sal wanted to walk before he could run, and despite his desire to add in an evolutionary rune to the gauntlet, he wanted to prioritize the functionality of the build first. An hour went by, with Sal making the tiny adjustments to the drone dock in the shoulder, and he was practically elated when Mythcrafter was finally satisfied. He always knew when he was close because Mythcrafter took a bit more time in finding problems to fix. It felt like it was scanning everything as a whole, or running a simulation of sorts, before giving him another suggestion. Another pleasant surprise was a trove of suggestions that the visor provided for the drone's protocols. Sal guessed it was a result of Cypher using that redundant file from when he was first learning how to make the essence chip for the Arkwright.

When Sal put down the stylus, he smiled to himself. He wasn't sure whether it was the influence of Mythcrafter, or his visor…but the materials that were being suggested were all high-end. To Sal's delight, one of them was the venomstone. It was suggesting that he use it to power the drone, and Sal had no objections, particularly if he had a ready supply of them. He wasn't exactly sure how a drone would benefit from the Assimilate ability, but he guessed that it would maybe collect essence on his behalf? It was a tough one to estimate, but it wasn't worth agonizing over.

Sal lifted the page and held it up to the light. He smiled as he looked over the design and details, when his visor suddenly flickered. Through the parchment, Sal could see a new screen appear on the Arkwright's interface. Lowering the page to get a better look, his visor relayed the information as though he were only a foot away from the machine.

Blight Core has been successfully researched
Blight Core has been added to Material Storage

Sal let out a relieved sigh as he got to his feet, his hands still gripping the page. He'd be able to upload the blueprint and see whether the Arkwright was able to manufacture it. However, the moment his eyes caught the page, everything had changed. Dozens of errors appeared all over the design. Sal faltered as he looked at it in confusion. *How had they just appeared suddenly?* All the dimensions were off, certain essence plates needed to be removed, and the shoulder dock needed to be reworked. Biting his lip, Sal sat back down, frowning, and picked up his stylus.

"What just happened?" Sal muttered as he started to make the changes that Mythcrafter was now suggesting. It was practically a complete rework of the design, and there were a lot of changes that needed to be made. The biggest pain was with the drone, which had suddenly taken up nearly five times as much space. Sal was worried about the feasibility of the armor as he continued.

If he wasn't able to move his arm, then it would be practically useless. He wondered whether he needed to add Feather to the mix to give him a range of motion, but that just complicated what he had been trying to achieve. Because the visor had four specific abilities, Sal wanted to give the equipment as much breathing room as possible. He had seen how screwed up the Ultimate Argento set was with its dozens of abilities, and he didn't want that for this gauntlet. He wasn't exactly sure it would work as he intended, but he wanted to see whether the high-grade materials would forcibly evolve the Pocket ability when he was finished Crafting. If he could hard-code the Arkwright into keeping it as the main ability, then there was a good chance of it happening.

Another hour of tweaking passed, and Sal finally realized what the issue was. It had been staring him right in the face the whole time. The blight core had registered to his visor after the research completed. Seeing as the venomstone was an integral part of the build, the visor decided to upgrade it to the best version possible with the newest material. It had to be massive as it was dramatically increasing the size of the small hover bot.

What had previously been a single circular groove for the rotary blade had suddenly become a mass of tendrils that looked remarkably similar to a leecher's tentacles. The grooves were woven around the arm, from the shoulder to the wrist. It meant that every essence plate had to be realigned or resized to accommodate the new pattern.

It took far too long for Sal to get everything right, and it only resulted in more doubt. This was the very definition of scope creep, and he had fallen victim to it once again. It still looked like a good design, but Sal wasn't exactly sure how he felt about the new material requirements. Abyssal steel for the tendrils felt like overkill, when he had previously been content with a small rotary blade made of silver. With it being a much bigger body for the drone, he guessed it would require a lot more essence to run.

Still, he wanted to see it through to completion. If the blight core was able to give him the Subsume ability, then he'd be a happy man. He didn't know how it would work, especially when factored into a drone, but he was curious…and that was enough to keep him focused on the task at hand. One of the things he was coming to terms with was that the Arkwright's design choices weren't perfect.

The best result so far had been the Vendetta Macclemark, but that was only because of Fabi's original designs. If Sal wanted to continually improve as a Crafter, and he wanted better outputs, then he'd need to be in the driver's seat when it came to the design of equipment and weaponry.

Sal glanced up at the Arkwright with a wry smile. "But you can handle all the boring stuff." He looked back at the gauntlet design and chuckled to himself. "Because I'm sure as shit not making these essence plates." He kept up with the corrections until he eventually got to the point where he was happy. Well, that was a bit of a lie. He went until Mythcrafter was happy and had no further improvements to make.

When that was done, Sal finally got to his feet and checked the time on his tablet. It was close to five in the morning, and he'd be sparring with his parents in the early afternoon. With an inward groan, Sal pledged to set an alarm to stop him from constantly jumping into the deep end on projects.

Just before he powered off the screen of his tablet, he saw a few notifications.

Fabrizia: Sorry Sal, but I can't run dungeons tonight. Currently working on getting Figment under control, so need to do a bit of solo-training. Will be free tomorrow?

Fabrizia: Also, have you picked out your classes for next semester? The Savior classes are already up. I'd highly recommend taking anything that Forge teaches.

Fabrizia: Essence Programming is taught by Upgrade, so you should absolutely sign up for that one. Happy to talk you through which classes suck and which were great!

Sal scheduled a message to send when she woke up, just wishing her luck with Figment and telling her that he'd take a look at the class list. She must have been awake, because when he finished his message, he got another one instantly.

Fabrizia: You're awake? I had a bit of an epiphany and was working on a new set of protocols. I've sent them on as an attachment and can run you through them when I next see you.

Fabrizia: Go to bed. I know you're not up early. You pulled an all-nighter!

Sal smiled as he typed out a quick response.

Salvatore: I'll show you the drone arm thing I've been working on when you next come over.

Fabrizia: I'm not even going to ask what that is. Sleep well.

Just as he navigated back to his messages, Sal saw another one from Barry that had been sent to him hours ago.

Barry: Salvatore Argento wants to run a dungeon? Who is this?
Barry: No, seriously…who is this?

Barry: Assuming it is actually you, and you're asking for my help, I'm guessing Divinity said no?

Barry: Apparently you didn't ask Divinity. I may have gotten you in trouble there. Maybe tell her it was a joke?

Barry: You know, I'm used to you not replying…but this is a little excessive, don't you think?

Barry: I can't run any dungeons at the moment, I'm staying with my dad and he's been giving me an informal masterclass on how the world works.

Barry: It's literally him and his friends telling me what's wrong with the current generation.

Barry: Seriously, if you could save me, I'd really appreciate it.

Sal continued to scroll through Barry's stream of consciousness before it finally ended with him signing off for the night. He sent him a short message, apologizing for the lack of responses and a quick recap of what happened in the dungeon. Unlike Fabi, there was no instant reply, and he guessed that Barry was very much asleep.

When he returned to his messages, he noticed there was one from Divinity. He hesitated for a moment, unsure whether she was going to tell him it was a terrible idea for him to go into a dungeon, or whether there was a threat with the red prowler. His uncertainty continued for a few seconds before he clicked on the message to read it.

Divinity: Barry said you were looking for help with a dungeon. I'm free tonight and the next few days if you want to go together?

Divinity: Guess tonight didn't suit. Another time maybe.

Sal sighed as he looked at the messages again. His first instinct had been anxiety that she was going to quote some vision, but she had apparently just wanted to help. Placing his tablet back on the workbench, Sal picked up the blueprint and scanned it with the visor. He wanted to send it across to the Arkwright to see whether it could handle some of the more tedious parts of the Crafting. Specifically, the essence plates.

When he put the parchment back onto the table, he moved over to the screen of the Arkwright and navigated to the Research tab. His new blueprint design appeared after a few seconds, and rather than going straight into production, he asked it to start researching what a full suit would look like. It was just a moment of curiosity to give it something to work on while he slept.

Arkwright Upgrade Required

Sal stared at the words, not really sure how to process them. He just wanted a blueprint for a suit version of the gauntlet. When he navigated into the error screen for more context, he was met with a surprise.

Mythcrafter Crafting Algorithm is unable to complete this request
    o   Mythic-Grade Blueprints cannot be simulated

Whatever Sal had been expecting, that hadn't been it.

He numbly moved back to the workbench and picked up his tablet in a dazed state. Going to his messages, he replied to Divinity's message.

Salvatore: Hey, I'm really sorry. Ended up going to the dungeon with my dad instead.

Salvatore: Really appreciate you offering to help. Are you free tomorrow? We can do Dungeon, Coffee, or Sparring?

Salvatore: Long story, but my parents are apparently badass and they're teaching me how to fight properly.

Sal pocketed his tablet and glanced over at the Arkwright one more time, not sure what the next steps were. If he was reading it correctly, the gauntlet he was attempting to make was Mythic grade? What didn't make sense was that he had all the materials to make it. There was no fabled missing piece, and everything looked feasible for him to Craft. The biggest question he had to ask himself was how his first ever Mythic-grade blueprint was somehow a left-handed gauntlet with the Pocket ability…and a drone embedded into the shoulder?

With a chuckle, Sal left the workshop to collapse on his bed. There was a lot to do tomorrow, and he'd hopefully get to see Divinity, too.

Just as he was about to close his eyes, he felt a small vibration in his pocket. Pulling out the tablet with a groan, Sal squinted at the illuminated screen in the darkness.

Divinity: Sounds fun! Sign me up for all three. :)

CHAPTER 82: DRIVE

"Did you tell her to wait at Memorial Square?" Petro asked as he turned the beautiful Panther De Ville down a narrow street. The windows were rolled down, and more than a few people had turned to look at them. It was a novelty to see a fully operational classic car driving on the road. Rather than avoiding the stares, Petro gave onlookers a friendly wave, which they ultimately returned.

"Yeah, she said she's at the entrance." Sal double-checked the tablet that rested on his lap. "Thanks for doing all this, by the way. You didn't have to drive me out here to pick her up."

Petro smiled as he continued down the street that had long since been pedestrianized. "Sending a private car or encouraging them to get a train is just bad manners. If you're going to invite someone, you should pick them up instead of putting all the hassle on their shoulders." He turned his head to give Sal a wink. "Besides, I rarely get to find an excuse to drive this beauty. Two birds with one stone."

Sal returned the smile as he looked out the window at the surrounding streets. There were no high-rises here, with all the buildings being three or four stories tall at best. The dominant feature of the area was the Memorial Square. The open skyline allowed anyone to see the towering marble structures no matter where they were in the district. Each shard of marble stretched about eighty feet into the air, and even though Sal wasn't up close, he knew that there were thousands of names engraved into them. Each obelisk of marble was intentionally visible, so nobody would forget the sacrifices of the men and women who first protected them from the demons.

The car smoothly turned another corner, and it was finally aligned in the direction of the square. Petro didn't needlessly accelerate as he allowed people to walk ahead of the car. Pedestrians had full priority on the streets, with personal transport vehicles being very far down the list. He drummed his fingers against the white steering wheel while hanging his elbow out the car window. "You can tell her we'll be there in a few minutes," he added as he glanced at Sal's tablet. "Hope she likes lukewarm tea."

"I'm sure she'll be delighted." Sal tapped out a quick message to Divinity. In the back of the car, they had a collection of pastries, teas, and coffees. Sal had even elected to get some fruit as he guessed that Divinity would prefer that. He had a hunch after watching her eat countless salads over the first semester.

"How are things going with the Arkwright?" Petro asked him out of the blue. It was the first topic that really referenced the last few months, as most of their car ride had just been idle chatter and pleasantries.

Sal looked up from the tablet and let out a sigh. "Honestly, I think I've hit a bit of a wall with it." He leaned back into the leather seat and looked straight ahead at the people walking around them. "It's excellent for material discovery and production. Like, I can feed it scrap and it'll discover some super useful metal. All those leecher cores have ended up being combined into things like venomstone and most recently a blight core."

"You made a blight core?" Petro repeated slowly, his eyes not leaving the road. "An actual blight core?"

"Oh, you've heard of them?" Sal asked impressed. "Yeah, it looks like an evolution of the leecher core. That's why I needed all those cores from the dungeon, because I wanted to make something with the Subsume ability."

Petro's fingers stopped drumming against the steering wheel. "Sal…when we get back, would you let me Appraise it?" He glanced over at Sal for a second before looking back to the road. "A blight core is a big deal, if it's the same thing that I'm thinking of. The Paradox Guild almost killed themselves bringing one of them back from a portal expedition over in Pinnacle about twelve years ago. The whole Hunter Bureau lost their shit over it."

"What did they do with it?" Sal asked nervously. He did not want to paint another target on his back. If he put aside the issues with the production, and the clear limitations of making higher grade equipment, the Arkwright was unparalleled when it came to material research and production.

Petro smiled humorlessly as he shook his head slightly. "Only have rumors to go by. Some say that Doc Ameye ended up taking it, but others claim Robert Locke commissioned Doc to make him a piece of gear with it. No matter who you believe, it's a pretty bleak picture. People died retrieving that, and it either went to the reclusive Crafter, or to a greedy non-combatant. Squandered resources isn't something new."

"I've seen how powerful Robert is," Sal said after a few moments of silence. "When we did that tower exercise, I saw him wipe out an entire building of demons with just a wave of his hand…it was insane."

"Likely a trick of some sort," Petro answered, and there wasn't a shred of doubt in his voice. "Robert Locke is many things, but he's not strong enough to subdue a wave of demons like that."

Sal couldn't help but wonder whether that was truly the case. Assimilation was the ability that the venomstone gave, and it allowed for the permanent increase in stats and ability grades. If Robert had access to a heightened version of that, in Subsume, would that have allowed him to build up his innate ability to something ridiculously powerful?

"There's something else I want to tell you," Sal said finally. "But you need to promise not to crash the car."

Petro nodded as he placed both hands on the steering wheel. "Am I going to be a grandfather?"

Sal barked a laugh before shaking his head. "No! It's in relation to the Arkwright. I made a design last night, that requires the use of the blight core. The Arkwright isn't able to make it, but I know for a fact that it's perfect. I mapped it out and used Mythcrafter along with the visor and Perfect. There's not a single thing wrong with it."

Petro frowned as he glanced over at Sal. "That's not something to crash over."

"It's Mythic grade," Sal stated flatly, waiting for his father's reaction. When nothing dramatic happened, he continued. "It's a remodeled gauntlet, similar to the Silverson one…but it uses a drone and a load of cores."

Petro smiled. "Sounds complicated."

"You don't sound surprised. It's *Mythic grade*," Sal insisted, as though he wasn't reacting correctly.

Petro shrugged as he glanced at Sal. "And that's incredible, but we knew you'd be able to make things at that level eventually. Your ability is literally called Mythcrafter." He offered a reassuring smile. "If you want me to crash the car, then you're going to need to come to me with more than just a drawing. I'll go crazy when it's done, how about that?"

Sal was flummoxed as he sat back in the seat with a resigned sigh. "Seriously, why am I the only one who can't believe this? It's Mythic! We've never seen one of them before, and this could be the first ever registered Mythic grade in the entire city!"

"Or it could just end up being another drawing," Petro countered. "I will say, though, that it would be a lot easier to disguise a blight core if you had it fashioned into a piece of equipment. We have a few of those headbands that block Appraisal and Analysis. All Sight can still see through them, but it would stop the majority of people from snooping into your abilities."

Sal frowned at that. "Wait, is that what Robert wears? I've never been able to use Analysis or Appraisal on him."

"Probably. It's mostly worn to keep people like Neuro out of your head, but it's a nice bonus when you want to hide your capabilities." Petro chuckled as he angled the car to the left. "Your friend is looking far healthier than she did at the party."

Sal looked forward to see Divinity at the entrance of Memorial Square with a small bag clasped in her hands. She was dressed in the same leather jacket and jeans that she had worn at the mixer party. Before he lost his train of thought, Sal looked back at his father. "Can I take one of those headbands? My arms might not get shattered this time around if I wear one."

"Why do you think your mother ordered them in?" Petro remarked dryly as he parked the car, his friendly smile appearing in a flash. "Are you the Miss Khan I've been hearing all about?"

Sal rolled his eyes as he opened the door to get out of the car. He walked around to greet Divinity, and while he went for a hug, she had gone for a hand-shake. It was an overly awkward affair that had Petro laughing.

"Sorry, I—" Divinity started as she accepted the hug. "Nice to meet you again, Mr. Argento." She peeked out from under Sal's shoulder to greet Petro awk-wardly.

"Petro is fine. I bought pastries, but Sal insisted you'd want fruit." He gestured at a collection of white boxes perched in the back seat. "Also, your tea is getting cold, so hop in." He smiled before looking at Sal meaningfully.

Sal disengaged from the hug and opened the back door so Divinity could get into the car. "After you," he said, laughing.

Divinity obliged, thanking Petro and making a beeline for the pastries. "You didn't have to go to all this trouble for me. I could have easily gotten the train or a cab over to Silver Sanctuary."

"Don't be absurd. You're the first friend Sal has actually invited to the auction house," Petro remarked, which apparently caught Divinity by surprise.

"Really? I was sure you'd have had Barry or Blathnaid over at some point." She looked at Sal, as if not sure whether Petro was joking or not.

Petro turned in his chair to look back at both Sal and Divinity. "Are you joking? He literally locked himself in the workshop and we've seen him a handful of times since he's been home."

"Dad…" Sal began, in a tone of voice that indicated his father should stop talking about it now.

Petro not only ignored the hint, but took it a step further. "It's our own fault, though. I told him to try making a vending machine for equipment, and it looks like that single project stole him away from his friends for the entire break." He grinned at Divinity and gestured at the box in her hand. "So, I'm bribing you with pastries as a peace offering, for us keeping Sal away from his friends all this time."

Sal knew what angle his father was going with. He was trying to cover for Sal being shit when it came to keeping in contact. There was no way that Divinity was going to fall for that, though.

Divinity beamed as she opened the box in front of her. "Thank you so much, Mr. Arg—" She caught herself before continuing. "Petro. I'll happily accept the bribe." She closed the box and secured her seat belt, smiling. "I love your car, by the way."

Petro grinned as he looked between them. "Appreciates the pastries and the car. That's two for two."

Sal secured his own belt with a sigh. "I was positive she'd go for the fruit. I'm pretty sure she's just trying to make a good impression." He smiled at Divinity, letting her know that he was only teasing.

"And it's working wonders. She's already my favorite," Petro countered before pulling out of the parking spot and bringing the car back onto the street. "So, any music requests from Miss Khan?"

Divinity smiled as she perked up in her seat. "Don't suppose you have any classical music?"

Sal groaned as he leaned his head back against the headrest, while Petro laughed and pushed a cassette into the old player. "A girl after my own heart."

Divinity just beamed as she looked at Sal. "Your dad is awesome."

CHAPTER 83: STYLE

"With all due respect, Mr. Argento…I don't think that's a good idea," Divinity said with a note of uncertainty in her voice. She looked at Sal as though asking for backup, but all she received from him was a knowing smile.

Petro smiled as he stood in the center of the wooden floor. "Nonsense. You're just going to handicap yourself in the future if you train without using your powers. Come at me with everything you've got." He slid his left foot backward and lowered his stance, raising his arms up as though inviting her to attack him. "You're not going to leave a bad impression by trying your best. Give me everything you've got."

They had arrived back at the auction house not too long ago, and Divinity had gone off to the staff bathrooms to change into her sparring attire. The ride in the car had been an experience, where Sal heard the same stories for the thousandth time about the different families who lived in each landmark. Petro had a captive audience in Divinity, and if she was feigning enthusiasm for all the wild auction stories, she did a masterful job at it. Now, their budding friendship was being tested as Petro squared up against Divinity.

Sal gave her a reassuring nod, communicating that it was okay. She still looked uncertain, and as though to prove her point, her eyes turned a milky white.

"Oh," Divinity said after a moment, her eyes snapping back to blue. "You're…really good."

Petro tilted his head slightly, looking at her carefully. "Really good? That tells me everything I need to know." He smiled before launching forward with a sweeping kick.

Sal could see that he was holding back his speed, and Divinity did not disappoint in the slightest. Her body was in the air as Petro's leg swung underneath her, and rather than focusing on evasion, she launched into a counterattack, with her right foot aimed at his head.

"Marvelous!" Petro laughed as he easily deflected her kick with his forearm. "Use your visions, just like you would in an actual battle."

Divinity landed and still hesitated. "Are you sure?" Her breathing had picked up, and it was likely from all the adrenaline. Her body shifted into a stance, and a smile graced her lips. "Would you like the first move?" Her eyes turned white, and unlike the previous instance, they stayed that way.

Sal watched in awe as Petro moved through the different formations of the Silverson Arts. He kept a low speed to start, with no surprises throughout the routine. Divinity danced around his attacks, and offered her own counters. It was like watching a practiced routine playing out live. There were no unnecessary movements, and each attack was blocked like it was predicted. With Divinity, that was to be expected, but with Petro, it was impressive. They continued their combative dance for close to two minutes before Petro increased the tempo. Sal could see him adding in feints to his attacks, and it actually caused a moment of uncertainty within Divinity, who seemingly dodged prematurely for attacks that never came.

"You're going to have to look a little farther ahead for these," Petro instructed as he continued his barrage of feint attacks, followed by real ones. Each time he connected an attack, he pushed Divinity away with the flat of his hand, or with a slight touch of his foot. None of them were designed to be particularly destructive, but rather, to prove a point.

Divinity's face was a mask of concentration as she, too, upped the tempo. Her attacks were far less controlled than Petro's, but she was getting progressively faster. Her arms flowed like water, pushing away his incoming attacks, while she bounced over his legs whenever they struck out. Sweat was visible on her brow as she continuously threw attacks that met air, or Petro's palm.

"There's no opening." Divinity panted as she took a step back. "How are you doing that?"

"I'm reading your body." Petro smiled. "If you're looking at the outcome rather than the movement, you're going to be getting countless mixed signals. Your body will want to react to the feint, but your ability will tell you it's fake. Instinct can be a powerful tool, but it looks like you're relying on your ability to see the truth."

"I don't understand," Divinity said finally as she stepped back again. Her eyes returned to their natural blue and she looked at Petro quizzically. "If I'm not using my instincts, how are they confusing my ability?"

Petro smiled warmly. "You're relying on your ability to know the truth. By reading your movements, I can change the truth faster than you can react to it." He gestured to where Sal stood. "We ran a series of dungeons and I wouldn't let him use the Perfect ability until we went against prowlers. He had to learn how to regulate his own body, and he went into each encounter without a guarantee that his ability would help him or save him. Training through desperate times is how you can build a truly formidable psyche."

Divinity looked at Sal in disbelief. "You were in a prowler dungeon?"

"I needed cores for a project, and Dad decided to help me get them," Sal said sheepishly, not sure how to respond to Divinity's look of surprise. It was weird that she didn't already know everything. *Was she acting like she hadn't divined all of this already? Or had she really come to the Argento Auction House without looking at the future?*

"And you're okay? You didn't get hurt or break down?" Divinity asked again, this time a little more pressing.

It was clear that Sal's words had struck some sort of chord. *Was there an alternate timeline where he broke down in a dungeon?*

Petro stepped forward and gestured at Sal. "He was remarkable. Used just his hands and his feet, tearing through an army of leechers." With a laugh, he tilted his head and looked at Divinity. "You should have seen his face when he kicked a prowler to death."

Divinity's jaw dropped as she looked between Petro and Sal in disbelief. "You're both messing with me, right? Sal went into a dungeon without a weapon…and kicked a prowler to death?"

"I'd offer to bring you both to a dungeon to show you," Petro admitted with a sigh. "But, unfortunately, the venue we're using for those runs isn't friendly to outsiders. I'm not a fan of giving spoils to the Hunter Bureau or the United Guilds Association and prefer to keep our business off the books."

Sal shot his father a warning look, but Petro waved him away.

"I wouldn't have said a word if I didn't trust in your judgment, Sal," Petro remarked casually as he gestured at Divinity. "She's your friend, so I'm sure she can keep a few secrets. She didn't go around telling people about your abilities, did she?"

Divinity's eyes were wide as she looked between them. "Wait, so you've been doing dungeons off the books…to get materials?" She looked as though she had come to a sudden realization. "So, that's why you asked Barry and not me? You didn't want to implicate me in something that wasn't legal?"

Sal was being offered a golden opportunity to capitalize on the misunderstanding, but he didn't want to take it. Just as he was about to tell her she had misunderstood, she let out a sigh of relief.

"I don't care about being invited to a dungeon, Sal," she clarified, just in case that wasn't clear. "I was worried that you were upset with me." Divinity laughed as she looked around the auction house. "But you were training yourself hard enough to take on prowlers? That's just…incredible! I'm so happy to hear that you're actually putting your mind to being a Hero!"

Petro smiled as he looked between them. "We need to whip him into shape if he's going to make a half-decent guildmaster. I hope we can count on your help while he's at Quest Academy?" He looked at Divinity, as though he had just enlisted her to a worthy cause.

Divinity laughed as she nodded. "He looks out for me just as much as I help him, so you've got nothing to worry about there."

Petro nodded with a satisfied smile. "Then, it's my duty to make sure you're not falling behind." He got into a fighting stance and gestured at her feet. "I've looked at your combat style, and there are a few improvements that I think would make you a much more formidable fighter. I'll use your martial arts and you can tell me what you think afterward."

Divinity's smile dropped as she looked at Petro in shock. "Wait…you can replicate martial arts?" She looked at Sal almost accusingly. "You said he was an Auctioneer!"

"All Sight," Sal reminded her as he gestured at his dad. It was funny because the first time he had heard those words were from Divinity herself.

Divinity stared at Sal before realization dawned on her. Her eyebrows shot up as she looked at Petro in surprise, who was smiling at her reassuringly.

"Trust me, it's more practice than it is ability." Petro added the disclaimer as he waved at his eyes. "Let's see how much we can help you improve while you're here."

Rather than answering, Divinity grinned as she dove forward with a right hook.

Petro just laughed as he replicated one of Divinity's kicks, which tapped her on the side of the shoulder before she could even get into range. He went a step further by hopping like she did, repositioning himself to her left side, where he tapped her on the shoulder again. "So, are you ready to start learning?"

"Please," Divinity answered with a breathless laugh, looking at Petro in wonder. "If you can do this sort of stuff, does that mean that Sal can in the future?"

Sal offered a shrug, because he honestly had no idea whether it was even possible.

Petro scoffed at the suggestion. "Of course he will. If he puts in the time to train, then there's nothing he can't do." He smiled at Sal and gave him a playful wink. "Well, that's if we're able to drag him out of his workshop."

Divinity laughed at the comment and moved back into a fighting stance. "I've been trying that for months. If you find the solution, let me know."

Sal pointed at the workshop. "Do you want me to just leave you two to it?" He was smiling as he spoke, as he didn't mind the teasing. Having Divinity in the auction house was actually quite fun, and he was delighted that his father was helping her with her combat. It wouldn't have been right if the only interaction they had was when Divinity was anxious about getting drunk, or when his parents were in full-on entertainer mode. This sort of scenario was much better, where Divinity could meet them in a calmer environment.

"Don't suppose you've seen a future where he gives us some grandchildren, have you?" Petro grinned before launching forward with a kick.

Divinity faltered at the question before bringing her hands up into a guard. The impact was light, and wasn't designed to hurt her. So when she took the hit, her arm barely moved. "Do you actually want to know?" she asked breathlessly, as though unsure whether Petro was joking or not.

"He's just trying to throw you off guard—ignore him," Sal insisted from the sidelines. "If he desperately wanted grandchildren, he could always adopt one."

Petro laughed as he created space between them. "Are you watching my movements?"

Divinity lowered her guard as she stared at him in confusion. "That wasn't my kick." Frowning, she looked at the space Petro's foot had just occupied.

Rather than answering, Petro imitated the kick again in a painfully slow sequence. "Are you seeing what's happening?" he asked her in a gentle tone as he pointed at his torso. "This tends to happen with flexible people. You have so much range of motion, that you're bringing your leg back farther to give it more momentum. Which means that the entire lead-up to the kick is telegraphed for an additional second. Because you're trying to create more force with the impact, you're twisting your whole upper body in the process." Petro followed through with the kick in midair, highlighting with a pat of his palm all the exposed areas of his side. "This opens you up for a counterattack, while your body is still trying to compensate for the added momentum and strength."

Divinity's head tilted to one side as she looked at the kick in a whole new light. "If I keep my form, then I won't be able to draw out strength. It's a compromise that I'm already aware of, but I didn't realize how open it left me."

Petro nodded in understanding. "Bad habits will compound over time. If you just rely on the strength and mobility, you'll get punished for it." He brought his leg down and got back into his initial fighting stance. "My proposal would be to go back to the basics, and create a sequence of attacks that wears down your opponent. Death by a thousand cuts, rather than trying to end it with a single strike."

"But I'd need to have monstrous stamina to go with that sort of approach." Divinity frowned as she looked down at her own hands. "I can hold my own in a fight, but...not a drawn-out one."

Petro waved the concern away like it was nothing. "Stamina can be trained. It takes hard time and effort, but it's not unattainable for someone with a good work ethic. With everything Salvatore has told me about you, I know that you've got what it takes."

Sal had said nothing of the sort. His father was clearly trying to give Divinity a morale boost, and he wasn't going to be the one to shatter that. With a nod of agreement when she looked over in surprise, he was rewarded with a shy smile before she got back into her stance.

"Is this the style of martial arts that you've been teaching Sal?" Divinity asked.

"Nope." Petro shook his head. "He's learning a specific art that suits his frame. Strong kicks and keeping range." He pointed at where Divinity stood. "You're going to be learning an art that's perfect for you and your ability."

Sal perked up at that. He had thought that his father only had the Silverson Arts, but there were more fighting styles he was able to teach?

"You have speed and excellent mobility. Rather than putting yourself in front of an opponent to duke it out, you should be positioning yourself at their weak point." Petro spoke confidently before he burst forward at Divinity. It was like a flash of movement, and before her arms could even fully come up to block the frontal attack, Petro stood behind her with his fingers lightly pressed against the base of her neck.

"Whoa…" Sal breathed as he looked at his father in surprise.

Divinity looked absolutely horrified. Clearly none of her visions had prepared her for such an outcome.

"Style." Petro chuckled. "It's the combat arts that the Assassin class trains for." He patted Divinity on the shoulder as he walked around her to see her stricken expression. "Style is the perfect match for someone who can glimpse into the future."

Divinity looked at him in utter disbelief. "You think I should be an Assassin?"

Petro laughed as he shook his head. "Not at all…I just think you should fight like one."

CHAPTER 84: COMPROMISE

"I can't move my body," Divinity muttered with a heavy sigh. "How have you been putting yourself through all of this?" She gestured back in the direction of the lobby, where Petro was speaking with Sophia. After his mother had arrived, the sparring had started to wind down and they all had tea and coffee. Divinity had peppered Sal's father with questions relating to the Style Arts, and it had resulted in Petro gifting her a half dozen manuals for her to read over.

"You get used to it." Sal laughed as he led the way to the workshop. "Well, you get used to the training…not the surprises that keep coming up. I was not expecting him to just appear behind you like that."

Divinity clutched the gifted manuals to her chest, as though scared they might disappear if she let go of them. "They're so nice." She smiled. "Like, I didn't know what to expect at all…but they're a lot different than you've described."

Sal chuckled as he waved his hands. "Well, they're a lot different from what I remember, too. I wasn't aware of their background until a couple of weeks ago. I'm guessing you knew about the Silverson Group?"

Divinity shook her head in the negative. "No, actually. I never had any reason to look up a future regarding your parents. I always just assumed that the Argento Plaza happened because of their financial backing…I didn't expect them to be Heroes." She looked at Sal curiously. "I've been avoiding looking into your future for a while now. Because I don't want it to impact our friendship."

Sal led the way up the metallic stairs to the Arkwright. When he turned toward Divinity, he could see that she stood still at the base of the stairs, her eyes taking everything in; the carriage that contained a wealth of materials, the tracks, the marble platform that reflected the evening sun overhead. He smiled as he saw the look of wonder on her face.

"I'm sorry I've been a shit friend for the last few months," Sal said earnestly as he leaned against the railing. "I should have invited you over sooner."

Divinity broke out of her trance-like state and looked at him in surprise. "Your whole world came crashing down, and you're apologizing?"

Sal didn't know how to respond to that. He felt like it was a convenient way out of feeling guilty, but he wasn't going to take it. With a shake of his head, he pointed at the Arkwright against the wall. "I got a bit obsessed with getting this thing up and running, and everything else just faded into the background. Then, after the gala…yeah, there were a few revelations with my family, and the training started for real. Then there was the dungeons and the projects with Fabi. There was just a lot going on, and I should have told you about everything while it was happening."

"How are things going with Fabi?" Divinity started to climb the stairs, the training manuals still gripped tightly against her chest. "Are you working well together?"

Sal cocked an eyebrow, taking Divinity's trademark reaction to everything, and using it against her. "Really? You're not going to ask if we're set to get married? I told her about that vision and she laughed it off with Upgrade."

Divinity looked startled. "Wait, you actually told her?"

Sal nodded. "Yep, and everything is fine. We've just been working together up here and we've been experimenting with a few designs."

"The Mythmark?" Divinity asked hopefully as she moved over to the work-bench to set down the manuals. Her eyes locked onto the Arkwright, and her jaw practically dropped. "Why does it have a dungeon fragment in it?"

"Doc Ameye said the key problem with Crafting was that it didn't have the will of a Crafter. He put the dungeon fragment into it so that it could properly Craft the designs, but it seems to be locked at the Epic grade for the moment, until I upgrade it," Sal explained as he sat down in one of the chairs, looking at the Arkwright thoughtfully. He was wondering whether it would be unfair to ask Divinity about the Mythic-grade design blueprint. Although things were going smoothly between them, he didn't want to relegate her to feeling like a tool that could show him the future.

"But it's only supposed to manufacture materials," Divinity insisted as she looked at Sal in surprise. "It doesn't actually Craft things, right?"

Sal stared at her for a few seconds, letting her words sink in. "It Crafts weapons and equipment. But it also does the material research and blueprint research."

Divinity sat down heavily in the chair and put her hands over her face for a few seconds before peeking through her fingers. "That…definitely changes things."

Sal chuckled as he spread his hands, as though it were an inevitable outcome. "Come on, how many times have I accidentally changed one of your futures? This should lead to a better one, right?" He wasn't angry that Divinity had locked onto a specific future again. He imagined it was the only way she kept herself sane throughout all the compounded trauma the future showed her.

Biting her lip, Divinity nodded slowly. "It looks incredible."

Sal smiled as he got to his feet, groaning. "So…what would you like made?"

"What?" Divinity asked, her eyes going wide.

"I just told you that it can make equipment. I have it loaded up with materials, so I can make you a few pieces for the next semester. If they aren't done by the time we drop you home, I can bring them to Quest Academy for you," Sal insisted as he moved over to the Arkwright, tapping at the interface to remove the series of error reports around the Mythic-grade gauntlet.

"Wait…what was that?" Divinity suddenly appeared at his side, her head ducked underneath his outstretched arm to get a better look. "Mythic grade?" She looked up at him in wonder. "What is it talking about?"

Sal laughed as he offered a shrug. "I didn't want to ask you about it, in case it felt like I was using you to see the future." He was surprised to see a hurt look on her face. "Like you said to me before? That I kept asking to see the future, and it was cheapening our friendship?"

Divinity stepped back from the Arkwright, frowning at Sal. "That's not what I meant. You can always ask me about the future…I just didn't want that to be the sole basis of our friendship." She gestured vaguely off to the right with her hand. "And there are times that I'll need to refuse, because those visions will end up pushing you in a weird direction."

"What sort of visions did Fabi and Victoria come under?" Sal smiled, trying to lighten the mood.

Divinity shrugged. "I just wanted to see Barry look uncertain for a change. I threw in Fabi as a name because she's almost certainly going to be a part of your guild in the future. I didn't really expect it to blow out of proportion like it did. I don't know if it was because of what I said, but she now has a ridiculously powerful ability, and there's less reason for her to be in your guild." She grimaced as she looked at the Arkwright. "Like, one little comment about you getting married, and suddenly there's a future with countless drones on the battlefield. Insane, isn't it?"

"Oh…" Sal said finally. A part of him was sure that it had been a real vision from Divinity. But she had just been messing with him and Barry? When he thought about it, his actions with Fabi didn't have anything to do with Divinity's vision. He did everything that he would have done, even if he didn't know her. Just as that thought happened, he realized that he was wrong. In the moment that he was adjusting her weave, his emotional state of wanting Fabi to have the best possible ability was what caused him to make the changes. There were safer options to choose from, but because he had met her, he gave it his all. Still, that wouldn't have really been a result of Divinity…since Upgrade was the one who asked him to look at her weave, and Upgrade introduced them.

"You're overthinking it, aren't you?" Divinity asked quietly, as though uncertain of what outcome awaited when Sal eventually came up for air.

"I don't think you really changed anything," Sal finally said as he looked at Divinity carefully. "I'm going through all the thoughts I had leading up to the gala, and I'm sure I would have done the same thing. You don't need to feel guilty about anything like that. The drones aren't really a surprise, though. All you have to do is start a conversation with Fabi, and she'll end up talking about them."

"What was the Mythic grade?" Divinity asked again as she pointed at the Arkwright. "Did you make something?"

Rather than answering instinctively, Sal hesitated. "What do you think it is?"

Divinity smiled as she exhaled slowly. "Okay…you're fishing." She put her hands on her hips and thought about the question. After a moment of staring at the Arkwright, she turned to look around the workshop, as though looking for something. "You don't have what's needed yet…but you could probably build it. I'm guessing that you're not making the big drone yet?"

Sal wanted to say the word "yet" aloud, but he stopped himself and remained quiet. Hearing from Divinity that it was possible was incredible, and he had a thousand questions that he needed to stifle. Instead, he waited patiently for her to guess again.

Divinity's smile grew wider as she looked at the Arkwright. "It's the Arsenal, isn't it?" She looked at Sal, seemingly delighted with herself.

"Maybe," was all Sal could get out in a normal voice. His mind was going ninety miles per hour, trying to parse what the Arsenal might be. "What makes you think that?" There was a higher inflection than normal, but it seemed like Divinity wasn't aware of his voice change. Although Sal could lie perfectly during a negotiation, he was rarely ever this compromised when it came to the outcome.

Divinity gestured at her left shoulder and waved vaguely. "It's the one with the shoulder thing?"

Sal's face broke into a wide grin as he moved back to the workbench and picked up the parchment for the gauntlet. "Does this look familiar?" He handed it to her, and was pleased to see a look of recognition on her face.

"Ooooh, it looks way clearer here." She looked at the blueprint, excited. "Your drawing ability is incredible," she remarked as she looked closer at some of the smaller details. When she handed back the drawing, she looked at the workbench expectantly, as though waiting for something.

"Looking for something?" Sal asked as he caught the expression on her face.

"The rest of it?" Divinity answered, as though it were obvious. "The chest piece and the—" She faltered as she looked at Sal in surprise. "You haven't drawn those yet, have you?"

Sal smiled as he held up a finger, this time saying the word aloud. "Yet! But this is great. Since you already know what I'm making…you can fill in some of the blanks?"

Divinity's brow scrunched as she looked at Sal. "I'm not going to tell you anything else about it, otherwise it might ruin it." She looked thoughtful for a second as she glanced back at the Arkwright. "But I will say, it's a relief. I thought that you would stop Crafting if this thing was able to do the Crafting for you."

Sal waved the concern away. "It's going to be staying here while I go back to Quest Academy. I designed it so I could make stuff for the auctions while I'm not here."

"A little overkill, don't you think? If it's able to make Epic grades, then doesn't that kinda make a lot of Crafters obsolete?" Divinity asked cautiously, as though worried she might upset Sal with the observation.

"Not at all." Sal laughed. "If a Crafter can't use essence, but is able to make incredible blueprints…then this works perfectly for them. It would enable way more Crafters to test their inventions in a safe environment. But that's assuming I ever put it in a public workshop or space. Right now, it's going to be kept here for my parents to use."

Divinity nodded, smiling. "So, are you going to turn up to Quest Academy with a load of presents for everyone?"

Sal looked at the Arkwright and couldn't believe he hadn't thought of that. "That depends…would you be willing to help me out?"

Divinity laughed as though he were being ridiculous. "I'm not a Crafter, Sal. I wouldn't even know where to begin."

Sal tapped the side of his head. "I'm asking if we can use your power for evil. I want you to look into the future to see what gifts would get the best reaction from them."

"That's cheating," Divinity insisted as she crossed her arms, but there was still a smile on her face.

"No," Sal corrected her. "It's incredibly efficient bribery."

Divinity sighed in defeat as she threw up her arms. She walked over to the seat beside the workbench and grinned as she sat. "Okay then…who do we start with?"

Sal didn't even hesitate as he answered. There was one person he was more indebted to than anyone else at Quest Academy.

"Upgrade."

CHAPTER 85: CULMINATION

"Thank you so much for having me over. I had a lot of fun today." Divinity practically beamed as she clutched the manuals tightly to her chest. Her bag with the training outfit was slung over her shoulder as she stood in front of the private cab. "I had no idea that we'd end up staying up so late, but it was great. Please thank your parents again for the hospitality and for the training!"

"Of course. It was a pleasure having you here," Sal answered earnestly. She had insisted on getting a cab instead of having Petro drive her home, especially with how they ended up talking in the workshop well into the night. "Just message me when you get home safe, okay?"

Divinity laughed as she opened the door of the cab. "As if you'll even be able to read it. I know for a fact that you're going to start Crafting before the cab even gets into the air." She didn't sound upset at all, but rather excited by the prospect. "I want all the pictures of that gauntlet, and Upgrade's gift, okay?"

"It's a promise." Sal lifted his tablet to show her that it still worked. "You're more than welcome to come back for more of the training, before we head back. My dad insisted I let you know."

Divinity grinned as she hesitated at the door of the cab. "I'll see how I get on with the manuals first, and then come back if I've got questions. I don't want to end up distracting you from changing the world." She winked at that last part before getting into the cab, a wide smile still on her face as she waved from the passenger seat.

Sal waved back and watched as she set off into the dark night. The underside of the cab kept a bright-white light aimed at the ground, which was replicated in its upward trajectory, giving the black cab a continuous stream of light as it ascended. It looked like she was being summoned by the heavens, which was quite fitting when Sal thought of the wings that manifested with the full use of her ability. He needed to finish the Valkyrie set for her when he got back to the workshop at Quest Academy. All his insistence around making equipment for her had fallen on deaf ears. She was elated with her circlet, and she didn't even humor the notion of him making anything else for her.

When the cab's lights disappeared, Sal saw the beam of light focused in a straight line, aimed toward Memorial Square. He waited until the cab had made its way out of Silver Sanctuary before making his way back into the auction house. To his surprise, his father was leaned up against the bar in the lounge section, while his mother was fixing up a drink.

"She's lovely," Sophia remarked, smiling warmly. "I'm glad that we got to meet her properly."

Petro nodded in agreement as he took the whiskey offered by Sophia. "I would have dropped her home, no problem." He spoke earnestly, as though trying to convince Sal that it wasn't a burden.

Sal waved it off. "I appreciate it, but she was adamant that we let her get a cab. Thank you so much for the sparring with her. It's rare to see her that ruffled or surprised, so it was definitely worth it."

Petro smiled as he swirled the whiskey in the glass tumbler. "She looked like she was holding herself back. They're the fun ones to train." He glanced at Sophia with a knowing smile. "Would have been great to get you into the ring with her, but it would have been an overload for the poor girl."

"Holding herself back?" Sal asked in confusion. "She looked like she was trying her best, though?"

"Poor choice of words, sorry." Petro responded with an almost dismissive wave. "It was great to have her here. What did she think of the Arkwright?"

Sal wasn't letting him off the hook like that. "What did you mean by holding herself back?" He wanted to understand what they were talking about, especially if it was something to do with Divinity. If she was unconsciously putting herself into difficulty, then he'd want to prevent that at all costs.

Sophia smiled as she uncorked a bottle of white wine. "Your father has trained countless people back at the Silverson Group. He has a lot of insight from that experience, and they're not always based on hard facts." She started to pour herself a glass as she glanced at Petro. "Go on, give him your verdict."

Petro looked at Sal, who gave him a simple nod, as though it were permission to continue.

"When learning a fighting style, there needs to be a baseline," Petro started as he traced an invisible line with his finger. "You need to create a stable foundation of basic movements. You then introduce new movements while continually refining the basics." He traced a new line slightly higher than the first. "Incremental gains over time, which then opens up sequences like combination attacks. Everything depends on a stable form that can be built upon."

Sal nodded in understanding. It was a completely logical approach.

"When you introduce an ability that can look into the future, you're suddenly met with advanced techniques…that have been created from experience. Forms that have evolved to cover weaknesses, and routines that have been refined against new enemies." Petro looked at Sal carefully, and the finger that traced an invisible line abruptly spiked up. "If the fighter suddenly tries to emulate future techniques without the basics, foundations, or experiences…then they'll create a paradox for themselves. Because their new future will be based around the limitations they've put on themselves in the present. That skewed style will become farther and farther from the ideal solution that it appeared to be."

"And you saw that from a simple spar with Divinity?" Sal asked in disbelief.

Petro shook his head. "No. I saw her resisting the movements. Hesitation in knowing that her kicks can have more reach, movement that can put her into better spaces, punches that contain incredible force…I watched as she fought against herself." He smiled as he glanced at Sophia. "That's why they're the fun ones to train. They know there's no shortcut to success."

Sal thought about it for a few moments. He recalled the time when Divinity was frustrated in Professor Lombardi's Skill class. "I told Divinity she could get ahead in one of the classes by using her power, but she adamantly refused. She wanted to learn it herself, rather than cheating by looking into the future." He looked at his father. "So, you think she's doing the same with fighting?"

Petro's eyebrow was raised as he looked at Sal in surprise. "Wisdom at such a young age is quite remarkable. I think you've made quite a friend for yourself,

Salvatore." He chuckled as he knocked back the last of the whiskey in his glass. "I'm more excited to see how she'll adapt to Style. It's a framework that will give her that explosive growth, without risking the basics."

"Is there a special martial art that you think would suit me?" Sal asked out of curiosity. "Like, Style sounds pretty cool."

Sophia rolled her eyes as she looked at Petro. "I told you he'd ask."

Petro laughed as he got to his feet with a shake of his head. "I just told you about the basics and building foundations…" With a feigned sigh of exasperation, he gestured at Sal's body. "You're built like a Silver, and your kicks will be formidable. You're learning the basic combat of the Silverson Arts, and then when you're comfortable with it, we'll build on that with the officer training. Everything is separated into rank, and you're at the beginning of your journey."

Sal smiled as he held his hands up. "I wasn't criticizing…Style just sounds a little more badass."

Petro placed his hands on his hips and looked at Sophia for backup. "Are you hearing this?"

Sophia just raised her glass in salute to Sal. "I'm with you, a hundred percent."

Sal laughed before pointing toward the workshop. "I'm thinking of doing some Crafting before heading to bed. Sparring tomorrow?"

Petro gave Sophia a wide-eyed glance. "First, he besmirches the Silverson Arts and then he asks for training. Has the boy no shame?"

"See you tomorrow, and don't stay up too late," Sophia warned him as she shooed him off to the workshop. "We'll start sparring in the afternoon…but then we'll have to finish up prepping for the upcoming auction."

"Perfect." Sal started to move. "I'll see you both then. I can't wait to learn more of the Silverson Arts, Dad."

"Yeah, yeah…" Petro waved him off, smiling. "Want me to get you some fancy manuals like I gave Divinity? Would that make you feel better?"

Sal blinked as he looked back at his dad. "You have something like that?"

Petro gave him a flat stare. "Have them? I wrote the damn things." He chuckled. "I'll bring them in with me tomorrow, but I expect some incredible pieces for the next auction. Something with obsidian will suit the theme!"

Sal laughed as he saw his mother swatting at Petro from behind the bar. "I'll work on something."

With that, he made his way down the stairs and couldn't help but notice that the traces of prowler blood were nowhere to be seen. He hadn't cleaned it up himself, and wondered who managed to get to it before him. He hadn't even thought to look while Divinity was around.

When he strode through the doors to the workshop, he was quite excited. Having had Divinity over for the day was a weight off his conscience. A part of him thought that they were going to be at odds with each other, but there had been nothing like that. Everything went smoothly, and they laughed and talked for hours while looking into the future. He had a detailed list of items that he'd be able to make for everyone back at Quest Academy, and some of them were surprisingly simple.

Sal had thought of just using the Arkwright to make a chunk of them, but Divinity told him that it would be better received if he made them by hand. He wasn't sure how true that was, but he agreed with the sentiment. Outsourcing gifts wasn't going to make anyone feel particularly special. He had a wealth of materials to draw on, and it was nice to have a focus for his last days at the Argento Auction House.

The thing he needed to focus on more than anything was the Mythic-grade gauntlet that he had designed. Sal wasn't sure how long it would take him, but he was absolutely going to outsource the material production for that one. Just the thought of manually carving out forty armor plates of pure essence was a nightmare. The Arkwright would get the heavy lifting done, and then he'd focus on the assembly. He was going to commission Fabi to work on the essence programming component, because he did not want to write anymore code for at least another few months. He desperately hoped that the Introduction to Essence Programming class would start out easy, and that he'd be allowed to use his tracker.

Sal picked up the blueprint for the gauntlet and smiled. It was an exciting prospect, knowing that Divinity had seen a positive future where he had built it. He didn't understand what she had meant when she said it was the Arsenal, but it sounded pretty cool.

With that thought in mind, Sal placed the blueprint to one side and slid on the tracker. It was time to create blueprints for the materials. Because the Arkwright couldn't process the blueprint as it was, he'd need to break it down into more manageable parts. Picking up the stylus, Sal drew out the small plates that would be made from the prowler cores.

Each core would be shaped into a condensed plate that would operate like a battery. He'd then stack each of them into the fabric like scale armor, allowing them to operate as one massive essence source. Then he'd need to make the mesh that would go over the cores, protecting them from impact. Silver was the original plan because of the Silverson gauntlets, but Sal had to compromise when he realized he'd need to break down the heirlooms his father had given him.

When Sal was happy with the composition of materials, he sent the details straight to the Arkwright and intended to get production underway immediately. Unfortunately, he was hit with a prompt asking him which core he'd like to use for the plates. If he had to pick each of them manually, then he'd be there for the rest of the evening.

Instead, he instructed the Arkwright to use the best cores available, with the exception of those that had been Crafted. After a few moments with the Arkwright processing his instructions, he went in to double-check that it wasn't going to accidentally use the blight core or venomstone for the plates. Neither of them were in the drop-down list.

A few more messages appeared, and Sal reviewed each of them diligently. He realized that each of the cores were being summoned to the screen to see whether they qualified for Crafting. Rather than painstakingly going through fifty messages, Sal made a new stipulation that it wasn't to use anything considered Legendary grade as a material, for the core project. Everything else was fair game. That protocol seemed to do the trick as all the prompts disappeared and the Arkwright started up in earnest. The last of the prompts that appeared was for confirmation that he'd like to use the best possible materials, while abiding by the protocols set.

Sal accepted and waited to see whether anything else would appear. When it didn't, he let out a sigh of relief and returned to the workbench. It would take a while for the prowler cores to be refined, but it would be worth it. He looked at the rest of the materials that he needed and asked the Arkwright to place them into the loading tray. Sal smiled in excitement as he saw chunks of metal and cloth being sent down the conveyor belt.

It was going to be a long evening, but there was nothing else he needed to worry about. He had everything he needed right there.

He was going to make his first Mythic grade.

CHAPTER 86: RECREATION

Sal stared at the Arkwright in disbelief. "Why are you like this?" He was at his wit's end. All the parameters he had put in place had been misinterpreted to the highest degree. His hope to have a series of higher quality prowler cores used for production had been thrown out the window. Now, he was left with the stupidest interpretation of his own request. Sal looked at the workbench in front of him and couldn't help but sigh at the glittering plates that shone back at him. Most of them were different colors, but cut the same way. They were plates, yes. Just like he had asked for. That wasn't the problem.

Task Complete: (40/40)
- o   Venomstone x 12 (Epic Grade)
- o   Wraithstone x 3 (Epic Grade)
- o   Shadow Glass x 14 (Epic Grade)
- o   Veilstone x 2 (Epic Grade)
- o   Bloodstone x 4 (Epic Grade)
- o   Scuttler Core x 2 (Epic Grade)
- o   Ether Crystal x 3 (Epic Grade)

The best conclusion Sal was able to take from all of this was that there were four plates that came from the prowler core. It wasn't any of the normal ones, but instead the big one that his father had procured from the red prowler. It was apparently called a bloodstone. The leecher cores had been used to produce the higher-tier venomstone material, which hopefully didn't result in the blight core being scrapped. Sal would have been furious with the Arkwright if that was the case.

With a quick check of his visor, he saw that there was a blight core still in inventory. It was a massive relief. He hadn't been sure whether researching and production were the same, but it turned out that each of the materials he researched, there was at least one of them in storage within the Arkwright.

Putting the thought to one side, he wondered whether all the conflicting cores would cause an issue or whether they'd play nice with each other on the gauntlet. All he needed was their essence capacity, rather than anything else. If the whole project turned out to be a failure, he'd find another use for them or feed them back into the Arkwright with the most crystal-clear instructions of what he wanted it to do.

"Let's get started," Sal said quietly, as though it would psych him up for the task. He didn't like the idea that the project was doomed from the very beginning. So rather than immediately jumping into the Crafting, he used the new materials against the blueprint of the Mythic grade, just to see whether it was all compatible.

It was not a quick process as Sal had to simulate each combination of the plates, with various layouts, just to see whether they would take to the gauntlet. Thankfully, after eighty-three simulations, according to Cypher, there was a positive match. That was enough for Sal, and he saved it as the new order for the blueprint. Just to ensure he wasn't working off the wrong information, he made the new notes on the physical blueprint so it would match the visualization.

His bad mood dissolved the moment he started to channel his essence into the abyssal steel. There was no room for useless thoughts as he had to give his full concentration to the task at hand. It was an entirely new experience compared to any material he had worked with before, as the metal felt ridiculously reactive to his essence. Sal instinctively knew that if he poured everything he had into the abyssal steel to make it malleable, it would likely shatter.

So all his efforts went into giving it a gradual but steady stream of essence, warming it up and pulling at it with his fingers to make the frame of the gauntlet. It was as slow as it was meticulous, and Sal became fully absorbed into the task at hand. It was like goading a reluctant snail, pushing against the resistance and ushering it toward an unseen finish line.

The abyssal steel lumbered into the new shape, and Sal had to fight every desire to rush the process. It was slow and steady, and he didn't break his concentration at any point throughout the exercise. The only instance where he nearly screwed up was when he forgot to breathe; that slight jump-start of his lungs almost caused the soft metal to shatter.

When the mesh started to properly form, Sal looped it around to create a cylindrical shape. It would house his arm, and he needed to give enough space to allow for the inner lining and the essence plates. There also needed to be plenty of space to mount the custom drone dock.

Sal didn't overthink how much was left to do; he simply got on with the task and achieved a flow-like state. He was so engrossed in the task that he ended up forgetting to use Perfect. Instead, he used his eyes and essence to guide the abyssal steel into the desired shape. A goofy smile appeared on his lips as the wrapped metal joined up perfectly, allowing him to meld the joints together in a seamless fashion.

At least an hour passed, with Sal coaching the steel into the frame he wanted. And when it was done, he was positively elated and couldn't wait to move onto the next part of the process. Before the abyssal steel even cooled, Sal had the storm steel and starlight steel in his hands. He was going to blend them into a new alloy to create the fist of the gauntlet. The palm would be made with the nightshade leather, as well as the interior layer. Sal was almost playful in melding together the storm steel and starlight steel, turning it into a singular ball of putty.

His essence didn't need to do any refining with the material at all, as both ingots had no impurities. Instead, he focused on making sure they were blended properly. His visor registered that the new alloy was perfect for the gauntlet, and Sal paused only for a moment. He was sure that it had been a part of the overall design. When he double-checked the instructions, he saw that the blending of materials wasn't referenced at all. He had just done it instinctively.

Sal noticed that the glowing ball of essence-infused metal in his hands was starting to cool with his hesitation, so rather than overthinking, he continued with the Crafting process. It reminded him of the first gauntlet that he had made, with Hannah sitting on his bed as he made his first ever Rare grade.

The memory brought a smile to his face as he started to create the fingers, using his essence to shape and form the new alloy. They were hollowed, blunt instruments that looked like they'd never allow movement, but that was something he could work on later. They just needed to be big enough to accommodate the nightshade leather.

The abyssal steel mesh had finished cooling off by the time Sal was happy with the gauntlet fist. There needed to be work done on it, but it was enough for the next part of the process. Plucking the leather from the workbench, Sal didn't even take notice of the lustrous sheen on the surface. It looked like a starry night, flickering through stormy clouds. All that beauty was lost on Sal as he stuffed it into the glowing metal alloy.

When that was done, it was suddenly a race against time. Sal used his right hand to keep the essence flowing into the melted alloy, while he tracked his left arm through the abyssal steel mesh. He lamely tried to pluck the end of the nightshade leather with his left hand before slowly pulling it through the mesh. Finally, when the mesh met the glowing alloy, Sal started to flood the leather with his essence. He was thankful that he could shape the leather with essence alone, and it blossomed around his arm, following his intent as it sank around the mesh frame.

Wiggling the fingers of his left hand, Sal was able to form the malleable leather into a perfect glove. With that done, he fused the combined alloy into the leather, while flexing his fingers to create natural joints. He didn't even need to look at the blueprint to know what part came next.

The essence plates would be slotted into place along the forearm, before the top layer of armor would be secured over it. Sal didn't even bother to bring his left hand out of the gauntlet frame. He instead used it to steady it while he placed the individual plates onto the glowing leather. They slotted in perfectly between the ridges of the abyssal steel mesh, clicking into place as they instantly fused with the frame.

"Thirty-nine to go," Sal breathed as he continued the painstaking process, glancing at the visor-approved blueprint from time to time to make sure he was coordinating them properly. The color scheme was awful, with a vibrant red alongside a glowing white, followed by a sickly green. There was no coordination and it looked like a mess, but the visor had pretty much said this was the only method to get them to function together properly.

Sal sighed as he continued to place each essence plate along the ridges. The whole project looked more and more ridiculous with each new palette, but Sal persisted until the job was done. An unexpected dilemma occurred when he was on the twenty-eighth plate…in the form of the previous plates forcibly jumping out of the mesh and clattering to the floor.

"What the—?" Sal almost jumped out of his skin when the sudden noise appeared beside him. He inspected the forearm of the frame and saw that three of the bloodstones had escaped from the gauntlet. There was even some sizzling along the nightshade leather, with a few flecks of abyssal steel peeking through. Ignoring it for the moment, Sal continued with the pattern for the other plates, telling himself that he'd go back to place the bloodstones more carefully.

That task crept up on him far quicker than he expected. Sal lifted the gauntlet frame off the workbench, keeping it on his arm as he bent at the knee to pick up the bloodstone plates. He was surprised at how light the overall frame was, but he assumed that it would be harder to move when he added in the drone dock and the outer plating.

Sal got back to his feet and went to sit at the workbench. With two of the bloodstone plates stacked near his chest, he carefully tried to adhere the third one to the gauntlet. The essence he had been using for each of the plates had been the same, and that was the key flaw. Sal must have missed it when he was doing them all at the same time, but they all had a wildly different adherence to the leather and steel. With an inward groan, Sal tested different levels of essence flow to see which would match the bloodstone. To his surprise, he had to use raw essence rather than the finely refined essence that had worked until that point. Once he had a grasp of it, he pushed through the discomfort of releasing such a raw output and got the remaining two plates fixed in place.

Sal then reviewed every other plate to ensure they were secured properly to the frame. He didn't want to have to do this again, and he was relieved to only have a dozen or so tweaks to make. It was a painfully slow process, but when it was done, Sal was both exhausted and elated. He was also ready to commit murder for one of Alex's coffees.

"Drone dock?" Sal asked as he referenced the blueprint in front of him. His gaze landed on the relevant part of the schematic and he slipped his left arm out of the gauntlet frame. "Drone dock." Sal wriggled the fingers of his left hand, dissipating the invisible essence that had caused it to numb.

This was the part that Sal was looking forward to, and also dreading. With how much fine-tuning went into the rest of the piece, this was going to be a bludgeoning of skill and essence. He would rely on his Perfect ability and the visor for this one. He paused for a moment at that thought. Perfect hadn't been activated yet.

"Oops," Sal muttered as he activated the weave with a rueful smile. "Let's just hope that the rest of it is fine." He glanced at the frame and dismissed any thoughts of redoing it. Those plates were painful. There were no immediate warnings from the visor that he had made an error, and no incoming suggestions, outside of patching up the singed piece of nightshade leather. Sal was happy to have that tiny piece of leather be the singular defect. Actually, being honest with himself, he was convinced he'd be able to smooth that out when it came to the final touches.

Sal pulled a small container from the floor up to the workbench. It was one he had taken from the carriage, and it stored all the materials he'd need to create the drone dock. He still needed to withdraw the blight core from the Arkwright that would power the actual drone, but that was the final phase of the project. There was still armor plating that needed to be done that would cover up the exposed essence plates.

Staring into the bucket of materials, Sal sighed and prayed that Upgrade would never find out about this. He flooded his essence into the bucket and kept his eyes locked on the image the visor was showing him. The drone dock was going to be a brute-force job of essence and Mythcrafter, with the outcome hopefully being functional. With a smile on his face, Sal focused on the task at hand.

"Please don't be shit," he breathed at the bucket.

CHAPTER 87: BLIGHT CORE

Sal sat in front of the Arkwright, waiting for the last of the load order to be completed. He had done enough for the drone dock to be considered a prototype. But rather than trying to fine-tune his essence into giving it the full functionality, he had deposited it into the Arkwright to cross the final hurdle. That endeavor, with all the heavy lifting done by Sal, had only taken thirty minutes. The Mythcrafter Algorithm and Cypher were far better suited than him to tackle the essence chip required for the drone dock. That wasn't something that could be shaped with a surge of essence and hope.

Next, he got the Arkwright to create the enclosures for the gauntlet, which would protect the essence plates from harm. His newly created alloy was perfect for the job, and by combining the paltry amount of storm steel and starlight steel, he had enough to make the cases for the gauntlet.

Bringing the second cup of coffee to his lips, Sal watched as the countdown ticked away. He used the full power of the visor to speed up the process, and he allocated a chunk of the unused prowler cores to give the Arkwright as much essence as it needed. It was the moment of truth. *Would the blight core take to the abyssal steel enclosure?* Sal had come to terms with the fact that the Arkwright wouldn't be able to manufacture the Mythic-grade blueprint, but it didn't mean it would be completely useless.

Sal was delighted to see that it was able to make mechanisms that would have taken an age to create by hand. There was clearly a limit to the minutiae that could be achieved with a flood of essence, and Sal hit that wall with the drone dock. Just reading from a visor wasn't enough to fundamentally understand what was happening, and even his flow state of concentration wasn't enough to overcome the required knowledge. That's why he needed to rely on the Arkwright to get it over the finishing line.

Sal got to his feet as the last few seconds counted down on the interface. He half-expected this to be a failure, or to be hit with an error report. But he still unconsciously held his breath for a positive outcome. The Crafting of the previous night had really been a draining experience. Constantly utilizing essence at various rates for different materials had been both physically and mentally taxing.

Blight Core Enclosure: Complete

Relief flooded through Sal like a wave, and he almost teared up at the sight of those beautiful words. The tiredness was getting to him, but the end was finally in sight. All he needed to do was put the pieces together and he would be finally able to get some sleep.

He pulled open the loading tray and was met with the most gorgeous sight he had seen in a long time. A sparkling emerald the size of his fist was nestled perfectly in a slightly scratched black enclosure. It was like a spider was upside down, clasping at the jewel from all sides with its eight legs. Sal tentatively lifted out the jewel and was delighted to see that the base of the jewel had various sockets, designed for the abyssal steel tendrils that had been produced earlier.

Sal wasted no time in picking up the drone dock with his other hand, bringing them over to the workbench. It was the final phase of the build, and it was very energizing. He practically skipped back to the Arkwright's loading tray with a grin on his face, plucking out the abyssal steel tendrils. They were solid and would need to be coaxed into the grooves of the gauntlet, but that was fine. Sal double-checked that he had everything he needed, feeling wide-awake at the prospect of being close to finished.

He was like a man possessed as he slotted in each of the tendrils. His essence regulation was ridiculously potent with the help of Perfect, and he fused each of them into place quickly and efficiently. The momentum carried through as he sidestepped to the gauntlet frame. Sal placed down the blight core and embedded the drone dock into the frame, paying special attention to rotate it to the correct angle. The tendrils would need to be lined up with the grooves. If he haphazardly socketed it, then they'd never be able to connect.

When he heard the satisfying click of the dock being secured into the frame, Sal grinned broadly. His heart rate picked up despite Perfect's best efforts. Nothing could stop him from feeling excited. Next came the blight core with its black base. The sparkling green was a gorgeous contrast to the black metal of the surrounding dock. When he socketed it, he carefully rotated it until the tendrils were matched up against the grooves. Another satisfying click told him that it was locked into position.

Sal channeled his essence into the abyssal steel, being careful to not alter the tendril's length, but instead to soften it enough that it could settle into the carved grooves. Each protective plate that was made with the alloy was a deep blue in color, with flecks of white light that seemed to peek through at random. Hints of green, red, white, and purple were visible at the edges…the result of having a multicolored set of essence plates. Sal didn't care about how it looked for the moment, as he was after the functionality it offered. The first tendril took Sal awhile, but each subsequent one took less time. When he finally got the last one embedded into the groove, Sal took a step back to give the entire gauntlet a proper look.

It wasn't an attractive sight, but Sal didn't care. The beauty of the blight core worked well with the nightshade leather, but the abyssal steel looked like a murky brown streaked with black. It looked closer to an amalgam of scrapped materials, and the glowing lights of the essence plates didn't help in the slightest. Sal bent at the waist and angled his body so he could slide his entire left arm through the gauntlet. It was awkward, but Sal grimaced and continued to force his arm through until his fingers found their leather sheaths.

Before he did anything else, he fished the tablet out of his right pocket and snapped a few pictures of the monstrosity on his arm. He sent them to Divinity, asking her what she thought with a quick message. Dropping his tablet onto the workbench, he gritted his teeth and tried to properly lift the gauntlet from the surface top.

Standing upright, Sal was keenly aware of the weight difference that was throwing him off-balance. His left shoulder was being pulled downward, and keeping the whole thing upright was a challenge. Grimacing, Sal leaned right and low to elevate the gauntlet. He then gradually fed his essence into the entire construct, with his visor and Perfect watching it intently.

Rather than sending it through his fingertips, Sal channeled the essence throughout his entire arm, soaking it into the nightshade leather, then through the abyssal steel frame, the essence plates, and finally through the protective alloy shells. An issue arose very quickly when the cores started to siphon off his essence, but Sal didn't let it faze him as he continued to send the essence everywhere else.

It slowly trickled into the drone dock and the abyssal tendrils, until it finally enveloped the sparkling green gem. Sal took a steadying breath as he compressed the entire build around his arm. It needed to be a snug fit that was molded for him, and bringing the padding around him would ensure that it wouldn't fall off if he stood straight.

The shoulder with the drone dock tightened against his skin, folding around his shirt and forming against his physical frame. Each of the spaces between materials was soaked with essence, pulling them tight and applying a coated finish. The essence plates slowly fused together, while the alloy shell melded perfectly against the frame.

Sal still felt a massive pull of essence being drawn into the plates, but he had plenty to spare. He didn't flood the gauntlet as there was far too much that could go wrong. He didn't want to upset the balance of the drone or the dock. If the essence screwed them up, then he'd need to wait for Fabi or Upgrade to help him get it right.

Sal slowly shifted his posture until he stood straight, with his shoulders level. The draw on his left arm was a lot less than before, and Sal guessed that the new fit was resting on his body a lot better. Wriggling his fingers, he felt the metal move fluidly. Clenching his fist was also satisfying, as it felt like it silently clicked into place, creating a perfect surface for attacking.

The elbow joint was a little rougher and Sal needed to focus more of the essence there to make it smooth. After a few more bends and rotations of his forearm, Sal was finally satisfied and started to raise his entire arm over his head. His range of motion was initially limited, but the shoulder adapted to the movement; after a few more attempts, Sal had the full mobility of his arm with the gauntlet attached.

Looking at it fondly, Sal was happy to see that the entire thing glowed in a haze of purple and white light. The Invention essence was doing its thing, and Mythcrafter was finding any inefficiencies that needed to be ironed out. His essence draw suddenly stopped, and Sal let out a sigh of relief. If the essence plates continued drinking up his internal reserves, then he wouldn't have been able to keep it going for more than ten minutes. His best guess was that the gauntlet was going to use the essence plates to complete any additional refinements.

Sal looked at the blueprint again to see whether there were any final touches he needed to implement before he finished up with the Crafting. But nothing on it caught his attention. So, he stood there in silence, sending excess essence through to inspect anything that might have been missed.

On the third check, he decided to coat the plates with another layer of essence, just to tighten things even further. He didn't foresee his forearm increasing in size in the near future, so he pulled the materials in closer to his skin, making the fit even more snug.

Restarting the checks, Sal went through everything a few more times until he had to admit that the gauntlet-sleeve-thing was as done as he'd ever be able to manage. When he looked at the shoulder, he had to turn a little extra to the left so the visor on his right eye would catch sight of the glowing drone.

New Device Found

The words that appeared in front of Sal's eye caused him to lift both arms in silent celebration. The drone signal had been caught by his visor, and it meant he'd have a safe method to input the correct protocols. If he got the files from Fabi, he'd be able to set the drone up without any sort of issues. Sal sat down heavily, sighing. It was actually done.

"Well fucking done," Sal said, to both himself and the Arkwright. He looked at the glowing essence and decided that it would be foolish to just pull his arm out before it was done. Unlike the time where his visor had scarred his face from a forced evolution, there was no burning sensation touching his arm. Rather, it felt like his arm was encased by a familiar and reassuring warmth.

Sal placed both of his arms on the workbench, folding his right so he could lean his head on it. He tried to keep his eyes open as he waited for the essence cooldown to finish, but the exhaustion and the lack of urgency caused him to fall asleep there and then.

Hours later, Sal awoke with a start. The first thing he saw was the glossy black surface of his new arm.

CHAPTER 88: MYTHIC

To say that Sal was hyperventilating would have been an understatement. He sat upright and moved his arm around in disbelief, completely stupefied at how dramatic the transformation had been. He had hoped for something that wouldn't be too bulky, but the reality was so far from his expectations. The glossy black metal encased his entire arm. It didn't look like armor at all, but rather like he had dipped his naked arm into a bucket of paint. It was ridiculously sleek, and he had the full range of motion at his wrist, elbow, and shoulder.

Sal looked at his left shoulder and saw no protrusion at all. What had previously been a bulky frame with layers of metal, padding, a drone dock, and then a drone…was now a sleek, flat surface that maybe came out an extra inch or two from his skin. The green jewel was still there, glowing like it was possessed. Each time it pulsated, ripples of green essence would track down the glossy black arm in a spiral formation. There weren't even any grooves, and Sal had to look with the visor to even see that the tendrils were locked in place. It was unimaginable to think that there was a drone embedded into his shoulder.

It took almost a minute of Sal marveling at the new sleeve, when his visor finally parsed what it was looking at. Sal was rewarded with a detailed Appraisal of the new piece of gear. He prayed inwardly that the drone was functional, and that it hadn't ended up just being a gorgeous but useless sleeve.

He was not disappointed.

Name	Mythical Blight Jackal
Origin	Crafted
Age	New
Grade	Mythic
Materials	Refined Mythcrafter Essence | Abyssal Steel | Storm Steel | Starlight Steel | Nightshade Leather | Bloodstone | Veilstone | Shadow Glass | Blight Core | Venomstone | Tempest Steel Alloy…
Attributes	**Arsenal:** Grants user access to a substantive private subspace that can store materials and goods. All materials in the subspace will be time-locked and preserved. • Jackal (Drone): Arsenal is synched with Jackal. Materials sourced by Jackal will be stored in Ar-

	senal subspace. Materials required for maintenance and repair of Jackal will be withdrawn from subspace. • Jackal Statistics: ○ Stored Materials: None ○ Withdrawn Materials: None ■ Repair Materials: None ■ Upgrade Materials: None **Subsume:** Chance to permanently acquire the unique ability of defeated demonic entity. Subsequent subsuming will increase the grade of the acquired unique ability. • Acquired Abilities (0/3) If no ability is acquired, subsumed essence will be allocated to user across innate abilities, base attributes, and technical proficiencies. • Growth Focus: Jackal (Drone) ○ Jackal (Drone): A portion of subsumed essence will be allocated to the development of Jackal. ○ Jackal Statistics: ■ Kills: 0 ■ Charge: 100% ■ Countermeasures Learned: 0 **Capacitor:** Rapidly generates and stores refined essence. Draws from atmospheric, subsumed, and internal essence. • Active Reserves: 5 **Nexus:** Central point of connection for a network. Marked equipment cannot be utilized by anyone other than user. All networked equipment can be secured and synchronized to user. • Active Network: ○ Arkwright ○ Scarlet Strategist's Visor ○ Argento Workbench ○ Quest Academy Tablet: S. Argento ○ Jackal (Drone) ○ Jackal's Arsenal
Abilities	Arsenal | Subsume | Capacitor | Nexus
Runes	None

Power Source	Capacitor Reserves: 5/5
Evolution	No
Quality	Perfect
Condition	100%
Value	Unknown

Sal sat down heavily as he read the words three times. He couldn't process what he was looking at. From the moment he lay in his dorm and was informed by Upgrade and Quest that he was a Mythcrafter…he knew the expectation was to someday create equipment at the Mythic grade. The sniper rifle had come close, and Sal guessed that it would likely be the first ever Mythic-grade item in existence. Yet, there he was, sitting in his workshop, wearing a Mythic-grade item on his left arm. He could only marvel at the glossy black arm, a stupid smile on his face as he shook his head in disbelief.

Subsume was far better than Sal had hoped. With the little that he expected from Assimilation, he guessed it would be a more powerful variant of the same ability. It definitely lived up to the name, and Subsume sounded like it would not only work on the Jackal drone, but also in elevating his own stats. Acquiring an ability from a defeated enemy sounded incredible, but it only looked like it would activate if he took down something strong. Sal wondered whether he'd have gotten the Cannibal ability if he had taken down that red prowler with the Blight Jackal.

The fact that Jackal had a kill counter was an excellent development. A part of Sal had hoped that it would have combat capabilities, but he was willing to just have it as a harvesting tool for materials. If he could send it ahead into a dungeon, he wondered whether it would be capable of taking out demons by itself. Sal hadn't built it to remove himself from the battlefield, but rather to have a sentry with him.

Sal had assumed he'd need to get Fabi to do the essence programming for the Jackal drone, but the essence chip seemed to be fully functional. He couldn't tell from the Appraisal if it was because of Cypher's influence or something else, but he certainly wasn't complaining about it.

He couldn't help but laugh at the ridiculousness of the situation. There he was, telling himself what he intended…when the reality was that he hadn't a clue whether it would work.

"Nice to meet you, Jackal." Sal laughed. "I'm Salvatore, but you can call me Sal."

To Sal's surprise, the green shoulder pulsated twice.

Jackal (Drone)
- o Vocal Signature Registering: 8%
- o Essence Signature Registered: 100%
- o Scarlet Strategist's Visor Registered: 100%

The visor reeled off the new information and it caused Sal to blink in surprise. "You're able to register my voice? Does that mean that you can understand commands?" He felt a bit stupid talking to his shoulder, but if there was a chance that it had this sort of functionality, then he would absolutely look like an idiot to find out.

Jackal (Drone)
- o Vocal Signature Registering: 21%

"Okay, I've got no idea if this is just a security protocol…or if you're going to suddenly understand commands. But, this is my voice. My name is Salvatore Argento. I made you with minimal levels of caffeine and supervision. I'm very surprised that you worked out as well as you did." Sal started talking aimlessly, spouting whatever nonsense came into his head to drive up the percentage counter.

"I need to send some pictures of your completed design to Divinity Khan. She's a friend of mine, so you better protect her if the opportunity comes up. Blathnaid Clean, Barry Francis, and Fabi Maccles—all of them are good friends of mine who we'll need to work hard to protect."

Sal laughed at the stupidity of what he was saying. It was clearly a security feature, that likely came through the Nexus ability. It was just going to lock his profile to the gear, like an advanced form of biometrics. Yet, he was talking to it as if it were a child. There was zero chance of it having any sort of comprehension without the protocols in place. He'd need to wait for Fabi to send him over some files for that.

Jackal (Drone)
- o Vocal Signature Registering: 74%
- o Protection Protocol List has been Updated:
  - Divinity Can (Verification Required)
  - Blahnid Kleen (Verification Required)
  - Bahree France Is (Verification Required)
  - Fabee Mackels (Verification Required)

Sal's heart froze as he looked at the names appearing. They were horribly misspelled, but that didn't matter. This was the first time that he had used his voice to interact with any of the equipment or machinery in his network. He took a slow and steady breath, and realized, just from the sound of his heart thundering, that Perfect was definitely no longer active. "How are you able to understand my words?"

Jackal (Drone)

- o Vocal Signature Registering: 79%
- o Quest Academy Tablet: S. Argento
  - ▪ Aural Communication: Enabled

Sal turned to look at the tablet that he had left on the workbench. "So, you're listening to me right now through my tablet…" Sal couldn't believe how advanced this was. Nexus had clearly added the tablet to the network, which gave Jackal access to the technology it needed. It was the best example of a network working seamlessly, but it was still unnerving. He wondered whether it would allow for him to take the visor back with him to Quest Academy but still allow the Arkwright to avail of Cypher through the network.

Sal glanced between the tablet and his shoulder. "Guess there's no harm in asking, but can you tell me if the Arkwright will be able to use Cypher if I take the visor to Quest Academy?"

Jackal (Drone)
- o Cannot Define

Sal stared at the words that appeared on the screen. He shook his head in wonder as a thousand questions flooded his mind. There was a protective protocol list, and he had seemingly added his friends to it. What would the verification process look like? Would they need to talk to it, or give it an essence signature of some kind?

Either way, it was an exciting prospect. Jackal was very much growing on him, and he desperately wanted to see how it would perform in a dungeon. He wondered whether he could go back to visit the Dragoons and their private dungeons with his father. It would be better to do a trial run with someone who could step in and help if everything went wrong. Sal also knew that his father would be able to keep it a secret. Hell, he could even go with Divinity or Fabi.

He flexed his arm a few more times, absolutely loving the fit of the new equipment. He couldn't really call it a gauntlet anymore because it stretched across his entire arm and shoulder. Pauldron and vambraces would probably apply if he was being technical, but Sal didn't really care about the terminology. He'd classify it as a gauntlet until he came up with a better word for it. The color scheme would make him look like a Healer class, or a poison-based Villain. Sal hoped he could incorporate the purple color that represented the Support class, but he could do that with the rest of his outfit.

That thought made him pause. Sal lifted his right arm, which was completely bare. He imagined what might be a good complement to the left arm, and started ideating on something with more offensive capabilities. The Blight Jackal was a storage, battery, network, and drone combination. As far as he could tell, Subsume didn't have an attack method and was more of a passive ability that worked on the gear. Sure, he'd be able to bludgeon things to death with a punch, but it wasn't exactly perfect for his fighting style.

As Sal was lost in thought, he began to wonder how the arm would come off. With a tentative grasp of the shoulder, Sal pulled at it, but it didn't budge.

"That's not good," Sal muttered as he tried digging his fingers underneath the shoulder attachment. They merely brushed between the slick metal and his skin. There was no gap between them. "That's really not good." Worry crept into his voice. "Jackal, how do I remove the…Mythical Blight Jackal from my arm?"

Sal waited for a few seconds, blinking and focusing on the visor to see whether it would give him some insight as to what was happening.

Jackal (Drone)
- o Vocal Signature Registered: 100%
- o Mythical Blight Jackal can be dismissed and equipped via Arsenal
    - Required: Create gesture or vocal command to open and close Arsenal

Sal laughed as he lifted his hands up like a maestro. "How about this?"

Jackal (Drone)
- o Gesture signature has been recorded for opening Arsenal
- o Ensure that you're connected to the network to open Arsenal

"It can't be that simple," Sal breathed in disbelief as he replicated the movement. Whatever he had expected to happen…it wasn't a void appearing in front of him at a size that rivaled the entirety of the mezzanine. Sal peered into the white space, seeing corners of the room in the distance. It was so disconcerting that Sal whipped his hands up again in the same maestro motion and the space disappeared like it never existed.

Sal stood there for a few seconds before opening the space again. This time, he picked up his coffee mug and placed it into the white space. He pulled his hand back and took a step back before closing the subspace. Looking at the floor where the cup should have been, it was completely gone.

Sal's visor flashed with a new message.

Analyze Material?

His mouth dropped open as he turned to look at the Arkwright, seeing the exact same message displayed on the interface. His coffee cup had been placed into the subspace, the thing that was called Arsenal…and the Arkwright asked to analyze it? *Was this the power of Nexus, in how it connected everything? Did it mean that the Arkwright could pull things directly from the subspace?*

Sal had so many questions that his head was spinning. He sat down unsteadily and looked at the arm in disbelief. Even if it had no combat capability, Sal was genuinely ecstatic that he had made it. Mythic grade was absolutely a step above Legendary, and he was ridiculously excited to see what else he could make to complement it.

"If you want to spar, you better get your ass moving, Salvatore!" Petro's voice called from the doorway below.

Sal blinked a couple of times, registering what was being said. He got to his feet and moved to the railing. His father was below, already wearing a light track-suit with rolled-up sleeves. Sal pointed at his black arm. "Look what I made."

Petro squinted as he looked at Sal's arm. "What in the world is—" His eyebrows shot up in surprise, but he didn't say a word. Instead, he just stood there and looked at Sal in a daze. "I…think I need to get that monocle."

Sal grinned, slowly nodding. "It'll be a good opportunity to see if it can Appraise Mythic-grade items."

He started to move when he suddenly faltered with what looked like a troubling realization. "Salvatore…"

"Yeah, Dad?" Sal answered in a chipper tone.

"Did you make a Mythic grade in a single day?" Petro's voice was strained. He looked positively aghast at the notion that such a thing was even possible.

"Yep." Sal wiggled his fingers in a wave. "I'll need to introduce you to Jackal, just so you can be added to the protection protocol list." A pulse of green light responded to Sal's words, which didn't escape his father's notice.

Petro raised his hand to his face as he slowly shook his head. "I'm not sure I even want to ask…"

CHAPTER 89: CAUTION

"This changes everything, Salvatore," Petro said as he pulled the monocle from his face. His expression was a mixture of bewilderment and excitement. "You've essentially pioneered a whole new level of equipment…and if I'm reading this properly, the abilities of that Mythic grade are far superior to anything we've ever seen before." He rotated the monocle in his right hand as he looked at Sal's face, finally tearing his attention away from the Blight Jackal. "Arsenal looks like it could make every warehouse or storage solution obsolete. If it could preserve food, then you'd be a one-man supply detail for any excursion."

"That's a little excessive, no?" Sophia asked from her lounge chair opposite Sal and Petro. She held a teacup in her hand, looking between Petro and the Blight Jackal in confusion. "Surely it has a limit."

Petro shook his head slowly. "It would need to be tested, but by my estimate, it's capable of so much more than the Pocket ability." With a resigned sigh, he leaned back against the lounge chair and looked at Sal thoughtfully. "The fact that you used an actual blight core for the build is the problem. People have died over that little green rock, and now you have it displayed in plain sight."

"You're not suggesting he dismantle it? It's the first known Mythic grade, Petro," Sophia insisted in incredulity. "There has to be a workaround where he can keep it secret, or disguise it somehow?"

Sal looked between his parents. "The blight core is a key component of it, and if I tried switching it out, it wouldn't function at all. Jackal and Subsume are tied to the blight core."

Petro nodded in agreement. "It's a truly remarkable piece…and I can't even fathom how you managed to build it. A drone that can operate independently of the user and access the Arsenal is, frankly, ridiculous when you read it aloud."

He pointed at the visor in Sal's hands. "Then when you factor in the Nexus ability, as well as Capacitor…I don't have the words for how valuable this creation is. Having a whole roster of essence reserves that you can call upon, an entire arsenal of equipment and supplies, and the ability to transfer items from the battlefield straight to the Arkwright…" The smile on his face just grew wider as he wiped at his tired eyes. "I couldn't put a value on it."

"The Subsume ability sounds powerful, too," Sophia added as she smiled at Sal. "If you're able to bolster your innate abilities by taking down tough opponents, you've essentially created a tool that helps you progress over time. It's like a personal evolutionary rune."

Sal returned the smile. "So, you're both in favor of me keeping it?"

Petro's nod was slower than Sophia's. "With conditions." He bit his lip before continuing, as though weighing his words. "Up until this point, we've been assuming that the key threats to your safety are with the Bastion, Hunter Bureau, and the Guilds Association." He gestured at Sal's shoulder. "But now, you'd be an open target to anyone with a base-level of greed. Mythic grade is something people would happily kill to acquire, and we have a ridiculous number of Hunters who wouldn't hesitate in making that choice."

"That's not reassuring." Sal attempted to make light of the situation, but only his mother smiled. Taking a different avenue, he looked at his father and tried a reassuring smile. "What are the conditions?"

"You need to get a lot stronger," Petro replied simply. "If we can make you untouchable, then the only method for people getting access to Mythic-grade pieces would be to ally with your guild. We fill your ranks with powerful people, and get you progressed through the tiers as fast as possible. We bring in outside help to bolster your fighting force, and create key alliances. Doc Ameye should be first on that list. Quest doesn't have as much power as Robert, and the Hunter Bureau is a tougher outfit to anticipate…so I think we should start with building up external forces."

"Like the Silverson Group?" Sal guessed with a hint of hesitation. From everything he had heard of them, they sounded powerful but also terrible.

"Fuck no." Sophia snorted as she shook her head. "I'd pick Shade and the Delvers before the Silverson Group."

Petro sighed as he gave Sophia a measured look. "They're not all bad, but as a whole, you're right…the Silverson Group aren't a good fit." He turned his attention to Sal. "I'd be more inclined to approach someone like Luke and the Dragoons. We could propose a partnership of sorts—get materials from their dungeons and use the Arkwright to help equip them. I know you've been insisting on the Arkwright for auction items, but we'll be fine as we are. I'd rather see those spoils go to an organization that will pledge their help."

"You're making it sound like *we're* going to war," Sal breathed as he turned the visor in his hands. "I'd have no issue with having the Dragoons on my side…but, do you really think they'd go for it?"

"Yes," Petro said, without a shred of hesitation. "He'd protect you because you're our son, and he wouldn't ask for anything in return."

Sal abandoned the levity approach at those words. As much as he wanted to loosen the tension in the room, he could appreciate how serious his father was being. "As long as we make a manageable split between the Argento Auction House and the Dragoons, then I'm fine with that deal."

"Salvatore," Petro began with a steady breath. "We don't care about the auction house. All of this was to create a comfortable environment for our family, and now it's time for us to adapt to the current situation. We'd happily shut down the whole operation right now if it helped keep you safe."

Sal's words died in his throat as he looked from his father to his mother in disbelief, but even she nodded, smiling.

"Exactly as your father said," Sophia said. "You told me that this is your safe space, and I'll ensure that it will always be here for you…but if we need to shift our focus, then we'll do that. We've done it countless times over the years, so this is just another obstacle we need to overcome."

"You can't just shut down the auction house." Sal couldn't find the words to describe how devastating it sounded, but both of his parents looked resolute. "There has to be another way."

Petro waved his hand as though he were dismissing their entire legacy. "Salvatore, you're more important to us than a bunch of artifacts." He tapped his finger against the Blight Jackal. "If we want to keep you safe, then we will need to shift focus. We can't maintain the illusion that you're from a Support family. If we're going to showcase you as a strong contender in this war, then we'll need to flip the narrative."

"What, like you're going to join the rankings?" Sal asked in disbelief. "Run some dungeons and show everyone that you can fight?"

Petro smiled as he offered a shrug. "That's an idea, but we have a lot more value we can offer. You'll need someone to help train your guild members in the future. We could throw everything behind the guild and make connections while you're studying at Quest Academy."

He placed a placating hand on Sal's thigh. "I know this is a lot to consider all at once, but we need you to step things up to ensure your own safety. We can do that through making your guild a force to be reckoned with. We can renovate that depot into a center of excellence, add a training academy aligned with the Dragoons. All you'd need to do is show your strength at every opportunity, and be someone people want to follow. We can do all the administrative bullshit in the background."

"Petro," Sophia said quietly as she watched Sal's reaction. "Wind back a little. It's an awful lot for him to process."

Sal closed his eyes and let out a heavy sigh. "Okay…let's just say that we keep the auction house." He opened his eyes to look at his father's reaction, and saw a sliver of disappointment. "We keep the auction house…what do I need to do to ensure that happens?"

Petro opened his mouth to answer, but Sophia interjected. Her eyes were locked onto Sal. "Power. You're already doing great with being the top-ranked Savior at Quest Academy, but after the gala, there will be countless eyes watching your every move. If you're staying cooped up in a workshop, you'll look like an easy target."

She swiveled the empty teacup in the coaster, making it line up with the floral pattern. "But if you go back to Quest Academy and start powering through the outings with the guilds, they'll see a completely different Salvatore Argento. Keep up the dungeon and scavenger runs, and build connections with powerful students. Get good grades, and make yourself untouchable. The trick is to make everyone want you as an ally rather than as an asset. Being powerful is the key distinction."

Sal nodded in understanding, his fists clenched as a reflex. "And if I do that, then you'll keep the auction house open?"

Petro's shoulders slumped as he raised a hand to his face. "Salvatore, your priorities are a little skewed here. I need you to understand the severity of the situation." He looked at Sophia for her help as he let out an exasperated sigh. "The auction house is just a collection of walls and artifacts. What makes the auction is us, not the location or clientele. If we close up to focus on building up your guild, then we can always recreate the Argento Auction House in the future. Hell, we could end up being a sub-branch of the Argento Guild or whatever you call it."

"I understand that you're conflicted," Sophia said in a soothing voice. "This is a lot to take in, and we don't want to be fearmongering when you've accomplished something so extraordinary. We're not trying to diminish that in any way or form. All we want to ensure is that you're protected and safe." She smiled at

Sal as she leaned forward in her chair. "So, I want you to be crystal clear about what it is you want to do going forward. You're not allowed to sit there and tell us what we want to hear. What way would you like to proceed?"

Petro sighed in defeat as she looked at Sal expectantly. It was clear from his body language that he was frustrated.

Sal looked at his father. "Moving away from the Argento Auction House isn't an option." He was adamant as he spoke, and it reflected how he felt. His entire life had been with the Argento Auction House, and he wasn't going to let that crumble because of a target being painted on his back. "I'll welcome all the support you two are able to give me with the guild, but I don't want that to be at the cost of the auction house." He raised a hand to stop his father from interrupting. "That's my feelings about it, and nothing you say will change that."

Glancing over to his mother, Sal smiled. "You said that for me to take ownership of this whole situation, I need to become more powerful?"

"Or represent a powerful entity, yes. It can be your guild," Sophia corrected herself.

Sal nodded. "Okay, then that's what I'll do. I'll take the combat classes and sign up to do the outings." He waved his hand in a rotation. "And if I need to break the entire Q-Cred economy, then that's what I'll do. We can add more students to the guild ranks as we move up the tiers. I'll find a way to get permission to use my Skill Master ability on students."

"No," Sophia interrupted with a panicked look on her face. "That's something you shouldn't do under any circumstance."

Sal looked at her carefully before answering. He could see the fear in her eyes, and he knew what she was concerned about. "Mom, if creating Mythic-grade items is going to paint a target on my back, and is something people would kill for…then I might as well use everything I have at my disposal to build up my reputation."

It was clear to Sal that his parents were concerned for him and wanted to put a plan in action to keep him safe. The problem he had was that they were willing to throw away everything they had built just for him. No matter what his feelings had been about the truth of their past, the fact that they were willing to give everything up just to protect him was too much. He didn't want that to happen, and he didn't want to lose the Argento Auction House because he had made a Mythic-grade item.

No, it was time for him to take accountability and stop making excuses. The whole concept of building a guild had felt like a good match when he spoke to Sergeant Head, but now that he was sitting with his parents, it looked like the guild would be the key to his own survival.

"Let me do my part," Sal insisted as he looked at them. "Right now, the only people who know I've made a Mythic grade is you two. We have time to prepare."

Petro got to his feet and walked toward the bar. "Okay…tell me then, what plan would you put in place?" He spoke with his back turned as he leaned over the counter to lift out a bottle of whiskey.

"First of all, I want you to stay sober for it," Sal replied with a smile as his father faltered at the bar. "Right now, we have time…and what I need more than anything are materials. I can create more blight cores."

The bottle nearly slipped out of Petro's hand as he stared at Sal in disbelief. "That's…quite literally, the worst idea I've ever heard. You want to make more of the insanely valuable material that people kill for?"

"Supply will decrease demand," Sal responded emphatically, gesturing at his own shoulder. "If I make more equipment with the blight core, then we can start selling them off and that would mollify the entities that would kill for it. Wouldn't it make people more likely to play nice to maintain the supply of rare materials? The value people are after is likely Subsume rather than the blight core itself. By us releasing them to the market, wouldn't that make us worth protecting?"

"That's a very dangerous line to thread," Sophia said with clear concern. "We'd be killed if we tried selling something like that."

"Then what about Lawrence Baron?" Sal countered. "He deals in all sorts of exotic materials. He'd probably be able to move the blight cores?"

Petro returned to his seat empty-handed. "Forget Lawrence and the blight core strategy for a second." He stared into empty space ahead of him for a few seconds. "Could you make more Mythic grades?"

Sal nodded quickly. "If I had the materials and the designs were good, then it's possible. What are you thinking?"

Petro turned his head and looked at Sal's shoulder. "The Blight Jackal isn't going to protect you in the long-term. It's a network, battery, and storage solution." His gaze moved up to Sal's eyes. "Can you make something with an offensive ability? Something that would make people second-guess their chances if they attacked you head-on?"

Sal blinked in surprise. "Wait, your solution is for me to make a weapon? We don't even know how good Jackal is in combat—it might end up being sufficient by itself." He looked over at his mother to see what her feelings were on the topic.

Sophia was smiling and nodding. "That could work. I said it myself—if you were powerful, then they'd need to be careful around you…so a weapon isn't a bad idea."

Sal laughed at the ridiculousness of the whole thing. "Wait…just so I'm clear. The plan is for us to get more materials so I can make a weapon, right?"

"Mythic grade," Petro corrected, sighing. "If you can do that, then it won't matter if people recognize you're wearing Mythic grades. They won't be able to do anything to stop you."

Sal folded his arms, a wide smile on his face. "Don't suppose you'll let me raid the storage room for materials?"

Petro shook his head. "Nope, I think it's time we went back to visit the Dragoons." He got to his feet, groaning, and looked at both Sophia and Sal. "It won't hurt to have an ally in all of this, especially if everything goes to shit. We can at least get an agreement in place for materials."

"Wait, right now?" Sal asked as he watched his father typing on a small tablet. "I haven't even figured out how to take this off yet."

"Keep it on," Petro replied as he pocketed his tablet. "The car is on its way, so we might as well get started. Luke can be trusted, so you can test your drone in the dungeon."

Sophia looked at the two of them. "Is this a father-and-son bonding thing, or can I come, too? I've got the equipment packed and ready to go."

Sal looked at her in surprise. "Wait, you were expecting this?"

"Fighting in dungeons? Yes." Sophia laughed as she got to her feet. "Encouraging you to make a weapon? Not so much."

CHAPTER 90: ALLIANCE

"You're back?" Luke gave a hearty laugh as he made his way over to Petro and Sophia. He waved down the soldiers who looked slightly on edge at their arrival. Seeing a trio of people turn up to their base wearing civilian clothing would have anyone curious. Luke looked past them to see Sal, and offered him a wink. "Here to get more materials, or have you given more thought to completing the circuit?"

Petro gestured at Sal with his thumb, not breaking eye contact with Luke. "We're here to do some equipment testing. He's made something and wants to work out the kinks in it. What dungeons do you have available today?"

Luke crossed his arms as he looked over his shoulder to the various dungeon entrances. "Fresh batch of recruits are being trained in the leecher dungeons, so they're not going to be available for another couple of weeks. We've got them on a fairly strict rotation." He tilted his head slightly to look at the prowler dungeons. "That red prowler really lit a fire under the asses of our more experienced soldiers. They weren't too pleased that their job was done for them by a civilian. They've been running the prowler dens nonstop since you two left with the spoils." Luke grinned as he glanced at Petro. "I owe you some thanks for that. It's good to see them fired up."

"So, does that mean you don't have anything free?" Petro frowned slightly. "We can always go to the Hunter Bureau if you're fully booked."

Luke waved away the suggestion. "Don't be absurd. We have 4-A under watch at the moment. It's an abnormal formation with a higher population of evolved and variant types…but the problem is that the voiders within have started teleporting past the barriers, and are appearing in 4-B. Since we don't know the full situation on how many of the dungeons have been compromised, we've been leaving them alone until our senior squads return from the Red Zone." He pointed off to the far right. "By our best estimate, 4-D has no such issues…but we've been wary just in case. I'd go in with you to ensure your safety, but it would be good to have solid backup."

Sophia twisted her head slightly to look at Sal as though trying to gauge his eligibility. "Strong opponents are likely to be in there, Salvatore. What do you think?"

Sal smiled as he jutted his chin in his father's direction. "That depends. Is he going to abandon me to take out the boss again?" He noticed a smile appear on his mother's face at that comment, but his father didn't say a word.

Luke whistled as he looked between the family. His voice turned to a whisper as he leaned in closer to them. "I don't know what your angle is, but if I were you…I'd pick a better lie than Salvatore here being a Crafter." He chuckled almost to himself as he started to lead the way to the dungeon. "What equipment do you guys need to go in? With it being 4-D, we can absolutely outfit you for the dive."

Sophia lifted a bag at her side. "We've already brought everything we need, and you can bring us to 4-A instead."

Luke froze on the spot before turning around, a look of horror on his face. "I don't think I've properly highlighted the severity of that dungeon, Sophia. 4-D is a much more appropriate level for someone with training wheels. You don't test equipment in something like 4-A, unless it's a weapon designed to kill everything." He gave Sal a wary look before shaking his head. "Two relics and a rookie aren't really going to cut it, I'm afraid."

Petro cleared his throat. "I'll ignore the relic comment, but you can trust us. We'll be able to handle 4-A without issues. Sophia is with us, so it'll be a fairly quick affair." He smiled over his shoulder at Sal. "And my son is full of surprises lately, so I think this sort of environment would be good for him."

Luke raised his chin and let out an exasperated sigh. "Will you at least let me go in there with you?"

"Nope," Sophia responded. "Sal's Crafting is all very top secret. We couldn't possibly have you seeing what he's been making…you know, unless you were officially affiliated with his guild."

Luke's eyes narrowed as he looked at Sophia. "What are you scheming? You know that we don't join hands with guilds or the bureau." His gaze turned on Petro. "I'm going to guess that this has to do with the materials we source in the dungeons?"

Pulling the jacket off his left shoulder, Sal revealed the ethereal glow of the Blight Jackal. He looked at Luke meaningfully. "This is what I'm going to test in the dungeon. It's the best grade I'm able to make with my ability."

Luke's eyes narrowed as he looked at Sal's shoulder, before they widened in shock. His mouth hung open as he looked between Sophia and Petro. As someone who could gauge a person's strength from their internal essence, there was no way he'd miss the overwhelming difference between Crafting grades. He looked like a fish out of water, with his mouth opening and closing in disbelief, the words not coming to him even after several attempts.

"My alias at Quest Academy is Myth," Sal said after an encouraging nod from his father. They had already established back at the auction house that Luke was a good man, who would be an ally in whatever was to come in the future. "I'm the guildmaster of a Trainee Guild, and we're hoping to have your support in the future."

Luke stared at Petro in astonishment. "I thought the Reavers had the only weapon that could go up to Mythic grade?"

Petro pointed at Sal. "He made that, too."

Sophia nodded in agreement. "And he'd like to make better equipment for the Dragoons. As a thank-you for the materials so far, and the future shipments we'd end up requiring."

"Rare grade at the minimum," Sal clarified quickly, smiling, just to set the expectations. "But there could be a few Epic-grade pieces on request. Custom abilities and even evolutionary runes."

Luke's face was priceless. His voice was barely a croak as he looked between all three of them, clearly wondering whether this was all some sort of elaborate prank. "Why are you telling me this?" He finally got his wits about him as he turned around almost frantically to check that nobody was in earshot. "You can't just saunter in here and start dropping terms like Mythic grade and evolutionary weapons!"

"Like you said," Sophia insisted. "Salvatore already has the support of the Hunter Bureau. They're gifting the old depot warehouses in Silver Sanctuary to him and Fabrizia Maccles for their joint operations. The Argento Auction House is the main financial backer to his new guild, so we're able to make these sorts of calls. Bringing you and the Dragoons into the mix will allow us to have a strong military backing for the future."

"Are you planning on going to war?" Luke asked eventually, his face paling ever so slightly. "It sounds like you're worried about more than demons at this point."

Petro gave him a slight nod. "It's a business decision for now, that solves a lot of the bottlenecks for Salvatore. He's created…a production method that will allow for a lot more output than we're used to. Building up the Dragoons is an investment over time. If there ever comes a time when people target Salvatore for his abilities, we'd ask for your help in keeping them at bay."

He lowered his voice even further and gave Luke a pointed look. "There's no way he's going to be left alone now that we know he can make Mythic-grade equipment. If you're not comfortable with this sort of arrangement, then we can just end the conversation here."

Luke took a few moments to gather his thoughts. He bit his lip and looked over Petro's shoulder into the distance, to where the soldiers were lounging around and talking to one another. "So, we give you a cut of the materials and you give us equipment?" He looked back at Sal. "And we pledge ourselves to protect Salvatore and his guild?"

"That's it." Petro smiled.

Luke stared at Petro. "We'd have done that anyway. We still have an old debt that needs repaying."

"Line in the sand," Sophia countered. "That debt is settled if you work with us, and we start from scratch."

Luke didn't even seem to think about it as he extended his hand to Sal. "I agree to those terms, Mr. Argento."

Sal took his hand and smiled. "I appreciate it, Mr. …" He faltered as he looked at his father for help, but Luke just laughed.

"General Lucion Drake." He introduced himself properly with a strong handshake. "I answer to all sorts of names, but Luke is fine." He looked at Petro and Sophia before exhaling. "Now that we're business partners, how about I join you all in 4-A?"

"Happy to have you along." Petro nodded as he gestured in the direction of the dungeon. "And thank you. We're likely being too cautious, but we'd rather be overprepared than caught unaware."

"Too cautious?" Luke chuckled as he led the way to 4-A. "I think I've really downplayed the severity of this dungeon. You'll need to really keep your wits about you because the evolved voiders are a nightmare to deal with." He looked over his shoulder at Sal. "I don't know what sort of specs you have on that thing, but punching isn't going to serve you well against this enemy type. Keep to the center of us as we move, and we'll protect you. Got it?"

Sal nodded in understanding. "Got it, sir."

"It's Luke. You're not a soldier," Luke responded, smiling as he led them across the man-made trenches.

If the security had been tight on the previous ones, with floodlights and guard towers…the 4-A dungeon was overkill. Rather than relying on technology to thwart any demonic escapees, the Dragoons had seemingly enlisted their own cohort of evolved creatures.

Sal's jaw dropped as he laid eyes on an enormous bird of prey. His visor told him that he was looking at a falcon, but the scale was completely wrong. With both of its wings tucked at its side, it leaned forward to stare at Luke with piercing yellow eyes. It was hard to ignore when it was bigger than his father's car. Sal could only imagine what it would look like in full flight, but it looked positively ferocious without doing a thing.

Each of its feathers looked like they had evolved at some point with a mottled black coloring, and sparks of yellow electricity dancing between them. Sal's eyes were drawn to the beak, and claws that had gradually started to grow in size. Each talon became longer and sharper, breaking the stone perch that it rested on.

When the feathers ruffled, Luke laughed. "Steady, Fig! They're friends."

The falcon flared out its wings, and illuminated the space for a short moment before it folded them back and bowed its head; a deep, rumbling noise came from behind its closed beak. Each of the talons shrank back and it pattered on the broken stonework to reposition itself. It was what was probably a second floor of a ruined apartment building, and it was stacked with straw and padded cushions. There were similar nooks on the upper floors, but they were all empty. Only Fig, the falcon, was visible.

"That's…the first falcon I've ever seen," Sal admitted hesitantly, not taking his eyes off Fig for fear that it would attack.

"She's a sweetheart," Luke responded with a proud smile. "Raised her from when she was a little nestling. Now she can pull lightning down from the heavens with just a flap of her wings." He grinned as he pointed at the empty nests. "The senior squad are all out with their mounts, but you should drop by to see them when they're home. I think you'll be far more impressed when you see them."

Sal just stared at Luke in surprise. "Wait, you have a Taming ability? I would have sworn that you were combat-focused."

Luke shook his head. "The Dragoons have always been a mounted force. We have a dedicated team for the nurturing of animals, but I'd be lying if I said that I knew how to tame them. We just bond with them when they're young." He looked over his shoulder at Sal. "Now, if you were to give up all the guildmaster stuff and join us, you'd get your own mount in no time. We've got a promising shipment of offspring coming in from the Brood Corps, so we'll have plenty to choose from."

"Oh, and what rank would he need to be to get something as ferocious as a falcon?" Petro laughed, already knowing the answer by the look on his face.

Luke sighed. "Okay, maybe you'd get there in three years…but still, it's something to think about."

Sophia snorted as she repositioned the bag on her shoulder. "Salvatore has a higher chance of building his own falcon than sitting here in a tent training for it."

"Ouch." Luke pretended to be offended as he placed a hand on his chest. "Don't listen to her, Fig…she didn't mean it."

A soft grumble emanated from Fig's nest high above, and Sal was surprised at the sudden revelation. "Wait, can she understand you when you speak?"

"Of course," Luke answered, as if it were obvious. "She's smarter than half of the soldiers here, and unparalleled when it comes to combat strategy."

"No falcon." Sophia looked at Sal meaningfully. She even went so far as to wag her finger at him, smiling. "Stick to the Crafting."

"Spiders match up well with Crafters," Luke offered casually. "Or snakes…they tend to shed or produce good materials, and they're very good at protecting their bonded partner."

Sal immediately thought back to Harlan's talk about evolved spiders and he could not for the life of him think of anything he'd prefer less.

Luke caught his expression and chuckled. "Seriously, you guys have no taste." He placed one hand on his hip and used the other to gesture at the entrance of 4-A. "Are you sure you want to do this?"

Sal nodded slowly. It was time to test out the Mythic Blight Jackal, and see how Subsume worked. If he wanted to see its effects, stronger opponents made the most sense to target. With both of his parents by his side, he felt like they could take on anything. The conversation from back in the auction house was still playing on his mind. There were so many variables outside of their control.

If there was one thing that Sal had control over, it was himself. If he needed to become stronger, then that's exactly what he was going to do.

Looking at Luke, he smiled. "Yes. We want to do this."

CHAPTER 91: JACKAL

"Well, isn't that a blast from the past?" Luke chuckled as he held up an essence lantern to get a better look at Petro and Sophia. "Are they the same pieces from back in the day? They look brand-new!"

Sophia smiled as she adjusted the polished silver bracers on her arms. "I might have buffed them up a bit with Restoration. Surprised you remembered them."

Luke glanced at Sal and pointed at the bracers meaningfully. "Stay the hell out of her way when she starts swinging those arms. We're going to have a tough time in this sort of lighting, and you don't want to get caught up in friendly fire."

"Understood," Sal answered him as he looked at his parents. He was pleasantly surprised at the sight of the Silverson officer uniform. The first thing he was able to tell at just a glance was that his parents had very different setups. His father's outfit was clearly tailored to his kicking power, and the entirety of his right leg was adorned in a soft silver plating. His left leg was only covered at the back of the heel, and the armor on his torso and shoulders was quite minimalist. It was a blue leather jacket with plated segments of silver on the shoulders and arms, that fused perfectly into a set of gleaming silver gauntlets. There was something about seeing his father in a stylish leather jacket that just felt wrong.

"Looks good on you," Sophia remarked teasingly as she gave her husband an appreciative look.

Her outfit was no joke either. Sal had to do a double take when he saw the grilled helm that she wore. It was only when she was pulling her hair through the back of it that he realized it was actually hers. It was gleaming silver, but had a pointed design at the face, coming out a few inches from her nose like an arrowhead.

"Lets me headbutt things to death." Sophia laughed as she flicked the front grill of the helm. "But these are the fun parts." She twisted her hands with the bracers, causing two identical silver blades to snap over her wrists. Then, with a practiced movement, she lifted her right foot and twisted it rapidly in midair, causing another concealed blade to poke out of the toe of the shoe. "What do you think?"

Sal just laughed. "Very old-school, but looks good!" There wasn't a trace of essence on anything they wore, and he was just a little concerned for their safety. If they were going into a dungeon with spring-loaded mechanisms, then it felt like they weren't fully prepared. Sal decided to give them the benefit of the doubt, especially considering he had seen them fight. There was also the fact that Luke wasn't worried for their safety. The beast of a man held his rapier at the ready and was standing guard of their position, likely to ensure that they weren't ambushed while changing.

"Your turn." Petro smiled as he zipped up the front of his blue leather jacket. He kicked the empty duffel bag to one side and gestured at it. "You can throw your jacket there."

Sal obliged by taking off his jacket, bathing the dark base of the stairwell in an eerie green light. His left shoulder practically pulsated in anticipation, and Sal checked his visor while throwing the jacket onto the discarded duffel bag.

Jackal (Drone)
- o   Protection Protocol
  - ▪   Add Users

Sal scanned his parents and Luke with the visor, and after a few seconds, he was rewarded with a notification that they had been successfully added to the protective protocol list. Thankfully, he had finished calibrating the vocal commands to Jackal, but he wasn't sure of its effectiveness while his tablet was in his pants pocket.

"Not going to lie, I was expecting something a little flashier." Luke chuckled as he glanced over at Sal. "It looks like a glowing sleeve. What does it do?"

"It's mostly a battery and storage device," Petro responded with a laugh.

Luke looked even more disappointed but shrugged it off as he started to lead them into the cavern. "There are three tiers to this dungeon, and the voiders will pop out from every surface imaginable. Keep your wits about you, and we should be fine."

Luke led them forward into the actual dungeon. It was dramatically different from everything Sal had seen in the past. For starters, there was a massive chasm in front of them that led down into a glowing fissure of red light. It cast a foreboding light to the ceiling, with various shadows showing movements of…something down below. Various pathways led down toward the red light, with many of them decayed and broken. In other words, there were plenty of ambush points in precarious locations.

"No commander, by the looks of it." Luke gave a sigh of relief as he looked over the edge of the chasm. "They're fighting one another, which makes things a little easier on us."

Sophia motioned Sal to come over and have a look, and he obliged with a few careful steps, making sure to look around him for any signs of an attack. His visor told him that there was nothing in the vicinity, but he didn't want to be complacent. When he peered over the edge, he was surprised to see an all-out war happening between a group of demons.

They were on a lower floor, but there was no mistaking the visage of the hulkers. Two of them were duking it out with each other, bludgeoning each other in the red glow of the fissure. They weren't obsidian variants, but instead looked to be made of a pale white rock. Each of them had chunks torn out of their bodies as they continued to throw heavy punches at each other. Surrounding the hulkers at a safe distance from both sides were two packs of prowlers, only visible with slight flickers of light in their direction. They all looked primed and ready to attack, with tentative clawing and retreating between hulker punches.

"Fuckers are waiting to kill the victor." Luke grimaced. "The variants are warring for supremacy, so we'll need to be quick."

Sal looked at him in confusion. "Isn't them killing each other a good thing? Less of them for us to fight?"

Luke shook his head, not tearing his eyes from the scenes below. "No, when they fight each other…the victor tends to gain an increase in strength from consuming the defeated. When they eat different types of demon, they develop weird evolutions that can be a pain to counter. The last thing we want is a hulker with Stealth."

Sal laughed, thinking it was a joke, but the deadly serious expression of Luke made him pause. "Wait…that can happen?"

"Yeah. It happens regularly in variant dungeons." His tone was flat as he stepped back from the ledge. "I'll take care of any hulkers we come across. Your armors won't be able to handle them." Luke looked at Petro and Sophia and gestured over the edge, like it was the only proof he needed.

Petro smiled as he wound back his arm and rotated it a few times. "Soph could take out a couple of hulkers, and I'm fairly sure I could take them on if it's a one-on-one."

"You're not fighting hulkers," Sophia said adamantly, in a tone that brooked no argument.

Petro sighed as he looked at Sal. "What about Jackal? Is your visor telling you anything about its chances?"

Luke frowned. "Jackal?"

Sal smiled as he tapped the glowing green part of his shoulder. "Part of the battery and storage. Let me check." Just as he was about to navigate to the drone settings with his visor, an idea popped into his head. Clearing his throat, he looked over the edge of the chasm again. "Jackal, can you start fighting?"

Jackal (Drone)
- o   Changing to Attack Mode
- o   Set Focus
  - ▪   Harvesting: Level 0
  - ▪   Learning: Level 0
  - ▪   Recharging: Level 0

"Learning." Sal spoke clearly as he looked over the edge with his left arm extended outward. He didn't want to risk Jackal by focusing on material gathering, and the charge was already full. His logic was that the learning focus might increase its survivability. He didn't really know what to expect, but he assumed that Jackal would detach from his shoulder and float in front of him while it properly calibrated.

Sal was very wrong.

"What the fuck?!" Luke shouted as he jumped back in shock.

Petro and Sophia also took a few steps back at the sight of the mechanical leecher that rapidly unfurled itself from Sal's arm. The green gem was visible only for a split second before glossy black metal snapped around it like a shell casing. The tentacles that dropped down from Jackal had initially glowed green, but the light evaporated as if it had suddenly lost power. Yet, it floated in midair and melded into the darkness like a prowler.

Sal stared at Jackal in a mixture of incredulity and pride. He had made it, and he wasn't sure it was going to be useful…but it looked incredible. As soon as the light disappeared from the tentacles, they rotated, propelling Jackal upward at a ridiculous pace before it angled itself toward the chasm.

Sal stared at it in absolute horror, realizing all too late what it intended to do. Without the visor equipped, he would have missed the blindingly fast speed of Jackal as it shot down into the midst of the fighting demons. Sal watched in a stunned silence as Jackal crossed the impossible distance in less than two seconds, and unfurled its abyssal steel tendrils like they were blades. The effect was as dramatic as it was horrific, with chunks of prowler being hurled in every direction. There was no stealthy finesse, or even subtlety as it massacred the first pack of prowlers with ease.

"A battery and storage device?" Luke repeated as he stood beside Sal. His expression was awestruck, and it was clear he was out of his depth. "Can you make more of them?"

Sal didn't even have a witty response for him. He was too preoccupied with watching Jackal butcher everything that came close to it. Although he was thankful that it had moved to the prowlers instead of the hulkers, he was still worried for how it would fare in terms of endurance. He glanced at the report on his visor to track Jackal's progress.

Jackal (Drone)
> o Kills: 7
> o Charge: 98%

There was a whole range of available information breaking down the demons it had killed. Apparently, the learning focus was creating countermeasures for each opponent that it faced. Despite all that information, Sal couldn't help but be astounded that it had only expended a couple of percent in killing seven prowlers. With how much he had struggled with the Dominion set and the amount of essence it consumed, Sal was at a complete loss when it came to the calculation for Jackal. *Was it siphoning the essence from defeated foes to sustain itself?*

Just as Sal was about to speak to his parents, his shoulder pulsated. Not with any sort of visual indication, but rather like a charge of electricity had just been sent throughout his entire body. It wasn't painful or unpleasant, but it left a sort of numbing sensation in its wake.

Sal faltered as he put his right hand to his chest in concern. Suspicion immediately consumed him. It had all been too perfect...the Mythic grade seemingly working as intended with no consequences? There was obviously a flaw of some sort that was claiming its price. Sal wondered whether the electrical charge was somehow depleting his essence or something. There had to be a payoff for the performance of Jackal. The minor ache that spread throughout his body was a telltale sign that something was wrong.

Jackal (Drone)
> o Subsume Notification
> > • Strength has increased by 0.08

"Sal, is everything okay?" his father asked in a concerned voice. Petro had torn his eyes away from Jackal for long enough to notice something was wrong with Sal.

Sal just stared at the words in amazement. *The aching was his Strength stat being forcibly increased? By Jackal…who was on the other side of a chasm, murdering prowlers?* He looked over at his father in complete shock. "It just increased my Strength stat." He pointed over the chasm. "From all the way over there."

Petro stared at Sal, then slowly his eyes moved to the glossy black armored shoulder. "You're positive?"

Sal nodded emphatically as he tapped his chest. "I can literally feel it. I thought it was some sort of kickback or something from the essence, but it's literally building my stats as it kills things."

"You might want to take a look at this," Sophia insisted, drawing both of their attention toward her. She pointed across the chasm. "I don't think we're going to find out which hulker won."

In the time that Sal had taken to inspect himself, read the notifications, and check on his chest…Jackal had murdered everything. It was like a helicopter blade of death, with vicious rotations that streaked lines of green blood across every wall. Yet, it looked like the little drone wasn't done, as it launched itself into the last remaining hulker.

"Wait, what happened to the other one?" Sal asked in confusion.

"Jackal happened." Sophia laughed as she shook her head in astonishment. "Watch and see…it's kinda disturbing how effective it is."

Sal looked at what she was talking about and could see Jackal planted on the back of the hulker. Each abyssal blade was assaulting it like a jackhammer in quick succession, plucking chunks of stone out with each attack and carving its way into the core of the hulker. Every time the lumbering demon tried to dislodge Jackal by throwing itself into walls, or onto the ground, Jackal moved seamlessly around its body. It was pathetically one-sided, with Jackal's barrage of quick and efficient attacks and the hulker unable to counter any of them. Then, when a large enough hole was carved into the hulker, Jackal crawled inside and disappeared completely from view.

"Wait for it," Sophia insisted.

Sal stared as an eerie green light poked through all the cracks of the hulker. Every gouged piece of rock suddenly became a pocket of light…before it dramatically erupted in a scattershot of rubble. Jackal hovered above the ruined husk of the demon with its green light visible once more.

Jackal (Drone)
    o   Subsume Notification
        ▪   Strength has increased by 0.11

"More Strength." Sal looked at his father in surprise. He pointed at his shoulder. "It's at like, point two more than before…just from those two hulkers, I think."

Petro opened his mouth to reply, but then closed it again. He frowned before looking over at Sophia. "I don't think he needs to make another weapon, Soph."

"Came to that conclusion about two hulkers ago." Sophia laughed as she watched Jackal dart into a crevice in the wall. "What sort of range does it have, Sal?"

"No idea," Sal responded as he kept an eye on the feed of information pouring in.

Jackal (Drone)
- o Hulker Countermeasure has been Learned
  - Confirmed Hulker Kills: 2
- o Prowler Countermeasure has been Learned
  - Confirmed Prowler Kills: 11

"It looks like it's still going strong. I'll keep you updated as we go." Sal gestured vaguely at his visor, laughing. "This is not what I was expecting."

Luke cleared his throat as he looked at the trio in front of him. "I'll ask again, because I think the question got lost in all the excitement. But are you able to make more of those things, Salvatore?"

Sal nodded. "Yeah, but you'd need a visor to go with it to give it commands and such. It requires some premium materials, but we can pro...cure them." Sal was about to say *produce*, but decided against it at the last moment. Even though his parents trusted General Drake, he didn't really know the man. Telling him about the Arkwright wasn't really going to help things along. "It's a lot of effort and time, though."

"I can imagine," Luke said almost breathlessly as he gestured at the massacred ledge at the base of the chasm. "There's no way you could produce something at this level of power in a short space of time."

Sal was absolutely positive he'd have caught his mother rolling her eyes if she wasn't wearing the pointed helm. He was about to answer Luke when another message popped onto the visor's screen.

"Oh, it found some voiders." Sal read the message aloud before his smile faltered. "It's too fast..."

Jackal (Drone)
- o Voider Countermeasure has been Learned
  - Confirmed Voider Kills: 2

The number of confirmed kills kept going up, and Sal wasn't sure whether he should call Jackal back or not. He didn't want to risk it running out of power, or attacking an opponent that was too strong. That said, if it was a choice between his parents and Luke fighting a demon or the drone, he'd always pick the drone. Sal finally appreciated Fabi and Upgrade's obsession with the drones, and found himself officially a fan of them, too.

"Are we just going to stand here?" Petro asked finally as he placed his hands on his hips. "I can't help but feel like we're being upstaged by a robot."

Luke nodded in agreement. "As destructive as that Jackal thing is, there's no feasible way for it to clear an entire variant dungeon by itself. We should remain on guard and continue deeper inside."

"Lead on, Luke." Sophia moved to stand beside Sal. With a practiced proficiency, she twisted her wrist to retract her bracer blades and tapped Sal's arm with her hand. Her whisper was almost conspiratorial, and he could imagine her smiling as she spoke. "Jackal is incredible."

CHAPTER 92: SLAUGHTER

One of the first mistakes Sal made in the dungeon was highlighting every single target that the visor could pick out. It was to avoid any surprise attacks hitting their group. That was his intention, as the impromptu Support of the group. He guessed his father would be able to do it, but he decided to be proactive. The problem that came from that was Jackal. Because the protective protocol was in effect, Jackal seemed to interpret the instruction very literally. It meant that any time their group even got close to a demon, the little bundle of abyssal steel and blight would smash through a wall to obliterate them before anyone could attempt an attack.

Petro and Sophia had even started to make a game of it, in trying to apprehend a demon before Jackal could get to them. They failed, miserably. It was interesting, though, to see how Jackal changed its death-dealing attacks to avoid hitting Sal's parents. No matter how many times he told them to just leave it to Jackal, they persisted with trying to kill a demon. Luke was far more realistic and seemed content to just walk through the dungeon with a bewildered expression on his face. He looked like he had given up on killing anything a while ago.

Jackal (Drone)
- o   Kills: 56
- o   Charge: 72%
- o   Focus: Harvesting: Level 8

Sal's attempts to switch focus had worked initially, but Jackal had learned very quickly how to kill things while preserving the loot. It took the drone a little while to adapt, but it started to clean up its murder techniques. There were still countless decapitations and dissections happening, but they were always followed by a notification from Nexus that materials had been added to Arsenal. No matter how much Sal tried to rationalize everything, he was at a loss for words. Jackal was far more impressive than it had any right to be. His original thought of having a little helper robot to pick up materials or act as a scout…seemed hilarious in hindsight.

"We could probably go to five million at a push," Luke said weakly from behind them. He was acting as their Vanguard, but in all honesty, he was just the last to walk through the devastation that Jackal left. His only attempts at conversation for the last twenty minutes had been around the cost of making another Mythic-grade Blight Jackal.

Luke winced and stepped to one side as Jackal floated past him, each of the tendrils plucking at the corpses on the ground. Each time it stalled over a particular corpse, Sal knew he was about to get a notification.

Jackal (Drone)
- o   Voider Heart has been added to Arsenal

Sal could only smile as he watched the drone going through each of the corpses. A part of him felt like he should be disgusted, but pride was seemingly overriding the nausea. Glancing over at Luke, Sal shook his head. "I told you already that the price of this is incalculable. I don't know how difficult it will be to secure the required materials…even my dad can't put a price on it."

"Can't or won't?" Luke asked gruffly of Petro, who smiled happily as he looked at the aftermath of Jackal.

"It's a blight core." Petro shrugged. "What sort of price would you put on that?"

Luke's jaw dropped as he whirled around to look at Jackal. "You can't be serious? Is that why you wanted the Dragoons to protect you?" He looked spooked by the revelation, and it took a few moments for him to calm himself. "Okay…can I ask how you came by one? It's not something that just turns up at an auction, Petro."

Petro's smile tightened. "I only tell you because of our history, and I know I can trust you." He gestured over at Sal. "He's found a method to create them from leecher cores."

"Fuck off," Luke stated flatly as he stared at Salvatore in utter disbelief. "The lowest value core on the market…is able to be turned into a blight core? You're telling me, that the item Robert Locke has absolutely killed people over, is derived…from leecher cores?"

Sal paused at that. "Okay, is that why we're really wary of Robert?" He looked over his shoulder at his father. "He's killed people for blight cores?"

Luke moved over to Sal, putting his hands on Sal's shoulders. "You won't get in trouble for telling the truth…I already promised to protect you, and I'll do that. I just need to know…where did you get the blight core?"

Sal stared into Luke's fierce gaze. "I made it. Leecher core can be synthesized into a siphonstone, which becomes venomstone, which finally becomes a blight core." Sal pointed past Luke to where Jackal was bobbing up and down over the corpses. "That's made with the blight core. There are also around a dozen venomstone plates in this arm." He tapped at the glossy black surface of his left arm. "I refined them down into plates that could be used as armor."

"That's what you meant by battery," Luke realized as he looked at Sal's arm in surprise. "And this…synthesis? How does it work?"

"Luke," Petro warned from ahead. "Salvatore is being very gracious in answering your questions, but he doesn't owe them to you."

Luke pulled his hands back from Sal's shoulders with an apologetic frown. "I'm sorry, Salvatore. I didn't mean to intimidate you." He turned his attention to Petro. "How are you so calm about all of this? You know better than anyone how fucked this situation is. If he can make blight cores, there's going to be an all-out war with the Hunter Bureau."

"We had a whole car ride to process the information, and we've seen how Jackal performs," Petro responded with an awkward laugh. "My best guess is that people will see Jackal and understand that it's by far the best use for a blight core. If people are going to keep killing each other over them, then my current hope is that they'll bring them to Sal to make more gear."

Luke glanced back at Jackal before letting out a sigh. "It'll take a lot more than that, but I understand where you're coming from. Rumors have been going around for years, and the one people seem to latch onto is that Robert is using the blight core to make himself stronger. I can't for the life of me understand how that would even be possible, but he's kept his position as president despite all the insurrections over the years."

"Subsume," Sal stated as he looked over at his dad. "That's what I was telling you. Just like Jackal's kills are increasing my stats, maybe Robert has it doing something similar? I'm sure Doc Ameye would have been able to make something for him with a blight core."

"Wait, what is it doing now?" Sophia lifted the grill of her helmet to get a better look.

Sal turned to see where she was looking, and saw Jackal suspended from the wall with all abyssal tendrils locked into the stone in an almost perfect circle. The gem was completely concealed by the black shell, and the tentacles weren't glowing anymore. Just when Sal was about to check the visor for clarification, the surface of the wall between the tendrils started to shimmer in the dim lighting.

Sal held his breath as he saw two clawed hands silently grasp at the edges of the shimmering surface. The voider poked its head through, but Jackal didn't react. It was only when half of the torso had come through the portal that the tentacles suddenly burst into light.

"Poor bugger," Luke muttered as Jackal cut the voider into pieces in less than a second.

Jackal (Drone)
  - o   Voider Heart, Voider Claws, Voider Eyes, Voider Skin have been added to Arsenal

Sal watched as the skinned chunks of the demon slapped onto the stone floor. Jackal went back to bobbing over the other corpses as though the sudden appearance had been nothing but a minor inconvenience.

"Are we going to talk about how it's becoming way more proficient?" Sophia asked as she pointed at the corpse. "What happened to the whirl of blades and everything died? It literally just waited for that voider to come out of the portal before attacking!"

Sal raised his hand as he unfortunately had the answer. "It's in Harvest mode, so it waited until it could get as many useful pieces as possible. It would have killed it instantly if it was in Attack mode."

"You're going to need to find a way to register everyone in your class on the protective protocol list, because I've got a feeling that Jackal might kill someone to end an argument," Petro said awkwardly as he looked at the corpse on the ground. "But on the upside, I don't think we really need to worry about you being kidnapped."

Luke looked between them and let out an exaggerated sigh. "So…back to the topic at hand. How many leecher cores do we need to give you to get something at that level?"

Petro intervened this time. "Luke, I know you're looking at the firepower and potential of Jackal…but it's too much of a risk. You don't want to give Robert any reason to turn his attention to the Dragoons. He'd use whatever excuse necessary to raze this compound to the ground." He put his hands up in a placating gesture. "But we've already pledged to provide equipment to your soldiers. While they won't be at the level of a blight core, there shouldn't be any issue with producing materials with the venomstone, is there, Sal?"

Sal shook his head. "No issue. I'd need to design something…but it would give you Assimilation, which is a lesser version of Subsume. It has pretty much the same effect of giving you stats for killing opponents, but you won't be able to steal abilities like Subsume can."

"Beg your pardon?" Luke stared at Sal. "Subsume can steal abilities?"

Sal waved his hand, like it wasn't anything to worry about. "It has a low activation chance and you'd need to take out something ridiculously strong. Like, I've only gotten the stat boosts from when Jackal took out those hulkers. Nothing from the prowlers or voiders." With a reassuring nod, he looked back at his father. "Venomstone would give Assimilation, and I think that would give you the desired effects. Could even throw on evolutionary runes and see if they progress to the blight core effects?"

Luke raised his eyebrows in surprise. "That sounds very good to me…what's the catch?" He looked at Petro. "There's always a catch with you."

Sal smiled as he offered a shrug. "Well, you did just tell us that you can afford up to five million?" He couldn't help but break with a laugh at the horrified look on Luke's face. "I'm joking…the materials and the support are what we want from the Dragoons. We'll supply the equipment."

"How much charge is left on Jackal?" Sophia suddenly asked, drawing everyone's attention to the small drone. Except it wasn't floating around the corpses anymore.

Sal looked around to see his mother pointing in the distance.

"It seems to have slowed down a bit." Sophia had a hint of concern in her voice. "Do you think it's starting to struggle?"

Jackal (Drone)
    o   Request to change to mode

Sal saw the request as he moved over to where his mother stood. "What's happening?" He asked the question, but realized he could see the answer in the distance.

The tunnel curved downward as a way to get to the lower floors, and it obscured a lot of their vision until they were at the top of the decline. There was no mistaking the green light that bobbed around evasively, but the light also illuminated an enormous claw that tore away a massive chunk of the tunnel wall. Jackal was evading it well, but there was a massive difference in speed compared to all the opponents it had up until now.

Sal accepted the request, and the green light below disappeared in an instant. All that could be heard were the shrieks and the faint sounds of the abyssal steel whirling around the enclosed arena. More tearing sounds followed, albeit a bit more erratic than before. Sal realized he was holding his breath with the anticipation. His visor was highlighting the red dot ahead as a particularly large demon, but the claws didn't look like a prowler or a hulker. The best guess he had was that they were up against a voider.

"Scuttler?" Petro asked as he joined them, frowning. "Sounds like it."

Sophia nodded in agreement. "Overgrown scorpion bastards…they're a nightmare to take on." She glanced back at where Luke stood. "You might need to get that sword ready." Then, she touched Sal on the wrist. "You should probably recall Jackal now."

Sal didn't answer her immediately as he was looking at the feed on his visor. "I think it's okay."

Luke shook his head. "Scuttler chitin isn't something that can be penetrated with a blade. It's ridiculously durable. You need to attack the exposed areas to have a chance against them. Your drone won't be able to determine that."

Sal nodded in understanding. "Except Jackal's blades are made from abyssal steel…which is made from scuttler chitin. Would that be enough?" He wasn't being sarcastic, and was genuinely curious whether the material would hold out. Judging by the blank expression on Luke's face, it likely was enough.

"I'm just…going to stop talking, I think." Luke sheathed his sword for the fifth time. "You made a drone, out of abyssal steel and a blight core. Are there any other surprise materials you'd like to tell us about?"

"Storm steel, starlight steel…and an alloy made from both of them. Nightshade leather, but that was upgraded from the prowler hide. I think that's it?" Sal answered truthfully, which seemed to give Luke a whole new level of discomfort.

"You…used storm steel, on a drone?" Luke repeated the sentence as though testing out the words for the first time. "You're right, that thing can't have a price." His sigh was one of defeat, and he gave Petro a bewildered shake of the head.

Sophia frowned as she continued to look down the decline. "I still think we should go down and help him."

"Him?" Petro smiled. "You're talking about the drone?"

Sophia shot him a look of disapproval. "He has done all the heavy lifting in this dungeon, and Salvatore made him. I think it's only fair that we give him the respect he deserves." She gestured down at the darkness. "Besides, if Jackal's going to be protecting Sal, then we should probably make sure he survives this."

Jackal (Drone)
- o Scuttler Countermeasure has been Learned
  - ▪ Confirmed Scuttler Kills: 1

"I don't think we need to worry. Just got the kill confirmation," Sal said after letting out an explosive sigh of relief. "I honestly wasn't sure how that one was going to go." Even though he knew Fabi was able to take down scuttlers without the use of her ability, he hadn't expected Jackal to adapt to such an opponent.

Sophia moved over to hold Sal's shoulder, a gentle smile on her face; her other palm rested on his back. "Just in case."

"In case what?" Sal asked with a confused frown. A half second later, a jarring bolt of electricity rocketed through his body with enough force to almost knock him to the ground. If it hadn't been for his mother holding him steady, he would have fallen into a heap from the shock alone.

Unlike the previous sensation that had been like a numbing tingle, this was much more akin to Vanessa's treatment…or more accurately, when he had downed the bottle of Kaizen. His arms and chest felt as if they were on fire. Squinting, Sal was able to read through the discomfort.

Jackal (Drone)
- Subsume Notification
  - Strength has increased by 1.21

"Is it bad that I'm relieved there's some discomfort?" Luke asked with an awkward smile. "Increased stats shouldn't be earned from a drone."

Petro gave Luke a steady stare. "At least wait until he's stopped suffering."

"Fair point." Luke approached Sal from behind, placing his palm on his back, just above Sophia's. "Take a deep breath, Salvatore."

"What are you—" Sal started before he felt a cool mist wash through his entire body. It was ridiculously soothing, and dulled the fiery sensation from Subsume. "Oh…that's nice," he finally uttered with a relieved sigh. "Thank you."

"Don't mention it. It's my penance for talking shit," Luke replied, grinning.

Sophia patted Sal on the back, giving him a reassuring smile. "So, do you want to see a dead scuttler?"

CHAPTER 93: CALLING

Sal stepped around the slop of blood and gore, his right arm covering his face to avoid the pungent odor that reeked throughout the enclosed space. Even with Jackal docked into his shoulder, the green light did not paint a pretty picture of the scene. What was once a scuttler had been picked apart by the little drone. There wasn't an ounce of chitin visible. The claws and all sorts of internal organs had also been harvested, to the point where Sal dreaded even looking at the once-pristine Arsenal. It was likely a mess.

Jackal (Drone)
- o   Kills: 61
- o   Charging: 52%
    - ▪   Estimated Completion: 2 hours

His body was still acclimatizing to the sudden surge of Strength, but it didn't impede his movement. It felt like there was a tightness throughout his body, that could only be relieved by a rigorous stretching routine. Maybe that and a cold shower would do the trick.

Sal was very aware of how valuable the Mythic grade was. Since entering the dungeon, his Strength stat had increased by almost a point and a half. When he considered that he was starting with less than five, it really put it into perspective how dramatic the effects of Subsume were. He thought of his peers, namely Darren Lenihan, who specialized in Body Manipulation…his Strength stat was thirteen. He hadn't checked the Strength stat when Darren was compressing those lockboxes with his hands, but if that level of growth was possible, then it would be fantastic.

"When I wanted you to see a scuttler, this wasn't what I meant." Sophia laughed as she skipped past the corpse, taking special care to avoid getting the blood on her shoes as she stayed close to the wall. "Are we going to take on the rest of the dungeon while Jackal has a nap?"

Petro gave her a curious look. "I'm starting to get concerned about how well you're treating the drone. Sal could end up dismantling the thing when we get back home."

"Don't you dare," Sophia said, but perked up in surprise as she looked over at Luke, who had said it at the exact same time.

He scratched at the back of his head, smiling ruefully. "I mean, obviously it's yours to do whatever you want with…but Jackal is outperforming more than a few of my senior guys. It would be a waste to dismantle something like that."

"No need to fear." Sal smiled at both of them. "I've got no intention of getting rid of Jackal. I'm just coming to terms with the fact that the improvements only really happen when it takes down strong opponents. My plans of sitting back and improving my stats while it clears through a leecher dungeon have kinda gone to shit."

"Any sign of it picking up an ability?" Petro kicked a chunk of scuttler out of his way. "Curious how much stronger an opponent you'll need to kill to get something like that."

"Nothing yet." Sal double-checked the visor to see whether there was any new information under the Subsume ability. "What's stronger than a scuttler?"

Luke shrugged as he pointed his sword farther down the tunnel. "Only one way to find out. I'd be very surprised if this was an elite. Even though it's just chunks at this point, it sounded like an average scuttler."

Sal nodded as he followed Luke, with his parents walking alongside him. It was oddly exciting for him as they went through the dungeon together. He didn't know whether it was the levity of their conversation throughout, or whether it was the reassurance of having Jackal with him…but Sal was actually enjoying himself. Maybe it would change when he had to fight, but it was doing wonders for his fear of demons. Seeing that they could be taken down by one of his creations in such a straightforward manner was an absolute delight. He couldn't help but wonder how different the tower exercise would have been if he had Jackal with him.

Luke led them through the tunnel until they entered a wide cavern. The rocky ground and blood-soaked sand had been replaced with a collection of otherworld-style plants. It would be disingenuous to call them trees as they were closer to an obstacle course made of thick red vines that shifted and swayed as though they were being pushed by an unseen breeze.

What made it all the more foreboding were the dead prowlers that were suspended in the center of the vegetation labyrinth. Sal wasn't sure what sort of creature would be able to create such a thing. His first thought had been a leecher, but the sheer scale of the maze was far beyond anything he had ever seen. It made the net exercise in the tower look like child play.

"Elite leecher?" Sophia looked directly up. "If it's been killing prowlers, then we can't discount it having a Stealth ability."

That sentence alone was enough to shake Sal back into the reality of the situation. He looked around with his visor for signs of whatever demon was hiding from view, and it didn't take him long to find the answer. Unfortunately, it was a horrible scenario. "It's the whole thing."

Sophia sighed. "You mean the maze itself is the demon?" She flicked her wrists to draw the bracer blades. "Guess it's up to Luke and me, then." She looked meaningfully at his drawn sword. "On the bright side, you'll finally get to show off your swordsmanship."

"Thank goodness. Was starting to feel like a passenger this whole time." Luke chuckled as he draped his sword low on his left side, the point aimed directly at the ground. "Let's get started then." He casually brought the blade upward in the slowest slash that Sal had ever seen. His form was perfect, but there was no force behind it.

A sickening crunch made Sal snap his head around to look at the maze folding in on itself. The impact lined up perfectly with Luke's sword strike. And rather than showing any sign of slowing down, it persisted all the way to the back of the cavern.

The sheer force of the invisible attack caused countless fragments of criss-crossed vines to shatter. While it was still sliding across the ground, Luke lazily swiped from left to right with his sword. The same controlled action, the same dramatic result. Two conflicting cuts into the maze created absolute mayhem, with the more resilient of the vines exploding under the pressure.

"Should show itself now." Luke held his sword at the ready. "My money is on it being below ground. Those vines didn't grow out of there of their own accord."

Sophia smiled as she started some basic stretches. "You going to let me get the kill?" Her closed helm was pointed at Luke as she spoke.

"All yours." He chuckled as he sheathed his blade. "I'd say you've got another ten seconds."

Sal could see with his visor that Luke was correct. Not about the time…he had no idea about that…but the leecher was indeed below ground. It was enormous. The largest he had seen was in his first ever dungeon run, when he had gone up against the leecher that fused with the train carriage. This one was about twenty times the size of that one. It was ridiculous to think that his mother would be able to take it out with such small blades. Sal was going to suggest that they leave it to Jackal, but his father made eye contact and gave the smallest shake of his head.

Sal gave him a nod of understanding. Now that he thought about it, this was probably the first demon his mother had killed in years. If his father's words were to be believed, she was ridiculously good at fighting back in the day. He never really questioned whether she enjoyed it or not. Looking at her hopping on the spot, he got the impression that she very much enjoyed it.

"And…there it is," Luke announced as the leecher emerged from the grassy floor.

It wasn't anything as dramatic as a demon burrowing through rock, but instead looked like the swelling of a diseased bubble, rising from a swamp. The remaining vines twitched and tried to support the body, but too many of them were structurally compromised and buckled under the massive weight. This caused the bubble to twitch and ripple as it rolled over, displaying the most horrifying vortex of teeth. Endless rows of triangular pointed teeth seemed to curl inward, as though inviting prey inside. A yellowy mucus oozed from the open mouth as it continued to twitch and ripple.

"Well, it certainly didn't starve," Petro remarked dryly as he looked at Sophia. "You sure you want your debut from retirement to be a demon that can barely move?"

Sophia slowed down her exercises as she looked at the twitching blob. Flicking open her helm, she stared at Petro for a few seconds. "You're going to compare this to the red prowler, aren't you?"

Petro nodded sadly. "And you won't hear the end of it."

Sophia sighed as she looked over at Sal. "Send Jackal to kill that, will you? I'll wait for something a little more exciting."

Sal stared at them in disbelief. "There's a massive leecher just lying on the ground and you're arguing over which kill is the most impressive?"

Sophia smiled as she offered a guilty shrug. "Suit yourself…I was trying to give you this lovely gift of more essence, but if you'd rather I take the kill, I'll take it."

Sal faltered as he thought about it for a second. It was a well-fed leecher and there was a good chance that it would increase one of his stats. Definitely not a mobility stat, if the gelatinous blob wasn't enough of a clue. Before he could vocalize that he had changed his mind, his mother had set off at full speed toward the enormous leecher. That singular movement was enough to render him speechless. He knew his mother was fast, but…she had clearly been going very easy on him back at the auction house.

He'd add it to the list of lies.

A laugh escaped Sal's lips as he watched his mother spin in midair, her arms doing an excellent imitation of Jackal's rotation attack. The key difference was the silver blades that burned straight through the yellow blubber. Sophia landed on her feet—or rather, bounced from her landing point—only to vault straight into another attack.

This time, her hands dug even farther into the leecher that could only flounder around on the spot, gnashing its teeth in a wordless rage. Each of the surrounding vines that had survived the ascent of the leecher and Luke's attacks tried to smother his mother in a thorny embrace. With just two rotations of spinning on her heel with both blades outstretched, the ambush was thwarted with ease.

Sal glanced at his father, who smiled with pride as he watched on from the sidelines. "I didn't think she actually enjoyed this sort of stuff."

Petro didn't even turn; his eyes were locked on Sophia. "It was never a job for your mother. It was a calling, and she answered it every single time." His voice was both proud and filled with respect as he continued to watch his wife dance around the leecher in a whirlwind of blades. "Seeing her able to do this again is just magic…and I know it means the world to her that you're here with her." Petro turned to smile at Sal.

"Pretend I'm not here if you two want to hug it out," Luke said from the wall behind them, where he was leaning with his arms crossed.

Sal chuckled as he glanced over at Luke. "It's my first time seeing her fight. I thought my parents were just Auctioneers until a few weeks ago."

"Ouch," Luke answered as he shot Petro a disapproving look. After a moment, he frowned and looked at Sal carefully. "Well, if you've managed to turn out this well…I'd say they managed to do a pretty decent job of raising you. My girls all despise me for the training I keep putting them through."

Sal smiled politely, not sure how to navigate that one.

Petro had no such issue. "You promised them a bird like Fig, didn't you?"

Luke grinned as he shrugged nonchalantly. "Of course. It's the only reason they haven't quit."

Sal couldn't help but laugh at the ridiculousness of the situation. He stood in an incredibly dangerous dungeon, listening to a story about kids being bribed with animals, while his mother was slaughtering a giant leecher. When he looked at his mom fighting, he could see that the leecher was in horrible shape. It was being seared and scorched from dozens of gashes along its quivering body, and the gnashing of teeth had slowed down to an irregular clench of resignation. Sal wasn't sure how it could be feasibly ended, but he had full faith that his mother knew what she was doing.

"Looks like we're wrapping up," Luke muttered as he slid off the wall and uncrossed his arms.

"How can you tell?" Sal asked out of curiosity.

Luke pointed at the mouth of the leecher. "See the faint glow back there? Your mother is carving her way into the core of the leecher. The fact that it's visible shows that she's detached enough of the sinew holding it in place. It'll collapse into a puddle soon, so we should probably find something to stand on."

Sal followed Luke's lead and moved onto a protruding rock that stood a few feet off ground level. When Petro hopped onto the rock beside him, he felt a reassuring hand on his back.

"Having fun?"

It was such a strange question, but Sal couldn't help but smile and nod. "Yeah, I can't believe it. I'm actually enjoying this."

Petro grinned as he patted Sal's back. "That's good. This is how it'll feel when you go into dungeons with a reliable team." He chuckled as he lightly tapped the Blight Jackal. "Although, I imagine you'll end up being the most reliable one with this thing floating around."

At that moment, a surge of congealed yellow slime washed across the floor as the leecher melted in on itself. Its teeth slapped against the ground, each falling out of the mouth as Sophia ripped a massive core from its corpse. She held it up triumphantly before letting it drop to her side, laughing. "That was not worth it." She scooped up the yellow slime that covered her body and slung it toward the pool of yellow at her feet.

"Absolutely not worth it." With a shake of her head, she suppressed an involuntary shudder before gesturing at Sal. "Can you send Jackal to pick up whatever is considered a material? I have no idea where to start with any of this."

"You were amazing!" Sal shouted back at her, earning him a wide grin from his mother, that was cut short by her helm slapping back into place.

"Thank you!" Sophia shouted in return as she pulled the helm off her face. "Any chance we can just let Jackal finish the rest of the demons so I can get a shower?"

Sal couldn't help but laugh as he sent the command to Jackal. His gaze returned to his mother. "Why don't you use Restoration to get rid of all the filth?"

Petro was the one who answered, albeit in a sagely voice. "Showers are apparently sacred, Salvatore. She claims she can always feel the blood after Restoration, so it's not worth arguing with her."

CHAPTER 94: PLANS

"Someone is eager," Petro joked as he poured two glasses of whiskey at the bar. He picked up his tablet and rotated it to show Sal the paperwork agreement with an unfamiliar logo on the top left of the page. "General Lucion Drake has just officially entered into an agreement with the Argento Auction House." He placed the tablet down on the table before lifting one of the glasses and handing it over to Sal. "Congratulations on becoming affiliated with the Dragoons of Remembrance. You were sensational today, Salvatore. I don't think it could have gone any better."

Sal smiled as he accepted the whiskey. "How many showers do you think she's going to have?" He laughed at the memory of his mother refusing to change at the Dragoon outpost. She had been wrapped head to toe in borrowed towels, which was seemingly enough for the taxicab, but the moment she entered the auction house, she ran at light speed to the staff showers. Her attempts at Restoration hadn't done anything to remove the blood and gunk under her armor.

"At least four." Petro smiled as he lifted his own glass. "I have her white wine chilling, so it'll be perfect for her when she gets out." He continued to look at Sal. "I mean it, by the way. You walked through that dungeon like you owned the place…it was a remarkable difference from our first outing."

Sal shrugged the compliment off. "It was because I had Jackal doing all the hard work. I doubt I would have been as comfortable if I had to face the demons myself." He corrected himself almost immediately. "That's a lie. I would have been terrified if I had to clear it with my fists."

Petro tilted his head to one side as he looked at Sal curiously. "But you made Jackal. It clearing the dungeon is the same as you clearing it…you know that, right?"

Sal stared at his father. "No? It's completely different. I didn't have to attack any of those demons."

Petro smiled as he shook his head slowly. "How is it any different from how Luke swung his sword? How would we have fared if you weren't there?" He chuckled to himself as he took a drink. "The contributions of that dungeon can't be allocated to an object. We don't celebrate guns or swords, but rather the people wielding them. Don't diminish what you accomplished today, Salvatore."

Sal tried to see it from his father's perspective. He understood the logic, but it still felt wrong to claim the credit of taking on that entire dungeon. Outside of Jackal, there were only a couple of kills handled by his mother and Luke. His father hadn't managed to take out a single thing throughout the day.

"By the way…I wanted to talk to you about something." Petro gestured to the lounge seats and tilted his head, indicating they should sit.

Sal followed him over and sat with a relieved sigh. He placed his whiskey on the table in front of him before looking at his father expectantly. "Are we revisiting the topic of the blight cores?"

"No, it was something a bit simpler than that." Petro hesitated as he placed his own glass down on the table. "I know that this break has been a rough time for you, with everything that came up…about the Silverson Group and all the craziness at the gala." He looked at Sal seriously. "I know that you've put yourself in the Support position because of your mother and me…when it's very clear that you could easily be a Controller like your friends. I just want you to know that we'd support you in whatever Hero class you decided to specialize in."

Sal stared at his father, a smile tugging at his lips. "I was expecting something serious." He lifted his glass and took a sip, enjoying the familiar burn running down his throat. It was a reassuring warmth. Sal thought about his father's words before answering. He wanted to be tactful in how he responded, but his answer was very clear. "Despite all the new developments, it doesn't change the fact that I was raised by two Supports. I want to make a Support guild that gets to Tier 1…and I honestly think we'd make it something incredible."

"Just wanted to check." Petro smiled. "Now, onto the actual serious topic." He lifted his glass and pointed his index finger at Sal. "We have the Dragoons on our side, which is a great start. I think that Jackal removes the need for you to make a badass weapon. Jackal alone is incredible, and we were wrong in underestimating the combat potential…but there's still more for you to do before you head back to Quest Academy next week."

"What do you suggest?" Sal asked, already anticipating what was coming next. He guessed that his father was going to tell him to keep the Mythic-grade Blight Jackal a secret. It made sense, as it would only lead to questions about the blight core.

"First thing. You made that with a venomstone." Petro pointed at the glowing green light. "There are no Appraisers lurking in Quest Academy who can handle up to Legendary grade. Strong people will know that it's more than Legendary, but you'll only bump into those types on outings with the guilds. Brag to your heart's content that you made it with a venomstone, but don't highlight anything to do with Subsume. There's no way they'll be able to identify it as a blight core. There are plenty of items that give off a green glow, so you shouldn't run into any issues."

Sal nodded in agreement. It was a good approach and he'd have no issue with maintaining that sort of lie. He guessed that his father thought of the solution while Sal was explaining the core synthesis to Luke in the dungeon.

"Next, I need you to work on a piece of gear that will protect you from Psionic interference," Petro said in a somber tone. "Neuro can't go poking around in your head anymore, nor should anyone else. Your safety comes first, and when you have secrets this big, we need to protect them." He gestured in the direction of the storage area. "You can probably engineer a better version of those crap ones your mother bought. It'll be easier than starting from scratch."

Sal couldn't argue with the logic. He had been putting off making a Psionic blocker because he felt like it would be admitting to Erika that he was scared of her. Now that he actually had something to lose from his mind being read, making a barrier for his mind was an obvious choice. "Okay, got it…anything else?"

Petro lifted his glass and took another drink. "I'm making this up as I go along, so bear with me," he muttered as he looked into space. "Just pretend that it was all incredibly sage advice."

"Seamless and profound." Sal chuckled as he nodded. "Let me know when you think of next steps."

Petro clicked his fingers. "Ah, yes… If you have time to do it before you go, a mock-up of the sort of weaponry you can supply to the Dragoons from the Arkwright would be great." He tapped his finger against the table. "And maybe you could write up a guide of sorts for us to use it while you're gone. Just a simple walkthrough should do it, and I'm sure we'll figure it out."

"Anything else?" Sal laughed as he made a mental list of everything he needed to do in the next week. "Anything that would reduce your worry while I'm gone?"

"If you were to make yourself a uniform out of this stuff, I think that would put us at ease." Petro tapped the glossy black metal on Sal's left arm. "I don't know how the Crafting works, but if you could make something that can heal you up from time to time, that would be an incredible weight off our shoulders. Your mother is terrified that you'll end up going blind because of my stupid ability, and you staying up until all hours using Mythcrafter isn't helping her relax."

Sal frowned as he thought about it. On one hand, he was exasperated at how his mother was in a position to worry about him when she was literally flinging herself at demons with nothing but a few silver blades. But on the other hand, he understood their concern and it was very real. He had experienced three Healers telling him that his eyes were deteriorating from using Mythcrafter—Rochelle, Dr. Bob, and the Healer in the infirmary after the excursion. If it was a piece of equipment that was going to heal his eyes, did that mean that he had to replace the visor? It was his second-best piece of equipment, and he didn't want to swap it out, especially with how great the abilities were on it.

Petro sighed as he looked at Sal with a weary expression. "I'm sorry, Salvatore. I know I'm not in any position to lecture you on this stuff. You didn't ask for any of this, and it probably feels like you're being punished for excelling with your abilities."

"Hmm? No…it's not that. I'm just thinking about how I'd make gear for Healing," Sal answered honestly as he lifted his glass and thought aloud. "I could try playing around with the Arkwright to see if something comes up. Fabi mentioned there was a leecher core that purifies, but I don't know if that would give the effect we're looking for." He shrugged as he took a drink. "I can play around with the materials we picked up in that dungeon to see if there are any blight core-level breakthroughs."

Petro grimaced. "For my own sanity, please don't tell me whatever you discover…or anyone else, for that matter. I don't think my heart can take it."

Sal laughed as he drained his glass and placed it back on the table. "No promises. I'll just brag about the tier of core before the final version… sound good?"

"Now you're getting it." Petro chuckled. "Venomstone sure is remarkable, isn't it?" He tapped the metal arm again before tilting his head. "You can take that off, right?"

Sal's smile turned into a grimace. "Yes…but it keeps telling me I can store it in the Arsenal, but it's the thing that gives me access to the Arsenal."

"Ah. So you're worried that it'll trap itself in a subspace that you've got no way of opening?" Petro realized the issue as he clapped Sal on the shoulder. "There's an obvious solution, though."

"Yeah?" Sal asked hopefully as he perked up.

Petro nodded. "Never take it off." He laughed at Sal's sour expression, and moved out of swatting range. "But seriously…why don't you just make something else that can access the Arsenal?" He thought about it for a few seconds before pointing at Sal's visor. "Why don't you try sending something to the Arsenal with just a visor command, and see if you can activate it within the subspace?"

"Like what?" Sal asked, not sure he was following his father's logic.

"You said that the vocal commands for the drone work via your tablet. Put the tablet in Arsenal, and then try giving a vocal command to Jackal to see if it responds. That would tell you if you can dismiss the Blight Jackal and summon it again from Arsenal." Petro continued to point at the visor. "Since they're all paired via the Nexus ability, then it should work. You said yourself that items in the subspace were being analyzed by the Arkwright, so even when it's closed, it's not cutting off the connection to what's inside."

Sal stared at his father. "Or I could just dismiss it, see what happens. Then make something else with Arsenal to open it up again."

Petro stared right back. "That's a very stubborn way to say that you didn't understand my example."

Sal smiled as he issued the command to his visor to dismiss the Mythic Blight Jackal to the Arsenal. In a very underwhelming fashion, the glossy black arm disappeared in a blink of an eye, revealing Sal's left arm with a very frayed shirt sleeve that had been burned to oblivion.

Petro dropped his glass and jumped to his feet. "You did not just send it into Arsenal!" He was clearly panicked as he looked at Sal as if he were demented.

"What? Doesn't this solve all our problems?" Sal asked innocently as he gestured at his bare left arm. "We won't need to worry about anyone trying to kill me."

Petro was clearly on the verge of insanity as he stared at Sal in utter shock. "You just threw a Mythic grade into the ether without knowing if you could get it back?!" His voice reached a high pitch that Sal hadn't ever heard before.

Sal sent the command to his visor, recalling the Blight Jackal, and it instantly reappeared on his arm. "Oh, you mean this?" He pointed at it in mock confusion.

Petro stared at Sal before he reached over and plucked Sal's empty glass from the table. "You knew that would happen, didn't you?"

Sal smiled. "It was worth it for the reaction. If it didn't work, I'd have just made something else with Arsenal."

With a resigned sigh, Petro picked up his fallen tumbler and inspected it for scratches. "Okay, smartarse. You've only got a week left. You better get back to your workshop." He smiled as he jutted his chin toward the workshop. "And I meant what I said earlier."

"Which part?" Sal asked as he reviewed their conversation in his head.

Petro smiled softly. "That you were sensational today. You and Jackal, both."

CHAPTER 95: RESULTS

Petro looked around the room, frowning. "Please tell me that you actually slept at some point over the last week." He started counting all the crates and boxes that lined the platform edge, nearly all waiting for collection by George. "What could possibly need eight crates? Are you intending on taking all the materials from the Arkwright back with you?" Petro finally guessed with a curious expression on his face.

Sal gave an imperceptible shake of his head as he pointed at the crate at the bottom. "That one is going to Luke and the Dragoons. I took your advice on making them rifles, and they seemed to work out well. We've got three Rare grades, and one Epic grade. I fitted the Epic grade with the venomstone and Tether so Luke can get the benefits of Assimilate, as well as an essence source for the evolutionary rune."

Petro nodded with a relieved sigh. "That will keep him happy for quite some time. Were you able to save it as a blueprint on the Arkwright?"

"Yeah, you'll be able to find it in the menu I showed you. They're under Argento, Dragoon Series." Sal pointed at the Arkwright up on the balcony. "You won't be able to do remote activation with your monocle since Nexus is tied to my devices, but you can do everything on the menu screen without issues."

"Perfect." Petro smiled as he clapped Sal on the shoulder. "He's promised a shipment of materials, which should be coming in the next few days. I insisted that he send a courier rather than taking them via Fig. Didn't want to scare the life out of the residents." He chuckled as he gestured at the boxes stacked on top of the Dragoon rifles. "And these?"

Sal chuckled at the thought of a falcon descending into Silver Sanctuary. It would likely cause mass hysteria, but it would definitely be a sight to see. When he reached the stack of crates, Sal tapped the next one up. It was a small decorative box similar in size to the ones they used for the obsidian daggers. "This is a present for Upgrade. I'll be taking it in the car with me, since I don't want to risk it going missing."

Petro clicked his fingers as though just remembering something. "Ah, you said that Fabrizia was going to take you to Quest Academy? What time is she arriving tomorrow? Your mother wanted me to ask if you'd like to have breakfast with us before heading off? Maurice is more than welcome to join, too."

"That sounds lovely. I'll let her know and see what she says. I think she mentioned leaving in the afternoon, but I'll double-check and let you know." Sal took out his tablet and typed out a quick message. "Oh, and before I forget, the ones on the top are for you and Mom."

Petro blinked in surprise as he pointed at the crates at the top of the pile. "For us? That wasn't part of the plan."

"Plans change," Sal muttered absentmindedly as he finished the message and sent it off to Fabi. "But in a good way. It was just something I wanted to try out, and there's no expectation on you wearing them. I'd almost ask that you don't Appraise it, because I know you won't like it." He chuckled as he pocketed his tablet before stepping over to the crates. Reaching up to the top, he pulled a small box down and handed it to his father. "Have a look."

Petro compressed the metal container on both sides to pop the lid open, revealing what looked like a golden circlet. "I'm guessing this one is for your mother?"

Sal peered into the box and smiled broadly. "Nope, that's the one for you." He pointed at the golden light that rippled across the surface of the metal. "I know it's not your color, but give it a shot."

Petro sighed as he plucked it out of the box. "Epic grade?" He gave Sal a steady look before raising his eyebrow. "Really though, why are you saying I'm not allowed to Appraise it?"

"Calibrate is one of the abilities I have on my visor. It gives me a boost to Mythcrafter and Skill Master. I managed to find a way to put that onto a small piece of jewelry." Sal smiled as he traced his finger along the smooth edges of the circular frame. "The frame is made entirely of essence cores, so it has the worst durability imaginable. I infused it with some of the Kaizen elixirs, and it worked better than I expected."

Petro frowned as he looked at the circlet carefully. "I can't help but question why you thought this would be good for me. Tapping into more of my ability isn't the problem, Sal." He smiled as he shook his head, passing it back to Sal. "I really do appreciate the effort, though."

Sal grinned as he held the circlet out to his father. "Calibrate and Regeneration. Those are the two abilities on this thing. I was trying to make a Healing item like you suggested, and this was the first attempt. I ran some simulations with Cypher using your scanned profile from the visor, and it estimates that your injuries will be completely healed in about three to four months." Sal shrugged slightly as he pointed at the thin golden material. "I couldn't find a place to put in any replenishing runes, so the long wait time is because of the recharging time."

Petro just stared at the circlet in a whole new light. "We should give this to your mother, instead! Would it work on her injuries?" His eyes were wide and his breathing had picked up. Both of his hands shook ever so slightly as he held the circlet, before he carefully placed it back into the box as though scared that touching it would cause it to break.

Sal smiled as he pointed at the other box that was on top of the pile. "I told you that yours was the first attempt. Mine was the second, and Mom's was the third. The reason that I don't think you should Appraise it…is because it's made of voider skin. I highly doubt she'll wear it if she knew that."

Petro barked a laugh as he reached up to the top of the pile to retrieve the other crate. "Salvatore, she would swim in demonic blood if it alleviated a fraction of the pain she deals with daily. Voider skin is absolutely nothing to what we've tried in the past."

Sal was caught off guard by that. He had known that his mother was in pain, but everything that his father had said to him in the past was that they had managed it with clinic visits. *Was the truth coming out now that a potential solution was in sight?* He found himself wondering just how bad her injuries were and desperately hoped this would work for her.

When Petro leaned back down, he repeated the process of opening the crate, only to reveal a laurel crown made of gold. He looked up at Sal, grimacing. "I knew they'd look different, but your mother gets a Greek crown…while I have a flimsy mesh?" With a laugh, he turned the box instead of the crown, trying to get a better look at it. "Where is the voider skin?"

Sal reached into the box and pulled out the crown, followed by a set of bracelets and anklets. Lastly, he withdrew a thin blanket. The sickly gray material thrummed with essence, and Sal had to hide his distaste as he pulled out a series of golden chains at the bottom. "Okay, this will sound really weird…but it was the only way I could figure out how to heal a Body Manipulator. You need to wrap her in the blanket and have her wear the crown along with the bracelets and anklets. If you wrap the chains around a fully charged core, and attach the other end to the bracelets, it will draw the essence into her."

Petro was completely lost for words as he looked at the assortment of equipment. "I don't mean to sound ungrateful, Salvatore…but I wasn't expecting something this convoluted. We have to wrap her like a burrito, and deck her out with gold trinkets, and finally hook her up to a battery? And will this ease the pain?"

Sal shrugged as he placed the blanket back into the crate. "Your regeneration will take a few months, but if Mom uses this every night and you have enough cores…then it should completely restore her body in about three weeks. The simulation that I ran was for her using it three nights a week, and it was closer to two months."

"Restore." Petro repeated the word slowly, as though testing out how it sounded. "You're saying that this will Restore your mother's body?"

Sal nodded as he pushed the crate into his father's hands. "Yeah, I had to go through a convoluted path in creating it, but hopefully the effects will be good. I think the main obstacle will be in getting her to try it. I've got a feeling she's going to leave it in a closet or something." Sal laughed at the thought of it.

Petro looked at the contents of the crate carefully. "It's a beautiful thought, Sal. We'll absolutely give them a try and report back to you. Even if they don't work, I appreciate you trying to make a solution for us." He smiled warmly at Sal. "I really hope you didn't spend the last days of your break working on this for us."

Sal grinned as he pointed at the base of the crates. "Rifles for the Dragoons took about two days." He raised his finger to point at the middle boxes. "Presents for Fabi, Upgrade, and a few others…that took three days." Finally, he reached the top. "And then the stuff for us took the last couple of days."

"Should I assume that you designed something that can heal you?" Petro asked hopefully.

"Yeah, but I won't show it to you because you'll be jealous." Sal laughed as he pointed at one of the boxes. There was another reason he didn't want his father to Appraise it. "I've got a black circlet that will protect against Psionic probing and attacks. It attaches to the back of my head and will be hard to see because of my hair. It was surprisingly easy once I saw the ones Mom bought."

"And the healing?" Petro insisted, as though worried that Sal was avoiding the topic.

Sal smiled as he gestured at his mouth. "It's a tough one. I made a ventilation mask that I can wear at night. I thought that it would make sense to have a piece of armor or clothing that would bolster it, but when I ran some simulations with

Cypher and the Arkwright, it proposed the ventilation mask instead. It's not perfect, but it's a good step in the right direction."

"And did you run any simulations with Cypher for it?" Petro frowned. "I can't imagine that a breathing apparatus would be much help when it comes to your eyes." He paused as he looked at the crate with his own circlet. "Why didn't you just make another one like mine?"

Sal tapped his chest. "I need more than just eye recovery. The ventilator is designed to help my body adjust to the new stats from Subsume, as well as working on existing injuries. It improves my natural healing, rather than pumping me full of essence to fix the problems. It's only a Rare grade, so I'll need to wait until I'm back at Quest Academy to find out if there's a better method I'm not thinking of."

Petro seemed to hesitate before he nodded again. "Okay, that's a good start. Thanks for humoring us and putting that in place. I'd still feel better if you go to the clinic at Quest Academy for regular checkups, too. Just in case." He pointed at the circlet Sal had just gifted him. "Also, if that would help you recover, you should take it with you, too."

Sal shook his head. "Nope. That was made specifically for you and your profile. Your injuries are far more nuanced than mine, and that thing is very much tailored for you. It would just be a paperweight if I took it."

Sal didn't want to tell his father that he had used the last of the Kaizen on making the equipment for them. He had already gotten a massive benefit from the elixir since he activated three-quarters of his available essence gates. It felt right to use the last of it as a material to create the pieces for his parents. The ventilation mask was something he had thrown together because he knew his father would ask about it. That was why he didn't want his dad Appraising it. It was nowhere near as good as the other items. Sal promised himself that he'd rework the concept when he got back to Quest Academy.

Petro sighed in defeat. "I really appreciate it. Your mother will, too. I'll send a picture of her when we wrap her up into an essence burrito." He grinned before switching topics. "So, is there anything else you'd like to do before you finish up your break?"

Sal just looked around the room. "Want to have a coffee with me?"

Petro nodded. "Sounds good to me. Anything you want to talk about?"

"Nothing really. I just miss the days where we could sit down and talk without a care in the world," Sal responded honestly. "So, no talk of the Hunter Bureau, Bastion, the Silverson Group, or anything like that."

Petro chuckled as he followed Sal up the steps of the mezzanine. "That I can do…but are you sure you don't want another spar before you go?"

Sal groaned as he looked at his father. "The manuals are already packed into my luggage, along with my sparring gear." He gestured vaguely at all the crates on the platform. "Besides, I think I've earned at least one evening of peace."

Petro smiled deviously. "Well, if you're not going to be sparring or Crafting, would you rather have a few real drinks instead?"

Sal paused as he thought about it, a smile appearing on his own face. "But we can't go crazy. I'm leaving tomorrow."

"Of course!" Petro said as he turned halfway up the stairs to start going back down. "It'll be a nice and relaxed evening. Nothing crazy."

CHAPTER 96: RETURN

Sal gave his father a baleful glare from the other side of the breakfast table. The bastard looked so chipper and unrepentant for last night's antics, where they had ended up going through three bottles of whiskey. Yet, if appearances were to be believed, only one of them was suffering through the pain.

Petro grinned at Sal and raised his coffee in almost salute, before turning and answering a question from Maurice.

What was even worse was how refreshed he looked. He wore the suit that Sal had made for him, and it looked immaculate. Even Sophia beside him looked more tired, and she had gone to bed after the first bottle.

"Don't worry, I'll drive extra slow…so just don't throw up in my car and we'll be golden," Fabi said in a low voice from her seat beside Sal, while she stacked more bacon onto her plate. "Did you have fun at least?" Her hair was pulled back into a ponytail, and she wore a blue turtleneck sweater with black jeans. The glowing necklace around her neck was still in place, and Sal wondered when she would be able to take it off.

Sal nodded, but regretted the action almost immediately as the throbbing in his skull flared up again. "Yeah, it was good…but I just can't believe he doesn't have a hangover." He thought back to the previous night where they had discussed everything and anything…brainstorming names for the new guild, and even making estimates on when Sal would learn the next phase of the Silverson Arts. Sal couldn't remember half of their conversation topics, but he could remember the laughs they enjoyed throughout. It was a genuinely great evening, and Sal had missed being able to hang out with his dad like that.

"Some people are just built different," Fabi remarked with a smile as she constructed a sandwich that consisted almost exclusively of bacon. "I had a quiet night in with Dad, and he wouldn't let me do any sort of Crafting. We had fun, but it was pretty tame in comparison to your evening. I'm glad you invited us over. I probably would have forgotten to eat and just hit up the canteen later."

"It was my dad's idea, but I'm glad you were able to come." Sal smiled. "Oh, and you don't need to worry about luggage from me, by the way. I had a sort of epiphany last night." He laughed at how stupid it had been, but he was taking credit for his father's idea. Arsenal would be able to handle all the crates, including Fabi and Upgrade's presents. He wouldn't need to manually transport them, and could just keep them in the private subspace. Petro had asked why he wasn't doing that from the start, and Sal inwardly had face-palmed at not even thinking of it.

"Really? Are you sending everything by courier?" Fabi asked in surprise. "You don't need to, because there's plenty of space. You might as well bring some of it with you so you can change when you get there."

Sal smiled as he shook his head. "I was going to tell you about it properly when we were on our way, but I've made a variation of Pocket that lets me store stuff."

Fabi held her sandwich in front of her face, not taking a bite. She slowly turned her head to look at Sal carefully. "Did you find a way to make a bigger subspace than Pocket? What was the material combination?"

"Eat," Sal answered, laughing. "We've got plenty of time to talk about it later, but the subspace is probably the least impressive part of the whole thing."

As though realizing that she wasn't going to get the answers she needed from Sal, Fabi turned her attention to Sophia. "Mrs. Argento, do you know what Sal made…that has a subspace?"

Sophia held her teacup and smiled warmly at Fabi. "You should eat your breakfast first. It's a conversation worth waiting for…I'm genuinely curious what you'll make of the newest addition to our family."

Petro practically choked as he looked at Sophia. "How many times do I need to tell you that Jackal isn't a part of the family?"

Sophia just shrugged as she took a sip of her tea. When she brought her cup back down, she smiled at Fabi. "Like Sal said, the subspace is the least impressive part of what he made."

"I think I'm missing something," Maurice said awkwardly as he looked at everyone around the table. "Is this about something Salvatore made?"

Petro sighed as he nodded. "Yeah. He's created a Mythic-grade item…and it is by far the most destructive and unorthodox thing I've ever witnessed." He looked over at Fabi. "I don't mean to spoil his fun, but I can tell you're not going to eat until you get your answer. Jackal is a drone that lives in his arm. It's a very useful little robot, and Sophia has practically adopted him since he tore up a dungeon."

Sophia's eyes lit up. "You called Jackal a him! See, I knew you'd come around." She laughed at Petro's apparent dismay at the slip-up.

Fabi's sandwich fell onto her plate, self-destructing in the process. She looked at both of Sal's parents in disbelief. "Wait…so, not only did he make a drone, it's Mythic grade? And you already tested it in a dungeon?" It was clear that a thousand thoughts were going through her head as she processed the information. It was a mixture of excitement, astonishment, and bewilderment.

Sal winced at the sudden onslaught of loud voices. "It has the same ability as the Vendetta Macclemark." He added a point of clarity. "The Assimilation ability. But it's a bit better at Mythic grade." His words were to provide context. He hadn't expected them to fuel the fire as much as they did. *Was it too much to wish that everyone would just calm down and enjoy the breakfast?*

Fabi's eyes sparkled as she looked at Sal. "Can you show me in a dungeon? We could make a detour on the way to Quest Academy. Students are returning over the next two days, so we'll have plenty of time to run a few."

Petro's laugh filled the room, fueling Sal's misery. "Would you believe, Fabrizia, that Salvatore predicted you'd say that? That's why he was intending on only telling you when you got to Quest Academy." He grinned as he pointed his fork in Sal's direction. "You won't be able to show it off at Quest Academy, so you might as well enjoy a little fanfare with friends and family who know your secret."

Sal smiled as he plucked his visor from the table beside his coffee cup. "Okay, but I'm not calling Jackal out." He set the conditions as he equipped the visor and summoned the Blight Jackal. His entire left arm suddenly transformed into the glossy black finish with pulsating green accents along the abyssal steel tendrils. Each groove was lit up, but paled in comparison to the rune-like circle that contained Jackal and the blight core.

"Whoa!" Fabi exclaimed as she practically flung herself out of the chair to get a better look at it. "This is amazing! And you had it stored in a subspace?"

Her hands cradled Sal's left arm as she ran her fingers along the grooves. "These are detachable, aren't they?" Fabi's smile was radiant as she looked at Sal eagerly. "The drone uses them, doesn't it?"

Sal nodded in agreement. "It's like a mechanical leecher, if…you know, it specialized in assassination." He finished the sentence lamely, not sure how to best describe Jackal without it sounding insane.

Sophia smiled as she watched from her seat at the table. "We watched it take out a scuttler in a variant dungeon. Also took out two hulkers, along with countless prowlers and voiders." She looked at the green glow affectionately. "Little guy murdered everything and then picked up all the materials. It was incredible to watch."

Maurice practically choked. "You went to the dungeon with him?" he asked in surprise. "A variant dungeon, no less?"

Sal piped up. "Since we're sharing family secrets…both of them used to be in a military group on the west coast, and they know how to fight." He pointed at both of them, grinning.

Petro sighed as he looked at Sal. "Okay, I deserved that." He chuckled and looked at Maurice. "Hey, don't go treating me any different because we know how to fight. We're still Supports at the end of the day, all right? Gotta keep up appearances for the sake of the auction house."

Maurice leaned back in his chair and crossed his arms, whistling as he did so. "Now, that is not something I would have been able to guess. I guess we can feel a little safer with Maccles Materials being aligned with the Argento Auction House." He looked over at Fabi and Sal with a warm smile. "And of course whatever the next generation of partnership looks like."

"Dad!" Fabi warned as she looked at him, causing a few eyebrows to raise. She shook her head in almost exasperation before turning her attention back to the Blight Jackal. "Ignore him."

Maurice held his hands up defensively. "I meant in a business sense…nothing untoward or presumptuous, I promise." He chuckled as he lifted his coffee cup, smiling.

Fabi pointed at the glowing green segment of his shoulder and looked at him intently. "What did you make this from?"

"Trade secret," Sal answered instantly. "Eat your sandwich, and I might tell you in the car."

Fabi held his gaze for a few moments before she begrudgingly got to her feet and sat back down. "This isn't over." She pointed at his arm almost threateningly before reassembling her bread and bacon. "I want to know absolutely everything about it…especially how Assimilation works in the field."

Sal chuckled as he dismissed the Blight Jackal. The action earned him a sour look from Fabi, who clearly regretted getting back into her seat.

"So…I think this is a good a time as any to bring it up," Petro started as he set his palms down on either side of his plate. "Salvatore has entrusted us with a sizable sum that he's earned from the auction over the years. With his permission, we're going to start renovating the old depot. Since it's a joint operation, we didn't want to steamroll Fabrizia into making decisions prematurely that she might later regret. We're still in the design phase, but wanted to see if there were any areas that were off-limits or things you'd like us to avoid?"

Fabi looked at Sal first and then at Petro and Sophia. "Did the funds come through from the Hunter Bureau?"

Petro shook his head. "No, this will just be from our own funding. We're not looking for help from the Hunter Bureau at the moment, and a lot of the work we'd be hoping to achieve would be restoration of the building itself before adding some much-needed modernization." He gestured at Maurice, smiling. "We were going to restore the shop fronts in phases. If you both aren't against it, I think having Maccles Materials relocating into one of them would enable your guild to have a steady income. I don't mind sharing my personal feelings, but I'd rather the rental income from Maccles Materials going to Salvatore and Fabrizia, rather than to Robert in the Hunter Bureau."

"I'm not opposed to that," Sal said earnestly. "Having a material supplier beside us would be great."

Fabi hesitated as she looked at Sal. "Are you sure? I'm okay with having it being deducted from my allocation of storefronts…just so you're not limited by us. I don't want it to look like I'm trying to monopolize the cash flow." She both looked and sounded conflicted, and her words at the after-party had been similar. It was like she was trying to find the line between compassionate and professionalism.

Petro snorted at the comment, which caused Fabi to look over at him in shock. Petro smiled and apologized. "Sorry, but Salvatore doesn't need to worry about cash flow at the moment. He's made millions in his first few weeks here, and with the Arkwright, that's likely just the start." He spread his palms farther away from his plate as he looked at them both. "We had a chat about what the guild could become in the future, and how we can level it up over time. One of the key things that we need to decide now is how the partnership between the two of you is going to work."

Sal caught Fabi's expression and understood that she was feeling pressured. Just as he was about to speak up, she surprised him by getting there first.

"I've seen how you designed Salvatore's workshop here at the auction house. I trust you to make something modern and stylish, which is very much my own aesthetic," Fabi said with a smile aimed at Sophia. "I also love how the Argento Auction House looks, so it's a no-brainer to give you the control of how it looks. I wouldn't even know where to start with that."

She held her hand up and started counting off her fingers, as though to remember the points she wanted to make. "My concern at the moment is that I'll end up being put into a corner, when I'll need a place to work and live by the end of the semester. Sal has another two and a half years to go before he finishes at Quest

Academy, but I just have another semester. Since I'm still learning how to use my ability, I don't know what sort of environment I'll need to Craft, but it can't be a small and intimate place like the balcony Sal had. I want a massive open space that will allow us to make industrial-sized machines. If we decide to start making cars or something even bigger, then we'll need the space to do it properly."

"You going to try to take on Doc Ameye?" Sal smiled.

Fabi nodded. "Yeah, but while he can control the rails…we could end up controlling the skies." She was deadly serious as she looked around the table. "I'd like us to never be limited by space, if that makes sense?"

Sal couldn't help but agree. "I think that it's best for you to keep in contact with Fabi and match the space to her needs for the moment. As she said, she's going to need it sooner than me. I've only really ever Crafted in small spaces, so as long as we have a setup where I can eat, sleep, and Craft…I'm good." As he finished that sentence, another thought popped into his head. "But when it comes to the storefronts…do you think it would be possible for us to sell goods from students at Quest Academy? But before they graduate?"

"What are you thinking?" Sophia asked curiously. "That Blathnaid girl?"

Sal nodded. "And Anderson Royce…if I can get his ability for material production, then we'll be able to make an Arkwright of elixirs. I don't know if he'll be up for it, but it's worth thinking about."

Petro smiled as he raised his right hand. "Let's not get ahead of ourselves just yet. We'll see what we can do, but everything you're talking about right now isn't really a fit for Silver Sanctuary. The auction is an exception because it attracts collectors rather than active Heroes. We have some from time to time, but they come for the big-ticket items. I don't think you'd have the customer base you're hoping for with those storefronts, especially if you're marketing it toward active Heroes."

Fabi shook her head. "I'm with Sal on this one. If we make good enough stuff, the people will travel to us to get them. I'd rather sell out of Silver Sanctuary than a pop-up store in Haven."

Sal smiled. "And if they only ever come for big-ticket items, then that's what we'll offer."

Petro let out an exasperated sigh but smiled before looking at his watch. "Isn't it time you both left?"

After the breakfast, Sal had hugged both his parents and promised that he'd visit them soon, joking that it would only be to check in on the Arkwright and the progress of the renovations. It had been a whirlwind of a break, with so much happening that he barely felt like he had a moment to relax. Building the Arkwright was a key highlight of the whole thing, and definitely worth the sleepless nights. He got to meet Fabi at the gala, and wouldn't have ever managed to make the Mythic Blight Jackal if she hadn't been so insistent on creating drones. He had his first ever Mythic grade, and he couldn't wait to see Upgrade's reaction when he got back to Quest Academy.

"What are you thinking about?" Fabi kept her hands on the steering device, smiling as she spoke. "I always hated leaving my dad behind when I went back to school, but we've gotten better at goodbyes over the years."

Sal glanced over at her before shaking his head. "No, it's not that. I'm just thinking about how much I managed to get done over the break. The gala, the Arkwright, the Mythic grade… It's just a pleasant surprise."

"Don't forget about how you've also turned into a bit of a badass," Fabi suggested as she stole a quick glance at him with a radiant smile. "You've learned some sick martial arts, and cleaved your way through more than five dungeons. That sounds pretty damn impressive, if you ask me."

Sal chuckled as he offered a slight shrug. "Leechers and prowlers were the limit, I think, with Jackal managing all the impressive kills in that last one."

"And you built him," Fabi corrected, echoing his father's words. "So, they're your kills too. Don't diminish the accomplishment, because it's pretty damn cool how much you've improved in such a short space of time."

"You're to thank for a lot of that." Sal smiled. "Pretty sure you told me that I couldn't be weak if we were going to be business partners?"

Fabi's smile turned guilty. "Did I? Doesn't sound like something I'd say…" She ended up laughing before extending her fingers forward, still gripping the steering yoke. "All I'll say is that you definitely stepped up to the challenge. I can't wait to see what you end up doing next."

"How are things going with your own ability? Figment still hard to control?" Sal asked, happy to change the focus of the conversation to Fabi rather than himself.

Her answer was an aggravated sigh, with Fabi clenching her fists around the steering yoke so much that her knuckles turned white. "It's a pain in the arse. It's like I've traded in all my finely tuned control for a tsunami of power. Every little thing I try to tweak ends up getting overloaded and it's taking a while to get used to it. I've been focusing on clearing dungeons the last few weeks, and restocking my dad's stores."

Sal thought about 4-A, the dungeon he had cleared with Jackal, Luke, and his parents. "Have you ever cleared a variant dungeon?"

Fabi nodded. "Yep, they're good for materials…and it's a bit thrilling not knowing what sort of enemy you're going to face. Did a couple of them last week."

Sal stared straight ahead. "And you went in alone, without using your power?"

"Yeah, but I used that void needle you gave me the blueprint for. It's ridiculously good, by the way." Fabi beamed as she turned to look at him. "They're not that difficult if you know what you're doing and you're prepared. A solid strategy and decent gear are all you really need to get through it."

Sal was stunned by this. He knew that she had come back with scuttler chitin after clearing a dungeon, but hearing her casual report really put Jackal's performance in perspective. Fabi was able to clear something like 4-A with just an Epic-grade weapon. When he thought about it, he wondered how ridiculous he sounded when he complained about going into a leecher dungeon.

"No overthinking allowed in this car." Fabi tapped his elbow before putting her hand back on the yoke. "If you're worried about doing dungeons in the future,

I'll do them with you. We're business partners, after all." She grinned as she looked over at him. "Sound good?"

Sal looked at her with a wry smile. "Are you sure you don't just want to see Jackal in action?"

Fabi let out a pained sigh. "I reeeeeaaallly want to see it! Would you be able to have it follow us in the car? What sort of range does it have?"

Sal shook his head. "What part of keeping it a secret did you miss?"

Fabi frowned as she glanced at Sal. "But you can totally let it out when we clear dungeons, right? You said it yourself that it has the Subsume ability, so it'll help you get stronger." She nodded, as though she'd just come to a conclusion. "That's what we're going to do. You're going to run dungeons with me for materials, and we'll level you up with Jackal. That way, you'll be more than fit to do the portal expedition if you decide to sign up for it."

"I forgot about that," Sal admitted with an awkward laugh. "And it's your final semester…are you sure you want to be running dungeons with me?"

Fabi laughed as she gave Sal an incredulous look. "Are you kidding me? You're going to be the guildmaster for two of my best friends. I need to make sure you're the best Salvatore Argento possible."

"No pressure." Sal chuckled as he looked out the window. It was becoming a beautiful day with the sun burning through the clouds, sending rays of light to the cityscape below. Quest Academy was visible in the distance with all its towers and amphitheater coming into view. It stood defiantly amid all the smaller buildings, and looked quite striking as it pierced the sky.

"Feels good being back." Fabi turned the car toward the private landing docks on the residential tower. "Are you looking forward to seeing your new room? Having a personal workshop is awesome."

Sal chuckled as he watched their descent toward the platform. "I've barely slept in my own bed since I went back. I practically lived in a personal workshop, but I am excited to be back. I've missed everyone, and I'm looking forward to seeing Upgrade's reaction to the Mythic grade."

"Please let me be there for that." Fabi checked the mirrors, lining up the car with the platform below. "What are you looking forward to the most? Alex's coffee? Canteen steak? Upgrade flipping out at useless Crafters?"

"All of it," Sal admitted with a smile as they finally touched down on the platform. As much as he had accomplished, there was still so much more that needed to be done. If he wanted to build up his guild, then he'd need to start boosting his own reputation beyond the accolades of Mythcrafter and Skill Master. He needed to showcase his strength and make a name for himself beyond the recognition of the Savior class. It wasn't enough that he was top of his class; he needed to prove that he was worthy of keeping that spot. Guild outings, dungeons, scavenger runs—he'd do it all. He'd continue to learn the Silverson Arts, and work on improving his base stats.

He looked at Fabi, who was smiling at him as she took the protective straps off her shoulders. "Thanks again for the ride."

Sal took off his straps and stared out the window at the city below. "It really does feel good to be back."

End of Book 4

REVIEWS!

So, how did I do? Did you enjoy reading Quest Academy? If so, it would be a massive help to me if you left a review for the story. With millions of books being published on Amazon, it's very hard to get any sort of traction and discoverability. If you share the book with people that you think might enjoy it, that would be incredible. I'd love for as many people as possible to have the chance to read the story, and for that, I need your help.

If the story does well enough, I'll be able to spend more time writing, which will cut down the time between releases... and fuel my coffee addiction.

If leaving reviews isn't something you can do, then I'd really appreciate you helping to share the story to people that might enjoy it. No matter what though, you've read my story and that's the most important thing to me.

Thank you!

<u>LEGION</u>

<u>Quest Academy Book 5!</u>

Quest Academy's second semester has begun!

Crafting the first ever Mythic-Grade piece of equipment should have made Sal a Legend. Instead, it might end up getting him killed. That's what happens when you use the most coveted demonic material known to man… to build an attack drone.

Secrets are piling up, and Sal is tired of hiding his abilities. If he wants to live without fear, individual power won't be enough. It's time to establish the guild. Sal has the headquarters and the funds. All he needs are the right people to bring them up the rankings.

Salvatore finally has the conviction to become a Hero, now he needs experience. To hold his place as the top ranked Savior, Sal must push himself harder than ever before. New combat styles, new modules and the most ambitious crafting projects imaginable.

It's not just about staying safe anymore.

Power isn't given. It's Crafted.

COMING SOON!

WANDERING WARRIOR: JUDGE

By Michael Head

A divine quest to deliver justice. One year to accomplish his mission. After nineteen planets, there's something different about this one.

James Holden has reached the maximum level there is for a human. That's perfect, since he's the only one of his kind: a wandering warrior, without control of his destination, tossed between universes by gods who've failed to tell him why. James is the lone Judge on a new world in need of someone to balance the scales. He isn't afraid to do so with extreme prejudice. As the Chief Justice, he has to right the wrongs the innocent can't fix themselves.

As James quickly discovers, the roots of corruption run deep. Guilds choose to protect themselves rather than the people. Monsters roam the wilderness unchecked. Judgment is usually a decision between right and wrong, but nothing is ever that simple. This time, being the strongest human won't be enough to punish the guilty. James might have to recruit some new blood, even if he prefers to work alone.

On his twentieth world, he is going to win, no matter the cost. James will have to find a way to break past the limits of the system if he's going to have a chance at making a difference.

https://mybook.to/WanderingWarrior

KNIGHTS OF ETERNITY: CALAMITY

By Rachel Ni Chuirc

When Zara awoke to find Valerius, leader of the legendary Gilded Knights, towering over her, she thought she'd gone mad.

She was the Fury, mistress of claw and flame—armies trembled at her name! Now she lay chained and broken, a prisoner in her own home. But that wasn't why she thought herself mad.

Only yesterday, she remembered a different life. She remembered her nephew in the local arcade, struggling to beat the villainous Zara the Fury in Knights of Eternity. She remembered her uncle and his big booming laugh.

…and she remembered the gun that changed everything.

https://mybook.to/KoE_Calamity

ARISE: ALPHA

By Jez Cajiao

When you steal a hundred grand from some very bad people, the best way to survive is to stay small and quiet…

Possibly it's not to save a pair of drowning girls, not go viral on social media, and certainly not to let the local police take your passport, trapping you on a small "party" island in the middle of the Mediterranean Sea.

But Steve isn't the average guy: he's ex-military, ex-enforcer, and ex-human. He's a one-man, nanite-fueled nightmare for those who cross the line, and he's decided that it's time to clean up his act. He's going to make up for the things he's done, and save "the little guys."

It's a nice fantasy, but even he has to admit, it's really just a justification, because he's a very bad man, with horrifying abilities, and he's only just learning what he's capable of. He needs a reason to not go to the dark. And if that's hunting down the creatures of the night and beating them to death with their own femurs?

Well, he's just the man for the job.

Stolen money. Greek Islands. Werewolves and Enforcers…what could possibly go wrong?

https://mybook.to/AriseAlpha

WELCOME TO THE DARK AGES

Morgan and Merlins excellent Adventures
Book One
By
Malory

When Merlin needs a hero to save the world, he gets... well, me.

Fan-bloody-tastic.

I was supposed to be dead. Instead, I wake up face-down in Dark Age mud, possessing some poor bastard's body, while the ghost of history's most famous wizard rambles on about being murdered, cosmic energy and the end of all reality.

Just one tiny problem: I know about as much about cultivation as a pig knows about particle physics.

Now I'm fumbling with mystical energy that feels like juggling nitroglycerin, trying not to get shanked by everyone and their grandmother, and dealing with Merlin's constant "helpful" commentary.

Something dark is rising in Arthurian Britain.

Something that made even Merlin scared. They say fate has a sense of humour. Turns out it's the kind that laughs while setting your hair on fire.

Welcome to the Dark Ages, where cultivation meets chaos, and the only thing sharper than a sword is my questionable wit.

Read Now!

THEFT OF DECKS

By Lars Machmüller

When the deck is stacked against you? Change the game!

In the frontier town of Isarn, Chase will never be more than the lowly Dark-born thief he is. Banned from training, banned from acquiring better cards, if the Lightborn had their way, he'd be banned from life itself.

He's not alone though, and the one thing he and his friends have is determination. Losing a hand to a brutal punishment only fueled his obsession to get access to his own amazing, reality-bending cards.

That is the path to power and a future for them all. Nobody cares where you came from when you're rich enough. For now, though, they're facing both established powers, churches and age-old prejudices. It's time to get to work, and if the Lightborn won't share and play nice?

Sometimes the only way to get dealt a better hand is to steal the whole damn deck!

Buy on Amazon

FACEBOOK AND SOCIAL MEDIA

If you want to reach out to talk about Quest Academy or just get to know me a little bit, you can find me on my swanky new author page on Facebook. There's a very high chance that you'll be one of the very first people to like it that wasn't involved in getting me published:

www.facebook.com/BrianJNordon

Alternatively, we've a new Facebook group to spread the word about cool LitRPG books, called LitRPG Legion. It's a fun space to share old and new books, and to discover great titles you might have missed along the way.

Only rules for joining are to spread the word about great new books, and not being a dick! As a bonus, if you join… you'll have access to dozens of author interviews conducted by me or Jez.

www.facebook.com/groups/litrpglegion

If you'd prefer to catch me over on Discord, here's a link:

https://discord.gg/GAN5RgNJGn

I created the Discord for my first ever series that I started over on Royal Road, called Wildcards: The Dread Captain. It's a fun story that I absolutely loved writing and will get back to after Quest Academy is established. I'm not the fastest at replying, but I do always reply!

PATREON!

Okay then, now for those of you that don't know about Patreon, its essentially a way to support your favorite authors, you can sign up for a day or a month or a year, and you get various benefits for it, ranging from my heartfelt thanks, to advance access to the books, to me sending them books, naming characters and more.

My Patreon was very focused on my time writing Wildcards, and I'll be incorporating new tiers in the future for advanced chapters of Quest Academy. I'm talking with Legion Publishers to find out what we could offer fans outside of more chapters, so it might be worth keeping an eye on. If not now, maybe in the future when there's more on offer!

All support is appreciated, but not compulsory. Honestly, a review or just recommending my story to others is more than I have any right to ask.

www.patreon.com/BrianJNordon

<u>RECOMMENDATIONS</u>

I'm not sure if they'll be your thing, but if you like reading my stories, then you might be interested in these books too. This is only from my own personal enjoyment though, so take my words with a pinch of salt.

Death, Loot & Vampires by Benjamin Kerei

Heretical Fishing by Haylock Jobson

Restarting The Apocalypse by Michael Chatfield

Portal to Nova Roma by J.R. Mathews

The Bad Guys by Eric Ugland

Shattered Dreams by Shawn Wilson

Iron Prince by Luke Chmilenko & Bryce O'Connor

See These Bones by Chris Tullbane

A Soldiers Life by Always RollsAOne

Isekai by Robert Locke

LITRPG!

To learn more about LitRPG, talk to other authors including myself, and to just have an awesome time, please join the LitRPG Group

www.facebook.com/groups/LitRPGGroup

FACEBOOK

There's also a few really active Facebook groups I'd recommend you join, as you'll get to hear about great new books, new releases and interact with all your (new) favorite authors! (I may also be there, skulking at the back and enjoying the memes…)

www.facebook.com/groups/LitRPGsociety/

www.facebook.com/groups/LitRPG.books/

www.facebook.com/groups/LitRPGforum/

www.facebook.com/groups/gamelitsociety/

www.facebook.com/groups/litrpglegion